THE RICH
SHALL INHERIT

ALSO BY ELIZABETH ADLER

Léonie
Peach

THE RICH
SHALL INHERIT

Elizabeth Adler

Delacorte
Press

F IC
A d L

Published by
Delacorte Press
Bantam Doubleday Dell Publishing Group, Inc.
666 Fifth Avenue
New York, New York 10103

This work was first published in Great Britain by Hodder & Stoughton
Ltd.

Book Design by Richard Oriolo

Library of Congress Cataloging in Publication Data

Adler, Elizabeth (Elizabeth A.)
  The rich shall inherit / Elizabeth Adler.
      p.   cm.
  ISBN 0-385-29727-0
  I. Title.
  PR6051.D56R53 1989
  823'.914—dc19   88-38684
                                         CIP

Manufactured in the United States of America

June 1989

10 9 8 7 6 5 4 3 2 1
BG

For Richard
with love

Blessed are the meek; for they shall inherit the earth.
MATTHEW 5:3–9

CHAPTER 1

The morning sunshine lightened the valley from green to gold as Mike Preston strode impatiently into the kitchen and flipped the switch on the coffee machine. To tell the truth, he was bored with the view of the Santa Ynez mountains; he was a man who needed the relentless pace and aggression of New York to spur him on—and yet it was to escape that same frantic life-style that he'd sought solitude in California.

Mike's talent as an investigative journalist had earned him a Pulitzer prize, seven years ago, for his daring exposé of corruption in high places. It was a snarled tale of armaments deals and contract payoffs that had eventually led to the dismissal, in disgrace, of a well-known general and Korean War hero, and the resignation of two members of the President's personal cabinet.

The book that had followed had swept him to fame and fortune, earning him far more money than he felt any man had the right to possess, and had opened up a whole new career as a guest lecturer in cities as far apart as Geneva in Switzerland and Stanford in California. It had also turned him into a reluctant television celebrity, and changed his life-style forever.

It wasn't just that he could now afford a lavish apartment in Sutton Place that boasted oak paneling and its own library, as well as a view of the East River, or that he was on every New York hostess's "A" party list, or that headwaiters in smart restaurants rushed to give him their most prominent table but, for a reason that still mystified him, fame seemed to have made him more attractive. Glossily beautiful women of the kind seen advertising perfumes on billboards, or pictured in *Vogue* magazine displaying dresses by Calvin and Oscar and Bill, blackmailed their hostesses to allow them to sit next to him at dinner; they stroked his arm and flashed him intimate glances as he sipped his wine, and they purred suggestions in his ear that would have shocked his aunt Martha back in Madison, Wisconsin.

If Mike couldn't understand what women saw in him, Aunt Martha surely could. His features were rugged and his battered nose the legacy of a boyhood tennis smash that had gone wrong, but his deep-set eyes were the color of a winter-gray sea and his thick dark hair was short and usually rumpled because he had a habit of running his hands through it when he was concentrating. Mike thought he looked like a thirty-seven-year-old has-been prize-fighter, but Aunt Martha understood women; she knew it was the unexpected combination of his six-foot-five truck driver looks, and his cultured mind and sensitivity, that caused feminine hearts to turn somersaults. And now, of course, to that was added his international success. "Mike Preston" was a name that could open any door.

Mike had earned a reputation as a man who could see beyond the public facades of the high and the mighty, to the raw emotions that burned beneath, motivating them to acts of folly that eventually caused their downfall. His three best sellers were written with that extra element of suspense—a who-done-it angle that had made them popular, whether he was writing about the real-life career of an automotive giant, a corporate scandal, or a spectacular murder. However, it was two years since his last book was published and he'd promised himself that here, at last, in Santa Barbara, he'd come up with the idea for his next. Yet he'd been here for six weeks and the typewriter still had its cover on, the wastebasket remained empty and the floor unlittered with balled-up sheets of paper. He had fallen prey to the California sunshine, the blue skies—and the sunkissed blondes.

Yesterday's L.A. *Times* was still lying on the countertop, unread, and Mike carried it out onto the redwood deck. Propping his feet on the rail, he began to read the usual daily reportage of stalemate politics, global terrorism, murder, property and automobiles, fashion and food . . . a quick summary of disaster, conflict, and consumerism in thirty pages. . . .

Flinging it to the ground, he stared down at it disgustedly . . . he'd promised himself he wouldn't read a newspaper for two months, just so he could confirm his theory that when he did everything would be exactly the same . . . he wouldn't have missed a thing. Or would he? He glanced again at the newspaper crumpled on the floor, his eyes drawn as though by a magnet to the black-bordered advertisement in the lower right-hand corner. It stood out from the pages as though it were written in scarlet letters. It read

SEARCH FOR AN HEIRESS

AS ASSISTANT TO THE PROBATE COURT OF GENEVA
IN THE ESTATE OF POPPY MALLORY
BORN JUNE 15, 1880, SANTA BARBARA, CALIFORNIA
DIED JUNE 15, 1957, IN THE VENETO, ITALY,
I AM SEARCHING FOR A DAUGHTER, OR IF DECEASED,
THEN HER ISSUE.
PLEASE ADDRESS INFORMATION TO ADVOCATE
JOHANNES LIEBER, 14, RUE GARONNE, GENEVA,
SWITZERLAND, OR TELEPHONE GENEVA 73-63-03

Mike forgot all about the coffee perking in the kitchen, he forgot the blue skies and the blondes and the temptingly slothful California sunshine. He knew a hook for a story when he saw one—and this was too good to miss. Poppy Mallory's name seemed to breathe mystery and intrigue. He could only imagine the dozens—maybe hundreds—of hopeful people who would reply to that ad.

He stared out to sea, trying to figure out a reason why Poppy Mallory, a woman born here in this very county, had died alone in Italy, so far from her home. Why had her daughter not come forward to claim her inheritance in all those years? And if, as was possible, the daughter was now dead, then who would be the heir or heiress? There was just one place to find out. Checking his watch, he reckoned it would be four-thirty in the afternoon in Europe. Picking up the telephone he dialed the number of Advocate Johannes Lieber in Geneva.

Mr. Lieber was obviously an important lawyer—it took three messages via his secretary to convince him to take his call, and only then because Mike had emphasized his familiar name.

"Mike Preston? The author of *Robbelard's Getaway*? I admire your work very much, sir," Lieber greeted him. "It was one of the best pieces of investigative journalism I've ever seen. Of course, we are all suspicious of corporate takeovers where people are making fortunes trading the market on insider information, but it took someone like you to bring it out into the open—and to name the culprits. I congratulate you, sir, on your courage in taking on the establishment—and in winning."

Mike smiled. "Well, thanks, Mr. Lieber. I'm always glad to meet a fan. But I'm calling you in the hope of a little insider information myself. About Poppy Mallory."

"Are you a relative then? Or maybe you have some new information?" Lieber was suddenly businesslike.

"No, sir, I'm just a writer on the scent of a good story. I was wondering if you could tell me who Poppy Mallory was, and how much her estate is worth?"

There was a long silence and then Lieber said, "I'm not sure of the ethics of this conversation, Mr. Preston. I must think of my client."

Mike ran his hand through his hair impatiently. "Since you haven't got an heir, do you in fact have a client yet?—sir," he added appeasingly. "You just said how good a job you thought I'd done on *Robbelard's Getaway*. Well, maybe I could do the same sort of job for you—with Poppy Mallory. After all, you could say I'm your man on the spot—I'm right here in Santa Barbara, where it all began. We could help each other. I follow up the Poppy Mallory story for you, and if I find your missing heir—or heiress—I get to write the book. If I don't succeed—or if the missing heir turns up anyway and there is no real mystery—then no book. What do you say?"

"We-ll." Lieber's voice sounded cautious and Mike frowned. He suddenly wanted this story more than he'd wanted anything in years. He had to find out about Poppy Mallory, his instincts were telling him there was something more than a missing heiress, there was something special about this woman.

"I can tell you that the Mallory estate is considerable," said Lieber, "yes, considerable . . . around five, six hundred—"

"Thousand?"

"Oh, millions, my dear man, *millions*. Maybe even more, when we are finally able to assess it all."

Mike whistled softly. "Then I guess you're gonna have a fight on your hands. You'll be inundated with claims from every con man or woman who sees a quick way to a fortune."

Lieber sighed heavily. "That presents a problem, of course, but we are still hoping to find Madame Mallory's daughter alive. The 'Madame' is a courtesy title, you understand. Poppy Mallory was never, to our knowledge, married."

"Okay," said Mike. "And if the 'heiress' is dead? Then who is in line for the millions?"

"Who indeed?" asked Lieber with a chuckle. "If anyone."

There was a short silence and then Lieber said: "I'm going to trust you, Mr. Preston, because I believe you can be helpful. I would appreciate your assistance—even though it is unorthodox. But then this is a very unorthodox case. Madame Mallory's will only came to light because of the question of the title to a parcel of real estate in Beverly Hills. She died at her home, the Villa Castelletto near Verona in Italy. She had lived alone for many years. Apparently she entertained no one—and had not a single friend. Apart from that, no one in the area seems to remember anything about her. The first my office knew of Poppy was when we were contacted by California lawyers whose clients wished to purchase a Beverly Hills property, apparently owned by her. Poppy's will had been prepared by a local country lawyer; he was an old man himself and neglectful. The estate just moldered on and eventually the old lawyer died too and his business was taken over by another, who later moved to Milan, taking all the old files with him. The Milan office became successful in dealing with international law and eventually, in 1968, merged with ours. When the question of the title to the property arose, a search through our archives revealed an unwitnessed will—and the mystery. As it was unwitnessed, the will was never probated and it can only be taken as an indication of who Poppy's heir, or heirs, might be. And that's why we are in the position we now find ourselves. It's up to us to find her true heir. So," he concluded briskly, "Poppy remains an enigma."

"I assume you ran this ad internationally," Mike said quickly. "Can you tell me what response you've had to it so far?"

Lieber laughed. "Let's just say, you are not *the first* to call."

"Thanks, Mr. Lieber." Mike was already riffling through the pages of the Santa Barbara telephone book and finding nothing under the name *Mallory*. "I appreciate your cooperation. Do you think you could fax me a list of all the claimants so far? I promise I'll guard it with my life," he added jokingly.

As he put down the phone he knew exactly where he was heading next.

CHAPTER 2

The old parrot ruffled his feathers against the damp, penetrating chill swirling in with the mist from Venice's Grand Canal. It oozed its way through the crumbling ocher stucco walls and brittle windowpanes of the Palazzo Rinardi, rising to the lofty beamed ceilings and clinging to the faded silk curtains that were now so fragile with age, they threatened to disintegrate into dust. The bird's plumage was the only blaze of color in the once sumptuously hued bedroom, but this morning even his gay jungle attire seemed submerged under Venice's watery November light.

He unfurled a leg from beneath his feathers, flexing it stiffly, and the emerald and diamond rings caught the light with astonishing brilliance. Poppy had had them made at Bulgari, instructing the jewelers to use only the finest stones, and for more than eighty years her beloved pet had worn a ransom in jewels around his stick-like legs. His thick perch was of solid gold, scratched and worn from his constant skittering up and down, and at each end was a knob the size of a tennis ball, clustered with fine jewels. An enormous gold cage shaped like a palace in a story by Scheherazade, its curves and arches battered by the bird's lifetime of use, stood on a table in a corner of the room. But mostly, nowadays, the parrot just sat on his perch, watching and waiting for Aria, the way he used to wait for Poppy.

The soft rustle of slippered feet sounded along the marble corridor and he cocked his head as the gilt door handle rattled and Fiametta, limping with arthritis, placed the breakfast tray on a seventeenth-century painted table. His weary, hooded eyes watched as the old woman tugged back the white linen hangings on the half-tester bed, tut-tutting as flakes of paint fluttered from its newels, adding more scars to the exquisite decoration of scrolls and flowers and trellises that had lasted for more than two hundred years.

"Aria," she called, shaking the girl's shoulder, "wake up!"

Her voice sounded different this morning, she was excited and the parrot scrabbled along his golden perch, flexing his wings. "Go away, Fiametta," replied Aria's muffled voice, "I don't want to wake up."

"But you must, it's your birthday!" The old woman's voice trembled with excitement as Aria stirred restlessly.

"That's exactly *why* I don't want to wake up," Aria mumbled into her pillow, "just go away and let me sleep."

"Now that's a fine thing to say!" Fiametta pulled the blanket back firmly.

"It's *freezing*," Aria moaned, pulling the covers over her pajama-clad shoulders. "Oh, go away, Fiametta, do. Just leave me with my misery!"

The old woman stared at her with an expression of mixed tenderness and exasperation. She never failed to be amazed by Aria's beauty, especially because as a child she could not even have been called pretty; her extreme thinness, along with her huge dark blue eyes and the thick fringe of curling lashes that dominated her tiny face, had given her the air of a badly nourished waif. Many a time Fiametta's heart had been in her mouth, fearing a broken limb, as she watched her charge climbing trees with the agility of a monkey, or surefootedly leaping the stepping-stones across the rough stream that bisected the parkland surrounding the Villa d'Oro. But Aria's delicacy had been deceptive. She was as strong as an ox, thought Fiametta proudly, and as graceful and fleet as a gazelle. There were those who compared Aria's gamine looks to the young Audrey Hepburn, and others who argued she had the pure beauty of Grace Kelly, but no matter, Fiametta knew that Aria resembled no one but herself. She was unique.

She arranged the pillows comfortably behind Aria's back as the girl wriggled reluctantly upright. "There now, that's better," she said as Aria flung a slender arm around her neck and kissed her affectionately on either cheek.

"*Ciao*, Fiametta" Aria murmured, a smile lighting up her smooth young face. "Why all this fuss? I haven't had breakfast in bed since I had my tonsils out when I was twelve!" She was smiling but her eyes were sad, and the parrot skittered along his perch squawking to catch her attention. "Luchay, *caro*," she called, "come here to me."

The parrot fluttered from his perch to the table and from there to the dresser, making his way toward her in a series of little hops. "Poor Luchay," Aria murmured sadly, "I think we are all feeling our age this morning, aren't we?" He hopped onto her outstretched hand, edging gently up to her shoulder where he nestled her against her cheek, nipping delicately at her earlobe and making soft cooing noises in his throat.

The breakfast tray was set with a worn white linen cloth edged with delicate Venetian lace, and on it was a chipped crystal glass of orange juice, a basket of fresh rolls, a dish of soft yellow butter, and another dish of the vivid scarlet jam made by Fiametta from the summer's lavish crop of wild strawberries that grew up in the hills near the Villa d'Oro. A neatly folded newspaper lay by the side of the beautiful blue and white plate—one of the last remnants of the Haviland service that had been made for the Baronessa Marina Rinardi a hundred and fifty years ago.

Fiametta's hand was trembling as she picked up the newspaper. "Read it, *cara*!" she exclaimed. "Here, read it quickly."

Aria took the paper from her, surprised. "But what must I read . . . it's just the paper, the same old news. Unless . . . *someone has died*?" She blushed, ashamed of the faint note of hope that had crept into her voice.

"Not the person you mean. But yes . . . in a way." Fiametta's finger, distorted with arthritis, pointed shakily to the bottom of the page. The ad for the Mallory heiress, outlined in double rows of black, stood out from the rest of the page.

"Well?" Aria asked, still puzzled.

"But it's *Poppy*!" exclaimed Fiametta. "*Poppy Mallory!* . . . Don't you see? *You* must be the heiress, Aria. *It's you!*"

Aria read the notice again, only now it looked like a beacon of hope. What if it was true? If she really was an heiress? It could resolve the fate that was hanging like the sword of Damocles over her head.

It had been just six months ago that her mother had dropped the bolt from the blue, that the Rinardi family trust had finally dried up; there was no more money and now she expected Aria to do her duty and marry a rich man, a man she had chosen for her—Antony Carraldo.

The name had sent a shiver down Aria's spine and she'd stared at her mother in horror. She had heard the rumors about Carraldo—everyone had, though no one had ever proven anything, or even tried. Her mother had told her she shouldn't believe the rumors, that they were just stories put about by people who were jealous of his wealth and success. "Think, girl," she'd said, "would your father have been his best friend if what they said was true?"

It was strange, Aria had thought, bewildered, that Carraldo had been Papa's best friend. Somehow he'd always been there, on the fringes of their lives, a shadowy figure, keeping his distance . . . she even remembered holding his hand at Papa's funeral . . .

"Don't worry," Francesca had said, "he promised he'll take good care of you. You will have everything in the world a woman could ever want."

"Yes—a woman like you!" Aria had retorted, tears stinging her eyes again.

Her mother had just laughed, a light, tinkling, mirthless sound. "Somehow I always thought Carraldo was waiting for you to grow up," she'd said.

Of course, Aria had refused to do it; she'd stormed, she'd cried, she'd protested that it wasn't the Middle Ages, that mothers didn't marry off their daughters anymore . . . she would run away, she'd said, anywhere . . . a million miles from Carraldo. And then her mother had stopped all her raging with a simple quiet statement.

"If you refuse," Francesca Rinardi had said icily, "then I don't know what I will do."

Aria had stared, terrified, into her clear blue eyes, and then Francesca had simply walked out and left her to think things over.

Aria had understood Francesca's threat, and she'd also known that she was capable of killing herself. To a woman like her mother, a world without the luxuries she considered to be the necessities of life was a world simply not worth living in. Frightened, she'd known then that Francesca had left her no choice.

And now it was her eighteenth birthday, the day she was to become engaged to Antony Carraldo. She stared again at the black-banded advertisement for Poppy Mallory's missing heiress.

"Poppy . . ." she whispered hopefully. "Have you come to save me? I don't even know who you are, only your name. Poppy."

"Poppy," repeated Luchay. "Poppy, Poppy cara, Poppy chérie, Poppy darling."

They stared at him in astonishment as he fluttered back to his perch, still cackling harshly.

"Poppy," he called again, more clearly as his throat, long unused to the sound of her name, seemed to remember the proper reflexes.

"Luchay!" Aria cried excitedly, "Of course. You knew Poppy. You knew all about her!" Her eyes widened as she realized exactly what the parrot knew. "And," she added quietly, "*you* know who is Poppy's true heir."

It was five-thirty in the morning and Antony Carraldo's sleek black Gulfstream III, with its distinctive raven emblem inside the gold circle, was waiting on the tarmac at Milan's Malpensa airport, its engines already warming up for takeoff to London. The long black Mercedes drew silently alongside, its smoke-gray windows hiding its occupant. The steward waiting by the steps drew smartly to attention in anticipation. He knew that Carraldo would be out of the car before the chauffeur even had time to apply the hand brake, let alone run around to open the door for his master.

Carraldo walked quickly up the flight of steps. "Good morning, Enrico," he said, nodding pleasantly.

"Good morning, sir. The captain is ready for takeoff whenever you give the word, sir," the steward replied.

Carraldo nodded. "Let's go." Without a further glance he sat down and fastened his seat belt, picking up the first of the dozen international newspapers that he read every morning. They were airborne within minutes and as he opened *Il Giorno*, Enrico appeared carrying a pot of coffee on a silver tray. He poured deftly, accustomed to his master's silence. He knew that Carraldo used every available minute of the day to work; even now, he would be checking the international money markets, as well as the art market. He thought to himself that Carraldo probably had a finger in every pie.

Nodding his thanks, Carraldo sipped the coffee. It was a blend made specially for him in Paris, thick, dark, and rich, and it never failed to jolt him into complete awareness, whether it was one, two, or five o'clock in the morning. But this morning he didn't need it. The ad, heavily bordered in black, jumped from the pages of *Il Giorno* with the impact of a time bomb.

Poppy Mallory. He stared mesmerized at the name from the past. It was a name that transported him back in time to a woman he'd never even met. But he knew it was a name that could have a devastating effect on his future.

Antony Carraldo was fifty-one years old. He was of medium height with a thin yet muscular torso, and his olive complexion had the light, year-round tan of the very rich. His thin face was prominently boned with a broad forehead and the sort of arrogant nose seen on ancient Roman statues. Carraldo would not have looked amiss in a toga on the steps of the Roman senate in Caesar's day, but in fact he always wore immaculately tailored suits—cream linen in summer and dark blue pin-stripe in winter, and always with plain light blue shirts of the finest Sea Island cotton. For such a formal man, his shoes were a slight eccentricity —tasseled loafers from Westons in Paris—but his ties were discreet, striped or spotted and fashioned from exquisite Italian silks. He had a firm mouth that rarely smiled, and he spoke in measured tones as though each phrase had been thought out carefully beforehand. His hands were slender and well manicured, and he wore no rings. A plain white-gold handcrafted Vacheron & Constantin watch was his only adornment— and that was for practical reasons, not vanity.

On the surface, Carraldo looked what he was—a rich, fastidious, and cultured man. Over the past thirty-five years he had made a fortune as an art dealer, and as a philanthropist he'd put a great deal of that money back into supporting his great loves: music, the opera, painting.

Carraldo traveled the world on his private jet to clinch major art deals. He owned a lavish turn-of-the-century villa in the hills above Portofino, a vast town house on the Via Michelangelo Buonarroti in Milan, and an ancient but beautifully restored palazzo in Venice. He also had a house in Belgrave Square, London, and kept a permanent suite at the Pierre Hotel in New York. Each abode contained a fortune in paintings, sculpture, and other art treasures and each was kept fully staffed and in immaculate order.

But there was another house, one that no one knew about—a large, shuttered villa near Naples that he visited once a month without fail. He always stayed exactly two days and two nights, and then he returned to his normal life in Milan.

Carraldo was not a partygoing man, but he was seen at the important international social functions, particularly those involving the worlds of art or music. He was involved in the Spoleto Festival and the Venice Biennale, and four or five times a year he entertained lavishly at his homes—a masked ball in Venice for the Lenten carnival; a congenial summer house party in Portofino; a gathering of eminent operagoers at dinner in Milan. Apart from these occasions his private life was exactly that—private. But it was also whispered about in the bars and cafés of half a dozen international cities.

They whispered that Antony Carraldo's smooth facade covered a thousand secrets, that his money was not earned only from his knowl-edgeable trading in art, that there were other, more sinister ways he added millions each year to his Swiss bank accounts. And despite his urbane appearance, they said that Carraldo's sexual appetite was insatia-ble.

It was rumored that Carraldo was a man of steel whose nightlong sessions left him still in control and his partners exhausted—and that he liked his sex rough. "Orgies," the gossip said, "week-long debauches with every vice and peversion imaginable . . ." But Carraldo, suave and with a faint smile, was impervious to gossip, and *no one* ever refused an invitation to his parties.

The only man in whom he had ever confided was his great friend Paolo Rinardi, but Paolo had died tragically fourteen years ago, and now there was no one who knew exactly how Antony Carraldo had amassed his great fortune, and *who* and *what* he was. *No one who knew the truth.*

As the sleek black plane swooped onto the runway at London's Heathrow, the pile of newspapers lay crumpled on the floor at Carraldo's feet. He frowned, pressing his fingers against his brow as the pain fluttered in his chest like a tiny saw-edged knife. Taking a silver box from his pocket, he removed a small pill and placed it under his tongue, lying back in his seat waiting for it to take effect and thinking of the extraordinary advertisement. He was quite sure that if Francesca Rinardi had anything to do with it, she would claim that Aria was the heiress to Poppy Mallory's fortune, whether she believed it was true or not. But if it was, then he stood to lose the one treasure he prized most in the world. And Carraldo wasn't a man who lost easily.

Calling Enrico, he asked to be put through on the radio-phone to the Banco Credito e Maritimo in Zurich, Switzerland. He spoke with Giuseppe Alliere, its president, instructing him to use his contacts to obtain from the offices of the lawyer, Johannes Lieber, a list of the purported claimants to Poppy Mallory's estate.

Claudia Galli decided she loathed Paris today. She hated its ancient tree-lined avenues and its beautiful buildings; she hated its tiled mansard roofs and cobbled courtyards; she hated its cafés and restaurants and its glittering shop windows displaying the most luxurious and beautiful clothes in the world. She hated it all because she was broke, and in her view, to be broke in Paris was a sin.

A small black cat ran between her feet, almost tripping her as she sauntered from the elevator of her elegant apartment building near the Avenue Foch. She aimed an angry kick with a slim foot, exquisitely shod in Maud Frizon's supple suede and alligator. "Bastard," she hissed. Broke or in funds, Claudia hated cats.

Emerging onto the street, she paused to scan the autumn sky. The clouds looked low and threatening and there was a chill wind lifting the last of the leaves from the black branches of the trees. Snuggling deeper into her collar, she thanked God that at least she still had a good fur—of course, it wasn't *sable*—her sables were long gone—but at least it wasn't mink. Fisher was a perfectly respectable compromise on the status scale. And, talking of scale and status, what was her life reduced to now?

Claudia lived in a tiny studio apartment at the rear of a smart building with a close-up view of the garbage cans. She supposed she could have found something larger for her money in a cheaper arrondissement, but here at least she had a good address, and that's what counted. And besides, she hadn't anticipated spending much time in her apartment. Right now, for instance, she'd expected to be sifting through a sheaf of invitations; she'd thought she would be spending Christmas at the Malinkoffs' villa at the smart new Mexican resort Costa Careyes, and then maybe a week or two at the Listers' chalet in Gstaad, and then on to Barbados . . . but somehow, this year, those invitations hadn't materialized. Her "friends" had realized she was on the lookout for a new husband and they weren't about to risk their own by having her around. Claudia was notoriously unscrupulous about these things. She was thirty-six years old and considered a beautiful woman—well, a very *attractive* woman—tall, with slender hips and high, round breasts that were larger than was fashionable but were one of her greatest assets. Yet sometimes, like now, being too attractive worked against her.

Biting her lip angrily, she searched the street for a taxi. Of course, Pierluigi would tell her she could no longer afford to take taxis, but damn Pierluigi, he'd never taken a subway in his life, so why should he expect her to do so? "Rue de Rivoli, Angelina's," she told the cab driver curtly, hoping she'd find someone there to pick up the tab for her breakfast coffee and brioche.

The chic café was practically empty except for two or three tables occupied by tourists. Of course, Claudia thought sullenly, everyone who was anyone was in New York for Pavarotti's concert and the Museum of Modern Art "Fashion" party . . . she would have been there, too, but the airlines had told her coldly that her Amex card was no longer valid and they had canceled her reservation.

It was all her father's fault, she thought angrily, blaming him, as she always did, for her own troubles. Aleksandr Galli had been a recluse and an eccentric who had rejected the family name of Rinardi in favor of his wife's name—Galli. He had refused to live in the family villa or the Venetian palazzo, waiving his claim to the properties and the title of Barone Rinardi in favor of his cousin Paolo. Claudia had never forgiven him for that; she could have used those houses, stocked full of expensive treasures. Instead, when he'd died, all he'd left them was the remote Villa Velata that nobody wanted!

She stared dolefully into her coffee cup, stirring in two spoons of forbidden sugar and deciding she would call Pierluigi one more time in New York. He would have to answer her calls eventually, even though he was angry with her. Pierluigi never could resist her for long. *He needed her.* Her twin brother was an immensely successful commodities broker, and even though there had been some disquieting reports in the papers about the market the last few months she was sure Pierluigi would be all right. He never let anything get in the way of his success.

It was while she was flicking through the pages of *Le Monde* to check the stock market reports that Claudia saw the ad for Poppy Mallory's heir. Her eyes widened as she studied it, and then she sat back in her chair, dunked her brioche in her coffee, and took a large and satisfying bite. This could be just what she needed . . . maybe, just *maybe,* her luck had changed . . . if only she could figure it out properly. And just maybe, too, she wouldn't call hateful Pierluigi. Not yet. Not until she needed him.

Pierluigi Galli's face was impassive as he sat at the elegantly appointed table in the Regency Hotel on New York's Park Avenue, listening attentively to what his breakfast companion had to say.

"Of course, it would have been better if you'd gotten out six months ago," Warren James told him, biting into the most delicious blueberry muffin he'd ever tasted, "but it's still not too late . . . just!" he added, chewing his muffin thoughtfully.

Pierluigi toyed with his beautiful bowl of fresh fruit salad. He was an abstemious man and fine food and wines held little attraction for him. He never drank coffee or tea and now he sipped a glass of Badoit water saying nothing.

"It was foolhardy to carry on when the metals market was that risky," declared Warren, signaling the waiter for a second basket of muffins, "and in my opinion you're damn lucky to have come out with your shirt. As it is, you've taken a hell of a beating . . . God damn it, man, at a time like this I expected you to get out of the market, like everyone else, not take a flyer on tin!"

"I know all that, Warren," Pierluigi replied smoothly. "And now that your lecture is over, we'll get back to the point of our meeting. I need your backing in order to get into my next project. *I need five million,* Warren—and *fast.*"

The banker glanced at him from beneath bushy gray eyebrows. "Sorry,

Pierluigi, but I just can't come up with that much. Look," he added reasonably, "we've had a good relationship for a lot of years and I respect your business judgment. Commodities is a risk business, and somehow you've always known instinctively when to get in and when to get out—but this time you blew it. On the strength of our old relationship, Pierluigi, I can go for a million. No more."

"Thanks, Warren." Standing up, Pierluigi adjusted the crease in his impeccably pressed trousers and buttoned his jacket. "I'm already late for another meeting," he said quietly, "so I'm afraid I must be on my way." His voice had an icy edge and Warren glanced at him warily. Pierluigi had the reputation of being a ruthless man in business and particularly with his enemies.

"Now, Pierluigi," he protested, "you couldn't honestly expect any more—under the circumstances."

"You are quite right, of course," he replied, unsmiling, "and I have no option but to accept your offer. Thank you, Warren . . . I'll take care of the bill on my way out." Turning on his heel, he left the banker with a mouthful of blueberry muffin and a frown on his face.

Outside the sky was gray and a cold wind gusted around the corner. Pierluigi turned up the collar of his dark blue cashmere overcoat as he strode smartly along Park Avenue. He wanted to walk for a while, think a few things out before heading for Wall Street. It was still only seven-thirty in the morning and normally he was in his office at five. Very little mattered to Pierluigi Galli except work—the specific type of work that he had chosen. He enjoyed being a commodities broker because it was all one great gamble and, until a couple of months ago, he'd always come out the winner. But now he'd lost a serious part of the considerable fortune he'd amassed, and if he didn't get backing—more than Warren was prepared to offer, and Warren wasn't his only banker—then he was in serious trouble. In fact, the sum he needed was closer to twenty million than the five he'd asked from Warren. He'd been hoping to raise it from several sources, but now it looked as though he'd be pushed to come up with even a third of that amount.

A cab swept into the curb in response to his outstretched hand and he climbed in, giving his office address on Wall Street. Pierluigi never had trouble getting taxis or the best tables in New York's many smart restaurants, or the attention of headwaiters. There was an air of command about his gaunt-faced, impeccably dressed figure that somehow placed him as a master of all he surveyed, triggering a response to serve him. Yet he never overtipped and rarely smiled. He simply expected service and he got it. The traffic was jammed solid at the corner of Fifty-second and

Lexington, and with a sigh he shook open *The Wall Street Journal* and began to check the market ratings.

Much later that evening, when he was alone in his designer-decorated office where the chic dark green walls were adorned with oil paintings of English landscapes and Italian virgins, and the pedimented walnut shelves displayed rows of leather-bound books, Pierluigi picked up the newspaper again. And this time he read the ad about Poppy Mallory. It gave him a great deal to think about.

Pouring himself a glass of ten-year-old Scotch single-malt whisky from Glenfiddich, he sipped it with a smile. So, he thought, the family skeletons were emerging from the cupboard—at last. How very, very opportune.

Orlando Messenger's thick blond hair gleamed in the fitful London sunlight as he navigated the zebra crossings at Sloane Square, heading toward the large W. H. Smith shop on the south side; but it wasn't just his smooth blond hair that turned every female head—the rest of him lived up to that Nordic-looking promise. Orlando was six feet four inches tall with a natural golden tan that made his light blue eyes look even bluer. His generous mouth turned up just a fraction at the corners and his nose was slightly long and very straight.

He was back in England for an exhibition of his recent works to be held at a smart gallery in Mayfair, and he was on his way to Smith's to pick up a copy of *The Times* to check that the announcement was in there. Without bothering to take his place in line, he grabbed a copy, thrust thirty pence at the girl at the cash desk and strode from the shop, oblivious to the withering glares of the waiting customers still standing in line to pay. Weaving his way back through the traffic, he walked up Sloane Street to L'Express.

Orlando nodded to the waitresses, scanning the tables casually for familiar faces, but the café was quiet this early. Ordering a double espresso, he eased himself onto a chrome and black stool at the bar and leafed through the pages until he came to the Arts section. Yes, there it was—not as big as he'd expected but nevertheless quite prominently displayed, *Art Exhibition of the recent oils, watercolours and gouaches of Orlando Messenger to be held at the Maze Gallery, Cork Street, Mayfair, London W. I. November 15–December 5.*

Well, that was that. All that remained now was for people to show up and buy his paintings. He was certain the opening would be crowded with international names—some whose houses he had stayed in, some whom he had painted, and some he had made love to. But these were not *buyers*. These people expected things to be *given* to them! What Orlando needed now were *real* customers.

There was no money left in the Messenger family. Before he died, his father had claimed it had all been spent on Orlando's expensive education, and on his late wife's thirst for gin and long cruises and losing large sums at bridge and in the casinos. Not that there had been a great fortune in the first place, but now there was just an old and not very grand house in an unfashionable part of the countryside that, after half a century of neglect, needed a fortune spent on it to make it habitable.

Orlando scanned the newspaper and sipped his espresso, thanking God that at least now they'd learned how to make decent coffee in England. There was no avoiding the large ad for Poppy Mallory's heir, squared off with black lines so that it jumped from the page, and he stared quietly at it for some time. Then, with a smile at the waitress that he knew would melt her heart and send chills through her body, he ordered another espresso and a croissant. But it should have been champagne he was ordering, because Orlando Messenger had just seen the answer to all his problems.

Even though it was autumn, the California heat bounced off the Ventura Freeway, sending distorting little wiggles of trembling light across Lauren Hunter's windshield, like ripples in a slow-moving stream. She swung the ancient Ford Mustang along the Encino exit ramp and headed down Ventura Boulevard, reaching automatically for a Kleenex to wipe the sweat from her forehead. A car without air-conditioning in this kind of California weather was the modern-day equivalent of Dante's *Inferno*, and Lauren knew quite a lot about the *Inferno*—not only had she studied Dante's work at Redlands High, but she'd been through her own personal version of hell, and sometimes she considered she would have been better off in the simple brimstone-and-fire version . . . but she had promised herself that she would try never to think of it again; that from now on whenever the events of the past few years came into her mind she would simply force them away. Of course, the psychiatrist had said she shouldn't repress them, she should let out all the memories and fears. He'd said she should tell her story at the group-encounter sessions the way the others did, but Lauren just couldn't. It was better nobody knew.

She turned the car off Ventura, making a quick left into the underground parking lot. Easing herself from the sticky heat of the plastic seat, she smoothed her short skirt over her slender legs. She pulled the shirt that had started out crisp and freshly ironed from her damp breasts, thinking disgustedly that she might as well have been sitting in a sauna. Feeling as limp as if she'd already done a day's work instead of just beginning, Lauren slammed the car door without bothering to lock it— who would want to steal that old heap anyhow? She doubted they'd get fifty bucks for it. Dispiritedly she walked up the steps from the lot and headed for Denny's Coffee Shop, where she worked as a waitress.

She knew she'd been lucky to get the job, but sometimes when she saw the young girls lunching together or just passing time having coffee, wearing cute workout clothes or Guess jeans and Reeboks, it made her even more aware of the difference between them and her. She envied their carefree lack of responsibility and their chat about classes and clothes and dates. Her face had once been pert and eager just like theirs, but now these girls would never even consider her as part of their crowd. If they did glance at her, they saw only a worn-looking young woman with tired blue eyes and clean reddish-blond hair skewered back into a knot. Lauren might have been any age between twenty and thirty, but in fact she was only eighteen.

She washed her face and hands in the ladies' room and tidied her hair, scarcely bothering to look in the mirror. She knew what she would see and she didn't like it. There had been times when she'd thought that if it weren't for Maria, she might have ended it all. But Maria, who could so easily have been said to have wrecked her life, was also her sole joy.

Lauren smiled as she thought of the baby; she was fourteen months old now and such a pretty little girl with round cheeks and the sweetest expression in her blue eyes, and she already had a cascade of thick dark curls. Of course, they'd told her the baby would have to be adopted or fostered, right away, but once Lauren had seen her and held her, there had been no question of giving her away. She was determined she would be loved. It had meant giving up her chance of college and instead getting whatever work she could, but she knew it would be worth it.

The cool vent from the air-conditioning relaxed her immediately. It was eleven-thirty and already the lunchtime crowd was pouring in, mainly men in business suits, jackets off and ties loosened, drinking coffee and talking deals. This was Hollywood and Lauren thought that most of them looked like agents or lawyers—or smart car salesmen.

She carried out her duties, serving efficiently and with a smile until two-thirty, when at last the crowd began to thin again. With a sigh of relief she began to tidy up her tables, arranging napkins and paper place mats neatly and setting the card with the day's specials in the exact center. Picking up a discarded copy of the L.A. *Times* from the red plastic banquette, she tucked it under her arm. It would save her twenty-five cents, and she could read it later.

The day seemed even longer than usual and at four o'clock, when she finally left to pick up Maria, she felt exhausted. She would just have time to shower and give the baby her supper, then bathe her and play with her for a little while, before beginning her evening job as a cocktail waitress at a Valley nitery.

It wasn't until much later when she'd finished her shift at Teddy's Barn for Night Owls and returned home sometime after two a.m. that Lauren finally had time to herself. She paid the baby-sitter, checked Maria and changed her, and then climbed into a washed-out nightshirt and poured herself a large glass of cold milk. With a great sigh of relief she propped her feet on a chair and unfolded the newspaper.

She was in the middle of a giant bite of the almost-cold slice of pizza she'd picked up for her supper on the way home, when she noticed the black-bordered ad. *Search for an Heiress* . . . What magic words, Lauren thought wistfully, surely everyone wanted to be an heiress! She scanned the rest of the ad quickly and then sat back, a puzzled frown between her brows. Her own middle name was Mallory—Lauren *Mallory* Hunter. Her heart beat faster as she remembered that her mother had always said it was a family name . . . but more than that, she felt sure that sometime, somewhere in the vague past, she had heard about *Poppy Mallory.*

CHAPTER 3

Mike walked slowly through aisles in the County Records Office inspecting the high wooden shelves filled with oversize leather-bound books, each numbered by a year. There was just a single slender book for the year 1880, and those for the earlier years were even thinner—a reminder of how recently the area around Santa Barbara had been settled. Dust bounced from the brittle, yellowed pages, floating in the beam of sunlight that penetrated the high window as he leafed through the volume until he found the entry. It was written in spidery old-fashioned script, faded to a mocha brown.

Record of birth of a child: June 15, 1880
Sex: female
Name: Poppy Mallory
Mother: Margaret Mallory (nee James) Age 33
Father: Jeb Mallory, rancher and gentleman of this
    county. Age 54
Place of birth: The Mallory House, The Rancho Santa
    Vittoria, Lompoc County.

He leaned back in his chair with a pleased sigh. At least now he knew where Poppy had been born, and where she had died—and the names of her parents. He flipped the pages of the record book, scanning the previous entry idly.

Record of birth of a child: June 1, 1880
Sex: female
Name: Angel Irina Ampara Konstant
Mother: Rosalia Konstant (nee Abrego) Age 35
Father: Nik Konstant, rancher and gentleman
    of this county. Age 42
Place of birth: The Konstant House, The Rancho Santa
    Vittoria, Lompoc County

He turned back the page, checking. . . . Yes, he'd read it correctly. There were *two* girl children, born within a few weeks of each other and living on the same ranch. Then surely the families must have been close; the children would have played together, maybe they'd gone to school together, as young girls they might have shared the pain and joy of growing up, shared their secrets . . .

With a triumphant thud Mike slammed the book shut and replaced it on the shelf. Quite by chance, he had found a clue. Now he was sure that there was someone right here in Santa Barbara, a daughter, or maybe a grandchild, of the Konstant family, who would know about Poppy Mallory. As usual in his business, he knew the simplest method was the best. All he needed to do was look in the telephone directory under the name "Konstant"!

Hilliard Konstant was cool and a little edgy on the phone. "I don't see many people these days," he told Mike, "and I don't see any good reason why I should see you, young man." It was only when Mike mentioned that he was an author in search of a story that his attitude warmed up. "A book you say? About the Konstants?"

"The Konstants *and* the Mallorys, sir," Mike added hastily.

"Be here this evening at five. Do you know your way to the ranch?"

"I imagine it'll be hard to miss," Mike replied, envisaging unbroken acres of pasture. He was wrong.

The wide Rancho Road, cambered to drain the heavy spring rains, split through the middle of sprawling housing developments on what had once been the Rancho Santa Vittoria. Walled tracts with names like Vittoria Oaks and El Rancho revealed glimpses of pretty suburban houses and neat lawns. Occasionally there was the massive spread of an ancient oak or the remains of a hazelnut thicket, or a hundred yards or so of split-rail fence around a paddock with grazing ponies, as a reminder that in Poppy Mallory's day, all this had been acres of pasture, with cattle and sheep, and real cowboys.

Mike drove the rented Suzuki four-wheel-drive through the endless winding suburban avenues until the paved road ended suddenly at the crest of a hill, changing into a single blacktop track bordered on each side with old poplars, so tall, they looked to be scraping the bright blue sky. A wrought-iron arch bore a sign THE RANCHO SANTA VITTORIA and the brand NK.

After half a mile the drive ended in a courtyard in front of an old white hacienda, with a riot of clematis and bougainvillaea spilling from its verandahs. A blue-tiled fountain sprayed sparkling arcs of water into the quiet sunlight and a Japanese gardener glanced up curiously, bowing to him before returning to his labor of love in the flower beds. As he walked to the house Mike noticed that everything was well kept; the grounds were immaculate and the worn terra-cotta tile steps had been polished until they shone like lacquer. The front door stood open, and as he peered inside a masculine voice called testily,

"Come in, come in. It's Mr. Preston, I assume?"

The cool tiled hall seemed gloomy after the bright sunlight, but still it would have been impossible to miss Hilliard Konstant—even though he was in a wheelchair. He was well over six feet, with the shoulders of an ex-football player. His sparse white hair had been combed carefully over his balding crown, and his pale blue eyes beneath their bristling white brows seemed to look into the distance beyond Mike, as though he were already impatient for him to leave.

"Come on in then, hurry up . . ." Hilliard said crabbily, wheeling himself through a pair of oaken doors into his sanctum. "I expect you'd like a drink while you tell me why you're wasting my time."

Books filled the walls from floor to ceiling, and some—obviously a valuable collection of ancient volumes—were locked safely behind glass doors. A fire burned in the enormous stone grate even though the evening was warm, and over the mantel hung a portrait of a tall, broad-shouldered young man with wheat-blond hair and Hilliard's pale eyes. He had his arm around a pretty Spanish-looking woman whose laughing dark eyes twinkled mischievously.

"I know, I know what you're thinking," Hilliard said irritably. "*Of course* I look like him. He's my grandfather—Nikolai Konstantinov—and that's my grandmother. He was Russian and she was Mexican—an extraordinary combination, don't you think, for that era? It was painted about 1885, I believe."

He handed him a small glass of dry white sherry. "Manzanilla," he said, watching eagerly as Mike took a sip. It was wincingly dry and Hilliard cackled with laughter as Mike closed his eyes, coughing. "It's not a drink for pansy-boys, but it's better than all your fancy whiskeys. That—and a glass or two of good wine with supper—are among the last few pleasures left to me." He fixed Mike suddenly with a pale blue stare. "Exactly what is it you want to know about the Konstants?"

Mike ran a hand apprehensively through his rough dark hair; Hilliard Konstant was a tough customer. "To tell you the truth," he said, "I'm a man in search of a story. There was an ad in the L.A. *Times* today—some lawyer in Geneva is searching for Poppy Mallory's heirs. . . ."

"I wondered when you'd get round to telling me," the old man commented dryly. "I can tell you this, Mr. Preston, there's not much I know about the Mallorys that you couldn't find out from the Santa Barbara Historical Society. The two families were friends. More than that—they were partners. But the Mallorys disappeared from here long before my time. I never asked why, I thought they'd just died off—the way we all do. I'm the last of the Konstants, y'know. We were never a good 'breeding' family. What there was of us have mostly perished in wars—World War Two, Korea, Vietnam—my own son died there, and *that* killed his mother. I've been alone ever since. No, no," he said anticipating Mike's question, "it wasn't a war that did this to me, it was a stupid, knuckleheaded horse. I was playing 'rancher,' you see, filling in my time here . . . after it had all happened."

The old man stared through the window at the view across the valley. "Sometimes I wonder, if my father hadn't sold off the ranch, what my life might have been like? I loved animals as a boy, loved riding horses, mending fences, playing cowboys for real . . . of course, all this was so big then—it was still a real ranch. It was only as I grew up that it became just a big backyard." He smiled approvingly as Mike finished the manzanilla. "Acquired the taste yet?" he asked with a grin. Without waiting for a reply he turned his chair abruptly. "Come with me," he commanded.

He stopped in front of a pair of framed documents hanging in the hall. Mike could see that one was written on cracked yellow parchment in the same sort of elaborate spidery writing as in the books recording the births at the Records Office.

"That is the original title deed to the Rancho Santa Vittoria. It amounted to just fifty acres. Exactly what we're left with now! Ironic, isn't it? You know the old saying—rags to rags in three generations?" His laughter had a hollow ring as he added, "Not that it matters anymore, when I die this'll all go to my grandmother's family, the Abregos. There's dozens of 'em out there somewhere." He waved a hand vaguely across the valley. "Rich as Croesus too. Of course, they don't need it—except maybe for family sentiment." He coughed impatiently, as if to hide an emotion he was loath to let Mike see. "Now this," he said, pointing at the other framed document, "this is the original partnership agreement between Nik Konstant and Jeb Mallory."

"They were partners?"

"Of course they were partners, why else would they live practically next door to each other and farm the same land? Read it, will you?"

The yellowed piece of card was headed, CLANCEY'S IRISH SALOON, KEARNEY STREET, SAN FRANCISCO, and underneath, AMERICAN AND IMPORTED BEERS AND ALES . . . A DOZEN DIFFERENT WHISKEYS . . . FREE LUNCH COUNTER NOON TILL TWO DAILY. In the center was written in a bold hand: *Jeb Mallory and Nik*

Konstant are equal partners in the Rancho Santa Vittoria and all its lands and livestock. Dated this tenth day of April, 1856.

Jeb Mallory had signed his name with a flourish, but Nik's name was written with the careful letters of a man just learning to write.

"My grandfather was fresh off the boat from Russia," Hilliard explained, "he was still learning English. Jeb Mallory Americanized his name. As you see, they became partners while drinking in a saloon. It's always been said that Nikolai learned a lot from Jeb Mallory—and probably more than he'd bargained for."

"Such as?"

He shrugged. "If I ever knew, young man, I've forgotten. I'm seventy-four years old and at this age you have enough trouble just keeping up with today, never mind the past. Still, I expect it's all in there, if you're interested enough to look." He gestured toward the library. "Everything the Konstants ever wrote is there, neatly bound and put away. There's probably an old journal or two— women always kept those things in the old days, y'know, gave 'em something to do, I guess, writing up all the births, deaths, and marriages. . . . It's no good for my eyes, all faded ink and crabby writing. I was a soldier, y'see, Mr. Preston, an outdoorsman, never had time for all this chitchat. That's why I'm so bad at it now."

Mike was itching to get his hands on all that untapped material, but the old man suddenly looked very tired. "Maybe I should come back tomorrow?" he suggested.

"Nonsense, nonsense." Hilliard's pale eyes were suddenly beseeching. "I haven't had a chat like this for years, and I don't mind admitting I've enjoyed myself. There's no one comes here much anymore, y'know," he added sadly, "just the Japanese gardener you saw—and he doesn't speak English—not *proper* English. And, of course, there's Mary, my housekeeper, a nice woman but she watches television all the time . . . I can't stand it myself. Have another sherry, won't you?" he said eagerly, wheeling his chair back into the library. "Tell you what, if you want to go through all this stuff, why don't you just come and stay a while? You can work late at night, all by yourself—isn't that what you writers like to do? And then you can ask me questions anytime you want."

"It's a deal," Mike said, hardly able to believe his luck. But as he shook his hand, the gleam in the old man's eyes made him wonder uncomfortably what he was up to.

The big old house was silent but for the ticking of a clock in the hall as Mike pushed the old-fashioned leather chair from the table. He frowned as the casters screeched from rust and long disuse. It was three-thirty a.m. and he'd been reading in the library since eight that evening, when Hilliard Konstant had retired to bed. The big oak table was littered with books and papers, mostly old ledgers and documents relating to the running of the ranch, but they were not what he was seeking.

He paced the plum-colored carpet restlessly, too alert to go to bed and sleep. The library was thirty feet long and twenty-five wide and lined wall-to-wall with books. Hilliard had given him no clue as to where to begin, he'd simply said, "It's all there somewhere, young man. Help yourself!" Sometimes Mike would catch Hilliard looking at him with a sardonic twinkle in his pale eyes, as though he was enjoying some secret joke, and he wondered if he knew more than he was telling—like *where* to look on those walls of shelves!

He wandered restlessly through the hall into the huge drawing room that ran the full length of the house. It was like being in a time warp. Hilliard had told him that the walls were still hung with the same faded blue damask chosen by Rosalia Konstant more than eighty years before, though the matching silk that had once covered sofas and chairs had been replaced sometime later by a mixture of cheerful flower prints. Mike stared at the twin portraits of a boy and a girl hanging over the mantel. These were Rosalia and Nik Konstant's two children: Gregorius—always known as Greg—and his sister, Angel, the girl who had been born within a few weeks of Poppy. He knew that Greg was Hilliard's father, but the old man had told him very little about Angel, except she was famous for her looks.

Even at nine years old, Angel had been a beauty. She was small, with fine bones, her father's enormous pale blue eyes and a cloud of softly curling blond hair. She was wearing a pink ruffled dress and held a tiny black dog with a matching pink ribbon, and she was smiling sweetly but confidently at the artist. *Angel and Trotty 1889* was inscribed at the base of the baroque gilt frame. Mike would have bet that Angel grew up to be a charmer; it was all there in the picture—the confidence in her beauty and in her position as daughter of the rich, landowning Konstants.

Sixteen-year-old Greg was tall, dark-haired, and handsome, with his mother's laughing brown eyes. He was a sturdy lad who had wanted his portrait painted outdoors so it could include his favorite horse. He was leaning on the paddock fence, holding a wide-brimmed Mexican riding hat in one hand, while the thumb of the other was linked jauntily through a leather belt with a chased-silver buckle, of which he was obviously proud. In the paddock behind him a beautiful chestnut gelding with a white blaze on his forehead, grazed contentedly. *Greg with Vassily 1889* was the legend at the bottom of the matching gilt frame.

Greg had a cheerful grin and that direct Konstant gaze, and Mike stared hard at the brother and sister, wondering what lay behind such confident facades, and whether life had lived up to their obvious expectations.

He walked on through the shuttered dining room in search of a cold beer, into the original adobe part of the house, built by the Indians two hundred years ago. Now it was a gleaming, efficient kitchen, but the old open fireplace where an Indian servant had once cooked Nik Konstant's meals still remained in the corner.

Mike poked the glowing embers with his foot as he settled in an old high-backed rocker, a can of Miller in his hand. Despite the modern appliances, this room felt different. Sitting here, staring into the embers, he might have been living a century ago . . . with Nik and Rosalia, Greg and Angel. *And Poppy Mallory!*

Mike supposed he must have been dozing when the answer came to him . . . but of course, it was quite logical. He had been looking in the wrong place. What he was seeking would never be found in a library. Where else did every family store its discarded treasures and its secrets—but in the attics!

"I wondered how long it'd be before you thought of the attic," Hilliard said, grinning maliciously. "Nobody's been up there for years, but anyway there's only a load of old junk. If there'd been anything of value one of the Konstants would have sold it by now!"

"I'm not looking for valuables, sir," Mike protested. "I'm searching for information."

"Information? Bah . . . you'll find nothing up there but a few old theater programs and dance cards—and a lot of moth-eaten clothes." He relented suddenly. "Still, if you want to . . ."

Hilliard was wrong—the clothes weren't moth-eaten. But there were lots of them, all beautifully folded away between tissue paper in enormous old chests and steamer trunks, plastered with the labels of long-ago Atlantic liners and continental hotels. Mike rummaged through trunks of lace tea gowns and stiff silk afternoon dresses, sneezing as he shook out a cloak of golden brown otter skins that had once been soft and supple but was now dry and cracked, though the taffeta lining had kept its gay, scarlet color. There were evening dresses embroidered with glinting beads and dulled pearls, and a magnificent blue silk chiffon gown with the label WORTH, PARIS sewn inside.

After a couple of hours he'd found nothing of any use and he slammed the last trunk shut exasperatedly. It was a collection worthy of a museum but it had got him no farther along the trail to Poppy Mallory.

Brushing a thick coating of dust from the lid of an old school desk, he ran his finger across the carved initials *AK*, imagining the pretty Angel, bored with her lessons, etching them into the soft pine with a hairpin. Inside was a collection of girlish mementos, a pile of old theater and concert programs, a bunch of dance cards with tiny gilt pencils still attached, a crumbling posy of pressed flowers. Then, at last, several batches of letters tied with ribbon. And underneath was a blue leather book imprinted in faded gilt: *Rosalia Konstant–Her Journal—Vol I, 1863.* There were more—*Vol II & III*—and then a thin pink velvet book: *Angel Konstant's Journal, Age 12–18.* And at last, a plain brown leather book inscribed *Margaret Mallory–Her Journal—1873.*

Margaret Mallory! Mike's hair stood on end as he ran his dusty hand excitedly over it.

Hurrying from the attic, he laid out his finds on the library table, arranging the dance cards in small piles alongside the packets of letters, and then the precious journals. With a satisfied sigh, he began to read.

Two days later, he refolded the final letter, retied the red ribbon carefully, and sat back gazing out of the window, puzzled.

"A glass of the finest manzanilla for your thoughts?" suggested Hilliard from the doorway.

Spinning around, Mike smiled at him. "Sorry, I was miles away . . . or rather years!"

"Well?" Hilliard wheeled himself across the room to the drinks table and poured two glasses of sherry. "Have you solved the mystery of Poppy Mallory's heir?"

Mike ran his hand thoughtfully through his hair, frowning. "No . . . but it's a beginning. . . ." The funny thing was that they had all written so much about Poppy, he felt he almost knew her—or at least the young Poppy. Because quite suddenly, she had disappeared from the pages of those journals as though she'd never existed.

He thought Hilliard would never go to bed, but as darkness fell the old man finally said good night. Turning his wheelchair at the library door, he smiled sardonically. "I think you've got your work cut out for you, Mike Preston," he said with an edge of bitterness to his voice. "Nothing in life is ever as simple as it seems—that's my experience, anyhow." Turning abruptly, he wheeled himself along the hall to his room.

Mike stared after him, puzzled. Then he looked at the little pile of letters and journals on the library table. "Okay, Poppy Mallory," he said determinedly, "you've hooked me. . . . I've got to know what happened. And when I do, I'm gonna tell the whole world about you!"

He knew he would have to use his imagination to fill in the gaps left by the journals, but now he had a pretty shrewd grasp of the characters involved. Inserting a fresh sheet of paper into his typewriter, he wrote, "In the beginning, there was Nikolai Konstantinov and Jeb Mallory . . ."

CHAPTER *4*

Jeb Mallory was celebrating his thirtieth birthday alone in Clancey's Saloon, Kearney Street, San Francisco. He drank his third Irish whiskey quickly, followed by a beer chaser, and signaled the bartender for another. The memory of his turbulent passage through the years from a raw fourteen-year-old lad in southwestern Ireland, learning his craft of a gambler the hard way, to a much traveled professional gambling man wise in the ways of the world, did not depress him, simply because he barely thought about it. Jeb was a man of the moment. When he was asked, he always claimed he had no past, but the truth was, he preferred to forget it—or at least to embroider it to suit the company he was in. Not that those years had been bad ones—there had always been plenty of excitement. He'd had a great many winning streaks and a few fast losses, as well as more than any man's fair share of beautiful women, most of them with the luxurious red hair and transparent white skin that was his downfall. And it was true that easy money ran all too quickly through his fingers. But the plain fact was, the highs had not been high enough and the lows had been merely boring, and Jeb still craved the ultimate excitement of the big game . . . the one where a fortune rested on the turn of a card.

Calling for another drink, he folded his lean height against the wall, watching the poker game in progress. His face was impassive, but inside he was seething with frustrated excitement. He had been playing poker since the age of nine, perfecting the art in the poor shebeens and shabbier taverns of his native land. Now he played on three levels: skill, intuition—and an uncanny ability to sense the underlying excitement of a man holding good cards. Jeb was a master of the bluff, a connoisseur of character—and a man for whom the game meant more than the money. His only trouble was that right now he didn't have *enough* money to join this game!

There was a certain man at the table whose progress Jeb had been following for three nights now—a rancher, up from the hill country near Lompoc. He'd been playing a flashy game, placing large bets and out-bluffing the others, guffawing loudly when he won—which he did most of the time. The sound of his winner's laugh was a constant irritant, and Jeb ached either to ram a fist into his florid face or to take him on at the tables. He turned away with a shrug; he would do neither. If he wanted to get back into any game around here, he'd have to get hold of some money—and fast.

He had exactly twenty dollars in his pocket and that didn't suit his extravagant way of life at all! He grinned ruefully as he remembered the girl who'd stolen his billfold from the hotel room a week ago. He couldn't blame her—after all, he'd left it lying around on the dresser, stuffed with bank notes. He'd just laughed it off as his stupidity and her good luck, thinking maybe it was a fair price anyway.

He turned his attention to a young man sitting alone at a table by the window. He was just a boy, really, but he was built like an ox, six feet four or five, with a massive torso and powerful shoulders. A lock of thick straight blond hair fell across his brow and his broad-boned face was clean-shaven. His eyes were of such a pale blue, they seemed to reflect the light, hiding his expression. Jeb could tell he was a foreigner—and not long off the boat. He was all alone and he guessed he had his savings from the old country strapped safely in a money belt around his waist. Sipping a beer, he thought out his plan before going over and taking a seat opposite him. "Jeb Mallory," he said, offering his hand with a friendly smile.

The young blond giant shook his hand warily. "Nikolai Konstantinov," he replied, "from Arkhangelsk." Just speaking the name of his hometown sent a throb of longing through Nikolai, and he blinked away the surge of emotion that threatened to crack his stoic facade.

"Arkhangelsk, eh? And where might that be?" inquired Jeb, lighting a thin cheroot and settling comfortably in the high-backed wooden chair.

"Is in Russia."

"Now there's a place I've never been. Tell me boy-o, what's it like?"

"Is better than here," Nikolai sighed, observing the gray fog pressing dankly against the windows of the smoky saloon. He recalled the small, cramped wooden house by the River Dvina that had always felt so cozy on the frozen black nights of Arkhangelsk's long winter. But he knew he was romanticizing things—there was no security in that house. The Konstantinov family was very poor and that was the reason he was here now, in San Francisco. "I am eighteen now and I will seek my fortune like other men," Nikolai had told his weeping mother as he left, "I've read of the gold out there in western Amerika—gold that is waiting for any man strong enough to take it. One day I shall bring all that California gold home to you, Matushka, and you will live like a princess, just the way my father always promised you."

"Let me buy you a whiskey," suggested Jeb.

Nikolai's ice-blue eyes returned from scanning the frozen plains of Russia and met Jeb's suspiciously. "Who are you?" he demanded. "Why you buy me drink?"

Jeb shrugged. "Just two foreigners in a strange town," he replied, "a friendly gesture, that's all. And you look as though you could use a friend."

"Where you from?" asked Nikolai as Jeb signaled the bartender for two Irish whiskeys with beer chasers.

Jeb Mallory grinned. "The west of Ireland . . . one of County Clare's finest sons," he replied. "But I'm a man of the world, Nikolai, a man of the moment. What you see—here and now—is what you get."

Nikolai tossed down the whiskey quickly and then studied his new acquaintance over the rim of his beer mug. He doubted that such fine, regular features and cheerful bright blue eyes could conceal anything really wicked in Jeb's past, though he had no doubt at all that this handsome black-haired man must have left a trail of broken hearts all the way from the west coast of Ireland to the west coast of Amerika. "Then you are here to seek gold also?" he asked, thawing beneath Jeb's friendly gaze.

"You've been out to the gold fields then, boy-o?"

"Not yet. First I earn money for living. Is a construction site on Union Street. I carry bricks up and down scaffolding. Is hard work and dangerous—a man could fall—but money is good." Nikolai sipped his beer, thinking of the dollars strapped around his waist in a webbing belt sewn for him by his mother. He'd discovered early that having money in your pocket brought its own kind of comfort and dignity, and to him that money belt felt warmer than a new jacket on his back or a grand meal in his stomach. "Soon I have enough to go search for gold," he added eagerly.

Calling for more drinks, Jeb gazed mournfully at the pattern of small circular stains on the polished surface of the table. "I hate to be the one to tell you this, boy-o," he said sadly, "but if it's your fortune you're seeking, you're looking at the wrong sort of field." Nikolai gazed at him blankly as he leaned closer. "You want to see a rich man?" Jeb murmured, "take a look at the rancher at the table over there, the one in the chamois jacket and high leather boots. Now there's a *rich* man! And you want to know how he got rich, my friend? He bought himself some land from the old Spanish grants down by the Santa Ynez River, and then he put sheep on that land and maybe cattle too—and then all he had to do was sit back and watch the profits grow. And with those profits he bought *more* land. *Land*, Nikolai Konstantinov. That's what you and I should be carving out for ourselves—a great chunk of beautiful California land . . . acres, hectares, leagues of land. Land to put cattle on, land to graze sheep, land for building houses and cities . . ." He waved his hand and fresh drinks appeared in front of them as if by magic.

Nikolai knocked back the whiskey eagerly. "But the gold . . . ?" he began.

"Boy-o, a handful of gold dust dredged up by the sweat of your brow and at the risk of your life is not going to make your fortune! Too many others have tried it before you. Believe me, Nikolai, that rancher over there is far wealthier than a hundred gold prospectors. Now, I'm telling you this in confidence . . . I aim to get myself some of that land . . . stick with me, boy-o, and you could be rich too."

Nikolai's pale blue eyes were fixed on Jeb's as he listened raptly.

"There's no more beauteous a sight than rolling acres of green," Jeb continued, "just waiting for a herd of cattle or a flock of sheep . . . and just waiting to put the dollars in a man's pockets. Sure now, you and I could buy ourselves a fine stake down there, boy-o. The Rancho . . . Rancho Santa Vittoria, we'd call it . . . and we could build a big adobe mansion on our land, with a grand piano in the parlor and a fine cook in the kitchen. I tell you, boy-o, we could have ourselves an Irish-Russian castle atop a California hill!"

Jeb paused for breath, tossing back the whiskey, his bright blue eyes gleaming with excitement beneath the strong straight dark brows. "And just wait till you see some of those Mexican girls, my friend—all lustrous dark hair and laughing brown eyes and skin the color of summer peaches." His eyes creased with merriment as he drank up and ordered another for each of them.

Nikolai didn't know whether it was the vision of the rolling acres dotted with cattle and sheep, or the adobe mansion with the grand piano —or even the beauteous dark-eyed girls—but somehow Jeb's ability to conjure up pictures in words made their future together seem a reality and his suspicions disappeared like the chill Bay fog under a hot sun. "How?" he demanded excitedly. "How you get land?" The barman had placed another drink in front of him and he downed it almost without noticing.

Jeb met his eyes with a sigh. *"That,* Nikolai, is a problem. You see, I know the rancher over there has land to sell, but I'm afraid I don't have enough to buy it. Not without a partner, that is."

"I be your partner," declared Nikolai. "I have money saved . . . one hundred and fifty dollars. Is enough for my share?"

Jeb's eyes narrowed as Nikolai began unstrapping the money belt from under his shirt. The sum was less than he had hoped, but it would have to do. "Boy-o, I couldn't possibly take your hard-earned money," he said solemnly, "it just wouldn't be right."

"But we be partners," stammered Nikolai, "this land—it will be ours . . ."

"Well, then, if you insist," agreed Jeb reluctantly, "but let's make that *equal* partners now, I wouldn't dream of having you take less."

"Equal partners," beamed Nikolai, his broad face flushed from the drink.

"Now wait just a moment," said Jeb, taking a pen from his breast pocket, "we'd better put this in writing so you'll be sure it's all above-board."

Taking a cardboard sign from the counter that proclaimed CLANCEY'S IRISH SALOON, KEARNEY STREET, SAN FRANCISCO, AMERICAN AND IM-PORTED BEERS AND ALES . . . A DOZEN DIFFERENT WHISKEYS . . . FREE LUNCH COUNTER FROM NOON TILL TWO DAILY, he turned it over and began to write . . . *Jeb Mallory and* . . . He paused, frowning. "It's no good you know," he muttered, "no good at all."

Nikolai choked on his whiskey as his dreams suddenly threatened to disappear. "What you mean is no good?" he demanded anxiously.

"Your name. It's too foreign-sounding, too confusing. You can't be a rancher with a name like Konstantinov!" Jeb thought for a while and then said, "Nikolas Konstant—Nik Konstant! Now that's a good solid-sounding name. An *American* name! How do you like it?"

"Nik Konstant," agreed Nikolai, his own voice sounding suddenly strange, ringing in his ears as if it were a million miles away.

"Agreed, then." *Jeb Mallory and Nik Konstant are equal partners in the Rancho Santa Vittoria and all its lands and livestock. Dated this tenth day of April, 1856.* Signing his name with a flourish, Jeb handed the pen to Nik. "Sign right here, boy-o," he urged, watching as Nikolai, still unused to the American alphabet, signed his new name slowly, forming each letter with care. Then Jeb handed the barman a dollar and asked him to sign as witness.

"There, that's settled," he declared, handing Nik the card. "You keep this document and meet me at Marco's Livery Stables tomorrow morning—at dawn. Order two horses to be ready and waiting and we'll make an early start." He glanced at Nik, whose face looked pale and spiked with sweat. "You're looking a bit worse for the drink, boy-o," he commented, "better get yourself back to your room and catch some sleep."

"Marco's Livery Stables," murmured Nik, stumbling from the table, his thick corn-blond hair falling over his eyes.

"At dawn," agreed Jeb, taking his arm and leading him to the door. He watched impassively as the young man, placing his feet carefully and with great concentration, walked slowly away down Kearney Street. "Good luck, boy-o," he murmured as he turned back into Clancey's Saloon.

The poker game in the corner looked as though it had settled in for the night and with a hundred and fifty dollars in his pocket, he was set to beat the big-bluffing rancher. After all, hadn't he just proven that luck was with him tonight? The luck of the Irish, he thought, grinning, as he took a seat at the table and lit a thin brown cheroot. With that and his talent with the cards, how could he possibly lose?

Nik had been waiting for more than three hours. The sun had long since dispersed the early morning fog and was painting the yard at Marco's Livery Stables a thin spring-gold as he peered down the road for the hundredth time for any sign of Jeb. He felt sick as he thought of his hard-earned money, of how much it would have meant to his family, and of how, filled with wishes and dreams, he'd handed over that money so trustingly to Jeb last night!

Cursing the liquor for turning him into a fool, he stared at the smart yellow brougham as it swung into the yard. The coachman hurried to open the door and Jeb stepped out, still elegant in last night's attire of crisp white shirt and black jacket, and with a large, fragrant cigar in his hand. With a nonchalant wave at Nik he turned to smile at the woman in the carriage. Nik saw that she had flame-red hair and looked about thirty years old, and she was amazingly beautiful. She looked flushed and out of breath, and as she leaned forward her yellow satin dress revealed such an expanse of soft white bosom that his heart lurched giddily.

Jeb ran his hand through her rich red hair and with a final smoldering kiss he stepped back and slammed the carriage door, waving as the coachman swung the elegant yellow brougham back through the gates.

"I . . . I thought you were not coming," Nik stammered, feeling the chill sweat of relief trickling down his spine.

"Just a bit late, that's all." Jeb pulled a crowded billfold from his jacket. "Here, boy-o, here's your stake money back, plus a little extra. I got lucky last night and I'd like you to share in it," he added magnanimously.

"But . . . is five hundred dollars!" gasped Nick, counting the money quickly. "You give me money so we are no longer partners?"

Jeb puffed his cigar uneasily as the boy fixed him with a stricken pale-blue gaze. "I like you, boy-o, so I'm going to tell you the exact truth," he said, narrowing his eyes against the curling cigar smoke. "I'm a gambling man," he said bluntly, "and, as you probably know, Nik, there isn't anything in the world can cure a man of that affliction! The barman tipped me off earlier in the week that there was this bunch of fellas, up from the ranches, spending money and having a good time in the city—and all of 'em big gamblers. And there was I, without enough to me name to join the easiest game in town! And there you were—and somehow I just knew you'd have a few bucks strapped in a belt around your middle. I'm telling you honestly, boy-o, I've never seen a real ranch in my life—but I'm a good man with words. It sounded pretty good to you, didn't it? Good enough to part you from your hard-earned money. My mother always said I should try for the priesthood—I'd have told a grand sermon."

Nik's face flushed an angry red and Jeb stepped back quickly as he raised his fist. "Now wait a minute," he pleaded, "to be sure you were taken for a fool—we all are at your young age. But let this be a warning because there's plenty more men ready and eager to part a fool from his money. Now, now . . . hold back there, boy-o," he said nervously as Nik grabbed him by the collar, "I'm here, aren't I? Didn't I just give you back your money—and more?"

Nik dropped his fist, staring at the money still crumpled in his hand. "Then we are not partners?" he whispered, his dream shattered. "There is no ranch?"

"A hundred and fifty bucks wouldn't buy you much land, boy-o," Jeb said dryly, "not even down there in the Santa Ynez Valley."

Nik turned away as a great surge of despair hit him and tears threatened to spill from his eyes. He'd been fooled not only out of his money but also into believing he'd found a friend—and a partner. . . .

Jeb watched him as he contemplated his luck last night. It had been strange, really, the way it had all worked out. Not only had he won a packet—but the dream he'd conjured up to part Nik from his money had been turned into reality on the last desperate bluff of a beaten man. He'd intended to convert it into hard cash at the bank, but now he wondered. He noted the breadth of Nik's shoulders, the sheer power and strength of his torso and arms, rippling with muscles. He knew the boy was honest; he was certain he would be trustworthy—and he sure as hell would be a hard worker. And when you suddenly found yourself the owner of a ranch, what better qualities could a man need in a partner?

"Come on, partner," he called, leaping onto the waiting horse. It skittered sideways across the cobbles, fresh and eager to be off. "I forgot to mention that your stake in the poker game also won us a ranch. . . ."

Hope dawned in Nik's eyes and then faded. "You fooling me. Again!" he said bitterly.

"No more fooling, boy-o. I told you, I'm a lucky man. Now come on, will ya—or do I get somebody else to be my partner?"

Nik was on his horse in a flash. He didn't know whether to believe the Irishman or not, but he would follow him anyway, because Jeb Mallory had that magical quality of *almost* making dreams come true. And even if they weren't quite what they seemed, somehow, when you were with him, it didn't seem to matter.

From the crest of the Santa Rosa hills to the Santa Ynez River snaking along the valley miles below, lay acres of rolling green pasture. Searching the horizon to the west, Nik could just make out a ridge of paler, golden-green young grain, while behind them were the dark shadows of canyons where grizzly bear lurked, emerging at nightfall in search of prey. In the distance, a coyote howled, and as if on cue, a breeze rippled the grasses, forcing dazzling silver reflections from the fast-moving river.

The valley was lush and green from the tumultuous early spring rains, and its spacious serenity seemed to promise a life impossible in ice-locked, darkly forested Arkhangelsk. Nik knew then that Jeb's words were not mere dreams. This was truly the land of plenty. *This* was the richness of Amerika.

As Jeb stared across the valley, for the first time in years he recalled the old cottage in Ilskerry, in Ireland. He saw in his mind the bare, malnourished earth, as poor and starved as the people who scraped their existence from it. He remembered his father—a hunched, defeated figure at only thirty . . . his own age now. He thought of his mother, struggling to grow a few flowers, a patch of pathetic beauty in the rutted earth by the cottage door. And he compared all of his memories with the lush greenness he saw before him. Sniffing the deep, moist fragrance of fertile earth, he imagined it dotted with sheep and cattle, seeing it productive—*earning him a fortune*!

Swinging from the saddle, he unfurled the roll of title deeds with a flourish. "We may not own all you can see," he said, grinning at Nik, "but fifty of these acres can now be called the Rancho Santa Vittoria." And then—because Jeb always played a big game—he added, "It's enough for a *beginning* anyhow." Nik grinned back at him as he shook his hand.

"You know something, boy-o," added Jeb with a laugh, "my old father used to say that nothing comes to you in this life without hard work. It seems I've been proving him wrong ever since."

CHAPTER 5

1 8 5 6 – 1 8 7 3 , C A L I F O R N I A

The old adobe house had been built under the curve of the hill. It was shaded with sycamore and oaks and had only two rooms. In one of them an old Indian, wrapped in a striped serape in heat and in cold, cooked smoky-tasting meals over an open fire; the other room was used for sleeping.

Nik spent the first few weeks just riding alone across their land and marveling at his luck, while Jeb went off to Santa Barbara to "scout out the scene" and to register their title deeds. Nik was not lonely, though he went for days without seeing another soul, camping under the stars at night with one ear cocked for the coyote's howl and the stealthy rustle of prowling bears. But nothing disturbed his solitude and he was happier than he had ever been in his life.

When Jeb returned, it was with the news that he was going to Missouri to buy sheep and that he would need Nik's five hundred dollars to do so. "How many sheep we buy for that?" demanded Nik excitedly.

"Trust me, boy-o," Jeb replied evasively, "we'll have plenty of sheep."

There were three thousand of them. Nik didn't bother to ask how this time, he just got on with the job of being a rancher and looking after his sheep while Jeb negotiated for more acres of grazing land.

At first Jeb seemed content with his new role, riding the ranch with Nik, but after a few months the old restlessness took over and he began to spend more time in Santa Barbara, and when that proved too genteel and small-town for him, he headed back to the bright lights of San Francisco. Sometimes Nik wouldn't see him for weeks and then suddenly he'd be back again, looking tired and pleased with himself, and more often than not with a wad of bank notes in his vest pocket. But he didn't talk anymore about the big ranch house with the grand piano in the parlor and the fine cook in the kitchen, and Nik realized that his friend was too restless ever to belong totally to life on the ranch. He shrugged off the problem easily. No matter, he was strong enough to do the work of two.

As the years passed Nik planted grain on his land and built huge barns in which to store it. He hired the best shepherds in the world—from the Basque country in Spain—to care for their sheep, and Mexican vaqueros to ride the range and tend their fine new cattle. He erected pens for the animals and he built long, low sheds to house the workers. He worked hard and for interminable hours and he loved every minute of it. He never felt tired, he was as strong as an ox, and the physical work gradually muscled out his body and his young, blond good looks hardened into those of an outdoorsman, with searching pale blue eyes in a stern, sun- and wind-tanned face. He sent money home to his family in Russia, but somehow he was never able to shake himself free of the constant round of work at the ranch to return home to visit them.

Most of the time Nik was too busy and too tired even to think about women, and when Jeb came to Santa Barbara he was always the perfect gentleman, raising his hat politely to the maidens and their mothers, and setting young hearts aflutter beneath demure high-necked blouses of white lace.

Jeb kept his women in San Francisco, but it was Nik who fell in love first—and with a girl who was not only lovely, she was a "catch"! He was just twenty-five and Rosalia Abrego was the eighteen-year-old daughter of the owner of one of the greatest cattle ranches in the Lompoc valley. And her father was not inclined to see her throw herself away on some strange Russian whom nobody knew anything about!

The two had met at Loomis's Saddlery Store in Santa Barbara and it took only one sidelong glance from Rosalia's lustrous, dark-lashed brown eyes, and a faint but charming smile in his direction, to break Nik's shyness and interrupt his seven-year love affair with the Rancho Santa Vittoria.

Lovesick, he spent all his time hanging around the saddlery store or lingering on the stoop of the small hotel on State Street, hoping for a glimpse of Rosalia. When he finally saw her again, he plucked up courage to pass the time of day and she surprised him by inviting him to a picnic she was giving with some young friends out at the beach. Rosalia's bubbling warmth made up for Nik's shyness; she seemed to talk enough for the two of them. And a few weeks later, when he finally kissed her in the shade of a grove of sycamores, they knew they were in love.

Don Jose was a very rich man and he viewed the romance with suspicion, but after investigating the young Russian and hearing nothing but praise for his hard work and the prospering Rancho Santa Vittoria, he gave the union his blessing.

The wedding, with Jeb as the handsome best-man breaking countless feminine hearts, was the occasion of a grand fiesta, but afterward Nik was unable to take his bride home to the Rancho Santa Vittoria because her father refused to allow Rosalia to begin her married life in a two-room adobe hut. Instead, they rented a suite of rooms at the Arlington Hotel, where Nik joined her as often as he could escape work on the ranch. Meanwhile, two new ranch houses were being built on the property, one on the site of the old Indian house for Jeb; and the other around an old adobe house in the middle of the extra two thousand acres of land, running concurrently with the ranch, given by Jose Abrego to his daughter as a wedding gift.

When it was finished the Konstant House at the Rancho Santa Vittoria was one of the finest homes in the Lompoc valley, but Nik's proudest possession of all was the partnership document, written on the old saloon card, now framed in gilt and hanging in the front hall for everyone to see. His joy was dimmed by the news of the death of his mother; but he still continued to send his sisters money regularly. The Konstantinovs of Arkhangelsk were no longer poor.

Rosalia often rode the ranch with Nik, sitting astride and wearing suede chaps like the vaqueros and helping with the new calves and lambs, but she also supervised her new home carefully. There was now a good cook in the kitchen and fine meals were served at their table and Nik lost his shyness and became an affable host to Rosalia's friends and family. Nik Konstant was a happy man—except for just one thing. He'd hoped for a child to be born quickly—a son to bear his name. But two years passed and still Rosalia did not become pregnant, and though she said nothing, there was a worried look in her eyes.

The Mallory House on the Rancho Santa Vittoria remained empty for most of the time—though there was now a grand piano in the parlor and fine dark mahogany furniture in its many rooms, just the way Jeb had said there would be. But Nik knew that, as usual, by achieving his dreams

Jeb had lost interest in them. Occasionally he would arrive from San Francisco with several carriage-loads of people and the big house would be lit up like a Christmas tree. Great banquets of food would be served at all hours while the wine flowed and singers—imported from the Italian opera or French revue companies appearing in San Francisco—would entertain. None of the local gentry would attend these dinners because it was said there were women at the Mallory House whose morals could only be described as loose—and who made no attempt to hide it.

Nik began to buy even more cattle for Rancho Santa Vittoria's ever-increasing acres and they were becoming richer, earning "leather dollars" by selling the hides to merchants in New England to make boots and shoes, and selling the horn for buttons, and the tallow for candles and soap.

By 1873—seventeen years after Jeb had won them their stake in the ranch, Nik Konstant and Jeb Mallory owned a hundred and forty thousand acres of land and more than eighty thousand cattle, as well as seventy thousand sheep. Nik worked hard on the ranch, and Jeb lived the life of a rich bachelor in his grand new house on Russian Hill in San Francisco. And to make Nik's happiness complete, Rosalia finally bore him a son. He was called Gregorius Aleksandr Abrego Konstant, and was known as Greg.

Oddly, with the birth of the child Jeb began to spend more time at the ranch. He would show up unexpectedly at the Konstant House and take lunch with them, watching the growing boy with narrowed, bright blue eyes and a faint smile. "I never thought I'd say this," he admitted to Rosalia one day, "but I'd give anything to have a son like Greg."

"That's easy," she retorted, laughing, "all you have to do is get married."

"Ah, Rosalia," he replied with a sigh, "*that* is the hard part. I'm afraid I'm too old to change my ways."

He met Margaret James a short while later, on board the ferry from San Francisco to Santa Barbara, where she had planned to take a little sketching holiday. Margaret had lost both her parents in the typhus epidemic of 1871, and to support herself worked as an art tutor at Belmont, a preparatory school for boys in San Mateo. She was quite surprised when the dashingly handsome Mr. Mallory, whom everyone on board seemed to treat with great respect, struck up a conversation with her.

She was on deck at the time, endeavoring to capture the changing hues of the sky with her watercolors. Naturally she was shy, but Jeb talked easily, asking questions about Belmont and making her blush by complimenting her on her talent for painting.

Margaret was twenty-six years old with smooth, dark-copper hair kept firmly in a knot on top of her head, and a flawless skin the color of fresh milk. She had cool gray eyes and a cool manner to match, and her full mouth drooped slightly at the corners, as though she were a little sad. But despite her somber manner, Margaret was quick to laugh at Jeb's little jokes, and her shyness soon melted under his expert charm. Still, she was the exact opposite of Jeb in temperament and it was totally unexpected on her part when he proposed to her . . . after all, Jeb Mallory was forty-seven years old and a well-known man about town, with a reputation for liking fast and fancy women. And he was very, *very* rich.

The Arlington Hotel in Santa Barbara was the scene of the grandest wedding reception held in those parts for years, and with Rosalia's coaxing, Santa Barbara society forgave Jeb his indiscretions, and everyone attended.

The long windows of the gaily lit ballroom stood open to the warm summer evening as guests wandered happily in the garden beneath the Chinese lanterns strung from magnolia trees that were filled with white blossoms as though decorated especially for the bride. Mexican mariachis serenaded the happy couple and the best French champagne flowed into hundreds of crystal glasses to be raised in a toast to Jeb and Margaret.

For Margaret, her wedding day was a triumph. And Jeb Mallory knew he had chosen well—Margaret was intelligent, cultured, and attractive; she was strong and healthy. She would make a perfect mother for his son.

CHAPTER 6

Margaret Mallory was never able to tell anyone about her wedding night. It was a memory she preferred to bury in the darkest recesses of her mind. Of course, she had known what her duty would be as a wife, but she also knew that no *lady* could be expected to *enjoy* it—the way Jeb had said they did. "Everyone but you," he'd shouted bitterly.

Afterward, she'd lain with her husband asleep beside her, thinking. Her bruised body ached but she was past feeling. After an hour, when she'd been quite sure he was asleep, she had gone to the bathroom and washed herself. Then she'd brushed her hair, put on a fresh nightgown, and looked at herself in the mirror. Surprisingly, she had looked very little different. No one would ever know about her shame and the terrible, humiliating experience she had endured that night. But there was no going back. She was Mrs. Jeb Mallory. And she knew that in the future, when her husband "needed" her, she wouldn't fight him off. Oh, no, she'd just lie there and let him do what he must; she would simply put her mind elsewhere . . . on the color of the new curtains or what to have for luncheon the next day.

A woman had her own weapons of revenge, Margaret had thought icily as she walked back across the room and lay down again beside her husband. And as she had watched the first light of dawn streak through the gap in the gold velvet curtains, she had known she would use them.

From then on Jeb spent most of his time away from home. Margaret didn't know where he went, or with whom, and she never asked. *But when he was home, he never let a day go by without claiming his rights as a husband.*

As the years passed, Rosalia Konstant wondered how Margaret put up with things the way they were between her and Jeb. "He's here one day and gone the next," she said angrily to Nik, "back to his real life— gambling and running around with fancy women in San Francisco."

Nik shrugged. "He married Margaret for the wrong reasons," he said, "and when he didn't get the child he wanted, he lost interest, the way he always does."

To make up for Jeb's long absences, he and Rosalia went out of their way to be kind to Margaret, but their home was always filled with noisy, cheerful Abrego relatives and it only seemed to make the contrast with Margaret's big lonely house worse. They watched her withdraw more and more into herself, filling in her days by creating a beautiful garden.

Tall locust trees now provided shade in the middle of her spacious lawns, and the drive to both the Mallory and the Konstant houses was lined with beautiful young poplars that were a marvel of delicate green-ness in the summer and a brassy gold in the autumn. Each year, at the first snap of cold they shed every leaf in a single shudder, leaving the trees mere black naked skeletons amid their fallen golden glory.

But what Margaret loved more than the bright-blossomed hibiscus, or the graceful oleanders and the enormous heavy-scented English roses, were the poppies. Every summer, the field behind the house changed from a bright spring green to a mass of silvery leaves, and then into a sea of trembling scarlet blooms. It was like a billowing red carpet with here and there, a patch of deep blue cornflowers for accent. She would sit alone on her verandah on the long summer evenings, just drinking in their transient beauty—for they lasted only a few days before the wind snatched their petals and scattered them, like confetti, over the hill.

Rosalia hardly dared tell Margaret when, in November 1879, she knew that she was pregnant again. Greg was already almost seven years old and she and Nik had prayed so long for a second baby, she was just bubbling with happiness. But when she finally did tell Margaret, she was stunned by her reply.

"As a matter of fact," Margaret said, casting her eyes down and blush-ing modestly, "Jeb and I are going to have a baby too—and about the same time as yours."

Things were different after that. Jeb sent crateloads of nursery furni-ture from smart San Francisco emporiums, along with an enormous rocking horse and toys of every description. He came home more frequently, and they noticed how considerate he was to Margaret, treating her tenderly, although he never kissed her or made any gesture of affection. And when Jeb was away, Margaret would chatter on about him and the baby, it was always "Jeb this" and "Jeb that" . . . as though they were quite a normal married couple.

Rosalia's daughter was born on the first of June, 1880. It was an easy birth and the baby had white-blond hair and eyes even bluer than her father's. She was baptized Angel in remembrance of the Russian town of Archangel, where Nik had been born; and Irina after his mother and Ampara for Rosalia's mother . . . Angel Irina Ampara Konstant.

When Margaret went into labor two weeks later, Jeb was as nervous as a cat. It was a humid June day and the sun boiled a dark, sullen red in the leaden sky as he paced the verandah, wincing as Margaret's helpless screams split the stormy stillness. He raged angrily at the doctor for letting her suffer and yelled at the midwife to hurry things up, terrified his son might be damaged by such a difficult birth. He sweated and stormed and prayed until, after eighteen hours of labor, the child was born. "A beautiful little girl," the doctor told him wearily. "You're a lucky man, Mr. Mallory, your wife had a very difficult time."

Without a word to Margaret, Jeb stalked across the bedroom and looked at the child in the crib. His hands were clenched into tight fists as he stared at the red crumpled creature he had been so sure would be a son . . . why, he'd even chosen the names—James Rogan Fitzgerald Mallory, after his grandfather, his father, and his mother. . . .

Silently, he walked over to the bed and kissed his wife on the cheek. But Margaret read the bitter disappointment in his eyes and knew that to him, she was a failure.

"You will be all right," he said stiffly, "Dr. Svensen assured me. Are you in pain, or uncomfortable?"

Margaret shook her head, closing her eyes, fighting back the tears. "I got this for you, a present . . ." he said, thrusting a sapphire brooch at her, "for the birth. . . ." Abruptly he walked back to the crib. The baby looked quite anonymous to him; she might have been anybody's child. He felt nothing—no emotion, no bonding with the tiny creature he had created.

The storm broke suddenly, and as thunder pealed across the mountains he stared blankly out of the window.

The rain fell in a torrent, turning the bright hill of poppies into a rippling scarlet and a silver stream. "We must give her a name," Margaret said tiredly.

Jeb shrugged, his eyes on the hill. "Call her Poppy," he said carelessly as he headed for the door. At dawn he left for San Francisco without saying good-bye.

A few days later Margaret lay on a chaise longue on the verandah with her baby in the crib beside her. Nik and Rosalia had been to see her, and though she'd made excuses for Jeb, she could tell they hadn't believed her. "I know he wanted a boy," Rosalia had whispered before she left, "are you sure he is happy—that everything is all right?"

"He adores the child," she'd lied, "why, he even decided her name."

"But why no family names, no remembrances?" Rosalia had asked, puzzled.

Margaret managed a smile. "You know Jeb, he's a man of the moment —he named her for the field of California poppies out there."

Though the doctors had warned her she shouldn't yet be out of bed, she felt much stronger and with a sudden longing to feel the sun warm on her skin, she picked up her baby and walked slowly across the smooth lawns to the foot of the hill.

Poppy lay quietly in her arms, gazing around her with wide, all-seeing bright blue eyes as Margaret waded knee-deep through the blossoms. With a feeling of pity she knelt among the flowers, holding out her child so that she might see them. "Look, little one," she murmured, "just look at the beauty of these California flowers—and know why your father named you for them. See how the petals dance on the breeze—like a host of scarlet butterflies." She held the child forward so that she might peer into the wondrous purple-black heart of the delicate flower. "Always remember this, my little one, your father named you for their beauty."

Lifting her head, she searched the land around her—all of it and beyond was owned by her husband and his partner. "And this will be yours, too, someday—all this wonderful, rich land," she murmured, but the baby was still staring wide-eyed at the flowers, seeming absorbed in the colors and the scent.

CHAPTER 7

1 8 8 0 ,   C A L I F O R N I A

Rosalia glanced sadly over her shoulder as she drove away from the Mallory House. The shades were drawn and the glittering windowpanes reflected only a blankness. There were no dogs lying lazily on the porch, no cats playing by the kitchen door, no mares with their foals grazing in the paddock as there were at her own home. And there was no baby lying in her bassinet taking the afternoon sun.

Whenever she visited Margaret, the drawing room would be neat and shiny, the heavy gold brocade curtains hanging half closed in pristine folds. There were never any books or journals scattered about and no children's toys littered the beautiful Turkish rug. The plump, overstuffed sofas bore no imprint where someone might recently have sat, and there was not even the sound of a buzzing fly.

It looked empty, Rosalia thought with a shudder, like a house no one had lived in for years. She flicked her little silver-handled whip, urging the horse into a trot, eager to leave it, and Margaret, behind.

Heaven knew, she'd tried her best to penetrate the defensive shell that Margaret had drawn around her, but she firmly refused to acknowledge the fact that Jeb had left her. He hadn't been home since Poppy was born six months ago, and yet she still talked about him as though he might return home tomorrow or next week, playing out the charade that everything was quite normal. "Jeb just felt the need to travel for a while," she'd said, fending off Rosalia's well-meaning queries as to his whereabouts. "He's always been a traveling sort of man." And she had poured tea from the heavy silver pot into fragile china cups as calmly as if she believed her own words.

Nik had told her this morning that Jeb's house on Russian Hill in San Francisco was still shuttered and that only the caretaker remained in residence in the basement. He'd also said that the lawyers had received a telegraph from Monte Carlo in France, commanding them to deposit a further substantial sum into Mrs. Mallory's household account. So at least Jeb was not neglecting his *financial* responsibilities.

Today Rosalia had deliberately asked Margaret if she'd had any news of Jeb, wondering if she would mention the money.

"Why, yes, of course. I almost forgot. I had such a nice letter from him, quite a long letter—from Monte Carlo in France. It sounds most exciting there." Margaret's voice had risen to a nervous pitch and she was so obviously lying that Rosalia had felt sorry for her. "Jeb is such a good letter writer, he has quite a way with words, you know. I almost felt I was there with him."

"He'll have seen no more of the sights than you or I," she'd retorted vehemently. "Gambling! That's what Jeb will be doing in Monte Carlo!"

Margaret's chin had tilted proudly. "Maybe," she had said softly, "but he still takes good care of me."

Rosalia's big brown eyes had filled with compassion. Margaret looked so tired and worn. Her rich red hair had lost its luster and her skin was translucently pale. She looked like a woman who didn't sleep nights, a woman who tossed and turned, tortured by her memories. And yet there was a look of shrewd patience in her eyes that somehow gave Rosalia the impression that she might also be a woman waiting for vengeance.

If it wasn't for the child, she knew she couldn't have forced herself to keep up her weekly visits. Margaret never seemed pleased to see her and it would have been so much easier just to let it slide, but as Jeb's friend and partner, Nik felt responsible for her and the child. And even though Margaret might be repressing her hate for the father, there was no mistaking she loved her daughter.

Rosalia thought that although Poppy couldn't strictly be called a beauty like her daughter, Angel, she had her own pixieish charm. She had a shock of red hair and her father's eyes, bright blue and alert and with a charming upward tilt at the corners. Still, it was one thing for Margaret to pretend that nothing was wrong and choose to live the life of a recluse, but quite another to submit her child to such loneliness. Why, she wouldn't even let Poppy come to visit with Angel.

The sandy lane dropped from the brow of the hill and the shining red-tiled roofs of her own charming hacienda came into view. Sensing home, the pony pulled on the shafts, eager for the treat of oats he knew awaited him and Rosalia's spirits lifted, too, as she thought of her family and the love and security of her own home. Leaving the Mallory House was like being released from prison, she thought guiltily, because no matter how hard she tried, she still couldn't find it in her heart to *love* Margaret.

The unseasonal warm weather persisted into December, bringing with it a plague of flies that swarmed around the cattle and the horses, and found their way in the house, buzzing around the kitchen despite the bright Mexican bead door-curtain that rattled in the dry, gusty wind. For the first time Rosalia was glad that young Greg had been sent away to the academy at San Mateo, he was well out of this dusty, disease-carrying heat. She kept Angel in the nursery, away from the hot wind and the marauding flies, and she neglected her usual visits to the Mallory House.

A few weeks later, the Mallorys' old Indian arrived on their doorstep at dawn. He lived in the original adobe house on the Rancho Santa Vittoria and had been Jeb's cook and caretaker from the very beginning. He had walked the fifteen miles barefoot with his old striped serape wrapped around his face to keep out the dust. The Konstants' house-keeper, Inez, was already in the kitchen tending the massive iron stove, and she stared at him contemptuously when he demanded she wake the Señor and Señora Konstant.

"The Señor is already up on the high pasture," she said, affronted by his cheek at asking such a thing, "and the Señora needs her rest."

"*Wake your mistress.*" The Indian's faded eyes gleamed maniacally as he stepped closer to her.

Fat old Inez backed away nervously. "I wake the Señora now," she gasped, racing for the stairs as fast as her plump thighs would allow.

Rosalia sat bolt upright as Inez shook her. "Is it the baby?" she cried, leaping from the bed and rushing to the door. "Has something happened?"

"No, no, Señora, is not the baby. Is the Mallorys' old Indian. He is here, in the kitchen. He says he must see you. I didn't know what to do." She twisted her hands nervously into her clean white apron, looking near to tears.

Pulling on a robe, Rosalia ran down the stairs to the kitchen. "What is it?" she demanded anxiously.

"Missus got sick two days ago," the Indian told her gravely. "She said she all right but I have seen this sickness before. Mr. Jeb's child should not be there. It is dangerous."

Rosalia's face paled. "How sick is Mrs. Mallory?"

"The sickness got worse quickly. Missus die last night. But Mr. Jeb's child will not die. I have brought her to you."

"Margaret? Dead?" Rosalia whispered, clutching her hand to her heart. "Oh, no . . . no, it's not true. . . ."

The Indian's strange opaque eyes met hers. "It is true," he said impassively.

"But why didn't you send for help?" she wept.

"Missus not need help. It is what she wanted," he said, "I know it." He turned to the door. "Come with me."

Rosalia followed him outside, staring at the basket, hastily made from grasses, placed in the shade of a young sycamore. In it lay Poppy, fast asleep.

CHAPTER 8

When he was in L.A., Mike always stayed at the Beverly Hills Hotel. He felt sure there were creative vibrations lingering there, left over from the early days when it was home from home for famous movie stars and flamboyant directors and hardworking writers. Or maybe it was just the calm luxury and old-fashioned glitz of the place that inspired him. Whichever, he'd written most of *Robbelard's Getaway* in a glorious, inspired two-month spurt in one of their pink "cottages," and he'd been fond of the place ever since. The hotel had been built in 1912 when the township of Beverly Hills consisted of nothing more than tilled fields and a few new, bare roads, and right from the beginning, it had fulfilled its role as the glamor hotel queen of Hollywood.

His breakfast was delivered at nine-thirty promptly, after he'd completed an hour on the tennis court with the resident pro, and was already showered and changed and ready for what the day might bring. Over his coffee and rye toast he studied Lieber's list of the claimants to Poppy Mallory's estate. The lawyer had divided it into two sections—the "Possibles" and the "Improbables." There were several hundred names in the last section—and just five in the Possibles . . . Aria Rinardi, in Venice; the twins, Claudia Galli in Paris and Pierluigi Galli in New York—who seemed to have a joint claim, though they had contacted Lieber separately; Orlando Messenger in London; and Lauren Mallory Hunter—right here in Los Angeles.

Might as well begin with the local girl, Mike thought, reading Lieber's brief résumé of Lauren's claim—at least she had the right name. Her great-grandmother was reputed to have been brought up on a ranch near Santa Barbara . . . both great-grandmother and -grandfather were deceased before she was born . . . mother's name Sonia Mallory Hunter. Mike checked Lauren's age again; she was only eighteen. Then why wasn't *Sonia* Hunter claiming the estate? Trouble between mother and daughter perhaps? Or maybe Sonia had simply missed the ad; after all, some people never read a newspaper from one month to the next.

Anyway, Lauren's story of the grandmother in Santa Barbara was the most tenuous claim possible, and completely unsubstantiated—although she did have a family Bible with proof of the name Mallory. Lieber had included her on the strength of that—and the fact that the dates fitted. And Mike thought that when you compared it with some of the fantasies in the Improbables list, maybe it wasn't so farfetched after all.

Picking up the phone, he dialed Lauren's number. He let it ring a dozen times but no one answered so he tried Denny's Coffee Shop on Ventura, thinking maybe she was already at work. The girl there told him it was Lauren's day off. "But she'll be at Teddy's Barn later," she told him brightly, "she works there as a cocktail waitress most every night."

Mike tried her number again, surely she'd be home if it was her day off. But there was still no reply and he put down the receiver irritatedly . . . there was nothing for it but to wait until tonight.

Lauren just let the phone ring. It couldn't be anything important, probably just Denny's to say they needed a relief waitress and could she come in? But not today she couldn't, not even if they paid her triple time . . . today was her day with Maria. She lay in bed, lazily contemplating what they might do. The baby was kicking her plump little legs in the air, making gentle noises as she tried to catch the gaily colored bird mobile over her crib. Lauren had heard of children who cried all the time and drove their mothers crazy, but Maria was such a quiet child and never a moment's trouble. She never cried when she was left at the baby-minder's during the day, or with a sitter at night; and she was always full of smiles when she saw her.

"Maria," she called to her, smiling delightedly as the child's lips seemed to copy hers and form the word; only the sound that came out of her mouth was strangely high-pitched and bore no resemblance to Maria. "You'll get there, honey," she said encouragingly, "just you keep on trying." But if she were truthful with herself, she wasn't at all sure she would. When the baby-minder had first heard Maria, she'd given Lauren one of those sympathetic looks and said, "Maria's just a bit 'different,' that's all."

Lauren had snatched the child away and hurried home, trying not to think of the look in the woman's eyes as she'd said it, because it only confirmed what she had suspected herself. She'd finally been forced to come to terms with the fact that Maria was different, lost in some private world of her own. She was "damaged," thought Lauren sadly, using the easiest word she could bear, because she would never ever say that Maria was "retarded" or "mentally disabled"—or any other of those awful truths, and anyway it just made her love even more fiercely protective. And it wasn't surprising considering what Maria had gone through before she was even born. In Lauren's worst nightmares Maria was old enough to go to school and the authorities had realized what was wrong. She'd be clinging to Maria, screaming as they tried to snatch her away. So many nights she'd woken sweating with fear, unable to see any way out of her dilemma. And she just knew that when it happened, as it surely would, both she and the child would die of broken hearts.

She lay back against the pillows, watching the little girl, absorbed in her game with the bird mobile, wondering how many times a heart could be broken. The first time it had happened she'd been twelve. Someone had telephoned from the Boeing factory where her father worked as a production manager to say that he'd had a coronary and that he'd been dead before he hit the floor. Her mother had repeated those exact words to her, and the awful image of her dead father falling to the ground had stuck in her mind for ever afterward.

She'd wondered then how she could cope with the leaden weight that had once been her heart but, like most things, with time nature had eased the pain, and after a while she'd gotten over it. The next crack in her heart had come two years later when her mom had told her she wanted to get married again. Up until then Lauren had been an ordinary conscientious student at Redlands High, doing all the usual things fourteen-year-old girls did—studying hard when she had to, and playing hard when she didn't. There had always been a party to go to on the weekend, or a sleep-over at one of her friends' houses. They'd shopped in groups in the malls on Saturday mornings and cheered the high school football team on winter Saturday afternoons. Now, of course, she realized that her mom had still been young, only thirty-four, and it was only natural that she should fall in love and remarry. But at the time, after all the grief they'd gone through together because of her father, it had seemed like the supreme act of betrayal.

She'd been wildly jealous and she knew now she'd behaved unreasonably and made their lives a misery, but it had been the only way she'd known how to make her opinion felt. "You never told me you were going out with him," she'd shouted at her mom, "you never said a word. I bet he doesn't even *know* about *me!*"

"Of course he knows about you," Sonia Hunter had told her soothingly, "why, I've told him every single thing about you . . . he knows you're a great swimmer and he knows you're doing well in school and you want to try for Stanford. He even knows you had chickenpox when you were three and how much the braces on your teeth cost."

"Why'd you tell him *those* things," she'd screamed, "those are things my *real* dad knew, not *him!*"

Sonia Hunter had sighed resignedly; people always said you could expect this kind of trouble when you told your kid that you were marrying again, but it surely didn't make it any easier. Sonia had shoulder-length blond hair, its lightness helped by regular visits to the hairdresser, and she had that very neat, burnished look of a woman who kept herself in shape. She took exercise classes at the gym and worked out on the Nautilus until she was aware of every muscle in her body. She drank lots of fresh juices and was passionate about health foods, and she'd brought her daughter up on the same healthy diet. Lauren's teeth might have braces, but they shone as whitely as if they'd been polished, her pretty blue eyes were clear and her skin flawless, and like her mother, she didn't have an extra ounce of fat on her body.

Sonia had put a brave face on Lauren's rebellious attitude, and on weekends when Doug came up from San Diego where he worked as an attorney, she'd tried very hard to keep things "family style" so that her daughter didn't feel left out. But Lauren had been fourteen and going through a tough adjustment into young womanhood. She'd hated the idea of her mom sleeping with Doug, and hated the idea that all the other kids at school would know that too. She'd begun to do badly in class and took to skipping her homework and going out instead, cruising along the boulevards with a bunch of other kids in some sixteen-year-old's hot rod.

Lauren had been a shy girl, happiest when she was part of a crowd. She wasn't even sure she'd know what to say to a boy if she went on a *real* date. She knew she wasn't beautiful, and she wished she were taller, but she was surely cute, with a limber, slender-hipped body, shapely legs, and small pointed breasts. Her mother always told her she had a "fresh, well-scrubbed look," with her polished skin and shining hair, and her natural California tan.

When her railway-track braces came off, all at once the boys' attitude toward her had changed and her own private phone never stopped ringing. She'd begun to wear shorter skirts to show off her legs and finally had enough confidence to go out on dates alone. She was still shy, but so were the boys, and mostly they would just eat at the coffee shop or the Chinese restaurant and maybe take in a movie. Then they'd cruise around for a while until they found a quiet spot to park and make out a little in the backseat—but she never let any of them get beyond first base. She didn't quite know why, because she knew some of the other girls did—or at least they *said* they did—but it just wasn't something she wanted. It was all too much responsibility—too much growing up. She'd decided that on the whole, she much preferred sleep-overs at her friends' houses and their gossip and hilarity, to a sweaty struggle fending off some overeager boy in the backseat of a car on a sultry California night.

When her mother and Doug finally got married, they said Lauren would have to leave Redlands High and move to a new school in San Diego, where they were to live. They'd watched stunned as she'd rampaged around the house in storms of tears, asking how could they do that to her. Didn't they know all her friends were here? Everybody she'd ever known, all her life? And now, just because they'd gotten married she was supposed to give them all up and begin again from scratch. And what about her exams? She was almost seventeen, her SAT college entrance exams were coming up . . . how did they expect her to pass if she went to a new school? With a new routine and new teachers who didn't understand her. They knew how important it was to her to get into Stanford. "It's unfair," she'd wailed, and she wouldn't go, she refused!

"She's right," Doug had told Sonia nervously, "the kid's absolutely right. It's *not* fair."

Lauren had stopped crying, staring at him suspiciously, wondering what he was up to. But then he'd said, "It's only another year, Sonia, she has to have her chance. I'll just have to commute to San Diego and then when she goes off to college, we can all move down there."

Lauren had looked at him, smiling; it had looked as if everything was going to be all right after all. And then all of a sudden, it all went terribly wrong. And she wished with all her heart she'd never complained, and that she'd just gone quietly to live with them in San Diego.

By seven o'clock that night, she didn't know who was more exhausted, she or Maria. The baby, surfeited on fresh air and the new experiences of the zoo, was already fast asleep in her crib. Lauren wearily applied her makeup and stepped into her leotard, black tights, and high heels. Teddy had been complaining lately that she looked too skinny. "You're losing all your curves, Lauren," he'd warned. "If it weren't for the fact that you've got a nice ass and a good pair of legs, I'd have to fire you."

"Thanks a lot!" she'd retorted angrily.

"You're a cocktail waitress," he'd said, shrugging, "you know why you were hired. Sure you can carry the drinks without dropping them, and give the right change, *and* you don't try to slide the odd ten-dollar bill into your pocket—but so can a hundred other girls. The guys like to look at you when you serve them. So you'd better get off whatever diet you're on and get yourself together."

Much as she hated to admit it, Lauren knew he was right; Teddy's Barn was famous for its attractive waitresses. She just never had the time or the money to eat properly, and she lived on cheap junk food.

The club was quiet when she got there, just a couple of guys up at the bar and one or two people drinking at the dimly lit tables in the back. The group who were to entertain that night were setting up on stage, testing the mikes, and the other waitresses were standing around gossiping. She combed her hair, added a touch more lipstick and a splash of Giorgio scent, and went to join them.

Mike Preston watched her from his seat at the bar, checking her appearance against the small color photograph attached to Lieber's notes. The picture looked as though it had been taken from her high school yearbook and in it she looked juvenile and sweet, with polished red-blond hair and wide blue eyes and a sparkling, if shy, smile. But the girl in the leotard was too thin; she looked tired and there was a little frown of worry between her brows. He wondered uneasily what had happened to change the eager young teenager into this careworn young woman.

She was setting ashtrays on the tables and checking the candles in their little red containers to make sure they didn't need replacing. Taking his glass, he walked over to her. "Lauren Hunter?" he asked. Her head jerked upward and she stared at him with huge, frightened eyes. "I'm sorry if I startled you," he said gently. "I got your name from Johannes Lieber, the lawyer in Geneva. He asked me to see you. There was no reply from your home number. They told me at Denny's you worked here at night."

"Johannes Lieber?" she asked, bewildered.

"It's about Poppy Mallory's estate."

Lauren's legs went suddenly weak and she sank into a chair. "Does that mean I really am the heiress, then?"

"I'm afraid we don't know who the heiress is yet," Mike said quickly. "Lieber just wanted me to see you and find out a few more details." Her disappointment showed in her eyes as she stared at him, and he added, "Of course, it doesn't mean you're *not* the heiress, I'm just here to help sort out your story."

"I see. Well, there's not much more to tell. I wrote it all in my letter to Mr. Lieber. I wasn't even sure whether it was worth it, but my mom always said you don't get anywhere without trying, so I did. Anyway everything I said in that letter was true!"

"I don't doubt that," he told her. "I'd just like to chat about it a bit more, if we could."

She glanced nervously at the rapidly filling room. "I have to get to work," she said, standing up.

"Could you meet me afterward?" Mike asked. "What time do you finish?"

"One o'clock. But I don't know . . . I'd have to call the baby-sitter."

"I see," said Mike, her background clicking suddenly into place.

"No, you don't," she replied, looking him straight in the eyes. "You don't see at all. I'll be here, at one o'clock."

Wondering what she'd meant, he finished his drink, watching as she moved busily and efficiently between the tables. She was obviously good at her job, conscientious and efficient. And she was a hard worker—he knew she had a day job at Denny's. She was young and she was bright, and she should have been in college, but of course now he knew. She had a responsibility. A child to bring up; another mouth to feed.

He filled in the time at a movie on Hollywood Boulevard, grabbed a bite at Musso and Frank's, and was back at Teddy's at a quarter of one. Lauren nodded when she saw him. "One o'clock," she mouthed across the room, pointing to her watch. Mike took a seat at the bar and ordered a drink, watching the milling crowd on the dance floor. The music was so loud, it vibrated through his chest and he wondered how she put up with it, night after night. And afterward she had to go home to her kid, who no doubt was up at six a.m. and raring to go, while poor Lauren would have to face another day's work at Denny's. He surely hoped she was Poppy Mallory's heiress, she certainly could use the money!

"Hi," she said, standing beside him. She wore blue jeans over her leotard and an old denim jacket. She had washed off the lipstick and the mascara and she looked about sixteen. With a shock, Mike remembered that she was only a couple of years older than that anyway. He took her arm, guiding her through the crowd. It felt thin through the denim sleeve, thin and fragile. It made him feel protective, as though he wanted to feed her. . . . "You hungry?" he asked.

"Sort of," she replied.

"What's your favorite?"

"Chinese," she said unhesitatingly.

He took her to the New Moon on Ventura Boulevard, and watched as she devoured egg roll, beef in black bean sauce, and Singapore noodles. "Feel better?" he asked with a grin.

"You bet!" she retorted with a satisfied sigh. "Thank you, Mr. Preston. It was awesome! The best I've eaten in a year."

He thought it was sad that her best meal in a year was in a second-rate Chinese eatery with Formica-topped tables, but at least she looked happier and more relaxed. And she was a whole lot prettier without that worried expression in her blue eyes. They were a nice shade of blue— deep and far too revealing. He felt he could read her mind through the changing expressions reflected in her eyes.

"Who exactly are you?" she asked, sipping her Coke. "I mean I know you're something to do with Mr. Lieber, but *what*, exactly?"

"Actually, I'm a writer," he said.

"*That* Mike Preston!" she exclaimed, her eyes round with astonishment. "But I've read your books!"

"Guilty!" he replied with a grin. Lauren studied him with new interest. "I've never met a famous author before," she said, "nor a Pulitzer prize winner. I thought at Teddy's that your face looked familiar—and, of course, now I remember seeing you on a couple of TV interviews. I thought you looked odd," she added. "Sort of beat-up, like Jean-Paul Belmondo . . . you're much nicer looking in real life." Her hand flew to her mouth as she blushed. "I always seem to say just what I'm thinking," she said apologetically, "and it's usually the wrong thing. Still," she added, smiling impishly, "this time it's true."

Their eyes met across the table as they assessed each other without speaking and Lauren felt a little shiver of apprehension run down her spine. There was something in his level glance that disturbed her, a look she wasn't used to seeing in a man's eyes . . . it wasn't the sort of come-on she got from the guys at Teddy's, it was deeper than that—and somehow more intimate. . . .

"How do you know about Jean-Paul Belmondo?" Mike asked without taking his eyes off her. "You're too young. . . ."

"Sometimes, when I get home from work at Teddy's, I can't sleep, I watch those old foreign movies on television . . ." His glance was disturbing and she turned away, sipping her Coke. "Where do famous authors come from anyway?"

He grinned at her ingenuousness. "This one hails from Madison, Wisconsin. I was raised by my aunt Martha, after my dad died and my mom ran off with a traveling salesman—now there's the basis of a good story for you!"

"What was it like, being raised in Madison, Wisconsin?" she asked. "I've never been farther than San Diego myself."

He shrugged. "You know, the usual—a small, ranch-style house in a middle-class suburb. Aunt Martha had all the good old-fashioned values —church on Sundays, respect for my elders and betters, devotion to the work ethic, and love for my country. I had to earn my allowance by cutting the lawn and taking out the garbage—and any other chores she considered suitable for a growing boy. We raised the flag on the front lawn every morning and lowered it every evening at sundown, and homework always had to be done before there was any chance of escaping to play basketball, or hang out with the other guys at the drive-in."

"I bet you had a car with *fins*," Lauren said with a grin.

"You bet I did. And I'll tell you what else I had—home-baked cookies when I got home from school, and the world's best blueberry pie—and my aunt Martha's Sunday roast—I can smell it now, that aroma'll live in my memory forever." She smiled at him, her eyes sympathetic and interested, and he said suddenly, "You know, Lauren, Aunt Martha was more than just a kind relative who took me in. I was nine years old, lost and frightened because I'd been abandoned, and desperately worried about the great blank of the future. It was her love that got me through it, and through those tough teenage years . . . I was always too tall and perpetually growing out of my clothes, it drove her crazy . . . 'The expense,' she would say sternly, 'can't you think of the expense, Michael, and stop growing?' "

Lauren laughed and he fell silent for a moment. "I don't know why I'm telling you all this," he said quietly, "but it feels good to talk about her to someone."

"Is she still alive?" Lauren asked gently.

He grinned. "She sure is. I call her once a week, no matter where I am in the world. We talk for an hour or so, just about this and that, her church meeting, my latest lecture tour, as though we were sitting opposite each other at the kitchen table over one of her delicious meals." He paused, looking at Lauren. "She's seen me through all the crises in my life," he added, "including a marriage that went wrong."

"Were you very young?"

He nodded. "We were both twenty-three, in the same year at North-western . . . I guess it was doomed from the start, but at that age you don't understand . . ." He stopped, aware again of how young she was.

"You're different," Lauren said softly.

"Different? From whom?"

"Oh, different from the guys I've been out with, I guess."

"That's because I'm older," Mike said with a regretful sigh, "although at thirty-seven I didn't expect to see myself cast in the role of 'the older man.'"

Lauren laughed and he liked the sound; it rippled joyously around the bare little restaurant so that the other customers turned their heads, smiling, to see who was having such a good time, and he saw what she must have looked like—before Maria.

"The older man chasing the young heiress," Lauren said mischie-vously. And then, suddenly sober, "But it's not me, is it? Things like that don't happen to girls like me."

He reached across the table and took her hand. It felt fine-boned and a little rough—all that hard work, he supposed. "We don't know that yet," he said, squeezing her fingers encouragingly. "We're just at the begin-ning of our investigations. I'm only involved in a roundabout way. I saw the ad in the paper and called Lieber to see if we could help each other. I'm a writer on the scent of a story—he's a lawyer who's inundated with claims from so-called Mallory heirs. I'm trying to help sort out the bogus from the real, and at the same time find out the true story of Poppy Mallory."

"Do you think I'm bogus, then?"

"Not bogus, Lauren," he said carefully, "but your story is, well . . . a bit thin."

She nodded. "It's all just hearsay really—you know, a story handed down in the family. Except for the family Bible with all the names in it. We're Mallorys, all right," she said, shrugging, "but then I guess so are thousands of others. Anyhow, I never knew my great-grandmother or my grandmother, but my mom always said that my great-grandmother had been brought up on a big ranch near Santa Barbara."

She stared down at her empty plate and he noticed, surprised, the sudden look of fear that crossed her face.

"They said that after she got married great-grandmother wasn't quite right in the head," she continued, her voice very low. "She had a baby and then ran away from her husband and so her baby was put out for adoption. That baby was my grandmother."

"Are you saying your great-grandmother was Poppy Mallory?"

"No," Lauren said simply, "she couldn't be. She wasn't old enough. But maybe she was Poppy Mallory's daughter."

"I see." He looked at Lieber's notes thoughtfully. "Yes, that would make the dates about right. Poppy was born in 1880, and the daughter was probably born around 1898 or 1900 . . . we're not sure yet."

"You're not sure? But I thought you knew; I thought you would be able to tell me. . . ."

"It's not that simple, I'm afraid. But that's where I come in; I'm gathering all the information and hoping I can sort out Poppy's story, so then we'll know who the heiress—or heir—is."

"I'm sorry I've not been much help," Lauren said wearily. "I don't think I stand much of a chance."

"There's always a chance, otherwise I wouldn't be here. There are lots of other stories that didn't even warrant looking into. You'd be amazed how many people replied to that ad."

She looked suddenly tired and dispirited. "I have to get home. The baby-sitter will be anxious. Thanks for the meal, Mr. Preston."

"It's been nice meeting you, Lauren," he said, meaning it. "Take care of that baby of yours."

"She's not my baby," she said abruptly. "She's my sister."

"*Your sister?*"

She nodded. "Mom had only been remarried a year. Doug was an attorney in San Diego, and we were supposed to move down there to live with him, but I wanted to finish Redlands High first—I was doing my college exams, you see, and I had all my friends. . . . Anyway, Doug would commute and sometimes Mom would go with him while I stayed with a friend. She was pregnant and real happy about it. Usually she'd fly down to San Diego to be with him, but she was eight months and the airlines don't allow it. They were driving down there one weekend and I was going off to some party and sleeping over at my best friend's. The police came by later that night to tell me the car had been struck sideways by a drunk driver on Route 101. Doug was killed instantly and Mom was on a life-support machine.

"I went to the hospital to see her. She looked so pretty, and sort of peaceful, and she was breathing into one of those ventilator things—it pumped her lungs up and down, I guess . . . I don't know. They said the baby was still alive and they'd have to do a cesarean. The baby was all right. . . . But after she was born they turned off my mom's life-support machine."

Her blue eyes were tearless and her voice matter-of-fact as she went on. "They wanted to give Maria away to be adopted. They said it would be no problem at all, that there were lots of loving couples longing for a baby, with good homes, money, everything she'd need. But I wouldn't let them do it. I fought and fought and finally they couldn't dispute that she was my half sister, they had to let me have her. I'd done real well on my SAT's, I'd been offered a place at Stanford—my ambition—but Maria came first. After all," she said with a choked little laugh, "I'll only be in my thirties when Maria's eighteen, I can always go to college later . . . there's nothing wrong with starting a little bit late, is there?"

"Nothing at all," Mike said quietly. "You're a brave girl, Lauren Hunter."

"She was all I had left," she said simply. "And I don't regret my decision at all. Maria means everything to me."

He walked with her to the parking lot, waiting while she got into her old Mustang. She switched on the ignition and rolled down her window. "I'll be in touch, Lauren," he said, leaning in to look at her. Their eyes met again. "Good luck, now."

" 'Night, Mike," she said, a little breathlessly. "Thanks again for the Chinese food—it was intense."

Mike found it hard to dismiss Lauren Hunter from his mind that night; her gallant smile haunted his dreams and he tossed restlessly in his comfortable bed. He woke up the next morning feeling tired and depressed, wishing he could tell her that all her problems were resolved and she was Poppy Mallory's heiress. But unfortunately for Lauren, real life was much tougher than that. Poppy couldn't have known what hopes and dreams her strange will would inspire.

The luxurious room seemed stuffy as he lay there thinking about the story that was emerging from Rosalia's journals about Poppy, and her father, Jeb. . . .

CHAPTER 9

1881, CALIFORNIA

Jeb Mallory disembarked from the coastal steamer *Santa Rosa*, swinging his malacca cane jauntily. The cane, with its silver lion's-head handle, had supposedly been made for a prince of Russia who had gambled away his inheritance and all his possessions. Jeb had bought it casually from the pawn shop in Monte Carlo intending it as a gift for Nik, but had decided that he liked the air of a boulevardier it gave him, and so he'd kept it.

He was wearing a pair of silver-gray worsted trousers and a black broadcloth jacket fashioned by one of London's finest Savile Row tailors. His soft black leather boots were handmade to his own last at yet another expensive London establishment, and the light cashmere overcoat slung around his shoulders had been purchased in Paris. His gunmetal-gray silk cravat came from Italy, and he had been assured by the Monte Carlo jeweler that the large pearl stickpin he wore came from the deepest waters of the South Seas. With his shiny top hat placed at exactly the right angle, he looked the perfect picture of a man in mourning.

Removing a fat Romeo y Julieta from a solid gold cigar case, he snipped the end neatly with a small gold clipper. Cupping his hands, he lit it with a wooden match taken from another small gold case and then, puffing luxuriantly, he smiled at the group of awed children who had gathered to watch the steamer from San Francisco dock, and who were now watching him instead.

As he boarded the horse-drawn Arlington Hotel bus waiting on the wharf, Jeb glanced around at the other passengers, tipping his hat as he recognized the wife of the local architect. She had been present at his wedding and he was surprised when she turned her face away as though she hadn't recognized him. He shrugged indifferently; after all, he'd been gone for some time and he guessed he looked like a foreigner in his new European finery.

The town looked even smaller than he remembered. The bus trundled slowly past the curve of the beach and Castle Rock, and past the stately white Diblee house, Punta del Castillo, with its wonderful ceilings painted by a French artist, and its beautifully landscaped gardens. It was Santa Barbara's masterpiece and exactly the kind of house Jeb would like to build. Only not in Santa Barbara, he thought with a smile. It was much too provincial. No, with his new fortune he would build his mansion along the banks of the Hudson River in New York, or perhaps at Newport, Rhode Island, alongside the railroad magnates and oil giants and captains of industry like Rockefeller and Vanderbilt and J. Pierpont Morgan.

The bus jogged past Larco's Fish Market where the same old white pelican picked among a pile of fish trimmings, just as he always did. On the right was Dr. Shaw's ancient blue adobe house encircled by an iron fence, and farther down the street the same bootblack plied his trade as usual in front of the Morris house. They passed Al and Seth Loomis's Saddlery Store where Nik had first set eyes on Rosalia, and Shaw's Grocery Store, and the blacksmith's on the left with a horse being shod at the glowing orange-red forge. In the single street that was Chinatown, the same old men with gray pigtails and black satin skullcaps sat in front of their shops thoughtfully smoking their long pipes, and women in silk coats and trousers clattered stiffly along the wooden sidewalk on tiny bound feet.

Nothing had changed—and it never would, Jeb thought, puffing on his cigar to dispel the cloying scent of Chinese incense. He noticed the red-brick Catholic church but remembered Margaret wasn't buried there; she was in the small Presbyterian cemetery up on the hill. And no doubt her face was turned to the wall, he thought bitterly. Naturally he was sorry Margaret had died, but in truth he felt nothing for her. She had blocked him efficiently from her bed and out of her heart. Who could blame him for seeking diversion elsewhere?

As the driver turned into the wide gates of the Arlington Hotel he felt as though he had been away years instead of ten months; he was a man of the world now, unsuited to Santa Barbara's leisurely pace of life. His vast new fortune, won at the tables in Monte Carlo, was burning a hole in his pocket and he was determined to enjoy it. But first he had a score to settle with Nik Konstant.

When the manager showed him his rooms, his face flushed with anger. It was the same suite he had shared with Margaret on their honeymoon night. "These rooms are not satisfactory," he said sharply, "kindly arrange something else."

"But, sir, Mr. Mallory, this is our very best suite," the man protested.

"Then give me the second best!" he snarled, heading for the bar. He hadn't thought that Margaret could ever upset him again, but, by God, one look at that room and all the bad memories had simply flowed back again. It was only as he sipped his second whiskey and chaser that Jeb allowed himself to think of Nik.

He'd been in another bar—the ornately decorated one at the famous Hotel de Paris in Monte Carlo—when Nik's letter had been delivered to him, and to his horror his hand had trembled and tears had pricked the backs of his eyes as he'd read it.

I have waited all these months for you to return and at least pay your respects to Margaret, Nik had written, *but all we have received is one telegram from you. I cannot tell you in strong enough terms that I consider the fact that you were not here—where you should have been—is the sole reason that her illness went unremarked and unattended. In short, I place the full blame for Margaret's death on you. I can never forgive you, Jeb, and I am writing to tell you that you must consider our friendship at an end. About our partnership, as you seem no longer interested in the Rancho Santa Vittoria I am willing to buy out your half share on whatever terms you and our lawyers consider suitable.*

Although you failed to mention your daughter in your telegram, nor have you expressed any concern as to her whereabouts or her welfare, we are taking good care of her. In case you are interested, she is a fine child. May God forgive you, Jeb Mallory, for I surely never can.

He had signed it *Nikolai Konstantinov.*

As he downed his third whiskey Jeb knew he had to see Nik that very afternoon.

He'd been waiting for an hour, alone in the library of the Konstant House, when Rosalia finally returned from the lambing sheds. She hurried into the room, her hair spilling from its braid, a tiny weak lamb called a *lepe* still cradled in her arms.

"Jeb!" she exclaimed, her brown eyes widening in astonishment. "We didn't expect you."

"The traveler returns," he replied lightly, kissing her soft cheek. "How are you, Rosalia?"

"I have to find this poor *lepe* a warm place near the stove in the kitchen," she said, backing away uncertainly. "He has to be hand-fed, you know."

"I'm here on more important business than *lepes*," Jeb replied, amused at having disconcerted her. "I'm here to thank you for what you did for Margaret. I wanted to give you this." Flourishing a sheaf of thousand-dollar bills, he held them out to her. "In repayment for your care," he said, smiling.

Rosalia stared at the wad of bills, horrified. "I only did what anyone would have done. I'm just sorry I wasn't there when she needed me. I don't need your thanks, Jeb."

"Indeed she does *need your thanks!"*

Nik strode into the room and threw a protective arm around Rosalia. His shirt was stained with blood from the lambing and, with his pale, angry eyes, his shaggy beard and his blond hair standing on end, he looked like a wild man. Jeb started forward, an easy smile on his lips. "Nik, boy-o, that's just what I was saying. Of course she needs thanks. Both of you do. I can never thank you enough for what you did for Margaret."

"Rosalia deserves your thanks," Nik said contemptuously, "but not your gambler's money. Did you win it when Margaret was on her death-bed, Jeb? Or maybe when she was being buried? Perhaps you'd like to hear a few more details? About how Margaret suffered? How she died alone? About how she was too worn and emaciated from the worry and turmoil you put her through to fight the typhoid fever?" He paced angrily across the room. "Still, you would have enjoyed the funeral, Jeb. Everyone came—all the same people who were at your wedding just a few years ago. Everyone—*except you!*" Nik's lip curled. "The perfect husband in his fancy European mourning clothes." He turned away wearily. "You had my letter. I'm willing to buy you out so you need never come to the Rancho Santa Vittoria again. Just name the sum and the lawyers will take care of it."

Jeb's face flushed an angry red. "So much for that fine *friendship* we had then, boy-o. And that fine partnership! Remember Nikolai Konstantinov? The lad fresh off the boat that I took under my care? Remember it was *me*, Jeb Mallory, who got us our stake in this ranch? *Without me,*" he added contemptuously, *"you would be nothing!* And now you say you want to 'buy me out!' "

"I remember this." Nik strode across the room, towering over him menacingly. "It was *my* money that staked your gamble for that first fifty acres, and *my* hard work that made the Rancho Santa Vittoria what it is today. Tell me what you have done to make it grow, Jeb Mallory. Where were you all those years? *Gambling and fornicating in San Francisco!"*

Rosalia forced her way between the two men, the lamb still clutched in her arms. "Nik, please, I don't like to hear you talk like this!"

He turned away with a disgusted shrug, but Jeb grabbed his arm. "I've put a lot of money into this place *Nikolai Konstantinov,"* he said through gritted teeth, "and by God if you hadn't done what you did for Margaret, I'd kill you right now for what you've just said!"

Nik's laugh was full of contempt, "That's typical of you, Jeb," he retorted, "you'll fight for your honor—even though you have none."

"God damn you," Jeb bellowed, raising his fist as Rosalia rushed in to separate them.

"Please, oh, please, don't do this," she wailed. "Don't bring violence into my home!"

Jeb stepped back, rigid with anger. He glared at Nik. "All I have to say to you is that you will *never* get my share of the ranch. By God, boy-o, I'll see to it that you never get another cent from me. *You'll never get your hands on anything I own."*

Nik folded his arms impassively. "We'll see." He shrugged. "We'll just see about that."

Jeb stalked from the room and Rosalia ran after him, the *lepe* still clutched to her breast. He couldn't be leaving, she thought wildly, just like that. Without even asking about his child? Without even seeing her?

"Jeb," she cried as he ran down the steps. *"Jeb. What about Poppy?"*

He stopped as though he'd been struck, then, turning his head, he stared at her. "Poppy," he repeated, like a man recalling something long forgotten. "Of course. *Poppy.* Where is she?"

"In the nursery, with Angel."

He leapt up the stairs, striding along the wide, galleried landing to the nursery wing. Thrusting the *lepe* at a maid, Rosalia hurried after him. Angel was fast asleep in the crib nearest the door, her blond curls fluffed into a fine halo around her head, and her golden lashes sweeping from fragile lilac eyelids across the smooth curve of her pink cheeks. Poppy was wide awake, her red hair was standing spikily around her ears, and her alert blue eyes stared at Jeb curiously.

He stared back at her with a jolt of recognition; she had her mother's hair and pale skin, but by God she was a chip off the old Irish block! Pulling the soft wool blanket from the crib, he wrapped her in it.

"Jeb!" Rosalia ran after him as he headed for the door, the baby tucked under his arm like a bundle of washing. "Where are you taking her? Jeb, Jeb . . . oh, please . . ."

"I told Nik that he will never have anything of mine. And that includes my daughter," he shouted as he crossed the hall.

"Nik! Stop him, stop him!" she cried.

"I can't," Nik replied sadly, "Poppy is *his* child, not mine."

"At least you're right about that, boy-o," cried Jeb from the top of the steps, *"and I'll tell you this. You'll never see me—or her—again!"*

Rosalia thought she heard the baby chuckle as he swung her onto his shoulder and climbed into the carriage. And then they were gone.

Mike pushed his chair from the desk and stretched wearily. The art deco desk clock said five-thirty a.m. and he was exhausted. The story had just poured from him; it was Poppy's beginning, but there was so much more to be written yet, so much more to be discovered.

As he fell into bed, he knew that he still needed to solve the enigma that was Poppy's character, and he wondered what a child born of such passion and such coldness would be like. Fire and ice, maybe?

CHAPTER *10*

1881–1886, CALIFORNIA

Poppy and Jeb stayed in the most extravagant suite the Sir Francis Drake Hotel in San Francisco could provide while the house on Russian Hill was being redecorated to include a nursery. As soon as they were established, Jeb called his longtime friend and mistress, Maraya Kent, singing and dancing star of the *Follies* revue and a woman with a heart of gold, and asked her to find him a nursemaid.

Maraya thought for a moment and then said, "I have just the girl for you. She'll be there tomorrow."

The next day Louise LaSalle came to be interviewed for the position of Poppy's nurse. Louise was a dancer who, for various reasons, had fallen on hard times and Maraya was doing her a favor getting her this steady work. She told Jeb she was a country girl, one of twelve children, so she knew all about bringing up babies. That, and the fact that she also had ravishing dark eyes and the pertest pair of breasts Jeb had seen in some time, secured her the job.

That first night, after she had put Poppy to bed in her fancy high-ceilinged room at the Sir Francis Drake Hotel, Louise put on her favorite red silk robe and went to Jeb's room to offer the poor widower a little comfort. Of course, it was accepted.

Jeb insisted that as Poppy's nurse Louise must wear a uniform, and thrusting a packet of money into her small, eager hand, he sent her off to buy whatever she needed. He roared with laughter later when he saw the result. Louise had stripped down to her black corselette and red silk drawers and as she bent down to pull on a frilled red petticoat, she waggled her bottom saucily at him. Propping one leg high on the table, she hitched up her new skirts and straightened the garter on her beautiful red silk stockings. Jeb groaned with lust as her plump breasts spilled out and she had barely had time to show him her white lace blouse before he ripped off all her new finery and flung her laughing on her back, spreading her legs and taking her fast. And if Poppy cried that night, neither one of them heard her.

Jeb Mallory's nursemaid, looking like something from a French revue, became the talk of San Francisco. She pattered along in her high-laced boots, red petticoats peeping from beneath her wickedly short skirts, pert breasts bobbing under her low-cut blouse as she pushed Poppy in her smart English wicker perambulator. Tilting her nose in the air, Louise acknowledged the stares with a wide smile, wondering if the scandal might get her a starring role in the *Follies*.

Jeb loved the notoriety she created, though he certainly didn't love Louise, and she was certainly not the only woman to lay claim to his bed. Despite his lavish tips and genial bonhomie, the management of the hotel were beginning to look askance on his roistering and wild parties, and it was with relief a couple of months later that they heard his house was completed and Mr. Mallory would be leaving.

He had given Louise the day off, and with Poppy on his knee, he drove in an open carriage through San Francisco's early June sunshine to Russian Hill.

The new English butler hurried down the steps to help them, but Jeb shrugged him off, hoisting Poppy under his arm in his usual fashion. She was wearing a white lawn dress with a French lace collar and tiny button boots made from the softest white kid. As he carried her up the steps past the waiting servants, her red hair blazed in the sunshine, and the new housekeeper murmured, smiling, that she looked like an autumn chrysanthemum.

Jeb marched up the grand marble staircase to the nursery, a cigar in one hand and Poppy under his arm. "I bet you thought I'd forgotten, didn't you?" he said to her with a chuckle. "Well, me darling, you were wrong! No one can ever say your father forgot your first birthday." Poppy stared at him wide-eyed and he threw back his head, laughing. "Sure, and I bet you know what I'm saying, even though you're only one year old. You've got a look in those fine blue eyes that I recognize. You're a chip off the true old Irish block all right! Don't worry, your old father knows exactly what a girl needs—whatever her age!" Flinging open the door, he plunked her down in the middle of the floor.

He had bought every toy he could imagine a child would like. There were regiments of dolls with porcelain faces and glassy blue eyes that opened and shut, and with real hair, blond and black and carrot red. There were baby dolls who squealed when Jeb tipped them over to show Poppy and rag dolls with painted faces. There were toy dogs with woolly coats and wheels, and patchwork cats and furry rabbits. There was a dollhouse crammed with furniture and toy soldiers and a farmyard, and piles of printed linen picture books. There were brightly colored rubber balls and skipping ropes with bells on. And at the back stood an enormous wooden rocking horse. He was glossy black with a white blaze on his forehead and he had a mane of real white horsehair. His flying hooves were lacquered a smart red and his saddle and bridle were silver and white.

Pushing aside the dolls, Poppy crawled toward the horse. Holding on to the stirrups, she pulled herself to her feet and stood for a while, wobbling uncertainly, glancing beseechingly at Jeb until he picked her up and set her in the saddle. "There you go, Papa's girl," he chuckled, "let's see how you can ride, then." A great smile lit Poppy's face and he grinned back at her. "You know what we'll call him?" he said slyly. "We'll call him Nik. Because he's a horse's ass too!"

His mood changed suddenly as he thought of Nik, and sweeping Poppy from the saddle he rang for the butler to bring him a bottle of champagne. Poppy sat in the middle of her new toys watching solemnly as he quickly drank his way through the first bottle and called for more. He was on his third bottle when he said suddenly, "Hey, it's bad to drink alone, y'know. Here, have a little sip," and tilting his glass he spilled a little into her soft mouth. She gasped as the fizzy wine hit the back of her throat, coughing and blinking the tears from her eyes.

"Well, what d'ya know, my daughter has extravagant tastes, just like her father," he cried, roaring with drunken laughter. "Poppy," he said, placing a kiss on her round cheek, "you know who you are, don't you? *You're Papa's girl. And don't you ever forget it.*"

The English butler lasted only a month in the Mallory household. Telling Jeb he found the position "unsuitable," he left, shocked by the wild parties and weeklong gambling sessions, and by what the housekeeper called the "criminal neglect" of Poppy.

"She's being brought up like a little heathen," the housekeeper told Jeb stoutly, "no regular hours and all those . . . those *fancy women* around. And that *nursemaid* who's no better than she ought to be. I can't put up with it any longer, Mr. Mallory, I tell you it's just breaking my heart."

"Well, we can't have a housekeeper with a broken heart, Mrs. Drake, so you must go. Immediately," Jeb replied coldly. "I'll give you a week's wages in lieu of notice."

Mrs. Drake bridled, her plump face red with anger. "By rights I'm entitled to a month," she retorted.

Jeb shrugged. "In that case, stay and work the month."

She glared at him furiously, but she knew he'd beaten her and she flounced off, muttering under her breath about "immorality and God's judgment on the wicked."

Jeb merely sighed and sent another message to Maraya. Soon the big house was staffed with sufficient out-of-work dancers and singers to form his own chorus line, and some nights he did just that, entertaining his friends royally with enough champagne and lobster to stock an ocean liner. The Russian Hill house became a rendezvous for theater people arriving in San Francisco, and Jeb hosted parties for opera singers and Shakespearean actors, variety stars and aerial artistes, musicians and playwrights. *And gamblers.*

But he still had sufficient charm and more than enough money to maintain his position in San Francisco's snobbish society. He appeared nightly at his box at the theater, immaculate in white tie and tails, and he was invited to all the cotillions and parties and musical soirées. Lovely girls from good families, intrigued by his reputation, flirted extravagantly with him, while Jeb flirted discreetly with—and quite often seduced—their mothers. And every one of them felt that only *she* could reform the charming black sheep and make him a respectable member of society. All he had to do was marry her.

Poppy was kept like the pampered little pet of the household. "A pretty little blue-eyed tabby cat," Jeb called her. When Louise grew too demanding, he replaced her with a new "nursemaid," and then another, and another. No one stayed for more than a few months. And he quite forgot Poppy's second birthday, and her third, but it made no difference because she knew no other children to invite, and anyway there were parties all the time where she was permitted to sip her own glass of champagne through a straw and to eat lobster and chocolate cake, and Jeb was proud of her because she didn't throw up.

When she was four, Jeb got the urge to travel again and he took her with him to France. Poppy dashed excitedly around Union Square Railroad Station, watching the great trains puffing and snorting steam, and when they boarded she found she had a little room all her own with a special bed that folded from the wall, while outside all the world rushed by. After two days and nights they woke up in Chicago and then took another train to New York. She and Papa and the latest nursemaid, as well as Papa's huge entourage of friends, stayed at the Waldorf Hotel overnight, getting up early to drive down Wall Street to the pier where the big ocean liner waited for them. Poppy thought the journey was quite the best part of traveling, because once she got to France no one understood a word she said. But she did get a lot of presents and pretty dresses from smart shops. And then, after another train journey south— there was Monte Carlo.

This time Jeb had rented a villa in the hills. Before too long her own nursemaid disappeared and a new, French nursemaid took her place, driving down with her each morning to the sea. Poppy thought it was bliss, running along the water's edge, wiggling her toes in the wet sand and digging with her little spade. But she missed Papa a lot because now he always went out without her. Sometimes when she was having her breakfast in the sunny dining room he would just be getting home. He'd come in to see her, his jacket slung over his shoulder, his stiff white collar and his white tie stuffed into his pocket. She thought he looked tired and very handsome as he called to her, "Hey there, me little darling, how's Papa's girl?" And he'd drop a big whiskey-scented kiss on top of her head before climbing upstairs to sleep away the day.

When she was five and back in San Francisco again, Jeb decided it was time Poppy had some book-learning and he hired a young woman called Mademoiselle Grenier to teach her the alphabet and numbers. Ma'mzelle Grenier was a Parisian soubrette with wondrously long slender legs who'd been stranded without a cent when the touring company she was appearing with went broke. Occasionally Jeb would wander into the nursery to see how the lessons were going and Poppy noticed that Ma'mzelle would pat her hair and blush and become even more "French." Jeb just smiled understandingly at Ma'mzelle and told her to come to his study that afternoon at two o'clock.

"Here *ma petite*," she said at five minutes to two, sitting Poppy hastily at a table with some pots of colored paints and a brush. "Paint a nice picture for your father, won't you? I'll be back very soon."

Poppy decided to paint a picture of her favorite friend, the rocking horse. She would give it to Papa and maybe he'd put it in a frame with some glass over it and hang it up beside all those dull, dark paintings in his study. When she'd finished, she regarded it, satisfied, and then looked around for Ma'mzelle. She had been gone a long time and it was awful lonely here in the nursery, even with Nik the horse to talk to. And she really wanted to give her picture to Papa . . . but Ma'mzelle had said to stay here. . . . She waited for what seemed like ages and then, wriggling from her chair, she ran to the door.

The red-carpeted corridor leading from the nursery wing was empty and Poppy tiptoed to the upper hallway and leaned over the banister, listening. The house was completely silent and suddenly she felt frightened. What if everyone had gone away and left her? She'd never been all alone before. . . . Clutching her painting to her chest, she stole silently down the grand curving marble staircase. There was still no sound as she crept along the corridor toward Papa's study because that's where she'd heard him say Ma'mzelle should go.

The big brass doorknob was quite difficult for her small hand but she finally managed to turn it, and pushing open the door, she slid inside. Papa's study was one of the largest rooms in the house, with a vast mahogany desk and a big leather chair that Poppy loved because it swiveled like a carousel. The walls were paneled in dark carved oak, and sofas and chairs were arranged around an elaborate gray marble fireplace. Tall glass-fronted cabinets held important-looking books bound in dark leather and heavy green velvet drapes were swagged and looped across the three high windows. At the far end of the room stood a full-size billiard table with massive bulbous legs and a green baize top. It was lit by a fancy chandelier, its red globes dripping with ormolu crystal drops that tinkled prettily whenever Poppy ran her fingers over them.

Only today they were tinkling anyway, and the pinky-red light glowed onto the green baize and onto Ma'mzelle, who had taken off all her clothes and was spread-eagled across the table, while Papa lay on top of her.

Poppy stared at them puzzled, wondering at Ma'mzelle's strange cries and Papa's odd behavior. Deciding it must be some new game, she smiled. "Papa?" she called in her low, sweet voice. "Can I play too?"

Ma'mzelle shrieked and sat up, clasping her hands over her large, wobbly breasts. Poppy put her hands over her ears, shocked. "You shouldn't scream Ma'mzelle," she informed her sternly, "it's rude."

"Oh, my God," exclaimed Jeb, climbing hastily from the table and adjusting his clothing. "Poppy, what are you doing here?"

"I came to bring you my picture, Papa. I waited and waited for Ma'mzelle to come back but instead she was here, with you." She stared at him reproachfully and Jeb groaned. Taking her arm, he led her to the other end of the room while Ma'mzelle gathered her scattered garments and dressed hurriedly.

"This was . . . er . . . grown-up business, me girl, nothing to do with the nursery," he explained sternly. "You should have stayed in your room as you were told. I'm very angry with you, Poppy."

Tears sprang to her eyes. "But I just wanted to give you the picture because I love you," she whispered.

Jeb stared at her. "Very well, then, Papa's girl," he said, ruffling her red hair that still reminded him of Margaret, "but I want you to promise me that you'll forget that you ever came into this room. Forget that Ma'mzelle was in here. All right?"

Poppy nodded. "I promise, Papa," she agreed. But she thought Papa must really have liked Ma'mzelle a lot because she stayed with them for a long time, and that's why the first language Poppy learned to read and write was French.

There was no "bedtime" for Poppy, no special times to get up or to have lunch. Quite often if there'd been a party the night before, she wouldn't even wake until the afternoon and then she'd have supper at eleven o'clock at night. Sometimes she'd be in bed and the noise would wake her and she'd wander downstairs in her white flannel nightdress, her glossy red hair in two fat braids and a plump rag doll clutched under her arm. The green tables in the card room would be filled with silent tense men, puffing cheroots or cigars, sending swirls of blue smoke into the low green-shaded lights. "Housemaids" in jaunty black soubrette skirts and high-button boots would be strolling around offering refreshment, and the smell of Irish whiskey and of southern bourbon hung in the air. Two sideboards groaned under enormous silver platters of meats and puddings and dishes of fruits and nuts, while opened bottles of fine claret stood neglected alongside decanters of rare vintage port.

Poppy would drift along the sideboards, tasting the turkey and the ham, running a casual finger through the cream on top of an elaborate dessert that had taken the French chef and his assistants all day to concoct. She'd stick a finger into the chocolate mousse or lick the icing sugar from the top of a cake. No one cared. And when she'd place her sticky fingers on Jeb's immaculate gray trousers, he'd merely brush her away irritably and tell her to go find the latest nursemaid.

Jeb would place a wager on almost anything—a thousand dollars on which carriage would turn the corner of the street first, a diamond ring from Cartier on which soprano could hold the high C longest, his ruby cuff links on which chorus girl in the new revue had the longest legs. He'd travel to New York, Chicago, Philadelphia, and Boston in search of a great poker game. But it was at the gambling parties in his own house that the stakes were highest.

The rumors started slowly at first but they soon gathered momentum. Some men had stopped going to Jeb's poker games, complaining that the stakes were becoming too crazily high. They said he was losing money, that he'd gone through his Monte Carlo fortune three times over and was spending a great deal more than he was winning. They said his share of the Rancho Santa Vittoria only made him land rich, not cash rich, and cash was what he needed to gamble. After a six-month run of bad luck the rumors had it that Jeb Mallory was broke.

"Nonsense," murmured the young ladies watching him through their tiny mother-of-pearl binoculars at the opera. "Why, he still looks wonderful. A man on the brink of disaster could never look like that, so calm and easy and smiling."

"Of course he's not broke," scoffed the guests arriving for Poppy's sixth birthday party, gazing in wonder at the banks of thousands of roses and carnations that Jeb had ordered to be specially dyed the same blue as Poppy's eyes. Blue damask covered the long tables, blue garlands were strung from the ceiling, and a small mountain of shiny blue-wrapped presents waited to be opened.

Poppy sat in her birthday chair at the top of the table wearing the beautiful blue organza dress scattered with tiny pink roses that Jeb had ordered from Paris. Sipping champagne, she watched the conjurer who was also their houseboy and the juggler who was a footman, and the dancing girls who were the maids, with large, solemn blue eyes. She noticed pretty young girls kissing red-faced old men, covering her ears as they shrieked with laughter. She watched people dancing gaily to the ten-piece orchestra, and she noticed how greedily they gobbled the roast quail and the sea scallops, the lobster and the caviar, as the expensive champagne spilled carelessly onto the pretty blue cloths.

At midnight Poppy's cake was carried in on a silver salver. It was the biggest cake she had ever seen, and then the funniest thing happened, suddenly it burst right open and out of the top popped two pretty ladies wearing nothing but ropes of blue beads and black net stockings with shiny red garters. They danced the whole length of the table, their breasts bouncing, kicking their legs high while Poppy and all the guests just laughed and laughed.

As the noise and music and laughter reverberated around the lofty room, Jeb suddenly called for silence. "A toast to my daughter, Poppy, on her very important sixth birthday," he cried, lifting her onto the table. "To Papa's girl." "To Papa's girl," chorused the guests, amused.

And then Jeb handed her a small blue suede box, and when she opened it inside was a beautiful sparkly blue necklace.

"Sapphires and diamonds," Jeb called loudly, clasping the inappropriate gift around her small neck. "I thought it was time my best girl had some jewels."

The men eyed him speculatively and the ladies ooh'd and aah'd as they inspected his gift, and Poppy's eyes sparkled as brightly as the sapphires.

Jeb smiled, satisfied that the lavish party and his extravagant gesture would put a stop to the rumors of his insolvency and increase his chances of credit. But this time there was a lurking glint of worry in his eyes.

A few weeks later Poppy was awakened before dawn by the sound of crashing china and the slamming of doors. Voices were raised angrily and, grabbing her rag doll, she ran to her usual vantage point behind the banisters, staring at the scene in the front hall. The heavy oak door stood wide open and she could see Ma'mzelle and some of the maids climbing into a hansom cab, piling wicker baskets and boxes in after them. The French chef stood in the hall shaking his fist and bellowing angrily, and by now Poppy knew enough French to understand that what he was ranting on about so murderously was money. She watched bewildered as he grabbed a pair of tall silver candelabra and marched from the house with them under his arm. The other servants quickly followed his example, grabbing expensive knickknacks, silver boxes and Chinese vases, even paintings from the walls—anything they could carry into the waiting cabs. Then the door slammed and the house fell silent again.

Poppy clutched the banisters waiting for Papa to come running to find out what was happening. Where was everybody going? And why were they taking all those things?

The long-case clock in the hall ticked ponderously and she heard the faint burr of the machinery as it prepared to strike the hour. "*Un, deux, trois, quatre, cinq, six,*" she counted. An hour for every year of her life. With a faint echo the chimes died away and she scrambled to her feet and ran across the hall and along the corridor to Papa's rooms. The little lobby with its gilt chairs and tall Italian rococo mirrors was empty. Papa had always warned her not to disturb him if he was sleeping, and she opened the door to his bedroom cautiously, peeking around and breathing as quietly as she could. But the vast mahogany four-poster was still covered with the black Chinese silk spread embroidered with dragons, and the bed had not been slept in. She remembered that sometimes, when Papa came home really late and he'd had a lot to drink, he'd just strip off his clothes and fall asleep on the daybed in his dressing room. She peeked in hopefully, but he wasn't there either.

Poppy thrust a tightly clasped fist to her mouth to stifle a sob of fear. Where was Papa? Had he left, too, along with everyone else? What would she do if he never came back? Panic lent speed to her legs as she flew back along the hall and down the stairs, flinging open door after door, searching for him.

Chaos reigned in every room, chairs and tables were overturned, curtains torn from their rails, valuable ornaments broken. She stared aghast at the kitchen. Bags of flour and sugar and other dry goods had been emptied into the middle of the stone-flagged floor and a metal churn of milk upturned over the lot. The big stoves that were usually kept stoked and hot twenty-four hours a day, in case Jeb or his guests called for a meal, were cold and dead ashes spilled from the grates. As she watched a small brown rat emerged from beneath the dresser. It scurried across her feet and she fled, screaming, back along the corridors to the front hall. Wrenching open the door, she hurled herself down the steps and into the street.

She ran and ran, sobbing with fear, her little rag doll still clutched under her arm—just the way Papa used to carry her when she was very small. It was only six-thirty and the sun had yet to burn away San Francisco's morning mist, and between her tears and the fog Poppy failed to see the man until she bumped into him.

"Hey, hey, now, little lady," a concerned masculine voice said gently, "what's the matter? How come a little girl like you is running around the streets at this time in the morning? Alone and barefoot, and in your nightgown?" Taking her hand, he said encouragingly, "Come on, now, it can't be that bad . . . look, your doll's not crying."

Poppy's red hair stuck out wildly, and her face was scarlet with fear and hysteria. She was sobbing too much to speak and picking her up, he said gently, "It's all right, little girl. You're just lost, that's all. Look, there's a police station over the way. Why don't you and I go and talk to those nice people about what we can do to help you?"

It was several hours before Poppy was calm enough to tell them her name. The police sergeant whistled softly. "Jeb Mallory's daughter," he commented in an awed voice. Between hiccoughs Poppy sipped a glass of milk and told them what had happened.

"Better send someone round there," the sergeant instructed, "see if Mr. Mallory's returned."

But the young policeman returned half an hour later to say that no, Mr. Mallory wasn't back and that he'd left someone on guard because all the doors had been left unlocked and you couldn't trust anybody these days.

Poppy spent the night at the police station, sleeping in a funny little bunk in a cell with bars and a big padlock, drinking lemonade and eating corned beef hash that the policemen brought from the saloon across the road. She might quite have enjoyed the novelty of it all if she hadn't been so worried about Papa.

When Jeb finally stormed into the police station demanding to know what they were doing with his girl, the police sergeant told him in no uncertain terms and a strong Irish brogue exactly what he thought of a father who left his six-year-old daughter all alone.

Muttering that it was a long story, Jeb pushed a wad of dollar bills into the sergeant's hand. "For the Police Recreation Fund," he said with a smile as he took Poppy by the hand and walked back with her to Russian Hill.

"It's all over now, darling girl," he told her, without offering any explanation as to what had happened, "we'll be leaving this house shortly. After all, it's too big for just the two of us, isn't it? Maybe we'll travel abroad again. How'd you like that?"

"Monte Carlo?" she asked joyously.

"Why not?" he replied, grinning.

Poppy sighed contentedly, clutching her rag doll closer. Everything was all right again now.

The scandalous story of Jeb Mallory's forgotten little daughter spending the night in a police cell while he played poker, and the juicy gossip of how his servants had stripped his house and walked out because they hadn't been paid in several months, flew around San Francisco like a whirlwind. The rumors that Jeb had gambled away his fortune were refueled and the Mallorys were the chief topic of conversation at every society dinner party, and in every saloon and bar in the city.

Jeb and Poppy just stayed quietly at home together in the big, silent, wrecked house, avoiding everyone. Poppy thought it was wonderful having her father all to herself, though she did wonder why no one came to clean up the mess. Jeb opened endless bottles of champagne from what was left of his once vast stock, drinking constantly as he fixed boiled eggs and scrambled eggs and fried eggs in the littered kitchen, until Poppy complained that she couldn't eat another egg, and then he made a funny sort of stew from potatoes and bacon. It was all very odd, but quite fun.

One morning a week later there was a thunderous knock on the door and a severe-looking man handed Jeb a sheet of paper. Poppy watched in surprise as Jeb tried to thrust it back at him, but the man merely stepped back and said, "That's a court requisition, Mr. Mallory, you'd best not ignore it. This property has been legally claimed by Mr. Bud Mayhew in payment of an IOU held by him to settle a gambling debt. I'm sorry, sir, but there it is."

Taking Poppy's hand, Jeb led her upstairs and began to pack their things. A few hours later they stood on the grand front steps with all their bags stacked around them while Jeb locked the big oak door firmly and pocketed the key. Then he hailed a cab and told the driver to take them to the wharf. They were to catch the steamer to Santa Barbara.

On deck later, Poppy stared in astonishment as he took the big brass key from his jacket pocket and flung it into the water, watching silently as it disappeared beneath the waves.

"It's all right, me girl," said Jeb with a grin, "there's plenty more where that came from. All I need is for the luck to be with me. And we still have assets, you and I. We have each other, don't we? And we still own half the Rancho Santa Vittoria!"

CHAPTER *11*

Francesca Rinardi had the sort of cold classical beauty that commanded awe and respect. Her smooth blond hair, flawless features, and tall, blade-thin body had taken her to the top of her profession in Paris, where she'd been the perfect model, swirling haughtily around the pale green, crystal-chandeliered salons of Dior and Balmain.

"Modeling was different before miniskirts changed the profession in the sixties," she often told her daughter, Aria. "Top models were like royalty—always beautifully groomed and dressed. We only mixed with the best people; to the others, we were an unattainable vision."

What she didn't tell her was that her father had been a Belgian greengrocer in a village near Liège and her mother a plump, comfortable countrywoman, and that she'd discarded them both when she'd departed their three rooms over the greengrocery for Paris and a career. She'd spent the hard-earned money they'd given her so proudly and lovingly, on a first-class seat on the train to Paris because she knew she wouldn't meet anybody who was anybody in second class, and her gamble had paid off. The middle-aged man in the very next seat who had helped her with her bags had turned out to be a silk manufacturer from Como and he'd just happened to know the Directrice at Balmain.

After that it had been easy. Francesca invented a whole new back-ground for herself as the only daughter of a country squire, recently deceased, and she hadn't bothered to stay in touch with her real family. She had eliminated them from her life as neatly as if they were dead.

Francesca was twenty-six when she met Paolo Rinardi at a party in Paris. Every time she glanced across the room she'd caught him staring at her, until finally she'd asked her host who he was. "That's Paolo Rinardi," he told her, "the *Barone* Rinardi, his family have one of the oldest titles in Italy, as well as one of the most beautiful palazzos in Venice." He also told her Paolo had estates in the country and a grand apartment in Paris and that he was a bachelor.

Paolo was tall with a blond shaggy mop of hair that he wore longer than was usual in those days, simply because he was so absorbed writing his book *The Lives of the Romantic Poets* that he forgot to get it cut. He often spent weeks on end at work on the book, shut away in the big library of his country home, the Villa d'Oro, without seeing anyone at all. *Except Antony Carraldo.*

But after he met Francesca, Paolo forgot all about his work, all he could think about was her, and he stayed in Paris just to be near her. Francesca had assessed her position and decided that though he was not the international billionaire she'd hoped to catch, at least Paolo offered her comfortable family wealth and a noble name, and she would be the châtelaine of three great houses, and she'd agreed to marry him.

There was a sumptuous reception at the Palazzo Rinardi; the bride's ivory satin dress was courtesy of Balmain, and her family were not invited. *But Antony Carraldo was there.*

Immediately after the honeymoon Paolo buried himself again in the library of the Villa d'Oro; all he wanted was a quiet life in the country with his new wife. Carraldo was the only person permitted to interrupt his thoughts.

He would drop by out of the blue, and after a dinner passed in chilly silence from Francesca, the two would retreat to the library and stay there until dawn. She would pace her bedroom floor furiously, wondering what they were talking about, and sometimes she'd creep downstairs and put her ear to the door, trying to catch what they were saying, but all she heard was the low murmur of voices. The next morning the bottle of brandy would be finished and she'd find pages of scribbled notes on Paolo's desk.

"What were you two doing all night?" she'd demand icily.

"Carraldo's come up with some great suggestions for my chapter on Verlaine," he'd say enthusiastically. "I told him it's he who should be writing this book! The man is so talented, Francesca, there's *nothing* he doesn't know."

In Francesca's opinion Antony Carraldo knew too much. He always looked as though his dark eyes could see right through her. Besides, she thought, there was something strangely sinister about the man. Whenever his black Mercedes crunched up the driveway and she watched Paolo rush out to greet him, she would remember the gossip; and when he took her hand in his cold one and kissed it, a shudder would run down her spine.

It wasn't long before she realized that the Rinardi family fortunes were on the wane. Paolo was totally impractical and he'd allowed the family money to languish in unprofitable investments. When she'd asked him about it, he'd shrugged and said the lawyers looked after all that, then he just buried his head in his book again while the villa and the palazzo gradually crumbled around them.

Francesca was wondering whether it would be easier to get an annulment or a divorce and how she might fare on the international marriage market as the beautiful Baronessa Rinardi, when she discovered that she was pregnant. She would have to wait.

Paolo chose the names for their daughter. Aria, because he thought his child was as beautiful as his favorite operatic songs; then he added Maria for his mother and his idol, Maria Callas, and Angelina, for his grandmother. To her fury, he also insisted on asking Carraldo to be godfather, but thankfully, Carraldo refused.

Francesca hated being saddled with the child. Leaving her in the care of Fiametta, the nurse who'd been with the Rinardis for two generations, and who had been Paolo's own nanny, she shuttled between smart parties in Rome and Paris, and spent months away from home, staying with "friends" at summer villas on the French Riviera. Paolo understood, too late, that the classically beautiful facade he'd fallen in love with was all there was, and, disillusioned, he'd divided his time between his work and his little daughter, whom he adored.

Aria was six years old when Paolo contracted the rare virus that attacked his nervous system and killed him in just three months. For once Francesca was glad to see Carraldo, who, frozen-faced and showing no emotion, took care of the funeral arrangements and paid the bills. When the lawyers had explained how little money was left, she was stunned to discover that she couldn't even sell the villa or its contents, let alone touch anything in the palazzo. It was all entailed in a family trust to be handed down to Paolo's heir—Aria.

Francesca was furious. She was thirty-four years old, she was tied to a couple of expensive houses in places she didn't even want to live, and she was stuck with a small child. She'd quickly accepted Carraldo's offer of help, but to her dismay all he allowed her was exactly enough money each month to pay their living expenses.

Leaving Aria in the care of Fiametta, she had flown off to Rome where she'd rented a tiny apartment and found herself a job as a vendeuse with one of the top designers. The pay wasn't much, but she got wonderful clothes for next to nothing and the social contacts were terrific. She went to all the right parties and was busy from dusk till dawn, and her face soon became a familiar one in the international gossip columns and magazines.

On her fleeting visits home, to host a reception at the palazzo or a house party at her country villa, then, of course, she would see her daughter, but Aria was an annoyingly tomboyish child, more interested in climbing trees and playing with her pet rabbits and the dogs than taking tea in the salon with her mother's friends, and somehow she'd always managed to spill lemonade down the pretty smocked dress Francesca had bought specially to show her off.

Carraldo rarely called at the Palazzo Rinardi anymore, though he was meticulous about paying Aria's school fees and expenses. As a christening gift, he'd given her a priceless antique silver goblet fashioned by the famous eighteenth-century silversmith Paul de Lamerie, and Francesca often eyed it longingly, wishing she could sell it, but the thought of Carraldo's cold dark eyes if he ever heard it was back on the market had stopped her dead.

On her daughter's seventeenth birthday, Francesca had been forced to reassess her own position. Younger women were running off with the marriageable prizes now, not poor widows. She was "on the shelf"! It was then she'd thought of Aria.

Her tomboy child had emerged into a dazzlingly attractive young woman, and surely seventeen was quite old enough to find a rich husband. Picking up Aria's silver-framed photograph from her dressing table, she had decided, critically, that her daughter wasn't as beautiful as she was. Aria's was a strong face with enormous dark blue eyes set challengingly beneath winged brows, a straight nose, a wide mouth, and the sort of bones that gave it character. But there was something about the way she held her tall, slender body, her confident long-legged walk and the engaging way she faced the world, straight on, her chin held high, that turned heads along any street. Francesca knew that with grooming and the right clothes Aria could be the sort of unusual beauty who lasted in a man's memory.

But Aria was also stubborn and willful—she had never done as Francesca had wanted. She'd remembered with a sigh all those sabotaged tea parties with spilled lemonade, and realized this wasn't going to be an easy task. Aria was a typical teenager; she had a host of friends and boyfriends, yet she often liked to spend time alone at the villa, riding her horse or painting and playing music too loud on her record player.

Of course these days young people expected "love." But what Aria needed was an older, more experienced man; a man who knew what he wanted—and what he was paying for. Francesca sighed again; Aria didn't seem to give a damn if her friends were rich or poor—and she certainly wasn't going to marry a man her mother had chosen just because she said so . . . she was going to have to be much more clever about this. . . . It was then she'd summoned Antony Carraldo. What he had said had surprised her, but after thinking it over quickly, she had been thrilled. Still, it had taken a great deal of thought to plan how to get Aria to agree.

"Darling," Francesca had said the next morning. "I think it's time you knew something important . . . something . . ." Her voice had broken with a sob, and Aria had glanced up from her breakfast, her eyes wide with alarm.

"What is it, Mama? Are you ill?"

"No . . . well, not really, though the doctors have warned me . . ." Francesca's hand had trembled a little as she'd brushed it wearily across her eyes. "The fact is, Aria, we Rinardis have no money left. Of course, after working so hard all these years, I'm completely exhausted, but I explained to the doctors that I must carry on with my work, otherwise who would look after you? It's so hard for a woman of my age to commute between her work in Rome and a young daughter who needs her here in Venice, but I know it's my duty. Oh, Aria, if only you knew the *truth*! How much I've sacrificed in the name of 'duty'! How I've devoted myself to work in order to bring you up; why, I even had to sacrifice being here—with my own child—because your father left us penniless. . . ."

"No, he didn't," Aria had retorted defensively. "How can you say we were *penniless*, Mama? As though Papa left us out on the street, begging for a living? You worked because you enjoyed it and it meant you got a lot of pretty clothes."

"Aria! Did you want me to suffer in some job I hated? Make no mistake about it, I worked in order to bring much needed extra money into the house. I tried to keep it from you, to protect you while you were still so young, but the truth is that the money from the Rinardi trust wouldn't have kept your dreadful parrot Luchay in sunflower seeds! I'm afraid it's only because I've struggled to keep things together that you are dressed decently and went to good schools. *And now I'm exhausted.*" Pressing a fragile white hand tiredly to her brow, Francesca had sunk gracefully onto a frayed brocade chaise longue.

Aria had stared at her doubtfully. After all these years she still couldn't tell when her mother was telling the truth or when she was acting. Yet if what she said about the Rinardi trust was true, then where had the money for her schooling come from? And how had they managed to keep up the palazzo and the villa? Recalling the vast undulating roofs of the Villa d'Oro, she shuddered at the thought of what they must cost to repair.

She had thought wistfully of her father. To her, the Villa d'Oro was still the special place she had shared with him; she'd never felt as happy anywhere, anytime in her life, as in the times spent with Paolo. Their love had been so uncomplicated, so natural and easy, quite different from the complex range of emotions she felt toward her mother. Sometimes Aria wondered how she could dislike so many things about Francesca, and yet still love her. And how she could despise Francesca for her shallow, social-butterfly existence and yet still find herself anxious for her approval.

Her mother had dropped her hand from her brow and was gazing listlessly into space. She *did* look exhausted, Aria had thought, suddenly worried. What if she was *really* ill? She must do something to help. She would get a job. She'd thought longingly of her art studies at the college in Florence; painting was her passion and she'd intended it to become her life, but now it would have to wait. "Listen to me, Mama," she'd said, "you must go to Villa d'Oro, it's peaceful there and quiet, you can rest until you feel stronger. I shall leave college and get a job and look after you." She'd stroked Francesca's blond hair tenderly.

"Don't do that, Aria," her mother had complained, smoothing back her hair, "I'm just on my way out for lunch." Then she'd stared at her astonished. "A job? And what would you do? Sell carnival masks and Murano glass to the tourists? Work in a hotel as a waitress, or a chambermaid perhaps? You don't seem to understand, Aria. The Rinardi trust is virtually at an end. All it consists of is right here, around you . . . these crumbling walls and these faded antiques that we can't even sell because they belong to the same damned trust that has no money! *I tell you, Aria, I cannot go on!*"

Shrugging her jacket over her shoulders, Francesca had picked up her purse and headed for the door. As she flung it open she'd turned, staring back at her daughter still sitting at the foot of the chaise longue. "I want you to know, Aria, I'm at my wits' end. If this cannot be resolved properly, then . . ." She'd paused dramatically. *"Then I simply don't know what I might do!"* And turning abruptly, she'd stalked from the room.

Aria had clutched her arms across her stomach as fear gripped her. What had her mother meant, *she didn't know what she might do . . . ?* She couldn't possibly mean that because they had no money . . . *she would kill herself?* Tears had spilled down her cheeks as she'd considered the possibility that to her mother, a world without the luxuries she considered to be the necessities of life was a world that simply was not worth living in. But there had been a new, desperate look in Francesca's eyes and a shrill nervous edge to her voice that had a terrible ring of truth. Springing from the couch, Aria had run terrified from the salon in search of Fiametta.

No one knew exactly how old Fiametta was—not even Fiametta herself remembered, and with her wrinkled walnut face and her swollen arthritic hands, she might have been anywhere from seventy to a hundred and seventy! By title and employment—though it was many years since Francesca had actually paid her any wages—she was Aria's nanny; but to the Rinardi family she had always been much more than that; Fiametta was more like a beloved grandmother, as well as being Aria's friend and confidante. Aria told Fiametta all the things she could never tell her mother, and she loved her dearly.

The old woman was sitting at the scrubbed pine table in the center of the lofty, antiquated kitchen that had once required a staff of fifteen to run. Her coarse gray hair was scraped back into a knot at her neck, and she had the comfortable full-bosomed matronly body of the eternal grandmother. She wore a starched white apron over her black dress and was chopping herbs for a lunchtime risotto, her swollen arthritic hands making painfully slow work of the job.

Her bright, birdlike glance changed to a frown of concern as she saw Aria's tears. "Whatever's the matter, *carina?*" she'd asked, lumbering to her feet as Aria hurled herself into her arms. "Now child, tell old Fiametta all about it," and she'd patted Aria's back gently, the way she might a tired infant's.

She'd frowned ominously as Aria had poured out her story. She had known Francesca for more than twenty years and there was something about this that didn't ring true. Francesca wasn't the sort to kill herself, she was far too cold and calculating.

"But Fiametta," Aria had wailed, "that's what she said! And she *looked* different, I've never seen her like this before, so . . . odd and nervous."

"Your mother is never nervous," she'd snapped, "she's no more penniless today than she was six months ago. All it means is that now she's decided to do something about it!"

"Do something about it?" Aria asked, puzzled. "But *what* will she do?"

The very next day, her mother had told her she was to marry Carraldo. And she'd made it clear that there was no choice.

"Marriage!" Aria had leapt to her feet, overturning her glass of water. "Whatever are you talking about, Mama? I'm only seventeen! I don't want to get married. I've never even fallen in love yet."

"Love!" Francesca had snorted derisively. "Love has nothing to do with marriage. Love is merely infatuation, it never lasts. *But money does.* You'll have houses, fabulous jewels, couture clothes and furs; you'll travel the world on private planes and yachts. You will be a star of the international set."

"You mean I'll be everything *you* would like to be!" Aria had retorted. *"Don't you understand? I'm not like you.* I'm like Papa, I want to be an artist, I want to create great paintings that will bring pleasure for generations. . . ."

"Very well, Aria," Francesca had said coldly, "why not think about your father? Remember how *he* felt about this beautiful palazzo, remember how many generations of Rinardis have called it home. *Your Papa revered the history of this palazzo. He loved every stick and stone and blade of grass of the Villa d'Oro.* Your father would have done *anything,* Aria, to keep the Rinardi history and the Rinardi name alive! So don't imagine it's for *me* you might be sacrificing your freedom . . . it's for Papa, and all the Rinardis who served to make our name a proud one."

Aria had sat for a long time, alone at the supper table, thinking about her father.

She could no longer remember his face clearly, but she could recall little incidents and things they had done together. And her most vivid memory was of the day he'd brought home the parrot.

It was a bleak February afternoon with a threat of snow in the yellow-gray sky over Venice, and the bird's carnival colors had delighted her.

"His name is Luchay," Papa had told her, "and he is much older than you or I. He was born in the depths of the Amazon jungles in a faroff country called Brazil, but I doubt he remembers that now. He used to live with your great-aunt Helena and before that he belonged to someone called Poppy Mallory. Luchay can say Poppy's name, so don't be surprised if you hear him."

"Will he say my name?" she'd asked, running a tentative finger along the bird's soft green wing. She'd pulled it back hurriedly as the parrot turned his head, watching her with his sharp little topaz eyes.

"I daresay he will, someday," Paolo agreed, "when he knows you better and knows that you love him."

Then, lifting Aria up, he'd shown her the precious emerald and diamond rings around Luchay's scrawny legs, and his bejeweled stand, and his wondrous golden cage, and she'd clapped her hands laughing in delight. The parrot had suddenly mocked her laughter, and then she and Papa had laughed even more at the parrot laughing at them. From then on Luchay and she and Papa had shared a special relationship, one from which Francesca had been excluded, and to this day her mother hated the bird.

Aria clasped her hands to her aching head; the emotional pressure from her mother and the memories of her father were all too much; she simply had to get out. Snatching up a jacket from the hall, she'd run from the house.

The streetlamps had cast pale pools of light across the Campo Morosini and puffs of cotton candy mist drifted in the shadows as she'd run through the Campo San Vidal and past the church of San Stefano, threading her way through the familiar cobbled alleys until she emerged opposite the Teatro La Fenice. The strains of a symphony orchestra playing Vivaldi's *Four Seasons* filtered from its brightly lit facade, the urgent beat of the "Summer" music matching that of her own heart. Aria had thought of the times her father must have walked up these very steps and into the lovely old rococo theater to listen to the great opera stars. She thought of how much her father had loved music, how much he'd loved Venice, and of how much he had loved her, and she knew she couldn't bear to let him down. Nor could she risk what might happen to her mother. She must accept her responsibilities.

Turning despairingly from the theater, she'd plunged back into the shadowy alleys. The shops were still open and people jostled busily past her, heading for the cafés and restaurants. She stared at the smiling young girls clutching the arms of their boyfriends, or out shopping in laughing, gossiping groups, and realized with a stab that she was no longer part of their world. She had been forced to grow up. Just then a woman emerged from a brightly lit beauty salon, a small dog clutched in her arms. The jaunty red bow holding back the hair from the dog's beady-bright eyes exactly matched the bow in the woman's own hair, making Aria smile. The optimism of youth had lifted her spirits temporarily. She might have to do as her mother asked, she'd thought, striding into the beauty salon, but she didn't have to make it easy for her!

"Yes, we can fit you in now," the receptionist had told her. "Giorgio will take you."

"I want you to cut it all off," Aria had said, her voice wobbling uncertainly.

"But Signorina, it is so beautiful," the hairdresser had protested, running a thick silken strand through his fingers. "Just an inch, maybe, no more . . ."

"All of it," she'd commanded, tears brimming again in her eyes. "Now."

CHAPTER *12*

A week later, she had stopped crying and finally agreed to meet Carraldo. He was never late and Fiametta answered his knock at eight p.m. precisely. Aria had told her what was happening and she'd offered at once to give her all her life-savings. "It's not a great deal of money, darling child," she'd said, weeping, "but it's enough to let you run away and begin life somewhere else. And it's better by far than selling yourself to Carraldo!" But Aria had been resolute. "There's really no other way Fiametta," she'd said loyally, "it is my duty."

A shiver ran down her spine as Carraldo took her hand in both of his.

"The naughty girl cut off all her beautiful hair," her mother gushed into the silence. "She looks like a street urchin. But hopefully it will have grown a little, in time for the wedding."

"I want you to talk to me quite openly," Carraldo said, ignoring Francesca. "Your mother has agreed to allow me to ask you to marry me, but of course only you can give me the answer. I can quite understand that this may be a shock to you, and I don't want you to feel under any pressure. All I can say is that I genuinely loved your father, he was my dearest friend. And that I've loved you since the day you were born. If you say yes, then I will do everything in my power to make you happy."

Aria felt as though she was an onlooker in a play; she seemed to be floating in limbo between her brief past and her unknown future, and though Carraldo was being gentle, she sensed it was just a crust over the surface of a volcano.

"Aria?" her mother prompted anxiously.

"I accept, Signore," she said, lowering her eyes. Carraldo's hands were on her shoulders and then his lips brushed her cheek in the lightest of kisses. "Thank you, Aria," he said.

He took a small dark blue box from its packet and flicked it open, offering it to her. Aria stared, dazzled at the immense flawless emerald inside. There were no extra decorative strips of diamonds surrounding it, because it needed none. It was just a single densely green jewel whose size and simple setting proclaimed its rarity and importance.

"It came from the treasure chest of a maharani," Carraldo told her. "I liked its magnificent color and its lack of ostentatious decoration. I thought it might please you."

She shrank back; the huge emerald looked to her like a symbol of bondage. "I can't do it, I can't wear it," she whispered.

"Whatever is the matter with you, Aria," Francesca cried shrilly. "Why, any girl in the world would be thrilled to wear such a ring."

"Please, Antony," she pleaded, "can't we wait a while . . . until I'm eighteen . . ." Eighteen seemed like light years away, an eternity.

"As you wish," he said quietly, "I can wait a few months. But we must marry soon after that."

Carraldo's eyes had looked suddenly anxious and she'd agreed hurriedly. "Yes, yes, I promise. Just give me time."

"You've made me a very happy man," he said, standing up. "My plane is waiting at Marco Polo Airport to take me to New York, there's an important art auction tomorrow. Will you have dinner with me when I return?" She'd nodded silently, watching, as her mother saw him out. Carraldo had been gentle, he'd been charming and kind. He'd treated her as though she were some rare and precious object to be handled and admired, and somehow she'd felt that as the wife of Antony Carraldo she would be just another part of his famous collection.

For two weeks Aria had gone to bed every night filled with relief that the day had passed without Carraldo's return, and she'd woken each morning filled with dread that he would call and demand that she keep her promise to have dinner with him. She became so tense and nervous at the prospect that when he finally did telephone, it was almost a relief.

Ignoring Francesca's instructions to wear the slick new little Ungaro silk suit she'd made her buy, she put on a simple white skirt and a black silk knit sweater, snapping the two together around her slender waist with a wide black leather belt. She wore flat black pumps and no stockings on her tanned legs, and Francesca was furious.

"At least put on some jewelry," she pleaded as Aria remained adamant about her choice, "my pearl and diamond earrings perhaps?" Aria clipped an enormous pair of black-and-white-speckled ceramic earrings onto her small flat ears and stood back to examine the effect. She ran her hands through her short hair, making it stand up spikily, and Francesca groaned.

"Mama!" Aria exclaimed irritably. "Will you please stop trying to make me into something I'm not. I am who I am and I wear what I like, and if that's what Carraldo wants, then that's what he will get. But I'm not changing to please you—or to please him."

They heard the roar of the launch outside and Francesca hurried to the stairs, waiting as Fiametta opened the big doors onto the Grand Canal. She returned a moment later clutching an envelope in her gnarled hand. "The Signore Carraldo had been delayed, Signora," she called. "The boatman is waiting to take Aria to meet him now."

Francesca snatched the envelope from Fiametta. It was addressed to Aria, but she opened it anyhow.

My darling girl, Carraldo had written in a large, firm hand. *Forgive me for not coming for you myself, especially on this—our first time together, but unfortunately I realize that I will be delayed. My boatman, Giulio, will bring you to me and I await seeing you with much pleasure.*

He'd signed it simply *Antony Carraldo.*

Aria's casual appearance hid the trembling sensation she felt inside as she stepped into Carraldo's sleek black Riva launch. His personal flag, the black raven in a gold circle, fluttered at the bow as the boatman, in a crisp white jacket and naval cap trimmed with gold braid, swung the launch into the busy canal. She'd expected to be taken directly to Carraldo's house to wait for him there, but instead the boat picked up speed and surged, with a deep-throated roar, across the lagoon.

"Signore Carraldo asked me to take you to the airport to meet him," the boatman told her, and Aria thought nervously that Carraldo must be impatient to see her if he wanted her to meet his plane.

A chauffeur was waiting for her at the jetty and they drove in the large black Mercedes through the airport to where a small, powerful, black Gulfstream jet waited on the tarmac, again emblazoned with Carraldo's raven insignia.

The waiting steward saluted her and escorted her up the flight of steps into the aircraft, and into a gray suede–padded saloon.

"The Signorina Rinardi," he announced.

Carraldo glanced up from his auction catalogue and then leapt to his feet, smiling. "Aria. Can you forgive me for not coming to you? I sent Giulio because I knew we would be late."

"I don't mind if you're late," she replied shyly. "I'm not very punctual myself."

"I'm afraid punctuality is one of my habits. My father was a stickler for time; I think he organized our lives on a minute-by-minute schedule."

Aria glanced at him, surprised. Somehow she had never thought of Carraldo having a real father; perhaps he was human after all. She became aware of a noise outside as the steps were wheeled away, and the muted purr of engines. Then the doors were closed and the engines roared as they began to taxi down the runway. "But where are we going?" she cried, alarmed.

"Sit down, Aria, and fasten your seat belt," Carraldo told her calmly, "I'm taking you home for dinner."

"But I don't even know where you live." She clasped her seat belt obediently, "I thought we were having dinner here, in Venice."

"I have many houses," he replied, "but I suppose I must consider Milan my home, because it's also the center of my business. It will be your principal home, too, Aria, and I thought you might like to see it." He smiled. "Don't worry, you'll be back in time for bed."

The plane was surging effortlessly into the air and suddenly all that lay below them was the blueness of the lagoon and the sea. Aria looked at Carraldo nervously; they were finally alone and Venice might have been a million miles away.

He showed her his aircraft proudly. It was the smallest of his Gulfstreams, he said, and the one he used for hopping from city to city. The other two were Gulfstream IV's with a transatlantic capability. One was kept at Kennedy Airport in New York and the other at Charles de Gaulle in Paris. Each was painted the same glossy black and bore the Carraldo raven emblem, and the interior of each was decorated in the same way. The walls, window shades, chairs, cabinets, mirror frames, beds, were all in the same padded steel-gray suede. Carraldo had not allowed even a single touch of color, and he told her he found the monochrome effect restful after feasting his eyes on so many exciting canvases during the course of his work as an art dealer.

He asked about her painting and why she had given up her courses in Florence. "It's because I'm to be married," she replied, lowering her eyes.

"Then we must arrange new courses for you," he said quickly. "Leave it to me, I'll find you the best teacher."

Aria wondered why he didn't understand that it wouldn't be the same. It wasn't only the teaching she would miss, but her friends; she'd miss their laughter and the fun together in the cafés and at parties.

The steward appeared to ask if they wished anything. "Champagne?" Carraldo suggested.

"Thank you, but could I please have a Coca-Cola instead?" She blushed as he smiled, stealing a look at his profile as he asked the steward to bring two Coca-Colas. She thought his hawkish nose made his bony face look arrogant and the purplish shadows beneath his deep-set eyes made them look even darker. She supposed some women might find Carraldo an attractive man, but he made her feel uncomfortable.

"Did you know I also have a house in Portofino?" he asked, meeting her eyes.

"No," she replied, "but then I know so little about you."

"We must rectify that," he said quickly, "but I think you'll be happy there, Portofino is always full of young people. And then, of course, there's the house in London and the apartment in New York. Do you enjoy travel, Aria?"

"I haven't had very much opportunity." She sipped her Coke uncomfortably. It was served in a delicate Baccarat crystal glass with smooth rounded cubes of ice and wafer slices of lemon, but she would have traded it for a simple can of Coke shared with her college friends any day.

As the plane prepared to land, she thought, surprised, that the half-hour flight had passed quickly. Another long black Mercedes was waiting to whisk them from Malpensa Airport to the city. "Are all your cars the same then?" she asked. "Like the interiors of your planes?"

Carraldo shrugged. "As always, there is a good reason. I was once in a bad accident—I was almost killed. I was driving my father's old Mercedes, a car he'd had for years because he loved its style. The steering was such perfection, I was able to spin the car out of danger. I've driven Mercedeses ever since, and this particular model suits my needs."

Of course, she thought somberly, a man like Carraldo would always have a reason for everything, he would never act on impulse. Every single act would have been considered and planned. But if so, then what was his real reason for marrying her?

A butler in black jacket and white gloves flung open the door as the Mercedes purred to a halt. Carraldo had turned the tall, gray-stone eighteenth-century town house into a twentieth-century home. The floors were of bleached wood and the only carpets were the two antique Chinese silk rugs glowing quietly on the walls, like a pair of exquisitely subtle paintings. He had opened up the downstairs rooms to make one vast area with lofty double-height ceilings, and twin fires blazed in the unadorned marble fireplaces at each end. The walls were a plain cream and the deep sofas were all in a simple taupe linen. All the lighting was indirect, from recessed downlights or spindly high-tech lamps that cast pools of light, and a wonderful Bang & Olufsen hi-fi whispered the sounds of Ashkenazy playing Mozart through speakers as tall as Aria herself.

She stared around the room expecting to see Carraldo's famed art collection, but apart from the beautiful rugs, the walls were bare. There was not a single painting, not a single piece of sculpture or decorative object.

"Everything in these rooms has a function," Carraldo said. "As I mentioned before, I look at so many works of art each day that I need to allow my mind to rest in absolute simplicity. Except for one favorite painting kept in my bedroom. It's the last thing I look at each night before I go to sleep. It stays for a month and then I change it. I don't like to get too attached to any one possession."

The girlish posy of flowers arranged in the center of the steel and glass dining table seemed out of character, lily of the valley and baby's breath, stephanotis and freesia, and tiny cream rosebuds. Like a bouquet for a young bridesmaid, Aria thought, surprised.

"I chose them for you," Carraldo told her. "I thought they might be the kind you'd like."

Aria flushed angrily; did he think she was such an infant, then? The butler offered her a glass of champagne, and she took a large gulp, suddenly determined to behave as badly as she dared.

The meal was a simple one of Italian food, exquisitely presented and served, but Carraldo ate little, sitting back in his chair, sipping his champagne and watching her with that faint sardonic smile. Avoiding his eyes, Aria drank her champagne as if it were water, saying nothing.

They sipped their coffee in silence, and then finally he took her hand and said, "I have something to show you before we go."

Her head was swimming from all the champagne as she stumbled beside him down the hallway and into a room that was obviously his study. An eighteenth-century oaken *cartonnière*, its leather drawers faded from burgundy to rose, contrasted with the modern simplicity of the slab of speckled black granite that served as his desk. Everything was immaculately tidy, with papers in neat piles next to important-looking books. The telephone was black and the simple pale cream shades on the windows matched the color of the walls. Aria thought it looked as though Carraldo had pared his personal life down to a minimum, and she shuddered, wondering what his bedroom must look like, imagining some cold, monastic cell. A small, gilt-framed landscape was displayed on an easel, and she recognized it instantly as a Manet.

"Ohh . . . How beautiful," she gasped, bending forward to look at it more closely.

"I thought you'd like it," Carraldo said quietly, pleased.

Aria hovered over the painting, thrilled. "However did Manet do it?" she whispered, forgetting for a moment where she was and who she was with. "How did he create such a magical feeling with just a brush and some paint? This is so . . . so intimate, I feel as though I am there, in that meadow by that river, on a sunny Sunday evening."

"When Manet submitted this painting to the Paris Salon in 1860 they rejected it," Carraldo told her, "they thought it was odd, and ugly."

Aria stared at him, shocked. "How sad not to know that someday his painting would be appreciated, even though he must have known the Salon was wrong."

Carraldo turned away with a shrug. "Van Gogh never sold a single painting in his lifetime. What I try to do now, Aria, in my own small way, is to find young artists of talent whom I can help by nurturing them along, and eventually finding a market for their work. Nevertheless, it's a hard life for them. It takes a great deal of courage to be an artist, and a long time to build a career."

"I didn't know that's what you did," she said, surprised.

Carraldo took the Manet from its easel and offered it to her. "I bought it for you," he said abruptly. "Please take it."

Her eyes widened in amazement. *"You bought this Manet—for me? But that's impossible . . . I mean . . . nobody does things like that."*

"I didn't succeed in impressing you with the maharani's emerald," Carraldo replied curtly, "but obviously you find this more appealing. It's yours."

She hesitated, staring at the painting, stunned by his magnificent gift. "I can't," she said finally. "Please don't ask me why, but I just can't accept it. Not yet."

Carraldo replaced the Manet on its easel without another word. "It's time to leave," he said curtly. Aria glanced nervously at him as she hurried through the door; he seemed so cold suddenly, she was afraid.

As the Mercedes sped silently back to the airport, she told herself she was just being silly, she was just a little drunk from all that champagne. Of course, Carraldo would never harm her. But she'd felt he was angry with her for refusing his gift, and Carraldo's anger was an unknown force.

She lay back in her seat on the plane, her eyes closed; when she finally peeked at Carraldo, he was immersed in his art catalogue and the journey passed in total silence.

The black car was waiting to take them to the launch, and as the boat nosed its way back along the canals, he finally said to her, "I'm glad we had this opportunity to talk. I feel that we know each other better now."

But as Aria watched the sleek black Riva speed into the Venetian night, she knew it wasn't true. She knew no more about the real Antony Carraldo than she had before. And she was still afraid of him.

CHAPTER *13*

Today was the opening of Orlando Messenger's exhibition at the Maze Gallery in London, and though a great deal of not very good champagne was being consumed by a lot of very rich people, there were still very few of the little red stickers that denoted a sale. Orlando smiled charmingly at everyone, accepting quick double kisses from chic women whose dresses had probably cost more than his paintings, and at the same time keeping an ear open for the international gossip that everyone seemed to find more interesting than his work. Damn them, he thought angrily, they can talk about who's screwing whom over their endless lunches, they don't have to do it now!

Ever since he was an infant Orlando had been told how beautiful he was, how extraordinary his coloring, how charming his nature. The odd thing was that it didn't seem to have gone to his head. For a time he'd enjoyed the benefits of several of Britain's top public schools, where for some inexplicable reason he'd acquired the knack of getting himself thrown out—too frequently to please his parents. It had turned out that Orlando hated school. The child psychiatrist had told his parents his nature was totally opposed to its day-to-day small disciplines, though the larger discipline of learning was no problem to him at all. In fact he was extremely bright, with an IQ of 158.

Orlando had proven to be artistic and with a sigh of relief his parents had sent him off to spend three years at art school in Florence—on condition that he boarded with his mother's relatives there and kept to certain rules—after all, he was then barely sixteen. In Florence, he had managed to give the social impression of a well-brought-up, good-mannered, charming young art student while at the same time carrying on a series of affairs with his aunt's friends. "At least they were all females," his uncle had said with relief when his aunt had found out and was denouncing Orlando bitterly. "With those English boys you never know!"

Somehow his sojourn abroad had lengthened—after Florence there had been Paris, and then the south of France, and a detour to the Greek islands. But he wasn't the sort to paint wilderness—his terrain was urban chic, the villas and opulent apartments and homes of his many acquaintances. He had a facility for capturing a likeness and soon learned that there was no better way to flatter a woman than to tell her he simply *had* to paint her portrait, or her house. Women were no problem for Orlando Messenger. No problem at all.

"Orlando! Lovely to see you again. We haven't met in ages . . . it must have been, what? Two years ago?" The small and deadly chic woman was dressed in black and her large mouth was a glossy red gash in her white face as she smiled at him.

"At least that, Pamela," he replied taking her hand and turning on the charm. "I've missed you."

"Me too, darling." Her large brown eyes under their burden of gray shadow and black mascara stared knowingly into his. "I have a new chalet in Gstaad," she murmured, allowing her hand to linger in his. "Come spend Christmas—we're having quite a house party, twenty-six, I think. . . ."

"Sounds great," he said, smiling into her eyes.

"Lovely, you can do a painting of the new chalet."

She strutted across the room on the impossibly high heels that she always wore to give her the necessary extra inches, flinging her arms around another man, a writer Orlando knew, and he heard her repeating almost identically the conversation she'd just had with him. Pamela made a habit of "creative" conquests, and Orlando thought bitterly that with her money she usually had her choice. He'd go to Gstaad for Christmas and she'd expect him to entertain her in bed—if and when she felt like it—and in return he'd do a nice little watercolor of the house. Singing for his supper again!

He stared moodily at the unsold paintings; they were charming and colorful, and they were just a touch commercial because he'd tried to gear his talents to what the customer liked instead of giving himself free rein and painting what *he* wanted, the way *he* wanted it. It had to stop, he told himself bitterly, he was an excellent artist, maybe even a great one. The trouble was he was no good at starving in a garret, he enjoyed the high life too much. And that's where Poppy Mallory's money came in.

He'd called the lawyer in Geneva right away and told him his story. Lieber had listened and then he'd said: "And what documentation do you have to back this up, Mr. Messenger?" What could he say? He'd searched his father's study from end to end, looking for birth certificates or family letters and documents, and found nothing.

Lieber had sounded doubtful. "Send me a written statement, Mr. Messenger. Let me know if you come up with anything substantive," he'd added, not quite dismissing him because after all, his story might be true.

Orlando sighed frustratedly, staring at the smart, laughing gossiping crowd; with Poppy's money he could be one of them instead of always on the outside, and then there'd be no more having to be charming to the Pamelas of the world. It would be their turn to try to charm him—and by God, he'd make *them* sing for their supper!

"Well, well," said Peter Maze, the gallery owner, "just look what the wind blew in! My word, Orlando, the gods are visiting you! That's Antony Carraldo."

He bustled away, beaming as he held out his hand to the dark, hawkish-looking man standing by the door. Orlando's eyes lit up; he knew that not only was Carraldo a major art dealer, but that from his bottomless wealth he'd already sponsored two decades' worth of young artists, establishing several as major names. Carraldo was an artist's savior, a true patron in the old-fashioned sense, and he was exactly what Orlando needed. Nor was Carraldo a man who wasted his time. He knew Carraldo wouldn't have come here unless he was interested in him. He sipped his champagne coolly, watching and waiting for Peter to introduce him, but Carraldo was pointing at the painting displayed in the window.

He saw Peter Maze beam delightedly and then a red sticker was affixed to the painting. *Carraldo had bought his watercolor of Portofino.*

Putting down the champagne glass, Orlando made his way through the crowd toward them. "Ah, Orlando," cried Peter, "come and meet Antony Carraldo."

"I just bought one of your paintings," Carraldo said.

"I'm flattered that someone as discerning as you liked my work enough to buy it, Signore Carraldo," he replied.

Carraldo's hooded dark eyes met his broodingly for a moment. "Your work is charming," he said at last, "you have a nice touch."

"It's not what I really want to do, though, sir," Orlando said eagerly. "It's commercial, geared to these people's pockets. If I were able to give myself free rein, let myself go and do the work I really want to do . . ."

"Then why don't you?" Carraldo asked.

He shrugged. "The usual thing, money. Or lack of it. I have to make a living."

"As do we all."

"Carraldo! Is it really you? I thought you were in New York for the Van Gogh sale." A tall, thin American woman, still swathed in her magnificent sable coat even though it was hot under the gallery's lights, insinuated herself between them. "Did you know that Harry was here? You must come over and say hello to him."

"Perhaps we'll meet again someday," Carraldo said as the woman urged him away, "and good luck with your work."

"What's he doing here?" Orlando asked Peter Maze angrily.

"He was just passing the window and saw your painting of Portofino. He was amused to see his own villa in it, that's all."

God damn, Orlando thought savagely, even the great Antony Carraldo only wanted a picture of his house! He was destined to go on painting villas forever!

"Have you heard the latest gossip about him?" Peter asked, his small eyes gleaming with malicious mirth. "Carraldo's in love! Her name is Aria Rinardi. She's beautiful and juicy and not quite eighteen—and he's asked her to marry him. Apparently she's as poor as a church mouse and so of course she agreed. Who could turn down *that* kind of money? Anyhow—the thing is that now her mother is claiming she's the Mallory heiress—and so despite all the parental pushing, Aria's having second thoughts. After all, with her own fortune what girl in her right mind would marry the mysterious Signore Carraldo?"

Orlando stared at him, shocked. "The Mallory heiress? But who is she?"

"Didn't you see the ad? I thought everybody had. That's the trouble —it seems nobody knows who Poppy is . . ."

"Not that, you fool," Orlando snarled. *"Who is Aria Rinardi?"*

Peter eyed him huffily. "Don't get so emotional, Orlando, it doesn't become you. Anyway, if you really must know, she's the daughter of an Italian baron—a deceased baron and also an impoverished one. Hence the need for the rich husband. She lives in Venice in a wonderful old crumbling palazzo that probably needs a million or so spending on it to put it to rights. So she'll be no good for you, old boy. What you need is a woman as rich as Carraldo!" He laughed his high-pitched laugh as Orlando glared at him.

"What I need is for you to sell a few more of my paintings," he said, shouldering his way angrily through the crowd surrounding Carraldo. Sipping a glass of champagne, he studied him covertly, thinking about what he'd just heard. He had to find out about Aria Rinardi, but he knew he couldn't ask Carraldo.

"I'm sorry I must leave," Carraldo was saying. "I should be on my way to Paris right now. Yes, I'll be in New York next week." He shook a few hands, kissed a few scented cheeks, and as he turned to go, he caught Orlando's eye.

"I enjoyed seeing your work." He paused as a thought crossed his mind. "I bought the Portofino painting to give to my fiancée," he told him. "She was at art school in Florence for a year and her chosen medium is watercolor. She misses her work now, and I think she would benefit from some tuition. If it would help you, and if you are interested, I could offer you the job of tutoring her for a couple of months. It would be in Venice, of course, but some arrangement could be made for your board and lodgings in a *pensione.* I don't think you'd find the hours too arduous—it should leave enough time to paint *what you really want.*"

It wasn't quite the stroke of luck Orlando had expected when Carraldo walked through the door, but it surely was a gift from heaven. He was being given Aria Rinardi on a plate! "I'd be delighted, sir," he said, smiling. "And just to be in Venice will be a bonus!"

Carraldo nodded. "I'll have my secretary contact you. Good-bye then, Mr. Messenger."

Even though the room was hot and crowded, Carraldo's hand felt cold as Orlando shook it. He met his gaze uneasily. It was true what they said: There was something sinister about the man.

Carraldo was as good as his word; his secretary contacted Orlando the following day to make arrangements for his stay in Venice; the plane ticket was economy class and the *pensione* that would be his home for a couple of months was a modest one, but the salary was generous. He would be expected in Venice the following week, if that was convenient for him. It certainly was, he thought, packing his bags and calling in at the Maze Gallery to check how sales were going and pick up a little ready cash. It gave him just enough time to go to Geneva first and meet

Mr. Lieber and find out exactly what was going on. If there were other claimants to the estate of Poppy Mallory, he intended to find out who they were.

The law offices of Lieber & Lieber in Geneva were ultramodern and very smart, and the young blond receptionist had obviously been chosen to match. She glanced up inquiringly from her sleek telephone console on the rosewood reception desk, smiling prettily as her eyes met Orlando's. "M'sieur?" she said.

"Hi," he said, moving closer and leaning on the counter. "I'm Orlando Messenger, I'd like to see Mr. Lieber."

"Do you have an appointment, Mr. Messenger?" she asked, patting her short, swingy blond hair self-consciously.

"Sorry, no appointment; I just got in from London. It's about the Poppy Mallory estate—I'd thought he'd be able to fit me in, just for fifteen minutes or so."

"I'm sorry," she said, her blue eyes wide with sympathy. "I'm afraid Mr. Lieber doesn't see anyone without an appointment. He's a very busy man, you know."

"I'm sure he is," Orlando replied, "and he's obviously a man of good taste."

She put her head on one side, looking at him questioningly. "To have chosen you for a receptionist," he added with a disarming grin. She sighed, shaking her hair at his brashness, but she was smiling. "Look," he said quickly, "I've flown in from London especially to see him. I'm sorry I didn't make an appointment, I just didn't think about it. Isn't there any way he can squeeze me in, even just for ten minutes?"

"If you like, I'll ask his secretary," she suggested.

He knew she was aware he was watching her as she walked across the bronze-colored carpet, swinging her hips and displaying a pair of very pretty legs, and he grinned. She tapped on a door and disappeared inside, emerging moments later with a red book under her arm.

"I forgot Mr. Lieber's secretary took an early lunch today, but here's his appointments book. Let's see what it says." He looked over her shoulder as she ran her finger down the list. "I'm sorry," she said doubtfully, "but his day is really full. As you can see, he's marked how long he expects each meeting to take . . . there's not even a minute's gap. I told you he was a very busy man."

Orlando nodded. "I see," he said slowly. "Then I guess I'm going to have to try for tomorrow."

She turned to look at him, frowning as the intercom line buzzed. She picked it up quickly. "Yes, Mr. Lieber?" she said. "I'm sorry, your secretary is not back yet, but I can get the call for you, sir. Yes. Mike Preston, Santa Barbara, California. Yes, sir, right away." Whispering "Wait a moment" to Orlando, she dialed the number. "Mr. Preston? I have Mr. Lieber on the line for you, calling from Geneva. One moment, sir." She put the call through and turned back to Orlando quickly. "I'm sorry, Mr. Messenger," she said sympathetically. "I wish I could help. Maybe you should speak to his secretary when she gets back."

"Fine." He sighed, but then his face brightened and he smiled at her. "How about taking pity on a poor lonely young man who's feeling very hungry? I'd love to have your company for lunch."

She laughed. "A consolation prize, Mr. Messenger?" she asked.

"Not at all," he replied gallantly. "I would consider it an honor."

She stared at him consideringly; he looked handsome and boyish and he was so charming . . . "Why not?" she agreed finally. The phone buzzed again and she picked it up. "Yes, Mr. Lieber? Fax another copy of the list of Poppy Mallory's claimants to Mr. Preston in Santa Barbara? The one with the European telephone numbers. Yes, sir, I'll get it from your secretary's desk and do it right away." With a smile at Orlando, she hurried back into the office, returning with several sheets of paper that she placed in the fax machine, dialing the number. Picking up her purse, she smiled eagerly at him. "I'll just tell one of the other girls that I'm going," she told him, disappearing down a corridor.

Orlando glanced at the machine. It had stopped humming and the pieces of paper were right there—the list with the names of the claimants to Poppy's fortune and their reasons. Glancing around quickly, he picked it up and flipped through the pages, but there was no time to read it; he could already hear the girl returning along the corridor. Without a second's hesitation he stuffed the list into his pocket and walked across to meet her.

"I hate eating alone," he said, "and besides, I don't know where to go in Geneva." He smiled at her winningly. "I can't wait to find out more about you. *Who are you?* And what are you doing working in a boring legal office when you should obviously be modeling in Paris? I have some very good contacts in that world, you know."

"Really?" she asked, forgetting all about the fax and the list, her eyes sparkling as they walked together to the elevator.

CHAPTER *14*

Carraldo sat alone in the study of the big empty house in Belgravia. He'd been in London for four days now, and he was still undecided about what to do. He had meant simply to deliver the Renoir to his London client, celebrate the man's purchase over a leisurely lunch at the Connaught, and then fly back to Venice for Aria's birthday dinner—and their engagement; but the advertisement for Poppy Mallory's heiress had jangled in his memory all that day, like a nagging ache that refused to go away. He'd contemplated telephoning Francesca to see what she was up to, or even asking Aria herself, but he'd been afraid of the answer. It wasn't the kind of deep physical fear that he'd felt in the early years as a child, nor the kind of intimidation he'd felt later when his circumstances had changed; this was a much more subtle fear, and a much more tortured one.

Francesca would want to claim Poppy's money, and he could guess how she would do it, though he knew she still wouldn't want to lose him as a catch for her daughter—two fortunes were better than one to Francesca. But if Aria had an alternative source of money to funnel to her mother, he knew in his heart she wouldn't marry him. There were two courses left open to him: He could sit back and let fate take its chance, or he could take steps to ensure they were never able to prove Aria was the heiress.

He had called the Palazzo Rinardi after reading the ad. The Baronessa was out, Fiametta had informed him sullenly, and Aria was out, too, and no she didn't know when they would be back.

"Tell them urgent business keeps me in London," he'd said, "and that I'll be back sometime next week. And please tell Aria I'm sorry about our engagement dinner, but as we've waited so long already, no doubt it'll wait a bit longer."

Then he'd called the florist and ordered six-dozen white roses to be sent to Aria.

Swirling the brandy moodily in his glass, he listened to the sounds of silence in the vast house . . . the crackle of the log fire in the grate, the mellow voice of Pavarotti, turned low on the CD deck, the faint distinctive rumble of a London taxi as it turned the corner. And then his thoughts turned, as they always did when he was alone, to the past.

There had never been any love lost between Carraldo and Francesca Rinardi. She had realized when she'd married Paolo Rinardi that Carraldo knew her for what she was—shallow and superficial. But when Paolo had died, he'd hidden the depths of his sorrow for his only true friend and taken charge, seeing that Paolo was buried with all the proper respect in the Rinardi tomb.

Tiny six-year-old Aria had clutched his hand trustingly as the funeral procession had sailed across the misty Venetian lagoon to the burial island of San Michele, and he'd felt somehow as though they were sharing their grief. As he carried her, weeping, from the church, he'd been overwhelmed by a feeling of strong possessive love. Afterward, he'd kept his distance because of Francesca, but he'd always seen that Aria was looked after financially. On the odd occasions when he did see the little girl, she'd seemed afraid of him, backing nervously behind Fiametta, and he'd wondered what Francesca had been saying to her.

It had been five years since he'd last seen Aria, when Francesca telephoned asking him to go to the Palazzo Rinardi, and the photographs dotted about the salon showed that she was becoming a beauty, in a contemporary delicate-boned fashion—and yet there was a look of her father about her. He'd listened to Francesca and realized with a shock that she was grooming Aria for the marriage market—to be sold to the highest bidder. Of course, he knew he could simply have given her the money she wanted and washed his hands of the whole situation, but he also knew there was no way to satisfy the greed of a woman like that. She would always want more—and he was sure she would use Aria to get it.

He'd thought over the situation that night, telling himself that there were two good reasons for marrying Aria Rinardi. One was because he couldn't let the daughter of his old friend Paolo be humiliated by Francesca. The other was a much more personal reason, but one he knew would be to her benefit. But there was also a third reason. Aria was too young to be used as Francesca's bait; she needed time to grow strong, to mature—to become a woman. And when he thought of the woman Aria would become, he suddenly knew he wanted her with the same kind of possessive passion that made him bid millions for a Rembrandt or a Monet. Aria was youth and innocence personified—and right now, he needed her.

He'd sat alone all night with a bottle of brandy, just the way he was now, staring into the fireless grate in his lonely house, thinking about his old friend and worrying about what to do, wondering whether Paolo would approve, and remembering that night, thirty-three years ago, when he'd confessed the truth about himself to Paolo.

He had first met Paolo one memorable evening at the Teatro La Fenice in Venice, at a performance of *Norma*, sung by Maria Callas. Carraldo had remained in his seat after the rapturous audience had departed, still under the singer's dramatic spell, and finding that his neighbor was still in his seat and equally in love with "Norma," he had suggested they share a bottle of champagne to celebrate.

When Paolo had told him about his great interest in the romantic poets, Carraldo had invited him to his apartment to inspect his collection of rare books and manuscripts. A friendship based on mutual interests had bloomed quickly, and they had spent many evenings together, discussing art and music as well as poetry, continuing their conversations by letter when Carraldo was at one of his many homes or away on his business travels.

Carraldo knew that the Rinardi family was an old one, but Paolo told him that after four centuries the family money was running out. His parents were both dead and he was hopelessly impractical, and when he received his allowance, paid from the family trust every three months, he spent it all immediately in a joyous whirl of old books, art objects, and good wine. But Carraldo thought he had a magic way with words. He had a beautiful resonant speaking voice, and just to hear him reading the poets in Italian, or reciting a Shakespeare sonnet in English, and Virgil in Latin, was like listening to music. He found him fascinating, and Paolo was equally intrigued by Carraldo's air of mystery and his inexplicable wealth—the paintings in his house alone were worth a fortune. It was an attraction of opposites. They enjoyed each other's company and they never asked each other personal questions. They were good friends.

Occasionally, in the dark hours before dawn, over a bottle of good brandy, they talked about their innermost feelings—about women and love . . . and sex. And on one such night Carraldo realized he could no longer live with his conscience; he either must tell him the truth about himself—or else end their friendship. It was a momentous decision because Paolo was the only man Carraldo had ever allowed himself to come close to, and the only person with whom he'd ever dropped his guard and expressed his feelings. Now he stood to lose the man he loved as a true friend and brother. He knew he had no choice. Paolo must be the judge of that friendship.

The two were at his villa in Portofino. It was a chilly autumn evening and they had been out sailing all day. They had dined well and now, relaxed, were sitting companionably in front of a blazing log fire, drinking an aromatic marc brandy, when Carraldo said suddenly, "There is something I must tell you."

His face was pale and his dark eyes serious, and realizing that it was important, Paolo listened, asking no questions while Carraldo related the story of his life.

He said he thought he must have been born in 1937, though he couldn't be certain of the exact date because all the records had been destroyed. He hadn't even been sure who his parents were as, from the time he was old enough to remember, he'd lived with a woman called Antonella in a dank, sunless tenement in Naples. He remembered that he had never called her "Mama"—it was always "Antonella," so he assumed that she wasn't his natural mother, but she must have been a cut above the other tenement dwellers because she had always kept him clean and neatly dressed. And for some reason, she had always called him "Antony," and not "Antonio," the Italian version of the name.

Benito Mussolini and fascism had already taken control and, swept along in the wave of hysterical enthusiasm for the German leader, Hitler, in April 1939, Italy invaded Albania. A few months later Italy, now aligned with Germany, was at war with the Allies and later with Russia.

As World War II raged through Europe, life became more difficult; food was in increasingly short supply because all the farm workers were sent to fight, but to young Antony, who knew no different, everything seemed quite normal. His playground was the grimy, littered streets of the *bassi;* his friends were the children of peasant tenement dwellers; and he learned the dialect and coarse language of that environment. By the age of five, he had the vocabulary of a street urchin and knew his way through the maze of alleys and steps between the tall tenement buildings that were his home territory, and he could recognize whose apartment he was passing by the lines of washing strung overhead.

In September 1943, under the command of Lt. General Mark Clark, the U.S. Fifth Army invaded the western shore of Italy at Salerno, and as the fighting gradually came closer, Naples was under constant bombardment. The city was a shambles, but somehow daily life went on. On a sunny morning in late September, the American forces shelled the city and within minutes Antony's entire block of tenements had been wiped out, leaving only burning rubble and bodies behind. One of those bodies was Antonella's. Antony had escaped death only because he had been sent on an errand to the baker's to fetch fresh bread for lunch. He was six years old, skinny, with large brown eyes and a shock of dark hair; and he was alone on the wartime streets of Naples.

That night he discovered he wasn't totally alone—there were other children in the same situation, dozens of them—hundreds maybe. He couldn't yet count beyond twenty, so he wasn't sure how many, but there were a lot. The other children warned him that the American soldiers were coming and they would take him away if they found out he was an orphan. Many had been taken by the authorities already, they said, and never seen again. The next day the city fell to the Allies and, terrified of the tanks and the guns and the marching foreigners, Antony lurked in the ruins of the bomb-scarred city, learning from the others how to beg for coins and food—and how to steal. They stole anything they could get their quick hands on—washing from the lines to be sold to dealers who funneled it back into the markets; purses from old ladies and food from careless grocers and bakers. They were small and sharp-witted and innocent-looking—who would suspect such tiny waifs? At night they slept among the ruins on the remnants of what were once mattresses and chairs. They were a group of twenty or more, united by a single aim—to survive.

After a year of dodging the authorities and learning to become a petty criminal, Anthony could barely remember any other way of life. One day, he stole a shoeshine kit from behind the back of its owner, who was sitting in a café enjoying a glass of wine with his lunch. This time, instead of hurrying back with his loot to their headquarters in the ruins, he hid it behind a dusty velvet curtain in the vestry of a nearby church. That night he thought long and hard about his next move. He was seven now and he had learned a lot in the past year—he was a quick and accomplished thief, he knew where to get rid of stolen goods and how much they were worth; he knew how to steal and how to get enough food so that he could survive. And he knew what it meant to be alone. With that shoeshine kit he could have his own little "business," earning proper money, not just the few odd coins he was permitted in the group. It meant abandoning his comrades, but it was an opportunity he could not afford to miss.

Antony was smart enough to move from his *bassi* to another, farther west. Italy had surrendered, and in no time he'd learned that a painfully thin, knobby-kneed, ragged waif with an orphan story could make a fair bit of money shining the shoes of the young GI's who sat around in the cafés in the squares. He did a good job and they often tossed an extra coin into his outstretched palm, offering him chocolate and ruffling his untidy, louse-ridden hair genially as he departed. But Antony didn't realize that he was being watched.

He was marching confidently up the steps at the top of the alley toward the particular ruins he'd adopted as his new home, when they pounced from behind. An arm was flung around his neck and he felt the chill of sharp cold metal against his ribs as his attacker forced him to the ground. He was scared but he was not going to give up his shoeshine kit without a fight, and arching his back, he leapt to his feet. Turning swiftly, he kicked his attacker in the groin. With a scream of agony the boy crumpled to the ground, but immediately two more took his place, kicking and punching him until the blood ran. "Okay, kid, *now* are you prepared to listen?" they growled. Antony was amazed that they were still there and hadn't simply run off with his shoeshine kit, and he peered at them in bewilderment through rapidly closing blackened eyes. They were much older than he was and much bigger, and he knew he was beaten.

"Listen to what?" he snarled back. "Why don't you just take the kit and leave me alone?"

"That's not what we want," the boy hissed, placing his foot in a soldier's heavy boot on Antony's chest. "Now just shut your mouth and listen."

His eyes fixed on that dangerous boot, Antony did as he was told, learning that he was to go out as usual with his shoeshine kit, but that in future for every lira he made, half would go to his new associates. There was to be no choice in the matter—these fourteen-year-olds were now his masters. In return, they told him that the area around the church square where he worked would be protected . . . no other shoeshine boy would be allowed to work there. His captor ran his thumb along the edge of his knife, resting the weight of his booted foot on Antony's chest. "Do you agree?" he asked, holding the knife closer. Antony nodded. "I agree," he choked.

"You will meet us every afternoon at two," said the boy, "and again at eleven at night to make your payments. And don't think you can cheat— you will be watched. If you try anything"—he ran the knife along Antony's throat with a menacing grin—"you know what you can expect. *This* was just a warning, to let you know we mean business."

As they disappeared into the night Antony struggled to his feet. He wiped the blood from his face with a grimy rag and, with his shoeshine kit clutched under his arm, limped back into his refuge. It took him only a couple of weeks to realize that he was on the wrong end of the deal— *he* did all the work and *they* profited. *They* were using their *brains*—he was only using his *hands*! For the first time he understood what it meant to be a boss—and he vowed that before too long, that's what he would be.

One night his associates failed to show up for their take, and he heard that they had been rounded up in the latest attempt by the military to get the orphaned young criminals off the streets. He was free again—and ready to expand his business.

Antony's "home" was adjacent to a ramshackle funeral parlor and on cold nights he shared the straw bed in the stable with the decrepit pair of black funeral horses who somehow—through superstition and fear—had survived being made into steaks. With black plumes on their heads, they still pulled the ancient hearse to the local graveyard. Though the horses were worn and puny, the funeral business was thriving, and Antony would watch as the hearse, followed by its tribe of wailing, black-robed mourners, wended its way through the streets to the church. He noted that many of the old people, suffering from the privations of war, were now dying off, but there were also many children's coffins. Disease in war-damaged Naples was rampant and there was still a shortage of food. And, too, there were many accidents in a newly remechanized city. Only the strongest survived.

No plans were made by the families of the deceased for their funerals —it was a question of what was immediate and convenient, just the closest funeral parlor to home. It would be easy to channel their business, Antony thought, if the director of a funeral parlor arrived opportunely and offered to remove the final burden of arrangements from their shoulders in their time of sorrow. But obviously, only the local funeral director ever heard of the death. Someone would have to get the information about who was dying or had just died, and then he could quickly tell a rival funeral parlor so that they could claim the business. And if he,

Antony, could be that person, then he could demand a percentage of each funeral. It would be easy enough to scout the neighborhood—everyone always knew everything about everyone else, the neighbors gossiped incessantly in the market or at the baker's, or from their tenement windows—but speed was of the essence. He would need to be *fast* if his plans were to work. *He would need a bicycle.*

The next day, a young GI, hot and sweating in his khaki T-shirt, heavy wool pants, and boots, locked his bicycle securely to the iron grill of a doorway before stepping inside a bar in search of a cold beer. Emerging from the shadows, Antony glanced carefully up and down the empty street. Kneeling, he juggled with a bunch of keys "traded" for the day from an acquaintance in return for a day's use of his shoeshine kit. After six tries the lock turned and he was on the bike and away.

He made his first "deal" with the funeral parlor next door and he asked only five percent. Flashing up and down the tenement's mean alleys on his bicycle, he became an expert on the health of the inhabitants of the *bassi.* Business was brisk at the funeral parlor and soon he was able to sell his shoeshine kit for a handsome sum—plus a weekly percentage of the take—and expand his activities to include a second funeral parlor. His first client upped his percentage to ten, fearing the competition, and it was then Antony knew that the tide had turned. *He was now a boss.*

He recruited boys in other *bassi* to work for him, until he had a team of a dozen covering the city. Before too long he was making more money than he knew what to do with.

When Antony was ten, he looked like a stocky fourteen-year-old, and he decided to add a convenient four years to his age. He had a rent-free apartment over a funeral home with a woman who came in to clean and cook occasional meals, and a good deal of money that he kept concealed beneath the floorboards. By the time he was fourteen, and claiming eighteen, he had arranged through a lawyer to buy a small two-room apartment of his own. He paid for it in cash.

He was walking back alone one night when a car drew up beside him and two men jumped out. He felt the snub of a pistol thud painfully against his ribs and knew this was no ordinary robbery. "Get in," commanded the taller man, "and take it easy. We're just taking you to meet someone, that's all."

His eyes were blindfolded, and they seemed to be driving in endless circles before the car finally crunched up a gravel drive and stopped. Antony stumbled up a flight of broad stone steps between his captors, and it wasn't until they were commanded by a soft-voiced man that they finally removed his blindfold.

He was in a lamp-lit room of an opulence he hadn't known existed. His entire apartment would have fit in a corner of this sumptuous room. The walls were paneled from floor to ceiling, and pale soft carpets were spread across the polished oaken floor. There were many silk brocade sofas and chairs, small tables held bowls of sweet-smelling flowers, and a log fire burned in the enormous grate. A small, dark man, his face furrowed with age, sat in a high-backed chair near the fire, watching him as he stared openmouthed at the fine paintings that adorned the walls.

"You like those, do you?" the old man asked in a tremulous voice. "The one on your left is Ghirlandaio. The nude you are admiring is a Titian; the painting on your left, by Veronese . . . and on the wall opposite, my favourite Canalettos." He tapped ash from his cigarette into a silver ashtray. "All looted, of course—not by me, by the Führer's army." He shrugged. "If I gave them up, they'd probably end up in the storage vaults of some museum. I feel they are better appreciated here."

Antony stared at him in amazement. "What do you want with me?" he blurted at last. "Why am I here?"

"I've been observing you for some time, Carraldo. You are a very enterprising young man. I understand that, though you claim otherwise, you are still only fourteen?"

Antony eyed him angrily; what did his age matter to this man unless he was the police? But of course he wasn't . . . this man was rich, he had power. *Suddenly he knew who this man was* . . . he'd heard his name mentioned in awed voices tainted with fear. His legs turned to jelly and he clutched the back of a chair with shaking hands. But anger soon took over from the fear. "You want to muscle in on my business," he said flatly, "that's why I'm here, isn't it? So you can take it from me. . . . I've worked goddamn hard for all I've got, *Signore,* and I'm fucked if I'm gonna give it to you . . . you can do whatever you want, beat me up, *kill me* . . . I'll never give it up, *never!*

His face was purple with rage, but the man smiled serenely. "Calm yourself, Carraldo," he said, lighting a fresh cigarette, "we are here to discuss the matter like gentlemen. Your business nets you a nice little profit—and I know *exactly* how much. Of course, we could have taken it over easily, had we wanted, *you know how things are done.* But I'm afraid it's too trivial to bother with." He shrugged, flicking his cigarette ash, and Antony stared at him wide-eyed, his anger gone. He was scared now. He knew what the man had meant, but still had no idea why he was here.

"Sit here, opposite me, Carraldo," he said, indicating a pale brocade sofa. "I have no doubt you've heard certain things about me—about my businesses. And my methods." Antony nodded. "Then all I can say is that you must not believe *everything* you hear. But I have also learned a lot about you. You are here, Carraldo, because I need young men like you around me. Oh, there are more than enough thugs and brainless idiots available for the more . . . mundane . . . work, and they would be only too eager to take what I'm about to offer you. But there are not enough *brains*, Carraldo, not enough young men who can think on their feet, who can make decisions, who can take charge. I think that with training, *you* may have that capability. You are alone in the world, and I like that—no family ties or attachments. I have no sons, Antony Carraldo," he continued, stubbing out the half-smoked cigarette, "and I am searching for an heir to my . . . empire." His iron-gray brows rose in his furrowed forehead as he stared at him. "Well, boy? What do you say?"

Antony swallowed nervously. "I know nothing about your business," he muttered. "I just know what I do . . . I've never been to school . . . I don't know about paintings—those names you said meant nothing to me. I've never been in a room like this before, I've lived on the streets since I was six. What can you possibly want with someone like me? You can get yourself an educated man, someone who knows how to behave. I've got nothing to offer you—or your business."

"That's exactly my point, Carraldo. I employ university graduates—accountants and lawyers—elsewhere in my business. I've watched you closely. *I know you.* You are young, you can be tutored, you will learn . . . *but there is no school where you could learn what you have on the streets of the* bassi. One day my business will *need* you, Antony Carraldo. And the rewards will be big—more than you've ever dreamed of."

Antony ran his hands bewilderedly through his mop of dark hair. He was being offered the world on a plate . . . but he knew this man's business, he knew he was a top man in the criminal network that riddled Italy. He was a frightening man—yet what he was offering was infinitely tempting . . . riches . . . position . . . *power.* But what was he going to be asked in return? "I'll never kill a man for money," he said, contemptuously pushing back his chair.

"My dear Carraldo, no one will ever *ask* you to kill anyone," the man said with a knowing smile. "You forget, it will be *you* who will give the commands."

Antony nodded in agreement. He understood. "What happens to me now?"

The man settled back in his brocade chair, smiling. "You have made a wise choice. Let us hope you will never have cause to regret it. You move in here tonight—your room is already prepared. Tomorrow a tutor arrives from England and you will begin your education."

"But my apartment, my things . . ."

"You will need nothing from the past. Your apartment will be sold and the money placed in your new bank account. You will earn *nothing* until your education is finished and I am satisfied."

Antony stared at him doubtfully; he was making a deal with the devil —and if he failed? He shuddered at the thought of what might happen. But the lure of that ultimate power was very strong. . . .

"One more thing before you retire to your room." The man's voice was almost shrill in its coldness as he lit another cigarette. "You are a young boy, barely fourteen, yet there is already much talk about your sexual prowess—and inclinations. From now on you will exercise control over your needs. I will have no scandal attached to my Family." Turning away, he picked up a book, opening it at a page marked neatly with a silver bookmark. "You may go now," he said coldly.

Antony knew he'd sold himself into some kind of strange slavery, but he found himself eager to learn. He devoured the books provided by his tutor, exhausting him by refusing to quit when lessons for the day were over. Mathematics was easy for him, he'd been putting it to constant practical use since he was six. But now the world opened up to him geographically, and the past became reality through brilliant history teaching. And the beauty of the written word, of music and art, provided whole new avenues of knowledge and pleasure. When he wasn't studying, he spent his time in the man's library, discovering with delight rare volume after rare volume. Taking them carefully from the shelves, he marveled at their age and the fragile hand-illuminated pages. He touched the soft leather covers with sensitive fingers, imagining the bookbinder creating these works of art to last for centuries. He studied the paintings of the masters that adorned every room in the mansion, learning about each artist's qualities and techniques, and he soon formed strong opinions about those he liked and why.

Dressed neatly in gray flannel trousers and a blue shirt, with a plain dark blue silk tie and a gold-buttoned blazer, he dined nightly with the man. Although, of course, he addressed him by his name, Antony always thought of him as "the man," as though subconsciously he wanted to keep his identity secret. The man always questioned him shrewdly about his day's lessons, nodding, pleased, when he answered quickly and intelligently. He decided that Antony was not getting enough physical activity, and that he should take lessons in tennis, swimming, and fencing. Antony enjoyed fencing the most. Wearing a white uniform and a fencer's mask, brandishing his foil, he felt like Douglas Fairbanks in one of the old movies the man enjoyed several times a week in the small private cinema in the basement.

He was amazed how easy it was to slip into a life of luxury, where things are always done for you. The mansion and its grounds were kept immaculately by a silent band of servants and gardeners; his clothes were washed and pressed; his breakfast was brought to the schoolroom where he would already be studying at six in the morning, and where he also ate lunch. Dinner was always with the man, beautifully served by a white-gloved footman, and always with a fine wine whose excellence and characteristics the man was at pains to explain to him. Of course, there was a price to be paid. The beautiful gardens were surrounded by high walls, and patrolled by armed guards with fierce, snarling black dogs. There were more guards at the gate and by each door. There were alarm systems and floodlights. The mansion had held the man a prisoner for almost half a century. But there was also a constant coming and going of people, some official-looking, some sinister, and some humble from the bassi. The man saw them all.

It was a solitary life for a young man, though, of course, Antony was used to that. But it was rich and interesting and he wished it could go on forever, except for one thing. Sex. Or rather the lack of it. Life on the streets of Naples had not allowed sex to be a private matter, and he'd observed his first coupling in a darkened doorway at the age of six. Some of the boys had offered themselves for sex with older men for money, and others had seemed to have frequent sexual encounters that they described graphically and with a great deal of exaggeration. Antony had listened to their talk of what it felt like and how good sex was, and felt the stirrings in his own loins. When he was thirteen and already looking seventeen, he'd gone to an apartment where he'd heard an old man was dying, hoping to get there first and sell them the funeral. The woman who'd opened the door was young, twenty-three or -four, full-bosomed and wide-hipped. Her curly dark hair tumbled about her shoulders, and as she opened the door she stared at him suspiciously, clutching her cheap silk robe across her breasts. With an effort Antony averted his eyes from her bosom and explained that he'd heard she would be needing to make funeral arrangements. "Oh, yes, he's dying all right. *Thank God!*" she exclaimed. Then, staring at him, she added, "You'd better come in so we can discuss things."

She'd sat next to him on the worn velvet sofa. Through a half-opened door opposite, Antony could see a man lying in bed, his gray-white face turned in their direction. It was shriveled and old, but his eyes were alert and he was watching them. "I don't know how he's hanging on," she commented, glancing indifferently across the room, "the doctor said he should have been gone a week ago. He's old—he's had his day . . . it's time he went to his maker and left the field open for a younger man." She eyed him thoughtfully and then went into the kitchen and came back with an open bottle of red wine.

"How old is your father?" Antony asked politely.

"*My father?*" she exclaimed with a mocking laugh. "That's not my *father! That* is my *husband!*" Filling two glasses, she handed him one. As she leaned toward him her robe fell away from her breasts and Antony gulped his wine quickly, crunching his knees together desperately as he felt himself harden. Her breasts were like two heavy pears and her olive skin looked smooth, the nipples dusky and pointed.

"Have some more," she said, refilling his glass, "and then you can tell me what you are doing here." Her plump hand rested deliberately on his thigh as she edged closer, staring into his eyes and making no attempt to cover herself. Draining her glass, she said hoarsely, "Do you have any idea of what it's like to make love with an *old* man? To climb into his bed at night and have his cold hands crawl all over you while he fumbles to achieve his own pleasure? Can you imagine what it's like to have *that*" —she glanced viciously at the half-open door—"kissing you with his spittle running down his face? God," she moaned, her hands suddenly roaming across Antony's body, "you don't know how I've *longed* for him to die, *longed* for warm young flesh next to mine." Antony put his hand on her breast and she trembled. "Ohhhh, God," she cried, "I just want to be made love to, the way a woman should . . . is there anything wrong with that?"

Her robe slid from her shoulders as she fell back on the sofa, pulling Antony on top of her. Automatically, he buried his head in her breasts, and it was as if he suddenly became another person. He felt strong, powerful, as though he possessed every woman in the world. The woman moaned again with delight when she saw his erection. As he thrust into her Antony thought he heard a faint cry from the half-open bedroom door, and turning his head, he saw the old man's eyes fixed on them. "More," she begged, "harder, harder . . . go on, *hurt me* . . ." He slammed into her, increasing his rhythm, biting at her nipples as her nails clawed his back. Even though it was his first time, he outlasted her, permitting himself the ultimate luxury of ejaculation only when she begged him to stop.

Antony threw on his clothes quickly. Still tauntingly naked, she walked across to the bedroom and stared at the old man. "Well, that finally did the trick," she said in a voice tipped with ice. "The old bastard's dead." Her shrill laugh had followed Antony through the door and down the stairs as he'd fled back to the familiar street.

Once he'd known about it, it had been easy enough to find sex—it was for sale on any streetcorner, or to be had, like the first time, from a casual encounter. Suddenly it had seemed to Antony that the whole world revolved around sex. It had certainly absorbed him, and soon he'd found the parties where sex was the name of the game. And he'd discovered that he liked two girls or even three . . . and that first time had marked him well . . . he liked it rough . . . he wanted to hear them moan with pain as well as with pleasure, to beg him for mercy . . . he wanted ultimate power over them. He was their master and they were his slaves.

Now, at the villa, he was expected to remain celibate and direct his thoughts to learning. Strangely, after a while he began to enjoy the self-discipline. He felt like a novice monk and simply put his energy into ferocious games of squash and swimming and fencing.

There was no doubt that the man was becoming fond of him. When Antony complained of violent pains in his stomach, the man summoned a doctor anxiously, and when it was diagnosed as appendicitis, he personally went with him to the hospital in the big, chauffeur-driven black Mercedes with an escort of police and wailing sirens. He remained at the hospital throughout the operation, leaving a pile of half-smoked cigarette stubs in the ashtray of the private waiting room. When Antony was wheeled from the operating room, the man satisfied himself that he was no longer in any danger before he left. He returned later that evening with enormous baskets of fruit and flowers, and a carton of books he had selected personally, that he thought Antony might enjoy.

After that, he began to keep Antony with him more during the day, and gradually he began to teach him his business, explaining how it was structured and what his specific areas were. By the time Antony was legitimately twenty-one years old, and still claiming an extra four years, he knew all the man's secrets, and he knew what would be expected of him as his heir.

Two months later the man had his first stroke. It wasn't a serious one, but he was confined to a wheelchair. He looked suddenly fragile, and Antony realized that he cared deeply for him. The man had taken him from the tough city streets and made him into a civilized being; he had educated him, he'd seen to it that he became cultured and knowledge-able. But when Antony prayed that he wouldn't die, it wasn't only because he cared, but because he didn't want to take over the man's position as head of "the business."

One evening they had been sitting quietly reading after dinner, when Antony closed his book and said good night. He felt tired and wanted to get to bed early. "Don't leave me yet, son," the man said in his thin, tremulous voice.

"Of course not, sir." Antony sat down again beside him. "Is there anything I can get you? Anything you want?"

"There's a document over there." He nodded toward the circular inlaid marble table near the window. "Bring it to me, would you?" Antony carried it across. "Now read it," the man said quietly, "and tell me what you think."

Antony read the Deed of Formal Adoption. *The man wanted him to become his legal son.* He stared down at the paper, unwilling to meet the man's anxious eyes. He had always imagined that if he could stand this way of life no longer, or when he was called upon to take part in "the Family," somehow he'd find a way out. He would leave this house, leave Italy, find a new life. But if he signed this document, he would become the man's legal son. And there would be no escape.

"It's the only way, you see," the man said. "If you are my son"—he flung out his arm stiffly, encompassing the room, the house, the paintings and works of art—"all this will be yours." He sighed tiredly. "There are others, waiting like sharks to snatch it all when I'm gone. We can't allow that to happen, Antony, can we? My collection . . . so many treasures . . . so much beauty . . . to them it's only the monetary value that matters. But I know that *you* will love them as I have. *You are truly my son.*"

Antony signed the deed with a trembling hand, stunned by the look of pure joy in the man's eyes as he handed it to him. "I once said that I hoped you would not regret joining me here," the man said quietly, "and now I can assure you that you will not."

Two months later he suffered a second, massive stroke and was dead within minutes. And Antony found himself owner and master of all he surveyed. And the new head of "the Family."

The funeral was held with discreet pomp and was attended only by Antony and the man's top "executives," and a dozen silent, black-coated, somber-eyed men who were total strangers to him. After the ceremony they told him courteously that it was time to discuss business. Hiding his nervousness, Antony listened while they outlined the role they now expected him to play. Because of his inexperience, they said smoothly, he would find it difficult to run such a complex business. They proposed to help by taking over certain "situations"; it would be much better all around if he simply left it to them . . . there would be no problems, no fights. . . . The man's personal fortune was Antony's outright, they said; but, of course, the paintings and works of art had never really *belonged* to the man and would now be incorporated into the business.

Antony stared at them contemptuously. They had made the mistake of taking him for a fool and he seethed with pent-up anger—not for himself but for the man. They were simply carving up his business into handy slices—a share for each, and the crumbs for him. He held back, letting them have their say until silence finally fell on the imposing room, and they gazed at him expectantly, awaiting his response.

It was ironic, he thought, that what they were offering him was the way out he had always thought he'd want. But now he knew he couldn't take it—not because he wanted to be "Godfather" of the Family, but because he could not let down the man who had turned him from an uneducated streetwise kid into a civilized human being, someone who could take his place beside his intellectual peers in what Antony always thought of as "the real world." He knew these unsmiling crime barons were not in the same league as the man, and he also knew this was the test of loyalty the man had banked everything on when he'd made him his heir.

Keeping his voice low, he thanked them for their offer and told them that he had no need of their help, and that there was no question of his relinquishing any part of his inheritance. Before they could reply, he added, "I think you should remember, gentlemen, that I was trained to take over this business, and trained well. My Family is loyal and will do as I command. I think you will find that things will be run as efficiently as when my father was alive." It was the first and only time he'd ever called the man his "father," and he choked on the word, wishing he had been able to bring himself to say it to him before he died. "As to the paintings and works of art," he went on, "they were my father's personal collection. It was his specific wish that it be kept intact. I promised I would see that his wish was fulfilled."

Each man embraced him as they filed from the room, offering condolences and good wishes for his success, but Antony knew he had not heard the last of them. He also knew he could not allow himself to become a prisoner in the mansion, the way the man had done. He would rather be dead. The man had been old, he'd already lived his life when the trap had snapped shut, but Antony was still young. He intended to fulfill his promise to the man, but he would also live his own life, without guards or guns. He knew he would have to earn that freedom, and the respect of the other Families.

A week later, he was driving the man's big black Mercedes saloon along the winding coast road when he noticed in the rearview mirror that he was being overtaken by a truck carrying crates of vegetables. The road was narrow, falling away steeply down a massive cliff to the sea, and the truck was approaching fast, deliberately forcing him to the edge. There was no doubt that whoever was driving that truck meant to kill him. Instinctively he pressed his foot on the accelerator and, as the truck struck him broadside, the powerful car surged forward, its tires squealing as it swerved across the narrow road. The truck shuddered to a stop and, thrusting the Mercedes into reverse, he spun around fast, facing back the way he'd come. Putting his foot on the gas, he slammed into the truck, sending it crashing through the barrier and down the cliff. He pulled on the hand brake and sat for a few moments, sweat pouring from him, his whole body trembling. Then, wiping his forehead with a handkerchief, he climbed from the car and peered over the edge. The emerald sea boiled at the foot of the raw sienna-brown cliffs, with only a crate or two of purple eggplants bobbing on its surface. He knew now he hadn't lost that old street-gang reaction to strike first before he got hurt, and to strike with force. To be the winner—or not survive. In future, his entire approach to life would be based on this concept.

The following week there was a fire at the villa. It was only because Antony had been unable to sleep and had gone down to the library in search of a drink and something to read, that he saved the building—and his own life. He rescued the Titian, and the Veronese, but among other valuables lost were the Ghirlandaio and the man's favorite Canalettos, and Antony felt bitterly that he'd already let him down.

Then one night he went alone to the theater, arranging for the car to pick him up afterward. Suddenly he decided he couldn't stand the loneliness of the villa another night. He needed life . . . women . . . *sex.* Sending the chauffeured car home, he disappeared into the *bassi* in search of his particular pleasures. When he emerged two days later, looking pale and with deep circles under his eyes, he learned that the car had been found at the bottom of the driveway, riddled with bullets. The driver was dead. He knew then that it was war. He knew who his enemies were—and it was him, or them.

The old instinct for survival, learned from a childhood in the wartime ruins of Naples, gave him strength as he summoned his executives and ruthlessly made his plans. Within a few months each of the men who had attended the man's funeral had found his own grave. And from then on no one questioned Antony Carraldo's fitness to inherit the man's empire. With a wry smile he remembered that first night when the man had summoned him and he'd said so contemptuously: "I'll never kill a man for money." "No one will ever *ask* you to kill," the man had replied with a knowing smile. "You forget, it will be *you* who will give the commands." And Antony knew that if he needed to, he would give those commands again. But he had won his freedom.

By then he was locked into the business so deeply, there was no going back. He was a superb administrator, but he hated what he was doing. Watching huge amounts of money steadily amassing in international banks never gave him the sort of pleasure that the little pile of notes hidden under the floorboards of his own first small apartment had. He sought diversion in his two true loves, music and art. He went often to the opera and he haunted the galleries, making trips to special exhibitions and sales and buying shrewdly. He was at an auction at Sotheby's in London when he fell into conversation with an aristocratic-looking old man, and over a drink at his club he told Antony that he still had a houseful of paintings, though he'd been forced to sell all the old masters long ago. Impressed by Carraldo's knowledge, he invited him to spend the weekend at his country house so he could see the paintings for himself.

There were many large, pale gaps on the walls where the old masters had once hung, but as they wandered along endless corridors and through chilly, echoing rooms, Carraldo found several paintings of great charm and decorative value. He offered Lord Beston a fair price for them, which he instantly accepted.

They were taking a drink of whiskey in the library afterward, to celebrate their deal and unfreeze their bones after the trek through the unheated mansion, when Carraldo spotted a pair of small paintings half hidden in a dark corner. A massive cabinet shielded them from direct view, but he recognized them at once as rare Canalettos, painted during the artist's sojourn in London. He told Lord Beston that he was quite certain the paintings were authentic and that they were very valuable, and then he offered him ten percent more than he knew they might currently fetch at auction, knowing that he could resell them before too long for thirty percent more. Telling him to check with another dealer before accepting his offer so he could be sure he was not being cheated, Antony returned to London. The two paintings were delivered by Lord Beston to his hotel the next day and, flushed with the thrill of his first great find, Carraldo felt that not only had he at last vindicated the man's faith in him, he'd also discovered his true role in life.

Milan was a rich industrial city not noted as an international art center, which was exactly the reason he decided to set up his gallery there. He would be the first. Buying premises on a discreetly elegant street, he had the interior redesigned to create a superlative modern gallery. It was divided into two separate sections—one for paintings from the past, and the other for the new young artists he discovered, and whose careers he sponsored in return for representing their work. He had learned his lessons well, and with his knowledgeable eye and his instinctive feel for what was good, he soon attracted the attention of collectors, who commissioned him to find works by the particular artists they were interested in. The Carraldo Gallery was a success and a year later he opened a second one in Paris. Within two years the name "Carraldo" ranked with the majors of the international art world in New York, London, and Paris.

He traveled constantly, seeking out hidden treasures, long lost in dusty old palaces and mansions; and he spent weeks wandering happily through the shabby makeshift studios of hungry young artists in the hopes of finding just one with that extra-special jolt of impassioned genius. And, on those rare occasions when he came across such a talent, it was worth more to him than anything else in the world.

But on a certain day each month, he returned faithfully to Naples. At first he would spend a long time there, ten days or at least a week, but gradually as he tightened his grip on the Family business, he was able to delegate more duties to his executives—though never enough to give any one of them too much control. The man had taught him well. But there were three men—and only three—who knew where to get in touch with him at any time—anywhere in the world.

The fire was dead and only dusty gray embers remained in the massive grate as Carraldo drained the last drops of brandy and looked at his friend. Paolo had simply listened to his story in silence, and now Carraldo noticed that his hand was clenched so tightly around his glass, it was a miracle it didn't break.

"For years," Carraldo had said, "I've veered between two different lives, changing from one persona to another between Naples and Milan. But there's one thing the man was never able to change in me. My need for *sex. Sex has dominated my life!* Sometimes I think I'm owned by my body and its needs even more than I am by the man's 'business.'" He'd shrugged. "Of course, I try to keep my affairs discreet, but I'm aware there's gossip. So, Paolo, now you see why I can never allow myself the luxury of a close relationship with a woman. I could never tell her *any* of my secrets. The man once warned me never to fall in love. 'It will destroy you,' he said, 'as it almost did me.' *Love* can never have any part in my life."

He'd walked over to the fireplace, kicking at the dead embers in the grate. "One other thing," he'd said finally, "I was the 'good son' not the prodigal one of the parable. There are now many more millions from the business, scattered in banks around the world, than when the man died." He'd paused, his shadowed eyes fixed on Paolo's face. "But I swear I've never touched a cent of it. The personal fortune left me by the man I considered a proper inheritance from father to son. I used it to finance my galleries and my art-dealing. I am a very rich man, Paolo. *But nothing I own—not the houses, the cars, the boats, the treasures—has in any way touched the business.*"

Leaning an arm along the mantel, he'd stared into the dead fire, afraid to look at Paolo, afraid of what he was going to say . . . he couldn't bear to hear it. "Please feel free to leave," he'd said, choking on the words. "I have no right to ask your friendship."

Paolo had walked toward him and put an arm around his shoulders. "My dear Antony," he'd said softly, "when a man has the courage to bare his soul to another, that is a sign of true friendship. I'm only glad that you felt you could tell me this story."

Carraldo had felt the tension drain from his body, like a tightly coiled spring relaxing. He was aware that tears were trickling down his face but he was helpless to stop them. "All my life I've been alone," he'd said brokenly. "When I met you it was like finding my brother."

"And it will always be that way," Paolo had assured him. "I only know that you are Antony Carraldo, my friend."

Neither man ever referred to that night, or that conversation, again.

Carraldo sighed deeply, staring at the dead coals in the cold fireplace, just the way he had when he was with Paolo. But Paolo had died long ago. He was in the past, and Aria was the future.

Lieber's list of the claimants to Poppy Mallory's fortune lay on the table by the window, and pouring himself another glass of the fine marc brandy, he glanced again at the name "Orlando Messenger." He hadn't realized when he'd offered to help him that he, too, was after Poppy's money, though his story seemed more farfetched than anyone else's—except maybe Lauren Hunter's. He'd sensed a grain of despair in Orlando about the waste of his talent and impulsively he'd decided to give him a chance. Of course, he didn't know enough about his true work yet to warrant sponsorship; Orlando would have to prove his worth before he could expect serious financial help.

Staring out of the window into the empty London night, Carraldo thought that it wouldn't make any difference that both Orlando and Aria were claiming the estate—but it would make Francesca furious when she found out. He smiled grimly at the thought. He hoped Orlando got the money; he hoped Pierluigi got the money; anybody—except Aria.

CHAPTER *15*

Claudia stretched languidly, glancing at the pretty lapis and gold Cartier bedside clock, one of the few trinkets remaining from her last marriage. It was ten-thirty in the morning, the telephone was ringing, and she was very annoyed. Her friends knew never to call her before eleven; she needed her beauty sleep, especially now that she was getting older.

Sighing exasperatedly, she flung a tiny lace pillow at the phone, burying her head beneath the covers . . . she must have forgotten to turn on the answering machine last night! Whoever was calling was very persistent, and it certainly wasn't any of her friends because they knew her routine too well—therefore it could only be someone demanding money from her. Philistines.

The ringing stopped at last and she breathed a sigh of relief. She stretched luxuriously, running her hands the length of her smooth body, wondering how she felt to a man when he caressed her that way. Sometimes she wished she could be someone else making love to her, just so she'd know how sensational she was. She'd almost achieved it once, she thought, smiling, almost . . .

Since the age of thirteen, Claudia had been only too aware of her sensuous allure. She'd been a wild child—too wild, she now thought bitterly. Had she known then that her looks and sexual attraction were to be her only assets, she might have used them better. Instead, she'd run away from the quiet aristocratic life in a rambling marble villa in the middle of nowhere.

Sitting up, she lit a cigarette with a gold Cartier lighter, wafting away the smoke with an elegant manicured hand. Damn! One of her nails had chipped. That really was the last straw! She leaned back against the pillows, smoking sullenly and thinking of her parents.

Aleksandr Rinardi had been fifty years old when the twins were born in 1952, and he'd stared mistrustfully at the scraps of humanity he'd fathered, wondering how he was going to prevent them from upsetting the calm arrangement of his life. He'd been married to Lucia Galli for only two years and she had been the first woman to penetrate the icy sheath of loneliness that he'd formed around himself since he was nine years old. He cared nothing for these babies, he'd told himself, *nothing*! But they made Lucia happy, so he was prepared to accept them.

Tiny, soft-spoken Lucia was the golden glow in Aleksandr's heart that made him look forward eagerly to waking each day and finding her curled in his arms, and to going to bed each night with her sleeping soundly beside him, while he, an insomniac, read his way through the night by the light of a flickering candle so that the glare of the lamp wouldn't disturb her. He wanted only Lucia: no babies, nothing else— not even a dog. He'd even taken on her maiden name of Galli, giving up his own hated one of Rinardi, as well as the title of Barone.

As the twins Pierluigi and Claudia grew up, they had realized that effectively they were a one-parent family; Lucia was both mother and father to them and she'd treated them indulgently, letting them run wild in an effort to make up for their father's neglect.

Claudia stamped out her cigarette angrily. There was no doubt that if her mother had gone back to the hospital when complications had set in after gallbladder surgery, she would be alive today. And how different life might have been then! But she'd wanted to be there, at the Villa Velata, safe with Aleksandr. *Safe!* After she'd died, their father had devoted himself to his gardens, planning an immense new lake that never seemed to be finished being dug, and mapping fantastic visions on paper of follies and gazebos, miniature English and French and Italianate gardens and landscapes, and paying no attention at all to his growing children.

Rebellious and curious, Claudia had had her first sexual encounter at the age of thirteen with one of the stable lads. She'd been hanging around, eyeing his muscular chest and small, tight buttocks longingly for some weeks, and every now and then he'd turn and catch her eye, giving her a knowing little smile. She'd smile back breathlessly as she busied herself brushing her bay mare, watching him all the while. Then one day he'd leaned over the edge of the stable door, just watching her as she worked. It was a hot summer morning and she was wearing a shirt and riding breeches and nothing at all underneath, and she knew excitedly that he was staring at her breasts bouncing under her shirt. Putting down the brush, she'd turned to face him, stretching her arms upward so that he could see them through her thin shirt, while she pretended to fix her hair. His eyes had roamed boldly over her body, and then with a sardonic laugh he'd walked into the stable and unbuttoned his pants. As she watched breathlessly, with a mocking glance at her he'd peed a beautiful clear arc into the straw on the stable floor.

It was the most erotic act she could ever have imagined, and feeling a hot, moist excitement between her legs, she'd put her hand there instinctively. When he'd finished, he turned to look at her, her hand clutched between her legs, her eyes fixed on his member, swelling now as he gazed at her. Still with that knowing smile, he'd walked toward her and stood there, exposed. "Touch it," he'd said to her. "Go on, touch it, that's what you want, isn't it?" Her eyes were riveted on his thick, springy penis and she'd known he was right, she wanted to touch it . . . she wanted it so very badly. . . . It had felt warm and hard and smooth in her hands, and he'd unfastened her shirt and was caressing her breasts, pulling at her hard nipples lustfully; she'd wanted it and him and anything he wanted to do to her; she wanted to do it all and to feel it all. She wanted to fuck so badly, it hurt.

In retrospect he hadn't been a great lover, but he'd been young and big and hard and she'd let him do whatever he wanted, learning how to use her assets to the utmost until gradually she became the one in control of the situation. They met every day in the stables, sometimes twice or even three times; she couldn't get enough of him. Claudia smiled as she lit another cigarette. Of course, she hadn't known then that she was being watched, but that was a whole other story.

When she was sixteen she had run away with the son of a beach concessionnaire at Forte dei Marmi, the resort on the Tuscan coast that good Italian families always patronized in the summer. There had been no indecisiveness about her father then; he'd acted immediately. She was cut out of his will, he never wanted to see her again. And he never had—not even on his deathbed three years later.

By then Claudia was on her fourth—or was it her fifth—lover. The beachboy hadn't lasted very long—just long enough to give her a comprehensive education in the art of sex and a taste for gutter language during it, and after that her craving for change and luxury had led her into the clutches and the beds of some very odd men. There had been the British army officer who had loved her youth and made her dress up in the gym tunics and navy blue underpants that he'd had sent especially from a school-outfitters in London; and the riding master in Vienna who liked a taste of his own whip; and the French couturier who liked to watch her making it with someone else . . . but they'd all kept voluptuous young Claudia in the style to which she was accustomed.

It was all so long ago, she thought dispiritedly. Thank God she'd progressed from that misspent youth into a more lucrative line in men, establishing her name via a couple of wealthy ex-husbands as a prominent member of the international set. Only now, the last alimony settlement had somehow run out, and with it her entrée into the only society she cared about.

The phone rang again and she glanced at it exasperatedly. Heaving a sigh, she rolled over and picked it up, clutching the sheet around her nakedness. *"Allô?"* she said huskily.

"Is this Claudia Galli?"

The man's voice was deep and pleasant but totally unfamiliar, and she stared suspiciously into the receiver. *"Sì, pronto,"* she said sharply, afraid that it was someone calling about another unpaid bill.

"Claudia, I'm sorry if I've woken you," he said. "My name is Orlando Messenger, I'm a friend of Bibi Mouton's. I saw her in London last week and when I mentioned I was going to be in Paris, she said if I was going to be alone, why didn't I give you a call? I was wondering if perhaps you were free for lunch."

"Lunch?" Claudia thought rapidly . . . if she said yes, he would know her engagement book was empty; but if she said she was too busy, she'd miss a really good restaurant and the chance of meeting someone new—and his voice sounded very pleasing, a nice, cultured upper-class English voice. . . . "Thank you, Orlando," she said sweetly. "It's so kind of you to invite me, but I'm afraid I already have a lunch date."

"That's a pity," he said, sounding very disappointed. "I was looking forward to meeting you. Bibi told me so much about you . . ."

Claudia hesitated. "Still, I hate to think of you all alone in Paris, especially as Bibi asked you to call me . . . wait a minute, let me think what I can do." She paused, tapping a nail reflectively on the receiver. "I know this is naughty," she said with a little giggle, "but for Bibi, I'll do it. I'm supposed to have dinner with some people tonight—to tell you the *truth*, Orlando, they are *boring* people! If you are free tonight, I could put them off . . . make some excuse. In fact, the more I think about it, the more relieved I am at the prospect of *not* seeing them. You know how it is sometimes?"

"Indeed I do," he said, laughing, "and I appreciate the sacrifice."

"The Ritz bar, then, at nine?" she said, smiling.

"I'll be there," he promised.

Claudia always enjoyed making an entrance; she never just *walked* into a room, she *swept*. Tonight she was swathed in dark furs that set off her creamy complexion, and her chocolate-brown hair was pulled back into a velvet Chanel bow. Underneath the fur she wore a black wool Alaïa dress whose complicated swathings curved around her body like a second skin. High-heeled black suede pumps and beautiful black suede gauntlet-gloves with a cuff of rich fur completed her outfit. There was a magnificent diamond ring on her right hand, a fake emerald of enormous proportions on her left, and glittering double *C* Chanel earrings and bracelet. She knew she looked wonderful as she posed just inside the doorway, letting her coat fall casually open, one hand clutched to her beautiful bosom as she scanned the room. Naturally, everyone turned to look at her, but her eye caught that of a devastatingly attractive blond man sitting alone in the corner. Half smiling, he stood up and came toward her.

"Claudia Galli?" he asked, holding out his hand.

"Orlando?" she said, her bright blue eyes lighting up interestedly. My God, he was a hunk! What had Bibi laid on her tonight! She certainly owed her a favor for this one . . . "I apologize for being so late," she said in her husky drawl, "but maybe Bibi told you it's my failing. I simply have no conception of time."

"Not at all," Orlando replied courteously. It was nine twenty-five and he was so relieved she was here that he discounted the anxious minutes spent nursing his drink, wondering if she was coming.

"I always love the Ritz bar," she said, snuggling into a chair and letting her fur fall from her shoulders becomingly. "It's a sort of home from home."

Orlando smiled. "And where is your real home, Claudia?" he asked, signaling the waiter.

"My real home?" She heaved a sigh. "There have been so many, too many to think about . . . it's depressing. But I suppose the Villa Velata is 'home'—at least it's where I was born and I own it, along with my brother. Not that I've any great love for it. And, of course, I also have my apartment on the rue des Arbres. And you, Orlando?"

"Madame?" the waiter asked.

"Oh, a champagne cocktail, please," she ordered.

"And m'sieur?"

"Make that two," he said. "There's a house in the country where I spent most of my childhood. It's mine, now my father's dead, but I rarely go there. I have a small apartment in London—a studio, where I do my work."

"But you're *an artist*? How fascinating. What sort of an artist are you, Orlando?"

"Oh, right now, portraits, landscapes." He shrugged modestly. "A bit of everything really. But next year I plan to specialize more."

"Portraits," Claudia breathed excitedly. "How *interesting*. I've always meant to have my portrait painted, before it's too late."

"Too late?" he asked with a smile.

"A woman must be painted *before* she has her face lifted," she told him seriously. "Afterward she'll have lost that youthful flexibility of expression. She'll be stiff and . . . unlined . . . without character. Not that we need *too much* character—no ugly lines or crow's feet, but enough for the real person to shine through."

Their drinks arrived and he picked up his glass. "To you, Claudia," he said, "and your character shines through beautifully, without the need of any lines—or any face-lifts."

She smiled as she raised her glass. "To a very happy chance meeting, Orlando," she murmured.

Dinner at Jamin, where Claudia had thoughtfully managed to secure a table, was exquisite and expensive. As he paid the bill Orlando thought that it was the price of one of his small paintings, but he didn't regret it. Claudia was a bonus; she was beautiful, she was charming, she was sexy as hell, and she was a talker. Words spilled from her pretty, pouting lips as easily as breathing, and among the gossip and the chitchat were small nuggets of information. She had already hinted twice about the fact that she expected to be very rich, very shortly, without his even mentioning Poppy Mallory; and now he was biding his time.

"Would you like to go dancing?" she asked, snuggling her fur collar prettily under her chin and gazing into his eyes as they waited outside for a taxi. "Or perhaps you'd prefer to come back to my place . . . for a nightcap?"

"Yes," he said simply. "I'd like that, Claudia."

"It's just a small apartment," she said as the cab dropped them on the rue des Arbres, "a pied-à-terre . . . as I said, I live in so many places, I'm always on the move. But this is where I keep my clothes!"

The curtains were drawn, shutting out the view of the garbage cans, and the apartment looked cozy and elegantly cluttered with a hundred expensive knickknacks and soft-shaded lamps.

"Brandy, darling?" she drawled, tossing her fur over a chair. Pouring two glasses she sat beside him on the sofa. "Of course, when I get my inheritance," she said, gazing at him dreamily, "I shall buy a bigger place, just so I can have more closets for my things. Personally I take up very little space, but it's my possessions that need a larger home." She laughed. "Pierluigi will be furious, of course, he hates it when I spend money. But he's so rich anyway, sometimes I tell him he's just a miser. He gets so terribly angry with me, Orlando." She gazed at him with perplexed blue eyes. "Can you understand that?"

"No," he said, reaching over and smoothing out the frown between her brows with his finger. "I can't imagine anyone getting angry with you, Claudia. But will he inherit the money, too, then?"

"Yes." She sighed. "He will. It's a strange story . . . you may have seen the advertisement in the newspapers. 'Search for the missing heiress . . . Poppy Mallory . . .'? Well, that's me—and Pierluigi. We are twins, you see, and our father was Poppy Mallory's son."

"Your father was Poppy Mallory's son!"

She laughed at his shocked expression. "I know, it's amazing, isn't it? But it's true, you know. Papa's real name was Aleksandr Rinardi—the Barone Aleksandr Rinardi, only he hated the Rinardis so much that he dropped the name and the title. My grandmother wasn't his real mother —Poppy was. And so of course Grandmother's husband always hated him because he wasn't his own son. It's all so logical when you think it out . . . that's why Aleksandr was alienated from the rest of the family and was always a loner. The real mystery is why Poppy never came back for him."

"I suppose you must have evidence to back up your story," Orlando asked casually, sipping his brandy.

"Oh, I think there's enough evidence to be found at the Villa Velata and the Villa d'Oro to confirm it all," she said, stretching luxuriously. "There's no doubt the money is ours." She laughed huskily. "And this time I'm not going to let Pierluigi get his hands on any of my share. I intend to go on one, long, glorious spending spree!"

"How much is the estate, then?" he asked curiously.

"Millions," she said dreamily, "hundreds of millions, Orlando. Can you just imagine it?" Leaning forward, she kissed him lightly on the mouth. "When I'm rich," she said, smiling, "I'll commission you to paint my portrait. As an odalisque, an exotic nude."

"I see you as a Goya," he murmured, putting his hand under her chin and tilting her face to the light, "cream and chocolate and blue . . . you're a very beautiful woman, Claudia."

"And soon to be a very rich one," she murmured, smiling as he kissed her.

Claudia was one of those rare women who are more beautiful unclothed than clothed, and Orlando's artistic eye appreciated every delicious curve, as much as his body appreciated her lustful enjoyment of their lovemaking. It was a long, languorous night and he almost regretted when morning came and he had to leave.

"Shall we meet again?" Claudia asked drowsily as he dressed quickly and kissed her good-bye.

"Of course we shall," he assured her, "do you think now I've found you, I'm going to let you go?"

She smiled impishly. "As long as it's not my money you're after."

"No, Claudia," he replied, kissing her again, "it's not your money. I'll be back in Paris next week. I'll call you."

"I may go to Italy, to the Villa Velata," she said. "I'll leave a message on the answering machine for you."

"Promise?" he asked, straightening his tie.

"I promise." She smiled. "See you soon, Orlando."

CHAPTER 16

Mike read the postcard Lauren had sent him for the fifth time. The picture was one of Hockney's swimming pools, aquamarine and white and filled with ripples of golden sunshine. On the back she had written, *. . . My mother always said it was polite to write and say thank you, but anyway, I really wanted to. It was really nice meeting you. Good luck on your trip to Europe, and I hope you find the missing heiress.* She'd signed it *Love Lauren,* and for some silly reason Mike found himself touched.

Picking up the telephone, he dialed her number. It rang and rang but no one answered, and disconnecting, he dialed Madison, Wisconsin. This time the phone was picked up on the second ring.

"Hi, Aunt Martha," he called, "how're things?"

"About the same, Michael, though no doubt you'd be able to see that for yourself if you ever managed to get off that social merry-go-round you're on and come home."

Her tone was sharp and he grinned; Aunt Martha always got that off her chest first, and then—like now—she'd go on to tell him the faults of the new preacher at the church, and about Joanna Handspacher's outrageous new hat, and that Mary Griffith's daughter had just made her a grandmother for the third time—and so when was he going to find himself some nice respectable woman and make her a great-aunt? Then at least she'd have something to boast about at the next Ladies' Lunch

Circle, instead of everybody always asking her to get his autograph. In her opinion, autographs were ridiculous and why anybody should want his, she didn't know . . .

"Come on now, Aunt Martha," he protested, laughing, "you know you're proud of me."

"Proud? Of course I'm proud . . . what's that got to do with your getting married? Everyone keeps reminding me you're thirty-seven years old now—as if I need reminding!"

He could just imagine her smiling as she talked to him; her short dark hair would be smooth and softly curled, the silvery wings at her temples proudly displayed—though she was even prouder that the color was real. Most of her friends were already completely gray, or, as she'd said caustically, were wasting their money at the beauty parlor tinting it some ridiculous blue color. "Age is a state of mind," she'd always told Mike, "it's got nothing to do with the way you look." He remembered that now, thinking of Lauren.

"What's on the stove, Aunt Martha?" he interrupted her. "It sure smells good."

She laughed, a robust, jolly sound that always made those around her join in. "Silly boy," she said indulgently, "as a matter of fact it's your favorite—pot roast."

"Aunt Martha, I haven't had pot roast in years, be sure to make it next time I'm home, okay?"

"I miss you," she said quietly. "When will that be?"

Mike sighed. "Sorry sweetheart, it'll be a while yet. I've got to fly to New York this afternoon and from there to London and Geneva, and then Venice. It's business."

"Hummph, some business, all those wonderful cities. It must be a new book then?"

He explained, "It's a strange story and I'm just getting to grips with it —or at least the beginning of it. I'm on the trail of the missing heir, or heiress, to a mysterious fortune."

"What's so mysterious about a fortune?" she demanded. "It's either a fortune—or it's not."

"It's the story of how she made the fortune that's still a mystery," he said, laughing. "I'm going to Europe to try and track it down."

"Well, good luck then, son. Come and see me when you get back, will you?"

Mike hesitated. "Aunt Martha?"

"Yes? What is it, Michael? I can see Millie Hutchins coming up the path; she's coming for supper . . . never mind, the door's open, she'll let herself in."

"Aunt Martha, I've met this girl . . . here in L.A." There was silence at the other end of the phone and he hurried on quickly. "I mean, I scarcely know her, I've only met her once, but, well . . . there's something about her . . ."

"Well, thank the Lord for that," she said laughing, "bring her home with you when you come."

He grinned in relief; he didn't know why he'd told her but somehow he felt better for putting what he felt into words. "I'll keep it in mind," he said cheerfully as she hung up.

Still smiling, he glanced at the suitcase on the bed, waiting to be packed; his plane left in two hours, he'd better hurry. His notes on Poppy Mallory's life, composed with the help of Rosalia's and Angel's journals, lay on the desk and he walked across, staring down at them thoughtfully. It was funny, but he had the same feeling of tenderness for Poppy as he did for Lauren, and, God knew, both were deserving of compassion.

CHAPTER 17

1 8 8 6 , C A L I F O R N I A

Nik studied the little red-haired girl browsing along the counter in Mrs. Price's Candy Store, biting her lip in concentration, contemplating the shiny glass jars of aniseed balls and gobstoppers. There was no mistaking she was Jeb's daughter, she looked exactly like him.

"Two twists of licorice, please, and one gobstopper," the child decided, holding out her two cents anxiously.

"You're short one cent, little girl," Mrs. Price replied kindly. "I'm afraid you'll have to choose again."

"Allow me." Nik placed the extra cent on the counter and Poppy glanced up at him in surprise.

"But how can I pay you back?" she asked doubtfully. "I don't know you."

"But I know you—and I knew your mother," Nik replied, smiling. "It's Poppy, isn't it?"

She smiled back at him. *"How* did you know?"

"You look exactly like . . ." Nik hesitated; he didn't want to mention Jeb. "You have your mother's red hair," he said finally.

"Do I really?" Her eyes were round with pleased astonishment. "No one ever told me my mother had red hair!" Nik frowned, surprised by what she had said, as Poppy licked her gobstopper. "What's your name?" she asked.

"I'm Nik Konstant."

She burst into peals of laughter. "But I've got a rocking horse called Nik. Papa named him that because he had a friend who—" She clapped a hand over her mouth suddenly; after all, she couldn't tell him he was a horse's ass, could she? "Oh, well, he's a beautiful horse," she added lamely, "and I love him. He's in San Francisco, though." She hung over the counter companionably, watching while Nik made several purchases and Mrs. Price wrapped them in a paper bag. "Who's the candy for?" she asked, licking her sticky fingers with a pointed pink tongue.

"It's a present for my daughter, Angel."

"Angel!" She frowned. "What a funny name. How old is she?"

"Just your age, six." He smiled, pocketing the candy.

"I don't know any little girls my age," Poppy said importantly. "I just know grown-up ladies."

Nik sighed. "Well, there are lots of little girls in Santa Barbara, maybe you'll meet some."

"Maybe I'll get to meet Angel," Poppy said hopefully, and then her face fell. "But I know I won't. There are no children at the Arlington Hotel and I don't expect there'll be any at the Mallory House. Anyway, Papa says he's going to buy me a real pony of my very own."

Her eager smile and bright blue eyes were so like Jeb's it hurt. Nik turned away. "That's nice, Poppy," he replied, stepping out onto the wooden porch.

She ran after him anxiously. "Mr. Konstant," she called. "I'd really like to meet another little girl."

Her wistful gaze stabbed him and he cursed Jeb once again for what he was doing to the poor lonely child. "We'll see," he called, waving good-bye.

"Nice to have met you, Mr. Konstant," Poppy called sadly, leaning over the porch, watching as he walked away.

Farther down the street, in Goux's Liquor Store, Nik heard the full story about Jeb's financial disasters from a man just disembarked from the steamer. And before the day was out the whole of Santa Barbara knew it. It only confirmed their opinion that Jeb Mallory was a bad lot.

"It can't be true," Rosalia gasped, horrified, when he told her. "How could he lose his fortune? He came back from Monte Carlo with millions!"

"Jeb could run through a million dollars so fast, you wouldn't even have time to blink," Nik replied with a shrug. "He's a selfish man. The world revolves around him and his needs. Don't you see he's like a child,

Rosalia? When he wants something he wants it *now*—and what he wants most is to gamble. He doesn't care what it costs—or who it hurts." Pouring himself a brandy from the decanter on the sideboard, he looked at her somberly. "Poppy has his eyes, you know, *and* his smile. There's no mistaking whose daughter she is. She's a lovely child, Rosalia. And a very lonely one."

Rosalia counted her blessings; happy little Angel, safely asleep in the nursery; and Greg, home for the summer vacation; and Nik. She thanked God that her home was more than just four walls that gave them shelter, it was a place that offered the warmth and stability, the love and security, of a true family.

"We must invite her to come here," she said quietly. "After all, we cannot visit the sins of the fathers upon the daughters, can we?"

Poppy scuffed her feet in the accumulation of dead leaves and dust on the porch of the Mallory House while Jeb rang the bell impatiently for the third time. It looked run-down and shabby; its white paint was chipped, and the faded green shutters hung lopsidedly at the grimy windows. The picket fence around Margaret's overgrown flower beds was tangled with ivy and the once baize-green lawns were brown and withered from neglect.

There was the sound of slow, shuffling footsteps, then the heavy bolts were drawn back, a key turned rustily in the long-unused lock, and at last the door swung stiffly open.

Poppy shrank terrified behind Papa as an Indian, looking as old as Methuselah, peered out at them. His nut-brown face was folded into a thousand creases and his eyes were clouded with cataracts that almost blinded him; nevertheless, he knew somehow that Jeb Mallory had returned, and he bowed. Jeb strode past him into the gloomy hall, switching back the drapes until sunlight flooded the room. Pausing by the hall table, Poppy wrote her name in large, straggling letters in the thick layer of dust. Then, telling the Indian that Lian Sung, their Chinese servant, was waiting in the gig to bring in the provisions, Jeb marched her up the oaken staircase.

"The child," the Indian called after him in his slow, sonorous voice, "has her mother's hair."

Jeb glared at him; the wily old bastard could still see exactly what he wanted to see, despite the cataracts!

"He's the second person to tell me that," Poppy remarked excitedly. "Did he know my mother too?"

"What do you mean? Who else has been talking to you about your mother?" Jeb asked, surprised.

"I forgot to tell you, I met a man in Mrs. Price's Candy Store the other day. He said he knew who I was because I had my mother's red hair. Papa, why did you never tell me she had red hair?"

"Who did you talk to?" he demanded, gripping her shoulder fiercely. "Who was it?"

Poppy's eyes were round with fright as she answered. "He said his name was Nik Konstant and he has a little girl my age. She's called Angel. I told him I thought it was a silly name, Papa—"

"I don't want you to speak to Nik Konstant again!" he commanded in an icy voice she barely recognized. "Or any other of the Konstants. You understand me, Poppy? *Never!*"

"But he seemed such a nice man . . ." she faltered.

"Just do as I say!" Jeb commanded, letting go of her so abruptly, she fell back against the banisters.

Poppy nodded. Her head drooped and frightened tears squeezed from her eyes; she just hated it when Papa got angry, it was even worse than when he drank a lot and just ignored her, or when he became involved in some card game and forgot to come home. She trailed despondently after him down a long, gloomy corridor to her old nursery.

It was a large room on the southeast corner of the house, with long windows on two sides, but even when the curtains were drawn back and sunlight filled it, Poppy thought somehow it looked unfriendly. She longed suddenly for her lavish satin and silk and lace nursery on Russian Hill, with all her familiar toys and books and Nik the rocking horse. She'd even be willing to put up with Ma'mzelle if only she could go back there. Blinking away her tears, she smiled bravely as she wandered around touching the neat white-painted iron bed with its patchwork quilt, thinking how hard it felt. She stared sadly at the little pine dresser and the straight rush-bottomed chairs and then, spotting a comforting old rocker by the window, she climbed into it. With her rag doll clutched to her chest she rocked gently backward and forward, taking in the details of her new—old—home. She tried to imagine her mysterious red-haired mother in here, putting her to bed when she was very small, and holding her on her lap in this very rocker, the way she knew from stories mothers did. And she wondered again why nobody ever talked about her mother. She turned to ask Papa but he had disappeared and she ran to find him.

He was standing at the doorway of a large dark room. A chink of light came from a gap in the curtains and a long mirror, spotted with gray where the silvering had worn off, reflected their distorted images. Everything in there was dark, Poppy thought, lurking nervously behind him, the big carved bed, the heavy dresser, the dusty velvet drapes . . . it wasn't a very pretty room. "Was this yours and Mama's room?" she whispered, because somehow the room had been too long silent for her to talk in normal tones.

"It was," Jeb replied abruptly, closing the door. She followed at his heels like a little dog as he strode along the corridor flinging open doors and opening the drapes. "I shall be sleeping in here," he said, choosing a room at the opposite side of the house, and Poppy thought nervously that it seemed an awful long way from the nursery.

It was getting late, and after a strange supper of Chinese rice made by Lian Sung she curled up in her chilly bed in the old nursery, her rag doll clutched in her arms and her eyes squeezed tight shut. Papa had left the door open and a night-light burning but even so, her mind was full of strange thoughts about the shuttered silent room that used to be her mother's, and the frightening Indian with the strange white eyes, and why Papa didn't want her to talk to Nik Konstant when he was such a nice man. Sadness filled her as she realized that now she would never get to meet the little girl, Angel, and tears of fear and bewilderment flowed from her eyes until, at last, exhaustion sent her into an uneasy sleep.

"Papa," she said a few weeks later as she paced up the hill at the back of the house beside him, "where are the poppies?"

His blue eyes narrowed as he glanced at her. "The poppies haven't grown here in years . . . not since you were born. Why, who told you about them?"

"No one," she replied innocently, "I just remember."

"Don't lie to me, Poppy," he said angrily. "It's impossible for you to remember. The old Indian must have been talking to you . . . or maybe it was Nik Konstant, eh?"

Poppy hung her head, saying nothing, mortified that he had thought she was lying, wondering why Papa wasn't behaving the way he used to, when everything was jolly and nice.

"Papa," she said a little while later, "why don't we invite all your friends and have a party, the way we used to at the other house? It's so lonely here and I miss everyone so much." She looked up at him hopefully, adding, "Don't you miss it, Papa?"

With a pang Jeb remembered the note he'd received from Rosalia asking if Poppy could visit them and his curtly penned refusal. But God damn it, *he* was lonely too. He was bored with the ranch and bored with Poppy, and he missed his extravagant life-style . . . he needed a woman, and he needed a poker game! And he surely wasn't going to find either at the Rancho Santa Vittoria.

"Tell you what, Poppy," he said suddenly, "what you really need is a pony. Yes, a snappy little black pony just like Nik the rocking horse—but a real one this time. How'd you like your old Papa to teach you to ride, me girl?"

Her blue eyes sparkled and she jumped up and down with excitement. "Oh, yes, Papa, yes. When? When can I have it?"

"I'll go right now and buy him for you," he replied, hoisting her onto his shoulders and jogging back down the hill.

"Can I come too?" she cried, clutching at his hair, laughing.

"Well, no, not this time," he said, setting her down on the porch. "It's better if Papa's girl waits here for him. That way it'll be more of a surprise, won't it?"

Poppy watched, disappointed, as he called instructions to Lian Sung and commanded the Indian to take care of her. And then he was off in the shabby little black and yellow gig, whisking the bay into a trot as he sped down the shady drive. "Be right back, sweetheart," he called, waving. But she sat on the front steps for a long time, watching the plume of dust raised by the horse's hooves die away into the distance.

Lian Sung was sweeping the hall when she finally went inside. "Can I help do that?" she asked, sneezing loudly, hoping she could make patterns in the dust, but he just shrugged and she remembered that Lian Sung spoke very funny English that only Papa understood. Hopefully, she tried a few words of French, but Lian just kept on sweeping.

Her tummy rumbled hungrily and she looked into the kitchen, but the scary old Indian was sitting in his usual place by the fire and she shrank back again. The nursery seemed empty and even more silent as she sat in the rocker thinking about her mother. Her father had told her that she had died when Poppy was still a baby and she thought it seemed such an unfair thing for a mama to do. Suddenly curious, she tiptoed along the corridor to the mysterious room.

The big brass key was in the lock, and by using both hands and all her weight, she managed to turn it. A chink of light came from the drapes and she stole across the room and drew them back cautiously, staring around in the bright sunlight, searching for a picture of her mother, wondering what she had looked like, what she had sounded like, and whether she had loved her. But there were no portraits or pictures on the walls, just a few gloomy woodcuts of saintly-looking men and women.

Under one window stood a small davenport desk made from some rich dark wood inlaid with patterns of mother-of-pearl. Poppy ran her hand over its surface, letting her fingers hover guiltily on the tiny gold key. She knew it was wrong to look at other people's things, but after all, this was her mother . . . turning it quickly, she peered inside. She rummaged through a disappointing mass of old papers and letters, and then turned her attention to the cupboard below. There was a whole shelf of sketch-books filled with pretty little watercolor paintings of the house and the gardens, and Poppy looked through them curiously for a while. Then she noticed a flat brown leather book in the far corner of the cupboard, and she recognized the name *Mallory* in gold letters on the front. Mallory! Her own name! Struggling, she deciphered the name *Margaret* . . . and beneath that *Her Journal.* Flushed with excitement, she held the precious book close to her chest . . . this was her mother's very own book and in it she would tell what she did, how she felt, what her world was like . . . maybe she'd even talk about *her.*

Poppy peeked eagerly at the yellowing pages but the writing was much too difficult for her limited reading ability. She ran her finger across the pages sadly, wanting to feel her mother's presence, and there, on a page near the end, she recognized one word: POPPY. Her own name written by her own mother!

She held the book close once again. She would treasure it forever and one day, when she was grown up enough and could read properly, she would know what her mother had said about her. Until then it would be her very own secret—she wouldn't even tell Papa because then he might want to take it away from her.

Tucking the book under her pinafore where no one could see it, she stole from the room and ran back to the nursery where she hid it at the very back of the old toy cupboard. Breathing a sigh of relief that no one had noticed her "theft," she dusted off her hands and went back outside to her place on the front steps to wait for Papa to return.

The first night he didn't return she told herself that he must be waiting for the pony to be ready. She was at her usual place on the front steps at dawn, peering down the road, and she didn't leave until it was too dark to see anymore. Even though she tried to tell herself that Papa was late because he was taking his time choosing exactly the *right* pony, she cried herself to sleep. The third day seemed endless. Lian Sung placed food beside her, but she couldn't eat. She just sat on the steps until darkness fell, waiting. The old Indian appeared suddenly in the gloom, grabbing her hand, and Poppy screamed, terrified as he forced her back into the house. But he merely shook his head and said, "Mr. Jeb come back when he come back. It is his way. You are child, you go to bed."

No one had lit her night-light or brought her a glass of milk, and stifling her sobs, Poppy tossed and turned in the dark listening to the barking of the coyotes in the hills and the eerie hoot of marauding owls, imagining she could hear the fluttering of strange, nightmarish creatures in her room.

Pale-faced and trembling, she was out of the house as the sun came up on her fourth day, hunched alone on the steps with her arms clasped around her knees and her chin sunk into her chest, waiting.

When Jeb finally returned just after four that afternoon, she was curled up on the wooden verandah, fast asleep.

"Hey there, Papa's girl," he called with his usual jaunty grin, "don't you think you should come and take a look at your new pony?"

"Papa!" she screamed, waking instantly and hurling herself down the steps and into his arms. "Oh, Papa! I thought you were never coming back. I thought you'd gone away and left me—forever and ever and ever . . ." Her arms snaked around his neck, gripping him tightly as tears of relief rained down her face.

He glanced bitterly at the window of Margaret's old room, wondering why she had to die, God damn it, and leave him with all the responsibility! Sure and he loved Poppy, but a man couldn't always be tied down by a little girl. "You needn't have worried yourself so, Poppy," he said, setting her back on the ground, "Papa will always come back. Now, let's go and have a look at that pony, shall we?" But as he walked across to the waiting horse, Jeb vowed that as soon as his fortunes changed for the better, he'd get the child a new nursemaid and a governess, and then he'd be off on his travels again. There wasn't a thing, child or woman, that could hold him down for long!

Poppy held out a cautious bunch of grass to the plump brown pony, patting his flanks excitedly. "If you're gonna ride a horse, you're gonna learn to do it well," he told her, hoisting her into the saddle.

For two days he held the pony on a lunge rein, first walking and then trotting her around in circles as Poppy learned to post up and down with the rhythm of the horse and how to use her knees for control and how to hold the reins as lightly as a feather and never to pull on the pony's tender mouth. Soon she was trotting round the paddock on her own, sitting easily in the saddle, straight-backed and relaxed and laughing with delight when the pony broke into a canter.

She named him Spider because of his long, spidery legs and she was up at dawn to feed and groom him and muck out his stable, and she thought that with Papa home and her new pony to love she must be the happiest girl in the whole world.

When Jeb told her that he was going into Santa Barbara on business and he'd be back the next morning, Poppy didn't even worry, she was so busy with Spider to look after. But when he hadn't returned by dusk on the second night, she felt that old gnawing fear in her stomach. As darkness fell on the third night her lonely, frightened tears flowed again. In search of comfort she crept from the house and curled up in the stable near Spider, comforted by his solid warmth and the clean stable smells. As the days drifted past she lost count of how long Jeb had been away. She just rode Spider in solitary circles around the Mallory House, afraid to stray too far in case she missed him.

When Jeb finally came back, he merely grinned his jaunty grin, his bright blue eyes sparkling with good humor, and demanded to know how the riding was going. He didn't say anything at all about where he'd been or what he'd been doing.

The third time it happened, Lian Sung walked out, muttering in his strange-sounding English that this was not a good house. Poppy followed him silently on Spider as he trudged down the sandy lane with his worldly goods strapped on his back, stopping at the top of the hill as he disappeared into a grove of sycamores. And then she walked Spider slowly back to the big silent house—empty now but for the terrifying blind old Indian.

The days dragged past and even the Indian seemed to have forgotten she was there, barely turning his head to stare at her with his strange opaque eyes whenever she sneaked into the kitchen in search of a piece of the flat bread he cooked on the open fire, or a hunk of cheese and an apple. Each morning she would saddle up Spider and ride to the top of the hill and she'd stare first at the dusty lane hoping to see her father riding jauntily home to her, and then along the sandy trail that Jeb had told her led to the Konstant House. Poppy wondered wistfully what it must feel like to have a father like Nik and thought how lucky Angel was, and she wondered again what Angel must look like.

Day after day she hesitated at the top of the hill, gazing intently down the sandy trail and conjuring up pictures of Angel, longing to ride down it and find her, but Jeb had made her promise never to speak to the Konstants. Still, she decided, he hadn't forbidden her to take a look at them, had he? Digging her knees into Spider's plump sides, she set off down the trail at a fast canter.

The trail seemed to go on forever and Poppy began to worry that she might be lost when, suddenly, beyond a stand of oaks she caught a glimpse of red-tiled roofs, and there below her in the valley lay the prettiest house she had ever seen.

The Konstant House wasn't in the least bit like their own gray weatherboarded home with the old adobe bit that was now the kitchen just stuck on one side. It was shiny and white and built around a court-yard, with a big arched gateway, and wrought-iron gates in a beautiful pattern like swans' wings. The spray from a blue-tiled fountain sparkled in the sunlight like graceful ropes of diamonds and the comfortable long chairs, grouped on the colonnaded verandah, looked just right for loung-ing in on hot days. And everywhere were terra-cotta pots of geraniums and lobelia, begonias and fuchsia, hibiscus, bougainvillaea and roses, spreading in a riot of color that dazzled Poppy's eyes. She could see gardeners at work in the shady flower gardens in back of the house and someone was picking vegetables in the walled garden beyond. And in a large grassy paddock a small girl with hair so light, it glinted like bleached gold in the sun, set her sleek black pony at a series of jumps, taking them steadily higher and higher until Poppy gasped in admira-tion.

She knew at once that this must be Angel, and even from a distance she could see she was beautiful. But there was someone else, a tall, dark boy in a checkered shirt who strode toward Angel and patted the pony's neck as he talked to her. Lucky Angel had *a brother* as well as a mother and father . . . oh, lucky, lucky Angel! Keeping to the shadow of the oaks, Poppy urged Spider forward, straining her ears to catch their voices, longing to know what they were saying, and wishing she were part of that charmed scene. A bell rang suddenly and Spider whinnied as she pulled clumsily on the reins.

A small, dark-haired woman was standing in the courtyard ringing a silver bell and her voice carried clearly up the hill as she called, "Angel . . . Greg . . . lunch is ready. *Vamos almorzar!*"

Sliding from her pony Angel loosened its girths and removed the saddle. Her brother gave the animal a hearty thwack on the rump and they laughed as it kicked up its heels and galloped off into the paddock. Breathless with envy and delight, Poppy watched as they climbed the paddock fence and, arm in arm, walked toward the beautiful house where their mother waited in the courtyard.

"Come on, you two," Rosalia called. "I swear that horses are more important to you than food!" And she ruffled Angel's blond hair affec-tionately as she followed them into the pretty house.

Poppy sat for a long time just staring at the house and thinking enviously about its inhabitants. She wondered hungrily if they had lunch at the same time every day and what they were eating. She wondered if they might come out again afterward and ride the pony, or whether Angel's mother would insist she take a rest. And as she finally turned away and urged Spider into a trot, she was quite certain that Angel's mother and father would tuck her safely into bed that night, and that every morning when she woke up, they would be there.

Walking softly so as not to wake the Indian, she foraged for her own supper that night, tearing off a piece of flat bread and pouring herself a glass of the frothy, creamy milk the Indian had taken from the cow in the apple orchard that very morning. Taking it to her usual place at the top of the steps, she munched it slowly, staring across the tangled garden to the road, wishing Papa would appear magically around the bend. But, of course, he didn't, and when it finally became too dark to see anymore, she turned wearily back into the big silent house.

She sat on the edge of her bed, her chin in her hands and her legs swinging, thinking about Angel Konstant again, remembering her bright hair and the sound of her joyous laughter. There was something so fresh and pure and beautiful about Angel—she had an aura about her, like a real angel. Scrambling from the bed, Poppy stared at herself in the long mirror. Her blue cotton dress was grubby and there were milk stains down the front. Her face was streaked with grime and a faint milky moustache bordered her mouth. She couldn't remember the last time she had brushed her hair because no one was ever there to tell her to do it, and now it was matted on top and the braids hadn't been undone in days. Holding out her hands, she stared anxiously at the black half circles under her bitten nails, and she compared her scratched, stockingless legs in the scuffed muddy boots with blond Angel's immaculate image.

Ripping off the dress angrily, she rummaged in the dresser for a clean nightgown. Then she unbraided her hair and attacked it with the harsh wire brush, trying unsuccessfully to remove the tangles. The water jug was too high for her to reach and anyway it was too heavy to pour, so she stood on a chair and dipped first one hand and then another into the cold water and rubbed them onto her face, wiping off the dirt on a harsh white linen towel. Finally she knelt beside her bed and, folding her hands, said her prayers, only tonight she didn't just pray for Papa to come home, she also asked God to make her like Angel Konstant. And that night, too, she dreamed about the pretty black pony riding over the jumps, and the brother and sister walking back together to the lady with the voice as sweet as her silver bell, only in the dream it wasn't Angel who was there, it was her!

When Papa finally returned, it was without his usual jaunty grin and bagful of presents. Poppy stood silently at the top of the mahogany stairs as he slammed into the house, his face bleak with anger.

"God damn it, Poppy," he groaned, noticing her suddenly. "I'd forgotten all about you!"

She stared at him, stunned . . . *how could Papa have forgotten her . . . it was impossible . . . she would never forget him. . . .*

He sighed again. "All right, then," he said grimly, and without even a kiss he marched past her into the nursery. "I guess there's nothing for it but to take you along with me."

Poppy watched silently as he dragged open her dresser drawers and began to stuff a small bag with her things, too upset that he had forgotten her even to wonder where they were going.

"Get yourself ready for bed," Jeb said brusquely as he closed the nursery door behind him, "we'll be off tomorrow at dawn."

Poppy lay unsleeping in her chilly bed, trembling with fear—not at the thought of *where*, or even *why*, they were going, but at the idea that Papa had forgotten her. She was up and dressed well before dawn, waiting outside his door with her small bag and her rag doll clutched beneath her arm, just the way Papa used to carry her when she was very small. When Jeb finally opened the door, he almost fell over her.

"I didn't want you to forget me, Papa," Poppy told him, her eyes wide with fear.

He glared at her silently. It was bad enough that he'd lost the house and his share of the Rancho Santa Vittoria to a cheap cowboy from Montecito, but now he was stuck with Poppy too. God damn, it was tough enough for a gambling man on the road without a kid tagging along! Grabbing her bag, he strode down the corridor so fast, she had to run to keep up with him. "What about Spider?" she asked breathlessly. "Is he coming with us?"

He'd forgotten all about the damned pony. "He'll be waiting for you, when you get back," he lied carelessly. "Come on now, hurry up."

The Indian, bundled into his serape, was waiting in the front hall. "I will not see you again, Mr. Jeb," he said, his once sonorous voice now faded to a whisper. "You and I will both depart this house for good."

Jeb looked at him steadily. The old Indian was always right. He had been here at the beginning and now this was the end.

The Indian bowed his gray head. "It will not be long now," he murmured as they filed past him into the pearly-clear dawn.

CHAPTER 18

1 8 8 7

Papa had told her they were to "travel" and Poppy had dreamed of returning to Monte Carlo, but it wasn't like that at all. This time they had only the tiniest cabin on the ferry back to San Francisco, in the lowest part of the boat where the waves slammed against the sides, making her feel sick. But even though she cried, Papa just lay on his bunk drinking Irish whiskey from a silver flask and snoring loudly when he finally fell asleep.

They disembarked at San Francisco on wobbly legs, and when she asked hopefully if they were going home to Russian Hill, Jeb merely grabbed her hand and loaded her into the horse-drawn bus that would take them to Union Square Station. Poppy pestered him with a barrage of questions, but he told her angrily to be quiet and she slumped sulkily in her corner.

There were no smart staterooms this time on the big train to Chicago, just a section of a harsh plush seat that scratched her legs, and when she complained that she was hungry, Jeb bought her packets of sandwiches and apples from a man with a large tray slung around his neck. Poppy finally fell asleep, with her head on Papa's arm, holding tightly to his jacket sleeve and dreaming that she was Angel Konstant riding her black pony over a hundred jumps, as the train rumbled and clattered across the vast country.

When she awoke, her head was resting on Papa's fine soft overcoat and he was gone. Panic clenched her stomach again as the thought crossed her mind that while she was sleeping he might have forgotten her again and got off the train without her. "Where's Papa?" she asked the dark, disapproving woman opposite as she rubbed the sleep from her eyes.

"By the smell of him, he'll be in the bar!" she snapped. "I don't know what a man like that thinks he's doing, leaving a little girl like you alone while he gets drunk!"

Poppy eyed her warily as she slid off the prickly seat and edged past her. "Papa is not drunk," she retorted from the safety of the door, "and he hasn't left me! He's the very best papa in the whole world!" And then she fled down the corridor, away from the woman's sharp tongue and her wrath at the impertinent retort.

She stopped to ask directions from a gray-haired man, who laughed loudly when she asked him for the bar, then she hurried on down the corridor, swaying from side to side and ricocheting off the walls as the train swung unexpectedly around a curve in the tracks. But when she finally found the bar, she understood why Papa liked it so much.

It was much jollier than the gloomy carriage and the disapproving woman in black. Pretty lamps in engraved glass globes shed a cozy glow over red flock walls, shiny wooden panels, and glittering shelves of bottles and glasses. Poppy stood just inside the door searching for her father among the line of pink-faced men at the mahogany bar, sniffing the familiar malt and mash smells of whiskey and bourbon and the bitter hops smell of beer. She spotted him at last, sitting at a table with four other men, shuffling a deck of cards.

Unconscious of the amused glances of the customers, she elbowed her way through the crowd to his table. "Papa!" she cried as silence fell. "There you are! I thought you'd left me again!"

Jeb's card partners raised their eyebrows, grinning as he threw her a cold glance. Laying down his cards, he said quietly, "Of course I haven't left you, Poppy. The nice lady in the carriage said she would keep an eye on you."

"I didn't like her," Poppy declared loudly as he took her hand and led her from the bar. "She said you had no right to get drunk and leave me all alone."

Guffaws of masculine laughter followed them down the swaying corridor and Jeb's hand suddenly gripped hers too tightly for comfort.

"Owww," she squealed, "you're hurting me, Papa!"

"You are just lucky I don't put you over my knee, me girl," he snapped angrily. Crouching until his eyes were level with hers, he said quietly but with an undertone of force that made her tremble, *"Don't ever come looking for me again, Poppy. You understand that?"* His voice shook as he added, *"You are never to come after me again! Never!"* Grabbing her hand, he dragged her silent and shaking back to the carriage, and giving her an apple and her doll, he told her to go back to sleep or to amuse herself looking out of the window, he would *"be right back."* But Poppy knew enough now to understand what *be right back* meant . . . it meant he would come for her whenever he had finished whatever it was that was so important to him—more important than her—and not before. And that might take days or weeks or even months . . . or forever.

As the train pulled into Chicago, Poppy thought Papa's mood had improved. He took her straight downtown to a smart hotel and she ran around happily inspecting everything, immediately at home in the velvet and brocade surroundings of the grand suite. She didn't get to see much of Chicago, though, because Papa ordered a card table sent up and he and some other men sat up all night playing poker and drinking whiskey, while she slept cozily in the very center of an enormous brass bed.

While Papa slept the day away Poppy amused herself wandering around the grand hotel chatting to chambermaids and waiters and especially the hall porter, who told her they often had important people staying there—stars of the opera and theater. "But I know them!" she cried excitedly as he reeled off a string of starry names, remembering how they used to fill the house on Russian Hill night after night.

"Sure you do," he chuckled, patting her head and ordering a passing pageboy to fetch a doughnut for the "cute little redheaded girl."

Poppy soon became quite well known in some of the smarter hotels in Philadelphia, Pittsburgh, Boston, and New York, as well as in Chicago. But that was only when Jeb was winning. When he was losing, they stayed in seedy rooming houses in run-down areas where Jeb hurried her through the grimy streets, his collar turned up, avoiding the angry stares of the hoodlums and bums and drunks on the sidewalks. She became used to silent, greasy breakfasts eaten alongside brawny red-faced construction workers and dockers smelling of sweat, and she soon learned how to hold her tongue when sharp-eyed landladies questioned her about when her papa was gonna pay their rent.

Soon she began to understand the pattern. When Papa was winning, he was jolly and pleasant and she could order whatever she wanted from room service, and when their fortunes dwindled again and they were reduced to a chilly room in some boardinghouse near the railway station or the docks, with cold brown linoleum on the floors and not even a rug for her bare feet when she stepped from the sagging bed in the morning, she would be lucky to get a sandwich. She wandered freely in the hotels, but in the boardinghouse Papa forbade her to leave her room when he was out. When she got bored, she'd sneak out onto the landing, listening to the sound of voices, often raised in anger, coming from the other rooms, and sniffing the strange odor of boiled cabbage lingering in the stairwell. And then somehow she knew she would never see her beloved pony, Spider, again.

They had been staying for a couple of weeks in a small midtown hotel in a city new to her, St. Louis; and as usual Jeb had gone out in search of a game, leaving Poppy sitting up in bed munching a slab of cake. Her eyes followed anxiously as the door closed behind him. She didn't like this hotel. Papa had said it was filled with traveling salesmen with cardboard suitcases, and the corridors smelled of disinfectant. The man at the reception desk had a bad cold and sniffed disapprovingly every time she wandered into the front hall in search of amusement, sending her scurrying back to her chilly room.

Still, tonight her bed was warm and she had her old rag doll to cuddle, and dreaming her now faded dream of being Angel Konstant amid her loving family in her beautiful home, Poppy was soon asleep.

The next morning she got up early and washed and dressed herself, hoping that Papa might have had a lucky night and when he returned he would take her to a coffee shop for her favorite breakfast of blueberry pancakes and maple syrup. She sat on the edge of the bed swinging her legs and singing a little jingle she'd heard the organ-grinder playing in the street when she'd fed peanuts to his sweet red-jacketed monkey. She waited for what seemed like ages, but still Papa didn't come. Disappointed, Poppy stared from the grimy window at the gray rain-slicked streets of the gray anonymous city.

As morning slid slowly into afternoon the rain changed to snow and her tummy began to rumble hungrily. She leaned despondently on the windowsill breathing on the panes now and again to clear the thin layer of frost. When it became too dark to see outside, she huddled in bed to keep warm, trying desperately not to cry. "Papa said never to go after him," she repeated out loud, jumping at the sound of her own voice in the cold, silent room. She repeated it over and over again throughout the long, sleepless freezing-cold night. *Be right back,"* Papa had cried as usual when he left, and Poppy was sure he would.

Her stomach was knotted with fear and hunger by the second afternoon and putting on her coat, she crept down the creaking shabbily carpeted stairs, hurrying past the reception desk praying the clerk wouldn't notice her.

"Hey you!" he called sharply. "Where's your father? Just tell him that he owes two weeks rent and if I don't have it in my hand by the morning —you're out!"

Poppy shrank against the wall, horrified. If Papa didn't come home tonight, they would just throw her out into the street—and then Papa would never be able to find her again!

"What's the matter then?" the clerk asked, eyeing her more kindly. "It's not your fault, kid. It's tough luck on you having a father like him, that's what."

"No, it isn't," flared Poppy, shaking her red hair until it sprang from its braids and flew about her head and stamping her feet in a rage. "My papa is the best papa in the whole world, the very best!" And then she burst into tears, sobbing uncontrollably as doors flew open on landings all the way up the stairwell and guests peered curiously at the scene.

"Whatever's the matter with that child?" demanded a stout woman in severe black bombazine with a large cameo brooch pinned at her neck. "Why is she behaving so badly?"

"I'm afraid I don't know, ma'am," replied the desk clerk worriedly, "but I haven't seen her father around for a couple of days and he owes more than two weeks rent. Looks to me like he might have abandoned her."

"Abandoned her? Why, the poor child. We must do something about it immediately." Sweeping authoritatively down the wooden stairs, she peered at Poppy, tearstained and bedraggled and still sobbing. "I'll telephone the city welfare officer," she decided, "there are homes for abandoned children and I'll see they find room for her, even if I have to take her there myself!"

Poppy kicked and scratched and fought as they thrust her into the carriage with the official-looking man from the welfare. "Don't," she screamed, "don't! Papa will never find me."

"Find you?" he retorted exasperatedly. "Of course he won't find you! He won't even be looking!"

The children's home was a granite-gray building set squarely in the middle of a snow-covered patch of shrubbery and lawn. Gloomy laurel hedges crowded against the uncurtained downstairs windows and Poppy thought it looked darker and grayer than any other place she'd ever seen in her life. Groups of drably clothed children shrank against the institution-green walls, staring at her, their pinched white faces looking shocked by her outburst of screaming as the man handed her over to a matron in a dark blue dress and white apron, saying, "She's hysterical. Father's a drunk and a gambler. He's run off owing the hotel bill—and he left her behind too."

"Nooooo . . ." screamed Poppy. "No, it's not true. He's not any of those things and he loves me . . . Papa would never leave me, never, never, never . . ." But she knew that he had before.

"Come, child," the matron said briskly, "you must take a bath and be inspected for lice, and then we'll give you some clean clothes and you can have supper."

Poppy had no idea what lice were, but she didn't want any supper, all she wanted was for Papa to find her. Her tears seemed to have run out, but her slight body still heaved with dry choking sobs as the matron dragged her reluctantly up the uncarpeted stairs.

She kicked and spat as a nurse inspected her hair and body and dunked her into a bath of lukewarm water that smelled of disinfectant. Then she was dressed in the same gray serge as the other children and her unruly red hair was braided so tightly, it hurt her scalp. With the fight gone out of her she was led exhausted back down the stairs to a room where rows of children sat on benches eating their supper. The woman placed her at the end of a table and a bowl of greasy brown stew was put in front of her. Poppy looked down at the stew and then up at the dozens of curious staring eyes. And then she vomited.

For the next two days she was confined to bed with a raging fever. On the third day as it subsided they fed her small bowls of hot gruel. She was sitting up in her narrow bed, clutching the unwanted bowl wearily when she heard a commotion in the hall.

"Where is she?" Jeb bellowed angrily. "Where is my daughter? How dare you take her away and put her in this godforsaken place?"

Flinging her bowl of gruel to the ground, Poppy leapt from the bed and threw open the door. "Papa, oh, Papa," she screamed joyously, "I told them you hadn't abandoned me . . . I told them you'd come . . . I told them I was Papa's girl and you'd never never leave me!"

"Sure and it was all a terrible mistake," he cried as her arms gripped his neck tightly. "I was a little *indisposed* meself for a few days or I would have been here right away. It's all over now, Papa's girl." He glared at the matron and her assistants and the curious children peering from behind classroom doors. "Don't you dare make a mistake like this again!" he roared as he carried Poppy out of the door and into a waiting cab. "I should take you to the courts for causing a child so much distress, and depriving her father of his daughter!" But of course he never would because he'd only just left the jurisdiction of the courts himself, after spending several uncomfortable nights there for being drunk and disorderly and causing an affray. But Poppy couldn't know that.

Jeb and Poppy crisscrossed the country staying in small towns as well as large ones, but they never again went back to St. Louis. Grimy industrial suburbs and railway sidings became a familiar sight from carriage windows as the trains steamed to their various destinations, and two surprise new words were added to her vocabulary: *Moonlight flit.*

The first time Jeb woke her in the middle of the night and told her to get dressed, Poppy thought it was an exciting new game. He told her to see how quietly she could steal down the stairs, across the hallway, and out of the door, and stifling her giggles she managed it as soundlessly as a mouse. They laughed out loud as they walked through the quiet night-time streets together, swinging their bags, and Jeb told her she would make a good cat burglar, whatever that was—it certainly sounded like something she'd like to be.

The times they spent in smart hotels grew fewer and fewer and there were no more new dolls and pretty dresses, and after a while Poppy began to wish they didn't have to play the Moonlighting game so often. The bitter winter weather was too cold and bleak to be dragged from a warm bed and made to trudge through the streets in the middle of the night. Papa told her not to worry, maybe next week they'd make it to Monte Carlo and the sunshine and the villa in the hills.

The next time Papa failed to return, Poppy was too frightened even to cry, she just stared bleakly at the landlady of the Pittsburgh rooming house as she told her she'd sent for the welfare officer. And this time when they took her away, she submitted silently to the humiliating search and the scratchy serge dress and droopy woolen stockings. But she refused to speak a single word, turning away her head when they questioned her and gritting her teeth together stubbornly until it hurt. This time Papa was gone for two weeks and she had almost given up hope when he finally came.

"I had the devil's own job finding you, me girl," he said cheerfully as she clung to him, trembling.

It happened again in New York, and again in Boston, and Poppy began to dread the moment Jeb walked out the door for fear he would never come back. She began to accept that every few weeks she would end up in a different children's home, submitting to its disciplines and privations either in silence or with screaming rage, counting the days and nights until Papa found her again. But he never once offered an explanation as to why he hadn't returned to the hotel, or told her where he'd been and what he'd been doing that was so important he couldn't come and get "Papa's girl."

Things suddenly began to get better. It was summer and they were back in Philadelphia, staying at a grand hotel. Jeb was wearing smart new clothes and he took Poppy to a store where she chose two new dresses and a bright blue overcoat and the prettiest little dark blue boots with scarlet laces. Later, she bathed luxuriously in the huge white cast-iron bathtub with the lion's-paw feet, drying herself afterward on enormous soft white towels, and sitting happily while Papa brushed out her long red hair until it dried in fluffy waves and curls.

When Papa went to the hotel barbershop, she sat at his feet, wincing as she watched the barber apply steaming hot towels that surely must have hurt. She watched fascinated as the man drew his long, gleaming razor across Papa's face leaving it smooth and pink, and she tried the aromatic gentlemen's elixir on her own neck, patting it in the way the barber did and sniffing its bosky sandlewood smell delightedly.

Then Papa surprised her by telling her it was her seventh birthday and he planned to take her to dinner in a grand restaurant. Poppy felt very important and grown up and pretty in her new blue silk dress with the French *point d'alençon* lace collar. All the waiters made a fuss of her and Papa said she might choose whatever she wanted to eat. Then they brought out a little cake just for her with seven candles and her name—POPPY—written in blue on the white frosting. She thought a little sadly that if all Papa's friends had been here, it would have been almost like old times on Russian Hill.

She was very sleepy when Jeb tucked her in that night. "That's my grown-up girl," he said grinning jauntily as she sank back on her pillows, tired and happy. "Here you go," he said, tucking her old rag doll inside the blanket and giving her a big hug and a kiss. Her eyes were already closing as he stole to the door. *"Be right back,"* he called, blowing her a kiss.

It was three days before the hotel staff realized that Poppy was alone. The manager was very kind to her; he put her in a small room of her own and saw that she was fed and looked after for another week before he understood that Jeb wasn't coming back. And then he called the city welfare officer.

Poppy didn't cry this time; she just huddled silently in the carriage waiting to be taken to her next place of incarceration. She wasn't angry with Papa anymore, she was just bewildered and frightened, and very, very lonely.

At the home she did as she was told, submitting to their rules without question. She kept her eyes on the floor, never looking at the other children or the matron and her assistants. She just counted off the days in French, the only language she'd ever learned her numbers in, and waited for Jeb to come and get her.

The weeks dragged by until Poppy could count no higher and the days became a gray oblivion of institution smells and cold greasy food and numbing lessons in reading, writing, and arithmetic that just made her head ache. Then one morning she stared around the large cold classroom and realized that this time Papa was not going to come and get her, she was going to be here forever. Pushing back her chair, she sent it crashing violently to the floor as she ran screaming from the room.

Matron O'Dwyer was a kindhearted woman who had come into the business of looking after children with the knowledge that her own spinsterhood was permanent, and therefore she would never have little ones of her own. She was a dedicated woman who had fought long, hard battles with the authorities for more and better facilities for her young charges, and she cared deeply that they were just ciphers in the institutional chain. When Poppy, red-faced and shaking, was hauled before her by an irate teacher, she told her to sit down and catch her breath and then tell her what was the matter.

"I don't want to stay here!" blurted Poppy, eyeing her angrily.

"Poor child," Matron said gently, "no one wants to stay here. But it is the only refuge orphans and abandoned children have. It's a place for the homeless, my dear."

"But I'm not *homeless!*" cried Poppy urgently. "I live in the Mallory House on my papa's ranch in Santa Barbara. It's called the Rancho Santa Vittoria. My papa is probably there now. . . ."

Matron peered skeptically from behind small gold-rimmed spectacles, but the child's face shone with truth. "That must have been a long time ago, Poppy," she decided, "and I'm afraid we are a long way from California."

Poppy's brow furrowed in despair as she thought about her papa, trying to place him in her mind at the Mallory House, but somehow the picture didn't fit. Matron was right. She remembered wistfully the happy scene she had observed secretly that day so long ago and her meeting with Nik Konstant in the candy store, and her face lit with sudden hope. "Nik Konstant will know where Papa is," she said eagerly, "he's my friend. *He* will know I'm not a homeless child. Please, oh, *please,* can't you just ask him? Can't you tell him where I am?" She had no idea if Nik would help, but he was her only contact with reality and her father, and the image of his strength and stability shone like a beacon of hope in her mind.

"We'll see, my dear," Matron said gently, as she handed her back to the waiting teacher, "we'll see."

But Poppy had lived long enough with those words to know that they meant exactly nothing.

Matron O'Dwyer couldn't sleep that night; somehow the image of the child's white face and passionate, blazing blue eyes kept appearing in her mind and she could hear Poppy saying over and over again, *I'm not homeless, Nik Konstant is my friend.*

The following morning she went to the rarely used telephone in her office and, cranking it, asked them to put her through to the Santa Barbara exchange. After a long wait she was put through from there to the Konstant House and she found herself speaking to a charming woman who said she was Rosalia Konstant.

A week later Poppy was told to wash her hands and face and to brush and braid her hair neatly, and then to be downstairs at Matron's room at twelve o'clock. Wondering what she had done wrong this time, she knocked on Matron's door precisely on the hour.

A look of wonder crossed her face and she stared at Nik and Rosalia as though they were gods who had come down from Mount Olympus to find her.

"It's all right, Poppy," said Nik quietly. "We're taking you home with us. You'll never come back here."

Poppy's face crumpled and she thrust her fists into her eyes fiercely, trying to stop the tears from coming. But her tears were not for relief at being saved from the children's home, and not for joy that her dream was finally to come true and she was to live with the Konstants. She was crying because she was no longer *Papa's girl.* Her childhood had been sacrificed to his whim and the turn of a card. And she never wanted to see him again.

CHAPTER *19*

Lying in bed on the morning of her seventeenth birthday, Poppy thought that the past ten years had been the most idyllic childhood anyone could ever have, and she was loath to leave it behind and grow up. Seventeen was awfully old! She glanced at Angel, still fast asleep in the other bed. The morning sun, beaming in through the open windows, caught her bright hair, turning it to pale spun gold. Her fair skin was flushed from sleep and Poppy thought with a sigh that she looked as though she'd just taken a long walk in the fresh air, whereas with her own pale skin she probably looked as though she'd slept under a stone like a frog! Of course, everyone acknowledged that Angel was a beauty, but even so, Poppy had never been jealous of her. They had been friends from the moment they met.

When she had left the children's home with Nik and Rosalia, Poppy had made a decision: From now on there would be no more tears—ever. She was going to stand up for herself and fight! She'd glared belligerently at Angel, the girl whose place she had dreamed of taking for so long, daring her to hate her, and Angel had stared back at her with those wonderful clear, astonished eyes. Poppy had felt herself blush because even though Rosalia had bought her new clothes, she was painfully thin and still had that pinched, beaten look of an orphanage child.

"My goodness," Angel had said, amazed, "you look exactly like a stick insect with red hair!" And she'd giggled, a low infectious chuckle that was impossible to resist, and Poppy had laughed too—for the first time in as long as she could remember. Then Angel had rushed forward and hugged her. "I've been waiting and waiting all week for you to come," she cried. "I just know we're going to be best friends."

Poppy had fallen in love with Angel right away. She'd wished her hair could be a smooth moonlit blond like Angel's instead of her stupid fiery fizz of tangled curls; she'd wished her eyes could be the same confident pale blue like a crystalline pond whose depths held a magic secret; she'd wished her complexion was pink and white instead of pale and freckled; and she'd wished she could be petite and delicately boned like Angel, instead of tall and gangling.

She had begun to talk with Angel's slight lisp, she'd tilted her chin in the same way when she laughed, and crinkled her nose when she didn't like something. She'd even tried to curb her own long, eager stride to Angel's graceful stroll, until finally Rosalia had taken her aside and explained that no two people were alike. She knew she admired Angel, but Angel was one person and Poppy was another. "And we love you because you are you," she'd added, smiling.

Of course, Poppy had realized how foolish she'd been, but it hadn't stopped her longing to be Angel Konstant instead of Poppy Mallory.

When they were eight years old, Nik had decided they were running too wild at the ranch and instead of their galloping off on their ponies to avoid the governess, they were sent to school in Santa Barbara, where the Konstants had built a lovely white clapboard house with bay windows and tall Victorian gables on De La Vina Street. There was a tennis lawn and a croquet lawn, and wonderful gardens with an orchard and trailing arbors of clematis and roses. There were stables for their new horses and a huge log store to fuel the enormous kitchen stoves and fireplaces; there was a white picket fence at the front; and there was school.

Angel thought it all great fun and slid into her new life with her usual ease, but Poppy loathed it. She hated having to be at school every morning when she would have much preferred to ride her horse, and she was suspicious of the camaraderie of the other girls. She found it easier to make friends with boys and soon learned from them to throw a mean punch, and then nobody teased about her red hair anymore because they knew her quick temper and the power of that small balled-up fist.

Angel was one of the most popular girls in Santa Barbara and even though everyone remembered that Poppy Mallory's father was "a bad lot" and knew the Konstants had taken her in, no one ever spoke of it.

The only time Poppy knew she was better than Angel was on a horse.

Angel rode well for a girl, but Poppy rode like a man. She looked so lazily confident in the saddle that it wasn't until you watched her helping Nik and Greg on the cattle roundup that you became aware of her superb horsemanship. Wearing an old white shirt of Greg's and a black buckskin riding skirt with fringed chaps to protect her legs from the brush, she'd spur her bay mare up the steep sides of the mesa chasing after a steer, then plunge precipitously back down again to guide it into the herd of bellowing cattle already waiting below. With her black sombrero tilted insolently over her eyes, she'd sit quietly on her horse waiting with the vaqueros while the buyer pointed out his choice for the stockyards. Then, rearing her horse onto its haunches, she'd be there as quick as any of the professional vaqueros, herding it through the sweating, angry animals to a holding point along the riverbank.

"You should have been a boy," Greg Konstant used to tease her, "in fact you'd even look like one if we cut off all that awful curly red hair!" And he'd tug the ribbon that held it back, sending her hair tumbling around her shoulders so that the wind tangled it and sent it flying into her eyes.

Greg had square white teeth and brown eyes that crinkled at the corners as he smiled and he was one of the handsomest young men in Santa Barbara. Poppy felt very proud that he was her brother—or almost her brother.

Occasionally, the dark memories would come back to haunt her and she would wonder where her father was. She would dream that she was "Papa's girl" again, and she'd remember as clearly as if it were yesterday the look in the hotel manager's eyes as he told her that her father wasn't coming back and that he had sent for the city welfare officer . . . it had been a mixture of sympathy and contempt, and humiliation crept anew down Poppy's spine. Waking cold and clammy from her nightmare, she'd rush down to the stables and saddle the beautiful Arabian mare she had been given for her fourteenth birthday. Then she'd gallop across the hill, trying to rid herself of the fear that one day Papa would come back and take her away again.

Ignoring the lane, she'd take a now familiar shortcut, slowing as she crested the hill that overlooked the Mallory House. Nik had told her long ago the story of the visit by the boastful, swaggering cowboy from Montecito who had claimed to be his new partner. Jeb had gambled away everything—and he had also put Nik and the Rancho Santa Vittoria in jeopardy. Nik had been forced to mortgage everything he owned to buy back what her father had so casually thrown away. It was the land that should have been Poppy's inheritance.

The Mallory House was unoccupied, but Nik always made sure it was well maintained. It gleamed with a fresh coat of white paint and its windows sparkled in the sunlight. Leaving her mare to graze, Poppy wandered slowly down the hillside that she still remembered as a blaze of scarlet poppies, even though they told her the poppies had never grown there since the storms the year she was born.

Anger would boil inside her as she looked at the Mallory House and at the beautiful rich acres spreading as far as the eye could see, and she would hate her father even more for gambling away not only her childhood, but everything that should have been hers. She told herself that if her worst nightmare came true and he ever returned and tried to take her away from here, she would fight and scream and kick . . . she would die rather than go with him!

"Penny for your thoughts?" Angel yawned as she sat up in bed, and ran her hands through her fall of pale silk hair. "You look too solemn for a birthday girl."

Poppy hugged her knees, staring ahead reflectively. "I was just wishing my father had died," she said bitterly.

"What a thing to say!"

"But it's true, Angel. Being an orphan would have been easier to accept than being abandoned. It's a thousand times worse knowing you weren't wanted. I swear to God that if I ever have children, I will never *never* leave them!"

Leaping from her own bed, Angel snuggled in beside Poppy. "Look at it this way," she said sympathetically. "Your father's leaving you the way he did was our luck. Greg and I got you for a sister and Mama and Papa have an extra daughter. You'd never think that you were the same girl who arrived here that winter's night ten years ago. I remember looking at you and thinking that this must be a special look that children from orphanages have, you were so pale and pinched and frightened. And you were so skinny, you really did look just like a stick insect with wild red hair."

Poppy sighed, running her hands through her unruly tangled mane. "I haven't changed much, have I?" she said, laughing.

Their faces were side by side on the pillow and Angel studied her carefully. Poppy's skin was the color of new cream. A faint dusting of freckles ran across the bridge of her small straight nose and under her uptilted bright blue eyes fringed with dark copper lashes, and her brows rose in two straight wings, giving her a strangely insolent air. She had high, flaring cheekbones, a wide, somehow vulnerable-looking mouth, and strong, even white teeth. And at just seventeen Poppy no longer looked like a stick insect, she had high pointed breasts, a tiny waist, and a deliciously curved derriere that Angel envied. Of course, she was unfashionably tall, but she had a natural grace and a kind of . . . Angel struggled to find the right word . . . style! Yes, that was it, even on a horse Poppy had style!

"You've changed a lot," she said seriously. "Truthfully, Poppy, all you have to do is look in the mirror to prove it. I think you are wonderfully pretty and elegant."

"Pretty? Elegant?" scoffed Poppy. "You must be talking about someone else . . . that's more a description of you than me, Angel."

Angel sighed. "You know that's not true," she replied loyally.

"Angel," said Poppy, "do you suppose now that we're seventeen we shall fall in love?"

"I hope so." Angel stretched luxuriously. "I just can't wait! But what do you suppose falling in love feels like?"

"I imagine it must be so exciting," Poppy murmured, clasping her knees and resting her chin on them as she thought. "It'll be thrilling— like flying on great eagle's wings, arching and soaring with happiness . . ."

"Oh, Poppy, how different we are." Angel laughed. "I imagine falling in love must be warm and dreamy . . . I shall feel gentle and wonderfully content and just carry this little warm glow of happiness in my heart every single day."

Poppy frowned, staring at the wide oaken beams running across the ceiling. "Angel," she said after a while, "how do you suppose babies get inside your belly?"

"It's a mystery to me." Angel sighed. "Mama says she'll tell us when we get married and not before. I mean it can only be something simple like what the rams do with the sheep and the cows with the bulls."

Their eyes met and they grinned at each other conspiratorially.

"Ugh!" exclaimed Poppy.

"Ugh!" agreed Angel as they burst into laughter. "I know what," she said suddenly, "let's whoever gets married first promise to tell the other what it's like, I mean exactly what you do and how it feels." She offered her small hand, pinkie finger outstretched.

"I promise to tell," Poppy agreed solemnly as she hooked her little finger with Angel's.

"There now, it's a solemn pact," said Angel. "You must never forget it, Poppy."

"I won't," she replied, "but anyhow you are sure to marry first. Every boy in Santa Barbara is already in love with Angel Konstant," she added wistfully.

It never failed to amaze Rosalia how two such opposite personalities could get along so well. Angel was so calm and feminine and sweet-natured. Poppy was volatile and a tomboy. Angel was amenable and easygoing and she looked on almost everything as "fun," while Poppy was rebellious and suspicious. Angel was confident and Poppy was the shy one, though she often hid it under some outrageous act that made it look as if she was trying to claim attention. And, of course, they looked so different, the petite cool blond beauty and the tall flame-haired vibrant firecracker!

She shook her head in amazement as with feminine shrieks and giggles and masculine shouts and laughter, two-dozen young people piled into the haycarts for the ride to Hope Ranch and the picnic on the beach. Poppy had clambered excitedly to the very top of the hay and hitching up her white skirts, she teetered along the bale, her usual black sombrero tilted over her eyes and her red hair already escaping from its grown-up pompadour. Her blue eyes sparkled with mischief as with a triumphant scream she pushed one of the boys off the cart.

Angel lounged back lazily against a bale of hay, a wreath of wildflowers threaded by an adoring young man crowning her upswept blond hair. There was a haughty look in her eyes as she dismissed him with a shrug, turning to flirt with yet another.

Rosalia looked at Nik, her eyebrows raised despairingly. "They are too wild," she said. "I'm afraid it's time they were tamed and I know just the place. Mrs. Diblee told me of this wonderful finishing school in San Francisco that absolutely guarantees to turn wild young daughters into charming young women."

They arrived at Miss Henderson's Academy for Young Ladies in Berkeley, with a trunkful of new clothes fashioned by the local dressmaker, Miss Matthews, and with handsome twenty-four-year-old Harvard graduate Greg Konstant as their escort. Angel swept confidently into the hall with Poppy following reluctantly behind her. The big house was gracious and elegantly furnished, with many gilt-framed paintings on the walls and lace curtains at the windows. There was a red Oriental carpet and flowers everywhere, carefully arranged by the pupils as one of their "feminine arts" courses. But despite their fragrance, to Poppy the smell was still that of an institution.

There was a flurry of stifled giggles and whispers from the stairwell and she glanced up to meet the curious stares of a dozen girls, who disappeared hurriedly as the principal herself came forward to greet them. Miss Henderson had smooth white hair, she wore a sensible gray skirt, a high-necked white silk blouse with a large topaz brooch clasped at the neck, and Poppy already hated her. She hadn't wanted to come here at all, but for once Angel had let her down.

When Rosalia had first told them they were to go to school in San Francisco, Poppy had stormed around her bedroom, tossing her long hair back angrily and demanding to know why they must go. "It's sure to be terrible," she'd raged, "all those silly society girls, and no ponies, no ranch, none of the things we love, Angel!"

"Oh, I don't know," Angel had replied, brushing her hair and staring dreamily into the mirror, "it might be fun. Mrs. Diblee told Mama that we'll be taken to the opera and to art galleries and museums, and we'll learn to speak a little French, though of course you already speak that, and maybe some Italian so we can converse with any foreign diplomats who might just happen to pass through Santa Barbara. We'll learn how to greet royalty—just in case we should ever meet any—and how to give a proper dinner party for them." She laughed at Poppy's mutinous face. "Oh, come on, Poppy," she said, "I'll bet we get to meet all sorts of nice girls there. And maybe even some suitable boys to fall in love with!"

Poppy had climbed into bed and pulled the sheets over her ears. She didn't want to hear what Angel was saying, she didn't want to go to San Francisco and she didn't want to go to finishing school. She just didn't want anything in her life to change.

"Mr. Konstant," Miss Henderson said, offering Greg her hand, "how very nice to meet you. Of course, everyone in San Francisco knows your father and the famous Rancho Santa Vittoria. Why, they say it's the biggest ranch in California."

"Indeed it is, ma'am," Greg replied courteously. "But my father arrived in this country a penniless immigrant from Russia. He worked hard for his success."

Miss Henderson's eyes flickered as she weighed the Konstants' wealth against their lack of breeding, but she was a quick thinker. "Ah, but your mother's family, the Abregos, are one of California's oldest." She smiled, offering her cold hand to Angel. "And this is Angel. What an unusual name, my dear."

"I was named for my father's birthplace, Archangel, ma'am," she replied shyly.

Miss Henderson's brows rose slightly in surprise. "How very quaint," she replied. "Still, my dear, I'm sure you are going to make lots of suitable friends here." Her glance took in Poppy, standing behind Angel. "And this is the Mallory girl?" she said icily. She hadn't been at all keen to take her into her school, but the Konstants had insisted that the two girls stay together.

"Another well-known name in San Francisco," retorted Poppy, tilting her chin defiantly. "Everyone knew my father."

"Indeed they did!" Miss Henderson turned from her dismissively. "Mr. Konstant, may I offer you some tea? It must have been a long and tiring journey."

"Thank you no, ma'am," he replied curtly. "I must leave. And I shall trust you to take good care of *both* my *sisters.*" Poppy shot him a grateful glance as he kissed her good-bye. "Be brave," Greg murmured with an encouraging grin. And then he was gone.

There were twelve rooms at Miss Henderson's Academy, each shared by two girls, and Poppy's heart sank as Angel was shown to a room she was to share with Dorothea Wilkes Frazer and she realized that they were to be separated. "Of course, you'll know of the Frazers, such a well-known San Francisco family," gushed Miss Henderson. "I feel quite sure that you and Dorothea will get along well."

"Of course we will," Angel cried, beaming at the dark-haired chubby Dorothea, "it'll be fun."

Poppy's head drooped as, with Angel's favorite phrase "it'll be fun" ringing in her ears, she was shown into a room with a sullen-looking copper-haired girl who glared at her unwelcomingly. "You are to share with Laura Banks," Miss Henderson informed her. "Oh, dear," she added, surprised, "I hadn't realized you both had red hair. I hope there will be no clash of 'temperament.'" Her glance rested warningly on Poppy as she closed the door, leaving her alone with Laura.

"The bed near the window is mine," Laura told Poppy abruptly, "and the walnut chest. We share the wardrobe and my stuff is already in there, you'll just have to make do with whatever space is left." Folding her arms, she stared at her icily. "And another thing, my hair is not a common *red* like yours. Mine is *auburn.*"

Poppy threw her a cool glance as she flung open the wardrobe. Laura had dresses for every possible occasion and they completely filled the space. Lifting out a lettuce-green organza evening dress, she gazed at it critically. "Only such a filthy color would go with your *auburn* hair," she commented, casting it to the floor. Then, ignoring Laura's outraged gasps, she threw out an armful of clothes. When the wardrobe was half empty, she said calmly, "Now we have equal space. I'm afraid you'll have to find somewhere else for all your rubbish."

Laura's cheeks burned as she glared at Poppy. "Do you have any idea what those dresses cost?" With a contemptuous glance at Poppy's new garments from Santa Barbara's most popular dressmaker, she announced scathingly, "Obviously you wouldn't. Don't think I won't complain to Miss Henderson about this," she added. "You are here five minutes and already you're causing trouble."

"If you do that, Laura Banks," Poppy said, clenching her small fist threateningly, "then I'll punch you. And I warn you, Greg says I punch pretty good."

"Who's Greg?" asked Laura, backing away nervously.

"Greg's my brother," Poppy replied with a triumphant smile.

"Oh, no, he's not," retorted Laura. "Greg Konstant is *Angel's* brother! We all know who *you* are! Just wait till my father hears that I'm rooming with Jeb Mallory's daughter, he'll have a fit."

Poppy felt the hot blood rush to her face. No one had ever mentioned her father in all these years, but this girl *knew.* The door flew open suddenly and Angel stood there beaming at them.

"Hello, you two," she cried. "Oh, what a heavenly room, it's much nicer than mine." She held out her hand to Laura. "I'm Angel Konstant," she said, smiling.

Poppy bit her lip to stop it from trembling as she bent over her trunk, hauling out her clothes and flinging them into the wardrobe.

"Oh, Poppy, isn't everyone just so nice?" beamed Angel. "I told you this would be fun!"

Most of the staff and the girls were quite kind and polite, but Poppy felt they knew she was "different." And everyone wanted to be Angel's friend. Was it Angel's beauty, her smile, her charm? Poppy wondered as she stood to one side watching the girls jostle for a place next to Angel at supper or passing little notes asking to be her very best friend. Or was it also the Konstant money? She hadn't realized until now that the Konstants were so very rich. She watched jealously as the teachers preened under Angel's smile, forgiving her instantly for being a duffer at French and for not remembering the exact placement of wineglasses for a banquet or the names of the painters of the Renaissance period of Italy. Even Miss Henderson went out of her way to be nice to her, and for the first time Poppy realized that Angel was not only a beautiful girl—she was the powerful Nik Konstant's daughter. Angel was an "heiress."

Each evening after roll call, the girls were permitted to read and converse genteelly in the "salon," as Miss Henderson called the big front parlor on the first floor. They took turns playing Chopin nocturnes on the ebony Steinway grand, and occasionally someone would sing or they would read romantic poetry, but mostly they just chattered and gossiped.

As usual, Angel was the center of a small group of girls, giggling together and whispering secrets, and Poppy watched jealously from her seat by the window where she was pretending to read a book. She and Laura never spoke to each other, and though the other girls were friendly, no one was "her friend." And now it seemed Angel no longer was either. Unable to bear it any longer, she grabbed her coat from the closet, ran down the stairs, and unlocked the big front door. She hurried down the street and around the corner, not thinking where she was going, just glad to breathe the fresh air of freedom.

The clock in the hall said eight-thirty as Poppy slid back through the front door of the Academy, wondering whether she'd been missed. Tossing her hat and coat into the closet under the stairs, she walked into the drawing room, glancing around apprehensively; but she needn't have worried. Meredith McGuinn was playing the "Moonlight Sonata" for the hundredth time and still getting it wrong, and the other girls were gossiping in small groups. It seemed no one had even noticed she was gone.

"Poppy!" Angel thrust her way through the small crowd of girls around her. "Poppy, where on earth have you been? Miss Tremaine was looking for you and I had to tell her you had a headache, but the house-maid said she'd seen you slipping out the front door!"

Silence fell as twenty pairs of eyes contemplated Poppy in amazement.

"Did you really go out?" Dorothea asked, awed.

Poppy shrugged. "Of course I did," she said casually. "I don't know how you can all bear to be shut up in this boring dump day after day. I just thought I'd pay a visit to . . . to a place I know."

"But Poppy—where?" breathed Angel excitedly.

Poppy knew she had their attention now and she smiled secretively. "I can't tell you," she replied, "but I'll be going back there again soon. It's so much more fun than here." Standing up, she yawned exaggeratedly. "I'm dreadfully tired," she said, throwing them a superior glance. "I must go to bed."

Angel couldn't imagine where Poppy might have gone, she was quite sure she knew no one in San Francisco. Leaving the other girls talking in hushed voices about her escapade, she followed her upstairs into her room.

Poppy was sitting on the edge of her bed, her hands in her lap and a hopeless look on her face. "I was so worried," Angel confessed, hugging her. "Why did you disappear like that? I was so scared when Miss Tremaine called the register for bed and I had to lie for you. I just said you had a headache."

"Well, it's true, I do." Poppy trailed a hand across her furrowed brow.

"But *where* did you go?" Angel asked, exasperated.

Poppy shrugged again. "I just walked," she said bleakly, "that's all. Anything to get away from here."

"How can you say that?" demanded Angel, surprised. "Why, it's such fun here."

Poppy sighed. "Of course it is, Angel," she said grimly. "Of course it's fun—for you."

"Do you know what sexual intercourse is?" Poppy asked one evening as the girls sat around chatting as usual. An awed silence fell over the room as she added, "I do."

"You do?" they gasped, edging closer.

Angel watched her warily. It seemed that ever since she'd come home from her walk, Poppy had been trying to behave more and more outrageously.

"Sexual intercourse is what bulls do to cows," Poppy declared, "only it's men and women."

The girls gasped at her daring even to speak such words. "But how?" whispered Dorothea eagerly. "*How* do they do it, Poppy?"

She grinned at them. "Well," she said, "the man has a thing like the bull and he puts it inside the woman."

"Inside where?" Meredith asked, bewildered.

"Down below," Poppy said brazenly, "you know." She pointed with her finger and their eyes followed in amazement. "I know it's true," she added, "because I read all about it in Miss Henderson's medical book in her study. It has pictures too . . . really strange pictures. I mean it shows the man's penis and everything. . . ."

The girls' hands flew to their mouths as she said the word, and they stared at her, shocked. "I don't believe a word of it," scoffed Laura, "you're just making it up, like you do everything."

"No, I'm not," Poppy retorted belligerently, "and what's more I've got the medical book upstairs. Anyone who wants to see it, can," she added magnanimously.

"Oh, Poppy," murmured Angel, distressed, "you shouldn't . . ." But Poppy was already leading the eager girls upstairs.

"Only one at a time," she ordered as Dorothea followed her giggling into the room, "the rest of you can wait outside."

A few moments later Dorothea emerged, scarlet-faced and looking subdued. "What's it like?" the others whispered. "Does she really have pictures?"

Dorothea just nodded and then, clapping her hands to her mouth, she ran down the corridor to her room, and threw up.

There was a buzz of excited speculation and giggles as they waited for the next girl to emerge. . . . "What's it like?" they chorused as she appeared a minute later. She laughed, her face pink with embarrassment. "Goodness, I had no idea I looked quite like that," she said, "and as for men! Ugh!"

Miss Henderson heard the commotion as she crossed the hall on her way for her usual nightcap of hot cocoa laced with a strong dash of French brandy, a little recipe that had helped put her to sleep without fail for the past twenty years. As she mounted the stairs she patted her smooth white hair into place and adjusted her topaz brooch, wondering angrily what the girls could be up to now. She stared in surprise as she saw them huddled together outside Poppy's room. "What is going on here?" she boomed, making them jump. "Is something wrong?" she added with a touch of alarm. *You just never knew with that Mallory girl. . . .*

"No, oh, no, Miss Henderson . . . sorry, Miss Henderson," they murmured, edging away along the corridor toward their own rooms.

"Ah, Miss Henderson, there you are," cried Angel, desperately trying to divert her, "I've been meaning to ask you a few questions about a trip to Europe that Mama is planning for us next year. I wonder if it would be convenient to come to your study now and discuss it?" She flashed Miss Henderson a brilliant smile, heading for the stairs, praying that she would follow her.

"Certainly not child," Miss Henderson snapped, thinking of her cocoa; then, remembering who Angel was, she smiled genially. "Why not come to my study tomorrow at three," she suggested, "we can talk then." She glanced up in surprise as Meredith McGuinn dashed from Poppy's room, her shocked face bright scarlet.

Flinging open the door, she marched in, "What's going on in here?" she demanded, purpling with rage as her eyes fell on the book open at a certain page. Poppy made no attempt to hide it, staring insolently as Miss Henderson slammed it shut and tucked it under her arm.

"You wicked girl," Miss Henderson shrieked, her prominent Adam's apple wobbling as she struggled for words to tell Poppy what she thought of her. *"You little slut! You are a disgrace,"* she spat finally, "but then with *your background* it's only to be expected. I knew I should never have taken you in. If Mr. Konstant had not been so insistent, I never would have done it!"

Poppy stared at the floor saying nothing, but Angel noticed that her fists were tightly clenched.

"You will be removed from this school immediately," fumed Miss Henderson. "I shall telephone Mr. Konstant right now and tell him so. Laura," she barked, "you will sleep in the room down the hall tonight. No one is to go near that . . . that *disgusting* girl!"

"Oh, Poppy," wailed Angel desperately, "just look what you've done! Now you'll be expelled."

"Good," Poppy replied sullenly, "that's exactly why I did it." But the expression in her eyes was bleak and Angel flew to her, clasping her in her arms. "I won't let them take you away," she promised, "we'll never be separated Poppy, *never.* I promise you . . . I just won't let them do it."

Poppy's pleading eyes met hers. "Do you mean it, Angel?" she whispered. "Do you really mean we won't be separated?"

"Of course I do. I shall telephone Papa right now," she promised. "I'll tell him it wasn't your fault, the stupid woman should not leave books like that lying around where girls can just find them. It'll be all right, Poppy, I promise you."

By noon the next day Miss Henderson was forced to take a small snifter of brandy while she contemplated her dilemma. Nik Konstant had castigated her roundly for possessing such a book, even though she'd protested that it was purely medical. "Then if it's medical," he'd said logically, "what is the great harm? It's just a little human biology, Miss Henderson, and every woman knows about that. I had thought your establishment would be better supervised but now I'm almost of a mind to remove *both* my girls. I'm quite sure you can understand what a scandal it would cause if I were forced to do such a thing—and for such a reason. I imagine the other parents would be none too pleased about this little affair, now would they?"

Sipping her brandy carefully, Miss Henderson knew she had no choice but to let Poppy stay.

Poppy had been moved to a single room and Angel went along to see her later that night. She was sitting up in bed with her wild hair tamed into two braids, and Angel thought she looked somehow pathetic and vulnerable despite all her bravado. "Poppy, now you've got to behave yourself," she said sternly, "because next time Miss Henderson really will expel you."

"I don't care," Poppy replied, "don't you understand, Angel? I can't stand it here. I just want them to send me back home where I'm happy!"

"Happy?" snapped Angel. "And how *happy* do you imagine you'll make Mama and Papa if you are expelled from here? Hasn't Papa already come to your defense once? Think how *unhappy* you'll make *them*, Poppy, before you do anything else stupid."

"I didn't think about it that way," Poppy confessed, staring at Angel miserably. "I'm so selfish and stupid, I only thought about myself."

"I'll help you," Angel said, her flash of temper gone as quickly as it had come. "We're here together. Just try and enjoy yourself. I promise you it really can be fun," she added wistfully.

Poppy really tried hard to redeem herself in Nik and Rosalia's eyes. She began to keep her room tidy and her clothes neat. Her hair was swept up and secured with a thousand pins so it was impossible for it to stray. She was attentive in class and behaved impeccably on their visits to the theater and to the great houses of San Francisco, whose portals were opened to Miss Henderson's smart girls so they might study the collections of paintings and sculpture and fine antique furniture. The other girls admired her daring and were now much friendlier toward her, and she and Angel were once again sharing a room. Despite Miss Henderson's disapproval she was beginning to feel that at last she had carved a place for herself at the Academy and that she might even begin to enjoy it.

Each week certain girls were delegated to arrange the flower displays in the house, and on a cold December day, dry and crisp with a promise of Christmas in the air, it was Poppy's turn to do the front hall. She had chosen sprays of holly and mistletoe, thick with shiny red and white berries. The woody stems were proving difficult, so she had borrowed a knife from the kitchen to split them. It was hard work, but she intended it to be the grandest Christmas display yet seen at the Henderson Academy. She was so engrossed in her task, she scarcely noticed when the doorbell rang, but as the young parlormaid hurried past her to answer it she tucked a spray of mistletoe mischievously into her dark hair.

"Oh, miss, whatever will people think!" the girl giggled as she scurried to open the door.

"Mistletoe, eh?" said a familiar voice from the doorway. "Well, now, we all know what that means, don't we, me girl?"

Poppy swung around just in time to see Jeb plant a kiss on the parlor-maid's astonished mouth.

"Hi there, Papa's girl," he cried, with that same jaunty grin, just as though nothing had ever happened.

Poppy felt herself grow faint as she watched him walk toward her. He looked just as she remembered—and yet he didn't. He looked older—much older; his eyes were puffy and his face deeply lined, and the hands he held out to her shook with a faint insistent tremor. But his eyes were still the same bright sparkling blue as her own and his face was the one she saw in her own mirror every morning.

Remembered hate swept through her as she backed away from him, and the other girls gathered curiously on the stairs as the frightened little parlormaid ran to fetch Miss Henderson. "I'm not 'your girl,'" she cried in a voice that trembled.

"Sure and you are . . . you remember, don't you? You were always Papa's girl. And didn't I always say I'd come back and get you? Well, here I am, me darling, your old Papa is finally here!"

Angel ran along the landing toward the group of silent girls. "What is it?" she cried. "What's going on?"

"It's Jeb Mallory," hissed Laura excitedly, "he's come to fetch 'his girl' . . . oh my, what a story *this* will make!"

Angel stared horrified at the scene in the hall. Poppy's voice was quavering as she repeated, "I'm not *your girl*. Please go away. I never want to see you again. *Ever!*"

"Sure and you do," Jeb replied, walking toward her. "Now don't tell me you're gonna turn out to be as unforgiving as your mother just be-cause a man made a few mistakes. What d'ya say you put on your coat and we'll go for a bite of lunch and get reacquainted? I'll bet you won't want to be staying here now that your Papa's home, will you? And I guess the Konstants'll be glad to get rid of you now that I'm back. I've rented a suite at the St. Francis; it'll be just like old times, me and Papa's girl!"

"I'm not *Papa's girl*," Poppy screamed as he held out his arms. "I'm not, I'm not, *I'm not!*"

"Poppy, oh, Poppy." Angel hurtled down the stairs toward her just as Poppy lifted the kitchen knife in her clenched fist and, panicked, threw it at her father.

"Oh, Poppy," Angel whispered again as Jeb sank to the floor at their feet, his blood making a dark stain on the red Oriental rug.

CHAPTER 20

1898, ITALY

Aunt Melody Abrego had been pleased when Rosalia asked her to chaperone her two girls on their European visit. She had listened to Poppy's story and her heart had gone out to the poor child—though of course she wasn't really a child anymore; she was a young woman, and a very attractive one in her own strange, almost catlike way. She couldn't compare with Angel, of course, but then Angel was so especially beautiful. Aunt Melody just hoped all those wicked Frenchmen and romantic Italians wouldn't be chasing after them.

She and Greg were shepherding the excited girls through San Francisco's Union Square Station en route for their European Grand Tour. Settling her large straw hat more firmly on her piled white hair, Aunt Melody straightened her worsted jacket and eased her new shoes. Her feet had always had a tendency to swell and now she was sixty and plumper than she used to be, they were the bane of her life; she just couldn't wait to board the train and take off her shoes in the comfort of their private stateroom. She only hoped her girls wouldn't want to do too much walking in Paris, and that they would behave themselves. Not that she anticipated any trouble with Angel, but Poppy was unpredictable.

Rosalia had told her that what Poppy had done had been unintentional, she had just been frightened by Jeb; she had said that the scars of her childhood would never heal, and that they could thank God that no one could brand Poppy a "murderess" (Aunt Melody flinched even thinking the word) because Jeb Mallory had survived. But even though his wounds had healed, the doctors had told them Jeb's liver was so damaged from drink, he would need constant attention for a long time. Nik had arranged to pay all his expenses and in addition had settled a large sum of money on Jeb, to be paid in monthly installments for the rest of his life—on the understanding that he stay away from Poppy and the Rancho Santa Vittoria.

Nik had been away when the "accident" had happened, and it was Greg who had rushed to San Francisco after Miss Henderson's horrified telephone call. He'd told them how the girls had been banished to Miss Henderson's study and forbidden to speak to anyone. Their clothes had been packed and the trunks were waiting in the hall when he arrived, and the other girls had peered curiously from the salon hoping to catch a glimpse of the notorious Poppy before she disappeared forever.

Miss Henderson, grim and white-faced and fearing the ruin of her lifetime's work building up the Academy, had been forced to make a telephone call to one of San Francisco's most important citizens, whose daughter she'd had the privilege of "finishing." He'd understood her predicament instantly and had arranged for Jeb to be transferred to a private nursing home, and he'd also ensured there would be no police inquiry.

Miss Henderson had flung open the study door. "Your brother is here, Angel," she'd said coldly. "I already explained to him that there was no need for you to wait in here with . . . with this girl, but that you insisted."

"Oh, Greg," Angel had whispered, hugging him, "it's horrible, horrible . . . I'm so frightened. Just look at her . . . I can't get her to talk, or even to move. . . ."

Poppy was huddled in a cold, slippery leather chair with her knees drawn up to her chest and her face buried in her arms. "I've come to take you home," Greg had told her, running a comforting hand over her springy hair. "Everything is going to be all right now, you'll see. Come on, Poppy, look at me . . . talk to me?"

Moving her arm an inch, she'd gazed at him with one bleak tearless blue eye. "I can never go home again," she'd whispered, "don't you see, Greg? They think I tried to kill my father!"

"Thank God your dreadful father is still alive," Miss Henderson had snapped, "and it's no thanks to you, you wicked girl, that we are not all in jail!"

Angel had turned angrily. "Be quiet, you miserable woman," she'd cried, "you know nothing about this situation. It wasn't Poppy's fault."

"It wasn't her fault? Did someone else stab Jeb Mallory then? Is that what you are trying to tell me? I'm afraid there were too many witnesses for you to get away with that lie!"

"It's not a lie," Angel had cried despairingly. "Oh, you just don't understand."

"Poppy," Greg had said gently, "your father is not dead. He's very much alive. But I promise you this, he will never bother you again. We'll make sure of that this time. He's gone from your life, forever." Lifting her easily into his arms, he'd said, "And now I'm taking you home. Your family is waiting for you. We need you, Poppy—and you need us."

Greg's brown eyes had held more than just sympathy for Poppy; he had been in love with her as long as he could remember. He'd just been waiting for her to grow up, hoping that when she was eighteen and out of finishing school she might begin to look at him with more than just sisterly affection. He'd wanted her to see him as a woman sees a man she loves, and who loves her.

There were gasps of shock from the other girls as, with Poppy's face hidden in his chest, he'd carried her through the hall. "Good-bye, Angel," some had called, and a few brave ones had added, "Good-bye Poppy—and good luck."

Over the next few months Greg and Poppy had become inseparable. She'd clung to him as though he were her lifeline, telling him the secrets of her painful childhood as she'd been dragged from city to city, rooming house to hotel, always alone and always ending up in the children's home. She told of her nightmares that Jeb would return and try to take her away, and how shocked and frightened she had felt when he walked through the door. She confessed that she didn't remember hurling the knife at her father; she'd just wanted to get away from him, she couldn't even bear him to touch her . . . and how she hated the fact that she looked like him.

"You are the wounded one, Poppy," Greg had reassured her tenderly, "but now it's all over. You'll never see him again. And I promise you, one day I'm going to make you forget all this. We'll be so happy, it'll be as though it never happened."

Walking through the gardens with her on the night his mother had told them of the planned trip to Europe, he'd been filled with sudden foreboding. "You'll be gone for six months," he'd said worriedly. "I don't want you to forget me. You know the old saying, out of sight—out of mind."

"How could I forget you?" she'd asked, looking at him puzzled. "Why, I bet Angel and I will talk about you all the time. I just wish you were coming too."

"It's just that—well, I don't want you to go falling in love with someone else, Poppy," he'd said. "I guess what I want is for you to fall in love with me."

She'd stared uncomprehendingly at his familiar handsome face. "But how can you say that? You are my brother."

"But I'm not your brother, Poppy," he'd cried, gripping her hands tightly, "Don't you see? *I'm Greg Konstant and you are Poppy Mallory. And I love you."*

"And don't you see," Poppy had whispered, her eyes anguished, *"that I really just* wanted *you to be my brother?"* And she'd rushed back to the house, her red hair flying in the wind, as though she couldn't wait to get away from him.

She'd avoided him after that, staying close to Angel until it was time for them to leave, but Greg had insisted on taking them to San Francisco to see them off.

The giant steam locomotive puffed even louder and the porter hurried along the train slamming doors. Angel kissed Greg good-bye, wiping an excited tear from her eye as she climbed aboard, and he smiled as Poppy's eyes finally met his. "Please don't go away not friends," he said, "after all, I only said I loved you."

"I know." She lowered her eyes. "I'm sorry, Greg. It's just that I never thought . . . I didn't realize . . ."

"Just promise you'll think of me," he pleaded, "don't dismiss me yet, Poppy."

As Aunt Melody called her again to hurry his eyes held hers for a moment, then, planting a hasty kiss on his cheek, she turned and climbed on board.

"Good-bye," they shouted, hanging out the window, as the train pulled away from the platform, "good-bye . . . we'll write . . ."

"Greg," Poppy called across the din of the departing train, "Greg . . . I promise . . ."

Paris was everything Poppy had ever dreamed it might be. The May skies were a clear cloudless blue, the chestnuts were in blossom along the *grands boulevards,* and the spring sunshine gilded the café tables where they lingered over a *citron pressé,* watching the Parisian world go by. Shuffling dazzled behind their guide, they saw the wonders in the Louvre and gazed admiringly at the Mona Lisa and the Winged Victory. "Be sure to take notes, girls," commanded Aunt Melody, taking a seat on a marble bench, and fanning herself with the guidebook as she eased her aching feet in their too tight shoes. "Your papa will want to know what you have learned."

They sat in the awe-inspiring nave of Notre Dame Cathedral listening to a soaring anthem sung by cherubic choirboys, and they lingered excitedly in front of shops selling rich dark scented chocolates and creamy pastries, or pâté de foie gras and strange pungent cheeses. They shopped for trinkets in the smart stores and worried over their choices in a chic little hat shop on the rue de la Paix. They even became accustomed to taking a small glass of wine with their dinner, under Aunt Melody's eagle-eyed supervision—though she herself always had three or even four. Then invariably she'd complain of how sleepy she was, saying that they must go to bed—just when Paris was waking up!

Every day they walked and walked until Aunt Melody cried for mercy and even Angel admitted she was tired, but still Poppy hadn't had enough. The city seemed to shimmer with excitement, like a mirage, and she wanted to see it, to grasp it . . . to know it was real before it all disappeared. Or before she had to leave.

Aunt Melody had refused to take them to Montparnasse, saying it wasn't "suitable," and Poppy was determined to find out why. One afternoon when Aunt Melody was sleeping off her lavish lunch in the comfort of the Hotel Lotti and even Angel was dozing over her book, Poppy put on her jacket and went off to explore by herself. She sat in a café, sipping lemonade beneath a striped awning, ignoring the bold stares of the men passing by, and wondering what was so unsuitable about such a jolly place. And she wandered alone through the pretty streets and squares near the Sacré Coeur, peering admiringly over the shoulders of artists busy at their easels, capturing so skillfully the scene she saw around her. She lingered in front of the facades of small music halls plastered with lurid posters and photos of the latest "artistes," and she climbed the steep Butte, staring at the bold-looking women loitering in the doorways, quickening her step as they stared back at her contemptuously. Once a man jostled her elbow and spoke to her, but she just glared haughtily at him, and murmuring *"Pardon, mademoiselle, je m'excuse . . ."* he hurried off. Her feet fairly skipped along as she crisscrossed the pretty bridges, stopping to admire the barges laden with vegetables fresh from the countryside; often there were whole families on board and even a little dog perched on the stern, and she waved to the children, who waved back, calling, *"Bonjour, ma'mzelle."*

Of course, she never spoke to anyone and she was back at the Hotel

Lotti long before Aunt Melody awoke and poked her head around their door, saying brightly, "Well, girls? Did you enjoy your nap? I'm sure you feel as refreshed as I do and ready for the theater tonight."

They wore their best dresses. Angel's was fondant-pink silk trimmed with rosettes of ribbons and flowers, and Poppy's was butter-yellow satin with swirls of tiny jet beads. At the theater the audience was more exciting than the Molière play, which was all in French anyhow. "Did you ever see so many smart women," Poppy whispered to Angel, as they peered through opera glasses at the chic audience gradually filling the tiers of red plush seats.

"All of a sudden I feel like the country cousin," Angel murmured, glancing down at her pink dress ruefully. "And I had thought Miss Matthews's dress was the finest I had ever seen—until now!"

"You look exactly as young girls should look," Aunt Melody commented approvingly, "and quite suitable for Santa Barbara."

Angel's eyes met Poppy's exasperatedly. "But Aunt Melody, this isn't Santa Barbara," she hissed, "this is *Paris*!"

They sat up half the night composing an urgent telegram to Nik and Rosalia: "Unless you wish your daughters to be known as mere country bumpkins, severely lacking in style and overloaded with culture, imperative attend the salon of Monsieur Worth to purchase several new Paris gowns."

They waited anxiously for a reply, shrieking with delight as they read: "One gown and one day outfit each may be purchased from M. Worth but am assured by those who know that Madame Marcel on the rue de Valence is just as good and less expensive. You may purchase anything else from her Aunt Melody thinks suitable. Love Mama and Papa."

M. Worth's salon on the rue de la Paix was very grand with pale green *boiserie* and long Louis Quinze mirrors. A haughty-eyed vendeuse asked them to take a seat and Poppy and Angel perched uncomfortably on little gilt chairs on either side of Aunt Melody, waiting for the Maître to be free.

"Jumped-up little dressmaker," fumed Aunt Melody after fifteen minutes had ticked away. "This is intolerable!" she snapped after half an hour; and finally she commanded the vendeuse to tell Monsieur Worth that if he could not see them immediately, they would leave.

"Oh, Aunt Melody, no," cried Angel, agonized, "no, *please*, we *must* stay . . ."

"Aunt Melody, it's so important," wailed Poppy. They were so close to their Paris dresses, they couldn't let anything stop them now.

"The Maître is with the Princesse de Vignes," the vendeuse informed them loftily. "She is ordering her wardrobe for the autumn."

"For the autumn," Angel said, astonished. "But my goodness, it's still only spring."

"In Paris, mademoiselle, we order our wardrobes a season ahead. The Princesse already has her wardrobe for the summer."

The great double doors at the far end of the salon were flung open suddenly and a stately woman wearing a navy silk coat and an enormous hat trimmed with lavish pink roses swept across the room, with the Maître himself in tow.

"Remember, Worth," she commanded. "I shall need everything in time for my Russian trip in October. And take particular care with the sables. After all, we don't want the Russians—*who really know about furs*—saying that M. Worth is second-best, do we?"

Her malicious laugh tinkled through the chandeliered salon as she paused and, lifting her gold lorgnette, peered first at Angel and then at Poppy.

"Who are they?" she asked the vendeuse in French.

She shrugged. "They are nobody, Princesse," she replied. "Just visiting Americans."

"*Ah, les petites Américaines!*" She peered closer as Aunt Melody glared at her uncomfortably, and then she said something in rapid French that made the vendeuse laugh.

Summoning all her remembered French, Poppy thought she'd managed to translate it properly, and she stared at her, puzzled . . . "They are charming," she'd said, and "the contrast is magical! The blonde is exactly like a rose that flowers at Christmas, pale, rare, and exquisite. Men will want to guard her, to treasure her, to admire her. And the other—the fiery one, she's just like a ripe cherry in a summer orchard; men will certainly want to steal her from the tree and devour her—and lick the juices from their fingers!"

"What is she saying?" Aunt Melody demanded angrily. "Poppy, you speak French, what did she say?"

Dropping her eyes, Poppy studied her dusty shoes, blushing uncomfortably. "I'm . . . I'm not sure, Aunt Melody," she murmured, as with another merry malicious laugh the Princesse wafted from the salon, leaving the scent of lilies of the valley hanging in the air. Of course she knew exactly what the Princesse had said, she just wasn't sure she *understood* what it meant—but somehow she sensed she shouldn't tell Aunt Melody.

The vendeuse showed them into a smaller mirrored salon and Aunt

Melody watched irately as, without speaking, the Maître inspected first Angel and then Poppy. Clapping his hands, he summoned half a dozen waiting assistants. "Bring the sapphire blue chiffon for *la petite*," he cried, pointing to Angel. "And for the other"—a faint gleam of amusement lit his eyes as he glanced at Poppy—"for *la cerise*, the cherry, something more subtle to cool her hair. The moss-green satin perhaps . . . ah, no, she is too young. I have it . . . the dove-gray velvet, *oui, c'est parfait!*"

Again Poppy blushed with embarrassment as Aunt Melody grumbled loudly, "Such appalling manners and not one of them speaks God's English."

"Madame," the Maître said in perfect English, *"my father was an Englishman."*

"Then why not say so?" boomed Aunt Melody irritably. "You've kept us waiting long enough, young man, it had better be worth it."

"There are those," said M. Worth, spinning yards and yards of sapphire chiffon from an enormous bolt of fabric, "who would willingly wait a year even to enter the doors of the Salon Worth. When you are dressed by the Maître, everyone knows it. My clothes add distinction to even the gauchest of young women."

He draped the silk skillfully around Angel, pinning and adjusting, testing it first one way then another, and then he summoned another assistant to take Angel's measurements. "As the Princesse noticed," he said to Aunt Melody, "both your girls are charming, the cool beauty of the blonde and the fiery charm of the red. But in *my* dresses they will become sensational."

"Mmm," she sniffed, unsure of what he meant. Still, she could see he'd been right about Angel. The blue did wonderful things for her pink and white complexion and deepened the color of her eyes, and even though he'd only draped the material around her, it was undoubtedly with the touch of a master. And Poppy, in silk velvet so fine that it slithered from the bolt like a river of mercury, clinging as softly as a dove's feather to her high bosom and tiny waist, and making her creamy skin glow like alabaster, already looked sensational.

"Well," she sniffed haughtily, "at least you know your trade, Monsieur Worth. And at least you girls will be a credit to me."

CHAPTER 21

When he arrived in New York, Mike called Pierluigi Galli immediately to suggest a meeting. He'd read in *The Wall Street Journal* that the Galli empire was shaky, and now the rumors had spread to the *Times* and the other major newspapers. They now said that the Galli empire wasn't just shaking, it was about to topple.

At first, the harried-sounding secretary said he was definitely not available, not to anyone—no matter who they were.

"Look," Mike said, "tell him I want to talk to him about the Poppy Mallory estate—tell him Johannes Lieber, in Geneva, asked me to call him. I'm due in London tomorrow, but I'm willing to stay here in New York until he can see me."

"I'll call you back, Mr. Preston," she said crisply.

Feeling rattled, Mike went to his club, swam thirty lengths of the pool, had a massage, took a cold shower, and, after checking that there were no messages, took a walk down Fifth Avenue to F.A.O. Schwarz, where he bought Lauren Hunter's kid an enormous teddy bear, telling them to gift-wrap and mail it. On the card, he wrote, *I don't know which of you deserves—or needs—this most, but no doubt Maria will let you share him.* Like her, he signed it *Love—Mike.*

There was a crackle of Christmas excitement in the frosty air as he walked back down Fifth Avenue. Saks' lavishly decorated window with its animated Christmas tableaux was the star attraction, with the enormous sparkling tree at Rockefeller Plaza and the crowded skating rink in second billing. There was nowhere quite like New York at Christmas, he decided, buying a bag of hot roasted chestnuts from the vendor on the corner of the Plaza; there was just that certain extra shot of excitement in the air. He surely hoped the teddy would help make Lauren's lonely Christmas a happier one.

There was a message on his answering machine for him to call Mr. Galli when he returned. The secretary sounded even more harassed. "Mr. Galli is too busy to see you this afternoon and he's leaving for Paris tomorrow," she told him. "He asked if you could come around to the office this evening, about seven-thirty."

Pierluigi's offices were as luxurious as Mike had expected; dark walls, soft carpets and good paintings. Nothing was overdone, but there was the unmistakable air of opulence that goes along with great success. The secretary was working late, looking even more harried than she'd sounded on the phone.

"I'll tell him you're here, Mr. Preston," she said tiredly.

"It must have been a hard couple of days," Mike said sympathetically.

She nodded as she buzzed the intercom. "Worse for him than for me, poor man. I don't know how he's holding up . . . all those stupid reports in the papers . . . Oh, Mr. Galli, Mr. Preston is here to see you." Putting down the phone, she said to Mike, "You're to go right in, sir."

Pierluigi was standing by the window staring down at the Manhattan traffic, thirty floors below. He was wearing an excellently tailored double-breasted suit in dark blue pinstripe, and a somber tie. His face was as colorless as ashes in a grate, and as he turned to look at him, Mike thought his eyes had that same dead feeling.

"Mr. Preston," he said, offering his hand, "how can I help you?"

"I'm sorry to interrupt at such a difficult time, sir," Mike said, "but Johannes Lieber asked me to see you."

"Have a seat, please." Pierluigi took his place behind an antique tulip-wood desk that looked as though it had come from an Italian nobleman's salon. "Johannes Lieber? Are you employed by Mr. Lieber then? Or am I to understand that we may be featured in a book at some future date?"

"I must admit there is a possibility of that," agreed Mike, "it all depends how the story evolves."

"I see. And how exactly is it 'evolving' at the moment?"

"Like Poppy herself, it's an enigma. I've found out about Poppy's parents and her early life—but nothing yet that's led me to any satisfactory conclusions."

"Like *who* is the heir—or heiress?"

"Exactly, sir. Lieber told me why you considered yourself—and your sister—to be the beneficiaries. I'd like to know if there is anything more you can add to that." Pierluigi stared broodingly at his desk and Mike thought uneasily that he looked like a man containing himself with an effort. There was a lurking quality of emotions too long repressed, of brooding violence searching for an outlet. . . .

"I have nothing to add to the story you already know," Pierluigi said at last. "Everything I told Lieber, I believe to be the truth. You can see the logic of it yourself. Poppy Mallory was my grandmother." He stood up dismissively and Mike realized that the interview was at an end. If he knew anything more, Pierluigi wasn't telling.

Pierluigi didn't accompany him to the door, and when Mike turned to look at him he was standing by the window again, staring down at the traffic. He looked like a man abandoned on a sinking ship.

The memory of Pierluigi's gaunt face and stricken dark eyes haunted Mike through the movie he went to in an attempt to escape, and through the snack at the Carnegie Deli, where he attempted to divert himself, watching the young cashier arguing on the phone with her boyfriend while he tried to pay his check. "Don't give me that shit, man," she hissed, juggling Mike's change. "I've been through all that before, I don't need it no more." Slamming his change onto the counter, she sank to the floor, the receiver glued under her chin. "I know you're married . . ." she was saying as he left.

A cab screeched to a halt in response to his outstretched hand. "Where ya going?" growled the driver, an edgy young Hispanic with a razor cut down one cheek.

"Park and Sixty-first," Mike told him.

"Fancy shit," the driver exclaimed contemptuously, slamming his foot on the gas and jockeying with the cab next to him as to who was to rule the road. Bouncing on the raveled plastic backseat, Mike tried to close his ears to their exchange as they shouted at each other, windows rolled down, as if it were High Noon. "What yuh driving? A fuckin' ambalence?" screamed his driver.

"Fuck you, cowboy," the rival driver yelled back.

" 'Scuze my language," the cabbie said companionably, "but he's a fuckin' pain in the ass." Mike sighed as they jolted over the Manhattan potholes; the exhilarating morning feeling of Fifth Avenue at Christmas was melting like the steadily falling snow, disappearing into dirty water on the sidewalks. It was time he left.

Back at the hotel, he studied Lieber's list again before he went to sleep. There were three people he had yet to meet: Orlando Messenger, Claudia Galli, and Aria Rinardi. Calling British Airways, he confirmed his seat to book him on the morning flight to London.

Aria unwrapped the painting Carraldo had sent her, hoping it wasn't the Manet and wishing that her mother wasn't breathing down her neck. "What is it, Aria, let me have a look." Francesca grabbed it from her and inspected it critically. "I should have thought the famous art-dealer could have done better than this," she said contemptuously. "It's worthless!"

Aria looked at the painting carefully; it was a small pen-and-watercolor wash of Portofino and whoever the artist was, he had a light touch and a way of conveying the outgoing warmth of the little Italian fishing village in its summer finery. "I like it, Mama," she said. "It has charm. I'd like to keep it."

Francesca leaned across on the breakfast table and, with her chin on her hand, stared at her daughter. "Sometimes, Aria," she said slowly, "I think you were born without brains. You turn down a Manet, you refuse a maharani's emerald worth a ransom—and you think this is 'charming' and want to keep it. This *cheap* watercolor is what you should return! Really, my girl, where is your common sense!"

"If you're so convinced I'm Poppy's heiress, Mama, why are you still insisting I marry Carraldo?" Aria brushed her hair from her eyes, glaring at her mother.

"Just a precaution, darling," Francesca said airily. "I mean, what if those lawyers should decide you weren't the heiress? Not that it would be true, of course, but you know how tricky they can be. They're not prepared simply to take my word for it, they want 'evidence.' And when you make the sort of mistakes Poppy Mallory made, the one thing you don't leave lying around is *evidence*. I told Lieber that. 'What do you expect? Birth certificates? The woman had an illegitimate child that was brought up by the Rinardis, and Aria is a direct descendant of that child. The money is obviously hers.' "

"And then he told you that Angel Rinardi had brought up three children, two girls and a boy, and the question was which one was Poppy's." Aria finished off her story wearily, she'd heard it all before—a dozen times.

"There were the twin girls," said Francesca crisply, "and everybody knows that Helena never married, so your grandmother, Maria-Cristina, is the only logical heiress. After all, the will specified an 'heiress'—a *daughter,* not a son, so any claim that Aleksandr Rinardi was Poppy's child is ludicrous, I don't care what Pierluigi and Claudia Galli say."

"What if Helena, the daughter who never married, was really Poppy's child? Who gets the money then?"

"That's hypothetical nonsense," scoffed Francesca, "besides, everybody knows that Maria-Cristina was the wild one—just like her mother, Poppy."

"And how do you know so much about Poppy, Mama, when no one else seems to know anything?" Aria asked scornfully.

"Intuition, my dear girl," Francesca retorted confidently as she sauntered to the door. "I understand women."

Aria laughed mockingly. "I think you'd better start looking for those birth certificates, Mama," she called, "Mr. Lieber's not going to like your 'intuition.'"

"Send back that worthless painting!" Francesca commanded, sweeping angrily from the room.

Aria opened the note that accompanied the painting, wondering what Carraldo would have to say this time. He seemed to have accepted the postponement of their official engagement calmly, far more calmly than her mother, who'd gone crazy; but she had the feeling that she'd hurt him, and that worried her. She hadn't thought that Carraldo was a man who could be hurt by anything; he'd seemed too powerful, too invincible —and when someone was that rich you never thought of them as being able to be wounded.

When he found the time, Carraldo would fly to Venice to see her, and they'd have lunch or dinner together, but Aria always insisted on going to a restaurant, so they were never truly "alone." He'd talk to her about the paintings he'd seen that week, or works that he'd sold or bought, and especially about his young artists, and she got the feeling that they were a true source of pleasure and pride in his life. But he rarely touched her, or even held her hand, and, thank heaven, she thought with relief, he never attempted to kiss her.

My dear Aria, he'd written in his fine bold hand, *I hope you will like this charming little sketch of Portofino. I noticed it in the window of a gallery in London last week and saw that my own villa was in it. Knowing your talent for watercolor, I thought you might enjoy having it. I haven't forgotten that you told me you'd have to give up your studies at art school, and my promise to find you a teacher. I think this young artist shows ability and therefore I asked him to come to Venice to tutor you for a few months. I know you never accept gifts from me, but this is also a round-about way of helping the artist earn some much needed money, and at the same time keep his self-respect. His name is Orlando Messenger, and he will be in touch with you in a day or so. Please say yes this time.*

He'd signed it simply *Antony*.

She folded the letter thoughtfully: maybe Carraldo wasn't as bad as people said he was, after all. She remembered that her father, Paolo, had liked him and trusted him, but yet there were all those rumors—everyone said he was a cruel, heartless man. She sighed again; she didn't know what to think, but of course she couldn't refuse his gift this time, because she'd deprive the artist of a much needed chance to earn money.

Orlando Messenger called her the next day and she arranged to meet him at Florian's for tea. He'd surprised her on the phone by speaking Italian, though with a charming English accent, and then he'd told her he'd spent two years at the same art school in Florence that she herself had attended. "So you see," he'd said with a laugh, "we already have something in common."

She hurried through the cold, gloomy gray afternoon to the Piazza San Marco, her portfolio under her arm, and pushing open Florian's door she stepped into its steamy warmth. Florian's Tea Rooms had been established for more than two centuries, and when Venice was occupied by the Austrians in the early nineteenth century, the Venetians had always taken their coffee at Florian's while the enemy patronized Quadri's, the café opposite. Byron had taken tea there and Elizabeth Barrett Browning her chocolate; the mirrored walls had reflected the famous and the notorious and Florian's hadn't changed its decor of red velvet banquets and marble-topped tables since the day it first opened.

Aria glanced around the tables, expecting to see a thin, half-starved, bearded artist and she was surprised when a tall, handsome young man with thick blond hair met her eyes expectantly.

"Aria?" he asked, getting to his feet.

"You must be Orlando," she replied, her heart thumping as he took her hand. "But I didn't expect you to look like this!"

Orlando laughed as he sat opposite her at a little marble-topped table. "And neither did I expect you to look like this!" he replied. And indeed he hadn't; she was tall and young and stylish, and very beautiful in an offbeat way. She had the sort of bone structure that any artist would long to paint and those startlingly winged eyebrows and heavily lashed blue eyes were devastating. Surely this girl didn't need to marry Carraldo. With those looks she could marry anybody! And then he remembered that she might not marry Carraldo; the betting was she was the Mallory heiress and would be a rich woman like all the others he knew, able to pick and choose at will. But like him, she still had to prove it. He sighed;

it would be a pity to lose such innocence and charm beneath the self-indulgence of too much money.

"You're staring at me," Aria said uncomfortably.

"I'm sorry. I was just thinking I'd like to paint you," he said, and for once it wasn't just a come-on line, he meant it.

"I didn't realize you did portraits."

"I work in oils and gouache as well as watercolor. Usually I'd do a portrait in oils, but I'd like to sketch you in charcoal first, and then maybe try a watercolor. But that's not what I'm here for, is it. Signore Carraldo asked me to help you."

The waiter came to take their order and she asked for tea with lemon. "I've brought my portfolio to show you," she said shyly.

He took it from her, inspecting each sketch carefully. They were soft, mystical views of landscapes, but in each she had caught the essence of the scene. She had talent, there was no doubt about that. "These are good," he told her, "but I think I see where you need help. It's a question of structure, you see, here—and here." Leaning closer to her, he pointed out what he meant. "If this had been the focus, then all the rest would have radiated from it. It's a question of seeing it a certain way, that's all."

"Of course," she cried, "now I understand. It seems too obvious, I can't believe I was so stupid not to see it right away."

"No problem." He shrugged. "We'll begin tomorrow and you'll soon develop an eye. And then we should talk about using pen and color wash to get a little more definition. But that will come later."

"Is it really difficult, being a professional artist?" Aria asked, putting the drawings and the sketches back in her portfolio. "It's what I've always wanted to be."

Orlando looked at her; he never met girls like this who gazed at you so trustingly and sweetly with eyes that could melt your heart, and he felt like a stranger in a strange land. She was light years away from those tough, glossy women who lived on gossip and diets and champagne. "It's hard," he admitted, "and I'm having to come to terms with that now. It's easy enough to make a living painting the sort of stuff people like to hang on their walls as part of their interior decor. No one will ever make a fortune at it, but it's enough to get by and it's an easy trap to fall into. I've decided that if I'm ever going to paint the way I really want to paint, I'm going to have to do it *now*—even if it means starving in a garret! That's where Carraldo comes in. I suppose he told you that we met at the Maze Gallery in London. I was having an exhibition there and he bought the Portofino picture. We got talking and I told him my ambition—he offered me this job as a way to help me." Orlando laughed. "Two months in Venice, teaching a beautiful girl! How could I refuse? Oh, but I'm sorry," he said quickly, "I shouldn't talk like that, I know you're engaged to Carraldo."

"I'm not engaged to Antony Carraldo," Aria said quietly, "but I did say I would marry him. Now, I'm not sure."

"But why?" he asked seriously. "Why are you even considering marrying him? You're obviously not in love with him or you wouldn't have to think about it. A lovely girl like you could marry anybody . . . anybody at all."

"My mother doesn't think so," she said, blushing. "She said nobody would want to marry a poor girl, even with the Rinardi name. You see, we have no money. We have the palazzo and the villa, but everything belongs to the family trust. My mother . . . well, my mother is a very special sort of person; she's worked hard, she says, to bring me up properly and keep up our standards. She . . . well, I suppose she *arranged* the marriage for me."

Orlando gazed at her, stunned. "I didn't know that sort of thing still went on. But surely you didn't have to agree?"

"My mother is ill. I'm all she has. I have to look after her. Carraldo was an old friend of my father's."

Orlando whistled in disbelief. Leaning back in his seat, he said, "So Aria, when's the big day?"

"I don't know," she murmured, staring down at her steaming glass of tea. "I was hoping that maybe now I won't have to marry him after all."

"Why is that?" He leaned forward, fascinated by the curve of her eyelids and the shadow her long lashes created on her smooth cheek. Her dark tousled hair shone with chestnut highlights under the red-shaded lamps, and her blue eyes were wide with new hope as she glanced back up at him.

"Maybe you saw the ad in the newspapers, about the search for Poppy Mallory's missing heiress?" she asked. She smiled as Orlando nodded. "It seems as though everyone read it. Well, Mama thinks *I* am the Mallory heiress. She says my grandmother was her daughter. If I inherit Poppy's money, I will give it to my mother—and then I'll be free."

"Free of Carraldo, you mean?" Orlando asked gently.

She shook her head. "It would be unkind to put it that way. Sometimes Carraldo is . . . oh, I don't know, I just don't understand him. Sometimes he frightens me."

Orlando reached across the table and took her hand. "Don't worry," he said protectively. "There's nothing to be afraid of."

She smiled gratefully at him across the table. Her hand felt safe in his; he made her feel secure. With his blond hair and rugged masculine beauty, he was like a knight in shining armor come to save her.

"Shall we begin our lessons tomorrow?" he asked, squeezing her hand comfortingly.

Aria nodded, smiling up at him. "I'll look forward to it," she said simply.

CHAPTER 22

Orlando's claim was interesting, Mike thought, walking through the chill, dank rain up London's Cork Street, toward the Maze Gallery. Like Pierluigi and Claudia, he was claiming that Poppy's child had been a son, not a daughter. But the story of Aleksandr Galli was based on sound psychology, while as far as he could tell, Orlando's was based on pure conjecture.

He studied the paintings in the window before going in; they were pretty and decorative and had a definite appeal, but he could tell they were not great art. The gallery was warm and brightly lit and Mike stepped thankfully inside, shutting out the damp gray afternoon. A small, plump man eyed him inquisitively, assessing if he was a potential purchaser or just another browser, and Mike smiled.

"Good afternoon," he called, "is Mr. Maze here by any chance?"

"That's me," the man said, bustling toward him. "Peter Maze. What can I do for you?"

"Mike Preston," he said, offering his hand. "I'm looking for Orlando Messenger."

"What's Orlando been up to now?" Maze asked apprehensively.

Mike laughed. "Should he have been 'up to' something then?"

"You never know with Orlando, he's all over the place. And he has a terrible way with women . . . I thought you might be an irate husband looking for revenge." He laughed apologetically. "Of course I didn't mean that, Orlando is a nice guy, and he's a fine painter."

"A good artist maybe, Mr. Maze," Mike agreed, "but not great."

"Well, you know, you're basing your judgment only on what you see here. But I mean what I say; Orlando is a fine artist and he could be a great one, if only he'd give himself the chance. Let me tell you, if he ever does, then these pretty little daubs here will be worth a fortune as 'early Orlando Messengers.' You should buy, Mr. Preston, while the price is right, because now that Antony Carraldo has taken Orlando under his wing, we might yet see a masterpiece from him."

"Carraldo? The famous art dealer?"

"He was in here a couple of weeks ago, at the opening of Orlando's exhibition. He bought a painting and then he offered him a job in Venice, tutoring his fiancée—apparently she dabbles in watercolors. But it was really an excuse to get Orlando away from the rat race he was in, and allow him to earn some money and still have the time to paint 'the way he really wants to paint'—to quote the artist himself. Of course, Orlando was thrilled, came in here to get an advance on his money and took off right away. I'm hoping when he comes back we shall see a marked difference in his work." He glanced shrewdly at Mike. "And now I've told you all this," he said, "maybe you'd better tell me why you want to see him."

"Oh, I was passing through London; it was just the suggestion of a mutual friend that we should meet," Mike said quickly. "I guess I'll catch up to him some other time. One thing, though, Mr. Maze, what did you mean 'the rat race he's been in'? What is it? Drugs, booze . . . ?"

"God, no! Orlando's straight-arrow on that score! No, his problem is that he likes the good things in life and he hasn't had the money to buy them." He shrugged, throwing his arms in the air graphically. "He's young and very good-looking, women like him . . . you can imagine the rest. But I think young Orlando's becoming bitter, he's tired of having to 'paint' for his supper—and believe me some of those rich international ladies can be true bitches. They know how to wield the power of money over someone like Orlando—and they enjoy every little humiliation along with every little gift they bestow on him. It's a tough price to pay, Mr. Preston, and I think he's just about had enough."

"Money and power," mused Mike, "they've always ruled the world."

"Yes, well, I get the feeling Orlando thinks it's time *he* was the king. Now, can I interest you in one of his paintings, Mr. Preston?"

"I wish I could say yes," Mike said, smiling, "but they're just not my style. Still, thanks for taking the time to talk to me."

"It was a pleasure meeting you," said Peter Maze as the door closed behind him.

Mike stopped off just long enough in Geneva to meet Johannes Lieber. The lawyer was a small, plump man, but nevertheless had a commanding presence. He was about sixty years old, his face was lined, and the eyes that assessed Mike across his desktop were used to seeking out the flaws in a man's character.

His sharp expression melted into a smile and Mike smiled back in relief. For a minute there, he'd felt himself in the dock, ready for sentencing, but now Lieber looked like everybody's favorite uncle.

"You're doing a good job," he told Mike, "at last we know *who* Poppy Mallory is, even if we don't yet know what she did to amass such a fortune." He paused. "You say you're off to Venice tonight?"

Mike nodded. "I was going to go to Paris first, to speak to Claudia Galli, but when I called, all I got was a message on her answering machine, saying she was out of town and wouldn't be back for a week. I thought I'd go straight on to Venice instead."

"An interesting claim, the Gallis," Lieber said reflectively. "Don't you think it strange, Mr. Preston, to find such intrigue within a single family?"

Mike shrugged. "In my experience, it's far from strange. The only thing that rivals a family for duplicity and machinations is a large corporation. Believe me, there's not much to choose between them. Let's not forget that most murders are committed within the family circle."

Lieber chuckled. "Well, at least Poppy didn't murder her father, though God knows he sounds as though he deserved it."

"I prefer to think she threw the knife at him in panic," Mike said soberly. "From what I know of her, Poppy Mallory wasn't that kind of woman."

"Ah, but then what kind of woman was she?" demanded Lieber. "*That* is the enigma you still have to prove, Mr. Preston."

On the plane to Venice, Mike knew he was right. He still didn't know the real Poppy Mallory. Poppy—the woman.

It was the week before Christmas and Mike had decided that if he was going to have to spend the festive season alone in Venice, then he might as well do it in comfort at the Hotel Cipriani. The hotel's private launch met his flight and soon he was speeding across the lagoon to the island of

Giudecca. As he disembarked he turned to gaze at the hauntingly beautiful view across the lagoon of the Doges' Palace and the Piazzetta looking like a medieval stage set in the bright afternoon sunlight.

The Cipriani welcomed him into its unostentatious luxury and over a sybaritic late lunch of spiny-shelled crab and melt-in-the-mouth tortellini filled with a mousse of chicken, Mike thought about Aria Rinardi and Orlando Messenger. Two of Poppy Mallory's would-be heirs, brought together by a catalyst in the shape of Antony Carraldo, the mystery man of the century.

The one thing all the claimants had in common was that they all needed the money. Orlando was sick to death of pandering to his rich lovers, and yet he was unwilling to give up that same rich life-style. He wasn't about to "suffer" for his art. And although Mike hadn't met her yet, it seemed that Aria Rinardi wanted to buy her way out of marriage to Carraldo by giving Poppy's money to her mother—she wanted freedom. Lauren Hunter needed the money so she and her baby sister could lead decent lives, and maybe she'd get to go to Stanford. Pierluigi Galli needed that money to shore up his toppling business empire. While, according to Lieber, Claudia had "needed" it the way she'd always needed money—just to enjoy it.

The one question that no one seemed to ask was where Poppy got all that money. If the story that she'd had a baby and been disowned by her family was true, then what had she done, alone in Europe?

Returning to his room, he called Francesca Rinardi.

"Pronto?" a clear, impersonal voice answered.

"The Baronessa Rinardi?" he asked.

"Sì. Who is this?"

"My name is Mike Preston. Johannes Lieber asked me to contact you."

"Lieber?" she asked, a sharp edge to her voice. "What is it you want, Mr. Preston?"

"Mr. Lieber wanted me to discuss the situation with you, about Poppy Mallory's will," he replied briskly. "Obviously nothing has been resolved yet, but we are investigating each story closely."

"Be here this afternoon at five," she commanded, hanging up abruptly.

Mike approached the Palazzo Rinardi on foot through the Campo Morosini rather than from the Grand Canal, but he thought it beautiful, despite the peeling rose-colored stucco. A fierce old woman, in a black dress covered with a crisp white apron, answered the door, acknowledging him with a nod of her head. "This way, Signore," she said, hobbling through the entrance lobby to the hallway, grumbling about her arthritis as she went.

"It's up the stairs," she told him, "the big double doors facing you at the top. The Baronessa is waiting for you—but it'll save my legs if you can announce yourself."

"There's no need to come up, Fiametta," Francesca called in a silvery voice from the top of the stairs. She smiled dazzlingly at Mike. "Please come up, Mr. Preston. Fiametta will bring us some tea, won't you, Fiametta."

The old woman hobbled away, still grumbling to herself, and Francesca sighed as Mike walked up the beautiful marble stairs toward her. She was wearing a green woolen dress with a fuchsia cashmere shawl slung carelessly over her shoulders. Her cool, symmetrically beautiful face was perfectly made up—not too much that it was obvious, and just enough to enhance her beautiful green eyes and rather tight-lipped mouth. Mike thought she looked very expensive.

"Poor Fiametta," she said, "I'm afraid she's getting too old for the job. But you see, she's been with the family for more than half a century, and when you have a servant that long you can't just dismiss her. She has no life other than with the Rinardis." She held out her hand. "I'm Francesca Rinardi. I'm afraid I don't know exactly why you are here, Mr. Preston, but welcome to the Palazzo Rinardi."

"You have a very beautiful home, Baronessa," Mike said, looking around the shabby, elegantly proportioned room, noticing the painted ceilings and the portraits, the heavy, worn silk drapes, and the priceless bibelots scattered on the tables.

"An inheritance like this can be a great burden," she sighed. "As you can see, the palazzo needs a fortune spent on it to restore its original beauty. I'm afraid the Rinardi family no longer has that kind of money. So you see," she added, smiling disarmingly at him, "what a good cause Poppy's fortune would go to."

Mike took a seat on a yellow brocade sofa opposite her. "I suppose that if her claim is successful, then Aria would be the one to decide what to do with her money."

"Aria is a child!" Francesca snapped, her smile fading. "I am her legal guardian. But naturally she would want to restore the palazzo that has been in her family for four centuries."

"But if she didn't?" he persisted.

She shrugged irritably. "Aria always does as I think best—ultimately."

Fiametta appeared in the doorway, a tea tray in her gnarled hands, and Mike leapt to help her. "Thank you, Signore," she said, glancing at him with her sharp, blackbird eyes.

"There was no need to help," Francesca said coldly. "Fiametta is perfectly able to carry a tray of tea. Of course, when we have Poppy's money, then her life will become easier too. We shall be able to afford proper servants again. Fiametta was my husband's nanny; she knew Paolo's mother, Maria-Cristina. Of course she's an old woman and her memories are a bit vague now, but perhaps you'd like to talk to her later."

"That would be helpful," he said. "Tell me, Baronessa, do you have any other evidence on which to base your claim? All we have is your statement that Maria-Cristina was Poppy's daughter, but you don't say why you believe that—other than that the other daughter, Helena, never married."

"As a girl, Maria-Cristina was wild," she said, pouring tea, "like her mother, Poppy. Always doing the wrong thing, marrying the wrong men, making the wrong decisions. Although I hate to say it about my own child's grandmother, she was no better than she ought to be. Helena never went anywhere. Angel, her mother, kept her by her side; she doted on her. There was no doubt that Helena was the favorite and now you see why. It was because Maria-Cristina wasn't Angel's own child at all, she had simply tried to help her old friend Poppy Mallory. And as for Aleksandr's claim, it's nonsense. There was no reason for Poppy to leave any money to 'her son' in her will, because she didn't have one."

"But you have no written evidence?" Mike persisted. "No documents?"

Francesca sighed again. "Mr. Preston," she said, "all we have is a parrot! Come with me and I'll show you."

He followed her up another flight of stairs to a spacious room on the next floor. Two easels were mounted by the window and a big table was littered with an artist's paraphernalia. And, on an immense golden stand by the window, was a large green parrot.

"This is Luchay," Francesca told him. "He was Poppy Mallory's parrot. Apparently when she died some old country lawyer showed up at the Villa d'Oro and gave the parrot to Helena and Maria-Cristina. Eventually my husband Paolo had it and now, Aria."

"But that stand," he exclaimed, "and the cage—they're works of art!"

"Solid gold, Mr. Preston, and those stones are real. Those rings around the bird's legs are emeralds and diamonds! These finials on the stand— made by Bulgari, I believe—are studded with sapphires, rubies, and emeralds, as well as lapis lazuli and turquoise. Poppy must have been besotted by that damned bird. And the ridiculous thing is that none of it can be sold because that was what Poppy had decreed. Besides, they are too famous ever to try to break down and sell off the stones separately."

Mike frowned as she bent closer to the bird. "Luchay," she called. "Say 'Poppy,' Luchay." But the bird just shuffled on his stand, turning his head away.

"Of course the parrot is very old now." She shrugged. "But occasionally he speaks her name."

"Thank you very much for talking to me, Baronessa," Mike said. "I think I understand the situation better now. It's always easier to meet people and discuss things face-to-face."

"Are you employed by Mr. Lieber then?" she asked. "He said he might put a private detective onto the case."

"As a matter of fact, no. I'm a writer. Mr. Lieber and I thought we might be able to help each other."

She glanced sharply at him again and then smiled warmly. "Mike Preston! Well, forgive me for being so businesslike. Of course, I didn't realize you were the famous writer. You must come to dinner and meet my daughter, Aria. Where are you staying, Mr. Preston . . . or maybe I'd better call you Mike, now we intend to get to know each other better."

"I'm at the Cipriani, Baronessa."

"No more formality, please, just call me Francesca. How about tomorrow evening, about nine? Would that suit you?"

"That suits me fine, thank you," he replied. "I'll look forward to it. Just one more thing, though; you mentioned I might have a word with Fiametta before I leave."

"Of course," she cried. "Better come to the kitchen, though, it'll save time. Follow me."

Fiametta looked up in surprise; Francesca rarely came down to the kitchen and she glanced around now, her nose wrinkling at the smell of the garlic Fiametta was chopping.

"Mr. Preston would like to have a few words with you about Poppy Mallory," Francesca called loudly, though Mike hadn't noticed that the old woman seemed deaf. "Mr. Preston is from Mr. Lieber's office—the lawyer in Geneva," she added, emphasizing the words. "I told him you knew Maria-Cristina."

Fiametta nodded. "Very well," she said, wiping her hands on a cloth and sitting down at the table.

"Fiametta will show you out when you've finished, Mike," Francesca said conspiratorially. "I'm afraid I have to fly. I have an appointment. Until tomorrow then?"

"Tomorrow," he agreed, shaking her cool, smooth hand.

"What is it you want to know?" the old woman asked, glaring at him. "Why can't those lawyers just take her word for it. Maria-Cristina was Poppy's daughter, she was Paolo's mother, and she was Aria's grandmother, and that's that."

"I wish it were that easy, Fiametta," Mike said, sitting opposite her at the kitchen table. The garlic smelled good and strong and there were little piles of chopped herbs and vegetables on the table next to it. "Smells great," he said appreciatively.

"I'm a good cook," she told him, "I learned as a young girl. Of course, Venetian cooking is different from the rest of Italy. Better! Lots of good rice instead of always pasta. You should try my risotto, Signore, it's the best in Venice."

"Maybe I will," he told her, "the Baronessa invited me for dinner tomorrow night."

"Huh, then you'll not be getting risotto; she'll want something fancier to show off with, she always does."

Mike nodded; it seemed there was no love lost between the old woman and her employer. "Tell me about Maria-Cristina," he suggested. "How old was she when you knew her?"

"She was a grown woman, and a selfish one; full of her own self-importance and too busy with her own affairs to bother much with her boy, Paolo. Maria-Cristina was flighty, always running off with some man or another. She'd been married once, you know, to an American—Bill Aston, he was called. 'Paul' was his son—until she got divorced and brought him to live here. Then we always called him Paolo. Bill Aston was a wealthy man and he cut them both off without a cent. Of course, she didn't care, her family was as rich as his. So you see he wasn't even a Rinardi by name, until his cousin Aleksandr refused to take the title. And then it went to Paolo as the next living male relative. This was before Pierluigi was born, of course, and before Aleksandr married. I'll bet *she* didn't tell you all this, did she," she said, jerking her head toward the door. "No, of course she wouldn't; it's not true to think that Paolo's name goes back centuries, along with this palazzo. And poor Helena, Maria-Cristina's sister. She was always a strange one, under her mother's thumb, I thought. She never spoke much, and they said in the end she'd gone completely off her head."

"Was there ever any mention of Poppy?" he asked.

Fiametta shook her head. "Not that I can recall, though everyone seemed to know the rumor that one of Angel and Felipe Rinardi's children was not theirs."

"Were you there when the lawyer brought Poppy's parrot to the house?"

"Oh, yes," she said eagerly, "I was there. He was a little countryman in an old-fashioned black suit. It was a hot day and he was sweating like a pig—I can see him now, the sweat dripping down his face and the parrot cage clutched in his hand." She laughed at the memory. "What a sight to turn up on your doorstep. Anyway, he told his story to Maria-Cristina about Poppy Mallory's dying and wanting to give the parrot to the Rinardis. 'What on earth do we need with a mangy old parrot!' she exclaimed. And then she saw the cage! She swung it around, inspecting it greedily—she liked jewels, that one, and the poor bird began to screech. He was making a terrible racket. Just then Helena appeared from the garden. 'What is it?' she asked. 'What sort of bird is that that's singing so beautifully?' 'What do you mean, *singing*,' Maria-Cristina asked her scornfully. 'The damned bird's making an infernal row!' Helena looked at the poor frightened bird and her big blue eyes were full of tenderness—she was a nice girl, good-hearted, you know, even if she was doted on and spoiled by her mother. But I'll never forget what she said. 'No, Maria-Cristina, you're wrong,' she said, 'he is singing. He's singing especially for me.' Her sister looked at her and I could tell by the look in her eyes that she thought that at last she'd gone completely mad. But she was always gentle with her. 'Then you take him, Helena,' she said, 'the parrot is yours. It's a present from Poppy Mallory.' And that's the only time I ever heard Poppy Mallory's name mentioned in that household."

"Thank you, Fiametta," Mike said, standing up to leave. "Your memories have been very helpful."

Her bright old eyes inspected him for a few seconds and then she said, "Have you met Aria yet?" He shook his head. "She's worth all the Rinardis put together," she told him. "I brought her up, and I know. She has a good heart, Mr. Preston, and it's not fair that she has to marry the Signore Carraldo." Her expression was sad as she added, "And that's why she needs the Mallory money so badly, so she'll never have to marry that man. Never!"

CHAPTER 23

The Villa Velata seemed to have settled even deeper into the brooding valley at the foot of the Dolomites. An early December frost had already left a coating of white over the shrubs and lawns, and painted a film of ice across the neglected gravel drive. Pierluigi knew from experience that it would never lift because the house was built in the shadow of the mountain, and at this time of year the sun never rose above its great bulk. The frost got thicker, the ice firmer, and then the heavy snows would cover the lot and the villa would become a prison again for four months. Just the way it had always been in his childhood.

The chauffeur negotiated the icy drive cautiously in the hired Fiat. Its tires refused to hold on the slippery surface and he wished he could curse, but he was afraid of his silent passenger. He hadn't spoken a word the entire journey from the airport at Trento, where he'd been told to meet him; he'd just stared out of the window instead, looking like a man going to a funeral. And for all the chauffeur knew, maybe he was.

He stopped the car with a sigh of relief in front of the somber ocher-colored villa, hurrying to open the passenger door, but Pierluigi was already out. The chauffeur unloaded his bag from the trunk and carried it up the steps. "Shall I ring the bell, Signore?" he asked Pierluigi, who was standing in the drive, just staring at the house.

"Thank you, no. You'd better get back quickly, it looks like snow," he said, handing him a tip.

"Thanks very much, Signore." The chauffeur examined the money quickly. It was fair but not generous, and he sighed; he'd expected more from this obviously rich man. As he drove off, Pierluigi was still standing where he had left him, staring at the villa as though afraid to go inside.

Pierluigi knew that the image of his childhood home would never leave him; the flat stucco walls and the unsymmetrical facade, the ocher color that had turned an ugly brown from damp; the windowpanes so distorted with age, they seemed to let in every blast of cold from outdoors; and the empty silent gardens. His father seemed to have chosen to live in the bleakest house he could find, to match the bleakness of his soul.

Only for a few brief summer weeks had the Villa Velata ever come to life, and then there'd been the smell of hay from the valley and the scent of the flowering shrubs his father had planted experimentally—those that had survived the cruel winter in his greenhouses—until he brought them out into the garden for their few hours of glory. The horses had galloped in the fields, kicking up their heels and biting each other playfully in an ecstasy of delight as the warm sun rippled along their backs, enjoying the freedom from their stables. And young Claudia had run wild too, shrieking in delight and kicking up her heels like the horses, casting off her clothes and rolling over and over in the grass, trailing garlands of daisies like a midsummer fairy.

He pushed open the heavy front door and went inside at last. The big hall was in darkness, but he knew it so well, he could have negotiated it blindfolded. Dropping his bag, he walked straight through to the big kitchen at the back of the house. The woman tending a pot on the ancient stove jumped with surprise as she turned and saw him. "Signore Pierluigi!" she exclaimed. "We weren't expecting you!"

"How are you, Giulietta?" he asked with a smile. "I'm sorry if I startled you."

"That's all right, Signore. I expect you've come to see the Signora Claudia. She'll be surprised, too, no doubt."

"No doubt," he said sarcastically. "Do you know where she is?"

"In your father's study, Signore. She's been busy in there for a couple of days now; she says she's looking for something."

"Yes," he said, "she would be."

He walked along the hall, through the library to his father's study. Claudia was sitting at the big old-fashioned rolltop desk and she stared up at him in surprise. Then a little smile curved the corners of her mouth. "Well, well, the prodigal son comes home!" she said mockingly. "And what are you doing here, Pierluigi? I thought I heard you say you were never coming back to the Villa Velata again."

"And didn't you say the same?"

She shook her head. "My memories were obviously less painful—or more attractive than yours, Brother."

"I can guess why you are here," he said coldly. "I thought you might have contacted me about Poppy Mallory. I telephoned you in Paris before I left, but got no reply. I flew there first, thinking I'd see you. Of course, when you weren't there I realized where you'd be and I flew down here—via Geneva."

"Does Poppy Mallory's money mean that much to you?" she asked contemptuously. "To Pierluigi Galli, the millionaire genius of Wall Street? Why can't you just let me have it *all*, Pierluigi? What will a million or so from the past matter to you? When you *know* that to me it means *everything*."

Unbuttoning his coat, Pierluigi folded it neatly. He placed it across a chair and took a seat opposite her. "You obviously don't know what you are talking about," he said calmly. "Poppy's money is not a mere million or two—it's hundreds of thousands of millions. There will be enough even for you, Claudia, though God knows you'll go through it faster than a hot knife through butter. You don't seem to acquire any sense as you get older."

"We are the same age," she cried, stung. "I'm only as old as you are!"

"It's different for men, though, isn't it? I'm sure you are well aware of that, Claudia."

"So, now you know why I need the money." She shrugged. "For my old age. Not just because I'm greedy, like you."

"Look, Claudia," he said with a sigh, "let's stop this stupid bickering. We've always been led to believe that our father was Poppy Mallory's son, and that we were her grandchildren, and we're both here now for the same reason—to find the evidence to prove it. Lieber showed me a copy of the so-called will. It quite definitely states that she leaves her money to her daughter. I explained that the story was that Poppy never actually saw her baby; Angel whisked it away at birth before she'd even held it. And Angel led her to believe it had been a girl because she was afraid one day she might come back and try to claim the child as hers. I also explained how Felipe Rinardi hated the boy because he was not his own, and made the child's life a misery—and that's why, when Felipe died, Aleksandr abandoned the family home and refused to take the title. He wanted nothing that had been the Rinardis'. He came here, bought the Villa Velata, and much later married Lucia Galli, whose name he took instead of his own. Lieber agreed that the story sounded valid but said he must have some documentary evidence to back it up. That's why I'm here."

"Oh? I thought maybe you'd come to visit your beloved sister." Claudia leaned back in her chair, stretching. "Don't you miss me, then, Pierluigi? All alone in your ivory tower of an office on Wall Street? Or that museum you call home on Park Avenue?"

"I *never* miss you, Claudia," he said icily.

She grinned; she knew better. "How's your sex life these days?" she taunted. "Or don't you stoop to such basic acts anymore?"

"You're being ridiculous," he said coldly as he opened the door. "I'll see you at supper."

"I can't wait!" she called mockingly as he walked away.

The vast unheated dining room was icy, and instead they ate supper at a round table in front of the fire in the small sitting room. Giulietta, who lived in the gatehouse at the end of the drive, served them minestrone soup, and Claudia chatted incessantly throughout the meal, grumbling about her Amex card being canceled and his lack of care for her. "You've got all that money and you never give me a cent," she cried angrily. "Here I am practically starving in Paris while you live in the lap of luxury!"

Giulietta offered Pierluigi the veal but he shook his head, waving the dish away. "You are quite wrong, Claudia," he said calmly. "I've bailed you out of every financial scrape you've ever gotten yourself into. Now it's time you took care of yourself. It's the only way you'll learn the value of money."

"The value of money!" She poured herself another glass of wine, spilling some on the white cloth. "And what value does money have to you, Brother? You just switch it from one bank account to another, playing games with it—buying this and selling that . . . you never do anything *real* with your money, Pierluigi! It doesn't bring you pleasure or comfort, any of the *physical* pleasures. To *you* money is the end result; for me, it's what I can buy with it that matters."

Giulietta removed their plates and carried in the chocolate mousse she'd made that afternoon. Claudia attacked it greedily, pouring herself more wine.

"You never think of the consequences of anything, do you?" he said contemptuously. "Not even the effect of two helpings of chocolate mousse on your hips."

"God damn you," she cried, throwing the plate violently across the table. "You are a bastard, Pierluigi, I hate you!"

Giulietta picked up pieces of the plate and retreated hurriedly to the kitchen. There had never been any love lost between these two and now they were at it again, hammer and tongs. Carrying in the coffee, she placed it on the table, glancing at them worriedly. "I'll go now, Signora, Signore," she muttered.

"Good night, Giulietta. Thank you," he said, but Claudia was sunk sullenly over the table, her head buried in her hands. Giulietta sighed; she was glad she was going home to her husband and a bit of peace and quiet.

"You're just jealous, that's all," Claudia said flatly.

Pierluigi poured a cup of coffee and carried it to the door. "I'm going back to father's study to see what I can find," he said, ignoring her remark.

He had been there for over an hour, sorting through the tightly packed drawers and compartments of the rolltop desk, when he heard her footsteps in the hall. The door was flung open and Claudia leaned against it unsteadily. Her hair fell untidily over her face and her cream satin blouse was stained with wine. "I want to talk to you—*Brother!*" she snarled.

He glanced up at her coldly. "You're drunk, Claudia," he said. "Why don't you go to bed and sleep it off. We can talk in the morning."

"*We can talk in the morning . . .*" she said, mimicking his precise tones, "and *what* shall we talk about in the morning, Pierluigi? Shall we talk about you and me?" A little smile played around her full lips and she licked them enticingly. "About 'old times,' Brother?"

Pierluigi's hand tightened on the sheaf of papers he was holding. "Go away, Claudia, will you?" he said, turning back to the desk.

She sauntered toward him. "Don't you want to remember then, little brother? *Don't tell me you don't dream about it,* alone in your narrow bachelor bed, high above Manhattan. Come on, now, Pierluigi, you and I both know you do." Standing behind him, she snaked her arms around his neck, kissing the top of his head. "You do love your sister after all, don't you, Pierluigi? And I never knew how much—until that day in the stables. You never told me how long you'd been watching us, Brother. Was it twice, three times . . . a dozen perhaps?" She laughed as he untwined her arms and pushed her away.

"Stop it, Claudia," he commanded, "stop it right now!"

"That's not what you said then," she mocked, "you just wanted it to go on and on. . . . Remember that afternoon, Pierluigi? He'd just left me, still lying there on the straw. I knew you were up there, in the loft, watching . . . and I called to you. You came down that ladder so slowly, you couldn't take your eyes off me, could you? Lying there half naked, my skirts tumbled to my waist . . ."

"Claudia, for God's sake!" he screamed, pushing back the chair and facing her.

"And then it was your turn, wasn't it, Pierluigi? Your turn to touch little sister's breasts, your turn to slide between her legs, your turn—"

Raising his hand, Pierluigi struck her across the face, jolting her head back with the force of his blow. "You cheap little whore!" he snarled. "All you've ever done is sell your body!"

"And you were *never* the highest bidder," she said bitterly, her hand on the livid red mark on her cheek. "You got it for free, *Brother!*"

"I'm leaving," he said, striding from the room. "I refuse to stay here with you."

"Afraid I'll seduce you?" she taunted. "Is that it?"

Ignoring her, Pierluigi strode up the stairs to his room. His bag was still packed and putting on his coat he picked it up and walked back down the stairs. Claudia was waiting for him by the telephone in the hall. "How do you propose to leave here?" she asked. "Have you forgotten, Pierluigi? You don't drive."

"I'll telephone the village for a taxi," he said, reaching for the phone.

She grabbed it first, laughing hilariously. "Oh, no, you won't," she said. "We've been cut off."

He stared in amazement at the scissors in her hand and then at the dangling ends of the telephone wires. Then, picking up his case, he brushed past her. "I'll walk to the village," he said icily.

"Walk?" she cried, running after him. "It's five kilometres, it's snowing out there . . ."

"Go away, Claudia," he told her savagely. "I want nothing more to do with you. I never want to see you again."

"Damn you, you bastard!" she cried, lunging at him drunkenly with the scissors. "I'll kill you." She stopped, staring horrified at the blood on his hand where he'd put it up to protect himself. Their eyes met and then without another word he walked out the door, slamming it behind him.

Claudia stared around her in a panic. What had she done, oh, God, what had she done . . . ? She hadn't meant to hurt him, she'd only meant to jolt him out of his icy complacency, force him to be nice to her . . . he *owed* her, dammit! She paced the chilly hall frantically, sobbing and wiping away the tears and smudged mascara with the back of her hand. It had never been as bad as this before—of course, they'd always fought, but this time she'd gone too far. And they'd never talked about that time in the stables, not even immediately afterward—but she'd always thought somehow that Pierluigi really loved her, that he was like a stern parent, keeping her on a tight rein because he knew she was wayward and unpredictable.

Still brooding about Pierluigi, Claudia didn't notice the passing of time until the long-case clock in the hall boomed the hour, making her jump. It was ten o'clock and he must have been gone for over half an hour, trudging through the snow to the village. It was a long, dark walk on a treacherous icy road, he might fall and break his leg, and then he'd just lie there in the road and nobody would find him until the next day— he'd be frozen to death. . . . She couldn't bear that—she loved Pierluigi, and she knew he loved her. . . .

Terrified, she flung on her coat and ran outside. It was slippery and the snow stuck to her high heels, making her skid as she struggled across the courtyard to the garage. The doors were open and the snow was blowing in and she looked at it, puzzled. Pierluigi must have tried to start the car, but he never drove—he had a phobia about it. . . .

Switching on the headlights, she backed out into the driveway, bumping over the frozen ruts until she came to the road leading to the village. It led downhill beneath a shelter of arching lime trees and so far not much snow had managed to penetrate the canopy. The windshield wipers flickered angrily back and forth as she peered out, searching for him in the darkness ahead, afraid she might not see him. She wiped away her tears again, sobbing as she murmured his name. "Pierluigi," she whispered, "I didn't mean it. I love you, truly I do. I don't know what makes me say these things to you." But there was still no sign of him. She fumbled in her purse on the seat beside her for a tissue to wipe her tears, keeping her eye on the road.

There! What was that? Yes, that must be him . . . look, he'd stopped and was staring into the headlights . . . "Pierluigi," she called. And then suddenly the back of the car seemed to slide away from her and the steering wheel was spinning under her clutching hands. Instinctively, Claudia pressed her foot to the brake, trying to steer into the skid, but there was no response; she was going faster and faster, sliding sideways across the road, over the bank, into the woods below. There was the brittle sound of breaking glass as the car came to a stop, upside down under an olive tree. And then there was just a deep, unearthly silence.

CHAPTER 24

Aria stood in front of Van Dyck's seventeenth-century portrait of a gentleman dressed in black. He wore breeches and buckled shoes, and his white lace collar and cuffs peeked from his velvet jacket. He was leaning arrogantly against a marble column with an expression on his face that said he owned the world and anyone who tried to take it from him would receive short shrift.

"He's intimidating," she whispered to Orlando.

"Sinister, you mean," Orlando said thoughtfully.

She nodded. "Like Carraldo, sort of powerful and scary."

"Let's not talk about Carraldo," he urged, "try to forget him for a while."

They wandered on through the elegant galleries of the Ca' d'Oro while Aria pointed out its treasures, enjoying watching his serious, handsome face as he inspected the paintings, moving back a little to study each one from a different angle. Being with Orlando wasn't like being with one of her fellow students from the art college, he was so interesting and sensitive, and quite different from *anybody* she'd ever known.

It was almost like a miracle that Orlando should have come into her life when she was at such a low point. She didn't have to *explain* to him about how she felt about her mother, or Carraldo, or even Poppy Mallory—he just understood.

Like now, wandering through the museum, they were tuned into the same wavelength; she respected his judgment on the paintings, and he asked her own poor little amateur view of them, listening carefully while she explained, and then pointing out to her what she had missed—but nevertheless praising her own intuitive opinions. "All any painting is, is what the viewer sees in it personally," he told her. "If it means nothing to you, then it has no value to you. Van Gogh's irises can be worth millions to one person and another wouldn't want it on his walls."

The two weeks Orlando had been in Venice had been the happiest Aria could remember in a long time, and she'd been relieved, too, because she hadn't seen Carraldo in all that time. He was away on business, much to her mother's fury, because the emerald engagement ring was still not firmly affixed to Aria's finger. Francesca had glared at Orlando suspiciously when she first met him, and Aria had the feeling that if Carraldo himself hadn't sent Orlando to tutor her, she would have dismissed him.

"What is Carraldo doing, sending that good-looking young man here?" she'd asked, fuming. "You'd better behave yourself, Aria, that's all I can say. Carraldo is not a man who would take an insult lightly."

"Are you warning me, Mother?" Aria had challenged.

"Of course I am," she'd replied angrily, "and you'd better take heed, or you—and Orlando—might have cause to regret it."

Of course, she didn't care about herself, but it was what Francesca had said about Orlando that worried Aria. He'd told her enthusiastically how much Carraldo had liked his work, how they'd talked about his need to be free to paint, and how Carraldo had given him this opportunity. It would be awful if Carraldo got angry and refused to help with his career. She knew how very important that was to Orlando.

"What are you thinking about?" he asked.

"You," she said honestly.

He laughed. "I hope they were pleasant thoughts."

"Of course they were. I was just wishing there was some way I could help you in your career."

"That's up to me," he said quietly, "nobody can do it but me."

"But if I get Poppy Mallory's money I can be your patron," she said. "I'm serious, Orlando, you wouldn't have to worry about money anymore; you could have as much as you need. Then you'll be free to paint, instead of having to tutor girls like me."

He linked his arm through hers, laughing. "I'm enjoying tutoring girls like you. I've just realized that I never got to meet 'girls like you' before

. . . all I met were hard-boiled rich women who always wanted *more,* no matter how much they'd got. You never seem to want anything."

"Oh, I do," she said, looking at him with earnest dark blue eyes.

"Tell me what," he asked, but she just shook her head.

"It's a secret."

"And you'll never tell, is that right?"

She nodded again, her dark hair falling over her eyes. "Maybe never," she said firmly.

He laughed again. "Only you could have made that statement, Aria— *maybe* and *never* in the same sentence. I shall take it to mean that one day you'll tell me. Okay? Meanwhile, Carraldo is paying me very well for this pleasant job, so what do you say I take you out to dinner tonight? Where would you like to go? Harry's Bar?"

"Oh, please, let's go to Corte Sconta," she said. "But it's always so busy, I'm not sure we'll get a table."

"Leave it to me," he told her. "What time shall I pick you up?"

She hesitated. "I think it's better if I meet you there . . . I'm sorry, but my mother wouldn't approve," she added miserably. "Because of Carraldo, you see."

"Okay," Orlando said curtly. "Meet me there then, at ten."

Corte Sconta was tucked away down a tiny alley off the Riva degli Schiavoni in the Castello area, and Aria waited impatiently for the waterbus. It was a bitterly cold night and the fog was rolling in across the lagoon, muffling sounds and reducing visibility to twenty yards. Snuggling deeper into her jacket, she paced the *vaporetti* stop impatiently. She had been waiting ten minutes already and she was afraid she was going to be late, and she thought that a single minute less in Orlando's company was a minute wasted. Exclaiming angrily, she turned away from the canal and began to walk; she could be there in fifteen minutes if she took the shortcut.

The heels of her new tasseled cowboy boots rang on the trachyte volcanic-rock tiles of the Piazzetta, sounding lonely in the fog. The weather seemed to have kept everyone indoors and many of the cafés and shops were already shuttered. She turned into a side street and began to wend her way through the alleys, thinking about Orlando and the secret she couldn't tell him. How could she? He'd probably just laugh at her if she ever said she was in love with him. Orlando knew such sophisticated women, she must seem just a girl to him. But inside she wasn't; she was very grown up and she was yearning for him to kiss her. Of course, she'd kissed dozens of boys before, but with Orlando it would be different because she would be committing herself. Love was love. And it had nothing at all to do with Antony Carraldo!

She heard the sound of muffled footsteps on the bridge behind her and glanced quickly over her shoulder, but in the glare of a streetlamp all she could see was swirling fog and shadows. She was quite alone. Nervously she increased her pace, straining her ears for the sounds . . . yes, there they were again, ringing on the stones of the little bridge she had just crossed. It was ridiculous, she knew, because if it hadn't been foggy she probably wouldn't even have noticed the footsteps, but the mist made everything seem sinister. The steps sounded even closer, increasing their pace, and with a cry of alarm she took to her heels, running two at a time down the steps that led to a little square where she could see the brighter lights of a café.

She paused under the lights, her heart pounding, glancing back to see who was there, knowing now she could run inside and ask for help. A prickling feeling at the back of her neck told her that she was being watched. But it seemed after all there was no one, and she told herself she was being foolish and continued on her way.

The Calle Crocera seemed very dark after the bright lights and suddenly losing her nerve, Aria began to run, swinging around the corner into the Calle del Pestrin, stumbling on the uneven paving stones. She was almost sobbing with relief as she reached the restaurant; with her hand on the doorknob she turned for one last look, but there was no monster looking at her from the swirling fog, only silence. Shaking her head and telling herself she was an overimaginative fool, she went inside.

Corte Sconta was a pocket-size cafe that had become famous for its superlatively fresh, imaginatively cooked seafood. Fashionable Venetians had soon discovered it and it was now so busy, its simple red-checkered tables were hard to come by. Aria glanced around eagerly for Orlando, but he wasn't there.

"You have a reservation, Signorina?" the young proprietor asked her.

"I think so," she said hopefully. "Signore Messenger?"

He studied his list. "Sì, Signorina, at ten o'clock. The Signore is not here yet," he said, escorting her to her table. "You would like a drink while you are waiting?"

"Aria!" Orlando hurried toward her, his blond hair beaded with mist. "I'm sorry I'm late. I can't believe this fog! I stopped a dozen times to ask directions and I still got lost!"

"Well, at least now you're here," she said, so glad to see him that she'd forgotten all about her fright. "I should have warned you, it's a bit out of the way."

"That's okay." He grinned at her. "I'm too used to stepping into a taxi and just telling the driver to take me there. In Venice you have to use your own two feet and your sense of direction to get where you are going!"

"But that's half the fun," she told him severely, "no cars, no fumes, no noise . . . that's part of Venice's beauty."

"You're right," he said, taking her hand across the table, "and *you* are the other part. You look lovely tonight, Aria. You know, I've been meaning to ask if you'd let me paint your portrait . . . every time I look at you my hand itches to take up a brush and capture you on canvas, the reddish highlights in your hair, those wing-shaped eyebrows." Reaching out his hand, he traced her lips with his finger. "Your lovely soft mouth . . ."

"Signore?" The waiter smiled at them understandingly. "For starters, tonight we have fresh eel," he said, "and spiny-shelled crabs, mussels, sea scallops, and some very special shrimp . . . and for the main course . . ."

They were so absorbed in each other, they scarcely heard him. "What would you like?" Orlando murmured.

"Anything at all," she whispered.

The waiter sighed, raising his eyes to heaven. "May I suggest the mixed plate for starters tonight, sir," he said rapidly, "eel, scallops, mussels, and shrimp all together with two sauces, and then maybe a salad and the sea bass . . . is very, very fresh tonight . . . And to drink, Signore?"

"To drink? Why, champagne, of course."

"But champagne is too expensive," Aria whispered.

He shook his head. "It's the only drink suitable, because tonight you're going to tell me that I can paint your portrait."

"But of course you can," she cried, delighted, "you don't need to bribe me with champagne!"

"It's no bribe," Orlando said so indignantly that the other diners glanced up, amused, "it's a celebration!"

"A celebration because you are going to paint me?" She laughed.

"No," he said seriously, "because I think I'm falling in love with you."

It was as if the busy café just disappeared the way it did onstage when the spotlight shut out everything except the two principals; their eyes locked and their hands touched across the table, and Aria felt they were alone together, just she and Orlando. "You can't mean it . . . ?" she whispered.

"But I do." He gripped her fingers tightly, staring unwaveringly into her eyes. "I've never met anyone like you before; you've turned my whole life upside down, Aria. I used to think that all that mattered was dashing around the world from one smart resort to another, and going to the smartest parties with the smartest people. My life has been superficial and stupid, and it's taken meeting you for me to realize that."

"But you know so many beautiful women," she said, "all those famous faces in the magazines . . ."

"They're women like your mother, Aria," he said. "I'm sorry, but that's the truth. Only a few of them have a heart, the rest run on calculators. I feel like a new person here in Venice, with you. I feel as though the whole future is there for me to grab hold of—now I know I can do anything I want."

"Orlando, I love you too," she murmured, oblivious to the other diners, "that's what I couldn't tell you today."

"The champagne, Signore," the waiter said, showing him the bottle.

As the cork popped and their glasses were filled, Orlando said to her, "Tonight, let's toast to a new beginning. For you, and for me."

"A new beginning," she repeated, but at the back of her mind was the sinister image of the man neither of them had referred to. Carraldo. And her mother's words of warning.

CHAPTER 25

Carraldo's office was on a discreetly smart street in Milan, and it revealed one aspect of his personality. The walls and furnishings were gray, with minimalist steel and leather chairs; a slab of polished gray granite served as his desk, and thin metal lamps cast pin-spots of light onto the work surfaces and into the eyes of any person sitting opposite him. The gallery beyond revealed another aspect of him; here the bare elm floors were bleached and the stark white walls adorned with bold modern canvases from the young artists he was sponsoring. But there was another more dimly lit sanctum—the soft underbelly of Antony Carraldo, where he kept his recent acquisitions, the priceless Impressionists and old masters in which he was an international dealer, and which were the only things he truly loved. Or had loved—because now he was so insanely infatuated with Aria Rinardi, he could no longer concentrate.

Picking up the copy of *Il Giorno*, he reread the report of Claudia Galli's death, and that her brother, the world-famous financier Pierluigi Galli, had been arrested and charged with her murder. He was being held here in Milan without bail pending further inquiries. Carraldo knew Claudia; he'd met her several times at parties in Paris and New York. She was the sort of woman you always saw at those expensive "charity galas" and "openings," though she was more attractive than most because she wasn't merely a too thin clotheshorse. Claudia had had flesh on her bones and curves that she'd displayed honestly and flamboyantly. She had given him the eye once or twice and he'd known she was his for the taking, but Claudia was too indiscriminate a lover for him. Still, to die like this was sad. And it was also a little strange that it should happen now, when she and her brother were claiming the Mallory estate, and at last Claudia might be rich.

He sat back in his chair, his hands folded, thinking about Pierluigi. He'd heard he was in difficulties on the stock market, that he was drastically overextended. Only a few people in the business had suspected the depths of his troubles, but now, with Claudia dead, there seemed to be a motive for murder. Poppy's fortune.

He'd met Pierluigi briefly, just once, in New York with his sister, and he'd seemed to him like a man containing a deep anger, or possibly pain, under a veneer of coolness. Carraldo had recognized the symptoms— Pierluigi had reminded him of himself. Now he thought about him, and he wondered.

The waiter had delivered a copy of *Il Giorno* with his breakfast tray, and even with his limited Italian, Mike knew what the banner headlines were saying. Claudia Galli was dead, and her brother, Pierluigi, was in jail, charged with her murder.

Mike whistled in amazement. Who would have thought it? And with what motive? Poppy Mallory's money? But surely there would have been enough for the two of them. Then he remembered uncomfortably the look in Pierluigi's pained dark eyes, and he thought maybe it wasn't so hard to imagine after all.

When he went to the Palazzo Rinardi that night, Francesca Rinardi said she wasn't in the least bit surprised, Pierluigi had always been a strange man, but he was a proud one. "I suppose he just got tired of Claudia dragging their name in the dirt," she said unsympathetically. "She probably deserved it."

"Mama!" Aria cried, shocked.

"And what do you think then, Aria?" Mike asked.

She was sitting opposite him in the octagonal dining room, and her big dark blue eyes looked sad as she thought for a moment about her cousins. "I never really knew them, you see," she said apologetically, "they were so much older than me, and they lived so far away. I only met them once or twice. I remember thinking how pretty Claudia was . . . I'm just sorry it happened. Sorry for both of them," she added.

Fiametta served the risotto she'd prepared, despite Francesca's instructions to the contrary. She hovered in the background waiting for

Mike's opinion, looking like an aging blackbird in her frilly serving apron. "It's tragic," she sniffed, dabbing her eyes with a corner of her apron. "Claudia was such a pretty little girl, so full of life. And poor Pierluigi was always kept under his father's thumb. After their mother died, there was no love in that household. Aleksandr was a strange man, very strange. . . ."

"That's enough, Fiametta," Francesca said quickly.

"The risotto's delicious," Mike told Fiametta with a sympathetic smile, "you were right, it's the best in Venice." She nodded, satisfied, and hobbled back to her kitchen.

"I asked her to serve asparagus soufflé," complained Francesca, "but she's getting so old and doddery, I don't think she remembers."

Aria's eyes met Mike's across the table. "She's not *doddery*," she said, "and this is Fiametta's specialty. She just wanted to show off, that's all."

"Well, she certainly succeeded," Mike said with a grin. "I've eaten at the Cipriani, and Harry's Bar, and this is the best so far."

"We try to keep up our standards, despite the circumstances," Francesca said coldly.

"What *circumstances*, Mama?" Aria asked sharply. "I hate it when you talk as if we're forced to live on a crust of bread and a lump of stale cheese!"

Mike watched interestedly as they glared at each other. The two were so different—Francesca was a cold fish, and Aria was passionate and turbulent—and at loggerheads with her mother! She wasn't beautiful like Francesca but there was something far more than that, something that drew your eyes to her. It wasn't just that she was lovely, he decided; and he knew suddenly what it was that Antony Carraldo had fallen for: Aria had that devastatingly vital quality of glowing, passionate youth.

"I apologize for my daughter's rudeness," Francesca said icily as Aria smoldered silently at the other end of the table. "One's children never see things quite the way their parents do, do they? I suppose it's what's called the generation gap."

Fiametta removed their plates and served a dish of chicken cooked in lemon. "This is an old Venetian recipe," Aria told Mike; "it probably originated with the Moors or the Turks. Fiametta knows all that stuff, don't you?" she asked, catching hold of the old woman's hand as she walked by.

Mike observed the glance of affection that passed between them. "Tell me about your grandmother," he suggested. "Did you ever meet her?"

"Grandmother Maria-Cristina?" Aria said, surprised. "Goodness, no.

She died long before I was born. And I don't remember Papa ever talking much about her. Apparently she was a bit of a tart," she said cheerfully, tucking into her chicken, "always chasing after men."

"Aria!" Francesca exclaimed, scandalized. "You shouldn't talk about your grandmother in those terms!"

"Oh, come on, Mama, you know it's true," she said with a grin. "Maria-Cristina was a naughty girl, just like Poppy."

"And what about Luchay?" asked Mike. "Didn't he belong to Helena?"

"You've met Luchay? Yes, he was Great-aunt Helena's parrot. When she died, Papa brought him home for me. Isn't he beautiful?" she asked enthusiastically. "He was Poppy's parrot first, you know. He must be the only one alive who actually knew her. Don't you wonder what must be locked away in that tiny little head of his? It's like a jigsaw puzzle, we each have these little pieces that are part of the picture of Poppy's life, but there are all these bits missing. And Luchay knows them. I'll bet he knows who the real heiress is. I just hope it's me."

Mike laughed. "And what would you do with the money if you got it? I heard you want to be an artist. Isn't Orlando Messenger tutoring you?"

She blushed deeply, staring down at her plate. "How did you know that?"

"I happened to be in the Maze Gallery in London last week, and saw Orlando's exhibition. The gallery owner mentioned that Carraldo had bought a painting and that he'd asked Orlando to tutor you. I just wondered how it was working out."

"Fine," she said, "he's very good. And he'll be a great artist, one day, when he gets a chance to work properly."

"In my opinion that young man is too full of his own self-importance," Francesca said as Fiametta brought in fruit and cheese. "And personally, I don't see the value in his work. Still, Carraldo is the expert, I suppose he must know what he is doing. I certainly hope so," she added meaningfully. "I'm afraid we never have dessert in this household," she told Mike. "Teenagers put on weight so quickly, you know, and we don't want Aria to get fat before her wedding, do we?"

Aria raised her eyes to heaven, heaving a sigh. "Mama!" she groaned.

Mike grinned at her; having dinner with Francesca was like negotiating a mine field; whatever the girl did or said, her mother was one step ahead.

"I remember you said you have a villa in the country," he said. "I know you've searched it already, but sometimes an outsider can see something you might have missed."

Francesca looked up, interested. "That's true, it's a very large old house, it would be easy to miss something. Why don't you take a look?" she suggested. "You're almost like a detective—or at least your books read that way."

Aria stared at Mike thoughtfully; maybe he really could find some evidence that would prove her claim. Orlando had gone back to London for a couple of days and she couldn't see him anyway. She'd been so disappointed when he'd told her he was going; they'd been walking back across the same little bridges and narrow alleys she'd walked alone earlier, on her way to the Corte Sconta, but even though there were occasional footsteps behind them in the swirling fog, she hadn't felt the least bit frightened—not with Orlando's arm around her. To tell the truth, she hadn't even thought about it, they'd stopped so often to kiss.

Aria shivered happily at the memory of his lips on hers; she'd felt so warm and relaxed with him, not like when she was with Carraldo. And they loved each other so much, even though they'd only known each other a few weeks. Of course, she couldn't tell her mother yet, Francesca would never believe in love at first sight.

But now she was at a loose end and eager to do anything she could to help Mike because she so badly wanted Poppy's money. Then she would be free from her mother, and Carraldo, and she could help Orlando— because Carraldo surely wouldn't, once he found out!

"I'll take you to the Villa d'Oro, if you like," she suggested. "I could show you around."

"For once that's a good idea," her mother agreed. "Why don't you arrange a time with Mike. And I certainly hope you come up with something, because Aria really needs it," she added, smiling at her daughter.

Aria had had a dental appointment the next day and they finally met the day after at the car park at the Piazzale Roma. She was there before him, waiting in the little white Fiat, muffled up in an expensive sheared-beaver jacket dyed deep green, with a huge bright blue scarf that matched her eyes.

"Hi," Mike called as she opened the door for him, "my, you look pretty today."

"It's the jacket," she said with a grin. "Mama insisted I buy a fur so I could look 'respectable' when I went out with Carraldo, so I got this. Of course she was furious, she'd wanted me dripping in mink, I suppose, but this is my style. Anyway, it cost a fortune," she added, as she negotiated her way through the traffic on Venice's periphery, "so we'd better find something at the villa today that proves I'm the heiress, or else I'll have to marry Carraldo so Mama can pay for it!"

She laughed, but Mike could see she wasn't amused. He thought of Lauren Hunter, struggling to make ends meet in order to look after her baby sister, and wondered if after all, Aria was just a spoiled little rich girl. "I don't know whether I know you well enough to ask you this," he said carefully, "but exactly why are you marrying Carraldo?"

Aria glanced at him, wondering if she could trust him. After all, he was working with the lawyers in Geneva; perhaps she should be more careful what she said. But she liked him; there was something trustworthy about such all-American ruggedness, and he was attractive, too, in his own way. Not like Orlando, of course—but who could compete with his beauty? And of course Mike was an older man—he must be at least thirty-five or -six. Deciding it would be all right, she told him the story of Francesca's "illness" and the arrangement with Carraldo. "I haven't seen him in the last few weeks," she said finally. "We were supposed to announce our engagement the very day the heiress ad appeared in the newspapers. He was in London and called to say he couldn't get back in time, and so of course the engagement was delayed. Then when Mama and Fiametta told me that *I* was the missing heiress, I knew I might not have to marry him after all. I've only spoken to him once or twice since, and I told him I wanted to wait. He was very nice, he understood, but . . ."

"But?"

"I think he was hurt," she said softly, "I think he really cared."

There was silence for a while and then Mike said, "Fiametta told you you were the heiress?"

She glanced at him with a smile. "You don't think I'd believe my mother, do you?"

"And what about Orlando Messenger?" he asked, waiting for her to tell him that she knew Orlando was also a claimant to the estate.

She blushed, gripping the wheel tighter. "Orlando's very nice," she said quickly. "I know Mama doesn't think so, but I believe he'll be a really great artist one day. And obviously Carraldo thinks so, too, or else why would he help him?"

Why indeed? wondered Mike. He'd tried to contact Orlando yesterday at his *pensione*, but they'd told him he'd left for London and wouldn't be back for a few days. Aria obviously didn't know about his claim and he wondered why Orlando hadn't told her. Did he think Francesca would be angry and have an excuse to fire him if she found out? Or that Aria was so desperate to get the money, she wouldn't want him around? Surely not, because from the look in her eyes and those blushes, there was already romance in the air!

One thing was certain, though. Carraldo knew Orlando was claiming Poppy's estate—because Carraldo was the kind of man who would make it his business to find out; he'd want to know what chance Aria stood of receiving the inheritance, and if he wanted her as badly as it seemed he did, then he wouldn't want her to win. Mike would bet his boots that Carraldo would do anything rather than let Aria get Poppy's money. And from what he'd heard about him, he'd also bet Carraldo wouldn't take it lightly if Aria made a fool of him by running off with another man. She'd better be careful; she was playing a very dangerous game.

The little Fiat was skimming along Route 21 to Treviso when she said suddenly, "Mike, are you a proper detective?"

"I'm an investigative journalist," he told her, "but I suppose you could call me a sort of detective."

"Then will you help me?" she asked, putting her foot down and overtaking an enormous truck, waving to the driver as she pulled back into her lane. "I think I'm being followed. There's a black Peugeot behind the truck, he's been on my tail ever since the Piazzale Roma."

Mike glanced back over his shoulder just as the black car appeared around the side of the huge truck, and then swung back into the lane behind them.

"You see, I told you so. Every time I overtake so does he, and yet he never tries to pass me. I've been driving slower giving him leeway, just to test him."

Mike peered at the car again; the driver, his face hidden by a dark, peaked chauffeur's cap, was keeping a steady pace behind them. "It's a main highway," he said, "maybe he's just taking it easy on his way to Treviso."

"It's not only that—I think I'm being followed in the streets too." Aria's eyes were frightened as she told him about the footsteps in the fog. "And yesterday—even in the daytime—I had the feeling I was being watched. You know, that sort of eerie prickling sensation in your spine. I went to the theater last night with my mother and I swear someone followed us home. The streets were still busy and I kept looking over my shoulder, but how could I tell? It might have been any one of a dozen people. But I *knew* he was there."

"Did you tell your mother?"

"Of course not; she'd never let me out of the door if she knew."

"But why would anyone want to follow you?" he asked, thinking of Carraldo.

"It's common knowledge that I'm supposed to be Poppy's heiress," she told him, "it's been reported in all the Italian newspapers. I thought maybe somebody was trying to kidnap me!" She glanced at him, and then through the rearview mirror at the little black Peugeot, still keeping steadily behind them. "I'm scared, Mike."

He thought of Claudia, murdered just a few days ago, and Pierluigi in jail, and now Aria thought she was going to be kidnapped—or worse. All for Poppy Mallory's money. The inheritance that had seemed such a blessing was becoming a curse. "Let's put him to the test," he suggested, "pull into the highway café up ahead."

Switching on her indicator, Aria swung the car onto the service road and parked in front of the gas station and café. They both turned to stare behind them, waiting to see if the black car would follow, but it didn't appear. "Maybe I was wrong after all," Aria said with a nervous little laugh, "my mother always said I had too vivid an imagination."

"Let's take a break and get a cup of coffee anyway," he suggested.

They leaned companionably against the counter sipping foaming hot cappuccino and sharing a wedge of rich chocolate cake. "Let me ask you something," Mike said suddenly, "does Carraldo know about you and Orlando?"

Aria stopped in mid-bite; there was a little piece of chocolate icing on her lips and she licked it in nervously. "What about Orlando and me?" she asked defensively.

"You know . . ." He shrugged.

"No, he doesn't," she said in a small voice. "I've only known myself for a few days. Anyway, how did you know?"

He grinned. "I didn't, it was just a feeling. You have to do something about that blush of yours."

She blushed again, staring at her feet, and he debated whether to tell her about Orlando but decided against it. Maybe Orlando would tell her himself later; he certainly didn't want to interfere in the course of true love. "You don't think maybe Carraldo has you followed, do you?" he asked instead.

Her head shot up and she stared at him, astonished. "Carraldo wouldn't do a thing like that! He trusts me. As far as he knows, he has no reason not to."

Mike nodded. "Okay, then let's be on our way."

He kept an eye out for the little black Peugeot, but there was no sign of it, and Aria seemed to have forgotten about it by the time they arrived at the Villa d'Oro.

"It's magnificent," he exclaimed. The impressive driveway ended in a circle in front of the cream stucco villa. A flight of stone steps flanked by pediments supporting full-height classical busts of Roman maidens, their arms extended in welcome, led to a wide portico supported by four marble columns. There were three rows of square windows edged with dark green shutters arranged symmetrically on either side of the massive double doors, and four more classical marble statues stood at each corner of the flat roof.

"It's beautiful," she agreed, "but there are others far more magnificent. If you ever saw Palladio's 'Rotonda' near Vicenza, you'd know what I meant. But let's go in, we must get to work."

The villa was exquisitely furnished with Venetian antiques, but it looked dusty and unlived in, and Mike noticed that there were large, pale gaps on the walls where paintings had once hung.

"They're on loan to a museum," Aria explained. "We couldn't afford to insure them any longer and anyway the house is not kept at the right temperature and humidity level to preserve them."

A man in a cloth cap appeared in the hall and she introduced him. "This is Alfredo; he and his wife look after the place. I think it used to have thirty servants in my great-grandfather's day, but very few people can afford that luxury now."

"We were expecting you, Signorina," Alfredo said. "The Baronessa telephoned. She said to have lunch ready at one-thirty."

Aria laughed. "Trust Mama not to forget her social obligations. Well, Mike, where shall we start?"

"How about the study?" he suggested, but he knew as soon as he saw it that it was a lost cause. The study was neat and tidy and the desk was immaculate, with fresh writing paper and envelopes, and stamps in little drawers, ready for the serious business of letter writing.

"Why don't we walk through the whole house and see if you get one of your 'feelings' about things," Aria said, smiling mischievously at him. She really was so pretty, he thought, following her up the stairs; he couldn't blame Carraldo and Orlando for falling in love with her.

"The villa was renovated at the turn of the century," she told him. "That's when the Rinardis got their hands on the Konstants' money and boy, did they spend it. Apparently it was almost a ruin by the time Felipe Rinardi got to work on it. He restored all these wonderful wall reliefs and the ceiling frescoes, as well as taking care of the rising damp and the drains. It's a pity, really, that it's slipping back again. Mama wants to put it back into shape, though, when we get the money."

Mike noticed she'd said "when we get the money," not "if," even though there was no real evidence yet to back up her claim. He followed her through bedrooms and dressing rooms, bathrooms and sewing rooms, upstairs salons and downstairs morning rooms, gun rooms, boot rooms, sculleries and butler's pantries. . . . Not to mention the library, the grand salon, and the dining room with a table that would seat thirty and a chandelier that must have weighed several tons, where they ate a simple lunch of pasta and salad and cheese, with a bottle of the local wine to wash it down.

"What about the attics?" he asked as they sipped their coffee afterward.

"The roof is almost flat, so there are no real attics, just servants' rooms. I don't think anybody's been up there in years."

"I've heard that before," he said, thinking of Hilliard Konstant. But when she showed him the musty corridor and the series of small, boxy rooms furnished with decrepit iron bedsteads and cheap wooden chests, he knew she was right. Unlike at the Rancho Santa Vittoria, there was no treasure trove here.

The light was already fading as they climbed back down the pine staircase into the kitchen quarters. "Perhaps we should try the library," he said, "we may get lucky," but he didn't hold out much hope. The Villa d'Oro had been cleaned of its family debris over the years and little personal remained that was of interest.

"My father always used to work in here," Aria told him, sitting behind a solid, workmanlike desk in the library. "This was his desk. Mama hates it; she always wants to get rid of it or hide it somewhere less prominent, but I won't let her." She glanced at Mike, her mouth soft with sadness. "You would have liked my father. He died when I was only six, but I can still remember him. I remember sitting on his knee, here at this desk, and the day he brought Luchay home. And I remember going to his funeral, holding Carraldo's hand. Funny, I thought Carraldo was so strong then, and that he was there to protect me. It just shows how wrong you can be," she added bitterly. Shrugging away her memories, she walked to a shelf and removed a large leather album. "Would you like to see Angel's bridal photograph?" she asked. "And there are pictures of her children too."

"I sure would," Mike said eagerly.

"Here she is on her wedding day." Aria pointed to a faded sepia print of a lovely blond girl in a cloud of tulle veiling and a radiant smile. "She was very beautiful," she said with a sigh. "None of the children really resembled her at all, unfortunately. And this is my grandmother Maria-Cristina. And this one is Helena."

Mike stared at the elusive daughters curiously. They were alike and yet they weren't; Maria-Cristina was very blond with bright, sparkling eyes and a lively, alert expression; while Helena's huge, unfathomable eyes stared, unsmiling, at the camera. Her hair was blond, too, though a shade darker, and she had none of her sister's sparkle.

"And this is Aleksandr," Aria said, showing him a stained brownish photograph of a boy, aged about six, standing stiffly to attention in a Norfolk jacket and breeches, with a magnificent pair of shotguns in a case on the table beside him. There were several more pictures of Angel and her daughters as they grew older, but none of Aleksandr, and none of Angel's husband.

"I think she tried to divorce him," Aria said, "anyway the story is she went back to live in California and didn't return here until after he died. Nobody seems to know too much about it, more's the pity, because if they weren't so prudish about hiding their scandals even from their own families, we might know the truth now."

"It's beginning to come together, though," Mike said, assessing the scraps of information he'd gleaned from each of the people he'd met. All he needed was a few more clues and he'd be able to piece together the next slice of Poppy's life. He just knew there had to be *something* here, but he needed more time.

It was already dark outside and there was a sudden flurry of sleet against the windowpanes. "It's getting late," Aria said. "We must be getting back."

"Couldn't we stay?" he asked suddenly. "We haven't even started in here yet."

She hesitated. "My mother wouldn't like it, not without her or Fiametta here as chaperone. I'll tell you what, Mike, why don't you stay? I'll ask Alfredo and his wife to make up a room and look after you. Then you can work as long as you want."

"Maybe I'd better come back with you," he said doubtfully, remembering how frightened she'd been about being followed.

"Don't worry, I'll be all right," she reassured him. "I'll take a water taxi from the parking lot at the Piazzale." He waved her good-bye uneasily, feeling maybe he should go with her, but the library and the big house with its tightly kept secrets lured him too strongly. He needed to know about Poppy.

Alfredo had built up the fire and drawn the heavy green velvet drapes in the library, and there was a silver tray with a fresh bottle of Jack Daniel's and a decanter of brandy on a small table. Mike stood by the fire, trying to visualize the Rinardis here at the turn of the century. The beautiful Angel and her handsome husband, and later the children. He knew quite a lot about Angel now, and even Poppy—up to a point. The one person he knew nothing about at all was Felipe Rinardi.

He sat in front of the fire, sipping his Jack Daniel's and thinking about Felipe, the man who had masterminded the renovation of the Palazzo Rinardi and the Villa d'Oro—no expense spared, even though it wasn't his own money he was spending; and the man who had ruled his household with such a rod of iron, they'd all hated him.

Then he prowled the room, searching the leather-bound volumes on the shelves that ran from floor to ceiling. On a shelf under *R* he noticed several marbelized paper boxes, like small files, marked *Paolo Rinardi— A Study of the Lives of the Romantic Italian Poets.* Pulling out the boxes, he carried them to the desk, the very same desk where Paolo had sat to write these pages—his life's work. It had probably all been bundled up by Francesca and pushed away on a shelf, to be forgotten forever.

Opening the first box, he inspected the contents. The pages were handwritten in a tight, closely knit script and Mike's shaky Italian was no match for it. Putting them back, he opened the other two boxes, leafing through their contents. The third one seemed to contain Paolo's notes and references and he glanced through it, not expecting to find anything of interest, until he noticed that some of the pages were written in English.

It was a letter and the first page was headed *The Rancho Santa Vittoria*, in big, sprawling writing. It began: *My dear Maria-Cristina, it seems a long time since I heard from you. Please write and tell me that you and Helena are all right. I worry about you, I'm always wondering what you are doing. Today I'm feeling particularly sad and lonely because I saw someone who used to be my friend—more, she was a sister to me. I know I've never mentioned her before, but now I want to tell you about her. Sometimes you remind me of her, and I wonder what it is that makes women like you so different from women like me. Is it genetic; a link from your father or your mother? Or is it pure chance, or circumstance? I'm telling you about her now because I want you to know that although I always believed in true love, I'm now older and wiser. I know that love can fade, or it can die—killed by a cruel heart, and the unjust actions of another. Now I'm left with only my love for you and your sister, and poor sad Aleksandr. Look after your sister, Maria-Cristina, she needs your help. She's not like you, able to take care of herself. Because I protected her too much, she has never developed the tough veneer that you have. But now I'm going to tell you about Poppy, so that you will know what happened between me and your father . . .*

There were a dozen more pages and Mike turned them over quickly, searching for the signature at the end. *Your loving mother, Angel Konstant Rinardi,* she'd written, in the old-fashioned manner.

He held the pages in his hand, almost trembling with excitement. He had the answer at last, right here in his hands. Maria-Cristina had handed the letter on to her son, Paolo, and he'd kept it—in case his children should ever need to know the truth.

Pulling the lamp closer, he pored over the pages of flowing script, absorbed in what Angel had to tell her daughter. After half an hour, he sat back in his chair, analyzing what he had just read. It wasn't the complete answer, not totally, because it was from Angel's point of view and she hadn't told her daughter all of the truth. But it filled in the next chapters of Poppy's life.

CHAPTER 26

Florence had been hot and Rome impossible, and now even Venice shimmered under a breathless haze of heat as Poppy, alone again on one of her secret afternoon walks, crossed the Piazza San Marco and stepped into the cool, welcoming dimness of Florian's. Taking a seat at a little round marble-topped table by the window, she ordered a glass of iced tea and began to read Greg's letter again. It was a nice letter, she decided with a sigh, the kind of letter any brother might write to his sister—except for the end where he said: "Don't forget me Poppy. And don't forget I love you." The trouble was that she really *loved* Greg, too, but it wasn't with that soaring-on-eagle's-wings love that she'd always imagined existed. Sighing, she tucked the letter into her purse and with a questioning finger to her slightly parted lips, she turned her attention to the tempting array of pastries displayed on silver cakestands.

"I recommend the hazelnut torte, Signorina," Felipe Rinardi said in English.

Poppy's eyes opened wide. "But how did you know I was American?" she gasped.

"A simple process of deduction, Signorina. You are obviously not Italian—though you have the coloring of a masterpiece by Titian; you are not haughty and cold like the French—though you are wearing a very chic Parisian dress; you are not Nordic or German—though you have their height. And you are not English—though you speak almost the same language."

She laughed appreciatively. "That's very clever—and thank you for your recommendation, but I think it's too hot today for cake."

"Then why not try a dish of *granita*? It's the best water ice in the world. I should be delighted if you would allow me to order you some— after all, as you are a visitor to my country it's my duty to show you the very best it has to offer."

Poppy's eyes sparkled; of course, Aunt Melody had expressly forbidden them to speak to strangers, especially men—but then, Aunt Melody was sleeping away the afternoon in her shuttered room at the Gritti Palace and didn't even know she was here. And he was so *very* handsome. He looked the way she'd always imagined a starving artist might look, tall and slender with prominent cheekbones that left romantic hollows around his beautiful greenish eyes. His thick fair hair fell smoothly across his forehead and the hand he held out to her across the café table as he introduced himself was as fine and long-fingered as a musician's.

"Of course, it wouldn't be right for you to accept without first being introduced," he said. "The Barone Felipe Rinardi, Signorina." Then his firm fingers gripped hers and his lips brushed coolly across her flesh, sending a little tremor up her arm. "Obviously a lady doesn't usually speak to a stranger in a café," he added with a charming grin. "But I can offer two impeccable references. My family is one of the oldest in Venice; and I've been coming here, to Florian's, since I was an infant. If you wish, you can check with the waiters about my respectability!"

Poppy laughed delightedly as he waved an arm for the waiter. "Carlo," he called. *"Una granita cioccolata per la bella signorina."* Then he said, *"Permesso?"* And without waiting for her reply, he took a seat beside her on the red banquette. Poppy gazed at him warily. "Let me guess where you come from," he said. "It must be some deep forest glade in the northernmost part of America where the sun never penetrates to warm your skin? Or no, no . . . there is a hint of southern warmth lurking there, too, perhaps, in the Mediterranean blueness of the eyes and the shape of the mouth . . . and are those freckles I see like gold dust along the bridge of that perfect nose? It's the southern states then? The land of bayous and moss-covered oaks and plantation houses . . . but no, you do not have the proper 'lazy' quality of a true southern belle." He sighed dramatically. "I must confess—I am lost. And I don't even know your name."

"It's Poppy," she told him, dazzled.

"Poppy? But how wonderful, it's the perfect name for you. Poppy, *che bella*. But . . . Poppy who?"

"Poppy Konstant," she said instantly, blushing a fiery red as she did so.

"Konstant? That's a very unusual name," he said as the waiter placed a dish of chocolate *granita* in front of her.

Poppy stared down at it unhappily. She really shouldn't have said that, but it had just slipped out somehow, as though all her longings to be a Konstant had finally come true. "It's Russian," she murmured, "the original name was Konstantinov."

"Russian? But no, you don't look Russian either." Felipe smiled. "Taste this," he ordered, "and tell me if it is not the very best thing in the whole world on a hot afternoon in Venice." He lounged back against the banquette, arms folded, watching her as she took a tiny spoonful. Poppy glanced at him sideways with a catlike slyness that was almost flirting. "You still haven't guessed where I'm from," she said, licking the chocolate from her lips with a small, pointed pink tongue.

"California?" he hazarded.

She gasped, "But how did you know?"

"Where else could it be? Of course you are a true California poppy—and just as beautiful as the flower you were named for."

Poppy glanced at him shyly from beneath her lashes, unsure whether he was teasing her, but he looked quite serious. She wished desperately that she had watched the older girls more closely at the dances in Santa Barbara, so that she'd know what to say when a man told you you were beautiful, but instead she was tongue-tied. Despairingly she scooped up another spoonful of chocolate ice.

"Poppy," he said, looking serious, "will you please have supper with me tonight?"

"Oh, but I can't!" she cried. "Aunt Melody doesn't even know I'm out alone." She dropped her eyes, thinking, damn, now I've done it, he'll think I'm just some silly schoolgirl with a chaperone and that I'm much too young for him. . . .

"Then why not invite Aunt Melody along?" he suggested, smiling.

"No, oh, no . . . well, there's my sister, too, you see. Angel."

Felipe laughed. "Angel, Melody, Poppy? Where do you find such charming names? The Konstants must be quite a lyrical family! But why not invite Angel too."

"No . . . please," she whispered, agonized, "I can't. Aunt Melody wouldn't allow it . . . she'd never take her eyes off me if she knew I'd been out, let alone that I'd spoken to a strange man."

Removing the spoon, Felipe placed it on the table and took her hand in his. "But I *must* see you again, Poppy," he murmured, gazing into her eyes. "It would be unfair of you to say no. I've never met anyone like you before. Please, tell me when we can meet."

Poppy's knees felt weak; she couldn't breathe; it was as though the whole world had stopped and there were just the two of them, isolated in this corner of Florian's; nothing else existed. "Tomorrow," she whispered, "here in Florian's." Then, as panic swept over her at her daring, she gathered up her purse and hurried to the door.

"Tomorrow, Poppy," he called, rushing after her. "At the same time then . . ." He watched as she sped lightly along in the shadow of the colonnade until, with a last shy backward glance, she disappeared into the labyrinth of alleys off the Salizzada San Moise.

"Barone, *perdone* . . ." the waiter murmured, holding out a silver platter with the bill.

"Put it on my account, Carlo," Felipe replied casually as he sauntered through the door.

"But Barone, there is still last month's bill as yet unpaid . . ."

Felipe frowned. "Nonsense, Carlo, of course it will be paid . . . eventually, as always."

"*Sì*, Barone," the old waiter muttered, shaking his head regretfully as he pocketed Felipe's tip. He'd known several generations of Rinardis and their fortunes never seemed to improve!

"Poppy, whatever is the matter with you?" complained Aunt Melody, over dinner at the Gritti Palace that evening. "You've sighed three times in the last five minutes and I swear you've dropped your fork at least as many times!"

"Sorry." Poppy sat up straight and tried to concentrate on what she was doing, but somehow her mind kept slipping back to Felipe and their meeting that afternoon, and his wonderful greenish eyes, so deep and long-lashed that when you looked into them you felt you were drawing back the curtains on his soul . . . and somehow she knew that Felipe's soul must be a very romantic one. . . .

"Poppy!" prompted Angel as the waiter hovered, waiting to remove her plate.

"Oh, sorry . . . sorry . . ." she said again, startled from her dream.

"Well, girls, shall we take a stroll in the Piazza?" suggested Aunt Melody. "The evening is warm and I could use a breath of air."

"Oh, yes, yes please," cried Poppy rushing through the vaulted hall to the door before Aunt Melody could change her mind. Maybe, just maybe she might see Felipe there.

As they approached the Piazza, they could hear the little orchestra playing popular melodies and she hurried ahead, impatiently.

"I declare, Poppy," cried Aunt Melody irritably, "you are like a racehorse heading for the finishing post! We are out for a stroll, my girl, not a four-furlong gallop!"

"Sorry," she apologized again. "Angel, don't you fancy an iced drink, or maybe a *granita* in Florian's? It's so hot," she added, fanning herself extravagantly with her hand.

"Why not?" Angel agreed amiably. "I feel quite breathless with the heat."

"I think we'll try Quadri's," declared Aunt Melody, leading them firmly to the café on the opposite side of the Piazza.

"Ohh," wailed Poppy, throwing a despairing glance at Florian's long plate-glass windows.

"Whatever's the matter, Poppy?" asked Angel, surprised. "Both cafés seem about the same to me."

"Oh . . . it's just that someone told me they had the best chocolate *granita* at Florian's," she replied, forcing a smile.

"Chocolate *granita*?" inquired Aunt Melody. "What is that?"

"It's the most delicious water ice you ever tasted, Aunt Melody," Poppy said quickly, hoping she'd change her mind, "I promise you, you'll love it."

Aunt Melody's eyebrows raised a notch. "And how do you know so much about Florian's *granita*, might I ask? Since you've never been there?"

Blushing, Poppy tried to cover her tracks. "I suppose someone at the hotel must have told me . . . but of course they could be wrong. . . ."

"Never trust a recommendation unless you know the person's character," Aunt Melody said, settling into one of Quadri's comfortable basket chairs, "but if it's *granita* you want, I'm quite sure it will be just as good here."

"Poppy," whispered Angel as Aunt Melody turned her head to listen to the orchestra, "you're behaving very strangely. What are you so excited about? And where did you go this afternoon?"

Poppy hesitated; one part of her longed to tell Angel of her meeting with Felipe, but another part wanted to keep it to herself. Later, she promised herself, she would tell Angel everything, but for now it was her own magical secret.

"Oh, I just went to Florian's," she whispered back. "I suppose it's the heat that's making me restless." But as she spooned up her *granita* she tried to imagine again that it was Felipe sitting opposite, smiling at her with that confident faintly sardonic look, telling her she was beautiful as a Titian, and kissing her fingers lightly with his cool firm lips. And she simply couldn't wait for tomorrow afternoon to come.

Poppy tried the snug little cream jacket and tobacco skirt that Madame Monet had copied from an original Worth design and decided it was too elaborate. Flinging it aside, she tried a yellow ruffled dress made by Miss Matthews and decided despairingly that it made her look too young! A simple white silk shirt and a dark green skirt seemed the only answer, and piling up her red hair, she skewered it hastily with a dozen pins. She was late as she hurried along Venice's quiet afternoon alleyways and across the tiny bridges, pushing back the rebellious tendrils of hair that fell in her eyes and stuck to her cheeks, already moist with heat.

The clock on the Campanile tower showed ten minutes past three as she half walked, half ran into the Piazza, smoothing back her hair nervously and slowing to a discreet stroll as she drew nearer. With her heart in her mouth in case he wasn't there, she peered through Florian's glass-paneled door and then went in.

"Poppy! I'm so glad. I thought you weren't coming!"

Felipe's greenish eyes shone with sincerity as he took her hand in both his, looking at her as though she was just the most wonderful girl on earth. Again Poppy felt as though he'd swept her into his privileged, private world where only she and he existed. Her eyes locked with his, she murmured, "I'm sorry I'm late. It was for the most foolish of reasons. I just couldn't decide what to wear."

They took a seat at the same table . . . *their* table, thought Poppy, as Felipe called the same black-moustached waiter, Carlo, to bring *"Una granita cioccolata per la bella signorina."*

"I was here, in the Piazza last night," she said shyly, "I looked for you . . ."

"Ah, but I wish I had known!" Felipe exclaimed. "Last night I had dinner with my uncle at our country villa. It's my refuge from Venice's summer heat. It's a fairy-tale place, Poppy. It has the most beautiful gardens in the world, full of waterfalls and secret grottoes. And one day," he added proudly, "the villa and its gardens and all the estates will be mine." What he didn't tell her was that the wonderful gardens designed and planted by his forebears were overgrown, that the vast estates with their tumbling cottages and farms and vineyards were unproductive from years of neglect, and that the sagging roofs of the villa let in the rain.

"The fairy-tale villa will be yours?" Poppy repeated breathlessly. She thought he must have forgotten he was still holding her hand, and embarrassed, she let it lie there in his warm fingers.

He nodded. "My father and mother died when I was seven years old. Uncle Umberto brought me up at the Villa d'Oro, and at our two palazzi, here in Venice."

"You have *two* palaces?" she gasped.

He shrugged modestly. "One is the Rinardi palazzo, the other came to the family by marriage. Sadly, it has been allowed to crumble into disrepair. It costs so much to maintain these old buildings; the winter floods always take their toll and the ancient pilings, the very foundations on which they've stood for centuries, are rotting away. I'm afraid it takes all the family money," he added apologetically.

"But for such a good purpose," Poppy replied earnestly. "I can't imagine anything more wonderful than living in a palace with a front door onto the Grand Canal, and your own private gondola moored to one of those beautiful striped poles. Felipe, you must live in one of the wonders of the world!"

He squeezed her hand delightedly. "Then why don't you come and see the wonders of the Palazzo Rinardi from the inside, as well as from the Grand Canal," he suggested. "It's been there since the fifteenth century and I promise you, it has a magic all its own."

Poppy's small silver dish of *granita* melted into a chocolate puddle as she continued to gaze at him, entranced. "Fifteenth century," she breathed. "*Nothing* in California is that old!"

Felipe put up his hand to brush a strand of hair from her eyes. "Tell me about yourself, and about your home in California. I can't imagine what it must be like there."

A little tremor of pleasure shot through her veins as his fingers touched her face. And California seemed so far away, as she told him about the sparkling white ranch house with its flower-burdened courtyard, its tinkling Mexican-tiled fountain, the lavish stables and her wonderful Arabian mare, Rhanee, whom she missed dreadfully; she told him about the vast acres of the Rancho Santa Vittoria and the cattle roundups and the lambing. She told him about their house on De la Vina Street and the hayrides and beach picnics. And she told him about Rosalia and Nik. *"My parents,"* she said proudly, because by then, in her story they really were.

"And then there's Angel," she added. *"My sister."*

"Your younger sister?" Felipe asked lazily.

"No, oh, no. We are both eighteen," she replied without thinking.

"Both?" he said surprised. "Then you are twins?"

Poppy blushed uncomfortably, caught out in a lie that she'd almost believed. "I . . . yes . . ." she lied miserably. "Angel is the elder . . . by just a little."

"And?" queried Felipe, raising his brows.

She eyed him nervously. "And . . . what?"

"And . . . who else is there?"

Of course—how could she ever have forgotten him! "There's Greg," she added quickly, "my brother."

"You can't know how much I envy you," Felipe sighed wistfully. "When my parents were drowned in a boating accident in the Adriatic, I went to live with Uncle Umberto. You can't imagine how lonely I was, Poppy. My uncle is a bachelor and he spent more time in Paris and London than he did with a small boy in the depths of the countryside."

"I'm so sorry," she breathed, her blue eyes brimming with sympathy as she imagined the beautiful little boy, alone in his opulent country villa. She was so caught up in his life that she'd completely forgotten her own intolerable childhood.

Felipe shrugged, managing a brave smile. "But that's in the past. And today, I am here in Florian's with the most wonderful girl I've ever met in my life."

Poppy stared down at the chocolate puddle of *granita* in the silver dish, not knowing how to reply. "You must know so many girls . . ." she murmured, blushing.

"Indeed I do. But not one like you, Poppy." Embarrassed, she made no reply, and calling for Carlo, Felipe pressed a tip into his palm, dismissing the bill.

Taking Poppy's arm he guided her across the Piazza to the Riva degli Schiavoni and she sighed with both the pleasure of his touch and relief at the whisper of breeze that lifted her hair from her warm brow, as they strolled together beside the Canale di San Marco.

Clutching her wide-brimmed straw hat, she looked out over the lagoon, at the islands of Giudecca and San Giorgio floating like a mirage on the horizon. There was a timelessness about Venice, shimmering and dreamlike in the summer heat, that sent a shiver down her spine. "There's an ancient magic about this place," she whispered entranced. "Venice is like a lover who wraps his arms around you and promises never to let you go. Even though you must go away, you know you will always return—" She stopped suddenly, horrified by what she'd just said, not knowing where the words had come from, and hardly daring to look at him.

"Ah, Poppy," Felipe murmured, pressing her hand, "such love is *true* magic."

Poppy met Felipe every afternoon, but still she refused to allow him to meet Angel and Aunt Melody. When she wasn't with him she was torn by the web of deceit she was weaving, yet she wanted to keep him all to herself. For the first time in her life she had a person who was all her own, whom she shared with nobody.

Felipe took her to see the Palazzo Rinardi in all its fifteenth-century glory on the Grand Canal. A silent-footed servant opened the door, disappearing as quietly as he had come, leaving them alone in the lofty marble hall. They wandered hand in hand through the grand salons and Poppy gazed admiringly at the frescoes and the inlaid furniture made from precious woods. She ran a wondering finger across the cool marble surface of a statue unearthed from an ancient Roman villa, and stepped delicately across priceless silk rugs worn thin through centuries of use. Felipe told her that on festive occasions, such as a wedding, all the great Murano glass chandeliers were lit with thousands of candles and the palazzo was reflected in a million points of light in the Grand Canal . . . "like a diamond in the moonlight."

Poppy lingered at the top of the sweeping marble staircase, staring at the portraits of long-dead Rinardis, searching their faces for a resemblance to Felipe, seeing his fair hair in one, his greenish eyes in another, thinking how wonderful it was to be able to look at them and know exactly where you came from. She turned away with a pleased sigh.

"You are so beautiful, in that simple white dress," Felipe said as she walked slowly down the stairs toward him, "with your cool skin and fiery hair you look as though you had stepped from a Titian painting." His voice shook with emotion as he whispered, *"Poppy, you belong here, in Venice. Oh, my darling, I'm very much afraid I've fallen in love with you."*

Poppy's eyes were starry as his arms encircled her. "Oh, yes, Felipe," she sighed happily, "yes, I love you too." And as Felipe kissed her she knew this must surely be true love, because she heard the eagle's wings and her blood pounding as she soared to new heights of emotion.

Time was rushing by and their stolen innocent afternoons must soon come to an end. Poppy didn't know how to tell Aunt Melody and Angel, but she just put it from her mind, praying that some miracle would happen to make it all right.

She had discovered a whole new world of sensuality and she wanted nothing more than to be in Felipe's arms; she wanted the touch of his hands on her face, on her throat, the pull of his fingers in her hair as his lips claimed hers; and she'd found she wanted even more—her whole body craved his touch and she felt out of control. But though she felt him tremble with passion, Felipe never went any further than just kisses.

"You either seem on top of the world or down in the dumps these days," Angel complained. "I don't know what's the matter with you, Poppy. And where *do* you go every afternoon anyway?"

"Oh, just exploring," she said airily, "round and about Venice."

"You must know the city better than the natives by now." Angel sighed. "Personally, I shall be glad to get back to Paris in the fall when all the parties begin. It's so dull here—just old buildings, old paintings, old churches. And water! *I can't wait to meet some attractive young men.*"

There were only two afternoons left and Poppy was filled with despair. Only two afternoons of stolen kisses as they drifted along Venice's silent afternoon waterways in a curtained gondola, with only the swish of the gondolier's oar and the lap of tiny waves to disturb their privacy.

"Please meet me tonight, Poppy, I can't bear to be without you even for an hour," Felipe begged as they drifted back toward the San Marco Giardinetti landing stage.

But Poppy already told him it was impossible; they were to attend a reception and dinner at the apartment of the American consul that evening and she was already worried that Aunt Melody would have woken early to prepare herself for the party. Neither of them mentioned it, but they both knew as she hurried away across the Piazza that they had only one more afternoon together.

"It seems such a waste," complained Angel, surveying herself in the mirror as Poppy buttoned her into Monsieur Worth's fabulous sapphire gown. "I should be wearing this dress to some wonderful ball, not to dazzle some boring old diplomat."

"Never mind, you look quite gorgeous in it," Poppy replied, staring at her in admiration. "Oh, Angel, sometimes you are just *so beautiful,* it takes my breath away."

Smiling serenely, Angel clipped a tiny diamond butterfly in her smooth blond hair. "Then the dress is even more of a waste, just think of the effect it might have on some handsome young Frenchman." She glanced at Poppy in her molten gray velvet gown, her red hair sleeked into a gleaming topknot. "You look quite lovely yourself," she told her, "like a cascade of mercury warmed by your burning red hair . . . in fact you're positively *glowing* lately. *Exactly what* have you been up to on these hot afternoons while the rest of us are dozing in our beds? I refuse to believe you've been looking at yet more paintings and more statues. Come on now, Poppy, tell me! You look as if you're just *bursting* with a secret."

"Oh, Angel," Poppy gasped, her eyes sparkling. *"I'm in love!"* She heaved a sigh of relief as the truth tumbled out at last; she was sure suddenly that if she told Angel *everything*—about her stupid lies, about pretending she was her real sister, and about Felipe and how much they loved each other—then magically everything would be all right. "He's wonderful," she bubbled happily, "I met him in Florian's and we've seen each other every afternoon since and—"

"Are you two girls ready?" Aunt Melody swept into the room, resplendent in purple lace, five rows of large pearls clasped around her plump neck, and a confection of net and feathers perched atop her silver hair. "My goodness," she exclaimed, surveying them through her lorgnette, "I have to admit that Monsieur Worth is worth his money!" Her plump rouged cheeks quivered as she laughed helplessly at her own small joke . . . *"Worth* and *worth,"* she repeated, wiping her eyes. "Anyway, darlings, you both look wonderful. Come on now or we'll be late!"

"Tell me everything later," Angel whispered excitedly as she hurried them from the room.

The American consulate occupied the ground floor of a magnificent palazzo and the consul general's apartment was on the *piano nobile,* the first floor with the grandest rooms. The ceilings of his gilded salons soared to lofty carved beams, ornamented three centuries ago in brilliant blues and purples and gold that were still unfaded by time and Venice's damp. And beneath a dozen candlelit crystal chandeliers milled a throng of elegantly dressed guests, glittering with jewels.

"Thank God for Monsieur Worth," whispered Angel, awed. *"Imagine* if we'd been wearing Miss Matthews's frills and rosettes tonight!"

It was true, Poppy thought admiringly, each woman seemed more elegant than the last and they were simply dripping with rubies, emeralds, and diamonds. The tiny row of seed pearls given to her and Angel on their seventeenth birthdays faded into oblivion beside the baubles on display.

The American consul, Osgood Barrington, was waiting to greet them at the top of the curving marble staircase. "So pleased you could come, Miss Abrego," he said with a smile, "and I'm delighted to meet your charming nieces. I'm only sorry I was away and we didn't manage to get together earlier, I could have introduced them to the young Venetian society. Still, never mind, perhaps they'll come back again soon."

Osgood Barrington was a friend of Felipe's uncle and it had been an easy matter for Felipe to gain an invitation to the party. He was drinking a glass of champagne, but his eyes were on the staircase, waiting for Poppy to arrive. When he finally saw her, he realized she was no longer the breathless simple girl of those hot stolen afternoons; Poppy was a smoldering elegant vision in simple gray velvet that breathed Paris couture and money. His eyes dwelled on her creamy alabaster flesh, the thrust of her breasts, and the curve of her tiny waist beneath the dove's velvet. And then he noticed her sister. If Poppy was a sensual dream, then her sister was a vision—pale and blond as a moonlit night, petite and with a profile of such beauty, it made him gasp. Was it his imagination or did the whole room fall silent as they gazed at Angel?

He made his way toward them purposefully. "Osgood," he said, smiling calmly, "won't you introduce me to your charming guests?"

"Well, now, Miss Abrego," beamed Osgood, "*this* is exactly what I meant. Here is Felipe Rinardi—the *Barone* Rinardi, I should say, and he's just the sort of young person your girls should be meeting. Felipe knows *everyone* in Venice. Felipe, this is Miss Abrego, visiting from Santa Barbara, California," Osgood said, "and her nieces, Miss Angel Konstant, and Miss Poppy Mallory."

In the silence that followed, Poppy knew she would die; her heart was thudding so loudly she thought they would hear, and she shrank against an ormolu side table to steady herself, afraid she was going to faint. *Mallory . . . Mallory . . . Poppy Mallory . . . the hateful name rang over and over in her head.* Her lies were finally exposed and she stared at Felipe, desperately afraid of what he would say.

But Felipe's eyes passed over her without a flicker of recognition. He bowed deeply and almost, but not quite, allowed his lips to touch Aunt Melody's hand. "I am at your service, Miss Abrego," he said, "and I would be delighted to show you the sights of Venice."

Aunt Melody gazed approvingly at him through her lorgnette. "Young man," she boomed, "I've seen enough sights these past two months to last me a lifetime. A pity we didn't meet you earlier; it would have been a good deal easier on my feet! However, I'm afraid it's too late; we plan on leaving the day after tomorrow."

"Oh, Aunt Melody," Angel protested, quickly looking at Felipe, "perhaps we might decide to stay just a little while longer? After all there's so much we haven't seen yet, and who knows when we might be back in Venice."

Aunt Melody stared speculatively at her niece and then at Felipe.

"Hmm," she said, sweeping grandly into the salon, "we'll see my girl, we'll see."

" 'We'll see' always means no," Angel whispered to Felipe with a sigh.

"You could try a little persuasion," he grinned, taking her arm and following Aunt Melody.

Poppy stood as if turned to stone as they disappeared into the crowd. Felipe hadn't even given her a second glance; he'd simply gone off with Angel as though she didn't exist. It was as if all those stolen afternoons had never happened, all their kisses, the held-back passion, the words of love . . . had been meant for *Poppy Konstant* and not *Poppy Mallory*.

"My dear, are you all right?" Osgood Barrington asked worriedly. "You look awfully pale."

"Please," whispered Poppy, her blue eyes dark with anguish, "*please*, would you tell Aunt Melody that I suddenly felt faint . . . that I've returned to the hotel . . ."

"Why not let me call her?" he asked, alarmed.

"No! No, please. It's nothing really, I'll be all right . . . and I don't want to spoil their fun . . ." Poppy's soft gray velvet skirts swirled around her like a dove's wings as she fled down the stairs and into the night.

"Poppy? Poppy, are you awake?"

She shut her eyes even tighter, pretending to be asleep as Angel hovered over her anxiously.

"Oh, dear," wailed Angel, "*do* tell me you are all right, Poppy."

"Where is she?" demanded Aunt Melody, bustling into the room. "Darling girl, are you feeling better? What is it? Food poisoning, I'll bet, you can't trust this foreign food, you know . . ."

Poppy sat up wearily. It was no use feigning sleep; with Aunt Melody shouting in her ear only the dead could remain still. "I think it must have been something I ate," she admitted in a small voice, "but I'm quite all right now. Except for a headache." It was true, her head *did* ache, but it was nothing compared with the pain in her heart. She would rather have been mortally wounded in combat than die of the wound Felipe had just inflicted. And the terrible thing was that she couldn't even die, she would have to live and carry this pain with her forever.

"But you look terrible, child," exclaimed Aunt Melody. "I'll speak to the manager at once and ask him to call a doctor."

"No! No, please," she cried. "I assure you, Aunt Melody, I'm all right now."

"Well, you look to me as though you've had the stuffing knocked out of you," Aunt Melody said bluntly. "I wonder if we shouldn't leave Venice as we'd planned after all. This heat is really very unhealthy."

"Oh, Aunt Melody, you promised," cried Angel, bubbling with excitement. "Isn't it wonderful Poppy? *We're staying on!* Felipe Rinardi—the *Barone* Felipe Rinardi—has promised to show us the city. *'His city,'* he calls it, and from what he tells me he owns a good part of it. *Two* palazzi, Poppy—and a wonderful old villa with acres and acres of vineyards and farms. He's even asked us to stay there with his uncle Umberto. And, of course, Felipe inherits everything when his uncle dies."

"You certainly seem taken with him," Aunt Melody commented indulgently, "though I have to admit he's a very charming young man, and I suppose things have been a bit boring lately for you two girls." She glanced at Poppy again worriedly. "If you're quite certain you're all right, I'll take myself off to bed. My feet are killing me!" Wrenching off her tight purple satin slippers, she hobbled to the door. "Sleep well, girls," she called gaily, "tomorrow is another day."

"Oh, Poppy," Angel cried as the door closed behind her. "Felipe is *so* wonderful, *I'm afraid I've fallen head over heels in love.*" She threw herself onto the bed, laughing and kicking up her heels in a flurry of sapphire silk chiffon. "And I thought it would be a waste of time to wear my Paris gown! Didn't I tell you the effect it would have on some romantic Frenchman? Well, Felipe may not be French, but he's certainly romantic so it's the same thing. He has the most interestingly *haunted* face, Poppy, sort of like a starving musician. If only you could have seen the way he looked at me, as though I were the only girl in the whole entire world . . . oh, he's just wonderful, *wonderful.* The boys in Santa Barbara seem so juvenile compared with him. Didn't you think him handsome, Poppy? Did you notice that his eyes were a *true* green? 'Mossy' is how I would describe them . . . goodness, here I am talking like a Shakespeare sonnet, I *must* be in love. . . ."

Poppy turned her face to the wall, clenching her jaw to keep the tears from coming, the way she had years ago when Papa failed to return.

"Poppy? Aren't you excited for me?" Angel asked anxiously. "Oh, I'm so selfish!" she wailed suddenly. "*Of course,* your *poor* head. Wait, I'll get a cold cloth." She dipped a linen towel into a jug of cold water on the bedside table and held it to Poppy's head. "This will make you feel better, I promise you," she said. "Oh, Poppy," she added with a happy sigh, "it's all going to be *such fun!*"

There was no need for Angel to hold the cold compress to Poppy's head; she was already as cold as ice. Her web of lies and deceit had come tumbling around her ears when she'd been introduced to Felipe as Poppy

Mallory—that hateful, hurtful, *shameful* name! "Poppy Konstant" did not exist. And neither would she now ever become, as she had in her dreams, Poppy Rinardi. Felipe had chosen Angel instead. And how could any man resist her, Poppy asked herself wearily. She was so very beautiful. And, of course, she *was* Angel Konstant.

CHAPTER 27

1 8 9 8 ,   I T A L Y

Poppy lay in bed the next morning, one arm flung over her eyes trying not to watch Angel dressing in her best to meet Felipe, but there was nothing she could do to cut off her endless excited chatter.

"Shall I wear the yellow, Poppy?" worried Angel. "Or does it make me look too pale? Maybe the pink would be better. Or how about this plain white silk blouse and a dark blue skirt? Yes, I think after Monsieur Worth's extravaganza, it's better to be as simple as possible." Throwing a heap of clothes onto the bed, she changed her outfit yet again. "*Oh dear!*" she moaned, sitting in front of the mirror and struggling to capture her silken hair into a knot, "this humidity does impossible things to my hair; it simply won't stay up. Poppy, do you think it'll be all right if I just tie it back with a ribbon?"

"You're late," Poppy said quietly, "he's been waiting fifteen minutes already."

Angel glanced despairingly at the clock. "Goodness, then this will just have to do. Still, it's a woman's privilege to be late, and anyway Aunt Melody is with him. Do I look all right?" she asked anxiously.

"You look wonderful, as always," replied Poppy, burying her face in the pillows as the knife twisted again in the wound, remembering how *she had* worried what to wear, and whether *she had* looked her prettiest for Felipe.

Angel flung herself on the bed beside her. "Do you *really* think he likes me, Poppy?" She asked wistfully, *"Really* likes me, I mean? Last night seems so far away, almost as if I'd dreamed it all. Oh, *I do wish* you were coming too, it's too bad you have this hateful headache. I shall miss you so."

She hugged Poppy compassionately, then, bouncing from the bed, she hurried to the door, turning with her hand on the latch. "But I completely forgot," she cried. *"Of course!* You were going to tell me about the man you'd met. *Your secret lover!* Oh, my goodness, I can't wait to hear all about him! What fun that we've both fallen in love at the same moment, Poppy! Remember to tell me the *instant* I get back!" And blowing a handful of kisses, she flew from the room.

Poppy's breakfast tray remained untouched on the table in the stuffy darkened hotel room. The bitterness of her rejection and the desolation of her loneliness brought memories of her childhood, and she trembled as though she really had the fever she'd complained of, going over and over Angel's excited snatches of conversation again, searching for some small reference to herself in Felipe's words. She considered asking Aunt Melody whether Felipe had mentioned her, but it was so obvious that all his attention had been focused on Angel that she knew it was pointless.

There had been a posy of violets on Angel's breakfast tray that morning, and with it a note reminding her that Aunt Melody had given him permission to escort her on a tour of Venice's wonderful churches. Naturally, Aunt Melody had been invited along as chaperone, but there had been no mention of Poppy in that note.

The lonely morning hours ticked by as slowly as a funeral procession. A maid came to take away Poppy's tray, and another brought her the light lunch Aunt Melody had ordered, returning an hour later to remove it again, untouched. At last Poppy heard the excited sound of Angel's voice from the corridor and then the door was flung open.

"Goodness, Poppy, you're still in the dark," Angel cried, rushing to the window and flinging open the shutters, "and it's such a *beautiful* day! *Oh Poppy, it's the most perfectly wonderful day!"* She perched excitedly on the edge of Poppy's bed, her eyes full of dreams as she remembered. "We went to the church of San Sebastiano where Veronese is buried and saw all his lovely paintings, and then to Santa Maria della Salute on the Grand Canal, and San Giorgio Maggiore—you know, the one on the island that seems to float across the horizon—and Santa Maria della Pietà, where Vivaldi was concert master from 1709 to 1740. Poppy, Felipe knows *everything* about Venice. And you know what he said to me when Aunt Melody wasn't listening?" Her voice dropped to a whisper.

"He said, 'Venice is like a lover who wraps his arms around you and promises never to let you go, so that even if you go away, you know you will always return to his arms!' "

Poppy gasped in horror as she heard her own words repeated, but Angel didn't seem to notice. "Isn't that just too romantic for words?" she asked. "And then afterward, Poppy, we had this enormous lunch at a little restaurant he knows on the Zattare, just a trattoria really, with red-checkered tablecloths, but so charming. And oh, Poppy, the *food*—real Venetian risotto and tiny spiny-shelled crab and that delicious chocolate *granita* you told us about."

Pausing for breath, she regarded Poppy anxiously. "Are you feeling better? I do hope so because we are all to go to the Teatro La Fenice tonight for the symphony. *Do* say you can come." Her lovely eyes clouded with concern as she noted Poppy's miserable face. "But you still look so pale! Aunt Melody is right, you must see a doctor."

"No, really, I'm all right," Poppy replied, forcing a smile.

"Then please say you'll come, I'm just dying for you to meet Felipe, I swear he gets more handsome every time I look at him. And you know something," she murmured dreamily, "when he looks at me it's not the way men usually do—*you* know what I mean. It's not just that I'm a pretty girl—he makes me feel 'special.' " She sighed happily as she began to undress. "Well, I suppose I must rest before tonight. Perhaps I shall sleep and dream of Felipe. Oh," she cried suddenly, clapping a hand to her mouth, "but Poppy, you were going to tell me about *your* secret lover! Come on, now, tell all!"

"Oh . . . it was nothing," stumbled Poppy, "nothing like . . . like you at all. Just someone I saw in Florian's . . . someone I . . . admired from a distance. It wasn't important . . ."

"What a shame." Angel sighed. "Still, maybe it's for the better, falling in love is so *exhausting*. I can't wait for tonight . . . and Felipe . . ." she added, smiling dreamily as she climbed into bed.

Poppy tossed and turned, listening to Angel's quiet, even breathing as she slept the afternoon away. First she told herself yes, she would go to the theater tonight; she would force Felipe to look at her, to acknowledge that she existed, that what had happened between them was real . . . and then she'd tell herself no, she couldn't go through with it—she couldn't humiliate herself again. But in the end, she knew she must see him.

She wore a somber dark red silk dress that made her hair glow with subdued chestnut lights, and she looked pale and composed as she followed Aunt Melody and Angel downstairs to meet Felipe. She thought she saw a flicker of concern in his eyes as he noticed her, but decided she must have been mistaken when Aunt Melody said in her booming voice, "Did you meet my other niece last night? Poppy Mallory? Of course, she's not really a niece, but we all think of her as Angel's sister."

"Aunt Melody, of course Felipe knows all about Poppy!" cried Angel. "You remember? I told him over lunch."

"Oh, dear, I must be getting old," sighed Aunt Melody as Felipe bowed to Poppy without meeting her eyes. "I seem to forget so many things these days."

"I'm pleased you could join us, Miss Mallory," he said politely.

"Poor Poppy has been so ill," Angel told him as they walked through the foyer to the hotel landing stage where a gondola waited. "We're just so relieved she's feeling better."

"Venice in the summer can be very tiring," Felipe commented, adding cryptically, "and it can play strange tricks on people's perceptions."

Poppy bit her lips to keep back her tears as she and Aunt Melody floated off in their gondola, leaving Felipe to follow with Angel. She remembered the secret afternoon rendezvous and their passionate kisses and Felipe's declarations of love, and she told herself this couldn't be happening, it was all a bad dream. Soon she would wake and everything would be all right again.

The foyer of the beautiful little theater was already crowded as they made their way to their seats in one of La Fenice's painted rococo boxes. Somehow she and Aunt Melody had lost Angel in the crowd and she searched the aisles anxiously until she finally saw them. Felipe's hand was resting possessively on Angel's arm as he whispered something in her ear, and Poppy's heart sank even farther into despair as Angel turned to gaze at him. Her face was so radiant with love for him that her beauty lit up the theater, and Poppy had to bite her lips again to stop the sobs that threatened. She scarcely noticed the pain; her whole being was crying out that Felipe was *hers*, that he loved *her* . . . not Angel . . .

The orchestra was already playing the opening bars of Tchaikovsky's *Romeo and Juliet* overture when Angel and Felipe finally slipped into their seats beside her. She stole a sideways glance at them, but Felipe's eyes were fixed on Angel's delicate profile.

Poppy closed her eyes as the romantic, sensual music filled the theater, feeling each chord with every fiber of her trembling being; now she understood all the passion and the pain and the despair of Shakespeare's young lovers. She had no idea of how she got through the rest of the evening, torn between her desire to run as far away from Felipe as she could and a despairing need to be near him, even though he had eyes only for Angel. Sheer willpower kept her upright in her velvet chair, seemingly absorbed in a Bach symphony, but inside she was crumbling.

She remained in her seat during the interval while the others drank champagne in the lobby. Her hands were knotted together so tightly that the knuckles showed white, and she closed her eyes to block out the scene.

"I don't like the look of you at all, darling girl," Aunt Melody whispered when she returned. "I've given Angel permission to go on to dinner with Felipe and some of his friends, but I intend to take you back to the hotel and call a doctor."

Poppy hung her head wearily as their gondola drifted back through the warm darkness to the Gritti Palace. Lights sparkled along the banks of the canals and the cafés were crowded; she could hear snatches of music and conversation and laughter, but she felt isolated, as though all the city's beauty and happiness were meant for everyone but her. Without Felipe, Venice, and life, were meaningless.

"The Signorina needs a tonic," the hotel doctor declared, smiling at her good-humoredly. "She's obviously not used to the heat. A fresher climate might do her good, the lakes, perhaps, in northern Italy. Yes, yes, that should put the color back in her cheeks. Other than that, Signorina Abrego, I can find nothing physically wrong with her."

"The lakes." Aunt Melody sighed longingly. "I should be quite pleased to breathe a little cool, fresh air myself. But oh, dear, Poppy, Angel is not going to like this one little bit!"

Angel didn't like it; she stormed, she protested, she cried, and finally Aunt Melody capitulated, arranging for her to stay with friends of Osgood Barrington's, where the Contessa herself agreed to chaperone her.

Poppy couldn't decide whether she felt relief or horror as the train rattled its way north; she just knew that her heart was broken and she would never be the same again.

Aunt Melody settled herself contentedly on the terrace of Signora Rossi's small *pensione* on the border of Lake Como while Poppy wandered the gardens at the water's edge in a daze, trying not to think about Angel.

The *pensione* was delightful and its proprietors took her under their wing, cosseting her with good food and encouraging smiles, but she scarcely noticed. One morning three weeks later Signor Rossi appeared on the terrace waving a telegram, and as she read it Poppy could almost feel Angel's excitement. *Felipe has asked me to marry him,* she'd written, *we are so in love—hope you approve and will convince Mama and Papa that he is suitable . . . Love, Angel.*

A month later Nik and Rosalia arrived in Italy intent on quashing Angel's sudden romance, despite Aunt Melody's protestations that Felipe was a charming young man, and that all he lacked was money. "We're not about to lose our daughter to some European fortune-hunter," thundered Nik, but Angel just smiled at him confidently. "Wait till you meet him, Papa," she said.

At their first meeting Felipe charmed them expertly with exactly the right mix of respect and frankness. "Of course the boy has no money," Nik said as he walked with Poppy through the overgrown but still beautiful gardens of the Villa d'Oro a few days later, "but that's hardly his fault. This mess was created by his ancestors. Felipe has good sensible ideas, he knows what needs doing and he's prepared to work hard to achieve it. Yes, I must say I like his spirit." He glanced affectionately at Poppy, clinging to his arm as though it were an anchor in a stormy sea. "And what do you think of Felipe?"

"I . . . the villa is so beautiful," she murmured evasively, staring longingly at its faded rose-colored walls and mossy tiles, picturing herself as Felipe's wife and mistress of the Villa d'Oro . . . but that role was now assigned to Angel.

Rosalia and Nik gave their consent to the engagement and Angel flourished the beautiful heart-shaped diamond ring Felipe had given her. "It was his mother's," she told Poppy, "it's been in the bank vaults for years. Of course, they weren't allowed to sell it even though they needed the money because everything really belongs to the family trust. Lucky for me!" she laughed, twisting it admiringly this way and that to catch the light. "And Poppy, we're so in love, we want to get married right away. . . . *Do* help me to persuade Mama and Papa to let us have the wedding here instead of returning to Santa Barbara. Can you just imagine how romantic a wedding must be in Venice? Felipe says we'll sail to the church in a gondola and the reception will be at the Palazzo Rinardi —and of course *you* will be my only bridesmaid."

Poppy sank even farther into despair as a visit to the Paris salon of Monsieur Worth was hastily arranged to purchase Angel's wedding gown and her trousseau. She barely noticed that she was back in the city she had once thought so wonderful, and she no longer had the desire or energy for the solitary afternoons she'd spent earlier, discovering a different Paris from the one Aunt Melody and the tour guides had shown her.

In between fittings for her white satin and lace dress, Angel fretted about being away from Felipe, confiding in Poppy all the secrets of their romance until she thought she would go mad. Nik had been more than generous in his marriage settlement and she and Felipe would be able to begin work restoring the villa and the estates as soon as they returned from their honeymoon in New York, and the big reception in Santa Barbara, where she would introduce her new husband to her family and friends.

In Paris, Poppy burned with resentment as she endured the fittings for her pale green silk-taffeta bridesmaid's dress, imagining herself walking down the noble aisle of Santa Maria della Salute behind Angel, the beautiful bride. *Why?* she asked herself, angrily pacing her room at the Hotel Lotti while Angel was out on yet another shopping expedition with Rosalia. *Why* has he chosen Angel instead of me? Was it her beauty? But Felipe had been entranced with the way *she* looked. Hadn't he told her he was captivated by her white skin, the blueness of her eyes, her Titian hair? Hadn't she felt his body tremble with passion for her? Angel had told her that Felipe's kisses were so gentle that she wasn't in the least bit afraid . . . In fact Angel told her *everything*. Suddenly she knew the answer. Of course, it was simple! Felipe was poor and Angel was the heiress!

With a tremendous feeling of relief, Poppy rethought the sequence of events. It was all so clear now, she couldn't imagine why she hadn't realized it earlier. Of course Felipe still loved her, but he needed Angel's money! Oh, poor, poor Felipe, didn't he realize that with love as true as theirs, they didn't need money? They could manage . . . she would help him . . . surely there would be a way. . . .

She glanced helplessly out of the window. Paris had suddenly become a prison and she couldn't wait to get back and see Felipe; she wanted to tell him that there was no need to marry Angel, that she loved him and she knew he still loved her and that everything would be all right.

There was just a week left before the wedding as at last the train carried them back to Venice, and Poppy thought guiltily of Angel with her glorious wedding dress and her sumptuous trousseau packed into the brand-new Vuitton cabin trunks in the baggage van, and her plans for her future already bubbling excitedly from her lips. After all, Poppy reassured herself, wasn't it better for Angel *not* to marry a man who didn't love her? At Venice's Santa Lucia railway station she hung back silently as Angel flew into Felipe's waiting arms, only this time it was pity she felt, not jealousy.

Angel's extravagant trousseau and her lavish purchases overflowed from their shared hotel room until she was forced to move into a separate suite along the corridor. "It's all going to change now, Poppy," she said seriously as her new cabin trunks and valises, hatboxes and shoe bags, were wheeled down the hall by the porters. "Remember when you first came to Rancho Santa Vittoria? Mama had prepared a special room of your own and you told her you'd rather share with me. Oh, Poppy, I've just realized we shall never share a room together again and I shall miss you so. I'll miss all our secrets, all our silly girlish confidences in the dark. This has all happened so suddenly, sometimes it frightens me. Poppy, *promise* you will come back to Italy to visit me. I can't bear to be without you." Bursting into tears, she flung her arms around her. "I love Felipe so much," she sobbed, "but I love you, too, and suddenly California and home seem so far away."

"Don't cry Angel," Poppy murmured soothingly, "everything is going to work out just fine, you'll see. Maybe it'll all be a little 'different' than you expected, but it will be for the better."

Angel glanced up at her, puzzled. "Whatever do you mean?"

Poppy shrugged, turning away to avoid her clear, direct gaze. "Oh, I don't know . . . it's just that sometimes things are not really the way they seem, people do things for the strangest motives . . ."

"Poppy, you're talking in riddles," Angel cried, exasperated. "But whatever you mean, I'm still going to miss you. And Greg," she added soberly. "It's so sad that he can't be here for the wedding, but Papa says that someone has to be home to look after the ranch. Still," she added, cheering up, "I'll see him when we're home on our honeymoon."

Poor Angel, Poppy thought as she disappeared with the last of her packages down the corridor. *Poor, poor Angel, I do so hate to hurt her.* Walking to the mirror, she studied her reflection, pinching her pale cheeks to bring color to them and patting her upswept hair into an even smoother chignon, wondering if Felipe would still think her beautiful after Angel.

The whole week was devoted to a round of parties and receptions, but this time instead of avoiding Felipe, Poppy went out of her way to stay close to him, catching his eye across a table, touching his arm in passing, glancing sideways at him, a slight smile lifting the corners of her mouth as her blue eyes signaled her message. . . .

Uncle Umberto, tall, urbane, and immaculately tailored, had opened up the Palazzo Rinardi for its first grand party in years. An army of workmen and cleaners had been hard at work putting the palace to rights, ready for the ball and the lavish wedding reception, which would take place two days later, and which more than four hundred distinguished guests would attend. The palazzo's tall windows sparkled with the light of a thousand candles shimmering like a reflected moonlit dream in the dark waters of the Grand Canal, just the way Felipe had told Poppy it always did for special celebrations.

Poppy was frantic; she still hadn't managed to find an opportunity to speak to Felipe alone. Poor Felipe, she thought as she mounted the stairs where he was waiting to greet his guests, to be forced into marrying a girl he didn't love in order to save his heritage. But she would rescue him from all that. There was a desperate gleam in her eye as she smiled at him, because it was a fact that they had not exchanged a single private word since that terrible night at the consulate when his glance had seemed to wipe her from the face of his earth.

She wondered if it was her imagination, as she caught his eye yet again, or was he really glancing her way more often tonight? Hope lifted her heart and she thought desperately that maybe he, too, had finally realized that marrying Angel for her money was wrong. That he loved her as madly as she loved him, and that he couldn't live without her. Like a gray shadow in her molten velvet gown, she sat quietly amid the chattering partygoers, awaiting her opportunity. And when she finally saw Felipe murmur an excuse to Angel and make his way to the door, she headed quickly across the room, grasping his arm determinedly.

"Felipe," she whispered urgently, "I must talk to you . . . now . . . tonight."

"What is it you want?" he snapped, pulling her quickly into an alcove. "I thought you understood what had happened. After all, it was your own fault."

"*My* fault?" she cried, bewildered.

He pushed her farther behind the curtain. "I can't talk to you here," he whispered angrily, "but in any case there's nothing further to say."

"But I *must* talk to you, Felipe, *I must see you alone.*" Her blue eyes beseeched him and for a moment he hesitated. "It's no good," he said abruptly, "it's over. It never even began!"

Poppy's hand flew despairingly to her mouth as she watched him go . . . he couldn't mean it, she told herself, if only they'd had an opportunity to talk together alone then she could have made him see that marrying Angel was wrong—when they loved each other so.

It was very late when the family finally returned to the Gritti Palace in the gondola. Rosalia and Angel drooped tiredly against Nik, and Poppy sat opposite, watching them through hooded eyes. Such a happy family scene, she thought bitterly, the mother, the father, and the beloved beautiful daughter. Closing her eyes, she remembered her real father's arms around her and his whiskey breath in her face as he'd said, *"I'm back, Papa's girl . . ."* and then his blood spilling onto the rug as he'd sunk to the ground. And she realized that after all these years she still wasn't Poppy Konstant, she was just Poppy Mallory, and Angel possessed everything she'd ever wanted.

Afterward, she paced her hotel bedroom, thinking about Felipe until the walls seemed to be closing in on her. Unable to bear it any longer, she flung a dark cape over her shoulders and stole from her room, running down the flights of red-carpeted stairs as though she were pursued by demons.

"The Palazzo Rinardi," she told the gondolier, shrinking nervously behind the curtains. She was still not sure of what she would say as she tugged at the old iron doorbell, praying that Felipe was there. She just knew she had to talk to him, to explain, to tell him she belonged to him before it was all too late. Trembling with fear at her own daring, she rang the bell again and again until at last there was the sound of hurried footsteps and Felipe's voice called, "What is it? Who is there?"

"It's me . . . Poppy," she called, leaning weakly against the chill stone wall, her knees threatening to give way.

Throwing open the door, Felipe stared at her in surprise. He was wearing a burgundy silk dressing gown over his pajamas and his hair was rumpled from sleep.

"Quickly, before anyone sees you," he said, grabbing her arm and pulling her inside. "What do you mean by coming here at this time of night? Are you trying to ruin things between me and Angel?" His angry green eyes burned into hers. "That's it, of course," he said contemptuously. "You're jealous! You're just trying to make trouble."

"No, oh, no, it's not that," Poppy cried. "I understand why you want to marry Angel. But you see Felipe, it's all wrong when we love each other so . . ."

"Love?" he asked, his brows raised. "*Love?* Ask yourself this, Poppy, is it *love* that you feel for me? Ask yourself exactly *why* you are here. *With another woman's fiancé!* I think you are a girl who knows precisely what she's doing," he added, leaning so close to her, she could feel his breath on her cheek. "You know enough to drive a man crazy, Poppy Mallory. Oh, yes," he added, tilting her face up to his, "don't think I don't know all about your little charade. You played the role of the Konstant heiress very well, Miss Mallory, but not quite well enough to outsmart me!"

Then his mouth came down on hers with such crushing force that Poppy gasped. "Wait, no . . ." she cried, pushing him away. "It's true, what you said. I did play a charade, but I didn't lie to you deliberately, I didn't imagine you thought I had money . . ."

"Then why else would I have bothered with you?" he asked contemptuously. "Because of your beautiful insolent eyes and your delicious milk-white skin? You're a temptress, Poppy Mallory, and love doesn't enter into that world!" He pulled her close to him again, forcing back her head as he kissed her.

"No," she cried, terrified. These weren't the same gently passionate kisses of their afternoon gondola rides; these were hard, cruel kisses that she didn't understand. "No, Felipe! I came to tell you our love was strong enough to manage without money, all we need is each other."

He laughed harshly. "You must be crazy," he said, blocking her path as Poppy backed toward the door. "You haven't come here for *love*, Miss Mallory," he snarled, picking her up in his arms and carrying her to the salon. "You are here because you want me." His hands were upon her again, exploring her breasts. "God, your skin is as smooth as this velvet," he muttered, "it's smooth as cream . . ."

"Don't," cried Poppy, terrified, "don't, Felipe . . . I shall scream . . ."

"Scream all you like, there's no one to hear." He gripped her long hair, forcing back her head as he kissed her throat. "The servants are asleep in their own quarters and anyway the walls are so thick, they'd never hear a thing . . . and my uncle has gone for the night with some lady friend . . . someone of *your* breed, Poppy. Of course you're not a Konstant, are you? You're a slut, a temptress eager to try what men have to offer, and you and I both know that's why you're here tonight."

"No, Felipe, no," she screamed as the pins scattered from her hair onto the pretty yellow brocade sofa, and then he silenced her protests with his mouth, forcing her back onto the cushions. His body pressed urgently against hers and his hands sought their way under her skirts, violating her softness with cruel intrusive fingers. Poppy screamed silently with agony and despair, and the tears she had sworn never to shed again flowed from her tightly shut eyes, staining the beautiful yellow brocade as he thrust himself into her.

The bright morning sun filtering between the slatted green shutters of her room stirred Poppy from unconsciousness—it couldn't be called "sleep" because it had certainly been no restful dreamless slumber. As she woke she felt she was climbing from the depths of some nightmarish crevasse filled with fear and despair. The pain between her legs throbbed agonizingly and her swollen breasts burned where they had been bruised by Felipe's rough caresses.

She closed her eyes again, praying it was just a nightmare, that she could just forget it all, as if it never happened, but it was no good. No matter how she tried, she would never be able to forget Felipe's words as she lay destroyed on the pretty yellow couch, her beautiful gray velvet dress ripped and stained with her own blood.

"You teasing little bitch," he'd snarled contemptuously, "you asked for it!"

Then, bundling her cape around her, he summoned a gondola, tipping the gondolier lavishly and telling him to return her to the Gritti Palace. He'd gripped her shoulders, holding her close for a moment as if he were embracing her, but instead he'd whispered menacingly, "If you ever say a word about tonight to anybody—*anybody, Poppy—I'll see you dead!*" And he'd thrust her, trembling, into the gondola.

It was very late when she got back and only the concierge had noticed her hurrying through the hall. He'd peered at her curiously for a moment and then his attention had returned to his newspaper. In the safety of her room again, she'd torn off the ruined dress and, filled with self-loathing, had hidden it in the laundry basket along with her torn undergarments. Fighting for strength to turn the heavy brass taps, she'd filled the bathtub with hot water and scrubbed the imprint of Felipe's body from her fiercely. And then, in a clean cotton nightie, she'd curled into a ball in the middle of her bed and wished she could die.

Even now, with the sun shining on another glorious Venetian day—the day before Angel's wedding—she still wished she could die. She could never tell anyone what had happened, no one would believe her. She thought despairingly that she would kill herself—she would take poison . . . but she didn't know where to buy any. . . . She remembered longingly the gun room at the ranch where the rifles, with their superbly decorated stocks, were kept in locked cases, and Nik's collection of pistols with their chased-silver and mother-of-pearl handles were displayed in a glass-topped drawer. It would have been so easy there, and a bullet would have been so clean and so fast.

She glanced up apprehensively at a rap on the door. "Wake up, you sleepyhead," Angel called gaily, "we've some last-minute shopping to do, remember?"

"Oh . . . why don't you go on without me," Poppy called, searching desperately for an excuse. "I . . . I've got this stupid headache again."

"Oh, poor Poppy," cried Angel. "The Venetian air really doesn't suit you, does it? Shall you need the doctor?"

"No, no," Poppy found herself answering in quite normal tones . . . "I'll just rest awhile, don't worry." *She realized suddenly that Angel didn't suspect anything. No one did. Only she and Felipe knew the truth.* A shred of hope shone through her despair. If she were clever, then no one need ever know her shame. Yet surely it must show on her face. She stared in the mirror, but apart from the shadows under her eyes she looked just as she always did.

She was sitting up in bed trying her best to look composed when Rosalia and Aunt Melody hurried in to see if she was all right. "I'm really getting quite worried about you, Poppy," Rosalia said, feeling her brow anxiously for fever.

"Nonsense," boomed Aunt Melody, "the girl's just lovesick, that's all!"

Poppy's eyes widened apprehensively; what could she mean?

"It must be love," Aunt Melody went on. "After all, I thought Poppy and Angel always do everything together."

"Oh, I see," Rosalia laughed, straightening her hat in Poppy's mirror. "Well, I think there's a young man at home who's more than eager to see her again. Greg was most upset not to be coming with us, but I suspect it was *you* he wanted to see more than anyone. But enough of this matchmaking, we must be off. Angel mustn't see Felipe again until the wedding, so it's just a family dinner tonight. My goodness, I'm so nervous about the whole thing—all these princes and countesses! I have awful dreams of us all falling into the canal in our wedding finery. Bye now, Poppy, we shan't be back too late. Why don't you open your window, dear, and let in some fresh air and sunshine, I don't like leaving you in the dark."

Poppy sank back against her pillows, thinking about what Rosalia had just said, and the enormity of her own stupidity hit her like a blow. *Of course, the answer had been there all the time. She could have had everything she'd ever wanted. She could be "Poppy Konstant." All she'd had to do was marry Greg!*

At three o'clock on a September afternoon, looking ethereal in her wedding finery, Angel sailed in her flower-decked marriage gondola along the Grand Canal to the great church of Santa Maria della Salute. Clouds banked the wide expanse of sky, changing the weather from blue to gray, and Venice lay hushed in a breathless prestorm stillness where every sound seemed magnified. A Bach cantata, played on the great organ, reverberated from the ancient walls, echoing over the still lagoon, and only Angel's tremulous smile lit her progress into the church.

Poppy, in swirling green silk-taffeta with fresh wine-colored roses braided into her rich hair, thought that Angel surely looked the perfect vision of a bride. Her wedding dress was of heavy white satin with a long court-train covered with a layer of delicate lace, sewn with pearls and crystal beads. The same scalloped lace encircled her long slender neck and a silk tulle veil cascaded from the Rinardi diamond tiara perched on her sleek blond hair. The veil hid the expression in her eyes as she took her father's arm for the walk down the aisle, but Poppy knew they would be shining with happiness.

Gripping her small posy so tightly that the florist's wire sank painfully into her fingers, Poppy followed them slowly down the aisle, her eyes fixed on Angel's sweeping train. When she finally dared to steal a glance, she saw that Felipe had eyes only for his bride, as, with her veil thrown back, Angel repeated her vows.

Pretend you are an actress, Poppy had told herself earlier, as she dressed for the wedding, just a minor player in some stupid drama. And so now she signed the register in a hand that she willed not to shake; and she tilted her chin and smiled proudly for the wedding photograph, and she laughed gaily along with the others at Felipe's witty speech as he proposed the traditional toasts.

"And, of course, we must all toast a most beautiful bridesmaid," he said without a trace of mockery. He raised his glass to her, but he was smiling at Angel.

When she was alone with Angel later, helping her to change into her going-away outfit of pale blue silk, Poppy was determinedly cheerful.

"First we go to Paris," Angel sighed ecstatically. "Of course, Felipe knows it as well as he does Venice; he calls it his second home, but for me it will be like discovering a whole new city. Then London . . . and then New York . . ." Tilting the little cream straw hat with its veiling and pale roses at exactly the right angle over one eye, she spun around from the mirror and threw her arms around Poppy. "I do love you, Poppy," she murmured, "you are the dearest sister any girl could ever have." And later, as she descended the marble stairway, her arm linked with Felipe's, she made sure that Poppy caught her bouquet. "You're next—and I just hope it's Greg," she whispered as she kissed her good-bye. And then, in a hail of rose petals and joyous calls of luck and happiness, Angel and Felipe sailed in their bridal gondola down the Grand Canal to the Santa Lucia station, and the train that would take them to Paris and the beginning of their new life.

The smile that had been fixed to Poppy's face since early morning faded as they disappeared from sight. It was over. She wondered if what Felipe had done meant so little to him, he had already forgotten it, because there had been no trace of remorse or guilt in his demeanor. He hadn't even glanced at her. She trembled with sudden hatred; *she hated Felipe, and she hated Jeb Mallory. The two men to whom she had given her love had cared so little for her, they had both hurt her and left her without a qualm.*

"Come on, Poppy," Nik said, throwing a comforting arm around her shoulders, "don't look so sad. We haven't lost Angel, you know, we've gained a new son."

They were to set off on their return journey to California the next morning and Poppy suddenly couldn't wait to get back. Her answer, and her future, were dazzling clear. Greg loved her. She would marry Greg.

CHAPTER 28

1 8 9 8

Greg's handsome face, smiling at her with a look in his eyes that told her he'd missed her and he loved her, lit San Francisco's gloomy railroad station like a beacon of hope. He hugged her and kissed her, and Poppy's smile held such profound relief that he laughed. "I can see you're glad to be back," he said.

"And I'm glad to see *you*," she whispered, with a surge of hope that, after all, life might not be over.

The Konstant house had never seemed more like home. As she fed her Arabian mare, Rhanee, an apple from her jacket pocket, Poppy stared across the paddock to the rolling tawny hills and the distant blue ridge of the mountains, and she thanked God for not letting her do anything foolish that desperate morning alone in her hotel room in Venice. She was home again where she belonged, and she never wanted to leave it again.

Each night when she went to bed, she told herself that Greg need never know what had happened, and finally, convinced that she was doing the right thing, she told him she would marry him.

How sweet his kisses were compared with Felipe's impassioned brutal ones, and how gentle his hands were as they caressed her hair or held her arm. But she felt listless and tired, and not at all her usual self.

When she first missed her period, she thought it must be something to do with Felipe's brutal attack and wondered if he had damaged her in some way; but she was too ignorant and too frightened to consult a doctor. When it didn't appear the second month, she told herself she must be anemic, that her whole system had been thrown off balance. Didn't they say that was something that happened to newly marrieds . . . but, of course, she wasn't married, so she couldn't ask. And then, the week Angel and Felipe were due to arrive, she woke up one morning and was violently sick.

A grand ball was held at the Arlington Hotel as the Abrego family gathered for the homecoming of the new bride and her foreign husband. "We welcome our son to our land and to our home," Nik said, raising his glass to Felipe. "To a true *noble*man!"

Rosalia thought Nik looked very Russian tonight, with his thick blond hair streaked with silver, and his eyes as clear and frost-blue as if he still gazed across the frozen Russian plains that he now saw only in his memories and dreams. But we are *true Americans,* she thought, a mixture of Russian and Mexican—and now Italian. Glancing at Poppy's pale, shadowed face, she added to herself, and Irish too, because once Greg married Poppy, Jeb Mallory's Irish blood would eventually flow in Konstant veins.

Poppy sat with her eyes downcast, fiddling nervously with the stem of her champagne glass as Felipe made a charming reply to Nik's speech of welcome. The girl is unhappy, Rosalia thought intuitively; something's wrong . . . yet there was no doubt Poppy was glad to be marrying Greg, and she'd told her only the other day how happy she was to be back home again, and that she had no more desire to travel. Still, she looked restless, nervous . . . as though she couldn't wait to escape. But from what?

Just then, the ten-piece orchestra from San Francisco began to play. Rosalia watched as Felipe swept her lovely Angel into his arms and circled the floor while the guests applauded, and for the moment Poppy was forgotten.

Angel sat on her old bed in Poppy's lamp-lit room, her legs tucked under her, spilling tales of their travels; of the restaurants in Paris and the rain in London and the wonders of New York. Poppy busied herself nervously at her dressing table, brushing her long hair endlessly, her eyes fixed on Angel in the mirror.

"Poppy," said Angel shyly, "remember our promise? That whoever got married first should tell? We-ll . . . it's not a bit like cows and sheep! Oh, Poppy, it's *wonderful.* How can I tell you? It's the most tender,

loving . . . *gentle* feeling in the world—and at the same time, it's exciting. Felipe was so sweet and understanding . . . why, it took me a
whole week to get used to it but he never rushed me, he just held me
close and soothed me and then when we finally did it, it just seemed so
natural somehow."

Her eyes sparkled at the memory and Poppy thought she must be
talking about a different man from the Felipe she knew.

"Poppy, I want to tell you first before anyone else—except Felipe, of
course, but before Mama and Papa, or anyone. Guess what? I'm pregnant!"

Poppy dropped the silver hairbrush with a crash. "Pregnant?" she
whispered.

Angel nodded happily. "Isn't it wonderful? Of course, Felipe is longing for a son to carry on the Rinardi name, but I don't mind which it is
—a boy or a girl." She glanced at Poppy's white face doubtfully. "Aren't
you pleased?"

"Pleased?" Poppy repeated, dazed. "Oh, yes, yes, of course I'm
pleased. Why wouldn't I be—it's wonderful news, Angel. But tell me
. . . how do you feel?"

Angel sighed. "That's the unpleasant bit. I throw up every morning as
soon as I set foot out of bed. In fact some mornings I'm tempted just to
stay in bed so I don't have to go through the whole nauseous feeling, but
after a while I'm right as rain again. Of course, I'm only a couple of
months so I don't even show yet, I'm still as sylphlike as you." Running
her eyes up and down Poppy's thin body, she frowned. "In fact you are
way *too thin*, Poppy. Mama said she thought you were too. Is anything
wrong?"

Poppy shook her head miserably. She'd been eating as little as possible
the last few weeks, both because of the terrible nausea and because she
wanted to stay as thin as possible to guard her frightening secret. She
simply didn't know what to do. How could she marry Greg when she was
carrying another man's child—and that man his brother-in-law? She began to brush her hair again, with smooth, automatic strokes. She was
beyond despair. Her life was in ruins and there was no way out of the
mess. Her mind dwelled again on the pretty silver pistols in the gun
room.

"Poppy, I want to ask a favor." Angel tilted her head wheedlingly. "I
know it's a lot to ask you to leave Greg again, but oh, Poppy, I do so
want you to come and stay with me at the Villa d'Oro. I shall be so
lonely there, and Poppy, now I'm pregnant, I'm a bit scared. Please don't

give me your answer yet," she said, holding up her hand, "because I know you'll say no. Just promise me you'll think it over."

"I can't bear to think of you being frightened," Poppy said quietly, "of course I'll consider it, Angel."

She lay in bed that night, thinking of Angel in Felipe's arms in the guest suite along the hall, and as she tossed and turned the germ of an idea came into her head. She went over it again and again until, as dawn broke, the plan was formed clearly in her mind. If it worked, she would be free.

The next morning she told Greg that it was her duty to help Angel; it wouldn't be fair to let her go through the difficult months of her first pregnancy without her dearest friend and sister's companionship and help. She would stay with Angel until the baby was born and then she would return home and they would be married.

"Is that a promise?" Greg asked sadly. "You promise me you'll come back to me, Poppy?"

"*I promise*," she vowed.

A week later Angel and Felipe left for Europe and a month afterward Poppy followed them. She traveled alone this time, staying mainly in her stateroom on the ocean liner and emerging only for dinner. Several of the young officers tried to make conversation with her, asking her why she didn't attend the dancing in the Palm Court after dinner, but Poppy pleaded seasickness. She wanted nothing more to do with flirtations and romance and men.

She was four months pregnant when she arrived in Italy, but she'd starved herself so that it didn't show. Angel was pleasantly buxom and blooming, and of course she was thrilled to see her, but Felipe scarcely bothered to conceal his impatience. Leaving them at the villa, he departed for Venice on what he called "important business."

"I can't tell you what a difference it makes having you here," Angel said when they were alone in Poppy's room. "Felipe is behaving so strangely, I wonder what can be wrong. Not that he's inhospitable," she added hurriedly, "but I suppose it's difficult having a wife who's sick all the time . . . oh, Poppy, if only you knew how it feels, you'd never have a child!"

"Angel," said Poppy, "I do know. That's why I'm here."

Angel laughed. "Don't be so silly, Poppy, how can you? Wait till you marry Greg, I'll bet you soon find out though."

"Angel," Poppy repeated, grasping her arm and gazing determinedly into her eyes, "how much do you love Greg?"

"Greg," Angel repeated, puzzled. "Why, I love him more than anything."

"And me?" Poppy demanded, gripping her arm even tighter.

"Of course, you too," Angel cried, alarmed.

"Good, then you'll help us. Now listen to me carefully, Angel, it's a complicated story, but unfortunately it's true. I'm in desperate trouble and if you care at all for Greg's happiness, you'll help me."

"But what is it?" Angel asked, frightened. "Whatever is the matter?"

"You remember I told you about the man I met in Venice? My 'secret lover' as you called him? I can assure you, Angel, he never was that. Oh, I hoped he might be, I was infatuated with him, I couldn't bear to be without him . . . I couldn't see his weaknesses, his faults . . . Oh, Angel," Poppy wailed, "he turned out to be a demon sent from hell. One afternoon he lured me into his apartment and then he locked the door behind me and . . . oh, *Angel* . . . *he raped me.*"

Angel's face blanched. . . . "Rape?" she whispered.

Poppy nodded. "It was . . . *it was hell.* Remember when you told me about your wedding night?"

Angel nodded, her eyes brimming with tears.

"Well, it was nothing like that . . . it was . . . *brutal,* Angel, a terrible, frightening, humiliating act by a despicable man. When he'd finally done with me, all I wanted to do was die."

"Die?" Angel repeated, terrified.

Poppy nodded. "Oh, believe me, I looked for ways. I thought of how to get hold of poison, guns, knives, anything to kill myself." She gazed into Angel's stunned blue eyes. "But Angel, I knew I didn't want to die —*because I loved Greg.* Can you blame me for not killing myself?"

"Blame you?" Angel gasped. *"Of course not!"*

"Loving Greg as I did—and because he loved me—I just knew that this had been a foolish infatuation with the wrong man, a foreigner who had preyed on my girlish romantic notions and then taken advantage of me. Oh, Angel, I thought no one would ever know, that I could put it all behind me. After all," she said piteously, "I wouldn't be hurting Greg, would I? I was still *mentally* as I had been before. You see, *it wasn't my fault.*"

"Of course not," breathed Angel, loyally.

"And then I realized I was pregnant," Poppy said slowly. "And I couldn't think of what to do."

"Oh, my God!" exclaimed Angel. "Whatever *are* you going to do?"

"That's why I'm here. Listen to me carefully, Angel. I don't want you to make any comment until I've finished. Just let me tell you my plan."

Angel nodded solemnly. "I shall go stay at a *pensione* somewhere in the Italian countryside, far away from here—a quiet place where no one knows me. I'll arrange for the baby to be born there."

"You're not going to give him away?" gasped Angel, horrified.

Poppy shook her head. "You promised not to comment until I've finished," she said reprovingly. "Now listen carefully, Angel, because this concerns you. And Felipe," she added softly. "We are both pregnant; our children will be born almost at the same time. Angel, I'm asking *you* to take my child, to bring him up as your own . . . don't you see? No one need know—it would be as though you'd had twins." Angel's blue eyes widened with shock as she hurried on, "Don't you see it's just a baby, another dear, sweet child . . . *my* child, Angel. How can I give him to strangers when he could be brought up as part of our family? *Please,* Angel, *I'm begging you* . . . take my child. Free me from this hideous burden . . . I just don't know what to do if you say no," she added piteously.

Angel stared at her, terrified. "You can't mean . . . not *suicide?*" she whispered.

Poppy dropped her eyes and stared at the rug. "What else would be left?"

"My poor, poor darling Poppy," cried Angel, flinging her arms around her. "Of course I want to help you. I *must* help you. But what shall we tell Felipe?"

"Felipe is a charitable man," Poppy said softly. "Just ask him, Angel, and see what he says. I'm sure you'll find that, because he loves you, he will agree."

It was Felipe who came back to her with their answer. "Angel insists on taking the child," he told her coldly.

"*Your* child," Poppy said quietly.

"As you are aware, that cannot be proven. However, rather than have you cause trouble in the Konstant family, I have agreed that the child will be brought up as our own."

"As he should be," she replied coldly.

"There is a condition," he said, "and Angel agrees with me on this. After the child is handed over, you must go away from here and never return."

"Naturally, I shall go home. To Santa Barbara."

There was a gleam of triumph in Felipe's eyes as he replied, "That's not what I meant, Poppy. *You will disappear! You will never surface to bother our lives again.* And if you ever try to return, I shall make it my business to inform your family that their so-called daughter has turned out to be just like her blackguard father! I will make sure that *Greg Konstant* will never want to see you again. *He* will know the truth, Poppy —about how you threw yourself at me, how you came to me on the night before your dearest friend—your *sister's*—wedding and offered yourself to me . . . how you seduced me with your wiles. . . . *No, Poppy. You will never go home again!*"

CHAPTER 29

1899, ITALY

Instinct sent Poppy back to the small, welcoming *pensione* on the shores of Lake Como, and the Rossis, the kindly Italian couple who had looked after her and Aunt Melody so well. Even though she wore the thin gold wedding band she'd purchased in Venice, she knew by the look in Signora Rossi's eyes that the woman didn't believe her story of sudden sad widowhood. Still, the Signora took her to her heart and looked after her with the same motherly kindness she lavished on her own grown-up children and grandchildren.

Poppy was treated with the proper respect due to a guest, so that on Sundays when the large family gathered, she would sit alone at her table in the window and Signora Rossi would hurry to serve her first. Then she'd excuse herself and hurry off to attend to the demands of yet another small grandchild.

Poppy tried not to watch as the excited children ran in and out, while their mamas lavished them with food and attention and love and their adoring papas looked on fondly; but they would come and peek around the door at her, laughing, and she'd feel a pang of jealousy for the family's simple happiness. She'd hurry through her unwanted lunch and then wander into the little town of Bellagio, lingering in the dim candle-lit church, searching for answers that didn't exist, and finding only temporary peace.

As the long days drifted into weeks and weeks into months, she had endless time on her hands to contemplate Felipe's revenge. Though she hoped each day for a letter, there was no word from Angel, and on the long, dark winter nights loneliness would engulf her. She'd doze restlessly, dreaming of home and Greg, whom she knew she loved so dearly now and whom she would never see again. On the sharp gray afternoons she would brave the icy winds blowing across the lake, pacing the leafless gardens restlessly, wondering how she could ever have been so foolish.

Her meager supply of money began to run low, and anxiously, she cut back on her meals at the *pensione*, taking only supper. Her body was growing clumsier as the baby grew, but she made no attempt to consult a doctor or to provide for her confinement. Signora Rossi looked worried, questioning her in her few halting English phrases, but Poppy just shook her head and pretended not to understand. It was almost as if, despite the evidence of her distorted body, she still wanted to believe it really wasn't happening.

Showery April slipped into the soft balmy days of May and, as the *pensione*'s gardens bloomed with vines and scented blossoms, she contemplated her future with dread. She tossed and turned at night, wondering where she would go, and what she would do. She had only a vague idea of when the child was due and, when the first pain stabbed tentatively at her lower back in the middle of a warm May night, she just lay there not wanting to believe it. Then the pains began to come stronger and faster.

When this child is born, she told herself, in the lull between contractions, my whole life will change. And then her agonized screams brought Signora Rossi running.

"Ah, Signora," she said comfortingly, "I felt the child would come tonight, I saw the signs in your face . . ." and she hurried to her kitchen to fetch hot water for Poppy's torn body and sheets to tie to the bedrails for her to pull on when the pains struck.

Poppy thought the night would never end, and when the dawn breeze finally crept coolly through the window, the child had still not been born. Worried, Signora Rossi dispatched her husband to bring the doctor from Bellagio. She bathed Poppy's burning forehead and held her in her arms as she would her own daughter, as the pain ripped through her again and again.

"The child is breeched," the doctor told the Rossis, his face serious. "There is grave danger she will lose it—and maybe her own life as well. Where is her family?"

Signora Rossi shrugged, lifting her eyes to heaven. "The husband is dead," she told him. "She is alone." And she hurried to Poppy's side as she screamed yet again.

Night had darkened the sky again when, with a final agonized scream that made Signora Rossi cover her ears in horror, Poppy's baby finally emerged into the world. Contrary to the doctor's predictions, she wasn't born dead; she was screaming lustily and she weighed a fine six pounds and two ounces. Poppy was too ill even to open her eyes to look at her, and the doctor sent at once to the village for a wet nurse as he began the fight to save Poppy's life.

As she hovered the next few days between dreams and reality, it seemed as though Poppy would get her wish. With nothing left to live for, she knew that God was about to free her from her mortal misery. She dreamed she was drifting slowly backward into a dark, restful tunnel where there was no pain, only peace . . . it would be so easy, she thought as eternal darkness came closer and closer . . . then her child's cries penetrated her unconscious and with it the double pain of her torn body, and all her memories returned again to torture her.

"So, Signora," said Dr. Callonio three weeks later, "you have decided to live."

Poppy glanced at him sullenly. "The choice was not mine, Signore," she told him coldly.

"Remember, poor Signora," he said kindly, "things are never as bad as they might seem. And you have a beautiful daughter you haven't yet seen." He shrugged apologetically. "We were not sure you were going to survive and felt it urgent that we baptize your child in the name of God. The Signora Rossi took the liberty of choosing her name. Helena Maria Mallory."

Poppy stared at the bland blue sky outside her window. Her child was three weeks old, she had a name . . . she was real . . . Pulling the sheets over her head, she turned her face to the wall.

"Don't despair, child," Signora Rossi said understandingly, "remember God helps us all."

But not me, thought Poppy, biting her lip to keep back the weak, anguished tears. Never me.

She peeked fearfully at the child when they finally brought it to show her. There was no sign of her own telltale red hair—she was as blond as Angel herself. With a sigh of relief she knew no one would ever tell she was not Angel's child. But even though the baby was as sweet and as pretty as any infant could be, she felt not one scrap of affection or love for it. It was Felipe's child.

She thought jealously of how different it must have been for Angel.

When her child was born, it would be all joy and love and celebrations. Asking for a pen and paper, she wrote a telegram to Angel: *Daughter born.* And then, ignoring her baby, she turned her face back to the wall again and waited for Angel to come.

Each day she looked eagerly for the man from the telegraph office in Bellagio bringing her a message from Angel, and each day she was disappointed. With the baby in her crib beside her, she paced the floor of her room at night, returning worriedly to the dresser to count the money remaining in her meager purse. The wet nurse needed to be paid as well as the doctor, and Signora Rossi, good-hearted though she was, could not be expected to give her food and shelter for nothing. . . . Oh, Angel, Angel, she thought desperately, you promised you'd take her, you promised to help.

Ten days passed and she had just about given up hope when late one afternoon the pony trap from the station at Bellagio trotted up the path. It swirled to a stop and Angel stepped out. She was wearing a silk dress in a tiny springlike flower pattern and a large cream straw hat. Her blond hair was coiffed immaculately and she wore ropes of large lustrous pearls around her neck.

"Wait here, my man," she commanded, alighting from the trap. Shading her eyes from the sun, she glanced up at the house as Poppy came flying out the front door.

"Angel, Angel," she screamed. "Oh, God, Angel! I thought you were never coming . . ."

Angel hesitated for a split second and then she opened her arms and they hugged each other tightly. "Are you all right?" she whispered, her clear blue eyes anxious.

"I don't even want to remember," Poppy replied bitterly. "And you?"

"It was a girl," Angel said, "born a month ago, like yours." She linked her arm through Poppy's as they strolled through the gardens. "Felipe doesn't know I'm here. I waited until he'd gone to Venice for a couple of nights and then I came. He wouldn't let me write to you—of course, I did, but he intercepted my letters. He even wrote to Mama and Papa and Greg . . . I don't know what he told them, but since then, Mama has never mentioned you in her letters. Oh, Poppy, why don't you let me tell her what has happened? She would help you, I know she would."

Poppy just shook her head. She knew Felipe had finally destroyed her. And now she would rather die than face Rosalia and Nik with her shame. As for Greg, he would never believe her story. No, she could never go home again.

"Felipe told me I must never see you, that he didn't want the child.

He said I must have nothing to do with you. Poppy, Felipe said such terrible things about you, things that I know just can't be true." Her blue eyes searched Poppy's for confirmation. "Felipe said you were bad, he said you were a temptress and that you had even tried to seduce him." Her voice faltered. "Please, tell me it's not true."

Poppy stirred the gravel of the pathway with her toe, avoiding Angel's honest eyes, "It's not true, Angel," she said at last.

"Forgive me for even asking you, for even thinking it might be . . ." stammered Angel. "Of course, I was *sure* it wasn't true . . . but then why should Felipe say such *cruel* things? Sometimes I just don't understand him, Poppy. Sometimes I think he's not the same man I'd married . . . the gentle, carefree Felipe of those days in Venice. He can be so *cold*, so . . . distant. You know when he seems happiest? When I'm all dressed up and dripping with diamonds, playing the role of lady bountiful on the estate, or queening it from a box at the opera. Sometimes I don't feel real, Poppy, it's as though he's changing me into someone else. . . ." She paused, examining Poppy's shuttered face contritely. "But how can I complain?" she exclaimed, "when I think of you and all your troubles! Of course I'll take the baby, I promised I would." She hesitated again. "Are you sure you want to go through with this? There's still time to change your mind."

Poppy shook her head. "It's fortunate the baby looks nothing like me, Angel," she replied. "She's so blond and pretty, she might easily be your own daughter."

"Then from today she will be my daughter. I don't give a damn what Felipe says," Angel said vehemently. "I can promise you this, Poppy. There will be no stigma, no one will ever know . . . not even the child."

Poppy nodded, satisfied. She stared at the driver, whisking flies from the horse in the waiting pony trap. "Felipe is going to be angry with you for coming here. You'd better hurry back before he returns."

Angel glanced anxiously at the pretty gold watch trimmed with seed pearls and rubies, which she wore clipped to her belt. "The train leaves in an hour," she said anxiously. "Oh, Poppy, I hate to leave you." Tears brimmed from her eyes as she looked at her.

"I'll get the baby," said Poppy. She returned a few moments later and held out the child wrapped in a woolen shawl. "Signora Rossi is bringing her things," she whispered. "There isn't much, just a few clothes."

Angel stared at the baby's sleeping face. "But she's so lovely, Poppy . . . oh, how can you bear it?" Tears spilled from her eyes again and she pushed them away hastily with her finger. "I mustn't cry," she said, attempting a smile. "They say it's bad for a mother's milk." Carrying the baby carefully, she walked to the pony trap and laid her in the waiting basket. Signora Rossi hurried forward with a small bundle clutched in her hands and handed it to Angel.

"The baby will be baptized formally next month," said Angel. "Have you chosen her name?"

"Signora Rossi named her Helena Maria."

Still, Angel hesitated beside the carriage. "What will you do?" she whispered. "What's to become of you, Poppy? I only wish you would return home to Mama and Papa and Greg. Oh, Poppy, I'm sure Greg will never rest until he finds you."

"He never will," said Poppy distantly. "I shall make sure of that." She handed the sapphire engagement ring Greg had given her—so long ago it seemed—to Angel. "Please give this back to him," she said harshly, "then he will understand. It's over. And don't worry, Angel, it's easy for people like me just . . . to disappear."

Angel hesitated, staring at the ring, the symbol, recognizing the finality in Poppy's gesture.

Instead of taking it, she thrust a packet toward her. "It's all the money I could get," she said. "I only wish it could be more but Felipe takes care of all our financial affairs." Impulsively, she tore the pearls from her neck and thrust them at Poppy. "Take these—sell them. They must be worth a fortune. Felipe said they once belonged to Madame du Barry . . . 'a whore's pearls,' he called them! I've never liked them because of that. . . ." She climbed quickly into the carriage, tears raining down her face. "Oh, my darling Poppy," she whispered, "shall we ever see each other again?"

"Good-bye, Angel," Poppy replied quietly.

"Oh, Poppy!" Angel wailed as the driver whipped his lazy horse into action. "I can't bear it . . . I just can't bear it . . . there must be something I can do. . . ."

"Promise me one thing," Poppy said suddenly, clutching at her hand, "only one thing. Name the baby for me . . . call her 'Poppy.' Please, Angel."

Angel stared at her, shocked. "It will be difficult . . ." She faltered.

"Please, Angel," Poppy begged.

She nodded. "Very well, I promise."

Poppy looked at her gratefully, knowing it was for the last time, and then she turned and ran back down the path, into the peaceful gardens along the edge of the silent blue lake.

CHAPTER 30

1 8 9 9

Angel faced her brother fearfully; she'd never seen him angry before, at least not with this deep, biting anger that narrowed his eyes and hardened his voice.

"You're lying, Angel," Greg said icily. "And why mother and father believe Felipe, I'll never know."

"It's because of Jeb Mallory," she whispered, terrified, "they said Poppy was truly his daughter after all, no matter how she's tried to deny it to herself. And why else would she run away—just disappear—if it wasn't true? Poppy met someone else, Greg, and she ran off with him; someone she loved more than you," she added cruelly, because she needed to protect Poppy and the baby.

"What did she say to you when she gave you this?" he demanded, pulling their sapphire engagement ring from his pocket. "Tell me *exactly* her words."

Angel closed her eyes to shut out his anguished face. "She said, 'Give this to Greg . . . tell him I don't need it anymore . . .'" she whispered miserably.

"I'll never believe it," he cried, storming back and forth across the newly opulent salon of the Palazzo Rinardi. "You're not talking about the Poppy I know, you're talking about someone else."

"That's exactly right, Greg," Felipe said from the doorway. "Poor

Poppy, I'm afraid she was completely taken in by this blackguard, but"—
he shrugged—"you know easily young girls can be swayed into believing
a man loves her when"—he threw a sly glance at Angel—"when her
emotions are involved. And with Poppy's unstable history, well, it's not
too unexpected, my friend, is it? If you ask me, you're better off without
her!"

"*I did not ask you,*" Greg retorted angrily. "I believe that for some
reason you and Angel have invented this . . . this charade. But I intend
to find out why—and I'll find Poppy if it takes me a lifetime."

"Poor darling Greg," Angel wept as he stalked from the room, "and
poor, *poor* Poppy, it's better if he doesn't find her."

"Don't worry," Felipe said icily, "he never will. I hope you realize the
impossible position you have placed us in, Angel. If you hadn't taken the
child when I had forbidden it and then tricked the priest into baptizing
both of them in her name, we could have simply washed our hands of
the whole affair. Poppy was not our responsibility."

"Poppy was . . . *is* my sister!" she screamed. "I don't care what she's
done . . . and it wasn't her fault, she promised me she'd told me the
truth."

"Then why didn't she tell you the name of her so-called seducer?" he
asked, gripping her angrily by the shoulders. "I'll tell you why, because
she was having an affair with another woman's husband! I told you the
stories I'd heard about her afternoon activities. And after the way she
behaved at that school in San Francisco, doesn't it all make sense? Poppy
has bad blood, it's as simple as that. Your father said the Mallorys have
caused enough grief. We must forget her and pray that she has reached a
merciful death."

"No," Angel wept, "no, please, no . . ."

But she lay awake that night, remembering the cold, calm expression
on Poppy's face when she had last seen her four months ago in Bellagio;
she had known then it was the calm of absolute despair. There was no
future for Poppy and she wondered now if she was dead.

She thought of the two small babies, sleeping in the nursery down the
hall, both blond pretty children, neither of whom resembled her but
both of whom, oddly, had a look of Felipe. Not even her own mother
would ever be able to guess that one was not her own. She had been
stunned by the bitterness of Rosalia's reaction to Felipe's story. "We
tried, Angel," her mother had cried angrily, through her tears, "we gave
Poppy everything we could, the love of a family, a proper home, everything you had, she had too. But the blood of Jeb Mallory was too

strong." Rosalia had crossed herself devoutly. "Poppy must pay for her sins," she'd said quietly, "and we shall pray for God to forgive her."

The family had gathered for the baptism, but Nik had refused even to talk about Poppy. By then, even Angel had begun to doubt Poppy's story because Felipe was so convincing. Nevertheless, she'd kept her promise to name the child after her, even though she'd had to be devious to do it, and it had shocked them all. But she'd also made sure that Poppy would never know which child was hers, by giving *both* children her name.

She had gone to the priest the day before, and telling him that there was to be a change, she'd handed him a slip of paper with each child's new name on it. At the church she had stared steadily in front of her as the priest had lifted first one child and then the other saying, "Maria-Cristina Poppy, I baptize thee in the name of God the Father, the Son and the Holy Ghost . . . and Helena Maria Mallory, I baptize thee in the name of God the Father, the Son, and the Holy Ghost." She'd heard Felipe's shocked gasp next to her.

"Stop!" he'd thundered, white-faced with anger. "You cannot give our children that woman's name!"

"And why not, Felipe?" Angel had asked innocently. "Are we not supposed to forgive the sins of others, the way our Lord does? It's only right that my children should commemorate my poor sister's name."

Felipe had glanced questioningly at Nik, and after a moment's hesitation, Nik had nodded. "If that's what Angel wants," he'd agreed quietly.

So there it was. No one but she and Felipe knew which child was which. If Poppy were not dead and should ever return to reclaim her child, there would be no way for her to tell. The child's secret was safe, and the "twin" babies were hers and hers alone. Everyone said that Poppy must pay for her sins, but Angel had made sure her child would not bear that stigma. Poppy could never claim her daughter back now.

CHAPTER 31

Aria collected her ticket at the barrier and drove thankfully into the car park at the Piazzale Roma. It had been sleeting heavily all the way from the Villa d'Oro, reducing visibility to a minimum, and she'd been crouched over the wheel, peering into the slippery darkness for over an hour. She waited a few minutes before getting out of the car, listening until Van Morrison had finished singing her favorite, "The Best Is Yet to Come," and then she switched off the tape deck, smiling. Orlando had bought the tape for her: "This song could be meant for us," he'd said . . . She glanced up surprised as, with a squeal of brakes, a car swept around the curved ramp and swung to a stop in the bay next to the exit. It was a black Peugeot and even from here she could see that the driver was wearing a chauffeur's black cap.

Panic swept through her, and she glanced wildly around the almost empty car park. There was no one in sight; she was alone with the man in the black Peugeot. Quickly she reached out and locked all the car doors. Her heart was thumping so loudly, she could hear it and tremors of fear were running down her spine; she'd read too often about the victims of kidnap in Italy . . . some came out alive from their ordeal, but many didn't; fingers and ears were cut off and sent to the victims' relatives, girls were raped . . . and murdered . . .

She stared through the rearview mirror at the man; his face was in shadow, half hidden by the peaked cap, and he was sitting in the car with the engine running, sending gusts of gray fumes into the icy night. She couldn't just sit here, she thought, hot with panic; she'd have to make a run for it; but he had deliberately parked near the only pedestrian exit. The only alternative was to drive away, beat him to the ramp. . . . Switching on the ignition, Aria threw the car into reverse, backed quickly from her spot, and swung toward the down-ramp, glancing fearfully through the rearview mirror. He'd anticipated her move and had pulled out from his position, and was already racing the other way around the bay, heading her off. With a terrified whimper, she accelerated past him, up the ramp to the fourth floor, not knowing what she would do when she got there, but praying she might be able to jump out and get to the stairs before him.

The tires screeched as she swung the car onto the next level, stamping her foot on the brake as a group of workmen just climbing out of a van leapt hurriedly out of her way.

"What d'ya think you're doing!" they yelled. "Stupid woman driver . . . you don't look old enough to have a license, you could have killed somebody driving like that!"

They glared furiously at her through the window and Aria gazed back at them as though they were angels sent from heaven. "Oh, I'm so afraid," she cried, bursting into tears. "A man is chasing me . . . he's down there on the third floor, he blocked the exit so I couldn't get out . . ."

The four burly workmen glanced at each other uneasily and then back at her. "Chasing a kid like that?" the tall one with a beard said. "The bastard, what did he have on his mind?

"I've got a daughter her age!" exclaimed another.

"Don't be frightened, kid, where is he? We'll sort him out . . . Maurizio, you stay here with her, we three'll take care of the bastard. Wait a minute, you guys, better take these." Delving into the van, the tall bearded man handed them large metal spanners.

Aria leaned against her car, sobbing, as they strode belligerently down the ramp to the third floor. "Calm yourself, my girl," the man waiting with her said kindly. "Here, have a cigarette."

She shook her head miserably, wishing Orlando were here. She remembered the way his arm had felt around her that night, walking back from Corte Sconta, so secure, so . . . supportive. Orlando would protect her from everything. Oh, Orlando, Orlando, she wailed silently, why did you have to go away and leave me now?

The three burly men reappeared at the top of the exit ramp, shaking their heads and gesturing thumbs down. "No one there now, lady," they called. "He must have heard us and decided to do a disappearing act. It's a good thing for him he did, too, or we might have killed the bastard." Slinging their spanners back into the van, they stared at her kindly. "Where are you going now?" they asked.

"Home," she sniffed, drying her eyes on her green fur sleeve. "I'll get a water taxi. But thank you . . . thank you so much. I don't know what I would have done if you hadn't been here."

They glanced at each other uneasily, contemplating what might have happened to her. "Come on," they said, "we'll walk you to the taxi."

Glancing nervously over her shoulder, Aria followed them down the stairs, half expecting to hear footsteps behind them, or to have the madman burst upon them around the next corner. It was still sleeting heavily and hunching into the jackets, they marched, two on either side of her, to the taxi landing stage. "My name is Aria Rinardi," she told them, "and I'd like to know where you live so I can thank you properly." She'd sell her gold bracelet, she thought, and send them a reward.

"No need for that, Signorina," they said, embarrassed, "we would have helped anyone in that situation."

"Then here." She tipped the contents of her purse into the burly man's jacket pocket. "Have a drink on me. It's nothing, but I can never thank you enough."

"Signorina Rinardi?"

Aria jumped, her eyes wide with alarm, and then she recognized Giulio, Carraldo's boatman. "The launch is here, waiting for you, Signorina," he told her.

The men turned to stare at the launch, gleaming like ebony, and at its black raven emblem in the circle of gold. "That's Carraldo's boat," one whispered, awed.

"Carraldo?" They turned to look at Aria again, the expression in their eyes changing. "Carraldo!" they said again, edging away. "Well . . . good night then, Signorina, good night . . ." They hurried across the Piazzale, muttering together, and Aria stared after them, horrified. They had been so kind, so sweet to her . . . they'd saved her life . . . but as soon as Carraldo's name was mentioned, they'd run off. And she knew why; she'd caught the look of contempt and fear on their faces as they turned away.

She turned to Giulio, smart in his black double-breasted pea jacket with the brass raven-insignia buttons, and his black peaked cap with the white naval cover, waiting patiently for her to make a move. "Giulio?"

she asked as they walked to the launch, "how did the Signore Carraldo know I was going to be here?"

"The Signore is with the Baronessa, Signorina. She had telephoned the villa and been told you were on your way home. The Signore was worried about you traveling alone in this bad weather; he sent me here to wait for you."

Aria's heart sank. It had been almost a month since she had seen Carraldo and so much had happened since then. She wished she'd never set eyes on Carraldo; she wished she'd never even heard of him. But then, if she hadn't, she would never have met Orlando.

Francesca was waiting for her at the top of the stairs. "Whatever happened to you?" she cried, shocked by her mascara-smudged, tear-stained face. "Was there an accident . . . are you all right?"

"I'm all right, Mama," she replied, climbing the marble stairs wearily. "I've just had a fright, that's all."

Carraldo was standing at the fireplace, a glass of whiskey in his hand. "What happened, Aria?" he asked sharply.

She wanted so badly to talk about it, but she couldn't, especially to Carraldo and her mother. Between them they'd see she never left the house alone again, and that would give her mother a perfect excuse to spy on her. She would call Mike tomorrow and tell him what had happened; Mike had seen the black Peugeot, he'd know now she was right. And when Orlando got back, he'd look after her. He would see that she was never alone and at the mercy of whatever madman was chasing her.

"Answer us, Aria!" Francesca exclaimed. "You look dreadful. What happened, for God's sake?"

"Some stupid boys chased me in the car park at the Piazzale Roma," she said quickly. "They scared me. That's all."

"Chased you?" Carraldo asked.

"They were just a group of silly boys. I suppose they'd been drinking and thought it was fun. I thought they were going to crash into me. It's nothing really, it was silly of me to cry."

"Well, for goodness' sake, go and clean yourself up," Francesca said, relieved, "you look terrible. Then we can have a civilized dinner together. Antony has a surprise for you."

Aria glanced at Carraldo apprehensively, wondering what it was this time. "Are you sure you're all right?" he asked quietly.

She nodded. "I'm okay. I'll just go and wash my face and get changed."

They were already at the table when she came down, and Fiametta was serving artichoke soup. "Your favorite," she whispered comfortingly, her sharp eyes taking in her tear-swollen face.

Aria got through dinner somehow, though her head was aching and tremors of shock still ran up and down her spine. They must never know how desperately afraid she'd been.

"Well, now, I think Antony should tell you his surprise," Francesca said, smiling happily.

"We've seen so little of each other lately," Carraldo said. "I know it's my fault, I've been so busy. But it's almost Christmas Eve, and even I must stop work. It happens that I've some business to take care of in California soon afterward, and I thought it would be nice if we flew over and spent Christmas in Los Angeles. You'll enjoy it," he promised, with a faint smile, "a couple of weeks of blue skies, sunshine, swimming pools . . . Rodeo Drive."

"Los Angeles!" Aria exclaimed, thinking frantically of Orlando. "But we always spend Christmas here, at home. . . . And what about my art lessons?"

"I suggest we give Orlando a holiday over Christmas," Carraldo said quietly. "I think we need time to get to know each other better, Aria, and your mother agrees."

"I shall be coming too," Francesca told her, smiling as she thought of shopping on Rodeo Drive. "After all, I couldn't let you go unchaperoned, could I?"

Aria knew Carraldo was trying to be nice to her, to give her a special treat, to give her anything she wanted . . . and she hated him suddenly with all her heart. Because all she wanted in the world was Orlando, and he was taking her away from him.

CHAPTER 32

Mike had worked through the night at the Villa d'Oro, piecing together Poppy's story, but when he'd finished, he was elated rather than exhausted. At least now he knew the truth about Poppy's baby—it was a daughter, not a son, and that eliminated two contenders—Pierluigi and Orlando. He guessed that Pierluigi wasn't going to need the money anyhow, not now; and Orlando would just have to trust his talent to earn him the big money. He'd also have to choose either Carraldo's sponsorship—or Aria. Mike didn't envy him the decision.

The phone rang at eight o'clock the next morning. "Just the girl I want to talk to," he said, smiling.

"I want to talk to you too," Aria replied. "Oh, Mike, you're the only one I can tell . . ."

Her voice sounded muffled, as though she was crying, and he said quickly, "What is it?"

"The man in the black car . . . he followed me back to the Piazzale Roma, or at least I think he did, it was hard to tell in the sleet and the dark. I didn't even see him until I pulled into the car park."

In between sobs, she told him exactly what had happened—but it was what *might* have happened that was in both their minds. "I'm going to drive out now to see you," she told him. "I've got to talk to someone. Mike, will you help me? I'm so afraid."

"Don't go out alone," he told her urgently. "Stay right where you are. I'll rent a car and be back in a few hours. Wait there for me, Aria."

She was at her easel, painting, when he finally got there. The green Amazon parrot glared at him from his outrageous jeweled stand beside her. "I'm painting Luchay's portrait," she told him, managing a smile, but there were shadows under her frightened blue eyes and a look of tension in her face that hadn't been there the day before.

Mike ran his hands through his short hair. He was unshaven and his tie was loose over yesterday's rumpled shirt, unbuttoned at the neck. "You look like Philip Marlowe," Aria said with a grin.

"Okay kid," he said in an exaggerated drawl, "give me the lowdown on the car park scam, before the D.A. gets to know about it."

Aria laughed, suddenly looking like her old self again. "Just seeing you makes me feel better," she told him.

"And just seeing *you* makes *me* feel a whole lot better," he said, thinking she looked lovely even with smudges of green paint on her nose and her hair all over the place. "You look like a girl who didn't sleep well," he said, holding out his finger tentatively to the parrot. "Jesus!" he exclaimed, snatching it back again as it darted forward and nipped him with his sharp beak.

"Luchay always does that," Aria said calmly. "If you hold out your hand, palm upward, he'll expect food; but if you hold out your finger, he thinks you are going to touch him, and he doesn't let anyone do that except me. And sometimes Fiametta. He once bit Mama so badly, she had to have a stitch in her finger." She giggled. "He probably thought she was trying to steal his emeralds—and she probably was!"

"What about this guy in the black car, then?" he asked soberly. "Do you really think someone's trying to kidnap you?"

She nodded. "Why else should anyone follow me? It was more than that, Mike; he threatened me, he *terrified* me."

Mike knew she wasn't going to like it, but he had to ask her. "Don't you think you should tell Carraldo?" he suggested. "He's the only man I can think of who can help in a situation like this."

She shook her head emphatically. "If he knew, he'd never let me out of his sight."

"What about Orlando?"

"Of course I'll tell Orlando. But he's still in London. And now a disaster has happened—I have to go to Los Angeles for Christmas with Carraldo and Mama. That means I won't see him until I get back in about three weeks' time."

"I know you won't agree," he said sympathetically, "but getting away is probably the best thing that could happen right now. Who knows, by the time you get back, we might have an answer to the Poppy Mallory jigsaw puzzle. And all this will be over."

"Really?" Her face lit up. "Do you really mean that, Mike?"

He laughed. "I sure do. I found out quite a lot at the Villa d'Oro. Now I know for sure that Poppy's baby was a girl and she handed her over to your great-grandmother, when she was born. Angel had a baby almost at the same time and she brought the girls up together, as twins. Maria-Cristina and Helena."

Aria's hand flew to her mouth and she gasped with excitement. "Then it's me? I'm the heiress?"

"Well, it's sure looking that way right now." He grinned.

"Oh, Mike, Mike!" She ran into his arms, hugging him as though he was some huge teddy bear. "I can't believe it! You can't know what this means to me. I'll be free!" She stared up at him, her face glowing. "Oh, I can't wait to tell Orlando!"

"How much does Orlando know?" he asked casually.

"Oh, everything, of course. I told him the whole story. You see, when I get the money I want to help his career. He's never been able to work the way he wants to—and now because of me, he will. Isn't it amazing?"

"Not yet it isn't," he told her. "It's not sure yet. Remember?"

"But almost sure?" she pleaded.

"Almost," Mike admitted, "but there's a lot more story yet to come. We still don't have the evidence that it was Maria-Cristina who was Poppy's daughter. Until then, you're not the heiress. Okay?"

"Okay," she agreed, but she was smiling. "I won't tell my mother and Carraldo, I'll wait until we know for certain. But what will you do next, Mike? Where will you find the evidence?"

"At the Villa Castelletto," he said. "Poppy's house."

Lieber's office had tried to get in touch with the agent in Vicenza who had the key to the villa, but the man had gone away on vacation, and so Mike found himself at loose ends until he got back. It was the day before Christmas Eve and Aria had already left for Los Angeles. He still hadn't been able to contact Orlando Messenger, and he debated whether to try his number again, but he'd already called several times without success. Odds were he was still in London; still, it was worth a shot.

"Sì, sì, Signore, he is here," the proprietor of the pensione told him, "hold on, Signore . . ."

"Orlando Messenger," a deep, cultured voice said.

"Mr. Messenger, my name is Mike Preston. Johannes Lieber asked me to get in touch with you to discuss your claim to Poppy Mallory's estate. I wondered if we could get together over a drink and talk."

Orlando sounded impatient. "I'm off to Gstaad this afternoon. What was it you wanted to discuss?"

"Mr. Lieber asked me to meet certain of the claimants to the Mallory estate to go over their stories with them," Mike explained.

"I've already told Lieber my story," Orlando replied abruptly. "I'm afraid I don't have the time to see you today, Mr. Preston. As I said, I'm on my way to Gstaad. Why don't you call me again when I get back?"

"Sure," Mike said quietly. "When will that be?"

"I'm not certain, why don't you try again in a couple of weeks or so?"

Mike replaced the receiver, and taking out Lieber's notes on Orlando, he read them again.

He remembered what Lieber had told him in Geneva. "Like Lauren Hunter, Orlando Messenger has no evidence to back up his story that Poppy's child was a son and he is her descendant," Lieber had said, "but somehow I couldn't dismiss his claim, there was a certain ring of truth about it."

Mike knew that Orlando claimed his grandfather had been Poppy Mallory's son. His evidence of this was even more tenuous than Lauren Hunter's, because at least she had the Mallory family name written in her Bible, while Orlando had nothing except the story told to him, he said, by his father.

Mike shrugged. Orlando's claim was hardly worth pursuing now they knew the child was a daughter, and anyhow the dates were all wrong. Grandfather Messenger had been born too late. Not even a good try, Orlando, he thought, dismissing him. But then he remembered what Peter Maze had told him about his way with women; Orlando used women to get what he wanted, and now it looked very much as though he might be using Aria. She'd told him she was likely to be the Mallory heiress, and Orlando might be making sure he got the money, one way or the other.

It was almost Christmas and everybody seemed to be going somewhere except him. Mike debated whether to fly back to the States— there was still time, he could be there by Christmas Eve. He could spend it with Aunt Martha. Or Lauren Hunter, in L.A. . . . Somehow that lovely girl, with her gallant smile and fearless blue eyes, just refused to leave his thoughts.

In the end he spent Christmas at the Cipriani, working. He typed up his notes and tried to fathom what had happened to Poppy after she'd left the baby with Angel. He couldn't wait to get to the Villa Castelletto.

Aria called him from L.A. right after Christmas. "Great to hear from you," he said, "how are you?"

"I'm okay," she replied. "I think."

She sounded depressed and he tried deliberately to be cheerful. "Enjoy all that sunshine while you can," he said, "it's cold here, and raining."

"It's raining here too," she said, laughing. "Mama's furious!"

"How's Carraldo?"

"He's . . . kind," she said. "Mike, I wanted to ask you a favor. I was expecting Orlando to call me. I haven't heard and . . . well, I was wondering if maybe they had lost the number I left for him at the *pensione*. Every time I call they say he's not there—no message or anything. I haven't seen or heard from him since before Christmas, and I'm so afraid he's angry because I'm here with Carraldo. Could you telephone, Mike, and find out where he is? I've got to speak to him."

She sounded on the verge of tears, and he said quickly, "I'll see what I can do," feeling like a heel because he knew very well Orlando was in Gstaad. But she had enough to handle right now, alone there with Carraldo and her mother. There would be time enough to sort out Orlando when she returned.

"Thank you," she said, "all I want is to speak to him. Another thing, Mike, when are you going to the Villa Castelletto?"

"Soon as I get the keys; the guy's away at the moment, I have to wait till he gets back."

"If you leave before I get there, would you do me another favor? I know it may sound strange, but the villa was Luchay's home, too, you know. He lived there all those years with Poppy. I really wanted to take him back there—not because he'll talk or anything; but he's so old now, Mike, and I know Poppy must have loved him very much. I thought it would be nice for him to go back there, one last time, just to see the villa again. Would you take him with you?"

"If you insist." He sighed reluctantly, envisioning the journey with the parrot in the back of the car.

"Please?" she asked again.

"Okay, okay," he laughed, "of course I will. I must admit, I'm curious, too, to see how he reacts. Anyway, when are you coming home?"

"Nobody's saying," she said dispiritedly. "Soon, I hope."

"L.A. can't be that bad!" he replied with a grin. "Any mysterious footsteps and black cars?"

"None, thank God," she said firmly.

"Okay then, baby, take care of yourself," he told her.

"You too, Mike. If I don't hear from you—or Orlando—at least I'll know you tried. See you when I get back."

Orlando, you little shit, he thought as he put down the phone, you're living up to your reputation, all right.

CHAPTER 33

Luchay huddled in his big gold cage, fluffing out his feathers against the cold, as Mike paced the gravel driveway at the bottom of the steps leading to the Villa Castelletto, waiting for the agent to arrive with the key. There was a smell of wood smoke in the air and an edge of ice on the easterly wind that promised snow, and the tangled gardens looked bleak and lifeless, hiding the sweet juices of spring in their winter hibernation.

"Come on, God damn it," he grumbled as a blue Peugeot estate car crawled slowly up the rutted drive and parked next to his Fiat. A florid-faced man in a heavy tweed overcoat stepped out, locking the door firmly behind him, though God knew who he imagined was going to steal it, Mike thought irritably; the villa was completely isolated on top of its hill. It was a three-mile trek to the village where he'd stopped to pick up some provisions of coffee, milk, crusty bread straight from the baker's ovens, a large piece of Parmesan cheese, slices of ham, and several bottles of hearty red wine. Enough to last him through a smallish siege should the snows come and bury him in the Villa Castelletto.

"Mr. Preston?" the florid man called. Who the hell else was he expecting, Mike thought sourly, frozen after his half-hour wait in the cold. "Sorry I'm late," the man said, hurrying up the path, "but I got held up at the office. My name is Fabiani. I've brought the key."

He struggled with the enormous lock until, finally, it gave, and grabbing Luchay's cage, Mike stepped inside. To his surprise the villa was pleasantly warm.

"Mr. Lieber instructed us to keep the house at a constant temperature, sir," Fabiani told him, "there are still some valuable antiques in here belonging to the Mallory estate. Mr. Lieber also had us do some of the more necessary repairs on the house—the roof was leaking badly in a few places and no doubt you'll notice the stains on the ceilings, but that has now been fixed. The heating has been put back in order, and of course now there's a caretaker who comes from the village every morning to stoke the boiler and see that all is kept in order, and his wife cleans up the place a couple of times a week."

Mike trailed after the agent, the parrot's enormous cage clutched in his hand, as he showed him the dust-sheeted downstairs rooms and the vast kitchen with its ancient iron range. "The caretaker swears it works," he told Mike as he stared at it doubtfully, "but I can't guarantee that. Now let me show you upstairs. The cleaning woman has made up a bed for you and I think you should be comfortable enough for a few days." Throwing open a pair of tall doors, he stepped back to allow Mike to enter. "I believe this was originally Madame Mallory's own room, sir," he said.

Mike put the parrot cage on a table near the window, staring first at the view of the garden from the tall windows, then at the fire burning cheerfully in the grate with a deep comfortable wing chair and a little embroidered footstool beside it. He stared at the big lonely bed beneath its draperies of gray-blue silk, and then he looked at the parrot, imagining the silent, chilly nights when there were just the two of them . . . Poppy and Luchay. . . . The parrot must know every piece of furniture in this room, every corner and cupboard, he'd know what it looked like with the warm summer sun streaming through the windows, and under the iced January moonlight; he'd know its scents, her perfume, and the overwhelming power of the lavender in full summer bloom in the flower beds. He watched as the parrot stretched its neck forward eagerly, searching the room, as though he knew he was home again, and knew that surely Poppy must be here. . . .

Mike accompanied the agent to the door. "Thank you very much for all your help, Signore Fabiani," he said, "I'm certain I'll be comfortable here for a few days. Yes, I'll make sure to leave the key with the caretaker before I go." And then he climbed the stairs of the big silent house again, back to Poppy's room.

Luchay's head was tilted to one side, as though he was waiting to hear the light, eager footsteps he once knew.

"Well, Luchay, what d'you think?" Mike asked, standing in front of the fire, warming his frozen hands. *"Now* we're getting there, *now* we'll find Poppy, I feel it in my bones." He stared hopefully at the parrot as if expecting him to say something, but Luchay simply turned his head to one side and stared at him out of one unreadable topaz eye.

"Okay then, be like that," Mike said with a sigh.

He put away his provisions in the kitchen, fed the parrot his seeds, and then with a second mug of hot coffee clutched in his hand, he wandered slowly through the house. He was puzzled by the heavy red velvet drapes, fringed and tasseled in gold, the massive ornate pieces of furniture, the uncomfortable red velvet sofas and dark gothic-looking dining room chairs. Somehow none of this fitted with his image of Poppy; he'd expected a lighter touch in her home, imagining it would be furnished with the graceful painted Venetian furniture of the region, and the pale colors and soft silks of Italy. Poppy had lived in the villa for over twenty years, and yet the house felt as though it had been locked in a Victorian Gothic time warp, untouched by her own personal style. Only in the bedroom, with its faded wallpaper and golden mirrors, the pale Persian rugs and blue-gray silk curtains, did he feel the real Poppy.

He pulled open the doors of an enormous French marriage armoire, carved with flowers and love knots. It was twelve feet wide and seven feet high, and it was filled to overflowing with clothes dating back to the turn of the century. The faint scent of gardenias wafted from the cupboard, as Mike ran his eye along the rail of evening dresses and day dresses, and smart suits and coats. He pulled out an ice-gray satin ball dress swathed at its handspan waist with a cascading pink satin sash, staring at it curiously, wondering what the special occasion was when Poppy had worn it.

Pushing aside the long dresses, he searched the corners of the armoire for hidden journals, still hoping for a lucky find like the one he had at the ranch, but there was just a forgotten pair of blue satin slippers lying in the dust. With a sigh he let the clothes fall back into place, retrieving a soft tweed jacket that had fallen from its hanger. It was a man's jacket, and well worn, with the name of a tailor in Rome; and he could feel something bulky in the pocket. His fingers closed around the cool, smooth beads of a necklace. He pulled it out carefully, exclaiming as he saw the five perfect rows of enormous creamy pearls with a magnificent diamond clasp. And there was more . . . a pair of large ruby-and-diamond drop earrings that glinted in the firelight like a dozen little rainbows. Mike whistled. "It's a bonanza, Luchay!" he said. "They must be worth a fortune! Now I'm starting to believe that Poppy was seriously rich."

Pulling out garments one by one, Mike searched systematically through the pockets, but found no more jewels. Instead he discovered dozens of folded-up little notes, written in the spidery, rambling writing of an old woman. Laying them carefully on the desk, he puzzled over them.

Some made no sense at all, like notes written by a madwoman as crazy reminders to herself. But some were painfully clear.

"As I grow older," Poppy had written, "the better I understand that it is not *who* we are born that matters, but what we become. *Circumstances* are what form us—circumstances—and survival. For even when there is nothing left to live for, we struggle to survive. How odd is the human heart!"

And then there was another: "I'm content here, with my solitude and my jumbled thoughts, letting my mind wander along any path it chooses, picking a thought here, a memory there, like a bunch of mixed wildflowers."

They were the pitiful, desolate jottings of a lonely old woman, Mike thought sadly, as he searched through the many tiny compartments of the Louis Quinze desk for more. He found hundreds of them, written on the backs of envelopes or on scraps of paper, and even on the flyleaf of a well-thumbed book of Keats's poems. Intrigued, he opened the beautiful glass-fronted bookcases and searched the books, finding more scribblings . . . obviously, Poppy had written her thoughts down as they came to her, on whatever piece of paper she had in her hand at the time.

Setting his finds on the desk, he went to the kitchen to fetch a bottle of wine, and then he threw another log on the fire and began to read the notes, trying to sort Poppy's thoughts into some kind of order.

It was dark outside and the snow was falling softly and steadily. The only sounds in the room were the ticking of Poppy's little silver cherub clock and the falling of a log in the grate as he worked through the night, under the circle of light cast by a rose-shaded lamp.

He read for a long while, occasionally glancing up at the parrot; Luchay was on his golden perch, his head tucked under his wing, sleeping, Mike thought. He looked content, as though he could feel Poppy's presence even though he couldn't see her . . . maybe he was dreaming she was back with him in their lonely exile, stroking his feathers with her soft fingers, whispering her secrets to him in her warm, melodious voice. Just the way she'd always done right from the beginning, in that cold little room in Marseilles with the girl in the attic coughing herself to death and the widowed fishwife on the ground floor sweeping her children out of their way as they passed, afraid they might be contaminated. . . .

CHAPTER 34

1899, FRANCE

Poppy sat as long as she dared over the small cup of coffee in the little fishermen's café-bar in Marseilles thinking of the five francs and seven centimes left in her purse. Her expensive leather valise containing her entire worldly possessions was scuffed and dirty and intolerably heavy, and she dreaded the moment she would be forced to pick it up and trudge on her way again.

It was October and the burning sunny skies of summer that had plagued her wandering journey through Italy to the south of France had now changed to gray. A blustery mistral wind whipped the café awning until it crackled like the sails of a ship and she shivered, peering through the open door at the cozy interior where fishermen, in heavy dark blue sweaters and tall rubber boots, leaned against the zinc counter drinking rough red wine. They were dunking chunks of fresh, crusty bread into a hearty stew whose aroma had been torturing her for the past hour. Torn by temptation and hunger, Poppy reminded herself again exactly how little was left in her purse. For over a week she'd been existing on a small loaf, bought cheaply each evening when the bakery was about to close, and an occasional cup of strong milky coffee drunk for its warmth.

The café proprietor bustled toward her, whisking away her empty cup and staring at her inquiringly. *"Eh bien, mademoiselle. Vous désirez quelque chose?"*

"*Non, non, merci, m'sieur,*" she murmured, sliding reluctantly from the little cane chair and hefting her bag.

"*Au revoir, mademoiselle,*" he said, puzzled.

"*M'sieur?*" she called, turning back hopefully. "I wonder . . . well, monsieur, I need a job. I thought maybe you'd need someone to help in the café. To serve or to clean . . . anything at all."

She was so young and her expression so pitifully eager that he hesitated. "Well . . ." he began.

"Henri? What is it?" His wife glared at him from the doorway of the café. "What does she want?"

"Just a job. I thought she might help with the dishes. . . ."

"Dishes? *Her?* The woman's dark eyes raked Poppy shrewdly. "I'll vow she's never washed a dish in her life! Anyway, what does she want a job for? Those clothes she's wearing must have cost a fortune."

The café proprietor shrugged apologetically, avoiding Poppy's eye. "Sorry, mademoiselle," he muttered, wiping the zinc-topped table hurriedly.

It was always the same, Poppy thought, trudging dispiritedly down the narrow street. No matter how poor and worn she looked, there was something about her that told people she was different. No one wanted to employ her; not the women at the smart hotels in the fashionable resorts along Lake Como where she had inquired about a job as a lady's companion, nor at Lac Leman, in Lausanne, where she'd placed a discreetly worded advertisement in the local journal. She had given her address at the modest *pensione* where, for a sum that only a year ago she would have thought nothing of squandering happily on a small box of exquisite Paris chocolates, she was given a room and three meals a day.

To her surprise, a week later there'd been a letter by her breakfast plate. She'd ripped it open, scanning it eagerly . . . a Mrs. Montgomery-Clyde would be pleased to see her that afternoon at three o'clock with reference to the position of lady's companion.

She'd given the poor little drudge of a maid at the *pensione* a few coins, and asked her please to press her beautiful cream jacket and tobacco skirt. Then, brushing her red hair back as tightly as she could, she'd anchored it with a hundred pins, daring it to escape. She'd polished her shabby brown boots until they shone and steamed her battered straw hat over a hot kettle in the kitchen, tugging it anxiously back into shape.

She had invested precious francs in a brand-new pair of cream kid gloves, and pulling them on carefully, she'd examined the finished effect critically in the mirror, swinging around to peer over her shoulder at her back view. The jacket that had once fitted so snugly now hung on her thin frame and she'd tugged at it anxiously. Later, as she waited nervously in the foyer of the Hotel Beau-Rivage for Mrs. Montgomery-Clyde to send for her, she'd thought she looked the role of the "demure" lady's companion.

Fifteen minutes had passed, then half an hour and an hour. Leaving her seat by the potted palm nearest the door, Poppy had approached the desk nervously. "I wonder if Mrs. Montgomery-Clyde has forgotten?" she'd asked hesitantly. "I was supposed to see her at three o'clock."

"I expect she's still taking a nap," the clerk replied indifferently. "She usually does after lunch. No doubt she'll send for you when she wakes up."

Poppy had begun to droop in her blue velvet chair, then, reminding herself she should sit upright and look alert just in case Mrs. Montgomery-Clyde should spot her, she'd sat up ruler straight. It was five o'clock and she had almost given up hope when Mrs. Montgomery-Clyde finally sent for her.

"Come in, girl, come in then. I sent for you five minutes ago, where on earth have you been?" The enormously fat woman in a lilac silk dress and a lot of diamonds had peered at her with puffy, faded blue eyes.

"I came as quickly as I could, Mrs. Montgomery-Clyde," Poppy had replied, blushing angrily. She'd noticed the remains of a sumptuous tea on the table by the window and a half-eaten box of chocolates by the sofa.

"The least you could do is apologize," Mrs. Montgomery-Clyde sniffed, popping another chocolate into her pursed little mouth. "And what *background*, might I ask, do you have for the position of lady's companion?"

"None really, Mrs. Montgomery-Clyde," Poppy had said apologetically. "I mean . . . I was sort of companion to my Aunt Melody in California—"

"*California!*" the woman had snorted. "How barbaric! And where is your aunt now? Why are you here? Alone and seeking employment?"

Poppy had lifted her chin in the old defiant attitude. "Reduced family circumstances force me to look for work since . . . since my aunt . . ."

"I see," Mrs. Montgomery-Clyde had said hastily, not wanting to hear the boring details of her aunt's funeral. "Well, then, come over to the window. Stand here, in the light where I can see you properly." Screwing a large gold-rimmed monocle into her left eye, she'd scrutinized Poppy mercilessly.

"You are seeking a job as a lady's companion," she'd said icily at last, "in a Paris suit that cost more than you would earn in a year? And a

Worth suit, if I know my fashions. Now, how did you come by that, my girl? Not honestly, I'll be bound!"

"Not honest?" Poppy had gasped, burning with humiliation. "Not *honest?* Why you miserable, fat, greedy old woman! How dare you suggest I'm not honest!" Her blue eyes had traveled angrily over the fat woman's stunned face. "My mother and father bought me that suit, and I'll bet they could buy you ten times over. You are disgusting," she added contemptuously, "all *you* have, Mrs. Montgomery-Clyde, is money. And that can't buy everything."

"Why," the woman had gasped, purple-red with anger, "if my late husband, Mr. Montgomery-Clyde, had heard you speak like that to me, he would have thrown you out bodily. . . ."

"A pity he didn't throw *you* out bodily," Poppy had cried, stamping her foot furiously, "maybe he would have lived longer." And then turning on her heel she'd run for the door.

"You'll never get a job here," Mrs. Montogmery-Clyde had screamed after her. "Never! I'll see to it your name is blackened around this town. . . ."

That night Poppy had packed her bags again wearily. The elation of winning the verbal battle had drained from her and she was left alone to face the truth again. If she expected to get a job with the Mrs. Montgomery-Clydes of the world, then she must curb her tongue and submit to their petty disparagements.

On the hot, crowded train taking her to Florence she told herself she would dress more discreetly next time—and hold her tongue.

But in Florence the English Lady Anthea Glennis had not liked her accent, and the American, Mrs. Cornelia Fish, had wanted an English-woman, and in Rome the Contessa Milari had not liked her red hair. . . . "Too much temper," she had decided after a single glance in her direction.

It seemed to Poppy that the trains grew hotter and more airless as she'd sat crunched into a corner of the cheapest hard wooden seat in a hot, stuffy carriage smelling of garlic and sweat and rotting vegetables, on her way to Monte Carlo. She wondered what it was about her that told them she was not cut out to be a lady's companion. She had surely tried hard enough to keep up her appearance, despite her circumstances. She had wondered if maybe she would have more luck as a lady's maid.

She had touched her hand to her neck, feeling the solid warmth of Angel's pearls against her throat under her high-collared blouse. *"Whore's pearls,"* Angel had said . . . *worth a fortune* . . . But Poppy knew it was impossible for her to sell such a valuable heirloom; any jeweler would suspect at once that she had stolen them; he'd send for the police and they would trace them back to their purchaser, Felipe. And who knew what he might do then? Perhaps he would accuse her of stealing them and she would end up in jail. She knew there would be no limit to Felipe's vengeance, not only to her but to Angel for giving them to her. If she couldn't survive without selling the pearls, she told herself determinedly, then she was worthless.

In Menton, the Comtesse de Brillard had stared at her suspiciously, but when Poppy had spoken to her in French, she'd relented. *"Eh bien, Mallory,"* she'd said authoritatively, "you are too young, but I am desperate. You may begin at once on a week's trial."

For a week Poppy stumbled through a hundred different duties, washing the Comtesse's silken undergarments and pressing her expensive taffeta and lace gowns, struggling to arrange her hair and getting her knuckles rapped for stabbing her with a hatpin. She fell asleep when she should have been awake and alert, ready to help her mistress undress when she returned in the early hours of the morning from her parties. And then one terrible day, she forgot to spit first on her burning-hot flatiron and sizzled a hole in a fragile peignoir. She was fired immediately.

With barely enough money left in her pocket to eat, Poppy meandered along the southern coast of France, begging lifts from farmers and smallholders on their way to market, seeking lodgings in the meanest quartiers of the little towns, always asking in the shops and cafés if they knew anyone who wanted a maid, a cleaner, a dishwasher . . . anything at all. But they just shrugged her away, glancing suspiciously at her too smart though shabby clothes. She didn't belong in their world.

By the time she reached Monte Carlo, she looked worn and tired. Her red hair had lost its gloss, the soles of her boots had worn thin, and her once chic clothes were rumpled and shabby. The concierges at the smart hotels she approached hopefully, frowned and showed her the door, and the smart jewelry shops and elegant clothing establishments hurriedly sent her packing.

Leaving Monte Carlo's bright lights and glitter behind, she wended her way slowly west until finally, still jobless and down to her last five francs, she found herself in Marseilles.

Setting down her heavy valise, Poppy leaned wearily against the damp stone wall in a squalid tunnel-like street near the waterfront. At its far end through a maze of funnels and masts she caught a glimpse of the sea, silver under the gray October light, and the white flash of seagulls wheeling across a fragment of colorless sky. As the wind whipped the pins from her limp hair, sending it straggling into her eyes, Poppy knew that for her, it was the end of the road. There were no jobs, nobody who cared, there was no hope. Loneliness enveloped her like a shroud.

A snatch of raucous laughter wafted from the bar across the street and, as its bead curtain rattled in the wind, she saw the crowd of sailors inside. Fresh off the steamships that had taken them to all parts of the world, they were proceeding to get roaring drunk as quickly as possible. A burly black-haired stoker, the coal dust ingrained into his hands and face from his job tending the boilers in the hot bowels of a ship, was sitting at the bar. On the counter in front of him was a tiny ball of brilliantly colored fluff. There was yet another great burst of laughter, and Poppy stepped into the bar curiously, wondering what it was that they found so amusing.

"Come on then, you little bastard, talk!" roared the stoker, slamming his fist into the zinc counter so hard that the tiny ball squawked and flapped its useless clipped wings in an attempt to fly away.

"Why, it's a parrot!" Poppy cried in astonishment, blushing as silence fell and the drunken sailors turned to stare at her.

"That's an *Amazon* parrot," the stoker boasted, leering at her lecherously. "Why don't you come inside and take a closer look? Bought him myself, I did, five hundred miles up the Amazon River straight out of the jungle and his mother's nest . . . cost me a fuckin' fortune."

He slammed his massive fist down again, so close to the bird that Poppy felt sure he would crush it. "No," she cried instinctively, "no, please . . . don't do that. Don't hurt him!"

"Why not?" he asked. "Three months I've been trying to get the little bastard to talk and he still doesn't say a word. Useless little fucker . . ." Raising his hand, he sent the bird crashing to the floor with a hefty blow. "Waste of goddamn money," he roared as they all laughed drunkenly. "I should wring its fuckin' neck and be done with it!"

Dropping her valise in the street, Poppy rushed inside. "Please don't hurt him," she cried, "he's so little . . . I'm sure he'll learn to talk soon. After all, he's still just a baby parrot . . ."

Plucking the terrified bird from the floor, the stoker grasped its body in one massive fist and its tiny head in the other. "You wanna watch the little poor parrot die, lady?" He grinned. "You wanna see me do it?" His big hand crunched around the bird as Poppy screamed, hurling herself at him.

"No! No!" she cried, beating his iron fists hysterically. "Don't do that, you *can't* kill him! Give him to me!"

Holding the limp bundle of bright feathers aloft, he grinned down at her as the men in the bar crowded closer. "And what'll you give me in return then, eh?" he demanded as they burst into uproarious laughter once again.

"I . . . I don't have much money . . ." Poppy faltered, taking her purse from her pocket.

"That wasn't what I was thinking of, lady," he said, "but let's see what you've got anyway."

Setting the almost senseless parrot on the counter, he sent the contents of her purse clattering onto the zinc. "You're right, there's not much," he said, pushing the coins around contemptuously with his grimy finger. "You'll need to offer more than that, girl. Tell you what." He threw a hefty arm around her thin shoulders. "Why don't you join me for a drink and we'll talk it over?"

Poppy stared despairingly at the tiny jewel-colored heap of feathers. Suddenly the bird's eye opened and stared back at her. There was something familiar about his look of hopelessness, and she knew that the parrot was as alone and frightened as she was. There was no way she could just condemn him to death at the hands of this merciless lout. As the stoker turned his back to call for more brandy, she darted forward, quickly scooped up the parrot, and ran for the door. The sound of raucous laughter followed her into the street and she glanced wildly around for her valise . . . she had left it right here, outside the door. But now it was gone!

A furious bellow came from the bar, and thrusting the little parrot into the front of her jacket, Poppy fled, twisting and turning in the maze of narrow alleys near the waterfront until her heart was pounding so fast in her tight chest, she was forced to stop. Slipping into the shadow of a dark malodorous doorway, she leaned unsteadily against the wall. Her eyes were closed and she was panting for breath. The little feathery bundle inside her jacket stirred and she put her hand gently against it, thankful that at least it was still alive. She had no idea what she would do with it, or with herself. She had just lost the last of her money and all her clothes and possessions; she had nothing left—except the whore's pearls around her neck. But they would go to the bottom of the sea with her.

"Hey," a female voice said angrily, "what the hell y'think you're doing, this is *my* territory!"

Poppy's eyes flew open and she stared at the blond girl standing opposite her, legs apart, her hands on her hips and an aggressive glare in her eyes.

"Territory?" she faltered. "I don't understand . . ."

"Aw, come on," the girl sneered, "don't give me that! Of course you know." She eyed Poppy up and down again thoughtfully. "Maybe you don't, though. But then what the hell are you doing around here? Wearing that fancy suit and all . . ." She fingered the lapel of Poppy's jacket admiringly. "That's a class bit of material," she said, "real *high* class, the sort you see in the shops in the rue de la Paix in Paris." She stared, amazed, at Poppy's chest as the parrot stirred under her jacket. "What the hell you got there?" she demanded, backing away nervously.

"It's a young parrot," Poppy explained, unbuttoning her jacket to show her. "I stole it from a sailor in a bar. . . ."

"Stole it, did ya?" The girl threw back her head, laughing raucously. "Well, good for you. Those cheap sailors never give anything away; they'll always cheat a girl sooner than pay, it's time they got a bit of their own medicine."

"Not *really* steal," Poppy said hastily, "he took all my money. . . ."

"How much?" asked the girl suspiciously.

"Five francs," she admitted.

"*Five francs?* The cheap bastard, robbing you like that. God, I hate men!"

They stared at each other curiously. Poppy had never seen anything quite like her. She was middle height with plump breasts and a round face, a short pert nose and a generous mouth. Her untidy dark blond hair fell in a tangle of curls that she'd attempted to anchor in a knot, and her cheeks and mouth were rouged an unflattering garish red. Peering closer, Poppy could see that her eyes were lined in smudgy black and her eyelashes were stuck together in black clumps. "Are you an actress?" she asked finally.

"An actress?" the girl repeated, with a throaty laugh. "Yeah, in a way I suppose I am an 'actress'—but not the sort you mean."

"I just wondered," Poppy said politely, "because of your rouge and things."

"Yeah, it goes along with the profession, kid." She peered closer at Poppy. "You are just a kid too," she said thoughtfully. "So what the hell brings a young girl like you . . . a foreigner too . . . to this quarter of Marseilles?"

"It's a long story," Poppy said tiredly, "I've just lost the last of my money and now my valise has been stolen. I have nothing, and nowhere to go . . . there's just me and the parrot." She was quite calm as she clutched the tiny frail bundle closer, thinking of the immensity of the sea that they would both have to face that night, because the poor little bird would have to die with her. Still, anything was better than leaving him to die cruelly at the hands of the drunken stoker.

Anxiety flickered in the girl's greenish eyes. She glanced quickly up and down the empty street, but business was always slow at this time of the afternoon. "You'd better come home with me," she said, putting her arm around Poppy, shocked by the sharp jut of her shoulder blades. "I'll fix you a cup of coffee and you can tell me all about it."

Poppy followed her up the grimy wooden stairs to a room on the second floor. She stared around her curiously. A sagging iron bed took up most of the space, but somehow the girl had also managed to cram in a table, a dresser, a washstand with an enormous blue-and-white-pottery washbasin and jug, and a couple of ancient chairs with horsehair stuffing peeking from large rips in the worn burgundy velvet. Every available surface was filled with a clutter of objects that dazzled Poppy's eyes; flimsy silk scarves from cheap market stalls, bits of glittering jewelry and pots of rouge, amusement park trinkets and seaside mementos, picture postcards of fashionable music hall stars and actresses, tatty bits of fur and a molting red feather boa, a couple of battered straw hats on a lurching stand. And piles and piles of books everywhere.

"Oh, I'm 'educated,' you know," the girl said, following her gaze. "I can read and write. I had my schooling, my dad saw to that. And that's all he did, the bastard!" Filling a battered saucepan with water, she balanced on a rickety chair, and coaxing the single gas jet, that was meant to light the room, into flame, she held the saucepan over it. She grinned at Poppy. "It's forbidden, but we all do it. They say we'll blow ourselves up one day, but what the hell . . ." She shrugged her shoulders philosophically. "A hot cup of coffee is worth it."

Poppy's knees threatened to give way suddenly, and with a little moan she sank into a chair.

"What is it?" the girl demanded sharply. "Not pregnant, are you? If you are, I know just the person—but it'll cost you. That sort of thing doesn't come cheap."

Poppy shook her head and the girl inspected her once again. "Hunger," she said decisively. "I've seen those signs before." Pulling an earthenware crock from a curtained cupboard, she took out a baguette and a slab of cheese, and tearing a hunk from each, she handed them to Poppy. "Get this down you," she said roughly, "and a hot drink, and then we'll see what we can do."

Poppy glanced at the girl's poor room, certain that she had barely enough food for herself. "No, thank you," she said politely, "I couldn't possibly take your food."

"Couldn't possibly?" The girl laughed her throaty, raucous laugh again. "Such fancy talk, Miss! And where did you learn to speak French like that?"

"From my governess in San Francisco when I was five," she replied, eyeing the cheese hungrily.

The girl shoved it toward her. "Go on," she said encouragingly, "eat. We can talk at the same time. And I warn you, I want to know everything—about San Francisco, the governess, the posh clothes . . . the lot!

"First tell me your name," she demanded as Poppy slowly savored the rich creamy taste of the cheese.

"It's Poppy," she replied, taking another bite.

"Poppy! Mmm, that's pretty. Mine is Simonette . . . actually it's Berthe, but I always hated it so I changed it to Simonette. I'm usually called Netta."

"Netta, that's pretty too," said Poppy, absorbed in the delicious moistness of the bread—she had eaten stale, hard loaves for so long now, she'd almost forgotten how good fresh bread really tasted.

The parrot struggled feebly against her chest, and hastily unbuttoning her jacket, she held the tiny creature in her hands, smoothing his feathers with a gentle finger. "He's so soft," she told Netta eagerly. "Feel him? Isn't he softer than silk velvet?"

"I wouldn't know," said Netta. "I've never felt real silk velvet." But her hand and her eyes were gentle as she touched the bird.

"Look at his colors," Poppy exclaimed, "emerald, and scarlet here along his wing, and such a wonderful sapphire blue along the head. And his eyes are pure topaz. But I think he's prettier than any of those jewels." The parrot cocked his head, watching her through one topaz eye, and she smiled delightedly. "Why, look, Netta, he's already feeling better!" she exclaimed.

"He's probably as hungry as you are," she retorted.

"But what do you suppose parrots eat?" Poppy asked, staring at her, horrified. "I've no money to buy him food."

"Then for now he'll just have to eat what you eat, won't he?" Netta said, crumbling bread and cheese into tiny bits and offering them to him. The little bird's sharp beak hovered over her hand for a second and then he jabbed eagerly at the crumbs.

"Just look at that," said Netta. "I thought he was going to bite me, but he's as gentle as a babe." She glanced at the darkening window and turned the gas jet higher.

"It's getting late," said Poppy. "I'd better be on my way . . ."

"On your way to where?" Netta demanded. Poppy hung her head, saying nothing, and Netta hesitated for only a second. "Better stay here for a while," she said gently, "the bed's big enough for two—I know, I've tried it," she added with a saucy wink. "And anyhow, I won't be home tonight, what with three ships fresh in the harbor."

She glanced at Poppy hunched in the chair, her eyes half closed with fatigue. "Ah, the hell with the ships," she said cheerfully. "I'll tell you what, Poppy, you just curl up on the bed there and have a rest. I have to go out for a little while, but when I come back you and I are going to Victor's café for a good hot meal and a bottle of wine—but I warn you, I'll want to know your story."

Poppy stretched out luxuriously on the bed and Netta smiled as the tiny parrot, his green and scarlet wings clipped to restrict his flight, fluttered unsteadily onto her chest, huddling close to her. "Bloody little creature thinks you're his mother," she said. Her hearty laugh was the last thing Poppy remembered as sleep claimed her.

"Are you sure that's everything?" Netta demanded later, pushing aside their finished plates of delicious lamb stew flavored with rosemary and young parsnips, and emptying the last of their second bottle of red wine into Poppy's glass.

"That's all," Poppy assured her. "Now you know everything about me."

"*Merde!*" Netta said thoughtfully. "So that's how the rich live . . . I always wondered. Well, kid, you certainly learned about life the hard way. Still, my story is not much different from yours . . . seduced at sixteen by a friend of my father's, *and* accused by his wife of enticing him. My father beat me for it, ripping me to shreds until my back bled. And my mother just stood there and watched. They left me senseless on the floor. When I came to, I called it quits. I've never seen them again." She looked at Poppy shrewdly. "How old did you say you were?"

"I'm nineteen," Poppy told her.

"Nineteen, huh? And how old do you think I am?"

Poppy considered. "Thirty?" she guessed generously. "Thirty-four?"

"Thanks!" snarled Netta. "I'm twenty-two."

"Oh . . . I'm sorry." Poppy grinned suddenly, "No, I'm not sorry, because it means we're almost the same age—and I'm glad I've found a friend. Netta, I haven't talked to anyone in months; I haven't eaten a meal like this in . . . forever . . . and I haven't been anywhere as jolly as this in . . . years!" She glanced around the steamy little café. Its tables were packed with a motley assortment of cheerful neighborhood folk and a sprinkling of blowsy laughing women, and it felt cozy and secure. She never wanted to leave it.

Her eyes sparkled as she sipped the red wine, and she stroked the parrot, perched on the table, with a gentle finger. "You know what I think?" she said, scarcely recognizing the sound of her own laughter. "I think the parrot changed my luck. He brought me to you, Netta." Her face grew serious again as she said quietly, "I meant to . . . to kill myself tonight; I was going to walk out into the sea as far as I could and just let the waves take me . . . I didn't want to live."

"I know the feeling," Netta whispered, reaching out and grasping her hand, "I've had it too, Poppy."

"My problems haven't gone away," Poppy said quietly, "but you have given me strength to face them again. How can I ever thank you, Netta?"

"Thank?" she scoffed. "Rubbish! It's the parrot you should thank. He's the little ray of light that guided you here."

"A little ray of light," Poppy said, stroking his soft downy green breast. *"Luce,"* she murmured softly in Italian, pronouncing it "luchay." "Then that's your name—Luchay—my ray of light! And my poor little friend."

"We're all poor here," said Netta, gathering up her shawl and her purse. "And speaking of that, I'd better get to work. Come on, Poppy, you'll sleep well tonight after the meal and all that wine, I'll be bound."

Wearing a cozy old flannelette night gown of Netta's, Poppy curled up in bed with Luchay beside her, watching as she powdered her face and rouged her cheeks. "Netta," she said, puzzled, "where *do* you work? What exactly is it that you do?"

"Do?" repeated Netta, throwing on her shawl and marching to the door. "Why, I'm a whore, of course. I thought you knew."

"Oh," Poppy said. "Oh, yes, of course, how silly of me to ask. . . ."

As the door closed behind Netta and she heard the clatter of her high heels on the naked wooden stairs, she fingered the "whore's pearls" at her throat . . . maybe Madame du Barry wasn't so wicked after all, she thought as she drifted into a dreamless sleep.

CHAPTER 35

1 8 9 9 , F R A N C E

"Of course you'll stay," Netta insisted the next morning. "After all," she added, "I don't use the bed nighttimes, do I?"

Then she went out and canvassed the other streetgirls for a job for Poppy. "She's desperate," she told them bluntly, "and she's different from us; she's not suited to be a whore. Let her clean your rooms. Come on, girls, raise your standards—and your prices . . . think like *high-class* tarts for a change! Imagine the luxury! To come home to clean floors, clean sheets—for those who possess them—and clean underwear—for them that wears it. And all for a few sous. After all, we have to keep that bloody little parrot in sunflower seeds, don't we?"

To Poppy, the house had a familiar smell about it, like the cheap rooming houses of her childhood—a mixture of stale food, stale sweat, stale sex. It was tall and thin with a narrow dark staircase of splintered wood twisting upward to the very meanest room—an attic under the steeply sloped eaves, and in her new capacity as cleaner and laundress Poppy soon got to know its inmates well. With Luchay perched on her shoulder and her heavy bucket of hot soapy water, boiled over the ancient cauldron-like stove in the basement, she tried her best to wash away a century of grime.

The girl who lived in permanently stooped poverty in the sloping attic was only nineteen, Poppy's own age, and despite her desperate hacking cough, Poppy would see her swagger off into the misty night, an artificial flush of rouge masking her pallor and a cheeky grin distracting attention from her shabby thinness. And then she would see her again the next morning, limping, exhausted, back up the stinking stairs, often drenched from the night's rain and coughing as though she would never stop.

"Oh, she'll stop, all right," said Netta angrily when Poppy asked about her. "It's consumption—she'll not last the winter."

"But we must help her," Poppy gasped, horrified. "What can we do?"

Netta shrugged, but Poppy glimpsed the bitterness in her gray-green eyes. "You tell me," Netta suggested helplessly. And of course, she had no answer.

The ground floor was occupied by a fisherman's widow with four children. She worked at the fish dock scaling and gutting fish, and though she was the cleanest woman in the house and her children's school pinafores the whitest in the street, still the smell of fish permeated the hall. There were two rooms on each of the other three floors, each occupied by streetgirls, but the fishwoman kept well away from their kindhearted friendliness, whisking her children indoors whenever she heard their hurrying footsteps or their raucous laughter.

Poppy would hear their high heels clattering on the stairs as they hurried off to work in the evenings, and she'd hang out of the window, watching as, hands on their hips, they sauntered down the street on their way to the waterfront bars, their low-cut blouses displaying the maximum of their charms. And later she would hear them pattering back up the wooden staircase with some drunken sailor lumbering behind them, cursing as he tripped in the dark.

Alone in Netta's comfortable sagging bed, she'd try to close her ears to the grunts and curses that penetrated the thin walls, pouring out her heart to Luchay, huddled in the curve of her neck, going over and over again the events that had brought her to this . . . *if only* she'd obeyed Aunt Melody, she would never have met Felipe and how different her life would have been; and *if only* she'd seen how easy it would be to love Greg instead of being so foolish, how happy she might have been. . . .

"But then," she told Luchay comfortingly as his bright topaz eye watched her, "I would never have found you, Luchay, would I?"

The parrot fluffed out his poor bedraggled feathers as though he were doing his best to look his most beautiful to please her, and she smiled at him. "Luchay," she whispered despairingly as the creak of the bedsprings increased in tempo and the girl upstairs shrieked in either fear or pain. "Luchay, whatever would I do without you? You are truly the ray of light in my life. You listen to my miserable story and you look so wise." She glanced fearfully at the door as someone rattled the handle, but after a moment the footsteps stumbled past. *"Who knows,"* she went on softly, *"maybe someday we'll make our fortunes. And when we do, Luchay, you will have jewels as bright as your feathers, you will have a golden perch studded with emeralds and rubies and a golden house all your own . . . you will be the 'Prince of Parrots,' Luchay. And you will be my only companion and love, because I never want to know another man as long as I live."*

Netta never brought her customers back to her room. "It ain't much," she told Poppy, "but it's my home, and I don't want those cheap bastards to set foot in here! Besides," she added thoughtfully, "they don't pay enough for the comfort of my bed."

Remembering with a shudder her only experience of sex, Poppy tried not to think of what Netta did or where the "act" took place, but she'd seen enough ugly gropings in the tenement doorways and shadowy corners of the *quartier* to have a good idea.

Each morning when Netta came home she would go immediately to the washstand and fill the big washbowl with the icy water. Then she'd strip herself naked, and, shivering, she'd wash herself from head to toe. "Got to get their dirty fingerprints off me, don't I?" she'd say, walking, casually naked, across the room and pulling on a serviceable flannel nightgown—laundered and ironed by Poppy.

Poppy had never seen anyone naked before, not even Angel, and she was astonished by Netta's matter-of-fact attitude to her nudity and her full-bosomed, beautifully curved body. "You're too good for them, Netta," she blurted angrily, "you're too beautiful, and too nice for those bastards."

"Better watch yourself," grinned Netta, "you're starting to talk like me. Of course I'm too good for them, but I've got to make a living, don't I? For as long as it lasts," she added, yawning.

"What do you mean, as long as it lasts?" Poppy asked, puzzled.

"What do you see when you look out on the street? Dozens of young girls . . . *young* girls, Poppy. There ain't too many whores make a living after thirty—if they're still living and haven't been killed by the clap."

"The clap?" she repeated, bewildered. "I don't know what you mean."

"Never mind, girl," Netta murmured, closing her eyes sleepily, "you'll learn."

Poppy's hands soon became red and chapped from constantly being plunged in and out of water as she struggled with the washing, thumping her wooden stick against the few worn sheets and thin towels, the tired underwear and cheap blouses, in the big metal cauldron in the basement, hauling them through the rusty wringer and stringing them up to dry on the line across the narrow sunless street. She scrubbed the floors and swept the stairs; she dusted their litter of face powder and rouge and tidied their meager possessions. And sometimes in gratitude for their friendship, she would buy a small bunch of flowers from the market at the end of the day when they were sold off for a sou, and then she'd place a single blossom in a chipped mug and leave it in each girl's room to cheer her up in the morning when she got home.

The streetgirls were not much older than she was, but they recognized that she was different—"You're quality," they said admiringly—and they adopted her with motherly pride, dropping in to see her and making a great fuss over Luchay, whom they adored. They would peer at the little bundle of gaudy feathers with eyes as bright and beady as Luchay's own, nervously offering him a small gift of nuts or pumpkin seeds, afraid he would bite. "He brightens up the place," they exclaimed delightedly when he fluttered his little clipped wings, displaying a flash of scarlet underfeathers. Luchay was the pet they'd never had and he was something on which to lavish their love and attention and caresses, the way they never did with men.

But when they'd gone off into the night with their bright chatter and strident laughter, and the house fell silent again, Poppy would feel the familiar dark shroud of loneliness envelop her once more. She would think despairingly of home and of Nik and Rosalia, and Greg. In her mind Greg became a hero. Greg would never have behaved as Felipe or the sailors did. Greg was a man of integrity. He'd offered her his love and like a young fool she'd turned it down, until it was too late. She'd think of Angel and the "twin" babies, but she never thought of the child she had borne as being her own, nor did she conjure up a picture of her baby's face, wondering what she looked like. She was Angel's daughter and had as little to do with Poppy's own life as if she'd never borne her.

The past faded into the harsh reality of the present and instead of worrying about herself, she worried about Netta, sashaying forth in the bitter winter streets, her tatty bit of fur slung jauntily around her neck and her thin boots letting in the rain and sleet. "Netta," she said anxiously, "surely there's something better for you than this."

"Sure there is," Netta replied with her cocky grin, "there's a millionaire out there just waiting to sweep me off my feet." And she dragged Poppy off to the café for brandy and hot soup to cheer them up and keep out the cold that penetrated their miserable unheated room. Still, there were nights when even Netta couldn't face the street and, with poor chilled Luchay, far from his warm tropical jungle, huddled under the blanket between them, she and Poppy would cling together for warmth, whispering stories of their past lives. But they never, ever mentioned the future.

Netta had been wrong about Jeanne, the girl in the attic. She didn't die that winter. Somehow she clung grimly to life, coughing blood discreetly and flaunting her brave smile out on the bleak streets. But by January she was too weak to climb the stairs and she lay in bed, gazing quietly upward at the patch of sky that was her only view through the small, grimy window set high in the wall, smiling her thanks as the other girls bustled in to cheer her up. They brought blankets taken from their own beds to try to keep her thin body warm, and bowls of hot soup from the café to try to tempt her to eat, and bottles of patent medicines, bought with money they couldn't spare, which the pharmacist had promised would cure her; and they brought belladonna to ease her pain.

Alone in the house at night Poppy would sit by Jeanne's bedside, reading to her from one of Netta's pile of books, or sometimes just talking to her. Jeanne was too weak to respond in more than a whisper for fear of starting the coughing again, and with it the terrifying hemorrhage, but she'd gaze at Poppy with an expression of such sweetness and gratitude for her companionship that Poppy would be forced to turn away so she wouldn't see the sorrow in her eyes.

Luchay pattered backward and forward on his makeshift wooden stand fashioned from an old broomhandle, cocking his head on one side and peering at them both anxiously. He was growing bigger and stronger and when he flapped his wings fluffing out his beautiful green and scarlet feathers to keep himself warm in the icy room, Jeanne's glittering dark eyes would sparkle with delight as well as fever. "Poppy," Luchay would squawk hoarsely, "Poppy *cara,* Poppy *chérie,* Poppy darling . . ." And despite herself Jeanne would laugh, and that would set off the coughing again, and the blood.

When the cold in the room grew too much for Luchay's tropical bones to bear, he would huddle under Poppy's shawl, and with his tiny body close to hers, she no longer felt lonely and afraid.

The sun, shining from a hard blue sky through her high, grimy window on the first bright morning in April, was the last thing Jeanne saw before she closed her eyes and, with the tiniest of sighs, was gone.

Netta hurried around the *quartier* taking up a collection for the funeral, and a straggling line of weeping streetgirls, black shawls pulled over their heads, followed the refuse cart with Jeanne's cheap pine coffin as it was pulled slowly through the streets to the Church of St. Mary the Virgin.

Even the church was shabby, Poppy thought despairingly as the priest intoned a brief funeral service; the brass candlesticks needed polishing and there were no flowers on the altar. "Poor Jeanne," she remarked sadly as the coffin was lowered into the frostbitten earth, "how terrible to end like this . . . as nothing."

"She's lucky she died young and we were able to give her a decent burial," Netta said with a flash of bitterness, "most of us will end up in paupers' graves. And then you really *are* nothing."

The next day another girl moved into the attic room, even younger than Jeanne, maybe sixteen or seventeen. And pretty, too, thought Poppy, or she would be if she didn't paint her face and adopt such a brash manner. And she sighed because she knew that was the way she had to be if she was to make a living in the streets.

Netta had a special "friend," a sea captain who traveled the southern routes and who every couple of months would roll into Marseilles, as unsteady from his long weeks on board ship as if he were already drunk. The Captain had a wife in the Channel port of Cherbourg and a girl in every other port on his route, but he had a soft spot for Netta and never forgot to bring her a present. He was big and burly and jolly with a face that was more weather-beaten than suntanned and eyes like blue slits from constantly narrowing them into the wind.

Whenever she heard that the *S.S. Marquand* was coming into port, Netta would dress in her cheap finery and in a flurry of excitement watch the big ship slip into its dock, waiting for the Captain to swagger down the gangplank and into her arms.

Poppy wouldn't see her after that until the *Marquand* sailed again three or four days later, when Netta would return with a satisfied gleam in her eyes and wearing a new dress or a pretty necklace or a ring. With a happy sigh, she'd say, "Men ain't all bad, you know, Poppy. And when they're good . . . ooooh, they can be so *good!*" And with a happy wink, she'd hurry off to the pawnshop to hock her latest finery, and it would be brandy for everyone in Victor's café that evening.

This time when the *Marquand* put into port, though, it was different. Instead of disappearing for a few days as she usually did, Netta hurried back home with a gleam of excitement in her eyes, "Poppy, *guess what?*" she demanded. *"He's asked me to marry him! Me,* the best whore on the waterfront and he wants me to be his bride!"

"But . . . but what about his wife?" Poppy stammered, shocked.

"Died, two months ago," said Netta airily, "and there are no kids to tie him down. He says all he thinks about when he's lying in his bunk out under the southern stars—is me. Netta Fosquet . . . soon to be Mrs. Captain Georges Noiret! Oh, Poppy," she cried, her generous mouth splitting her face in a grin of triumph, "can you believe it? *Me, a captain's wife? And* a respectable married woman? And he's such a good man too," she added softly.

She looked so happy as Poppy kissed her and congratulated her and shopped with her for a dress for the wedding that was to take place two days later, that she couldn't bring herself to ask Netta what was to become of her and Luchay.

"You'll keep my room, of course," Netta told her at the riotous party in Victor's corner café the night before the wedding. "Here, take this," and she pressed some notes discreetly in Poppy's hand. "It's not much, but it'll pay the rent for a few months and with your washing and cleaning, you'll manage." There was a glimmer of doubt in her eyes as she said it, but still Poppy smiled bravely. The noise and laughter in the café seemed to fade into the distance as she gazed at her one true friend. "I'm so glad for you, Netta," she whispered. "I know you'll be happy."

"Mrs. Captain Noiret." Netta sighed happily. *"I've beaten the game, Poppy."*

There was no man to give her away, so she walked down the aisle of St. Mary the Virgin alone, with Poppy behind her as her bridesmaid. She and the First Officer of the *Marquand* were the only witnesses, and as Poppy watched Netta in her cheap new dress of blue China silk exchanging her vows, she couldn't help but make a bitter comparison with Angel's lavish wedding. But Netta and her Captain didn't seem to need soaring Bach organ cantatas and a thousand roses, and incense and candlelight to add to their happiness, and they were married just as surely as Angel and Felipe.

It wasn't often one of their profession was lucky enough to capture a husband, and Netta's friends were waiting outside the church to throw rice and rose petals on the beaming couple. Her laugh rang out happily as she and her Captain hurried back to the ship, which was to sail that evening for the Cape.

"I'll be back in a couple of months," she told Poppy, hugging her tightly. "Now don't you go do anything foolish, you hear me?" And Poppy smiled and waved as the captain swung her into his arms and carried her up the gangplank, piped aboard by the crew.

But there were no smiles on her face that night, alone in her room. With her uncertain future to face once more, loneliness settled over her again, as dark and mysterious as the night.

Luchay pattered anxiously back and forth on his wooden perch. "Poppy," he cackled, "Poppy *cara*, Poppy *chérie*, Poppy darling . . ."

"Oh, Luchay," she exclaimed, half laughing, half crying. "Of course I've still got you."

When the *S.S. Marquand* put into port three months later, Netta walked down the gangplank alone, and she was wearing black.

"He's gone," she told Poppy, weeping, "died four weeks ago. It was a hot night and we were in bed; there I was on top of him—doing what he liked best—and then he just sort of gasped and stared at me. And that was it—gone! He was buried at sea, just like an admiral."

Tears rained down her face as Poppy held her hand, unsure of how to comfort her.

"I knew it was too good to be true," wailed Netta, her pert face blotched from weeks of crying. "Damn that bastard, why did he have to die on me? Or *under* me!" she added with a hint of her old grin. "At least he went happy. Well, that's that," she sighed, drying her eyes and removing her hat. "I'll never find anybody else to marry me. I'm home again, Poppy, for good. But at least the old bastard left me his worldly goods. I don't know exactly what it amounts to yet, but he was a traveling man, so it can't be much."

Dignified in black, Netta and Poppy listened as the gray-haired lawyer explained Captain Noiret's bequest. "The Captain changed his will after his first wife died, leaving everything to you, Madame Noiret," he told her.

"Well, get on with it," Netta urged bluntly, "it can't be that much that we need all this legal fuss."

"On the contrary, madame," he said, glaring at her. "The Captain left a considerable estate. There is a house here in Marseilles and another in Cherbourg."

"A house in Marseilles?" gasped Netta.

"As I said, *and* the one in Cherbourg," he went on, "plus a small sum of money in the Banque Maritime de Marseilles. It amounts to just over three thousand francs, madame."

"Three thousand francs!" Netta repeated slowly, her eyes widening with amazement. "Are you telling me that I have *three thousand francs —and two houses of my own?"*

"Indeed I am, Madame Noiret. All you need do is sign these probate papers, right here, and the title deeds and the money will be yours. Of course, I must advise you to leave everything in the bank for safekeeping."

"Safekeeping!" caroled Netta, leaping to her feet. *"Safekeeping?* Poppy and me are gonna throw the party of a lifetime at Victor's café tonight." Picking up her pen, she dashed her name across the documents with a flourish. "Bet y'thought I couldn't write, huh?" she said, nudging the lawyer's elbow, with a cheeky grin. "The party'll be at Victor's on the rue Lesange if you want to come," she added, laughing as she headed out the door on her way to the Banque Maritime.

"Netta, you've got to be sensible about this money," cried Poppy, hurrying by her side. "You can't just fritter it away on parties and new clothes . . . it'll be gone in a month. The Captain wanted to make sure you were taken care of. You could sell the house in Cherbourg and put the money in the bank, and if you're careful it'll last you the rest of your life."

"But I've never been careful, Poppy," she laughed, "and it's too late to start now. Besides, what would I do all day?"

"Maybe you should consider starting a little business," suggested Poppy, "something you'd enjoy."

"Come on," Netta grinned, "you know there's only two things I really enjoy—a good man, and the good life. And I intend to have myself a piece of both right now."

"I have an idea," Poppy said thoughtfully as Netta walked from the bank later, brandishing five hundred francs in her hand. "I have an idea . . . I think you might like it. But you'll need all your money."

Netta glanced at her suspiciously. "What sort of idea?" she demanded.

Poppy explained it to her as they strolled back through the autumnal streets to the waterfront, and Netta's eyes lit with amusement.

"God, you're a clever one," she marveled, "why didn't I think of that? With your brains and my know-how, we'll make a fortune!" She shook Poppy's hand, laughing happily. "One last fling, though, tonight at Victor's? In memory of the Captain? He'd have liked that."

CHAPTER 36

1 9 0 0 ,   F R A N C E

Captain Noiret's old house was at the smarter end of the Canebière in Marseilles, conveniently located between the harbor and the hotels, and POPPY'S culled its clientele from both. But there were no wild, drunken sailors fresh from a long voyage and raring to go—the seven-foot, three-hundred-pound bouncer with the face of an ex-pugilist and fists like hams saw to that. A man couldn't get into Poppy's without a personal recommendation, and even then Poppy would run a critical eye up and down him before she grudgingly permitted him anywhere near her precious "girls."

It had been to protect Netta and the girls that Poppy had come up with the idea; and because she couldn't bear to see Netta squander her money as fast as it had come on parties and presents and what she called "the good life." The truth was that Netta had never known a good life; she had never considered either yesterday or tomorrow; she'd always lived for the present—the only way she knew how. The Captain had been her one chance to escape, and when his money was gone it would be back to life on the squalid streets.

The idea of running her own "house" had intrigued Netta, but all it had meant to Poppy was relief that at least her friend would be off the freezing winter streets and would no longer have to sell herself to dangerous drunken strangers in doorways. She knew Netta would never change, but at least now she wouldn't die of consumption like Jeanne, or end up in a pauper's grave—worse than a nobody. What Poppy hadn't realized was that inadvertently *she* would become a "madam."

Netta had chosen the girls, ruthlessly rejecting those she considered too old or too predatory. "This is going to be a high-class establishment," she told them haughtily, "I want a girl who's clever enough to give a man a good time for his money, not just a quick tumble. We're aiming to build up a regular clientele of 'gentlemen' and we need girls who are so pretty and so exciting, the customers won't be able to wait to come back."

Poppy had busied herself decorating the house, trying not to think about the acts that were going to take place in the bedrooms she was making so attractive. Hanging prim lace curtains at the windows, she'd thought wistfully of her youthful dreams of true love and the soaring, wonderful feeling of being lifted on eagle's wings that she'd always imagined making love would feel like; and now here she was selling sex in all its forms—none of which she knew anything about. Swagging great brass four-poster beds with deep blue velvet, she thought about the men who would lie in them, and she hoped they would be kind men, and gentle. Running a tentative hand over the black satin sheets Netta had insisted on, she tried to imagine what it would feel like to be a girl in the arms of a stranger, sharing her body for money. And placing rose-shaded lamps beside the beds, she hoped, naively, that maybe some of the girls might find happiness and love here.

Netta installed an enormous bar in the salon—like the one she was so fond of at Victor's café—but Poppy had persuaded her that it should be in mahogany instead of workmanlike zinc. They stocked its mirrored shelves with every kind of liquor and spirits plus, at Poppy's instigation, a selection of expensive champagnes. "Our customers will never be able to afford it," Netta protested, but Poppy simply added a hefty mark-up to the price and told Netta that if they couldn't afford it, they wouldn't be allowed through the door.

In an effort to make it all look more "elegant" and less like a bordello, Poppy hung the walls in burgundy silk and installed massive gilt-framed prints and etchings of classical subjects, but try as she might, she couldn't stop Netta from placing an oil painting of a reclining and very voluptuous nude over the bar. She filled the shelves with books on every subject, even though Netta told her, laughing, that men wouldn't be coming here to read. She bought deep, comfortable sofas and chairs, she placed an enormous urn of fresh flowers on the bar and scattered a selection of the day's newspapers on the small tables. She hired two maids—one to clean and tidy the bedrooms after each customer, and one to prepare and serve delicious little canapés to tempt their appetites. And when Netta brought home an armload of flimsy negligees for the girls to wear in the salon to facilitate the customers' choices, Poppy just stared at them, scandalized. "They may wear those in the bedroom," she said firmly, "but in the salon they'll be fashionably dressed young ladies." And she'd chosen their clothes personally, insisting that they would look just as alluring in a silk dress, with a pretty necklace and earrings and their hair immaculately coiffed, as they would half naked in a peignoir.

"This way they'll feel like pretty girls, not whores," she told Netta bluntly, "and it'll make all the difference in the attitude of the men, you'll see."

On opening night they waited nervously for their first customers. Netta was behind the bar and the girls, unaccustomedly elegant in their finery, were sipping champagne and trying to look nonchalant. Wearing a demure gray velvet dress buttoned to the neck, with her red hair pulled back severely from her young, unpainted face, Poppy waited anxiously in the hall, wondering what on earth she would say to the "customers" and praying she wouldn't blush.

When the first gentleman finally arrived, he stared at the elegant young madam in astonishment, and then he hastily removed his hat and bowed to her. Another customer followed on his heels, then another and then two more . . . soon Poppy found that she was too busy to be nervous, and she forgot to worry about what was going on upstairs. Netta supervised the bar and the "arrangements" in the salon; while Poppy greeted the customers pleasantly in the hall, asking how they were and commenting on the weather as she accepted their payment—in advance.

Word spread like wildfire about Poppy's and its strange combination of naiveté and know-how; its prim lace-curtained parlor and fancy bar; the beautiful, clever girls who looked as though they were attending a fashionable finishing school; and the very proper "young lady" in the front hall. In less than six months, Poppy's became the best-known secret in Marseilles. It was like an exclusive new club to which every man wanted to belong, but only those Poppy favored could gain entrance.

As she gained confidence the speculation grew about the lovely Poppy herself. That she was very young, there was no doubt—but no one knew exactly how young; of course she was foreign—some said from America —but with her impeccable French accent it was difficult to tell. Certainly she was educated and well-bred—a "lady," in fact—but no one knew her background. And with her sleek red hair and insolently tilted blue eyes, her creamy skin and long legs, Poppy was temptation itself. Her very unavailability in a house full of available women only added to her desirability, but she let it be known very firmly that any man who even dared to suggest such a thing would no longer be made welcome. Still, the combination of worldly-wise madam and beautiful young lady caused more than one man to try his luck.

"Aren't you ever tempted?" Netta asked her curiously. "Or are you planning on remaining celibate all your life?"

"Maybe," Poppy replied noncommittally, but her mouth set in a tight line.

Netta had her own room on the second floor with an enormous four-poster bed and a flurry of blue satin draperies. Poppy's room was on the ground floor and it contained a simple wooden bed covered with a throw of dove-gray velvet, a dresser, and a comfortable chair. The heavy curtains were of the same gray velvet that was becoming her trademark and she'd found a pretty, old Isfahan rug in pinks and faded blues in a secondhand shop in Marseilles. The lamps had matching rose-colored shades with trembling bead fringes and even Luchay had a new stand, not of gold, but of oak, fashioned by a craftsman. While Poppy was working the parrot would sit on his perch, accepting the admiration and tributes offered to him, but he always seemed to keep an anxious eye on her, and if she left the room he would flutter after her pathetically, crying her name, "Poppy *cara*, Poppy *chérie*, Poppy darling."

At the end of the first year Netta and Poppy assessed their progress. Poppy was running the house with an iron hand in a velvet glove, and the business was profitable. They were able to live well, better than Netta had ever expected—she no longer had to wonder where her next meal was coming from, and neither did her girls.

"So what's wrong?" she asked, observing Poppy's downcast face. "Are you still thinking about that bastard in your past? Or is it Greg still?" Poppy stared into her glass of champagne, saying nothing. "It's time you forget them all," Netta said brusquely, "*this* is your life now, Poppy, *this* is reality. You should try to enjoy it more." And with an exasperated sigh, she returned to her place behind the bar.

Poppy took a sip of her champagne, pushing the dark memories away and contemplating her future. At least now, she had a future—of a sort. Yet she still wasn't satisfied. Poppy's was making them a living, but it was never going to make her fortune; and if there was to be no love in her life then the only alternative was to be rich. She fingered the whore's pearls at her neck, worn flagrantly now instead of tucked away inside her blouse. Her mind was made up; if she was destined to be a madam, she wanted to be the *richest* madam in France.

CHAPTER 37

1 9 0 3 ,   F R A N C E

Franco Malvasi sat in his luxurious Mercedes coupe, one of the first ever seen in Marseilles, drawing on his cigarette and contemplating the exterior of Poppy's. It was a modest house with only a small flight of iron-railinged steps separating it from the street. Heavy lace curtains covered the sparkling windows and the steps were scrubbed clean and edged with yellow scouring stone. On the surface it looked like any well-kept provincial home, but Franco knew that Poppy's was the best-run bordello in the south, and he was here to find out why. Not that he wanted to buy a woman—he was far too fastidious a man for that—but any business that was successful enough to have its praises sung as far south as Milan and Naples and Rome intrigued him. And what *especially* intrigued him was the idea of Poppy, its unpainted, unattainable, ladylike owner.

Tossing away his cigarette, he stepped into the rainy night, glancing at his car admiringly as he walked up the steps. He was a man of many possessions, but for some reason that car gave him more pleasure than most. A massive doorman inspected him warily before permitting him to enter, and a uniformed maid took his coat, asking politely if he had been here before. When he said he hadn't, she told him to wait, Poppy would see him in a minute.

Amused, Franco paced the red-carpeted hall, inspecting the dozens of paintings that crammed the walls from floor to ceiling. He was a collector himself, and quite a connoisseur, and though they were inexpensive and sometimes amateurish, he thought that the buyer had good taste. The tinkling sounds of a Chopin piano sonata and a muted hum of conversation came from behind a half-opened door on his left, and he peered around it curiously. There were large bouquets of flowers every-where and their scent mingled with the subtle perfumes of the women in the rose-shaded room. Several couples were sitting in the deep velvet sofas, talking softly and drinking champagne, while a few well-dressed, attractive girls lingered at the bar, chatting to the pert, smiling blonde behind the counter. At the far end of the room another girl sat holding the hand of a dapper gray-haired man who had fallen asleep by the fire. The pretty girl at the ebony grand switched from Chopin to Paganini, smiling at him pleasantly, while a little maid bustled around offering small dishes of smoked oysters and salmon, pâté de foie and truffles. Apart from the bar and the fact that the girls were all attractive, he might have been at a country house party.

"Signore Malvasi?"

Franco spun around, feeling like a little boy caught out by the head-mistress. "Excuse me," he said, "I was curious . . ."

"Naturally," Poppy replied, showing him into her office, "everyone is curious about Poppy's. May I ask who recommended you, m'sieur?"

He watched for her reaction as he said quietly, "Monsieur Nobel . . . Jacques Nobel," but there wasn't even a flicker in her startling blue eyes as she nodded briskly and wrote his name in a black leather-bound book. The parrot fluttered suddenly from his stand and perched on her desk, glaring at him with eyes like topaz beads.

"You understand the rules here, Signore Malvasi," Poppy said calmly. "Our first commitment is to our girls, but of course by keeping them protected, you—the customer—benefit. The girls are intelligent as well as pretty, and they expect to be treated like ladies in the salon. Upstairs, alone"—she shrugged—"is a personal matter between the two of you. But one word of warning—there will be no violence. I'm sure you must have heard all this from Monsieur Nobel, but we do have rules. Obvi-ously we don't allow just anyone in here, and those we do admit to our 'club' all agree to answer a few questions . . . your name, age, address, and business."

Franco studied her, amused, as she waited for his response. She couldn't be more than twenty-two or -three and in her gray velvet dress she was devastatingly attractive, but she was running her bordello with the gall of an amateur.

"Isn't that asking a lot?" he asked with a cool smile. "Most men don't exactly want it advertised that they are patronizing a bordello—and they certainly don't want their names inscribed in a book for any amateur blackmailer to see."

Poppy snapped her black leather book shut briskly. "We consider Poppy's to be a club, not a bordello," she said curtly. "Many of our clients have been coming here since we first opened, three years ago—they know they can trust us, and we know that we can trust them. I take the names of all new clients for their own protection, as well as for our girls. For instance, a man arriving like you tonight, recommended, but still unknown . . . it's a potentially dangerous situation for a girl, and if by any chance something should 'happen' to her," she said, shrugging, "then we have some recourse against that man. There are some very important names in my book, Signore Malvasi, but I can assure you, I am the *only* one to see them."

She sat back behind the big oval desk, her hands clasped, assessing the man in front of her. He was of medium height, broad-shouldered yet slender, and very well dressed. He had a fine-boned Italian face with piercing dark eyes beneath heavy brows, and although he could be no more than thirty, his forehead was already furrowed and his dark hair was graying at the temples.

"As you came recommended by Monsieur Nobel," she said to him finally, "obviously you already knew our rules."

He nodded. "But I must confess that I'm here for more than just idle curiosity, or the need for a woman. I'm here because I'm intrigued by *you.*"

"Me?" Poppy asked, surprised, adding quickly, "there's nothing intriguing about me, Signore Malvasi. Now, do you still wish to stay, or do you prefer not to answer the questions? I quite understand if you'd rather not."

Franco took out a cigarette, tapping it against his silver case. *"Permesso?"* he asked.

Poppy shook her head. "You may smoke in the salon," she told him, "but I don't permit it in my room. I dislike the smell of smoke."

He nodded, replacing the cigarette in its case. "So, Madame Poppy, you are a woman of strong likes and dislikes, as well as high principles. It seems to me that for so young a woman, you know exactly what you want from life."

She flushed; for some reason this man had sneaked under the barriers she had so carefully erected between her and the clients. Pushing back her chair, she said angrily, "Signore Malvasi, my private life is my own and—though you are not the first to try—it stays that way. I'm afraid I must ask you to leave."

"I had no intention of prying into your privacy," he said calmly, "in fact quite the opposite. It's your business acumen that intrigues me."

Poppy rang a silver bell to summon the doorman. "I'm not interested in your speculations," she replied icily. "Michel will show you to the door."

"I had heard you were a woman of ambition," Franco continued, ignoring the enormous bouncer who had appeared at his elbow, "and I'm here to offer you a business proposition." He stood up with a sigh. "Of course, if you're not interested . . ."

Poppy stared after him as he walked to the door. He'd touched a sensitive nerve; business was now the only thing that interested her and she was no farther on in her "career" than she had been three years ago . . . "Wait, Signore Malvasi," she called, "just a minute. I'd like to hear about your business proposition. Of course, I don't believe that anything you have to say can be of interest to me," she added coldly, "but I'll hear you out."

Franco noticed that she had cleverly put herself back in charge of the situation and he smiled. Poppy was bright as well as beautiful, and that pleased him, though if the truth were known it was because he was beguiled by her red hair and her alabaster skin and those devastating blue eyes that he'd just dreamed up his "business" idea.

"This house does very well—for a small establishment," he told her. "I'm sure that for your partner, Netta Fosquet, that is enough, but for someone like you, Poppy, someone who knows better, who knows there is more to life"—he waved his hand around the room—"can this satisfy you?" He waited a moment but she said nothing. "I think you are a very clever young woman, Poppy Mallory," he said, and then added slyly, "and I've no interest in your past. It's your future that interests me."

Poppy blushed, wondering nervously what he'd meant . . . *her past* . . . but this man couldn't possibly know anything about her. . . .

Franco leaned closer across the desk, staring directly into her eyes. "I think you can do better than this, Poppy Mallory," he said softly, "*a lot* better than this. You are different. Just look what you've created here. But you and I both know what you could really do *if money were no object.*"

"*Money no object,*" she whispered, mesmerized. "What are you saying?"

"My dear," he murmured, "I am offering you the opportunity to open a house on one of the smartest streets in Paris. I'm offering you fame and fortune, Poppy. And I am personally prepared to be your backer."

Fame and fortune . . . the words hovered in the air between them, and her eyes glittered with sudden excitement . . . *a house of her own in Paris* . . . *the smartest street* . . . *money no object* . . . "And what do you ask in return?" she said, coming back to earth suddenly.

"I ask nothing except a return on my capital investment. It will be a business partnership. You will let me know your decision tomorrow, at lunch. Be at Ghiordes Restaurant at one-fifteen," he commanded, pushing back his chair and walking to the door.

"I can't do that . . ." gasped Poppy. "I never—"

"Never go out in public?" Franco smiled. "Then isn't it time you started? How else do you expect your fame to spread?"

"Wait," she cried as he turned the door handle, *"who are you?"*

"Let's just say I'm 'a friend,' " he answered. And with a wave of his hand he was gone.

Ghiordes Restaurant was the most fashionable in Marseilles and Poppy was nervous. She was wearing a tailored silk dress in her usual gray and a frivolous pink hat bought that morning, with a little net veil that made her red hair look peach-colored, and her blue eyes look mysterious.

"Signore Malvasi is expecting you, madame," the maître d' said, escorting her fussily through the crowded tables.

Franco was sitting by the window, a bottle of champagne in a silver cooler beside him, and Poppy thought he looked very distinguished.

"How charming you look, Poppy," he said, taking her hand, and she blushed, aware of the curious stares in their direction, wondering nervously if the other diners knew who she was.

"I took the liberty of ordering champagne," Franco told her, "because I knew that if you came, it was because you were going to say yes. Of course, if I'm wrong, then I'll just have to celebrate the pleasure of having lunch with you."

She laughed. "You were right," she admitted, "though I confess I was up all night worrying about what to do. You see, I'm very fond of Netta, she's my dearest friend . . . my only friend," she added sadly, "apart from Luchay, that is."

"Luchay?"

"The parrot . . . only to me he's more than that. He was my savior, really, my little ray of light, sent from God. . . ." She blushed again, aware she was revealing too much, and she had meant to be so cool, so calm, and so severe . . . she'd meant to keep the upper hand.

"I'm only sorry that it was Luchay who was your savior and not me," Franco replied gallantly, "but perhaps I can be counted as the 'second phase.' "

Poppy laughed, and she realized, amazed, how rarely she laughed these days. "The only thing is," she said suddenly, "I'm afraid to leave Netta. I'm sure she'll get into trouble and she'll be back on the streets in no time. And there's another reason . . ." He lifted his eyebrows questioningly, but she shook her head, staring embarrassed at her plate. "I . . . I can't tell you," she murmured.

"Very well then," he said, "Netta comes with you."

Poppy took a sip of champagne and decided that Franco had nice eyes, very dark brown, almost black, and sort of . . . compelling, was the right word she supposed. And the combination of his young face and gray hair was interesting . . . she wondered again what he did that caused the worried furrows on his brow.

The waiter flourished their menus and Franco watched as she studied hers intently . . . she was so *young,* he thought, and so very vulnerable . . . and she was a lady. And of all things that he had possessed in his life, not one of them had been "a lady."

She glanced up at him smiling. "I'm starving," she said, "aren't you?"

"How old are you, Poppy?" he asked abruptly.

She blushed. "I'm twenty-three . . . today in fact. It's my birthday."

"Twenty-three," he repeated, *"and* your birthday. Then it's a double celebration." He lifted his glass, "Happy birthday, Poppy."

Suddenly she remembered all those other champagne-filled birthdays with her father, which now seemed light-years away. That old life was gone forever, and she was here now, having lunch with Franco Malvasi . . . a businesswoman on the brink of her first big venture that would lead her to fame and fortune.

As they discussed Paris, Franco congratulated himself on being a quick thinker. He'd known there was no chance of getting close to Poppy Mallory personally because she rebuffed all men automatically; the only way had been through business. Like a lot of his best ideas, he'd dreamed it up on the spur of the moment, and he had no doubt that it would reap him his reward.

Netta polished the glasses behind the bar, glaring at Poppy doubtfully. "But who is he?" she demanded. "And how do you know you can trust him?"

"I just feel it in my bones," Poppy said simply.

"Huh! And where have *those* feelings gotten you so far?"

"That was different," she protested, "this has got nothing to do with *love*, it's purely a business arrangement."

"Is that so?" Netta asked skeptically. "You're sure this Franco Malvasi's not captivated by your big blue eyes? Or your reputation as the only chaste woman in the business?"

"Don't be silly, Netta," she replied primly, "besides, he was recommended by Jacques Nobel."

"*Nobel!*" exclaimed Netta. "Poppy, do you realize *who* you are dealing with? Nobel is one of the top men in the crime syndicate that controls the south of France!"

"But he always seems so pleasant," Poppy said, surprised, "he's one of our most charming and considerate clients. He can't possibly be involved in anything really bad."

Netta sighed. "Sometimes I don't know whether it's your innocence that keeps you out of trouble, or whether it gets you into it. I bet you don't even know what the syndicate really is, do you?"

Poppy shook her head. "No, and I'm not sure that I want to," she said firmly. "I'll keep my innocence, Netta. I don't care what he does, all I know is that I trust Franco Malvasi."

Netta stared at her, exasperated. "Sure you do," she said, "isn't he offering you everything you want? I may not be a good businesswoman, but I am smart enough to know that he'll expect something in return for backing you; after all, it's going to cost him a fortune."

"All he wants is a return on his capital investment," Poppy repeated. "It's my business head he admires, Netta, not my body!"

"Don't you believe it," Netta murmured. "Well, I can see your mind is made up, but I shall be sad to see you go."

Poppy stared at her, astonished. "Then you're not coming with me?"

Netta shrugged. "I like it here, my friends are here, my business is thriving. How can I leave it all for Paris when I know I'm not cut out for the big time? You'll need smarter girls than me, Poppy, at your Paris house."

"*But Netta, I need you,*" Poppy wailed, "*don't you see? I can't do it by myself, I know nothing about sex! You've always taken care of that.*"

"Then don't you think it's time you found out?" Netta cried, exasperated. "Just because you had one bad experience you shouldn't let it warp your whole life. Oh, I know you're not like me and the other girls, but you don't even allow yourself to meet a man, let alone fall in love with one." She sighed. "But *merde*, when you finally do, just watch the sparks fly."

"I'm not interested in love," Poppy replied pleadingly, "all I want is you to come with me to Paris. You're my best friend, Netta. There's just you and Luchay. Please?"

"Listen, little one," Netta said, taking her by the shoulders and gazing into her eyes, "I know my place. This is where I belong. You are different, you've always been too good for the rest of us. You don't *need* me this time, Poppy, you're better off on your own. Believe me, you know all you need to know—it wasn't me who made this place a success. Without you it would have been just another bawdy house. So, good luck, my friend. But remember, watch out for Franco Malvasi."

Poppy's things were packed and she was ready to leave. She stared somberly around the room that had been her home for three years; she had given these walls the breath of life but already they looked sad and empty, as though no one had ever lived there. Luchay fluttered nervously in his cage and she turned to soothe him. "We shall like Paris, Luchay," she reassured him as he made anxious little throaty noises, "everything's going to be just fine." But her hand shook as she picked up his cage, because she was as frightened as he was—and of what she had promised to do.

"Are you sure this is what you want?" Netta asked worriedly. "When you opened the house here, it was for me. But this is different. There'll be no going back from such a step, Poppy. You will always be known as a madam."

A madam . . . the words frightened Poppy and she stared uncertainly at her friend, the girl who had taken her in, who'd cared for her and helped her without question or judgment. For a moment she wavered, but then she recalled the feeling of helplessness as she'd trudged alone from Italy to France, searching for a job, and the shock of suddenly finding that no one wanted her and she was a "nobody." And she remembered Franco Malvasi's dark eyes burning into hers as he'd leaned closer across her desk, saying, *"It's your business acumen I'm interested in . . ."* She lifted her chin proudly. "I'm already a madam, Netta," she said, "and I've decided I like it better than being a nobody. Besides," she added with a brilliant smile, "this time I intend to make my fortune and then I'll never be a nobody again."

But as she sat alone on the train with frightened Luchay huddled in his cage beside her, she wondered exactly how she was going to go about it.

CHAPTER 38

Seeing Paris again brought Poppy both pain and pleasure—pain for the memories it caused, and happiness for pleasure at being once again in the world's loveliest city. Her eyes sparkling with excitement, she took a room in a small hotel on the rue des Saints-Pères in the unfashionable Saint-Germain area, and then she checked with the Banque de Paris that the money had been deposited into a new account in her name as Franco had told her it would. It had—and the amount frightened her. It was more than the Marseilles house could have made in forty years!

Eating a solitary meal in the hotel dining room that night, she glanced around at her fellow guests; there was an earnest-looking young man with his head buried in a guidebook; there was a pair of maiden ladies, eating silently and keeping their eyes firmly on their plates; there was an elderly couple obviously up from the provinces; and there was a scattering of spinsterish-looking ladies, dining alone, like herself. With a shock Poppy realized that, with her hair pinned firmly back, in her gray linen skirt and white blouse, she was exactly like them—except, of course, she was younger and she didn't have a pince-nez.

Taking a look in her mirror later, she realized that she was out of style and provincial—and she certainly didn't seem "grand." And how could anyone who looked like a spinster schoolmarm from Marseilles ever hope to run the grandest house in Paris? She lacked all credibility and identity,

and if she were to succeed she would need to establish both. Her customers would expect *style*.

She had expected to see Franco again before she left for Paris, to
discuss the details of her new venture, but there had been just a quick
note from him, confirming their business arrangement and informing her
that a sum of money would be placed at her disposal at the Banque de
Paris. "My only advice to you," he'd written at the end, "is to let your
creative and your business instincts merge. You did it in a small way in
Marseilles, but remember this is Paris; if you are going to make any
impact on that tough, jaded city, where they've seen and done it all
before, you must think *'grand.'*"

Poppy lay awake all that night worrying about what to do, and the
next morning, with circles under her eyes, she made a few discreet inquiries and then headed for the rue de la Paix and the haute-couture salons
of Doucet and Lucille. Her spirits rising, she ordered day dresses and
suits, and the lavish evening gowns for which Lucille was famous, all in
her now "trademark" color of dove-gray.

Stopping at a famous coiffeuse, she had her long hair cut to a fashionable shorter length, so that it curled on top and fell in waves to her
shoulders. One of the new "beauticians" showed her how to enhance her
features with a little powder, a dusting of rouge, a hint of pearl-gray
shadow on her eyelids, and a peach-color lip rouge. She shopped for fine
kid gloves and shoes and purses, and for indecently luxurious underwear
in gray silk trimmed with exquisite ecru lace. And then she went to the
great furrier, Revillon, and asked them to design a special floor-length
silver fox evening cape, and a soft gray squirrel jacket for daytime. Next
she went to the expensive Ritz Hotel and checked into a suite, ordering
her bags to be sent around from the rue des Saints-Pères.

Finally she sank, exhausted, into a huge, luxurious bathtub filled with
hot water and perfumed oils. "Now I'm ready for Paris," she exclaimed
out loud. "Now I'm thinking 'grand.'"

The next important step was the house. The gentleman she'd asked to
show her the properties he dealt with in Paris's most exclusive areas
looked skeptical, until Poppy showed him her banker's draft with the
amount left blank for her to fill in, and the words *unlimited funds available* in the bank's accompanying letter. "Of course, Madame Mallory,"
he exclaimed, as though he knew of her already, and suddenly he was all
smiles and deference. But when she finally chose the big old *hôtel par-
ticulier,* a private mansion in the fashionable sixteenth arrondissement,
and signed the bank draft for a small fortune with a trembling hand,

Poppy wished with all her heart that Franco or Netta were there to guide her.

An army of efficient workmen, recommended by the estate agent, swept through the old house, converting the rooms upstairs into lavish suites, and repaving the hall in marble. Biting her lip at the painful memories, Poppy ordered enormous crystal chandeliers from Venice; and she bought an entire library of carved oak paneling and shelves already filled with books, taken straight from an old English manor. She purchased carpets from Aubusson and silk rugs from China and Persia, so that when her "guests" stepped out of bed all they would feel on their bare toes would be softness and warmth. She ordered bathtubs made of onyx with graceful gold swan faucets with eyes of malachite and lapis; and she ordered brocade fabric for the curtains and the sofas to be specially woven in Lyons in a dozen cleverly "faded" shades of coral and peach, and mint and celadon, and the softest blues. She decided she wanted no vulgar matching suites of furniture; she wanted only the beautiful antique pieces that she saw in the grand shops and fell in love with. She felt like a crazy millionaire on a spending spree, but always at the back of her mind was the fact that Franco Malvasi expected a return on his investment.

Her own rooms on the ground floor were finally finished and, at last, she moved in. They were as simple and unfussy as her new couture dresses, and as elegant. Her bedroom walls were lined in pleated pale gray silk that matched the hangings on her big four-poster bed. The rugs were the palest blue-gray and the curtains were of ruched white taffeta. The paintings on her walls were her old favorites brought from her odd, inexperienced collection in Marseilles, and the few ornaments were her own. But thinking "grand," she had her portrait painted by John Singer Sargent to hang in the library.

She had paid for everything in the apartment herself—not a cent of Franco Malvasi's money was being spent on anything that wasn't strictly business. But she knew she must also be a little bit outrageous, and remembering her promise to make Luchay a Prince of Parrots, she called the grand jeweler, Bulgari, in Rome, and asked him to design a beautiful new gold and jeweled stand. "It'll be a long way from that old broomhandle and that cold little room of Netta's in Marseilles," she told Luchay fondly. And then, climbing into her big new bed with the parrot huddled into her shoulder for company, she cried herself to sleep, because she really didn't know what she was doing and she did miss Netta so.

Hiding her nerves beneath her new couture gowns, Poppy began to go out, always alone because she knew no men to escort her. She was aware of the ripple of interest as she sat in the stalls at the Folies-Bergère, dressed in a lavish gown and her sumptuous gray fur; watching the audience to see what it was about the performers they liked. She ignored the riffraff and concentrated on the obviously wealthy and aristocratic men who were there to see the girls in the show, not merely to solicit some little strumpet from the balcony. And she noticed that it wasn't merely the girl with the most stupendous breasts or the most beautiful derriere or the longest legs that they admired—though those assets helped—it was also the girl's personality and the touch of the unexpected. It was the comic little blonde with the face of a cherub who sang wicked songs with an innocent expression and the haughty milk-complexioned chanteuse clothed in a novice's pure white habit, which she finally flung open to reveal a daring black lace leotard that barely restrained her exuberant breasts, that sent a tingle down every male spine. It was the red-haired dancer with a limber, versatile body who sparkled with sheer verve and vivacity, and the mysterious Oriental girl singer dressed in opulently embroidered Chinese silks, whose main attraction was her air of mystery and the unknown. "Mystery," the unexpected, a touch of wickedness, the comic, the graceful energy . . . Poppy saw that these were all characteristics that men admired.

One night she made a sensational entrance at Maxim's, fussed over by the maître d' and obsequious waiters. She was wrapped in her sumptuous floor-length silver fox cape beneath which she wore Lucille's slithering gray chiffon gown, tight at neck and wrist. Her red hair looked vibrant against the cool color and the wonderful five strands of the whore's pearls glowed against her pale skin. Every man in the restaurant turned to stare and the women glared at her covertly, scenting some new rival in their fiercely competitive courtesans' ranks. But Poppy refused demurely the little notes and the bottles of champagne sent over by intrigued admirers, shaking her head and smiling her secretive little smile. She was there to learn, not to take part. But she was desperately worried because although she now knew what she wanted, she still had no idea how to go about recruiting her "girls."

Simone Lalage had been one of Paris's top courtesans for fifteen years —a kept woman de luxe who, though no longer quite as young as she used to be, was still very beautiful. Simone was not a clever woman, but she'd inherited an innate peasant shrewdness from generations of farming forebears in Languedoc, and she had a body to rival that of any seventeen-year-old starlet at the music halls. After a rough start in life she had managed to amass a fortune in jewels and cash, but she'd never forgotten her debt of gratitude to Jacques Nobel, who had started her on her glittering career. And as she drove the three blocks from her house on the rue Le Sueur to number 16, rue des Arbres, she was repaying his favor.

Ever since Jacques had called her four months ago and told her that Franco Malvasi wanted her to help Poppy, but without letting Poppy know, Simone had been keeping an eye on things. It was she who'd called the real estate salesman and guided Poppy to the right house on the right street; she who'd made sure that the right workers were sent to the house and that they'd finished in double-quick time; it was she who'd called her old friend, the maître d'hôtel at Maxim's, telling him about Poppy and asking him to seat her in a prominent position. Simone knew everyone in Paris who was anyone; she always had her inquisitive ear to the ground for the latest scandal and the newest trends, and she often seemed to know what was going to happen before it even happened. The word in Paris was that if you wanted to know *anything*, just ask Simone Lalage.

Her glossy maroon de Courmont limousine drew to a halt in front of number 16, rue des Arbres, and the chauffeur sprang to open her door before hurrying up the steps to ring the bell. A young maid in a demure black dress and frilled white organdy apron opened the door, bobbing respectfully as the chauffeur informed her that "Madame Lalage was here to see Madame Mallory."

Simone glanced around her critically, taking in the beautiful Persian rugs, the exquisite antique furnishings, the soft pleasing colors of the drapes and the masses of flowers—and the empty silver tray on the console table where normally a dozen or so little white calling cards would have been displayed, its emptiness betraying the fact that no one at all had yet called on Poppy.

She inspected Paris's soon-to-be "success" closely as Poppy walked down the blue-carpeted steps toward her. The girl was still breathtakingly young and as elegant as the best of couturiers could make her, and her choice of that clear dove-gray color was masterful. Her beautiful wild-looking red hair was swept up at the sides and fell in exuberant waves to her shoulders, and it had been cut by an artist. Her blue eyes had an arrogant tilt even though her glance was apprehensive. Poppy hadn't yet learned to mask her feelings, Simone thought, but she knew that before too long, she would. Jacques Nobel had told her that she was a very clever woman. And judging by this house and those incredible pearls, she'd already made her first conquest!

"My dear," she said, sweeping haughtily toward Poppy and offering her hand in an immaculate lilac kid glove that exactly matched her dress, "you simply can't have a young girl like that opening your door; you must get a butler at once."

"A butler?" Poppy repeated, astounded.

"Naturally." Simone smiled her famous smile, showing two surprising dimples in her soft round cheeks. "In a house this size you must have the proper staff, otherwise what will people think? And in Paris, my dear, it's what *people think* that matters. It's just so easy to be out of style." As Poppy stared at her, bemused, she added sharply, "Well, are we to stand in the hallway all day? Or are you going to ask me into the salon for some tea?"

"Tea? Oh, yes, of course." Poppy beamed; after all these weeks alone she was so relieved to have company, she would have been happy to take tea with almost anyone. Besides, she knew who Simone Lalage was and right now she seemed like a gift from heaven. Simone would be bound to know what she needed.

"I'm here because I was curious," Simone said, her sharp dark eyes taking in every detail of the luxurious room as she sipped jasmine tea from a beautiful Limoges cup. "And as I live around the corner, I didn't have far to come to satisfy my curiosity. You must look upon me as a neighbor, my dear," she said, leaning forward and patting Poppy's knee kindly with her lilac-gloved hand. "Of course, I noticed you at Maxim's —they tell me you've been there every night for a month now, and I've heard reports that you were seen at the Folies and the theaters and music halls. And always alone. Isn't that rather surprising, for someone of your obvious wealth and good looks? I take it we are in the same business?" She knew perfectly well what Poppy's business was, but from her innocent smile Poppy would never have guessed it.

"Not *quite* the same business, Madame Lalage," Poppy said carefully, "as a matter of fact I'm not in any business at all, right now."

"Call me Simone, my dear," she said, "and pour me some more of that delicious jasmine tea while you explain yourself."

Dare she ask her? Poppy wondered, inspecting her from beneath her lashes as she poured the tea. Simone was tall and statuesque, with an olive skin brightened cleverly with rouge, and masses of long dark hair that today she wore swept back into an elegant chignon. She was dressed beautifully and she was weighed down beneath what looked like several million francs' worth of diamonds—there were ropes of them slung around her neck, starburst brooches pinned to her chest, enormous pear-shaped drops in her ears, and half a dozen rings on her fingers.

Simone's eyes sparkled like her diamonds as she said merrily, "I'm a peasant at heart, my dear, I always carry some of my wealth on my person—I never feel one can totally trust *banks,* do you?"

Poppy laughed. "Simone," she said, "I have a problem. This house is not meant for me alone, it's meant to be the core of my new business venture."

"Is that so," Simone said interestedly, as though she was hearing it for the first time. "Then why don't you tell me all about it? Maybe I can help with the problem. After all, my dear," she added with a charming grin, "they say there's nothing I don't know about in Paris, or how to do it, or how to get it!"

For the second time Poppy knew she had to put her trust in a stranger, and again she felt she wasn't wrong. She began by telling her about Poppy's in Marseilles, and, without mentioning Franco's name, about how she had the backing of a rich man to open her own house, and that it was to be the grandest house in Paris—with her own particular style. "It's not a bordello," she told Simone firmly, "it's more of a gentleman's club, a civilized place where a man can come and relax, maybe he'll have dinner, or a drink with his friends, or conduct a little business. And if he also wishes the company of an attractive, intelligent young woman at dinner, for an hour or so—or for the night—he shall have it." She sighed heavily. "The only trouble is, I don't know where to find the girls."

"It's simple, my dear," Simone told her briskly, "once the girls know, *they'll* find you. And I shall personally make sure that the right sort of girl gets to know."

"It's important," Poppy said urgently. "She can't be the same sort of girl you would find in just any house. She must be intelligent as well as attractive—but of course beauty will be an added bonus. And, of course, she must be clever in bed, but she should also know how to entertain a man, how to make him feel happy so that he'll be glad to be here in our house, in our company. She must be able to learn; she'll need to read books and newspapers so she can talk on the arts and current affairs." She stared earnestly at Simone. "I want my girls to be able to sit down to dine with politicians, and businessmen, or with artists, actors, or writers, and to be able to talk to them intelligently about their own world. I want my customers to feel *at home* here, the way a man does in his club."

"I see," Simone said thoughtfully, "so you're a *clever* woman, Poppy, as well as a beautiful one. Oh, yes, you are beautiful, you know," she said as Poppy blushed, "especially when you are intense like that . . . all that energy and flashing blue eyes and wild red hair. And where is the man in your life? Could it be this mysterious financial backer?"

Poppy shook her head, blushing even deeper. "No, no, of course not . . ." she murmured, "I'm too busy for that sort of thing."

Simone put down her teacup and straightened her expensive little lilac straw hat. " 'That sort of thing,' as you call it, Poppy, is what makes the world go round," she said, laughing. Her grin was mischievous, and for a moment Poppy caught a flash of the young girl she had once been. "And besides, it's what keeps me young. Sex once or twice a day is still my recipe for physical fitness—and for putting a sparkle back into the eye and a blush of color into the complexion. And sex is also something that's going to make you a very rich and successful woman," she added shrewdly. "I shall put the word out, my dear, so you'd best employ that butler before the little maid is run off her feet answering the door. Of course, for an *understanding* butler, you must go to Smith's, the English agency. The English are always so tolerant of these things, aren't they?

"You must come to my next dinner," she told her as she stepped into her beautiful maroon car, "I give one every month, you know. They are quite famous. It's a coup to be invited to Simone Lalage's dinners—your first coup in Paris, but not your last," she added as she waved good-bye.

Poppy went to Smith's Agency the next day and interviewed butlers, choosing a dignified white-haired man whose noncommittal expression never changed throughout the interview. His name was Watkins and he was a polite Englishman, tall and discreet in his butler's black tails and striped gray trousers, and he came highly recommended by a duchess who was down on her luck and could no longer afford him. Poppy explained her "household" delicately, but he merely nodded and said gravely, "I understand, madame. The Duchess's household, too, was a little eccentric."

Over the next few weeks Watkins was kept very busy answering the door to a stream of young women, some of them beautiful but all of them attractive and dressed in their best, and all wanting to become one of Poppy's "girls."

Sitting behind the big leather-topped desk in her study, which she'd chosen because it looked impressive, Poppy questioned them all closely, and if they were too young or obviously inexperienced, she told them bluntly that she wasn't about to set young girls like them on the wrong path because they thought they could earn some easy money. "Believe me," she said, "it's never easy—you are better off going back to the little town or village in the provinces you came from, marrying that nice young farmer or salesman and have a houseful of children. That's where happiness lies—not here."

And she didn't choose only the prettiest girls; she wanted clever ones who could learn, she wanted girls who enjoyed sex, and she wanted girls who were different, who sparkled with personality, or wit, or humor. When she had chosen them, she told them they must attend lessons in manners and deportment and learn how to dress.

"The way you look is important," she lectured them, "as is your voice, and your demeanor. You may not have been born to the role, but you are about to become young ladies. In the salon, that is. Of course, upstairs is another matter. You know the old story, 'a lady in the drawing room and a whore in bed'—well, that should be you—if that's what the man wants. But always remember, you are in control of the situation—if you don't like the man or what he asks you to do, then just say so and we will ask him to leave. I'm not laying down any rules," she told them simply, "after all, we aim to please, and as you know a gentleman's pleasures can vary."

They looked at her expectantly as she got to the subject of sex, and Poppy struggled to remember what Netta and Simone had told her. Keeping the nervous tremor from her voice with an effort—because she was aware they knew more about it than she did, she skated lightly over it. "If a man wants more than one partner, and you enjoy that, then it's perfectly all right," she said quickly. "Some men enjoy dressing in women's clothes, or being treated like a naughty boy, and some just like to watch. Some will want nothing at all except the pleasure of your charming company," she went on, remembering Netta's words, "and maybe an affectionate kiss good night. Many men are *starved* for love and affection and while they can't expect to buy love, we can certainly offer the affection. And always remember," she told them firmly, "if you behave like a lady, you will be treated like one. . . ."

Thinking "grand," Poppy sent them to the top couturiers, telling them that she expected them to be well dressed and groomed at all times, even when they weren't working, because as "Poppy's girls" they would have to maintain a reputation for being the smartest in Paris. She found a diction teacher to rid them of their provincial accents and their harsh tones, until they spoke as softly and mellifluously as any of the great actresses; she hired tutors to teach them about the arts, and she sent them all to the latest plays; she plied them with the latest novels and biographies and books on philosophy, and she gave them tests to see where their natural interests lay. She paid for lessons in deportment and manners, etiquette, wines and food. In two months she'd covered everything and, at the end of her crash course in the social arts, she sent them out to the grandest restaurants—alone—to test their savoir faire. All of her girls passed the test with flying colors, returning elated with stories of obsequious maître d's and attentive waiters, and the interested attention of other diners.

Poppy was satisfied, her girls could go anywhere. Of course, she could give them no lessons for their work "upstairs," as she called it to herself; she would just have to trust Simone Lalage, who had promised her everything would be all right.

The house was ready at last. Sargent's full-length portrait of her in a cascading pale gray satin gown, her red hair upswept and dotted with diamond stars, dominated the library; and Luchay, on his wonderful bejeweled gold stand, waited in the hall to dazzle her guests.

With Simone's help, she organized an opening party, sending out engraved white cards from the very best stationery shop, stating that *Madame Poppy* would be *at home at numéro seize, rue des Arbres, on the evening of December 10th, between 9:30 and midnight.*

Two new chefs had been hired, one specializing in traditional French haute-cuisine, and the other in exotic foreign dishes from China and India. On the night of the party Poppy surveyed the groaning sideboards loaded with silver dishes, remembering herself as a child on Russian Hill, trailing her finger in the chocolate mousse and taking a bite out of a turkey leg while her Papa played poker and the showgirls danced. Now *she* was giving the party. I've come full circle, she thought sadly. They were right after all, like father, like daughter . . .

The girls were lined up in the salon awaiting her inspection and she walked down the line, removing a too ostentatious pair of earrings here and straightening a bow there, finally standing back and looking at them approvingly. The couturiers had done a good job and each girl looked true to her personality—the flamboyant dressed flamboyantly, the demure, demurely, and the more eccentric, differently—but they all looked, sounded, and conducted themselves like "ladies." "I'm proud of you," she told them simply. "Be proud of yourselves and you won't regret your decision to work for me."

Wearing trailing gray velvet and her pearls, with a scented white gardenia in her hair, she paced the beautiful Aubusson rug in the hall, throwing anxious glances at Luchay, skittering excitedly up and down on his stand, and at Watkins waiting impassively by the door. She wondered if Franco Malvasi would come. She'd sent an invitation to his villa in Naples but had received no reply. In fact she hadn't heard a word from him in the four months it had taken to put the house together, and she wondered worriedly whether he'd already lost interest in his new "business venture." But the money was still there in the Banque de Paris, as much as she cared to spend, though of course she made sure that every cent was entered into the immaculate ledgers kept by the very reputable accountants recommended by the bank.

She needn't have worried about her guests. Simone had let it be known that she would be attending the smartest party in Paris, and by now everyone was burning with curiosity. They came in droves, the rich, the aristocratic, the stars of the theaters and the music halls, the courtesans and a few curious—and daring—ladies. But Franco Malvasi wasn't among them. They marveled at Luchay, the proud guardian of the hall on his Bulgari stand with jeweled finials the size of tennis balls; they admired Poppy's portrait hanging in the library, and paid her extravagant compliments. They drank her champagne and ate her food. And they met her lovely girls, who were proving they had learned their lessons well and were mingling discreetly with the guests. Simone told her afterward that she was certain every man who'd been to the party wanted to come back. "Numéro seize, rue des Arbres, is on the map," she said gleefully, "you're *made*, Poppy."

Still, as she closed the door wearily on her last guest, Poppy wondered wistfully why Franco hadn't been there to witness her triumph.

CHAPTER 39

1 9 0 4 ,   F R A N C E

The discreet and very expensive "club" at numéro seize, rue des Arbres, became a password among those who knew in fashionable Paris. They said the food at Numéro Seize was out of this world, and that the fabulous library had books to satisfy anyone's curiosity—from a priceless collection of erotica, to books on philosophy and science as well as all the latest novels. They said a man could read the newspaper in peace in the library at Numéro Seize, and that he could eat a delicious leisurely meal —alone, if he so wished, or in the company of a delightful girl who understood what he was talking about when he boasted of his business successes. They said a man felt at home at Numéro Seize, he could relax and be himself—or anyone he wished. And if he wanted more, they said that beneath its elegant country house clubbiness, a man could almost *scent* the lust in the air at Numéro Seize. It was all there for the taking— at a price, of course, because the membership fee at Numéro Seize was outrageous.

Each girl's room was decorated to suit her personality: an exotic Chinese wallpaper and red lacquer for Han-Su, the half-Javanese, half-French odalisque, who was said to drive men wild with her long, shiny black hair, fine as spun silk, that fell to her knees, veiling her voluptuous body in the most tantalizing way. Han-Su entangled a man in that hair, they said, teasing him with its softness, tying her hair around his neck as she straddled him, and raking her long red lacquered nails along his flesh until he quivered with desire. Han-Su knew Oriental secrets of muscle control that could draw a man to new heights of passion, not once or even twice, but many times; and afterward she would play the obedient Oriental maiden, washing his body and tending him, bringing him jasmine tea as well as champagne.

Then there was Belinda, the small English blonde with the milkmaid skin in the fresh blue-and-white toile de jouy room, with her wide, appealingly innocent blue eyes, her carefully tumbled blond curls, her breathy little-girl voice and her charmingly fractured French. Belinda's waist was so tiny, a man could span it easily with his hands, and her breasts were so generous, she could tuck a man's organ between them and squeeze him until he almost fainted from pleasure.

There was yellow Regency-striped wallpaper for the elegant amber-haired Solange, who never wore any underwear and let every man know it. Solange had long legs and a curving bottom and as her exquisite Lucille chiffon evening dress flowed and clung to her every curve they would watch her speculatively, comparing her cool, ladylike image with their own private knowledge of what lay beneath—and it was said that Solange more than any of the others really enjoyed her work. Solange loved sex; she wore no underwear because she enjoyed the *frisson* of pleasure of her own naked body under the expensive dress; she was haughty and choosy, but when a man pleased her, she would make him feel like a king.

There was a mysterious room with black-lacquered walls and satin sheets chosen by a dusky-eyed beauty from Tunisia, who, it was said, had brought with her the ancient secrets of centuries of the harem. Mafelda never smiled, but her large slumberous dark eyes would sweep as hotly over a man as a desert wind, as though she couldn't wait to explore the secrets of his body. Mafelda had dark hennaed hair and smooth bronze skin and she had a ritual, before making love, of massaging her man with scented oils, smoothly rubbing and squeezing every part of his body, lubricating and retreating, until he burst with desire. And then she would take him like a wild lioness in heat.

Magda was a haughty Hungarian girl with elevated cheekbones, a passionate cruel mouth, and a mane of blond hair, who claimed to be descended from royalty and who always wore long white gloves, even when she was making love. She had an opulent white lace and dark blue satin room where she held court, tossing her satin slippers from her perfect slender feet and commanding her man to kiss them, pushing him back arrogantly with her foot when his hand slid eagerly upward from her slender ankle, to her silken calf, to her warm thigh. . . . She would command him to apologize and then make him prostrate himself at her feet before she would permit even the smallest caress. To make love to Magda was a privilege that few men actually achieved, but those who preferred her methods were satisfied with their particular rewards . . . that same haughty satin-shod foot on their private parts was enough to fill their cup of ecstasy.

Villette's room had a small stage lined with mirrors where she could watch herself dance. Villette was a flamboyant exhibitionist, a peasant girl with the body of a Venus who liked nothing more than to display it. Villette wanted to parade for a man—or men, because for her the more the merrier. She would dance for them, removing each chiffon veil from her wonderful alabaster curves and dragging it, still warm and scented from her flesh, across their faces and their bodies, slowly, tauntingly, until at last all was revealed. It could be said that Villette was more in love with herself than any man, but every man adored her "performance."

And then there was Chloe, who was slightly older and whose ample curves held a motherly charm; and Belkis, whose huge waiflike dark eyes and small-breasted, tight-buttocked body had a gamine appeal; and there were Martina and Floquette, who always liked to work together, and who knew each other's bodies as intimately as they knew their own, and who loved each other simply as sisters. And the special Véronique, who understood how to find out a man's secrets, and how to make his fantasies come true. There was someone to suit every taste at Numéro Seize.

And, of course, the woman all the men secretly coveted was the mysterious and beautiful Poppy. She was always there to greet them, always dressed in gray and always with a smile in her alluring bright blue eyes. Poppy was the success of Paris. Who she was and where she came from were the questions on everyone's lips, but they were questions that went unanswered. Poppy remained a charming enigma, always friendly, always smiling—and always alone.

It was a bitterly cold night in February and fires blazed cheerfully in all the rooms, filling the house with the comforting scent of applewood, while outside the snow and slush piled up on the sidewalks. Few people were out on the stormy streets and the great salon was quiet, just the sound of one of the girls playing Mozart on the piano, and the muted hum of conversation from the dining room where a few gentlemen were enjoying a meal and talking business, and the click of billiard cues from the library.

Poppy busied herself at her desk, running her pen over long columns of figures, assessing each month's income against the past and nodding approvingly. She glanced at the little silver clock on her desk. It was eleven-thirty p.m. and she sat back in her chair, yawning and running her hands wearily through her hair. She hadn't had a day off since Numéro Seize opened two months ago; she was exhausted, and afraid of what she was doing, though she never allowed it to show—except when she was alone, as she was now. If there had been any small glimmer of hope in her heart that maybe someday she might go home again to the Rancho Santa Vittoria and be forgiven, it was gone. She had burned her bridges to her past and her future was as Paris's smartest—and one day richest—madam. But even though she tried to tell herself that her girls were like Netta and that they would have been selling themselves anyway, reassuring herself about how much better off they were working for her, she knew it wasn't right. But she told herself wearily that there was no one who cared what she did, or didn't do, anymore. Only Luchay.

Nevertheless, Numéro Seize was an undoubted success. It would be a while before she recouped the initial investment, but with the deliberately high membership fee that also served to keep the club exclusive, it wouldn't be nearly as long as she had feared. Of course, her overheads were enormous—but so were her prices, and she'd found out soon enough that the more expensive things were, the happier the customers were to pay. They seemed convinced that anything that cost so much must be good. "And in our case, it is," she said, yawning again, so lost in her thoughts that she didn't hear the door.

"Well, and how is my business partner?" a deep masculine voice asked. Her eyes flew open and she stared, shocked, at Franco Malvasi.

"You look at me as though I'm a ghost," he laughed, "but I assure you I am real. Here, feel my hand, it's cold but the pulse still beats, the blood still flows in its veins."

"I wasn't expecting you . . ." Poppy stammered, at a loss for words. Her heart was thudding and she felt both excited and nervous at the same time.

Franco tapped his cigarette against his silver case. *"Permesso?"* he asked, and then, frowning, said, "No, of course not, I remember you don't allow anyone to smoke in your rooms."

He was wearing evening clothes and Poppy thought his hair looked grayer, contrasting even more sharply with his still-young face that was marked deeply with lines of worry and tension. She noticed, fascinated, the fine dark hairs along the back of his hand as he placed the cigarette case on the table and took a seat opposite her.

"Do you like the house?" she asked, rearranging her ruffled hair anxiously. "I'm afraid it cost an awful lot of money, but you said . . . think 'grand' . . ."

"Never be afraid of spending money on a good investment," Franco told her coolly, "as I'm sure you know from the ledgers in front of you; the figures are already very good for such a young business."

"I'm so glad," she replied, sighing with relief, "you can't imagine how many nights I've lain awake wondering why you never came to see me. I thought you must be angry, or that you'd lost interest."

Franco closed his eyes for a moment so she wouldn't read his expression. What other woman would have confessed her thoughts so innocently? In his world, every word that was uttered was fraught with dangerous hidden meanings; nothing was what it seemed. Poppy's guilelessness filled him with tenderness. He curbed his desire to take her in his arms and tell her that he'd thought about her every single day for months; that he'd paced the floors of his villa in Naples, smoking cigarette after cigarette, wondering what she was doing, and telling himself that he mustn't go to her, it wasn't time yet. He wanted to tell her that he'd dreamed of having her in his arms so often, he almost knew how she would feel, how she would respond to his lovemaking. . . .

With a great flutter of wings Luchay flew from his golden perch and settled on the desk between them, crouching low and glaring balefully at Franco.

"I'm not sure that your parrot likes me," he said with a smile.

"Of course he does. Luchay is very friendly." Poppy picked up the bird, stroking his brilliant feathers gently. "He's probably just hungry, that's all. I hadn't realized it was so late."

"Then is it too late to ask you to have dinner with me?"

She bit her lip, embarrassed. "The fact is I made a rule never to have dinner with any gentleman here. If they see me dining with you, they'll think I've changed my mind and then they're sure to get angry when I refuse to have dinner with them."

Franco recalled the beautiful portrait of her he'd just seen hanging in the library for everyone to admire—and to covet—and he burned with a sudden savage jealousy as he thought of other men dining with her, flirting with her, seeking her favors. He shrugged coldly. "As you wish."

"Of course, I could ask the chef to prepare something special and serve it in my apartment," she suggested, blushing, "that is, if you don't think I'm being forward inviting you there."

"My dear Poppy," he laughed, his heart flooding with relief, "you wouldn't know how to be forward, that's part of your charm."

Poppy wasn't sure whether it was a compliment or not, but feeling ridiculously pleased, she led the way to her suite of rooms. They were on the first floor overlooking a small courtyard garden and well away from the activities of the rest of the house.

Franco was surprised by the simplicity; there was none of the lavish opulence of the rest of the house here, though it was comfortable and pretty. Her only luxury seemed to be the pots of hothouse white gardenias whose subtle, heady scent lingered in his nostrils. A fire burned in the grate and next to the blue brocade sofa was a small table piled with books.

"Books are my escape," Poppy said, following his glance. She hesitated and then added, "I want you to know that I didn't spend any of your money on my own rooms. It didn't seem right to think 'grand' in here. After all, no one sees it but me."

He could have kissed her for those last few words, no one else came here but her. His Poppy was all alone, thank God, oh, thank God. . . . Picking a gardenia, he put it in his buttonhole.

She summoned a waiter and ordered an expert little dinner, selecting a wine from the list with a frown of concentration. Then she put Luchay onto his stand and gave him a small dish of seeds, turning to Franco guiltily. "I'm such a bad hostess," she said. "I forgot to ask if you would like a drink."

"No," he said, "but I'd like you to come here and sit next to me. Tell me, how you are enjoying Paris? Have you made any friends?"

She sat beside him stiffly. "Friends?" she asked, frowning. "Only one, Simone Lalage. She was so helpful, I don't know what I'd have done without her."

He smiled. "Simone Lalage? Isn't she a famous courtesan? I wouldn't have thought she was exactly the kind of person you would have chosen as a friend."

"I didn't choose her," she said, and told him the story of how Simone had arrived unexpectedly on her doorstep just when she was despairing of ever meeting anybody, and how she'd helped her find her girls. "I'm so proud of my girls," she told him, "they are all so nice, and so happy to be working in these wonderful surroundings. Most of them were on the stage, and when times were hard they'd drifted into . . . into relationships, or even onto the streets. Like me and Netta, they were living on just a few francs and hope. Through Simone they heard about Numéro Seize, and now here they are. They are so clever, when they dine with cabinet ministers they can discuss the latest political situation fluently, and when they dine with financiers, they can ask the right questions; and they know all the latest plays and books and fashions. So you see," she said, searching his face for approval, "they are not just . . . not merely . . ." She touched her pearls nervously, unwilling to say the word *whores.*

Franco tasted the wine, a Château Leoville Lascasse, nodding approvingly. "So," he said, "then are you all set to make your fortune, Poppy? I wonder, how much is *a fortune,* to a girl like you?"

"A fortune?" Poppy remembered Jeb's story of how he'd won a fortune at the gaming tables in Monte Carlo, and how quickly it had disappeared, but she had no idea of how much it was. "A million dollars," she hazarded.

"A single million? Such modest ambitions, Poppy, I expected better from you than that."

She blushed angrily, glaring at him as he ate the salmi of pheasant; what did he expect her to answer, then, ten, twelve . . . twenty million? How could she ever hope to earn that kind of money, even with Numéro Seize a raging success?

"Investments, my dear," he said, answering her unspoken question. "If you listen carefully, I shall tell you how to become a very rich woman. Not just one million, Poppy, but all the millions you've ever wanted. Naturally, it will take time, this is not just some get-rich-quick scheme, but in ten, twenty, thirty years you will be *very* rich."

The delicious food and wine lay untouched as Poppy listened to what he was saying, leaning forward across the table, her chin propped in her hand, her eyes fixed on his face. Time ticked by, the candle spluttered, and a little maid came in to bank up the fire, drawing the pale curtains against the snow falling steadily outside the long window.

When Franco had finished, she looked at him with respect. "It's all so simple, the way you tell it," she said, awed. "Is that how you made your fortune, then?" She sat back, startled as his smile faded. His face was masklike and suddenly he seemed like a different person.

"It's getting late," he said coldly. "It's time I was going. Just remember my advice, Poppy, and one day you'll be a very rich woman."

She glanced nervously at him from beneath her lashes as she followed him to the door; one minute he'd been relaxed and smiling, the next he was cold and indifferent. She wondered what she had said wrong.

"Shall I see you again?" she asked quietly. He stared at her broodingly for a moment. "I hope so, Poppy," he said. And then he opened the door and strode quickly away along the corridor.

She waited, hoping Franco would turn and wave good-bye, but he didn't, and she closed the door with a sigh, wondering when she would see him again. She wished she hadn't asked him such a foolish, personal question. She'd always avoided knowing exactly what it was he did, and despite what Netta had said, she was still convinced it could never be anything bad. Franco Malvasi had helped her when she needed it; why, tonight he'd even shown her a way to invest her money that would ensure her future. He was a kind man, and an interesting one, and she was suddenly afraid she found him very attractive.

CHAPTER 40

1904, ITALY

Franco didn't know how much longer he could go on playing the waiting game; Poppy Mallory was interfering with his life; she dominated his thoughts, she affected every move he made. He was manipulating his business empire automatically, and his executives began to look at him nervously as he paced endlessly back and forth in the library of his big villa. They needn't have worried; Franco's iron hand and steely brain still controlled his empire expertly. But on the table beside his bed lay a withered gardenia that he had forbidden his servants to remove. And locked in a private safe was a small file of papers that told everything there was to know about Poppy Mallory.

Franco Malvasi had been born to inherit an empire. His father had planned it that way. Enzo Malvasi was a self-made man who, by dint of a sharp brain and a single-minded ruthlessness, had clawed his way from the lower depths of the Sicilian underworld—via extortion, protection, ransom, and blackmail—until he "owned" a fair-sized piece of southern Italy for himself.

Enzo had started out in Palermo as a wild young lad of sixteen, eager to attract the attention of the local Cosa Nostra and gain admittance to their secret ranks. First he'd collected small sums of protection money for them, then he'd done a couple of revenge jobs of arson, and a few broken legs for those who "forgot" to pay. His work had gradually increased in importance, and in violence, and as his final test, before he could be admitted to the dreaded society, he knew he had to kill a man. It was a village barber suspected of passing secrets from one Family to another. Enzo had simply walked in and asked for a shave. He had sat in the chair and as the barber wrapped a white towel around him, he'd shot him. Enzo had felt no emotion about the act, only triumph that at last he'd proven himself and now he would become a sworn member of the Cosa Nostra. But he decided he would never again shoot a man in the stomach at close range; it was too messy.

He'd progressed rapidly, and by the time he was twenty-five he was living in a peasant's idea of luxury in Naples and was known as a hard man, even in a world as tough as his. He returned briefly to Sicily, to marry a nice local girl from a respected Mafia Family, whose father was murdered two weeks later by a rival gang.

By the time he was thirty, he was head of his own "Malvasi Family" with territories and businesses that had made him a rich and feared man.

His first child, a son, as he had decided, was born nine months later and named Franco for Carmela Malvasi's dead father. Enzo was himself a small man with preternaturally gray hair and a permanent worried frown, but as his boy grew and developed he thought disappointedly that he would have liked him to be more robust, taller, stronger—as befitted a future ruler. Still, his boy was intelligent even if he was small; he was interested in everything, he was affectionate, and his mother adored him.

Franco's godfather risked traveling from the safety of his territory in Sicily for his baptism, in order to show respect for his old friend and countryman Enzo. His other godfather came from the north of Italy, and Franco's aunts stood as godmothers. His early childhood was a happy one, running free in the palatial villa near Naples with its big, sunny walled garden. Franco didn't even notice that its walls were exceptionally high, nor that the men who patrolled them and manned the great iron gates were not really there as his "friends." All the other children he was taken to visit, or who came to see him, lived exactly the same way. His mother loved him and his father determined to make a gentleman of him. He had tutors from the age of four to teach him reading, writing, and arithmetic. He had a bright, acquisitive mind and he enjoyed his studies. In fact his tutors said he exhausted them, coming up with question after question and pursuing his train of thought with persistence and determination until he was satisfied with their answers.

"The boy needs other children," the tutor told Signora Malvasi when he was seven years old, "he needs school." Carmela wanted nothing but the best for her boy, but when she brought up the subject with Enzo he refused even to listen. "Too dangerous," he said flatly, "the boy stays here."

Carmela knew that Enzo was upset that she hadn't yet given him another child. Franco was all he had, but she couldn't allow the boy to be deprived of a "real" life because of Enzo's nervousness, especially as the Family were not in the business of kidnapping children; they were mostly religious men who feared only the wrath of God and their mothers. No member of a Mafia Family would stoop to kidnap a child for fear of his own mother's anger at such a barbarous act. Still Enzo wouldn't hear of it and when she finally found that she was pregnant once more, she took it as a sign from heaven.

The new baby was a cherub, with a mass of dark curls and enormous brown eyes. Enzo had his dream child at last. It was easy after that for Carmela to get permission for Franco to attend the local school with the other boys; after all, if anything happened, there was always young Stefano—named for Enzo's own father this time.

Stefano was spoiled by his father and babied by his mother, because with Franco busy in his own new world of school, all her maternal instincts were centered on the little one. And Franco loved his little brother, though he didn't always like him. Especially as he grew older.

When Franco was twelve, Stefano was still only five. Of course, he was just a baby so it was only right that Franco had to let him have his own way. Sometimes it was hard, though, because Stefano always seemed to destroy or lose the things that mattered to him, like his model battleship or his Swiss penknife, and once he'd even scribbled on the copies of famous paintings that Franco had admired and hung around the walls of his room.

When Franco was seventeen, he went away to a university and then to business school in America, and he missed a great deal of Stefano's growing-up years. When he returned, aged twenty-two, he found his brother to be a spoiled, petulant boy of fifteen, cosseted by his mother and protected by his father. There was no doubt that Stefano was handsome, but there was also no doubt that he was lazy and stupid.

Stefano's tutors had had an easy time of it; he'd asked no questions and avoided lessons as much as he could. He had no curiosity about the world beyond his own immediate boundaries, and his only strong urge was sexual. At fifteen, Stefano had already got one of the maids into trouble and though he'd been warned by his father, albeit with a conspiratorial wink and a reference to his manhood being "the Malvasi inheritance," he still pursued his urges as single-mindedly as a rutting stag.

It seemed to Franco that he'd always known what the "Family business" was and he'd accepted it and its special way of life because he knew no other. He'd gone to America armed with letters of introduction to the heads of other Families and, with an inborn wariness, he'd kept his social life within that clan. He'd made few real friends at the college itself, and none that would last, simply because he knew he couldn't expect them to understand. Whenever he was tempted by the carefree life-style of the other undergraduates, and especially the beautiful blond Anglo-Saxon Protestant girls who looked to him like the princesses in his childhood picture books, he reminded himself sternly of who he was: Franco Malvasi, son and heir apparent of a Mafia godfather. And nothing and no one would make him deviate from that responsibility.

The Malvasi headquarters was in a massive warehouse and office complex in the southwestern corner of Naples, close by the docks. Franco was surprised on his return to find that Stefano was already working in "the business." He even had his own office and a seat at the big oval table in the boardroom when the great meetings were called and all the "executives" attended. The fact that Stefano's seat was on his father's right hand, while his own was lower down the table, was not lost on Franco, but he kept quiet. He had been away so long, he thought it was only right that his father should expect him to prove his worth; as his heir he would be undertaking a great responsibility.

He had been home a month when he first detected the strain of cruelty in Stefano; he was walking in the garden, his head buried in a book on the life, works, and techniques of the painter Fra Angelico, when he heard the sound of a pitiful meow. Hurrying toward its source, he found Stefano holding a small cat aloft by its tail. He was clutching a long, open razor and he was systematically shaving the fur from the terrified creature. Each time it screamed and jerked in a desperate effort to get away from its torturer, the blade cut deep into its flesh. It was already a streaming mass of blood and fur when Franco snatched it away from him, glaring at him contemptuously.

"You young bastard," he snarled, "what do you think you're doing?"

"It's only a cat," scoffed Stefano, "what difference does it make?"

"And what right do you have to make it suffer?" Franco demanded angrily. "The poor creature is almost skinned alive! It will have to be put down."

"You should have just left it with me, it would have been dead in minutes," laughed Stefano. "You're too softhearted, brother, and that's not the stuff a godfather is made of."

"Nor is senseless cruelty," snapped Franco. "Use your head, Stefano, and try to control yourself."

He kept his ears and eyes open after that, ever alert for reports of Stefano's activities, and it wasn't long before he became aware that his brother was already notorious for his treatment of women in the cheap alleyway brothels of Naples. It seemed Stefano sought out the lowest of them all, a place where he could play the young lord, throwing money around, swaggering and drinking and boasting of his sexual prowess—though oddly enough the reports that came back from that section were dismissive. Young Stefano was no hotshot in bed despite his claims, but he more than made up for it with a crude display of sadism.

At home, though, he was Carmela's baby. He could do no wrong. He was tall, handsome, and always smiling, and he was as gentle and affectionate with his mother as he was coldly cruel to the helpless young women in the bordellos.

Franco was twenty-five and Stefano eighteen, when one night Enzo took them aside and told them that he was a dying man. Half a dozen different doctors had confirmed the diagnosis—cancer of the stomach. "This will go no farther than this room," he said, glaring at them both, his dark eyes already filmed with pain. "Your mother will not know—and nor will our enemies. The time has come for me to think of the future of our business, my sons. *Your future.* You already know what I feel for the both of you. Let a dying man make one last request. Make me a happy man . . . get married. Now. Give me a grandson so that I can die happy, knowing that the Malvasi family will go on and prosper. Give your mother her grandchildren so that she will have some happiness when I am gone."

Stefano proposed marriage through Emilia Bertagna's father the following week and was accepted immediately, though Emilia didn't find out about it until later when the family told her they were throwing a big engagement party—hers. She was to be wed within the month.

Emilia was also eighteen; she was pretty and vivacious and full of fun, and though Stefano Malvasi wasn't the boy she might have chosen, he was handsome. She accepted that it was a good match and went to her wedding like a dutiful daughter.

It was the most lavish celebration seen in Naples for years. The bride was beautiful in yards and yards of demure white lace with a retinue of twelve tiny dark-haired bridesmaids. She smiled happily, clutching Stefano's arm as they cut their cake, and Enzo Malvasi, beaming paternally from the head of the table, gave them his blessing.

At three the next morning Franco was woken by a telephone call. It was from Emilia, alone and distraught in her honeymoon hotel in Rome. Stefano had drunk a lot of wine that night and when it came time to go to bed . . . well, she said desperately . . . he'd tried to make love to her, unsuccessfully. Swearing and cursing and blaming her, he'd slapped her several times across the face, flung on his clothes, and departed. She'd fallen asleep exhausted and tearful, but had been woken later by noises coming from the drawing room of their suite. She'd crept to the door and peered through. Stefano was kneeling naked in front of a young boy—and he was— Emilia hadn't been able to go on but Franco had heard enough. Telling her to stay calm, he was out of the villa and on the road to Rome in less than five minutes.

Now he knew why Stefano's reputation with women was so unsuccessful; now he *understood* his lazy, self-indulgent mother-dominated brother! By the time he arrived at the hotel in Rome, he was ready to kill him. But Stefano had packed his bag and gone. Emilia said he'd left with the boy an hour before.

It took Franco two days to track him down, and when he finally found him it was in one of the lowest dives in the city, a sordid, dingy bar, wreathed in smoke and smelling of sweat and opium, with rooms above, patronized by deviates and their prey. In one of the rooms he found Stefano sleeping naked on a filthy torn mattress swarming with lice, while a young boy of eleven or twelve years cowered in a corner. Franco saw the opium pipe and smelled its sickly sweetness on his brother's breath as he hauled him to his feet, cursing him for the beast he was. Thrusting a fistful of money at the poor child, he pushed Stefano into some clothes and half dragged him from the room.

He took him first to the public baths, ordering them to strip him and to burn his clothes, and then he told them to plunge him into a hot bath filled with strong disinfectant. He went to buy some fresh clothes, and when he returned Stefano was shrouded in a white towel, looking furious. "What are you doing to me? Your own brother?" he snarled as Franco threw the clothes at him.

"You are disgusting," Franco said coldly. "You are worse than an animal. If our father were not dying, Stefano, I would take you to him and make him understand what you are. You know I can't do that. Still, you have married this poor innocent girl and I'll make sure you keep your marriage vows. Or I'll see you dead."

"You wouldn't dare," Stefano scoffed, "and I'll do as I please." But the cold, angry glint in Franco's eyes made him doubt his own brash words.

Franco reunited Emilia with her husband and she accepted him back meekly, even though she was now afraid of him. Franco made a point of going to see them every few days in their new home, a pretty house just along the road from the Malvasi villa and with the same high walls and ever-present guards. Emilia reported that Stefano was behaving reasonably enough, though he often got drunk and disappeared for the night. But she was used to the men in her family disappearing on business, and she thought nothing more of it. Franco knew differently. But Enzo Malvasi was growing worse, and Franco's mind was on his sick father, and on his responsibilities when the time would come for him to take over the business.

He was at work every day before seven, going over each sector of the business, drafting plans for new ways to expand in some areas and ways to conserve in others, deciding where to cut back and how to maximize profits. He drew up plans to send executives to South America to facilitate new drug connections, and outlined his new ideas for stepping up the pressure on the gambling and protection scenes. He used his business school knowledge to restructure the whole financial base of the Malvasi empire, planning new investments into industry and banking. "The Malvasi Bank" was his dream, a name he wanted to see not just in Naples, not just in Italy, but in the serious, international world of finance. Franco wanted the Malvasi business to have a legitimate facade in order to launder its illegal earnings.

When he had readied all his new proposals for the business he spoke to the family's lawyer, Carmine Caetano, telling him of his plans. Carmine had known both the Malvasi sons since birth and he had made his own assessment of them. The information he gave to Franco, confidentially, was not because he cared more about him than his brother but because he was concerned for his own survival and that was now in serious doubt. When he told Franco that Enzo had appointed *Stefano* as the next godfather of the Malvasi Family, Carmine was protecting his own business interests. He, and the other executives, knew that with Stefano at the helm, they were as good as dead.

"I'm telling you now, Franco," he said, "the old man is besotted with that boy. Don't ask me why; it's obvious to everyone else that the kid is the biggest piece of crap that ever fell to earth. He doesn't have a brain in his head, he's degenerate and he's dangerous. He'll ruin us all within a year. You must take control, son. It may be hard and there will be decisions that I pray you may never have to make again. But I am sure you will uphold the honor of the Family. And in return your Family will be forever grateful. You will have earned *our* loyalty."

There was no happier woman in Italy than Carmela Malvasi when

Emilia told her she was pregnant. It was a chill winter night and Enzo stood in front of the fire, leaning heavily on his stick now, trying vainly to feel some warmth in his pain-racked body. He watched tenderly as his beloved son Stefano kissed his mother, and as the boy walked toward him he threw down his stick, holding out both his arms to embrace him. "My son, my son," he cried, "you have fulfilled your duty. You have made me very happy."

Stefano's eyes met Franco's and he smiled mockingly. "I shall always do my best to make you proud of me, Father," he said.

Enzo was dead a few weeks later and the entire Malvasi Family, and all the godfathers of the leading Families of Italy traveled to be present at his funeral. As the two sons, Franco and Stefano, cast earth onto their father's grave, their eyes locked, and there was a triumphant glint in Stefano's.

As the funeral procession made its way back to the Malvasi villa for the wake, it was ambushed by a group of marksmen. The leading cars were raked with bullets and Stefano Malvasi and his young wife were killed instantly, as were two other leading godfathers. With his arm around his brokenhearted mother's shoulders, Franco had inspected the bodies. He was sorry about Emilia, but there had been no choice; she was carrying Stefano's son, and he had wanted no future rival to his position of godfather. He was now sole head of the Malvasi Family.

Franco declared afterward that the mysterious "assassination" would be avenged, that he would make sure that not only his own Family's honor was satisfied, but that of the other men who had come to pay their last respects to his father.

A few days later the bodies of half a dozen men were found locked in a garage in a Naples back street. They had been lined up against a wall and shot, as though by a firing squad.

It seemed Franco Malvasi had "avenged his honor," and he was now godfather of the Malvasi Family. He had earned a reputation as a man to be reckoned with before he'd even begun. And it had taught him a lesson. In his business, *in his world,* only the strong and the ruthless survived. Nothing—not family, friends, or love—could come between him and "the business."

He had never gone back on that decision.

CHAPTER *41*

Netta swept up the steps of numéro seize, rue des Arbres, the bright feathers in her new hat bouncing saucily. She put out her hand to ring the bell, but before she could do so it was flung open and a distinguished-looking man with a funny accent inquired what she wanted.

"I'm here to see Poppy," she said haughtily, "all the way from Marseilles."

"Madam is not available at the moment," Watkins said firmly.

"Oh, no you don't," she cried, thrusting her foot quickly into the door before he could close it. "Poppy's never too busy to see *me*. I'll just come in and wait!" She pushed past him into the hall, her eyes and mouth rounding with amazement as she stared at the luxurious furnishings. "Well, the girl's really done it this time," she muttered, "she's really burned her bridges with Franco Malvasi."

"Madame," the butler protested, "I'm afraid I must ask you to leave."

"Leave? Why ever should I leave?" Netta asked, surprised. "I just got here, didn't I?"

Watkins looked at her nervously; she was loud and she was bringing down the whole tone of the establishment. Luckily there weren't many guests around at the moment, but he knew Madame Poppy would be most upset to see this . . . this tart, in the middle of her beautiful hall, but he couldn't just throw her out forcibly.

"Would you please wait in the small salon?" he said politely. "I'll see if Madame will be available soon."

"Hoity-toity," mocked Netta, sauntering after him down a lengthy corridor, "where did Poppy find you, then? In the actor's emporium?" And her raucous laugh rattled through the high-ceilinged corridor.

Poppy was at her desk going over the week's menus and she lifted her head, listening in surprise. Luchay flapped his wings, running excitedly up and down on his stand, cackling in the same mocking tones . . . just like Netta . . .

"Netta!" she screamed, leaping joyfully to her feet and flinging open the door. "Netta, oh, Netta," she sobbed as her friend's arms closed around her. "I've missed you so."

" 'Course you have," Netta said gruffly, wiping away a tear, "and I missed you. Tell the truth, Poppy, I've missed you more than I ever missed the Captain . . . God bless him."

"Is everything all right, madame?" Watkins asked without a flicker of expression.

"All right? Oh, Watkins, everything is just wonderful now that Netta's here," she said tearfully.

"Some fancy place you've got here," Netta said, linking her arm through Poppy's as she showed her to her apartment.

Poppy grinned. "But what are you doing here?" she asked.

"Oh, I just felt like a little vacation," Netta said airily, "thought I'd do a little shopping in Paris."

"I know just the place to go," she promised.

Netta eyed her tailored silk dress shrewdly. "I'll bet you do, but it'll take me a month to earn enough for that frock."

"Only a month, Netta?" Poppy teased. "I thought you were going to say a year. You must be doing well!"

"I'm doing well, all right, but it's not the same without you there. *And* that bloody parrot. Oh, the girls are nice and the customers are faithful, and there's always plenty of new ones ready and waiting, but without you there," she said wistfully, "I guess I'm just a bit lonely."

"Then why not come here and join me? Be my partner again? By rights, half of what I've got should be yours anyway, because without you I wouldn't have anything."

" 'Course you would," Netta said loyally, "but I can't do that, Poppy. No . . . it wouldn't be right." She thought of Franco Malvasi and she shuddered. "I really just wanted to check and see if you were all right. Oh, I know your letters said you were fine and all, but I thought I read a little something between the lines."

Poppy took her into her sitting room and closed the door. "I'm all right Netta," she said nervously. "It's just that I'm worried about Franco Malvasi."

"I'll bet you are!" Netta plopped onto the sofa and flung off her hat. She wrinkled her nose. "Mmm, what smells so good in here?" She spied the pots of gardenias scattered around, their fragile petals like fresh cream against their dark, glossy green leaves. "Gardenias! Such extravagance, Poppy. You must have changed your ways since I've seen you."

"Franco sends them to me every week," Poppy said simply. Netta's eyebrows rose in astonishment and she added hurriedly, "Netta, is it possible to be in love with a man you don't even *know*?" Netta's eyebrows almost disappeared into her hair and her jaw dropped open as Poppy went on, "I can't stop thinking about him, Netta, I dream about him, I . . . I fantasize about him, that he's here talking to me the way he did that night . . ."

"What night?" Netta demanded quickly. "You haven't . . . ?"

"No . . . oh, no, of course not," Poppy replied, blushing, "he came here one night to talk about the business, we had dinner, alone. Netta, that's the only time I've seen him since I've been in Paris. That's why it's so strange . . . I mean, how can I fall in love with a man I've met only a few times in my life?"

"You can fall in love with a man you meet only once," retorted Netta, "but not when he's Franco Malvasi! Poppy, you *can't* fall in love with a man like that!"

"A man like what?" she demanded, bewildered. "Who can tell who is good and who is bad? He's kind, generous . . . a gentleman. Why, when I think of Felipe and how dishonest and vile he was . . . and yet *he* was an aristocrat."

"And what about when you think of Greg?" Netta asked shrewdly. "How does Franco compare then?"

Poppy closed her eyes, her heart plummeting. She never allowed herself to think of Greg anymore—he symbolized all she had lost: the wonderful handsome young man, the family, the love and the caring, the simple, uncomplicated happiness. Greg didn't exist in her new world. "Franco is . . . different," she said carefully. "But Netta, I've never felt like this about a man before. I mean with Felipe, I suppose I was just a stupid romantic little girl swept off her feet by a handsome young man, even though I thought it was love. And with Greg there was always that steady companionship, the sort of friendship and affection you feel for someone you care about deeply, whom you've loved all your life. But this time it's different, Netta. I've never felt like this before. Can this be what's known as being in love?"

"I hope not." Netta sighed. "Because if it is, you certainly have a knack for picking the wrong men! Now, come and sit beside me and tell me all."

They huddled on the sofa together all afternoon while Poppy talked and talked. Then they caught up on each other's news and Poppy showed her around the house, pointing out its beauty proudly, and introducing her to the girls as "my dearest friend."

Poppy arranged for Simone to come to lunch to meet Netta. The two women sized each other up quickly, their prying eyes taking in the details of each other's appearance as the silence between them grew and Poppy hovered anxiously. "You shouldn't wear that bright green, my dear," Simone said finally, "it's never good on blondes."

"I know that," retorted Netta, her hands on her hips, legs apart in best belligerent Marseilles streetgirl style.

"A rich ruby color," Simone said musingly, "and sweep back your hair a little more, you've got good bones, you should show them off." Smiling benignly at Poppy, she took a seat. "You didn't tell me your friend was this attractive, Poppy," she said. "If things go on at this rate, the competition in Paris will become impossible."

"*Merde*," exclaimed Netta, throwing back her head with a laugh, "I'll confess I wondered what you would be like, I thought you'd be stuck up and full of yourself, but I can now see why Poppy said you were so charming. You know just how to put a person into a good mood—no wonder men love you—and I can tell they do by that jewelry you're wearing."

Simone patted her diamond-studded bosom complacently. "You and I understand each other, Netta," she said, "we are both provincial girls who've made good. For us Paris is only a veneer. Poppy is the one who is different: I expect great things from Poppy."

Poppy didn't know what she meant, but she laughed, glad that her only two friends were getting along so well. Netta listened fascinated as Simone gossiped her way through lunch, but when she'd gone she confessed to Poppy that it would be a relief to get back to Marseilles. "I'd settle for just one diamond brooch and my little house," she said feelingly, "rather than have to play her sort of games." She looked thoughtful for a moment and then added, "Well, maybe a diamond brooch *and* a pair of earrings."

Netta's weeklong visit passed in a whirlwind of activity; Poppy took her, in her brazen green finery, to Lucille's and chose a half-dozen dresses to be placed on her own private account. She took her to the hat shops and the furriers and they lunched together at Maxim's. The maître d' greeted Poppy like an old friend and every head turned as she paused casually here and there, greeting people.

"You know something," Netta whispered as the waiter served blinis with caviar and champagne, "you are a *star*, Poppy. You don't need Franco Malvasi anymore . . . *everybody* knows you."

"That's just the trouble, Netta." Poppy sighed, her blue eyes wistful. "Now I really do need him."

When Netta had gone, Poppy found it hard to slip back into her old routine of simply work and more work, and she roamed the house restlessly, finding fault with everything. She complained that the fruit served at lunch had not been fresh enough, that the cheeses were too cold and the wine too warm. She told Villette she was wearing too much makeup and Solange that her dress was cut too low, and, seething with unexplained nervousness, she went for long, solitary walks. The chestnuts were blooming again, their pink candles weighing down the branches with beauty, and the springtime skies were as blue and clean as though they'd been freshly washed. She glanced at her reflection in the shop windows as she passed, thinking that she looked like any other smartly dressed woman out shopping—except she was different, because of *who* she was, she was always alone.

Despairingly, she returned to the house and shut herself in her room. Luchay huddled onto her shoulder making his affectionate little cooing noises in her ear and she stroked him automatically. "Poppy *cara*, Poppy *chérie*," he muttered, "Poppy darling . . ."

"Oh, Luchay," she sighed despondently, "I love you too. Whatever would I do without you to pour out my troubles to? I wish you could tell me what it is I feel for Franco Malvasi. Am I in love, Luchay? Is this what it feels like? This nervous, excited . . . *distrait* feeling? Not the soaring on eagle's wings that I expected? But I don't even know him, Luchay, and he barely thinks of me. What am I to do?"

"Poppy *cara*, Poppy *chérie*," he murmured comfortingly, nibbling at her hair, and she laughed, offering him some pumpkin seeds.

There was a knock at the door and Watkins appeared. "Madame," he said, "there is someone here to see you."

"Is it the Signore Malvasi?" she gasped, color brightening her cheeks.

"No, madame, this is a lady. I'm afraid she wouldn't give her name."

"I suppose it's a girl looking for a job, Watkins. Of course, we don't need anyone, but show her into the office and I'll speak with her."

Watkins coughed discreetly. "This is not our usual type of girl, madame, perhaps the office would not be the proper place for her. May I suggest you see the lady in the small salon!"

A "lady," worried Poppy as she tidied her hair and hurried to the small salon, hoping it wasn't an irate wife on the trail of her erring husband. She paused, her hand on the door, giving herself a moment to pull herself together, and then, tilting her chin arrogantly, she swept in, ready for battle.

"Good afternoon, madame," she said, "I am Poppy Mallory."

The blond woman dressed in discreet but expensive black swung around from the window and came toward her. *"Bonjour,* madame," she said in a low, cultured voice.

Poppy stared at her curiously. She was tall and very beautiful in a haughty, well-bred, understated way, with smooth blond hair, large green eyes, and a petulant mouth. She looked like any of a dozen women you might see shopping in the rue de la Paix, the sort with a rich husband and a title and a family tree that went back a couple of centuries. Poppy knew there would be a château in the country and a town house near the Parc Monceau and enough money to buy whatever she wanted. So why, she wondered uncomfortably, was she here?

"I'm bored," the woman said suddenly, "my life is driving me crazy. My husband is distinguished, charming, a gentleman—he would never come to a place like this." Her large green eyes were desperate as they searched Poppy's face. "I crave excitement," she whispered, "something to break the monotony of my days. I thought about this a long time before I came here, but now I'm offering you my services."

"Your services?" Poppy gasped, taken aback.

The woman stared at her somberly. "Where else could I get what I want? I want sex, Madame Poppy . . . sex with strangers where I don't have to be the 'lady' . . . I want delicious, exciting sex—not the routine embraces of a husband who is too busy thinking about his next business or political coup. I want a touch of illicit excitement in my life . . . I want to be a whore when I feel like it—and a lady the rest of the time. I came here because I heard that your house was exquisite, that a man could find superb food here, and wonderful wines . . . and the promise that whatever his pleasure, 'it all can be had,' they say, at Numéro Seize. At a price."

"Are you saying that you want to work here? Like the other girls?"

asked Poppy, amazed that any woman could talk that way. Up until now she'd thought that only men had those feelings about sex.

"I am." Sitting primly in a little gilt chair, the woman stared back at her.

"But obviously you are from a good family, maybe even a prominent one," Poppy protested, "aren't you afraid of being recognized? Fashionable Paris is a very small, very closed society. The word would get around in a minute."

"Naturally, I've thought about that. I plan to disguise myself, I shall wear a dark wig, and an eye-mask . . . and, of course, I shan't parade myself in the salon. I shall be available only for special clients . . . those chosen by you. And I shall be exorbitantly expensive, though of course I shall take only one franc for myself." She smiled aloofly. "But I promise you I shall give value for money." She stared hard at Poppy. "Well, what do you say, madame?"

Poppy thought of the whispers that would flash around Paris, and she knew the scandal would make her an immediate success. "We must design a special room for you," she agreed with a smile, "one to suit your mysterious dual personality. But tell me, madame, what is your name?"

The woman looked at her with hooded, unsmiling green eyes. "Why not just call me Cathérine?" she said.

Cathérine in her dark wig and with a veil hiding her face would arrive at the back door of Numéro Seize on three afternoons a week, flitting like a shadow to her own suite on the second floor. There she would change from her usual smart dress to black lace underwear, black silk stockings, and high-heeled shoes. Opening an exquisite Buhl cabinet she would remove a long-handled black whip and, stroking it lovingly, would lay it on the Empire chaise longue at the foot of the bed. "This will be my specialty," she'd told Poppy happily; "at last I can live out my fantasies."

"But we don't permit violence," Poppy had gasped, shocked.

"This isn't *violence*." Cathérine laughed. "This is *pleasure*." And she'd run the lash between her fingers longingly. "I had an English lover who taught me all about it," she said musingly, "he told me they liked it because of the way they were brought up, with sadistic nannies who always spanked them, and schools where they were caned—usually for the master's own pleasure. Now," she said, shrugging, "they can't do without it." She sighed. "It was the most exciting thing I ever did."

"Exciting?" whispered Poppy, curiously.

Cathérine's hooded eyes were full of the remembered thrill as she said huskily, "So exciting that your whole body quivers with it, lusts for it, you can't wait to see the lash slide over the skin, the drops of scarlet blood and hear the groans of ecstasy . . . and then afterward, oh, afterward, when he finally takes you . . . oohh, Poppy, then you really know what a man can do for you. Of course, not all men will want that." She shrugged. "And there are many other forms of sexual pleasure that are enjoyable to me."

Dragging herself from Cathérine's erotic fantasies, Poppy made a note that whenever an Englishman came to Numéro Seize, he was to be offered Cathérine's special services.

Cathérine was a well-kept secret, but it seemed she talked to her closest friends. Suddenly more society women arrived on the doorstep of Numéro Seize, swathed in high-collared coats and hiding beneath veiled hats, eager for a sensational escapade, and soon Poppy had a group of beautiful women who whiled away their afternoons masked and naked under satin sheets at Numéro Seize, instead of shopping at Poiret or taking tea at Fauchon.

The rumors that at Numéro Seize a man might be seduced by his own wife—or even his best friend's—reached as far as Naples, and Franco Malvasi laughed when he heard them. It was the beginning of June, almost a year since he had first met Poppy. Then she had been too young, too vulnerable, she was a small, wounded animal protecting herself from the old predator—man. Cleverly, he'd given her money and advice and he'd kept his distance, until now she was a rich, notorious woman of the world. Poppy was ready for him.

CHAPTER 42

1904, FRANCE

Luchay ruffled his feathers enjoying the August sunshine, stretching first one wing and then the other, preening his long tail feathers and fluffing out his chest. He was watching Poppy through one topaz eye as she fastened her pearls and inspected herself in the mirror.

It was stupefyingly hot. Everyone had retreated to their villas at the coast or to their country houses, and the city was deserted. Poppy had given her girls the month off, intending to go to Marseilles, but Netta was having one of her flings with her latest love, a textile merchant from Toulouse, and she'd disappeared on vacation with him. So she was alone and at a loose end in the empty city. However, today she'd woken up with a definite purpose in mind.

She stared at her reflection in the mirror. She was wearing a blue dress; it was the first time she'd worn any color but gray in years and it felt like coming out of mourning. In a mad moment, inspired by the sunlight and flawless blue skies, she'd hurriedly bought a dozen dresses in a rainbow of pale summer colors, and she was enjoying the youthful feel of wearing simple cotton voile, after so many nights in elaborate satin and velvet.

"I feel like a girl again today, instead of a twenty-four-year-old woman, Luchay," she laughed, dropping a kiss on his soft feathered head. Her car was waiting outside the front door, a long, glamorous dark green de

Courmont like Simone Lalage's, except Poppy had refused to have a chauffeur, and the sight of her at the wheel of her enormous car had created yet another sensation in Paris.

She sped down the rue des Arbres and into the Avenue du Bois de Boulogne, weaving her way through the maze of streets and heading for the suburbs. Half an hour later she paced a desolate tract of land in a scrubby straggling village on the southwestern fringes of the city, listening to the salesman extolling its beauty.

"Don't be ridiculous," she told him sharply, "neither the village nor the piece of land is beautiful, and the price you are asking is far too steep. No one but a fool like me is going to come along and buy this land, so you'd better take what I'm offering you and be done with it. If not"— she shrugged carelessly—"then I shall go elsewhere."

"Fifteen hectares, madame? At that price?" he asked despondently.

"Fifteen hectares," she said firmly.

"It's robbery!" he sighed, leading the way back to his small office. Poppy signed the deed with a flourish, handing him a check for the exact amount she had planned to spend.

Afterward, she walked back alone to look at her desolate fifteen acres and the distant view of the Paris skyline . . . "Find out which way a city is going to grow," Franco had told her, "study the planning permissions, the railway links, the needs of industry, then buy a piece of land in its future path. Snap it up for a song, and let your investment lie until the city catches up with you. Not just Paris, any city, any country . . . you won't get a quick return on your money, but as the city develops, your land will suddenly be in demand and it will be worth a fortune."

Poppy sighed with pleasure as she took a last lingering look at her fifteen unlovely acres. They were her first stake in her future, and they promised her a life in which she need no longer be a madam.

It was early evening when she drove back down the rue des Arbres, parking with a flourish outside her door. The windows of her apartment were open to the hot night, but the air was still and oppressive and without a breeze. Feeling lonely, she ordered a light supper and a bottle of champagne to celebrate her purchase. "But there's only you to share it with me, Luchay," she murmured sadly, throwing open the glass doors that led onto her little courtyard. It was filled with tubs and pots planted with roses and camellias. A stone Bacchus-head fountain embedded in the wall splashed soothingly, so that if she closed her eyes she could almost imagine she was back in the courtyard at the Konstant House, a child again with Angel and Greg, and Rosalia calling them all with her little silver bell for dinner . . . The old familiar shroud of loneliness enveloped her again and she shivered.

She was leaning against the open door, her head flung back and her eyes closed, when Franco walked in, and she looked as though her thoughts were a million miles away. "It's not good to drink alone," he said reprovingly.

Poppy stared at him with a little gasp, so filled with pleasure at seeing him there that she almost wanted to cry.

"I felt so alone," she whispered, "and now you're here."

He took her hand, holding it in both of his as he put it to his lips. "Do I assume the champagne was to celebrate my arrival?" he asked with his usual sardonic smile.

She shook her head. "It was intended to celebrate your advice. I bought my first parcel of land today. My first stake in my new fortune."

"Then we'll drink a toast to your success," he said, pouring the wine.

She smiled into his eyes, feeling as giddy and breathless as though she'd already drunk it. They tasted the wine, still gazing into each other's eyes, and behind them Luchay fluttered anxiously on his perch, skittering up and down and screeching.

"Poor Luchay, we didn't forget you," Poppy said, laughing, released from the spell; but the parrot still pecked angrily at his golden stand, glaring at Franco with his beady eyes.

"There's a little country inn I know, out in the forest near Rambouillet," Franco told her, "where they serve the most delicious food you've ever tasted. What do you say we leave this tired, hot city, and go where we can breathe fresh green country air and indulge ourselves in a wonderful dinner."

Poppy glanced down at her blue cotton dress. "But it's late and I'm not even changed . . ."

"It's only a simple place; you don't need to change, and anyway you look beautiful. Please say you'll come."

Luchay skittered angrily up and down his perch as Poppy put her hand in Franco's and they walked from the room. *"Poppy* cara. *Poppy* chérie. *Poppy darling,"* he screamed, *"Poppy, Poppy, Poppy . . ."*

The little inn was full of simple rustic charm, with ancient oaken beams and whitewashed walls and long, low windows flung open to the dusky summer evening, smelling of hay and roses. The innkeeper's daughter served them delicious pink trout fresh from the stream and a salad just picked from the garden, speckled with fresh herbs; and the innkeeper himself came to pour their wine, cool and straw-colored and smelling of fruit.

Poppy looked at Franco across the candle-lit table. "I feel drunk on fresh air." She smiled. "I'd forgotten what it smelled like . . . it's so good, I can even taste it!"

"You work too hard," he said, frowning. "You've let Numéro Seize become your entire world."

"But I have no other life," she replied, astonished. "What else would I do?"

He made no answer, merely summoning the waiter for more wine. But later, as they walked in the garden, he said, "why don't you buy a house in the country, a retreat of your own? Just see how much you are enjoying this place tonight, its summer beauty, its simplicity. You need the contrast, Poppy, if you are to keep your sanity."

She turned to look at the low, whitewashed inn lost in its soft green garden, alive with fruits and flowers and the sounds of chickens and birds, and fragrant with scents of herbs and blossoms. Suddenly her heart longed to own it. But there was just one flaw. "I'd have nobody to share it with," she said simply.

Putting his hands on her shoulders, Franco turned her to face him. "Share it with me, Poppy," he said quietly, "let me buy it; it will be *our* retreat, a place where we can escape, from my world and from yours. I promise you I've never said this to any other woman in my life. *Poppy, I love you.* I've wanted to tell you for so long, but I had to wait for you to heal from your wounds. Oh, yes," he added somberly, "I know everything about you, I know who you are and where you are from . . . everything."

Poppy's hand flew to her mouth and she stared at him, agonized. "Then how can you possibly love me if you know?" she gasped. "There are things in my life too terrible even to be told."

"Then we are equal," he said quietly, "because there are things in my life that are too terrible ever to be told. But surely, all that matters is that I love you. . . . Poppy, if you tell me you love me, I shall be the happiest man in the world."

"I don't know," she murmured uncertainly, "I don't know what love is . . . I thought I knew, but I've been wrong. What I feel for you . . . is that love, Franco?"

"I hope so, my darling," he said, taking her in his arms; and then her mouth was soft and pliant under his, and her body seemed weightless as he held her close, and he wanted to go on kissing her forever.

Poppy opened her eyes as he took his mouth from hers, gazing at him starry eyed with rapture. "Oh, yes, I do love you, Franco," she murmured. "I truly do."

"Then stay with me tonight," he whispered, "let me love you, Poppy."

"I'm afraid," she whispered, "I know nothing of 'love' . . . only . . ."

"We'll start anew," he told her, "there'll be no bad memories, just you and me in a little cottage room with our windows open to the clean night air and the stars. Oh, and I'll love you, Poppy, I promise you I'll love you."

Later, upstairs in that clean little cottage room, in a simple wooden bed with plain white cotton sheets and with windows open to the starred blue heaven, he helped her undress, removing each garment from her slender body as though he were uncovering a work of art, caressing her gently, wooing her with endearments and compliments until she was swooning in his arms. As they lay naked under the cool cotton sheets, her body responded to his practiced persuasions, trembling with a newfound passion as he stroked and cajoled her, until finally he entered her and they were one.

And it was as Poppy had always imagined after all; she *was* lifted on the eagle's wings . . . she *did* soar into another realm . . . and she knew at last that this was true love.

The next morning as they drove back to Paris, dizzy with happiness, Franco said enthusiastically, "We'll look for a country house together, it'll be an adventure." He glanced at Poppy, but she was staring straight ahead, frowning. "Is there anything the matter?" he asked solicitously. "Do you have a headache from the heat?"

"No," she said, "I was just wondering when we'll use this country house. With me in Paris and you in Naples? It just doesn't seem to work out." She glanced at him hopefully, out the corner of her eye, waiting to hear him say that of course she was right, she must give up the Paris house at once and marry him and come to live in Naples.

"Of course I'll make time to come to France," he told her calmly, "but anyway, it's time you had a place of your own, where you can escape from the pressure and the people. After all"—he threw a smile in her direction, keeping his eyes on the road—"I don't want you exhausted from overwork, do I?"

Poppy sighed. "I see," she said in a small voice. "It doesn't seem very much, though, for two people in love, does it?"

"I'm sorry, Poppy," he said, glancing at her sharply, "but I can't leave my business. I must be in Naples."

"And I must be in Paris," she replied quietly. "So, there we are."

Franco looked at her, reading her thoughts shrewdly. "It doesn't mean I don't love you or that I wouldn't rather be here with you," he said finally, "but my business is in Naples and that's where I must stay."

"Then why don't I come with you?" she asked eagerly. "Why don't I just give up Numéro Seize and live with you?" She'd almost said *marry*, but she was too proud to suggest it, and the thought lurked in the back of her mind that maybe having created her as Paris's most sensational madam, Franco wasn't prepared to marry her.

"That can't be," he said harshly, "my life there is separate. Don't ask me why, just believe me. And I do love you, Poppy, you know I do. I can't live without you. But we are both busy people, so let's take the few crumbs of time we can have together and enjoy them."

CHAPTER 43

The scraps of paper were scattered throughout the house as randomly as Poppy's thoughts. Mike found them in bedroom cupboards, and in kitchen drawers, tucked into books and stuffed into vases, but after a week he was still puzzling over them. They were fragments of her life and as he'd sorted them out, he'd gradually pieced together the story of Netta and Numéro Seize, and Franco Malvasi.

He stared at Luchay on his stand under the window, remembering that Aria had said the parrot would know the whole story—after all, he'd lived through it. "If only you could talk, Luchay," he said wearily, "it's *you* Poppy whispered all her troubles to . . . God damn it, bird, *you know* about Poppy. You'd know where a woman like that would keep her secrets, because she sure as hell wasn't going to broadcast them to the world."

But the parrot simply turned his head away and began to preen his feathers, and Mike groaned. "I get it," he said, frustrated, "you only talk to Poppy. That's it, isn't it?"

"Poppy *cara*, Poppy *chérie*, Poppy darling . . ." the parrot repeated, flapping his wings. "Poppy, Poppy, Poppy . . ."

The telephone rang, its old-fashioned tinkling sound interrupting the brooding silence of the villa, and Mike kicked the footstool angrily out of his way as he leapt to answer it.

"Mike? It's Aria."

The line was crackling and he could only hear her faintly. "Hi, Aria," he yelled, "how're y'doing?"

"I've just come back from visiting Hilliard Konstant at the Rancho Santa Vittoria," she said. "I didn't even know I had a great-uncle still alive until Mama said you'd told her about him."

"How did it go?" he asked, grinning as he thought of prickly old Hilliard dealing with Francesca's social elegance.

"It was sort of touchy at first. Mama insisted on renting the most enormous limousine she could find and so we arrived there like a pair of Hollywood starlets. I had the feeling it wasn't quite Great-uncle Hilliard's style. But he was very nice to me, he told me he remembered Angel and Maria-Cristina. And Helena, of course. He said Maria-Cristina was the extrovert, always partying and very glamorous, but that Helena kept all her emotions locked inside. 'Like Pierluigi Galli,' he said. 'And people like that are always unpredictable.' What do you think he meant, Mike?"

"I'm not sure, but Hilliard's a cagey old boy; first he tells you he doesn't remember, and then he feeds you these little nuggets of information. I get this feeling old Hilliard knows more than he's saying."

"I thought he seemed very lonely, I felt quite sorry for him," Aria said, "but anyway, despite Mama being so pushy, wanting to know about the Konstants' money and their land, he was very kind to me. I liked him, and I think he liked me."

"Of course he did, he couldn't help it. So how are things with Carraldo?"

Even over the crackling line he could hear her sigh. "Okay, I guess. He threw a big party on New Year's Eve. Actually it was fun, I met all sorts of movie stars, but the trouble was they all thought I was Carraldo's girl. It was like being royalty only worse—everyone was very polite and kept their distance. I think they were surprised that I wasn't loaded with diamonds and sables, but Mama more than made up for me. She's the toast of Hollywood!"

"I'll bet she is!" He laughed.

"Mike? I was wondering if you'd found out about Orlando."

He grimaced, wondering what to tell her. "I called the *pensione* a few times," he admitted, "they told me he's gone to Switzerland—skiing, I guess."

"I see," she said quietly. "Then I'll just have to wait until he gets back. Thanks anyway, Mike."

Her voice sounded very small, and trying to cheer her, he said, "I'm making some progress with Poppy, here at the villa. She sure led an exciting life!"

"Oh, of course, Poppy!" she exclaimed, as though she'd forgotten about her, in her worry about Orlando. "Have you found the evidence yet?"

"Not yet, but I'm trying. I keep asking Luchay to give me a break and tell me where the clues are hidden, but he's not talking. Except to say, 'Poppy *cara*, Poppy *chérie*, Poppy darling . . .' "

"Poppy *cara* . . ." the parrot began imitating him, and Mike laughed.

"But you were right about bringing him here, Aria. He looks as though he knows he belongs."

"I just wanted him to relive his memories, that's all," she said sadly. "I must go, Mike, Mama's calling me. We're going shopping—again. It's all anyone does around here. Carraldo's gone off to Houston—looking at paintings, he said, so I'm reprieved for a day or two. Oh, dear, I suppose that's unfair, he's been so kind—and especially to Mama because I have the feeling he really can't stand her. I'll see you when I get back—soon, I hope. Or you call me first, if you find the 'evidence.' I'll be praying for you!"

Hooking the old-fashioned receiver onto its stand, Mike lay down on the bed—Poppy's bed—his arms behind his head, thinking about Carraldo. What sort of man was he, he wondered. Did he make his billions legitimately through his art dealings? Nobody knew for sure, and probably no one ever would. But he hated like hell for Aria to be involved. No wonder she was praying he'd come up with substantive evidence.

Carraldo was on his plane, returning to Los Angeles. His face looked gray and there were lines of strain around his mouth. The past two days had been grueling, but no more than he'd expected. The doctors at the Southern Methodist Hospital in Houston were among the best in the world and this time they'd put him through a battery of tests that had left him weak with exhaustion. And he might as well not have bothered, because things hadn't changed. Their conclusions were exactly what they had been the last time he'd been there, and the time before that. The pain stabbed across his chest again, and with a sigh he took the usual little white pill from his silver box and held it under his tongue, waiting for the relief it would bring.

He thought about Aria in Los Angeles, wondering if their little holiday together could be termed a success. She was polite to him, but she was nervous and distracted and he felt she was counting the days until they returned to Venice. Of course, he knew why she wanted to go back; she had told him Mike Preston was at Poppy's villa and he knew she was hoping he'd found the evidence. He also knew exactly where Orlando was, and what he was doing, and he knew that when he wanted to, he could feed that information into Aria's ear—and that would be the end of Orlando. But he still didn't have all the information he needed. And he didn't want to use his usual methods. Picking up the intercom phone to the flight deck, he asked them to put a call through to Mike Preston at the Villa Castelletto.

"We haven't met, Mr. Preston," he said formally. "But I've heard quite a lot about you from Aria."

"Yes, sir," Mike said, surprised. "How can I help you?"

"This may sound strange to you, Mr. Preston, but I'm asking for your trust. Of course, I understand that the information you are searching for is essentially a private matter, between you and Lieber, but I need a favor. When you finally discover who the heiress—or heir—to Poppy Mallory's estate is, I want you to tell me first. Of course, I know you'll tell Aria, sooner or later, *but I need to know immediately.* I'm only asking, Mr. Preston, because it is a matter of life or death. That probably sounds very melodramatic to you, but believe me, I mean it."

Mike hesitated, thinking of Claudia's mysterious death, and then Aria's fears that she was being followed. With a pang of fear, he remembered Lauren Hunter alone in Los Angeles. . . .

"Please trust me, Mr. Preston," Carraldo urged. "I promise you won't regret it. That's all I can tell you right now."

Mike nodded. He didn't know why he should trust him, but he did. "I'll call you," he promised. "As soon as I know for sure."

"Thank you," Carraldo said, sounding tired, "I'll wait to hear from you."

He sat back in his gray suede chair, staring at the clouds floating by the windows of the plane like a range of snow-capped mountains. It was almost February—*carnivale* time in Venice. He would throw a big party —an *engagement* party. And then, if she would agree, he and Aria would be married the week after.

Orlando had finished the painting of Pamela's chalet and he propped it on a little table-easel, ready to surprise her when she woke up. It was almost noon and everyone else had gone out on the ski slopes hours ago. He'd heard them planning on meeting up at the Eagle Club for lunch, but he hadn't been invited. Somehow there was an attitude that he was

Pamela's property and therefore she would take care of him, when she felt like it.

The chalet was luxurious in a deliberately rustic, Alpine fashion; a log fire burned day and night in the enormous circular fireplace in the center of the vast living room and the triple-glazed plate-glass windows offered breathtaking views of snowy mountains on every side. The morning seemed to be crawling by and Orlando checked the time again on the gold Cartier watch Pamela had given him for Christmas—a good watch, but not the best that Cartier offered. Like a lot of rich women, Pamela was careful with her money.

The place was like a prison, he thought, prowling its polished floor-boards like a caged bear, but there was no point in going back to Venice yet, not until Aria returned. He calculated the time difference between L.A. and Gstaad, wondering whether to call her, but then, he decided angrily, she could wait. Climbing the stairs to Pamela's room, he flung open the door.

She lifted herself sleepily onto her elbow, pushing the hair from her eyes. "Oh, Orlando," she murmured, "just the man I'd like to see. Come here, darling."

He walked toward the bed, staring at her expressionlessly.

"Why are you looking at me like that?" Pamela cried sharply. "Sometimes you're so strange, Orlando, I feel I don't really know you."

"Of course you do," he replied, unbuttoning his shirt.

"Well, then," she said, watching him, smiling. "Why don't you join me, it's very cozy in here."

"I've finished your painting," he said as he put his arm around her.

"Good boy," she sighed, relaxing under his caresses. "We'll look at it later, shall we?"

Sure, Orlando thought, kissing her, of course we will, Pamela . . . whatever you say, Pamela . . .

Mike hadn't really expected Lauren to answer when he called her, she was always so busy working, and he smiled, pleased at the sound of her voice.

"Hi, Lauren Hunter," he said. "How're things in California?"

He heard her laugh, a little breathlessly. "Sunny," she replied, "as usual. But where are you?"

"You're not going to believe this, but I'm all alone—except for Poppy Mallory's parrot—in her crumbling Italian villa in the middle of no-where. *And* it's snowing outside!"

"Poppy Mallory's parrot!" she exclaimed, "and her villa! How exciting, Mike!"

"Not so exciting," he grumbled. "I can't find what I'm after."

"Then you don't know yet . . . ? You're still not sure who it is?"

Her voice sounded hopeful and he smiled. "Sorry, kid, I still can't tell you. This whole situation is even more complicated than it seemed at first. But listen, Lauren, how are you? And Maria? I mean, you're okay, aren't you? No problems?"

"No more than usual," she replied, sounding puzzled. "Why, what do you mean?"

"Oh . . . nothing," he said, then, "yeah, well, actually I do mean something, Lauren. One of the possible heirs has been murdered—you probably read about her in the newspapers, and now another thinks she's being followed. I'd just like you to keep your eyes open, be aware . . . you know . . ." He heard her gasp, and said quickly, "I don't mean to frighten you, and odds are it's nothing, but just take care of yourself. Okay, Lauren Hunter?"

"Okay," she said quietly. "Mike? When will you be back?"

He thought for a moment. "As soon as I can, Lauren. Okay?"

"Okay," she replied, and he thought maybe she was smiling. "How's Aunt Martha?" she asked.

"Great, and Maria?"

"Great. I've got to go to work, Mike, I'm late . . ."

"Talk to you soon, Lauren Hunter," he said, still smiling.

Replacing the receiver, he drew the gray-blue silk curtains, shutting out the snowy night, and threw another log on the blazing fire. Slumped in Poppy's deep comfortable wing chair with a glass of red wine in one hand and an enormous ham and cheese sandwich in the other, he finally admitted defeat. He was exhausted—and he'd exhausted all the possibilities of the Villa Castelletto. He ate his sandwich morosely, washing it down with the wine; there was no doubt about it, he was at a dead end and he didn't know where to look next.

Hooking his toe under the footstool he'd kicked away so angrily earlier that day, he propped his feet on it and stared into the fire, wondering how many long winter nights Poppy had spent alone like this, sitting here in this very chair, just gazing into the flames and reliving her past. Damn, he thought as the footstool wobbled, he must have broken it when he kicked it, and it was probably a priceless antique! Groaning, he picked it up and examined it. It looked like a normal enough piece of Victorian furniture, with a heavily carved mahogany base supported on four lion's-paw feet and a needlework top of pink roses on a dark blue ground. He wiggled it cautiously, inspecting it for damage. Then suddenly he noticed a small gold keyhole. "Luchay," he said, stunned, "I think I've found Poppy's hiding place!"

He rummaged quickly through the desk searching for the key, but without any luck, and then he thought about how long it would take him to search the huge house with all its cavernous rooms—and still maybe not find it. Hurrying to the kitchen, he slammed around in the drawers until he found a screwdriver, and then he headed back up the stairs, two at a time.

The lock was a good one; it took quite a bit of prising until, with a splintering sound, it finally gave. Mike stared at the neat little pile of childish exercise books, probably bought years ago from the store in the village. He hardly dared open them. "Is this it, Luchay?" he said, awed. "Are we finally going to know the rest of Poppy's secrets?"

CHAPTER 44

Greg Konstant was at the end of his annual pilgrimage to Europe and another round of useless visits to the embassies, the consulates, and the police of Rome and Venice and Florence. He had spent more futile weeks just wandering the streets, never seeing the beauty of the ancient cities, endlessly searching the faces of the passing crowds, hoping against hope for that miracle to happen when he would suddenly see Poppy. So many times he'd caught a glimpse of wild red hair, or a fraction of a profile, or a particular long-striding walk that seemed familiar, and he'd hurried after his dream only to find it once more in pieces as the girl turned, glaring at him suspiciously. He'd apologize quickly, saying he'd thought she was someone else, someone he knew . . . an American girl. "Her name is Poppy Mallory," he'd say eagerly, "she's about your age, perhaps you know of her?" But they always shook their heads and hurried on.

"I don't know why you keep on coming back," Angel had said to him tiredly. "Poppy has chosen to disappear and it's time you accepted that."

"I'll never accept it until I know the reason why," he'd replied stubbornly. "Poppy would never just 'disappear.' Something must have happened to her."

He was in the Ritz bar in Paris, sitting over a lonely drink and worrying about Angel. It was obvious that his sister was not happy with Felipe, though she did her best to disguise it. It seemed to him that Felipe became more autocratic and demanding each year, treating Angel as one of his beautiful possessions rather than as his wife, though he did make an effort to tone down his sharp, disparaging tongue when Greg was around.

"That's because he's afraid of you," Angel had said with a weary smile, "he knows which side his bread is buttered on and you and Papa control the purse strings. Without the Konstant money, Felipe is just another impoverished aristocrat, long on titles and short on cash."

"Do you still love him?" he'd asked angrily, ready to whisk her back to California on the next boat if she said no.

"Sometimes I wonder if I ever really did," she'd replied sadly. "But I can never leave him, Greg—because of the children."

He'd seen how Angel's face lit up whenever her two little girls were around, and now there was two-year-old Aleksandr, the apple of her eye. They were the only elements in the empty socialite life Felipe had imposed on her, that brought the old sparkle of true beauty back into Angel's face. She was a slender, elegant woman now, smooth-haired and haunted-eyed, and always immaculately dressed, but though she was only twenty-seven, she might have been any age. She had lost all her youthful bounce, her joie de vivre. Life was no longer "fun" for Angel.

The twins were eight years old. Maria-Cristina was the fairer one with sparkling dark blue eyes, while Helena had golden hair with Felipe's moss green eyes. Maria-Cristina was lively and alert, but Helena was quieter and more inward. And young Aleksandr was a sensitive little boy, very much under the domination of his father.

This time when he was staying at the Villa d'Oro, Greg had noticed that Helena was behaving strangely. At first he'd thought she was just being disobedient when she didn't answer him, but Helena was a polite, well-brought-up girl, and even allowing for childish pranks she would never have ignored a grown-up.

"I'm surprised you haven't noticed before," Angel had told him sadly when he asked. "It's quite simple. Helena is deaf."

"Deaf?" he'd cried, appalled. "But why . . . ? How . . . ?"

"I first noticed it when she was just a few months old—it was the contrast between the two girls, you see."

"But surely there's something that can be done! After all, she's only a child."

"If there were, don't you think I would have done it?" Angel had retorted bitterly. "I took her to the best ear specialist in Rome—and then to Milan, and then Paris, and London. I took her everywhere, Greg.

And every doctor told me the same thing. There is a malformation of the timpanic bone and the pressure causes deafness. By the time she is twenty, Helena will be totally deaf."

Greg had stared horrified at the lovely blond child romping on the lawn in front of them, laughing and shrieking with delight as she and her sister chased the brown-and-white spaniel puppies he'd bought them as a present. He recalled Angel, playing with her little black dog Trottie, dead many years past now, when he'd been the adoring older brother. How perfect she had been; she'd had beauty, charm, affection, the gift of love . . . the good fairies had given the young Angel every gift at her christening, only to take them away later.

"I've hidden it from everyone—except Felipe, of course," Angel said. "I didn't want anyone to know. I'm always around to help her, so no one really notices. I answer the questions she doesn't hear, or I turn her to face the other children and tell them to speak more clearly . . . I just can't bear anyone to know."

"But what about when she's older?" he asked worriedly.

"No one will ever hurt her," Angel cried fiercely, "she will live here where she's loved, surrounded by these beautiful gardens, I'll find tutors so she will learn to lip-read, we'll strive to keep her speaking voice as normal as possible . . . it *will* work, you'll see, *it will*!"

It was ever since that fatal Grand Tour of Europe nine years ago, Greg thought bitterly over his drink in the Ritz bar, that things had begun to go terribly wrong. Not even the Rancho Santa Vittoria was quite the same now.

"Greg Konstant? It is you, isn't it?"

Greg frowned at the man in front of him, puzzled. "Good God," he exclaimed, his face clearing, "it's Charlie Hammond, isn't it?"

"Charles James Hammond the Third, Harvard class of '95. You old reprobate, you mean you didn't recognize me? After all the carousing we did together in Boston? You can't say we didn't paint that town red once or twice—or maybe even thrice! And what are you doing, alone in the Ritz bar in Paris? Waiting for a lady, I'll bet."

Charlie Hammond took a seat opposite Greg and summoned the waiter for more drinks. He was a tall, good-looking man of thirty-three, with wavy brown hair and matching brown eyes, and he was very much at home in the cosmopolitan environment of the Ritz.

"My favorite watering hole," he said, glancing around to check who else was there. "This is always the first place I make for in Paris. You can always guarantee you'll meet someone you know in the Ritz bar; it's never failed me yet. Still, I must admit I didn't expect it to be *you*, Greg.

Why, we haven't seen each other since our college days—ten years, is it?
A bit of water has flowed under my bridge since then, I can tell you, and
yours too, I'll bet. I just got in today—here on banking business, old
fellow. You remember?"

"Of course," Greg replied, smiling, "the family bank in Philadelphia.
You always swore at college you'd never end up in it—you were going to
be a boat builder, if I remember right?"

Charlie grinned as he downed his whiskey. "Well, you know how it is
. . . just too hard to escape from the grip of the family, old fellow. But I
still build those boats—and sail them. On weekends and summers, of
course. But you were always going to be a rancher—never wanted anything else except to run that great estate in California."

"That's me." Greg shrugged. "I never changed."

"Then what the hell is a California rancher doing alone in Paris? You
can't pretend you're here to buy cattle or sell hides."

"I've been visiting my sister in Venice. I always come through Paris on
my way back."

"Ah-ha, Paris—the City of Light—and sin!" Charlie exclaimed happily. "I'll bet there's a pretty little wife waiting patiently for you back at
that ranch, and three or four children by now—just like me. Still, that
doesn't stop a fellow having a good time in Paris, does it? After all, that's
what it's for. And I'll tell you now, Greg, that I know the best place for
that. They say Numéro Seize, rue des Arbres, is unsurpassed in the
sensual delights. What do y'say you and I go along there and have a little
dinner and survey the scene? A bit of fun, eh, in the city of wine,
women, and song?"

"Thanks, Charlie," Greg replied coolly, "but I don't know that I'm in
the mood for a bawdy house . . ."

"*Bawdy house?* Cut out your tongue, old fellow, this is no bawdy
house! You practically need two sponsors and a banker's guarantee to get
into the place! Numéro Seize is like an excellent gentleman's club, all
elegance and refinement; *and* they say the restaurant rivals Maxim's. So
why don't you and I dine and split a few bottles of champagne and see
what it's all about? I'm told if we require the company of a couple of
charming girls to entertain us with a little feminine conversation, we can
have that too. You want to doze by the fire in the library? Do so. You
want to listen to Chopin or Liszt being played on the piano by a girl
who's a lot prettier than any concert pianist and who cares if she's not
quite as talented? A game of billiards? A business discussion? And upstairs, old fellow"—Charlie sat back, drawing in his breath appreciatively
—"they say whatever tempts you, it's yours. *And* the girls are the most

elegant, the most beautiful, and the most talented in town! Well? How can you turn it down?"

Greg laughed, relieved to be diverted from his own gloomy thoughts.

"Good fellow," beamed Charlie, "there's only one snag, though, the damned place costs a small fortune." He winked. "Still, it's worth it. And the other thing is that I've heard the madam is even more gorgeous than all of her girls, but she's totally unapproachable. They say no one's yet made it past *her* bedroom door." He grinned as they walked from the bar into the rue Cambon and summoned a cab. "Who knows?" he said. "With our charm, Greg, you or I might be the lucky one!"

There were times these days when Simone Lalage couldn't stand the company of "fashionable" Paris. She'd been part of it for twenty-five years and she told herself she was getting too rich, too comfortable, and too *old* to be bothered to make the effort to be charming and look her best, all the time, and so now, occasionally, she just liked to stay home. She would order her chef to cook a lavish dinner, and she'd banish all the gentleman callers who still sought her company, eager to say they'd had dinner with Simone and to spread the news of her latest witticisms and wicked verbal darts. The trouble was, though, that she soon became bored with her own company, and when that happened she'd order her maroon limousine and ride in style the two blocks to 16, rue des Arbres, to take supper with Poppy.

Simone was drinking her third glass of exquisite Pol Roger champagne, and listening to Poppy's starry-eyed stories of how wonderful Franco was and what a paragon of kindness and courtesy; how Franco made her feel like the most cherished woman on earth, and how ravishing and *ravished* he made her feel in bed; and she was fast running out of patience. "There's nothing new you can tell me about what happens between the sheets," she said tartly, "it's the emotion involved that counts. I've only felt it for two men in my life and both times I've regretted it. As soon as they knew I really cared, they began to treat me differently. They kept me waiting, left me biting my nails and wondering where they were. Sometimes they wouldn't come around at all, and I can tell you, Poppy, those nights are the longest in the world. They acted as though I *belonged* to them and even when my pride told me I'd had enough, I still went on taking it because I simply didn't have the will to break it off. Oh yes, even *me*, the *'indomitable'* Simone Lalage. Of course, eventually I came to my senses. I decided to put all that romantic nonsense behind me and settle for more comfortable relationships—ones where *I* kept the upper hand. Believe me, my dear," she said, patting her hair that this week was hennaed a dark mahogany to match her limousine and her Burmese rubies, "it makes for a happier life."

"But Simone, you are missing so much!" exclaimed Poppy. "I used to think that way, too, but it's different with Franco, it's *wonderful*! Just look at me!" She twirled in front of Simone, the skirts of her gray chiffon gown swirling around her pretty ankles, her champagne glass held aloft, and her face shining with vitality. "Don't I look different? Hasn't love changed me?"

Simone glanced at Poppy's portrait, which Franco had insisted on moving from the library to her private apartment, then she looked at her friend. "You are a changed woman, I'll admit that," Simone replied, refilling her glass, "and I hope it's for the better."

"Oh, Simone," Poppy cried despairingly, "how can I persuade you that love is worth everything? More than riches, more than fame . . ." Her face shone with sincerity as she added, "Being in love is life's champagne, Simone; it's to taste and get drunk on, and then . . . wheeee . . ." She flopped backward onto the blue brocade sofa, laughing.

Simone glanced at her shrewdly. "Isn't it rather a long-distance affair, this love of yours? With Franco in Naples most of the time, and you here?"

"Franco's so busy," Poppy replied defensively, "he told me he has sole responsibility for an enormous business. That's what's put those lines of worry on his face. He's only in his early thirties you know, like—" She almost said "like Greg," but she stopped herself in time, and she wondered where that stray thought had come from. She hadn't permitted herself even to think of Greg for years, or that other faraway world.

"And isn't thirty the right age for marriage?" Simone suggested, watching for her reaction. For all Poppy's newly sophisticated appearance, she was still naive and unworldly—though how she could run such a successful bordello and remain innocent, Simone didn't know—nor how she could be so madly in love with Franco Malvasi and not know that he was one of the coldest, most brutal kings of organized crime. If she hadn't been so sure that Franco really loved Poppy, she might have been very frightened for her safety.

"Maybe," Poppy replied evasively, "but we have our little farm at Montespan, where we meet, and get away from all the pressures of our work. It's such heaven there, Simone, just fresh clean country air, and milk still warm from our own cows to drink; we have fresh butter and eggs that we have to search for in the hedgerows where the hens have laid them, and vegetables from the garden. And a big feather bed to sleep in. We're like two simple country peasants when we're at Montespan."

"That's what Marie Antoinette thought when she played milkmaid at Versailles, and look what happened to her," Simone retorted acidly. "It sounds dreadful Poppy, cow's milk, ugh! Give me champagne any day!"

There was a knock on the door and Watkins appeared.

"There are two gentlemen in the dining room who would like to meet you, madame," he told Poppy.

"Who are they, Watkins?" she asked, glancing at Simone with a sigh. "Can't one of the girls act as hostess for them?"

"They've already dined with Véronique, madame. They are not our regular clients and one of them is, well, rather *noisy*. It's he who is insisting on meeting you, madame."

"Tell them I'm having dinner, Watkins," Poppy said with a sigh. "I'll try to see them later."

"Big spenders up from the sticks, no doubt," Simone guessed. "They want to be able to go back home and boast to their friends about having met the mysterious Poppy at Paris's famous Numéro Seize."

Poppy frowned. "They would have to be recommended by at least two people to get in here," she commented, "so I suppose they must be all right, even if they are noisy."

Greg watched indulgently as Charlie downed yet another glass of claret. "Your friend has good taste," smiled Véronique, "1896 was a very good year for the first-growth wines, though I would have recommended a Château d'Yquem with the foie gras, and a Tokay with the dessert."

"I'm afraid once Charlie gets started on a wine, he sticks with it," Greg said apologetically, "he's very single-minded, always has been."

"I understand," she said, nodding her head so that her heavy topaz-and-diamond drop earrings swung prettily, "that's why he is still insisting on seeing Madame."

Calling the waiter, Greg ordered a bottle of Tokay and Véronique smiled her thanks at him, toying with a tiny pot of *crème brulée*, the caramel of which almost exactly matched her wide, heavy-lidded eyes. There was a slumberous quality about those eyes, thought Greg, and she had a purring, soft sensuality, like the cat who'd got at the cream.

"So when are we gonna meet Madame?" Charlie asked, exasperated.

"A little later," Véronique soothed, "after we've finished our wonderful wine."

"Wait a minute," he said, frowning, "we can't just call the woman 'Madame' when we meet her. For heaven's sake, what's her name?"

"Madame's name is Poppy," Véronique said, with a smile.

The stem of Greg's crystal glass snapped in his hand and the beautiful golden, silky-sweet wine spilled across the cloth. Solicitous waiters hurried forward to mop up the debris, inquiring worriedly about his cut hand, as he stared white-faced at Véronique. "Did you say . . . Poppy?" he whispered.

"Why, yes. Madame Poppy. She is quite famous, you know," Véronique replied, her eyes wide with surprise.

"Tell me, where is she from?" he said urgently. "What does she look like? Has she red hair . . . ?"

"Madame is very beautiful, and yes, she has red hair. But no one knows where she comes from." Véronique smiled at him, puzzled. "Madame is an enigma. But you will see for yourself when you meet her. Why don't you let me take care of your poor hand? How sad that the glass broke, and now you are bleeding and the wonderful wine is spilled."

"I'd like to send a note to Madame Poppy," Greg said, summoning the butler.

His hand trembled as he wrote the short message. He was suddenly so sure it was she that he had no need even to question the truth. "Poppy," he wrote, "I must see you. Greg."

Even as he folded the note he began to doubt himself. He was in Paris's most notorious brothel and for the first time in years someone had mentioned the name "Poppy." He was being ridiculous. The innocent young girl he'd known couldn't be running a place like this. But he didn't know what had happened in the missing years; he didn't know the secrets Angel knew about Poppy; he didn't know what they had meant when they all claimed that she had reverted to type, that she was "like her father." . . . A million thoughts and hopes crowded through his mind as he handed the note to Watkins, pressing a fifty-franc bill discreetly into his palm.

"I will take the note, sir, but I do not accept gratuities," the butler said smoothly.

"Tips are not allowed here," Véronique explained, "it's one of Madame's rules. She says Numéro Seize is expensive because you are paying for the best. No more should be required."

But Greg didn't even hear her, nor did he see Charlie drinking his Tokay and attacking his towering chocolate and spun-sugar dessert with gusto. All he could see was Poppy's face.

Simone thought that when Poppy read the note it was as though a light had been turned out inside her. And when she looked up, the expression in her eyes was as bleak and chilled as though she'd just looked into her own tomb.

She rushed to Poppy's side, reading the note over her shoulder. *"Poppy, I must see you, Greg"* was all it said. They seemed like six innocuous little words to her, but it looked as though Poppy might never recover from their impact.

"I want you to do something for me, Simone," Poppy said at last. "Please, I beg you as my friend to say you will. This man has never been here before . . . he doesn't know you—or me. I want you to meet him and pretend you are Madame Poppy. Can you do that for me, Simone?"

Simone knew Poppy was in trouble. "It's someone from your past, isn't it? Don't worry, just leave it to me." She turned to the butler. "Watkins, take Véronique on one side and warn her what is to happen, and then bring her with the gentleman into the blue salon."

Poppy sank back into her chair as the door closed behind them. Her face was drained of color and she was shaking so hard, her teeth rattled. Luchay fluttered from his stand to perch on her shoulder, muttering anxiously as he huddled closer. But all she could think was that *Greg was here. He was in this house.* Hope sparked in her heart; maybe he'd come to find her, to take her home; maybe he'd forgive her and restore her to her proper place in life . . . *maybe he still loved her.*

She came back to reality with a jolt; his note hadn't said any of those things. How could it? She was the madam of a Paris brothel. "Poppy" was no better than a whore herself. She touched the heavy pearls at her neck despairingly. Greg was the past and she had no part in his world. She was Madame Poppy and Franco Malvasi's mistress, and wasn't it true that she loved Franco more than anyone? More than Greg?

"Gentlemen," Simone said in her husky voice, "I am *enchanté* to meet you. My Engleesh is not as good as it may be, but I bid you welcome to Numéro Seize."

Greg gazed speechlessly at the beautiful Frenchwoman . . . true, she had reddish hair, and she was charming . . . but she wasn't Poppy.

Simone's sharp dark eyes took him in from head to toe, and she liked what she saw. She thought Poppy was a fool to turn this man down for Franco Malvasi, but who knew the ways of women in love? "Were you expecting someone else?" she suggested smoothly.

"It's just that Poppy is an unusual name," Greg said, "it belonged to someone I knew."

"Belonged?" she asked sharply. "Is your friend dead, then?"

"I don't know, madame," Greg said honestly. "But thank you for seeing me. I'm sorry to have wasted your time."

"That is what my time is for—to be wasted by handsome young men." Simone smiled at him, unable to resist the urge to flirt. "And your name is?"

"I am Greg Konstant."

"Perhaps we shall see you again, Mr. Konstant?"

"I'm afraid not, I'm leaving for New York tomorrow. I shall never come back. There are too many sad memories here for me."

"It's a pity," Simone said as he shook hands and said good-bye, "that you find Paris *triste.*"

Poppy was standing by the fire, a glass of brandy clutched in her hand, and she stared apprehensively at Simone. "Well?" she whispered.

"Mr. Greg Konstant is handsome, he is a gentleman, and I have no doubt he is rich. He's everything you should have, Poppy, and I have the feeling that he must have been yours for the taking."

Poppy gulped the brandy, her hand still shaking. "Once upon a time, Simone, just like in all the best storybooks. But not now. Not ever." And then she sank into the sofa and burst into tears.

Véronique watched Greg intently as he walked back to the bar. He was not the sort of man who usually patronized Numéro Seize and he was a puzzle. He was handsome, and she had no doubts about his masculinity, but yet he hadn't shown the slightest interest in her—well . . . maybe just once when she'd caught that long, assessing glance, but it had gone no further. His friend Charlie was a type she knew well, jolly, a little drunk, generous and straightforward; he was out for a good time in Paris with a pretty girl. Charlie didn't really need her specialized services. But Greg Konstant was another matter.

"I want champagne and dancing and singing," Charlie cried loudly. "Bring on the dancing girls."

"You shall have your own special dancing girl," Véronique told him, "and I promise you will never have had an experience like this. Wait here while I arrange it."

She told Watkins to bring Charlie two bottles of champagne— nonvintage—because as a connoisseur she hated to see good wine wasted on a drunk, and to find Villette.

Charlie gazed bemusedly as Villette drifted across the room toward him. She was wearing a floating red chiffon dress, her long blond hair flowed past her shoulders to her waist, and her honey-colored flesh gleamed in the lamplight. Véronique whispered in his ear, "Villette will dance for you as no one has ever danced before. Go with her, Charlie, she will be your Salome."

Stumbling a little, Charlie linked his arm with Villette's and walked toward the stairs, a bottle of champagne clutched in one hand.

Véronique turned her attention to Greg. He was staring down into a glass of Scotch, lost in his own somber thoughts. "You seem a million miles away," she said touching his arm.

"I wish I were," he said bitterly. "I return here every year, and every year I realize that I'm just wasting my time."

"Then why do you do it?" she asked, puzzled. "What are you searching for?"

"It's not *what* I'm searching for, but *who*," he said, draining the Scotch.

Taking his hand, she said, "It's bad to drink alone, you know. Why not come with me to the little salon, it'll be quiet in there. We can talk."

Greg stared at her. She was tall, lissome, lovely; her skin was soft and her amber-striped blond hair sleek as a tabby cat's. Her soft lips were parted and her hooded eyes gazed deeply into his. She was very desirable. But she wasn't the woman he wanted.

"That doesn't matter," she said, reading his mind, "it's just that sometimes it's easier for a man to talk to another woman, about the woman he loves."

It was true, he realized suddenly. There was no one else he could talk to about Poppy. Angel and the rest of his family had simply dismissed her from their lives. It was tempting to be able to talk freely at last, to tell someone how he loved her, how he'd been so desperately sure that one day he'd find her again.

The little salon was quiet. A low fire glowed in the grate and there were pools of light and shadow thrown by the green glass lamps. "Come sit by me," Véronique said, patting a deep sofa invitingly. A waiter placed a bottle of Scotch on the low table in front of them and then disappeared discreetly. Apart from another couple, deep in conversation at the far end of the salon, they were alone.

"You are searching for something," she murmured, curling her feet under her and propping her head on her hand. "Tell me what . . . and why." Her hooded caramel eyes probed his sympathetically.

"My search is over," Greg said abruptly. "I've lost the girl I loved. She's just disappeared, no one knows where, or why. God knows I've *tried* to find her," he cried despairingly, *"believe me, I've tried."* He gulped down the whiskey to ease his pain. "She haunts me, Véronique.

Her face is always there in the crowd—and yet it isn't. It's never *her*. People tell me I'm crazy to come back year after year, simply to wander the streets, hoping that I'll see her. And maybe I am. But you see, I still love her."

"And now you're mourning a lost dream," Véronique whispered understandingly. "Tell me what she was like. Was she very young? Was she beautiful? What is it about her that haunts you, Greg? Is it your memories of the past? Or of what might have been?"

"I remember her when we were young, out riding on the ranch," he said, his eyes staring into space as though he could see her there. "Her long red hair is flying in the wind because I've stolen her ribbon—such wild, curling hair, but it feels so soft when I touch it. And her eyes are such a bright, bright blue and she always has this sort of arrogant, almost *insolent*, look. She is long-limbed and lean and graceful. I met her when she was seven years old and I knew even then she was the girl I'd marry. All I had to do was wait for her to grow up. She's so *innocent*, Véronique. What they say about her having bad blood, like her father, can't be true . . . I refuse to believe it!" He drained his glass and poured another.

Véronique's hand was resting sympathetically on his arm, her fingers were long and tapering and her nails buffed to a pearly pink. "Don't let anyone change your dream," she whispered, leaning closer, "let her stay as she was."

"I don't even know what she would look like now," Greg said broodingly, "I haven't seen her in so many years—she was just eighteen then."

"Then she would no longer be a girl," Véronique said in her low, husky voice, "now she would be a woman . . . the woman you were waiting for her to become . . ." Her hooded eyes glittered hypnotically in the shadowy room and as she leaned closer Greg smelled her scent—a smooth, green, ferny aroma of woodland flowers.

"She would be the sort of woman who'd want *you* as much as you wanted her, Greg, wouldn't she? You knew that, even when she was growing up. You told yourself she would be passionate, you imagined her in your arms, that slender body, those long lovely limbs entwined with yours . . ."

"Oh, God," he groaned despairingly, "I wanted her so . . . I dreamed how it would be on our wedding night, how innocently passionate she would be. She would make love to me as naturally as an animal in the woods because there was no dishonesty about her . . . no false modesty. She would have given me her body the way she gave everything . . . totally."

"Poor Greg," Véronique murmured huskily, but a little smile played around her mouth. At last, she had what she'd been probing for.

A noisy group pushed past the salon's doors, laughing and chatting as they took a seat by the fire, calling for more drinks. Uncurling herself from the sofa in a single graceful dancer's movement, Véronique held out her hand. "Come with me," she said huskily, "we can talk some more. I want to hear about your dreams, the private world in your head . . ."

They entered the small, caged elevator, designed to hold just two people and lined in soft amber velvet, which led directly from the salon to the third floor, and as the golden gates closed smoothly shut behind them, it seemed to Greg that he lost touch with the real world. Upstairs at Numéro Seize was fantasy in all its forms.

"You must understand," Véronique said huskily as they walked hand in hand down the silent, softly carpeted corridor, "that on the third floor at Numéro Seize, we make dreams come true, and I am here to help you find exactly what you want."

She unlocked a door, and taking his hand she whispered, "Come inside, Greg, come with me, I want to help you to find exactly what it is you want . . . exactly *who* you need . . ."

Hypnotized, he let her draw him into the lamp-lit room. A four-poster bed that looked as though it belonged in a Jacobean manor house dominated the pretty room. The high wooden headboard was black with age and intricately carved with roses and unicorns and heraldic medallions, and curtains of a gauzy peach-colored silk waited to enclose the bed's occupants into their private world.

"You must be exhausted," Véronique murmured. "Let me take off your jacket. And why don't you sit here, in this comfortable chair, while I get you a drink."

Greg leaned back and closed his eyes, loosening his tie and listening to the soft rustle of her dress as she moved around the room. Soon he felt her light touch on his knee. She was kneeling at his feet and the lamplight painted the curve of her breasts a warm cream. "This is for you," she said, handing him a pale, cloudy drink. He glanced at her inquiringly and she said, "Trust me, it will make you feel better. Drink it quickly, and then sit back and listen to me.

"There," she said with a small satisfied sigh as he drained the glass, "now let me take off your shoes. I want you to relax while I tell you what wonderful things can happen here, on the third floor of Numéro Seize." She took off his tie and unbuttoned his shirt, and then, standing behind him, she began to massage his neck. Her fingers were cool and firm as she circled the tense muscles, leaning close so that she could whisper in his ear. Again he was aware of her delicious scent, like woodland ferns and mossy flowers.

"This is a room of dreams," she murmured, "we are far away from the real world, far from all the worries, far from the past . . . far from the future. We are just here, now, together. . . . The woman you are searching for is here in this room, that lovely, vibrant girl with her long limbs, her soft silken skin, her wild red hair, her youth, her innocence . . ."

Her hands moved down his back, circling and massaging, and suddenly Greg felt weightless, he was floating on a pleasant sea of wellbeing. All he was aware of in the world were those soft hands on his naked flesh and her husky hypnotic voice murmuring into his ear.

"My darling," she murmured as her hands moved across his chest, circling his nipples until he ached with sudden sharp pangs of desire, "this is the land of dreams come true," she whispered, "this is where we grant your heart's desire." She came to kneel between his legs, and he heard her sigh with pleasure as she said, "Such a hard young body, Greg, so strong and tanned. But of course you are an outdoorsman, you love the wide-open spaces. You love riding with your dream girl and watching her wild red hair flying in the wind . . . Come, let me kiss you," she said, her mouth hovering teasingly over his. And she sighed again with pleasure, running the tip of her warm tongue across his lips, tasting him. And then she kissed him, and it seemed his entire life force was merging with hers in a great surge of passion. She freed her breasts from her dress as he put his arms around her, crushing her even closer, not allowing her to take her mouth from his. "Delicious," she whispered, "wonderful . . . I can't wait . . ." And then suddenly she slid from his knee and was gone. "I'll be back," she whispered as she disappeared through another door.

Greg just lay there, unwilling even to move. His limbs felt heavy and every nerve ending tingled with pleasure. He had no idea how long Véronique was gone, he just knew he would have waited forever . . .

"Come, Greg," she called from the bed, "come to me . . . I'm waiting for you."

The gauzy peach silk hangings were drawn and he pulled them back eagerly. She was lying against the pillows wearing a simple white nightdress fastened with tiny blue ribbons across her breasts. But was it Véronique?

"I promised I could make your dreams come true, Greg," she whispered, stretching luxuriously and spreading her hair across the satin pillows. "I am your dream, Greg, your lost dream. Look! Just look at this wild red hair. Isn't this the hair of your true love?"

He gasped, leaning forward like a drunken man to touch a glossy red strand, letting it fall through his fingers wonderingly.

"Look at this face," she murmured, smiling at him, "isn't this the face of your dreams?"

He peered closer, her face blurring with his memory of Poppy.

"It's our wedding night, my darling," she murmured, "the night we've both waited for, for so long. There's no need any longer to hold back your passion. And no need for me to hold back mine. You always knew I would love you as naturally as an animal in the forest, because I am as innocent as one. Isn't that true, Greg? Isn't that the way I am? I've come back to get you, Greg, and tonight we are together. This is our honeymoon. Come into bed now, and love me, my darling."

Her husky voice seemed to have taken on Poppy's familiar sweet tones as he took the hand she held out to him and slid into bed beside her.

"Dear, darling Greg," she murmured, her voice girlish and excited as she kissed his cheek. She leaned across him to draw the silken curtain, shutting them into their own private peach-colored world where all that mattered was a big feather bed and their two bodies, hot with desire.

"I've always wanted you, Greg," she whispered, unfastening the blue ribbons over her breasts, "but I'm just a girl, I know nothing. You must teach me how. Let me learn, so that afterward I can make love to you properly."

"Oh, my darling," he cried, his face alight with love. "I've waited so long . . ." His mouth sought her breast, and she sighed girlishly.

"Oh, Greg," she said, "I feel wonderful, I want you to do more . . . I want you to touch me . . ."

His lips traveled slowly across her body and she trembled eagerly, parting her legs as his mouth came closer. "Oh, Greg, oh, my darling," she murmured, "I had no idea I would feel like this, ah, Greg . . . !" She arched her back in response to his urgent mouth, moaning with delight. Her head thrashed from side to side and she clutched the satin sheets with anguished fingers, screaming her pleasure. "Ah, Greg," she whispered at the shuddering climax. He knelt over her, bursting with his passion. "Now I know what it means to be a bride . . ." she whispered, "your bride, Greg, you are my only one, the only man I've ever wanted . . . love me, Greg, oh, please, love me now . . . I can't wait . . ."

With a groan of pent-up passion he thrust himself into her. Véronique gasped in pretend pain, and then she wrapped her legs around him, gripping him tighter and tighter, circling him with her arms until their bodies were locked together and all his love and desire burst into her in a dazzling finale of mutual passion. *"Ah!"* he cried. *"Ahhh, Poppy, Poppy, my love!"*

Véronique's hooded eyes flew open in surprise. "Poppy?" she whispered.

Greg stared at her with clouded drugged eyes; at their bodies still locked together; at the red hair, the bright blue eyes, the long-limbed creamy body of his true love, and he smiled. "Poppy," he said again, stroking back her hair, "Poppy, my love, you are so sweet, so very sweet. You are exactly the way I knew you would be. You are my little forest animal."

Véronique's brain clicked the events of the past night rapidly into place: the refusal of Madame to see Greg . . . Simone masquerading as Poppy . . . she drew in her breath sharply. And then she smiled.

"Greg," she said in her warm, husky voice, "let's talk about our early life; we've known each other so long."

"Don't you remember?" he said, lying back against the pillows and holding her in his arms. "Riding together through the high pastures at the Rancho Santa Vittoria? How you used to try and beat me at the roundups, seeing who could get the most cattle down through the mesquite? Remember how I used to take you and Angel to school in Santa Barbara, and how you hated it at first and you used to punch the other kids on the nose? You thought you were so tough, but you were the most feminine little girl I'd ever seen. Even though we used to call you a stick insect! A stick insect," he repeated, his voice blurred, "oh, God, and just look at you now."

"Poppy loves you Greg," she murmured, twisting her body from beneath his. "Look, she's going to show you just how much she loves you."

She smiled slyly as Greg closed his eyes, immersed in the pleasures of his body and the images she had placed in his mind.

"They call me *the chameleon,* Greg Konstant," she whispered. "I get inside your head and then I can be anyone you want. *And now* I am *Poppy.*"

Poppy awoke, startled by the knock at the door. She was still huddled on the sofa, and she knew it must be late because the fire had died down and the room had grown chill. The clock on the mantel said four-thirty, and she sat up, pushing back her tumbled hair as she called, "Come in."

Watkins glanced at her in surprise. Madame was usually on duty until the last guest had gone home, or had disappeared upstairs, and she always checked the night book at four-thirty. She went to bed at five and slept until noon, and her energy was phenomenal. But tonight she looked washed-out and exhausted.

"I'm sorry, madame," he said, "I didn't realize you were resting. I've brought the night book for you as usual."

"Thank you, Watkins," Poppy said tiredly. "Is the house quiet now?"

"Yes, madame, there is just one group left, discussing business in the library, and the kitchen staff are preparing breakfast for them for five o'clock."

The night book was a record of the night's activities, which girl with which man, whether she'd had dinner with him, whether he'd stayed the night . . . and what it would cost him. Poppy flicked through the pages, running her finger down the list of the girls' names and checking their clients. She stopped at Véronique's name. "Véronique?" she gasped.

"She's with Mr. Konstant, madame, the American gentleman who was so eager to meet you. His friend, Mr. Hammond, is with Villette."

"Then he's still here? With Véronique . . . ?"

"That is so, madame." Watkins eyed her apprehensively. She was deathly pale and he was afraid she might faint. "Madame, are you ill?" he said sharply. "Can I get you something? Shall I send for the doctor?"

"Just leave me alone, Watkins," Poppy whispered brokenly.

With a single despairing blow she swept the black night book to the floor, then she leaned forward and rested her cheek against the cool leather top of her desk. Great shudders ran through her body and she wished she could cry, but it seemed that the font of tears had finally dried up. Instead there was just this tearing agony inside her. Greg was upstairs with Véronique . . . the cleverest of her girls; the chameleon who not only satisfied a man's body, she satisfied his head. She extracted his deepest dreams and darkest desires so that she could become them. For once Poppy was forced to think of exactly what was happening in that room on the third floor of Numéro Seize: *Greg was making love to Véronique.*

Her gaze rested on the black book on the floor. It was a book that damned her as equally as it proclaimed her success. It contained every sinful entry of her career. But surely God had chosen the cruelest way to punish her for her sins.

She walked across to Luchay's stand. He was sleeping, his bright feathered head tucked under his wing. "Luchay," she whispered, "I have done every bad thing a woman can do. You are the only innocence left in my life, like the true innocence of a child." She thought for a moment of her own child, happy in Angel's luxurious, protected world, and she shuddered to think of what she had done.

The beautiful Paris mansion with its hidden secrets seemed to trap her in its cushioned silence and, flinging a fur cape over her shoulders, she ran through the quiet corridors and through the green baize door that led to the kitchens. Ignoring the surprised glances of the staff preparing breakfast, she let herself out through the service door and into the courtyard.

Her footsteps rang eerily in the empty street as she sped down the rue des Arbres toward the Avenue du Bois de Boulogne. She hesitated, not knowing which way to turn, staring helplessly up and down the street. A hansom cab pulled up beside her and she climbed in.

The driver peered at her suspiciously. She was rich and well dressed, but she looked a little crazy . . . probably running away from her husband—or her lover, more likely, at this time of night.

"Drive anywhere," Poppy whispered. "I just want to think."

The cabbie shrugged; he'd been right after all.

Poppy huddled in a corner of the cab, staring blank-eyed at the empty Paris streets, analyzing again and again all the mistakes she had made in her life, thinking agonizedly that *if only* she hadn't gone to Europe with Angel, *if only* she hadn't met Felipe, *if only* . . . *if only* . . . *if only* . . . she could have been a whole person as Greg's wife instead of this creature she had become. "Riches!" she reminded herself bitterly. "Remember that's what you said you wanted . . . 'no more love'!"

The silver-gray ribbon of the River Seine unfurled itself alongside the cab and Poppy stared dully at its smooth, unruffled surface. Maybe the river was the only way she could ever escape from her past . . . away from all the tortured memories of what she was and what she might have been. Away from the reality of who she was now. She thought of how it would feel, of how the cold river would close over her head, leaving only a momentary ripple, and then it would be smooth and serene again, as though nothing had ever happened. It would be so easy, she thought longingly, so temptingly easy . . . There was no one who needed her, no one who wanted her now. . . . She gasped with shock as she remembered: Luchay . . . *and Franco!*

She clutched the pearls at her neck agitatedly; how *could* she have forgotten Franco? The man who loved her, the man whose passionate lover she was. She'd forgotten how happy she was when she was with him, and how kind and gentle a man he was. She had forgotten all the *good* things in her life. She must call Franco now and tell him she needed him, that he must come to her right away . . . only he could make her life seem right again. *Only Franco would understand.*

"Take me home, please, driver," she said urgently. "Numéro Seize, rue des Arbres."

The cabdriver's eyebrows rose as he swung around, making for the Avenue du Bois de Boulogne. So that was it. Of course, now he recognized her. She was the notorious Madame Poppy!

Greg awoke from a deep sleep, feeling refreshed. He stared, puzzled, at the massive carved wooden canopy and then at the peach silk hangings and satin sheets, and gradually the memory of the previous night came back to him. He'd thought he'd come here with Véronique, but yet he remembered vividly being with Poppy . . . or was that just a dream? A wonderful, sensual dream when he thought he'd finally found his lost love and that she was his at last. He could even recall his overwhelming feeling of happiness as he'd held her in his arms and their bodies had become one. Surely he must be wrong. It was only a vivid dream and the woman he'd held in his arms last night was Véronique.

The satin pillow beside him was smooth and uncreased and when he tugged back the curtains he saw that the room was empty. There was a tap on the door and a little uniformed maid came in carrying a tray.

"Bonjour, m'sieur," she called. "I was just coming in to wake you. Mademoiselle Véronique told me you were leaving for America today and that the boat train to Cherbourg leaves at nine. She said you must be woken at six. I've brought you some breakfast—coffee, toast, croissants, brioches. If you wish anything more, sir, I'm sure we can provide it. Oh, and the valet has been to your hotel, m'sieur, and collected a change of clothes; a fresh suit, a shirt . . . everything you need. The valet will be in to run your bath shortly, sir. *Bon appétit."*

Greg leaned back against the pillows wonderingly; this place was run like a great hotel. Whatever a man wanted, they could provide, whether it was champagne with your croissants, or a valet to ensure that you needn't return to your hotel in last night's evening clothes, or the perfect woman to make your dreams come true. Everything had been thought of to make a man happy, and it worked. For one night in his life, he had been a completely happy man.

He drank his coffee and contemplated what a fool he had been, wandering through Europe every spring, hoping to find Poppy. Too much time had gone by. It was bitterly obvious to him now that if Poppy had wanted to come back to him, she would have done so. Surely she must have known that there was nothing she could have done that would be so terrible he wouldn't help her. Angel had been right; it had been Poppy's decision. Poppy's choice. She had left him for another man and it was time he faced up to that.

Half an hour later, bathed and changed, he stood on the steps of Numéro Seize, rue des Arbres, waiting for the doorman to get him a cab. He saw one approaching; it seemed about to stop but then it went past quickly. Greg thought he caught a glimpse of a woman inside, but he was still lost in his thoughts.

The doorman signaled another cab and he climbed in. "Hotel Lotti, please, driver," he said, glancing back with a smile. Numéro Seize, rue des Arbres, was a house of dreams and, oddly, it had played an important role in his life. He was going home to Santa Barbara to begin a new life, one without Poppy Mallory. He was going to face the future now, instead of looking back to the past.

Poppy waited until Greg's cab turned the corner, straining her eyes for a final glimpse of him. He hadn't changed. She would have recognized him anywhere, the same tall, handsome Greg. He had looked so confident, so distinguished, standing there on the steps of her house . . . he'd looked like a man in control of his life. But she'd understood that it was too late to rush out and throw her arms around him and beg his forgiveness. Greg didn't belong to her, or to her world. And Franco did.

She ran to the telephone in her apartment and though she knew it would be difficult and the connection poor, she demanded that the operator put through a call to Italy. It was urgent, she said, holding back a sob, a matter of life and death.

CHAPTER 45

1907, ITALY

The boardroom at Franco's villa reflected his classical tastes. When his mother had died two years after his father, he had stripped the house of their heavy, gilded suites of furniture, their velvet drapes, and the hundreds of ornaments and knickknacks that were the mementos of their lifetime. When it was completely empty, he had walked through the rooms, seeing them with new eyes. They were his now and he intended them to reflect his choices, his taste, and his love of beauty.

An architect was brought in to remodel the interior; he had broken down some of the interior walls, opening up the rooms into grander proportions. He'd added tall marble columns and built two new wings, and a Palladian facade and entrance hall, and Franco himself had chosen the fine antique wall coverings rescued from ancient houses in France and England. The exterior had been washed a typical Tuscan ocher with white columns and shutters, and he'd bought more land so he could extend his gardens in tiers of terraces fringed with marble balustrades. And then an even higher wall was built, topped with cruel shards of broken glass and pointed iron spears to protect the villa and Franco from his enemies.

Franco had chosen each piece of furniture, each rug, each silver-bracketed lamp and sconce, with the utmost care; his home was an example of restrained, luxurious simplicity, of the kind only money can buy.

After the villa was finished, he had turned his attention to his true love, old master paintings, particularly of the Italian school. Franco never set foot in an art gallery or a sale room. He knew what he wanted and he simply employed a knowledgeable dealer to track it down and obtain it for him—money was no object. He began at the top with a Botticelli Madonna painted in 1486, which he hung in his bedroom. He placed a pair of antique Florentine silver candle sconces on each side of it, and beneath it a small table draped with a crimson silk cloth, with photographs of his mother and father. There was no photograph of his brother, Stefano. The pictures and the looped rosary and crucifix hanging over his bed—given to him by his mother at his first communion—were the only ornaments in his room. And no one else, other than the maids and his valet, ever saw it. The Botticelli Madonna gave him more pleasure than any woman he'd ever possessed, and she was his alone.

His collection grew over the years to include examples from Italy's finest periods: Giotto from medieval times; Paulo Uccello and Fra Angelico from the early Renaissance, a magnificent Raphael and a Correggio from the High Renaissance. And then he fell for the more sumptuous, theatrical, and fleshy pleasures of Tintoretto, Titian, and Veronese. He collected books, medieval psalters, and illuminated breviaries; he bought a pair of fantastic globes of the fourteenth-century world; anything rare and beautiful was welcomed in his house.

Art collecting was a solitary pleasure because Franco had no friends outside of business, and the business and his Family occupied his entire time. He lived in a world where no one could be trusted, and he never brought a woman back to his home—he had an apartment in Naples for that. He had always found his life sufficient, though one day, he'd supposed, he would marry a suitable girl and produce an heir. He'd thought he had built a system and a life-style that brought him sufficient beauty and pleasure to balance the stress and ugliness of his responsibilities and his position. No man should expect more. Or so he'd thought until he'd met Poppy.

He'd sat alone in his sumptuous library many nights, thinking about her; he had sat at his desk, staring into space when he should have been working, wondering what she was doing and who she was with; he'd lain, unsleeping, in his wide wooden bed that had once belonged in a Doge's palace, remembering the fresh, sweet smell of her hair and her skin, and the mischievous insolent upward slant of her smiling blue eyes. He'd paced the floor cursing Felipe Rinardi for what he'd done to her, wanting to kill him, and his anger was such he would have struck the lethal blow himself; but then he'd told himself if it weren't for Felipe, she would have been married to Greg Konstant and living in California, thousands of miles from his world, and light-years away from his comprehension. Because he would never in his life have met a woman like Poppy.

Even now, at this important meeting, when it was vital that he keep his concentration, his thoughts kept drifting back to her and to their life together at the little farm at Montespan, where they both pretended they were not the people they had become. He had called this meeting himself, summoning his top executives; the lawyers, the financial advisors, and the bankers, as well as the men who directed the operations at street level. Though Franco would never forgive his father for betraying him in his will and appointing Stefano his heir, he had been a dutiful son. He had increased his father's business more than a hundred times, until now he dominated the southern Italian underworld.

He looked around the table, assessing his men. On his left was Carmine Caetano, the lawyer who had warned him of his father's betrayal and who was still his top man, loyal to him and to the Family. He would never doubt Carmine, not because the old man loved him but because he had proven to him that he was a good leader. He had made Carmine into a very rich man.

Gaspari, the banker who he had personally chosen to head his bank, the Banco Credito e Maritimo, sat next to Carmine Caetano. He was a big gray-haired man who, with his striped suits and conservative appearance, gave an impression of solidity and respectability to his position. Franco had started his first bank the year his father died and now there were seven, including a branch in Marseilles. The banks were a useful legitimate tool for funneling the vast amounts of money earned from his many businesses, and now Gaspari, too, was rich; and he was loyal.

Salvatore Melandri was a Sicilian. Like Franco, he'd been to business school in the United States and he had an astute financial brain as well as a Sicilian peasant's street smartness. Salvatore always knew what was happening before it happened and Franco found him invaluable, and rewarded him accordingly.

On his right was Giorgio Verone, a young man not yet thirty years old who had climbed his way through the ranks to become Franco's right-hand man. Giorgio was tough and ambitious; he carried out orders to the letter with never a mistake. He listened, he learned, he understood, and he was a coldly ruthless killer who was not afraid to take up a weapon and do the job himself. Franco never confided all his plans, all his thoughts, all his worries to any one person, but perhaps of all his top men, Giorgio was the closest to a friend.

The other dozen men around his table were important each in his own field, but none of them knew the whole structure of the Malvasi Family business, nor would they ever. They each took care of their own sector and reported to Franco. Like Giorgio, they had all come up through the ranks, usually from the tough city streets. They belonged as closely to the Malvasi Family as they did to their own.

Franco was respected as head of the Family. He was just and generous. A man could go to him with a personal problem and Franco would invite him to sit by him, to talk to him, tell him what he needed. And if Franco felt it was justified, the man would not be turned away empty-handed. Franco paid for operations and for funerals for people he'd never heard of; he donated large sums to children's charities; he paid for candles to be lit and masses to be said. He went to first communions and was a godfather to many children. He gave supremely generous Christmas bonuses to each of his Family, and he kissed their wives and their children when they came to the villa to pay their respects.

And yet there was unrest. He felt it like the first faint tremor of an earthquake, and he didn't know what it was, or why. He shrugged his shoulders dismissively; he had learned to trust gut reaction, but there was something more urgent on his mind at the moment.

"Gentlemen," he said, "you are probably aware of the reason for this meeting. The word is out, even on the streets. The Palozzi Family is jealous of our power. You all remember the battle when we took over a part of their territory ten years ago. Now they want it back. Mario Palozzi came here himself to see me last week. His proposal was that if we returned to him the areas we had taken, he and his Family would be forever grateful; the Malvasi Family and the Palozzi Family would march side by side as allies. In other words, gentlemen, Mario promised to be good to us if we gave him what he wanted. Naturally, I told him that anyone on the receiving end of such a gift would consider themselves my friend. I told him that the Malvasi Family owned those territories legitimately, that they were won when his own Family lacked leadership and strength. 'We must go forward, my old friend, not backward,' I told him. 'And in friendship, not in war.' We embraced as he left and I sent my good wishes to his wife and children." Franco paused, glancing at the faces around his the table. "But I was looking into the face of my enemy."

"The Palozzi Family are Calabrian troublemakers," exclaimed Caetano the lawyer contemptuously, "always have been and always will be. If they weren't starting up with us, they'd be doing it to some other Family. Mario Palozzi is a fat, stupid peasant with delusions of grandeur. Even if you gave him the power, he wouldn't know what to do with it!"

"Mario is sick of being poor," Gaspari the banker said, "he's a big spender and he's lazy."

"He's too fond of playing the tycoon," added Melandri the business school graduate, "the word from the street is that he keeps his wife and seven kids in a modest house in his own village, while he lives it up with his women and his entourage in a palace in the city. I doubt that he can cause much trouble, though; he has neither the money nor the backing of his own men."

"It's true, Mario is a fool," said Giorgio Verone, the young man who'd risen through the ranks until he was close to the top. "But he's an angry fool. And it's true that his men are restless. There is less and less money coming into the Family's coffers because Mario has lost all control. Most of his people are on the take, from the kids collecting the numbers money, to the young hoods in protection; more money ends up in their pockets than in Mario's. His other business ventures have failed. Mario is broke. In my view the Palozzi Family could be taken over without too much trouble."

Franco glanced at him sharply. "You know what that involves," he said coldly. "And you know I'm against unnecessary bloodshed."

"I know, sir." Giorgio Verone's mouth curved into a smile. "But is *Mario's* blood really considered *necessary*?"

"Even though his affairs are not in order, his Family are pledged to support him," Franco replied coldly. "Inevitably there would be be another bloody battle. I am concerned not to let the image of the Malvasi Family become one of 'street thugs.' "

The telephone shrilled in the quiet room and Giorgio sighed as one of the men went to answer it. He was just getting into his stride; he knew if he had enough time he could persuade Franco that Mario Palozzi needed to be eliminated. Then, of course, the Palozzi Family would be given a new leader. And who better than himself? Giorgio had worked hard; he'd started distributing for the numbers racket when he was seven and it had been a long, hard, bloody climb to where he was now, at twenty-nine. He was in his prime; he was streetsmart; he had contacts; and he knew every single racket that existed. And he wasn't afraid to use a gun.

He watched Franco's face broodingly as the man told him who was on the phone. The frown that sat permanently between Franco's brows lifted and he suddenly looked ten years younger. He looked almost boyish, thought Giorgio, like a man who's just won a fortune at the tables. *Or a man in love.*

Franco glanced hesitantly around the table and Giorgio assessed his dilemma; he desperately wanted to speak to the person on the phone, but he was in the middle of a very serious meeting. A *life-threatening* meeting.

"Tell her I'll come to the phone," Franco said. He rested his hand on Giorgio's shoulder as he stood up, adding, "Please continue your discussion. I'll catch up with you in a few moments."

Savatore Melandri took up the cue, like the well-trained business executive he was. "Mario has lost all credibility with his men," he said angrily, but Giorgio was watching Franco walk from the room, sensing the effort he was making not to look hurried. If he could, Franco would have run to that telephone. And Giorgio knew who was on the other end.

Poppy's voice was so muffled that at first Franco hardly recognized her. "Poppy," he called sharply over the crackling line. "What is it? Are you all right?"

"It's Greg," she sobbed. "Oh, Franco, it's *Greg!*"

His grip tightened on the receiver. "What about Greg?" he demanded. *"What about Greg, Poppy?"*

"He . . . he's . . ." She dissolved into sobs again and he frowned.

"Try to calm yourself, please," he commanded. "What is the matter? Are you ill? Are you hurt?"

"I *saw* him, Franco," she whispered. *"I saw Greg.* He was here at Numéro Seize . . . here . . . *with Véronique."*

Franco leaned his forehead against the cool, pale green wall in front of him . . . Poppy had never told him about Greg . . . they'd never even discussed her past. But she knew he knew everything about her; he'd investigated her past before he'd even met her that first time in Marseilles; even then he'd wanted to know who the mysterious Poppy was . . . it was all in that secret file, kept locked in the safe behind his bed. "Has he gone?" he asked, suddenly afraid.

"Yes . . . oh, yes . . ." she sobbed.

Franco's relief was so profound that his voice shook. "It's all right then, darling," he told her, "calm yourself. Call Simone, ask her to go to the farm with you . . . you should get away from there for a while."

"But Franco, *I need you!*" Poppy wailed. "I'm *desperate*, Franco. I drove by the Seine today and I . . . I thought . . . oh, dear God, I don't know what I feel, what I think . . . *I just saw my past, Franco, and I realized what I've become."*

He glanced at Giorgio, standing by the door.

"We are waiting for you, sir," Giorgio said. "I think we have come up with some interesting possibilities."

Franco frowned. Giorgio was out of line suggesting that he was keeping them waiting; at any other moment he would have dealt with him properly, but right now Poppy was sobbing over the phone and his heart was breaking.

"*Please*, Franco," she whispered, "*please, oh, please come.* Only you can make it right. I love you, Franco. Tell me it will be all right, tell me we love each other, that we are all there is in the world. Tell me Greg doesn't exist. *For God's sake, Franco, come with me to Montespan.* At least there, when you are with me, I know I am *real.*"

"You are too distraught to drive; have someone take you," he ordered. "Wait for me there. I will be with you as soon as I can."

"Tonight?" Poppy pleaded.

He glanced at Giorgio, still waiting by the half-open door. "Tonight," he agreed.

Giorgio walked back to his seat at Franco's right hand. Now he knew exactly how the land lay.

CHAPTER 46

1 9 0 7 , F R A N C E

Montespan was the only place besides the Rancho Santo Vittoria that Poppy had ever felt was home. Like the Konstant House it had that same welcoming quality, the feeling that it belonged to her and she to it. It had been the first house they had looked at and she had fallen in love with it right away. "I don't want to look at any others," she'd told Franco, standing in the courtyard, admiring its low-sweeping slate-tiled roofs and twin symmetrical chimneys, its wide windows with their lop-sided green shutters, and the pink-washed walls and the ranges of out-buildings that extended on either side like embracing arms. "*This* house is 'home.'"

Inside were stone-flagged passages and floors of pale elm. The ancient fourteenth-century beams they'd expected to be blackened with age were their original pale weathered blond and the house felt light, wide, and airy. Franco had laughed as she ran from room to room exclaiming over new delights, a hidden store cupboard, an enormous stone fireplace, a pantry with an especially deep sink where she could bring her cut flowers to arrange. And their bedroom.

The blond beams tapered to an apex over the place where their bed would go, facing twin windows with a view over the tree-lined meadow to the sparkling Montespan brook that gushed and gurgled and rippled its way over a bed of polished stones, until it met up with the River Cher twenty kilometers away. Franco had roared with laughter—a sound none of his Family had ever heard—at Poppy's delight in the small, simple details. "You live in a palace, surrounded by beautiful things," he chided her. "How can you be so pleased over an old stone sink and a storage cupboard?"

"Numéro Seize is business," she'd replied scornfully, "it's not my home."

She'd filled the house gradually with simple things, but they were nonetheless beautiful. She had shed her trademark gray image and bought bright rugs from India and Turkey, crisp cotton curtains from Provence, and great baskets of scented dried flowers from the local marketplace. The sturdy farmhouse tables and chairs had seated generations of countryfolk, and their bed was fashioned from local clm—wide, simple, and comfortable—a place to dream in each other's arms, away from the truths of Paris and Naples.

Poppy's favorite piece was a sixteenth-century wedding armoire, a vast wardrobe of pale polished elm, hewn from the wood of a single tree, and lovingly carved with bouquets of blossoms two hundred years ago by a craftsman for his bride. And every time she came back to Montespan, Poppy would hang away her Paris clothes in its cavernous interior, change into a simple blouse and skirt, and think longingly of the day she, too, would be a bride.

She had never approached the house without a heady feeling of happiness, almost light-headedness, as though the guilty burden of her Paris life had magically lifted from her shoulders, and she was just a normal young woman coming home to be with her lover. But this time, as the dark green de Courmont swept into the graveled courtyard, Poppy was looking for comfort.

Old Madame Joliot, the housekeeper, lived in the cottage at the end of the lane. She looked after the house and the chickens and ducks, while her husband tended the garden, sawed the logs, and looked after the small herd of sweet-faced black-and-white Friesians. She had built up the fires against the chilly evening and their warmth slowly began to melt the ice in Poppy's veins.

She took off her smart Paris dress and, wrapping herself in a soft blue cashmere robe, she lay on the bed, staring at the flickering firelight, waiting for Franco. It was as though all life had stopped until he got there. She didn't allow herself to think of Greg or what had happened; she just forced her mind into a blank, seeing only the fire and Luchay on his old wooden stand, watching her with alert topaz eyes. Her life was suspended until Franco arrived, only then could she begin to feel again—

all of it, the pain, the love, all the anger. And the regret. And then Franco would kiss her and everything would be all right again.

The ticking of the clock on the mantel and the occasional shifting of a log in the grate lulled her into an uneasy doze. Dawn broke and still Franco hadn't come. Poppy ran barefoot downstairs, flinging open the front door as if expecting him to be there. Placing her hand over her eyes, she scanned the lane, hoping to see his car, but the lane was silent and empty.

Back in the house, she stared at the telephone, willing it to ring, praying it would be Franco to say he was in Paris, he was on his way to her now . . . but it, too, was silent.

Luchay fluttered to her side as she huddled back in their bed. "Tell me he's coming, Luchay," she whispered, "tell me it will be all right."

Madame Joliot fussed up and down the stairs all day with cups of coffee and bowls of steaming broth, but Poppy simply turned away her face and buried deeper into the blankets. As suppertime came and went and still she hadn't eaten or spoken, Madame Joliot hurried home to her cottage where her husband was waiting. "Madame is either ill or she's going crazy," she told him. "I don't like to leave her in this state, there's no knowing what she might do."

"And where is her husband?" he demanded, dunking a chunk of coarse crusty bread into his soup. "He's the one who should be here with her, not you."

"Husband!" sniffed Madame. "She wears no wedding band. Still, for all that, she's a fine lady. I'm afraid to leave her alone; I'll go back there after supper and stay with her. I'll sleep in the kitchen."

The house was dark and quiet and Madame Joliot went around lighting lamps and building up the fires. She filled the big iron kettle and put it on the stove to boil and soon its soft whistling blended with the crackle of logs and the fragrance of freshly ground coffee. She heated milk in a copper pan taken from a cow she had milked that morning; then she poured it over a bowl of soft white bread and added a sprinkling of sugar.

"Taste this, madame, please," she begged to the silent heap of bedclothes. "It will do you good. Nothing is to be gained by starving."

Poppy peered at her gratefully. "You are so kind, Madame Joliot," she whispered, "but you shouldn't be here. You must go home to your husband."

"Nonsense," she scoffed cheerily, "I can see you need looking after, that's why I'm here."

"Madame Joliot," Poppy said wearily, "I want to cry—and I can't.

Isn't that a terrible thing, madame? All my tears must have been shed in the past and God is permitting me no more."

"Grief takes you like that sometimes," Madame Joliot said kindly. "It's not Monsieur Franco?" she added worriedly.

Poppy was staring at her but Madame Joliot knew she wasn't really seeing her. "Maybe," she whispered at last. "Maybe it is."

So, it was man trouble, Madame Joliot thought as she tidied the kitchen and settled herself into the rocker by the fire with a cup of coffee. Well, in her experience a woman always managed to cope with that problem somehow.

As the long dark miles sped past under the wheels of Simone Lalage's maroon de Courmont, Franco listened to the rain drumming on the roof. The chauffeur was a good driver, steady and not inclined to take chances, but on such a stormy night Franco would have preferred to be at the wheel himself. The journey had been a long one; first the train to Rome, then to Genoa and Nice and from there to Paris. He had telephoned Simone from Nice and she'd sent her car to meet the Paris train as it crawled into the station, three hours late due to the violent electrical storms across the Midi.

Franco felt tired and dirty and unshaven, and he was desperately worried about Poppy. No one had heard from her since she'd called him. Simone had told him what had happened at Numéro Seize, but she'd added, surprised, "I knew Poppy was upset and didn't want to see Greg Konstant, but I hadn't realized *how* upset." Her car had been waiting in Paris to speed him to Montespan, and in the boot was a hamper of champagne and delicacies fit to tempt an invalid—or a pair of lovers. Simone always thought of everything.

As they sped onward through the night, Franco's thoughts drifted between Poppy and the tense situation he had left behind him in Naples. There was no hurry over the Palozzi Family situation, he reassured himself; his men were discussing ways to deal with it; when he returned they would offer him their suggestions and then he would make the final decision. War or no war? Death for Mario Palozzi or life? Poppy's vivid, sweet face replaced Mario's in his mind; her bright blue eyes sparkling, her cool creamy skin that never changed color in the sun, even though she wandered bare-legged and hatless at the farm. He remembered her hair tugged by the wind, a dazzling flame color in the sunlight, and tawny when it was spread across her moonlit pillow. Oh, Poppy, Poppy, he groaned silently. I can't bear it if you tell me you're still in love with him . . . I love you so much. I can't live without you.

The de Courmont limousine crunched quietly over the graveled court-yard and he peered through the blinding rain at the darkened house. Unlike the Naples villa, the doors were never locked at Montespan and he simply lifted the latch and walked in. Madame Joliot was dozing by the fire, a large ginger cat on her knee. The black-and-white border collie who had come with the house when they bought it, knew his footsteps and watched him silently from his position on the old rug near the stove, his tail wagging.

The uncarpeted elm stairs creaked as he hurried up them and opened the door to their room. Poppy was sitting up in bed looking at him and the red glow of the embers in the grate painted her flesh a warm pink. Her eyes looked dark in the strange half-light as Franco said, tight-lipped, "I'm here to know my fate. Poppy. Are you going to tell me that you are still in love with Greg Konstant? That you want to go back to him?" He gripped her by the shoulders. *"Tell me now,"* he said, his tone brutal with despair, *"Tell me now so I'll know the truth at last."*

"No! No!" she cried. "Don't you understand? The girl who was Poppy Mallory loves Greg. It's me, Madame Poppy, who loves you, Franco. Oh, I love you, I love you . . . Thank God you have come. I don't know what I would have done if you didn't . . . I need you, Franco. Tell me you love me, tell me I'm real . . . tell me I exist. I don't want to remember the past, I only want to be here, now, with you . . ." Tears welled from her eyes and she sobbed hysterically as he wrapped her in his arms, murmuring that he loved her, that they would always be together, that he needed her, he couldn't live without her. . . .

Luchay watched unblinkingly from his old oaken stand as Franco smoothed her pillows. He brought her a fresh nightgown and dressed her as tenderly as a child, and then he wrapped her in the blankets and went to build up the fire. He undressed and stood for a moment, naked, in front of the flames. His body was as hard and muscular and disciplined as his life-style. He was filled with desire for her, he needed to claim her again as his own, but he knew he must wait. Poppy must sleep away her fears and exhaustion and tomorrow they would begin a new life, without the shadow of Greg Konstant.

As the gray, stormy dawn broke, Poppy turned in his arms, feeling his desire. Her lips met his in a kiss that was more than just a symbol of her need; she loved him and he loved her and their lovemaking had a new intensity, as though they both realized they were finally committing themselves to each other totally.

The sudden spring storms vanished as quickly as they had come, leav-ing the sky a pure clean washed blue, spotted with cotton wool clouds.

The next two weeks were the happiest Poppy ever remembered. For the first time she didn't compare *where* she was with the Rancho Santa Vittoria, and she didn't compare *who* she was with the girl she used to be; and she put Greg Konstant completely out of her mind.

The worried frown had gone from Franco's face and he was like a boy again, laughing as he chased her across the meadow to the brook, stripping off his clothes and plunging into the icy pool created by the piled-up boulders. Together they herded the cows from their pasture at night, trying to milk them and getting covered in creamy froth as the animals kicked over the bucket, impatient with their amateur fumblings. They searched the hedgerows for the hens' favorite nesting places, collecting the eggs, and they drank Simone's gift of champagne sitting beneath a willow, holding an improvised fishing line in a vain attempt to catch trout for their supper. They refused to answer the telephone and they never looked at a newspaper. They dismissed the rest of the world from their lives while they played at being simple country folk whose only problem was to while away their days, filling themselves on good fresh food and passionate lovemaking.

Franco was sitting comfortably across the table from her after a supper of a vast fluffy omelet and a glistening fresh salad washed down with a little cool, brittle white wine. For the first time in his life he felt he was living the life of a normal man, with an everyday man's pleasures and longings—he could imagine himself married to Poppy and running this small farm. He could see himself returning to her each evening after the day's labors in the fields, and finding her waiting—maybe with a child in her arms. His son. Someone to inherit Montespan and the freedom and happiness it stood for. He could imagine no greater joy.

"Why does anyone need more than this?" he demanded. "I never want to leave here."

Poppy laughed, clutching his hands across the blue-checked cloth. "You wouldn't last five minutes here without a woman to look after you," she teased.

"There have been women in my life," he told her seriously, "but none I would have lasted a day with, alone. Besides, *you* are my woman. There's no one else. And never will be."

"Yes," she said smiling at him. "I know."

Madame Joliot and her husband always went to the Thursday market in the local town, arriving back after a hearty lunch at the café, laden with fresh produce—a special pâté cooked by the butcher, a prime piece of veal, a fine trout from the big river, and stiff, spiky artichokes wrapped in newspaper.

Sniffing the delicious aroma of the stock Madame Joliot was brewing from the bones she'd bought at the butcher's, Poppy and Franco ran to the kitchen to see what good things she'd brought home this time.

"Mmm," he complained, touching the silvery scales of the fish, "why couldn't I catch one like this?"

"You didn't use the right bait, M'sieur Franco," Madame said, hobbling backward and forward between the pantry and the stove, "and besides the brook is too shallow, the fish see your shadow. The only way to catch a trout there is to 'tickle' it."

"Madame Joliot, you're a mine of information," he said, poking at the newspaper parcel. "What's this? Artichokes! My favorite—" he stopped in midsentence, staring at the black headline running across the top of the page.

UNDERWORLD KILLINGS ROCK SOUTHERN ITALY, it said. MASSACRES IN CALABRIA AND NAPLES.

"I'll cook them for you now, M'sieur Franco," Madame Joliot said, "you'll have them cold for supper tonight, stuffed with fresh crabmeat."

"Wait!" Franco's voice was suddenly so icy and strange that she jumped in alarm.

"What is it?" Poppy asked, her smile disappearing as she saw his tense face.

The plump green artichokes spilled to the ground as Franco snatched away the newspaper. He folded it carefully, and then without another word he strode from the kitchen.

Sensing trouble, Madame Joliot busied herself in the pantry as Poppy stared worriedly after him. "Franco," she called. "Franco, what is it?" Her bare feet made no sound on the cool gray flagstones as she followed him through the hall, and up the stairs. They had spent the afternoon making love and her body still sang from his touch; everything had been wonderful, until just a few minutes ago. Suddenly Franco had changed.

He was standing by the window in their room, reading the torn newspaper. Crushing it into a ball, he stuffed it into his pocket and faced her. "I have to go, Poppy," he said. "Immediately. There is no time to be lost."

"But *why?*" she cried, anguished. *"You can't leave me now."*

Franco's face was as cold and shuttered as a stranger's, and there was an expression in his eyes Poppy had never seen there before. He looked a different person from her laughing, youthful lover of the past two weeks. "I said I must go. Men's lives depend on it," he told her abruptly.

"It's your business, isn't it?" she cried. "I know it is because your frown is back, and all the worried furrows. Don't go, Franco. Whatever it is, it's no good for you . . . it makes you hard, desperate . . . We don't need anything or anyone now. *Please*, stay here with me."

Franco had already put on a fresh shirt and was fastening his tie. He took his city jacket from the bridal armoire and his black overcoat. "I'll take your car to the railway station in Montespan-sur-Cher," he told her. "I'll arrange for one of the cabdrivers to get it back to you. I don't want you to come with me to see me off."

She watched silently as he picked up the leather document case he'd brought with him but never opened, and then he turned to face her.

"I'm going to ask you to make me a promise," he said quietly. "Over the next few weeks you may read certain reports in the newspapers. You may hear certain things discussed at the dinner tables at Numéro Seize; there'll be gossip in the streets and among the servants as well as the customers. I'm asking you not to read those reports, Poppy; not to listen to the gossip and the stories. *Not to believe any of it!* I'm asking for your trust. Can you promise me now, that you will give it to me?"

"I'll always trust you, Franco," she promised, frightened.

He gripped her shoulders, looking at her intently, as though making sure he would remember her. "That's all any man can ask," he murmured. And with a light kiss on her mouth, he was gone.

Poppy returned alone to Numéro Seize and a week went by, but she still hadn't heard from Franco. She was sitting at her desk with the day's selection of newspapers spread out in front of her. Every one carried a banner headline about the GANGLAND WAR raging in Italy and France. *The current spate of violence has spread from Naples to Calabria and Sicily, up through Italy, through all the gangs—and the major cities*, the report said.

> *And not just cities; small villages have become involved, taking sides in the underworld's greatest territorial dispute since it became known to "innocent" man. And this "war"—no other word will suffice—has been triggered by one man's greed. One man gave the command to his "soldiers" to take over another's territory and sparked off a chain of devastation whose casualties have decimated entire families, and whose repercussions will reflect on us all, forever.*
>
> *Up until now, the so-called Mafia have kept to their own particular code of honor; that there would be no killings outside the Families. This man has decided otherwise. Innocent women and children have*

been killed, alongside their men. Passersby in the streets have been mown down in their crossfire. Innocent workingmen have been crushed beneath the tires of speeding getaway cars. And in some villages, as well as in the great cities, there are people even now who are in fear for their lives.

The photograph you see displayed below shows that man. His is the face of evil that has caused deaths and destruction. His is the greed that counts lives as nothing in its need to be sated. This photograph, readers, introduces you to the devil incarnate: Franco Malvasi.

Poppy knew she shouldn't go on reading it; she'd promised Franco . . . but she couldn't tear her eyes from the cruel printed words. The reports seemed to know it all . . .

Enzo Malvasi, born in Sicily . . . created his own small empire . . . Stefano gunned down at his father's funeral alongside his pregnant wife and three other prominent members of Mafia Families. . . . The revenge killings—six men lined up and shot in a garage in Naples . . . though it was rumored Franco himself had arranged the death of his brother so that he might inherit the Malvasi empire. Within two years he had doubled his father's inheritance, within four, he'd tripled it. Franco Malvasi had created himself king of the Italian underworld and it was said he would stop at nothing, not even the murder of his own brother, to keep that position. It was his greed and his attempt to take over the territory of a small-time crook, Mario Palozzi, that had triggered off a chain reaction of territorial violence on a scale unseen in this century. The man in this photograph is a cold-blooded killer.

Poppy slumped forward across the desk, her head resting on the newspaper with Franco's picture. She remembered his boyish smile as they raced hand in hand across the meadow, his tender look as he'd helped a child across the stepping stones at Montespan brook, and the sleeping, innocent face of the man she loved, his brow eased of its tired frowns as they lay together in their big bed, at their "home." She wanted with all her heart to believe that those reports weren't true. Franco had warned her not to read them. He'd known what they would say. *But how could he have known unless what they said was the truth?*

"Well," cried Simone, sweeping through the door unheralded, "you've seen the papers, I suppose?" Lifting her head, Poppy stared at her, white-faced. "Of course, the newspapers are making a feast of it," Simone went on scathingly, "but I have no doubt that most of it is true. Not about Franco, of course. He's not a violent man. I suspect some double-dealing within his ranks. But I thought I'd better come over right away and make sure you are all right." Her sharp eyes took in Poppy's pallor and her trembling hand holding the newspaper.

"Don't take it too hard, Poppy," she said kindly. "All men have feet of clay—especially the ones we think are gods. You've been too naive for too long; I'm afraid this is a rude awakening to the realities of the world. Oh, I know you've had rough times, you've always found out about life the hard way. But you'd better believe this, Poppy. *Franco is the same man you loved yesterday. He hasn't changed one bit. It's only your perception of him that's changed.*"

She planted an affectionate kiss on Poppy's cheek. "There's nothing else I can say," she added, "except keep your faith in him."

Poppy stared down at Franco's familiar face, at the ugly black headlines, at the cruel, damning words. Then she looked back at Simone.

"Simone," she whispered. "I'm pregnant."

CHAPTER 47

1 9 0 7 ,   I T A L Y

The villa looked like a fortress. Thirty men with shotguns patrolled its perimeters and a further two dozen covered every entrance. A man was posted at each window inside the house and half a dozen more lingered by the door of Franco's second-floor study.

He turned away from the window, grim-faced. It was a month since the headlines had hit the papers, a month since he'd seen Poppy. A month that had changed the entire course of his life, and that had almost destroyed him.

He leaned back in the green leather chair, his hands clasped in front of him. His head was sunk onto his chest and his brow furrowed in thought. He couldn't deny that what happened was his fault, but it wasn't the way the newspapers had it. It was because as godfather of the Malvasi Family he had not been here, where he should have been. He had let other priorities come first, and in his world there were no other priorities. The Family was everything. He had allowed his mind to be distracted, playing house with Poppy as though he were an ordinary man. And because of that he had foolishly, and for the first time in his life, put his trust in another man. That man had betrayed him. Now he had lost face among his own Family and he was reviled as a savage by the rest of the world.

Franco walked back to the window and stared out again. This was his world—just as far as the end of his land. He was a marked man. From now on when he went outside it, he would ride in an armor-plated car with darkened windows, accompanied by bodyguards. There was no choice left for him now, he could not abandon his world because it would never abandon him. It would seek him out and extract revenge wherever he went. His only answer was to take absolute control, to dominate that world and punish all challengers. It was not what he would have chosen, but it was his only course.

He sighed wearily. The battles were over and won, Palozzi's miserable territories were his, along with two other larger areas whose godfathers had challenged him. Many were dead, wives had been left widows and children orphans. And now it was time for his revenge.

The meeting had been called for three o'clock. A glance at his watch showed that it was one minute before the hour. Taking a deep breath, he walked downstairs to the boardroom.

They were all there, waiting. Caetano, the old lawyer, grim-faced. Gaspari, the banker, apprehensive. The business affairs man, Salvatore Melandri, looked coldly pleased. And there was his right-hand man, Giorgio Verone, whose warm eyes smiled as he stood up and shook his hand enthusiastically. "We did it, Franco," he said triumphantly. "We won. Now you own it all."

"Yes, Giorgio, I do." He took his seat at the head of the table, motioning Giorgio to sit next to him.

"At our last meeting a month ago, gentlemen," he said softly, "we discussed ways and means of dealing with Mario Palozzi. I thought I had made my feelings clear. Apparently that wasn't so. Someone took it upon himself to use my name to start this war. Someone with sufficient power to claim that the orders came from me. One of *you*, gentlemen."

He leaned back and, folding his hands, stared at them. They shifted uneasily under his gaze. "Aw, come on now, Franco," protested Giorgio, "you knew it was the best way to go. It was the only way to keep your credibility within the Families."

"My *credibility*? And what credibility do I have *now*, among the Family? It would seem I have broken all the rules. Very well, gentlemen, if that is the case, I accept it. The Malvasi Family is now richer and more important. We must think of the Family. I plan to push ahead our interests in the United States within the next year, and to expand even further."

"The United States?" Giorgio said eagerly. He'd known he would get the position as head of the Palozzi territory here in Italy, but America was a golden career opportunity.

"You are an ambitious young man, Giorgio," Franco said, standing up.

"And a reckless one. It was *your* actions that caused this war. *I accuse you, Giorgio Verone, of the deaths of innocent people.* It is *you* who deserve the name they have given to me in the newspapers: *A savage, a ruthless killer, the devil incarnate . . .*" He placed his hand casually on Giorgio's shoulder, and Giorgio glanced up at him apprehensively.

"I did it for you, Franco," he said, smiling ingratiatingly. "I thought you needed help. You were disturbed by this woman; everybody agreed you were losing your grip; even the other Families were talking about it. There was even a rumor that they planned to take over the Malvasi Family . . . it was the right decision . . . everybody backed me; you saw that."

"*A Godfather never needs help,*" Franco said quietly, sliding a small, blunt-nosed revolver from his pocket. Snapping a silencer onto the barrel, he pressed it to the back of Giorgio's neck, and Giorgio glanced around him wildly. "Gentlemen, you are all witnesses that this important member of our Family disobeyed his orders and his code. It is my decision that he shall be dealt with in the proper way." They met his eyes, nodding in agreement. "A godfather himself deals with his own personal enemies," Franco said, "that is only right."

"No," screamed Giorgio, clutching the arms of his chair, his eyes rolling wildly. "No . . . no . . ."

Franco was an expert. There was no mess, no blood. You might not even have known Giorgio was dead if it weren't for the small neat black hole in the back of his neck. And the expression of terror still in his eyes.

A few nights later a black Mercedes armored limousine drew up outside a seedy warehouse in the dockland area of Naples. Four bodyguards jumped out, standing with machine guns at the ready as Franco walked quickly inside. The twelve men sitting around the table at the far end rose to greet him.

"Franco," said one, "my Family sends greetings. We are honored to have this meeting with you. We feel sure we shall be able to come to some satisfactory agreement over the new territories."

Franco sat down at the head of the table. "I won't waste your time, gentlemen," he said coldly. "I am here to see the faces of my enemies. I accuse you of treachery to your own Families and of murder. You are dead men . . . gentlemen."

He walked quickly away as his soldiers moved in rapidly from behind, and as the big black limousine sped around the corner the sound of machine-gun fire echoed through the night.

Gaspari, the banker, was lost in a boating accident at sea a week later. Salvatore Melandri, the bright young business school graduate, shot himself, accidentally, ten days later. And two months after that Caetano, the old lawyer, died at home, in bed. The doctor's certificate said it was a heart attack. Franco had decided, for the Family's sake, to be discreet.

The new chief executives he chose were middle-aged, tight-mouthed, and single-minded. And their loyalty was beyond question. And if it were not, they had the example of their predecessors as a warning.

CHAPTER *48*

1 9 0 7 ,   I T A L Y

Poppy leaned back against the comfortable blue velvet cushions as the
train rumbled onward from Genoa to Naples. She was staring out of the
window at the passing scenery, but she was thinking of Franco. It was
two months since their romantic idyll at Montespan. And she was two
months pregnant.

All her telephone calls had been answered by a cold, efficient-sounding
man who had told her that Franco was not there, but he would tell him
she had called. Netta had come to her immediately she'd read the news
in the papers, and she'd watched in despair as Poppy hovered near the
telephone, waiting for the call that never came. "You don't need a man
like Franco Malvasi," she'd cried angrily. "I warned you from the beginning, Poppy, but you were like the ostrich burying its head in the sand;
you didn't want to hear the truth."

"Franco told me the truth!" she'd retorted, her eyes flashing with anger. "It wasn't *Franco* who did this. He warned me not to believe the
reports; he asked for my trust."

"And of course you gave it to him. You always do," Netta said bitterly.
"And where has all this *faith* got you? You're pregnant and there's no
sign of Prince Charming."

Poppy had slumped into a chair, sobbing. "I don't know, Netta,"
she'd wailed. "I don't know where he is."

When she could bear it no longer, Poppy told her she was going to Naples to see Franco. Netta stared at her, horrified, and then she ran to fetch Simone.

"It would be very foolish to go to Naples, Poppy," Simone had said worriedly. "Forget about him; it's better just to keep your illusions and stay here."

"What do you mean, 'keep my illusions'?" she'd demanded. "You all act as though he's evil. And yet he's never been anything but your friend."

"You don't know anything about his world," Simone told her. "You have no idea of what it's like, Poppy. I'm *begging* you not to go." But she'd known by the expression in Poppy's eyes that her mind was made up.

It had been a long journey and even though she had stayed overnight in Nice, Poppy hadn't slept. She stood amid the whirl of activity in the railway station at Naples, waiting for her baggage and letting the familiar sights and sounds of Italy rekindle her old memories. Even the raucous cries of the porters and the fruit peddlers, and the emotional chatter of farewells and reunions, couldn't destroy the beauty of the Italian language. She stared at the black-shawled women clutching precious dark-eyed babies in their arms, and she wondered whether her child would have Franco's dark eyes.

Telling the porter to get her a cab to take her to the Villa Carmela, she followed him through the milling throng. She waited while he told the driver the address, but the cabbie just threw his hands in the air, shouting in a torrent of Italian that she couldn't understand. "What is he saying?" Poppy called, bewildered. "Doesn't he know where it is?"

"Oh, he knows, Signora," replied the porter, "but he says he is too busy."

She watched, surprised, as the driver slammed the door of his cab and stalked off to the bar on the opposite side of the street. The next driver listened to the address, then simply shrugged his shoulders and went back to reading his newspaper. The third refused outright to go to the Villa Carmela, glaring at Poppy with a mixture of contempt and fear, and she shrank back against the wall as the porter went down the line of cabs, without any luck.

Tilting her chin angrily, Poppy climbed into a cab. "Take me to the best hotel in town," she commanded haughtily.

Her suite was palatial in the usual red velvet, gilt, and mirrored provincial style, but all she saw was the black telephone waiting on a little inlaid table. At the other end of the phone would be Franco . . . he was here, maybe only five, ten minutes away . . . Her voice trembled as she asked to be put through to his number.

Franco glanced up from his desk as Alfredo, his secretary, answered the phone. "I'm sorry, Signora, he is not here," he was saying softly so as not to disturb him. "I will see that he gets your message. Yes, Signora. Here in Napoli. Yes, yes . . . Thank you, Signora."

Franco leaned back in his chair and closed his eyes. He knew it was Poppy calling again, and he didn't know what to do. He had thought not going back would be the kindest way of ending things. Easier on her, and easier on him. Because he loved her as much as any man had ever loved a woman. To see her sweet face again, to feel her kisses, to lie with her in their big loving bed in Montespan, would only weaken his resolve. It would only make him believe that he wasn't the person he knew he was. And that belief had almost been his ruin. He couldn't afford such a mistake again.

"What did she say this time, Alfredo?" he asked wearily.

"The Signora is here in Naples. She is at the Grand Hotel. No cabdriver would bring her here."

Franco's face was impassive; he couldn't afford to betray his emotions again in front of any man, but the frown between his brows deepened and a small pulse ticked nervously in his cheek.

"Thank you, Alfredo," he replied, turning his attention back to the papers on his desk. But his mind was full of Poppy . . . she was here . . . he could go and fetch her right now. In fifteen minutes she could be in his arms. He would bring her to the villa, beg her to stay, ask her to marry him. They could live here, surely they needed no one else, no friends, no dinner parties, no visits to the opera. All they needed was each other.

Pushing back his chair, he paced to the window. Already his firm resolutions were dissolving. He had no right to act like a lovesick fool; she didn't belong in his world and he must set her free. He knew of only one way to do it.

"Alfredo, you will call every florist in Naples, even in Rome . . . wherever you have to . . . and order them to send every available gardenia to the Signora's suite at the Grand. Then you will telephone and tell her that a car will call for her at nine this evening. I want you to send three bodyguards with the chauffeur." He thought for a moment. "Ruggiere, Fabiano, and the Dottore." He had deliberately chosen the Dottore because he was the most frightening man he knew—a failed surgeon whose specialty was the knife, and whose only desire was to use it.

Poppy shrank against the chill black leather upholstery of the Mercedes limousine as it moved through the outer suburbs of Naples and climbed upward into the hills. The chauffeur knew the road well and blared his horn warningly at the peasants in their haycarts. They turned to stare, crossing themselves as the big car went past. She had no idea where she was going and she stole a look at the men on either side of her. They had the low foreheads and brutish, bovine eyes that came from generations of peasant inbreeding, and they were crouched forward in their seats, staring intently at the road ahead, with small machine guns clutched in their hands.

The third bodyguard, sitting next to the chauffeur, had been waiting for her in the foyer of the Grand. He was tall and well dressed, and his skeletal head was almost bald. His eyes were an indeterminate color behind thin, gold-rimmed glasses, and a fine scar ran from his right eye to the corner of his thin-lipped mouth, puckering it into a permanent sinister smile. "I am Emilio Sartori," he'd told her, "usually known as the Dottore—because of my medical training. I had plans to be a surgeon, you see, before my interests became . . . diverted."

The big car slowed down, stopping in front of tall iron gates set in a massive stone wall. Moonlight glinted on the shards of glass and the iron spikes, and on the guns pointing at her as half a dozen men surrounded the car.

"It's all right," the Dottore called to them, "it's the lady he's expecting."

They peered warily into the car and Poppy closed her eyes, wondering if she had been captured by Franco's enemies, waiting for the bullet that she felt sure was coming. But the big gates swung open and the car moved forward again, crunching up the winding gravel drive and stopping finally in front of an impressive Palladian portico. Four more men with machine guns watched her as she walked up the steps beside the Dottore, and Poppy stumbled in panic. Averting her eyes from their curious stares, she told herself none of this mattered, not their guns, nor their cruel faces and their frightening, implacable stares . . . nothing mattered except that in a few moments she would be with Franco.

"Wait in here please, Signora," the Dottore told her. "The Signore will be with you as soon as possible. He is in a meeting."

The lofty, pillared room into which he showed her was formal and classical, and in perfect taste. The walls were painted a cool almond-green and the elaborate cornices picked out in white and palest terracotta. The beautiful marble columns by the double doors were from ancient Rome and no attempt had been made to restore their crumbled beauty. Poppy wandered nervously around, admiring the important pictures, touching the little silver boxes inscribed with the crest of Charles I, the exquisite Paul Storr candelabra, the Fabergé eggs, the Caffieri clock. She hadn't realized before how very rich Franco must be; his home was like a beautiful museum stocked with priceless objects. She thought of their little farm at Montespan, and its simple country furniture, its stone-flagged hallways and tilting beams and the great bunches of flowers picked from the meadow and stuffed into a copper milk churn. The houses belonged to two different people. Suddenly she was afraid. It wasn't the same kind of physical fear she had felt in the limousine when she had thought for a moment she might die; it was less simple.

"I didn't expect to see you here, Poppy. In my home."

She swung around to face him, her hand on the pearls at her throat. Franco was standing by the door, unsmiling. He looked thinner, gaunter, and the lines on his face were etched even deeper—but it was Franco at last. She felt weak with love for him. "I . . . I was just admiring your collection," she stammered, resting her hand on the porcelain statuette of a little dog.

"The statue is of Marie Antoinette's chihuahua dog, Papillon," he said, walking toward her. "She ordered it from Sèvres in 1790. It was found in her dressing room at Versailles . . . afterward."

Poppy shivered as she remembered Simone's prophetic words when she had first told her about their life at the farm at Montespan. *Marie Antoinette played milkmaid too,* she'd said. *And look what happened to her.* Poppy wondered wildly if the little dog had had its head cut off too.

She waited for Franco to put his arms around her, to kiss her, to tell her he was happy to see her at last. "I never intended you to come here, Poppy," he said pouring champagne into two brittle and beautiful Lalique glasses. "But since you are here, we must celebrate."

"Franco, I had to see you. I needed you!" she cried desperately.

"I'm afraid I cannot always be available when you *need* me," he said, offering her the glass.

Their hands touched and a flicker of longing sparked in his eyes. "You heard what happened?"

She nodded. "I read it, and there was talk . . ."

"Well?" he asked harshly. "And what do you think?"

"You asked me to trust you," she said simply.

He nodded, looking at her. "Faith is such a rare commodity," he said sardonically.

There was a knock at the door and the Dottore entered. "Dinner is served, Signore," he said in the smooth, high-pitched silken voice that sent chills down Poppy's spine.

The dining room was as big as the salon, maybe forty feet long by thirty wide, with a narrow oaken refectory table running down the center. "The table came from a thirteenth-century monastery," Franco told her, as though he were a museum curator. "It pleases me to think of those old monks sipping their simple broth where we now dine so sumptuously. Every piece in the house has a story; the library table over there belonged to Cardinal Richelieu, the vases were a Chinese emperor's of the Third Dynasty, this very silverware once graced the table of Queen Anne of England. I suppose I have this passion for pieces of other people's lives because I have no real life of my own. The four walls, you see, are my boundaries. The gardens—a mere ten acres—are my country. I am 'king' of this small empire, Poppy, though now it spreads across continents. But what you are seeing is my entire personal world. One third of this prison I inherited, and one third I created, but the bars of the final third have been placed around it by men who betrayed me."

A white-gloved footman placed a small crystal dishes of caviar in front of them and the tiny silver spoons tinkled against the glass.

"I'm glad you came here," Franco said, spooning the glistening black grains onto a small triangle of toast, "because now you can see for yourself what it is like. Do try the caviar; it's beluga, my favorite."

"I never knew you even liked it," Poppy blurted.

He smiled, nodding his head. "The man who fished for trout in the Montespan brook and enjoyed drinking milk warm from the cow no longer exists, Poppy. But there are compensations; a man in prison is allowed the best food that he can afford. So tonight we are having the best—the champagne, the caviar, the veal with white truffles, the wines from the best châteaux. What more can a man ask?"

Anger flared in Poppy's eyes as she swept the crystal dish, the Lalique glasses, and Queen Anne silver to the floor. "What game are you playing, Franco?" she hissed. "What is going on? I'm here because you didn't come to me. I waited. I was frightened for you, I cared about you. *I love you, Franco!*"

Her face was pale and her blue eyes glittered in the candlelight as she reached up, tearing the combs and pins from her hair. "Look at me," she commanded as it tumbled around her shoulders in a glossy rippling mass. She ripped the earrings from her ears, the pearls from her throat, the rings from her fingers. Tearing open her red chiffon dress, she let it slide to her feet. She had deliberately worn nothing underneath because she had known he would take her straight in his arms and make love to her, and now she stood naked in front of him. *"This is who I am!"* she cried. *"This* is how I was for you at Montespan. *This* was the woman in your arms, the woman you said you loved. You are talking to me about caviar and Cardinal Richelieu's tables, when all I want you to say is that you love me, that you are glad to see me." Her voice dropped to a whisper. "I want you to tell me that nothing matters in the whole world . . . except us."

Franco remembered all the cruel deeds he had done in his life and he knew that none was more cruel than what he had to do now. "I am no longer a free man, Poppy," he said quietly. "I can no longer say those words to you." Kneeling, he lifted her dress from her feet, drawing it slowly upward, over the lovely length of her thighs, past the tempting triangle of bronze hair guarding the precious secrets whose tastes and texture he knew so well; past the slope of her creamy belly, the delicate curve of her breasts, up to her long, graceful throat. With his hands on her shoulders he looked at the face he loved; the pink-flushed alabaster skin, the freckles across the nose, the soft, passionate, trembling mouth, and her blue eyes blazing with despair and tears. He ran his hands for the last time through her wild silken red hair, willing himself to remember the way she looked, the way she felt, the scent of gardenias on her skin.

"It's cruel to imprison a butterfly in a world of guns and evil and sudden death," he whispered, "it would never survive. You have finally seen the truth. Go home, Poppy. Go home. I beg of you."

She knew then that it was no good; there was nothing she could say or do that would change his mind. She thought of Franco's child in her womb. It was the winning card in love's poker game and if she told him, he might relent. But how could she? She would be condemning an innocent child to a life behind these four walls, and an inheritance no sane person would ever want.

Franco rang a bell to summon the servant. "Remember," he said quietly, "if things go wrong, if you ever need help . . . all you have to do is call."

She nodded, looking at him for the last time. And then she turned and fled from the room.

CHAPTER 49

1907–1908, FRANCE

Poppy left Paris and went with Netta to Montespan before her pregnancy became too obvious, leaving Simone to supervise Numéro Seize. It was the end of September and the farm looked idyllic under the pretty blue sky. There was a warm breeze and the orchard was full of apples, plums, and pears; horse-drawn haycarts trundled past them down the country lanes as she and Netta strolled to the village or drove in the bottle-green de Courmont to Montespan-sur-Cher, and sometimes even farther, to Orléans, where they bought things for the baby, exclaiming over tiny jackets and bonnets and cribs flounced in organdy and lace.

Poppy's cheeks were flushed from the sun and her body plump from good health and the growing child. She had forbidden herself even to think of Franco for fear her despair would hurt her unborn child, and instead she channeled all her energies toward it. She would lie for hours on the grassy bank watching the kingfishers dive into the swift little brook like points of brilliant jeweled light, feeling like the mother of all the earth, and wondering why she hadn't felt like this the last time. She knew the answer, of course. It was because she was carrying the baby of the man she loved. If she couldn't have Franco, then at least she would have his child, and she wanted it more than anything else in the world. She envisioned a daughter with her red hair and his dark eyes, but when the baby finally came, two days before Christmas, it was a boy.

She thought long and hard before she decided on his name; she couldn't call him Franco, after his own father, and though she would have liked to call him Nik, after the "father" she loved, somehow it didn't seem right. And she never even contemplated calling him Jeb, because that memory was better buried. She wanted a name that meant something to her personally. Finally she called him Rogan, for her own Irish heritage. But the family name she entered on his birth certificate was not Mallory, nor was it Malvasi, the name of the father. It was a name she invented because her son was never going to bear the stigma of either his father's or his mother's identity. When he grew older and began to ask questions, she would think of what to tell him, but for now he was just Rogan.

"We can't stay here forever, you know," Netta said lazily one evening late in February. "Simone says they need you at Numéro Seize, and from the sound of it, I'm being robbed right and left back in Marseilles." She sighed. "I've half a mind to give it all up and get married again." She glanced at Poppy, curled up on the sofa, gazing into the glowing fire, with the baby asleep in his bassinet beside her. "What about you?"

"Give up Numéro Seize?" Poppy said wonderingly. "I can't do that now, Netta, I have Rogan to think of. I have to make money to look after him. A boy needs good schools, a future. An inheritance."

"I mean about marriage, not money."

"Marriage?" Poppy looked at her in surprise. Netta knew how she felt about Franco. "You know I'll never marry."

"And why not? You could always fall in love again, if you'd let yourself."

"Don't be ridiculous," she replied, angrily, "I'm 'Madame Poppy.' Who marries a woman like that?"

"Two of your girls have married," countered Netta. "Solange married a prominent politician and now she's a *grande dame* at all those cabinet dinners. And Belinda married a title."

"He has a title and no money," sighed Poppy. "Belinda will be back when he fails to provide her with the luxurious life she's used to at Numéro Seize. That address blights you for life," she added bitterly.

"Still, the house is yours now, since Franco gave you the deeds. And you have the farm too," Netta said. "You're a rich woman, Poppy."

Poppy supposed it was true; she was rich. She had accepted Franco's gift of 16, rue des Arbres, and the Montespan farm, for Rogan's sake. The properties were his security in case anything should ever happen to her. Meanwhile she would continue with Numéro Seize because she still craved the comfort of great wealth. When she was *really* rich, she promised herself, then no one would hurt her. The rich never suffered, they never felt pain. They lived in cushioned isolation from the rest of the world, indulging their pleasures. Over the years, she had learned a lot about "the rich." Meanwhile she kept on steadily buying her small properties here and there around the big cities in France, and even in Italy. Of course, they were worthless at the moment, but she still trusted Franco's advice. She felt sure that one day they would make her the wealthiest woman in the world and she would have found a way to be happy without a man. And without love.

She waited another month until the baby was weaned and then she left him at Montespan in the tender care of a plump, motherly nurse who had already brought up two children of her own. "Rogan will never know about Numéro Seize," she sobbed, as they drove back to Paris, "he'll never know the truth about his mother!"

"Why not just give it all up?" Netta begged. "Leave it all and go home to your son, where you belong."

"I can't," she said, wiping away the tears and sitting up straighter. "I need the money, Netta."

The house looked as beautiful as she remembered it and her girls crowded around excitedly, glad to see her back. But, of course, neither they nor any of the customers at Numéro Seize knew about the baby.

Luchay screamed with delight at being back amid the noise and excitement and, worried that she had neglected him in favor of the baby, Poppy hurried to Cartier and commissioned them to make twin emerald and diamond circlets for his legs. "You are beautiful, my darling Luchay," she whispered when he peered at them disdainfully. "Didn't I tell you one day I would make you a Prince of Parrots?" She laughed. "This is only the beginning. *You* shall wear the jewels in this family, Luchay. *I* shall stick to my whore's pearls."

A few weeks later she returned after a happy day in the country with Rogan to find a letter waiting on her desk. It was in a plain cream envelope and addressed in a handwriting she didn't recognize. But she was busy and it wasn't until later in the evening that she found time to open it. It was printed in bold black letters on plain cream paper, and she gasped as she read it.

MR GREG KONSTANT OF RANCHO SANTA VITTORIA IS VERY ANXIOUS TO KNOW YOUR WHEREABOUTS. UN- LESS YOU WANT HIM TO KNOW WHAT YOU ARE AND WHERE TO FIND YOU OBEY THE FOLLOWING INSTRUC-

TIONS. PLACE TEN THOUSAND AMERICAN DOLLARS IN BILLS OF SMALL DENOMINATIONS INTO A GLADSTONE BAG. CARRY THIS WITH YOU WHEN YOU LEAVE FOR THE COUNTRY ON FRIDAY AS USUAL. STOP AT THE OLD DISUSED STABLES OUTSIDE THE VILLAGE OF LUZY ST PIERRE AND LEAVE THE BAG IN THE FIRST MANGER. DO NOT DO ANYTHING FOOLISH. YOU ARE BEING WATCHED AND SO IS YOUR CHILD. IF YOU DISOBEY THESE ORDERS WE SHALL TAKE OUR REVENGE.

It was the word *revenge* that stuck coldest at Poppy's heart. She thought of her sweet baby, helpless and happy with his nanny at Montespan, and her instinct was to fly to him, to wrap her arms around him ready to protect him from any threat. She was being watched, the note said. . . . Panic swept over her suddenly. *Who* was watching her? *Who* hated her enough to do this? *Who* was evil and cruel enough? *And who knew?*

It was no one here, she was sure of that. Only Simone and Netta knew the truth, and they were her friends. The only other person who knew about Greg was Franco. She still had no idea how he had got the information, but she knew he had it. Of course it wasn't Franco. Then who was blackmailing her? Suddenly the face of the Dottore came to mind; she could see him as clearly as if he were there . . . the thin, gold-rimmed spectacles reflecting back the light so you couldn't see his eyes; the fine scar bisecting his cheek and tugging at the corner of his mouth where the damaged muscles had shrunk; his thin-lipped smile and smooth, high-pitched voice . . . The Dottore was close to Franco; it was possible that he could have got hold of the information about her . . . and what was it Franco had said about being betrayed?

She stared at the telephone. It had been over a year since she'd gone to Naples. Rogan had been born, time had moved on. Still, Franco had said if anything went wrong, if she ever needed him, she should call . . .

She glanced at the letter still clutched in her hand . . . "we are watching you," it said tauntingly, "we will take our revenge . . ." And Rogan was alone at the farm with only the nurse and old Monsieur and Madame Joliot to save him.

Picking up the telephone, she called her bank and asked them to have ten thousand dollars ready for her by lunchtime. "In small denominations," she told them, and no, she didn't care what the exchange rate was, or how expensive it was to buy dollars with francs right now; she needed it today.

The approach to Luzy St. Pierre was tree-lined, making the gathering dusk even darker, as Poppy stopped the car opposite the old stables. With the black leather gladstone bag clutched in her hands, she stared nervously across the road. The stables had once belonged to an old *maison bourgeoise* that had burned down years ago and, like the rest of the outbuildings, they had simply been left to rot. The roof had been destroyed by years of winter gales and bad weather and now the walls were buckling alarmingly.

A faint aroma of horse still hung around the place as Poppy stepped through the mounds of straw and dead leaves, glancing fearfully over her shoulder. In the last of the daylight she could just make out the old iron manger. She put the bag hurriedly inside it and fled, twisting her ankle painfully on the treacherous overgrown path. Wrenching open the car door, she hurled herself inside, and half sobbing with fear, she switched on the ignition. Not daring to look back, she drove through the village of Luzy St. Pierre, heading home to her baby.

The nurse always kept Rogan up late on Friday nights so Poppy could see him before he went to bed, and he was waiting for her when she opened the door. He was wearing the little white rompers she'd bought him in Paris just last week and his blue eyes lit up when he saw her. His arms reached out and Poppy picked him up and crushed him to her. His tiny fingers tangled in her hair and he gurgled with delight and she knew without any doubt that there was one thing in her life that was more precious than money. Her son.

Luchay squawked loudly, as if reminding her, and Poppy laughed in relief. "You too, Luchay," she called, "you, too, are more precious than gold."

The next letter arrived on her desk exactly a month later. It was almost identical to the first.

TEN THOUSAND IS NOT ENOUGH TO BUY MY SILENCE. THIS TIME THE PRICE IS TWENTY THOUSAND. LEAVE IT AT THE SAME PLACE ON FRIDAY NIGHT ON YOUR WAY TO MONTESPAN. AND REMEMBER YOU ARE BEING WATCHED AND REVENGE IS VERY SWEET.

Poppy thought of what to do; it seemed obvious that the demands were not going to stop. They weren't satisfied with ten thousand, now they wanted twenty . . . and the more she gave, the more they would want. It was a never-ending cycle.

It was Thursday morning; she had until tomorrow night to act. Picking up the telephone, she requested the bank to have twenty thousand dollars ready for her the next day. Next she called the Hotel Bristol and booked a suite. She chose the Bristol because it was discreet and expensive and very proper, and she felt sure there would be no criminals staying at that hotel. Then she telephoned Montespan and asked the nurse to pack some things and bring Rogan to Paris. They should catch the three-fifteen from Orléans and a car would meet them at the station to take them to the hotel. She would meet them there.

It was a long time before she could bring herself to pick up the phone and call Franco and when she did, tears coursed silently down her cheeks.

"Poppy?" he said. She didn't know why it was that just hearing his voice saying her name could bring back all the emotions she had thought buried, but she knew then there was no way she would ever stop loving him.

"Franco," she whispered. "I hadn't meant to call, but you said if I was ever in trouble . . ."

"Tell me what's wrong," he said sharply.

"It's . . . I'm being blackmailed," she said. "I don't know what to do."

She told him someone was threatening to tell Greg Konstant who she was, and where she was living, and also to expose their relationship. She had already paid ten thousand dollars and was about to pay another twenty.

"Don't worry, Poppy," he said, his voice sounding distant. "I'll take care of it."

"Franco," she said hesitantly . . . "I wondered . . . well, I was trying to think who it might be and how they knew. It couldn't be anyone here, you see."

"Don't try to think who it is," Franco said harshly. "Let me do that. I just don't want you to worry anymore." There was a silence and then he said, "Poppy, I'm glad you felt you could call on me to help you." And then the phone went dead.

Poppy put down the receiver reluctantly, feeling as though she had been cut off from her life force. And then she lay her head on the desk and sobbed her heart out.

Keeping up the charade, she left for Montespan at her usual time. As before, she left the black bag containing the money in the manger. Then she drove on, as if on her way to the farm, but instead she took a circuitous route back to Paris. Once again, she had bought time.

* * *

Two weeks later a parcel arrived on her desk. It contained twenty-five thousand dollars in small-denomination bills and a check from Franco Malvasi for five thousand. There was a note from his bankers saying that Signor Malvasi felt responsible for the missing five thousand because he hadn't acted fast enough. And that Signor Malvasi had said that there was no need to worry, the matter had been dealt with.

Feeling like Atlas when the burden of the world was lifted from his shoulders, Poppy rushed back to the Hotel Bristol and swept young Rogan off to the puppet show in the Bois de Boulogne. Wearing a veiled hat, she pushed him in his smart little carriage through the leafy paths, smiling and nodding at the other mothers and nurses, feeling like a proper *maman*. Then she took him back to the hotel and told the nurse that tomorrow they must return to the farm. She would be home at the weekend, as usual.

Numéro Seize was flourishing. Poppy was forced to turn away more applications for membership than she liked, simply because there wasn't enough room, or enough girls. But she was loath to expand because the whole cachet of Numéro Seize was its exclusivity. And besides, she treasured her girls. They were not all the same ones who had been with her since the beginning; Belinda and Solange had married—and married well. Some of the others had made enough money to satisfy their wants and had returned home to their native towns and villages where they'd bought a house, and then, being quite a "catch," had had their pick of the local gentry. And others had simply gone into business for themselves as high-class courtesans. But there were still half a dozen of the old guard left and Poppy was surprised when Watkins informed her that Véronique was missing.

"Has there been some trouble at home?" she questioned the other girls. "Is someone in her family sick? Maybe she had to leave immediately and there wasn't time to tell us." No one knew.

A week passed and Poppy was really worried. Véronique had always been a loner and had no particular friend among the other girls. And though she was one of her best girls, Poppy realized, surprised, that she didn't really know her very well. Véronique had never confided in her the way the others did, and she knew nothing of her personal life or her problems.

She was shocked when Watkins brought the police inspector to see her in her study and he asked her to identify a body in the morgue that they suspected was Véronique Salbé. And when she saw poor Véronique's cold, gray face, which she remembered as alive and beautiful, she was sickened.

"She was found in the Seine, madame, tangled up in a mooring line near the Pont d'Iéna," the inspector said. "There are no marks of violence on her body and foul play is not suspected. She just drowned. It's obvious she committed suicide."

Poppy cast her mind back to the night Greg had been at Numéro Seize—with Véronique, and she knew that of course it was she who had been the blackmailer. She thought of the packet of dollars and the note saying "the matter has been dealt with by Signor Malvasi . . ." She thanked the inspector for his trouble and said she was bitterly sorry— Véronique's suicide was tragic. But now she knew the truth.

She walked the streets of Paris half the night, thinking of what had happened. And in the loneliest part of the night, when even Paris finally slept, she took a cab back to Numéro Seize, rue des Arbres. She had kept her faith in Franco, even when the newspapers had blackened him, calling him "the devil incarnate." She had told herself that it wasn't true, that Franco couldn't do those things. Now she knew different. Franco had dealt with her problem the way he dealt with everything. Her son's father was a ruthless, cold-blooded killer.

CHAPTER *50*

1914

Rogan was six and a half years old in June 1914 when the Archduke
Ferdinand, the heir to the Austro-Hungarian throne, was assassinated by
a Serbian nationalist. A month later Austria-Hungary, backed by Germany, declared war on Serbia. The repercussions rumbled around Europe and suddenly all the talk in Paris was of war.

Poppy had known that the idyllic private years with her son must
come to an end soon. When he was still a baby, she'd kept him tucked
away at Montespan, dashing down there on Friday evenings when she
would take over from the nurse and devote all her time to him, returning
reluctantly to Numéro Seize on Monday afternoon. She hadn't forgotten
her ambition to be the richest woman in the world and she never neglected her business; but now it was even more important because she
didn't want to make money just for herself, she wanted it for Rogan. She
had an heir.

When he was four she'd been forced to face the fact that Rogan
needed more than the companionship of the local village boys; he
needed to be in Paris. She'd bought a small apartment near the Bois de
Boulogne and enrolled Rogan in the local school, and from then on
Poppy divided her time between her two apartments and the two per-
sonas she had invented. At Numéro Seize she was the ever more glamorous businesswoman, Madame Poppy, of the famous tumbling red hair

and slinky silvery-gray gowns, whose insolent blue eyes promised everything—and gave nothing. And at the apartment in the Bois de Boulogne she was the demure, widowed mother of a young son and, like all the other proper mamas, she was always there to collect him from school.

She could always pick Rogan out of the crowd of boys charging out of the schoolyard once lessons were over, because he already stood head and shoulders over his classmates and also because of his bright orangy-blond hair. She thought her heart would burst with love and pride when his blue eyes lit up as he saw her, waiting beside the long bottle-green de Courmont—the latest and smartest model. She was always home to see that he had prepared his lessons, and always there for the birthday parties and the fun trips to the parks or the river; and always there for the Christmases together at Montespan, with Netta.

No one could have faulted her in either of her roles, but sometimes Poppy wondered despairingly *who* she really was, and she felt a bitter, creeping envy for the ordinary young mothers with their simple, straightforward lives; she even envied the girls who worked for her at Numéro Seize, because at least they had chosen that role and they knew who they were.

Most of the time all that mattered was Rogan, and she counted the years since he had been born as the happiest of her life. His innocent, childish love was hers instinctively. He loved only her and she adored him. He was her friend and companion; he made her laugh and he made her cry; he made her feel tender and he made her feel protective. Rogan was everything her treacherous lovers had never been. Everything she did was for him. All the time spent at Numéro Seize, all the hard work, all the hours playing the charade of being someone she wasn't, all were for him. Rogan was her future.

Of course, Numéro Seize counted cabinet ministers and politicians among its clients, as well as financiers and industrialists, and sometimes Poppy would join them at dinner, listening to their talk of mobilization and armaments with fear in her heart for her child. When she understood that war was inevitable, she quietly converted her money into gold. At the beginning of August she took young Rogan to Switzerland, and transferred her gold and the deeds to all her properties to a vault at a bank in Geneva. The following day Germany declared war on France.

She stayed just long enough in Switzerland to settle Rogan into the school she had already chosen—by asking a series of carefully convoluted questions of various clients as to what school they thought would be best for a boy of a good family; and then she returned to France because, for

Rogan's sake, she couldn't just let her business fall into the hands of the enemy.

Rogan had smiled bravely as they waved good-bye and Poppy thought the matron looked kind and would take care of him, but the memory of the dormitory and his tiny white bed with its lone teddy bear almost broke her heart. All the way back on the train she told herself it was for the best, that she couldn't let Rogan stay in a country at war, that in his Swiss mountaintop aerie he would be safe no matter what happened to France; but she still had to stop herself from rushing straight back again to get him.

In September the French, together with the British Expeditionary Force, confronted the Germans at the Marne. The battle raged for four days until the enemy was finally forced to retreat across the River Aisne, but the casualties were high and many brave young men failed to return.

Numéro Seize underwent a drastic change; khaki and blue uniforms replaced the dinner jackets and black ties, and the usually quiet country house atmosphere became charged with desperate excitement. The young officers back from the front wanted fun and excitement; they wanted to dance and laugh, and to flirt with a pretty girl; they wanted to forget the war, and they wanted a magical night at the famous Numéro Seize to remember on those cold evil nights in the trenches. And Poppy provided that magic.

She converted the big salon into a nightclub, with one of the best bands in Paris for dancing; she improvised little tables where champagne and canapés were served, and candlelight to add an illusion of romance to the girl's eyes so that each young man felt she cared only about him.

There were those who said that what went on at Numéro Seize was immoral, but in Poppy's eyes it would have been immoral to profit on men who were prepared to give their lives to save hers and her son's. The girls earned the same extravagant amount they always did, but Poppy took no money for herself. Of course, Numéro Seize kept its exclusivity; the same politicians and financiers, the arms dealers and the industrialists, all paid exorbitantly to subsidize the cost of entertaining the fighting men, and her accounts still balanced out. She was still a good businesswoman.

She sold the flat in the Bois de Boulogne, but she kept the farm and old Monsieur and Madame Joliot looked after it. Her whole life became Numéro Seize and she spent all her waking moments supervising every detail, from searching out fresh supplies of the food that was becoming steadily scarcer as every man and boy was called to fight, leaving the farms neglected in the strife-torn countryside; to ensuring that the girls' wardrobes were kept as extravagantly glamorous as restrictions would permit. Female cooks replaced the chefs in the kitchens and there were now maids instead of valets. And if Numéro Seize got a little shabbier, no one noticed in the candlelight.

It was only in the few short hours she permitted herself for sleep that Poppy allowed herself to think about her boy. And about Franco. Because no matter how she forbade it, he still crept into her dreams. And to her shame, in those dreams he made love to her.

Poppy had taken no lovers since Franco; she had never had a lover as such, only the two men she had been in love with. Though she sold sex, she wasn't promiscuous and the idea of sex without love filled her with despair. Celibacy was her only answer and though she adorned herself each night, it wasn't for any one man—it was for all the young men who came to her house expecting to find beauty and glamor.

As the months passed, the brave hopes for an early victory faded and the fighting settled into a bitter line of trenches stretching from Ostend to the borders of Switzerland. Poppy was desperate to see Rogan, but the only way she could have obtained a travel permit was by asking someone in a position of power to pull strings. She knew a dozen men who could do it, but when she asked they said they would need to know her reason. After all, they said, she was a notorious woman. Everyone knew she was making a fortune; and they would suspect her of smuggling money out of the country. Naturally, *they* didn't suspect her, but she must see their point . . . Now, if only she could give them a legitimate reason . . .

But of course she couldn't; no one must know about Rogan. All she could do was pray that her letters reached him occasionally, and that she would hear from him, via the address of her bank. He wrote, too, now and then, small, scribbled notes saying he was well, that he was busy and school was fun and his friends terrific. Oh, and that he missed her . . . sorry, he had to rush, a group of them were going climbing—not the north face of the Eiger yet but he hoped to scale that one day and make her proud of him.

Poppy was so proud already of his prowess at sports as well as his studies, that she couldn't imagine being any prouder. One day, she promised herself, when she had made enough money and Rogan was old enough to be aware of certain things, she would close Numéro Seize and go to live in Switzerland, or England—or maybe even California—with her boy.

The year 1915 passed under a banner of mourning for the huge loss of lives at Neuve-Chapelle and Ypres, sliding miserably into 1916 with a crippling attack on the French at Verdun and then the ferocious and crucial battle of the Somme, where the Allies suffered some 600,000 casualties and the Germans, more than 650,000.

There was a new philosophy of life at Numéro Seize; no one spoke about it, but it was there. Today you were alive and therefore you lived for today. Who knew about tomorrow? And who cared? The aura of gaiety became a little more brittle, the pace a little more frenetic, and the lovemaking a little more necessary. Poppy felt like an illusionist, conjuring up a facsimile of prewar times for her soldiers. When they came to Numéro Seize, she looked after them like a mother, finding rooms for them in the crowded hotels, sending them to the best barber in Paris for a haircut and a shave, seeing that their laundry was taken care of and their uniforms cleaned and pressed. Their shoes were shined for them, food and drink was placed in front of them—free of charge—and when they finally left it was with one of Poppy's little "care packages" of cigarettes and chocolates and homemade pâté de foie. "Come back soon" she'd say, relaxing her own rules and kissing them good-bye, watching the expression in their eyes change and their young faces set in remembered lines of strain as they faced the future again. And she thanked God it wasn't her own son she was sending off to the war.

The year 1917 drew to a close with the British taking Passchendaele at enormous cost of life and then finally in the summer of 1918 the French forced back the Germans at the second battle of the Marne. In September the German line was broken again, and by October, Germany was petitioning for peace.

Poppy took the first train to Geneva; she counted the minutes to when she would see her son again, half afraid that he might treat her like a stranger after four years of separation. As she drove through the vista of snow-capped mountains and green valleys dotted with cows, she wondered what Rogan would look like. After all, when she'd last seen him he had been six years old, and now he was almost eleven.

Rogan must have been waiting on the steps because as the car rolled up the driveway in front of the neat Swiss manor house that was Le Rossant school, he ran to meet her.

"*Mother!*" he called. "*There you are at last!*" And as she stepped out he threw his arms around her in a great bear hug.

"Be careful," Poppy gasped, laughing, "you'll crush me!" She stared, amazed, at the eleven-year-old son she'd last seen as a lanky little boy. Rogan was already taller than she was, his shoulders were broad, and his young body looked hard and strong, but his shock of orangy-blond hair still fell engagingly over eyes that were as bright a blue as hers.

"Mother, you're just as beautiful as I remembered after all," he cried. "Come on, I want to show you off to my friends, I've been boasting about you for years. Now, they will see I told the truth!"

"Rogan," she said tearfully, "I've missed your growing up. I've missed all those years between the little boy and the big one! I think I'm going to cry."

"No tears, Maman," he said gently. "At least we're together again now."

Poppy thought of all the other mothers whose sons would never be returned to them, and she thanked God again.

She enjoyed meeting Rogan's friends and being shown around the school that had been his home for the past four and a half years, and afterward she took him away for a few days privacy together so they could get to know each other again.

The Hotel Beau-Rivage in Lausanne brought back memories of the fateful day she'd applied for the job as companion to Mrs. Montgomery-Clyde. She remembered hiding nervously behind that same potted palm near the pillar in the foyer, and recalled how the woman's pursed lips had folded greedily around a chocolate while she'd eyed her up and down, as though she was some lower form of life. But now, she thought proudly, she could match the wealthy Mrs. Montgomery-Clydes of the world, franc for franc, dollar for dollar.

Le Rossant had done a good job in her absence. Her son was clever, he was quick, he was handsome. Rogan spoke three languages fluently and would be at home anywhere in the world. He had the air and manners of a gentleman. Somehow, with a mother like her and a father like Franco, he had acquired "breeding."

It was miraculous to have dinner with him and have him take care of her as solicitously as any lover. And it was wonderful to shop with him in Geneva, indulging herself giving him all the things she'd been deprived of giving for so long—mundane things like shirts and socks, and a tweed sports jacket he liked, as well as the expensive gold watch he coveted in a jeweler's window that told the time in half a dozen countries as well as the phases of the moon.

They drove up into the mountains so he could show her the village of Gstaad, where the school migrated in the winter months, and he told her how much he enjoyed skiing on the clumsy wooden skis, and how thrilling it was to climb those dizzy heights. They took the little rack railway up the mountains and hiked together through forest trails, and they slept in tiny Alpine inns that brimmed with good fresh food and hospitality of the sort not seen in France since the beginning of the war. And they talked and talked.

Poppy asked him about his classes, about his sports, about his tutors and his ambitions. She asked him what his favorite food was and what music he liked and what books he read. And then, quite casually, Rogan asked her who his father was.

They were lunching at a little wooden mountain restaurant overlooking the village of Gstaad and Poppy had watched fondly as her big son devoured his favorite *rösti Oberlanderart*, which he told her consisted of ham, bacon, and onions topped with a gratiné of cheese and a fried egg.

"I never knew what happened to my father and I was afraid it might hurt you to talk about him," Rogan said humbly. "But you see, Maman, I have to know."

Poppy stared silently down at the valley, trying to gather her wits. "Your father was a fine man, a *good* man," she said at last. "He died before you were born, Rogan . . . he was killed in an accident. A car accident in Italy."

"Were you with him . . . when it happened?" he whispered, horrified.

She shook her head. "He was alone. It was a business trip, you see. I loved him very much, Rogan."

"Poor Maman." His hand covered hers comfortingly.

"At least I had you. When you were born I thought you were like a little messenger sent from heaven to help me. Just like Luchay," she added.

"Luchay?"

"You remember, the parrot?"

"Of course." He beamed. "*Luchay!* The magical green parrot . . . 'Poppy *cara*, Poppy *chérie* . . . Poppy darling . . .' Of course I remember that wise old bird. He must be very old now."

"Luchay will outlast us all," she said firmly, "and he knows all the family secrets."

"Do we have secrets, then?" Rogan asked lazily as the waiter poured her coffee.

She shook her head. "You wanted to know about your father. He was an Englishman. His name was Franco . . . Frank, I mean. We met in Italy when I was on my Grand Tour. . . ."

"Grand Tour?" he asked, astonished. "But I thought you'd *always* lived in Europe!"

Poppy felt herself blushing as one lie followed another. "No . . . no,

I was born in America. My father had emigrated from Ireland to California. Don't you remember, I told you that you were named for your Irish ancestors? Anyway, my father—your grandfather—was a bit of a gambler. He did well at first in California, but he later lost a lot of money. He had a big ranch there with cattle and sheep. I used to help with the roundups . . ."

"*You* did?" Rogan said, astonished.

Poppy almost laughed, except it was so sad. Rogan knew so little about her, and now even the stories she was inventing were lies, or half lies . . .

"Anyway, when Jeb—my father—died, there was nothing left. The ranch was sold . . . I don't know what's happened to it since. I'd fallen in love with your father and we were married. He died so young, but he left us the farm at Montespan, and enough to live on comfortably."

She felt as though his bright blue eyes were pinning her against the wall as he said, "But Maman, I remember you had a business. Wasn't that what you always told me when you left me with the nanny? You were away so much."

"Ah, yes," she lied quickly, "for a long time I ran a little fashion shop close by the rue du Faubourg Saint-Honoré. Hats and things . . . women liked it. It was a success—until the war came."

"But what about now?" Rogan asked anxiously. "Do you have enough money? If only you can wait until I'm able to work, Maman, I'll take care of you."

She smiled, he was so protective, so tender with her. "I've been very lucky with my investments, Rogan," she replied demurely. "I think you will find that when I die, you'll be a very wealthy young man."

"Don't even talk about dying!" Rogan exclaimed, a frown of horror crossing his handsome young face. "Besides I don't care about the money. I plan to make lots of my own."

"Really?" Poppy laughed. "And how will you do that?"

"I'm not sure yet," he replied, subdued, "but I know I will."

He was so painfully young that her heart went out to him. "Of course you will, Rogan," she said gently. "You are just like your father."

"Am I *really*, Maman?" he asked eagerly. "I know so little about him. I've never even seen a photograph."

"All the pictures were destroyed in . . . in a fire," she said, searching desperately for a story. "But I didn't mean you were like him physically. Frank had dark hair, although it was going gray when . . . anyway, he had dark hair and dark eyes, and he was sort of middle height, but you have other qualities that are like him." She hesitated, thinking of

Franco's charm—and his ruthlessness—and she was suddenly afraid for her son. "You know, Rogan," she said fiercely, "what we *are born* is one thing, what we *become* is quite another. I want you to remember that."

He nodded, thinking about what she had said. "I think I understand, Maman, I'll do my best to make you proud of me."

"To be able to be proud of yourself, that's all I ask," she said quietly, and they smiled at each other.

"If my father were English, then we must have family there. I'd love to meet them, now that the war is over," Rogan said eagerly.

"Yes . . . no," she cried, inventing another story hurriedly. "Frank was much older than me; there was only his mother—your grandmother —and she was already an old lady, in her eighties I think. She died at the beginning of the war. I'm afraid you are the last of the line. There are no estates or anything . . . your father's family had been rich once, but in the end they were reduced to modest means. I'm afraid that Frank didn't have much of an inheritance."

"It doesn't matter, Mother," he said quickly. "Let's not talk about it anymore, I can see it upsets you. I've got you, and that's all I need."

Poppy smiled wanly. "That's what I said to you when your father died," she whispered. *"At least I've got you."*

It was their last night together. She was to leave for Paris the next day and Rogan had asked if they could entertain some of his friends. "Of course," she'd said gaily. "Bring them all to dinner at the Beau-Rivage. They shall stay the night with you and we'll have a grand time."

Poppy felt as nervous as if she were meeting a lover as she dressed for dinner in a plum-colored silk dress with a demure high neck. She swept her exuberant hair up on top and secured it with a sprinkle of diamond stars; she clasped a ruby-and-diamond bracelet around her wrist and matching pendant earrings in her small pretty ears, and then she examined herself anxiously in the mirror, wondering if she was suitably dressed for her role as Rogan's mother. She wondered if she needed a little powder on her nose, and she pinched her cheeks to bring a blush of color to them. And, of course, she was much too early, Rogan and his friends weren't expected for half an hour yet. She paced the floor of her suite anxiously, wondering how she would compare with their mothers.

The restaurant at the Beau-Rivage was crowded with international businessmen and politicians, army generals and bankers, all in Switzerland to talk high finance business deals and peace, and Poppy felt proud of her table of schoolboys, laughing and chatting easily as they enjoyed the lavish meal she'd ordered. Glancing up, her eye caught that of a man opposite. She paled as he lifted his glass in greeting. He was a world-famous financier who supposedly had made an even bigger fortune dealing in arms. He was also one of Numéro Seize's best clients and Poppy knew him well; she knew his taste in wine and food, and in women. He'd asked her more than once to dine with him, even though he knew her rules; and unlike the others he'd refused to take no for an answer, until finally she'd told him that if he persisted, she would have to ask him not to return to Numéro Seize. He had obeyed, but Poppy knew he'd resented being put in that position.

"Are you all right, Maman?" Rogan asked anxiously. "You're very quiet and you look so pale."

"I . . . yes . . . no, I'm all right. It's just a little hot in here . . ." She glanced wildly at the door, seeking an escape, but it was too late, he was getting up, coming toward her . . . oh, God, this was the end. . . . She waited like a cornered animal, unable to move.

Their eyes met as he walked toward her table and Jacob Le Fanu paused almost imperceptibly, then, with the merest flicker of a smile, he walked on.

"I say," one of the boys cried excitedly, "isn't that Jacob Le Fanu? The arms dealer? His son is at Le Rossant. They say Le Fanu made a pile of money in the war."

"Really?" Poppy said brightly, but inside she was trembling. She had always thought she would be able to keep her two lives separate; she'd never imagined a situation like this. Now she realized how dangerous it could be. Le Fanu had been discreet, but another man might not be so sensitive. Funny though, she'd never liked Jacob Le Fanu, but she was grateful to him now.

On her way back to Paris the next morning she thought about what to do. Time was passing quickly; before she knew it Rogan would be eighteen. He would leave Le Rossant and go on to a university. He would be out in the world of young men—and young men knew all about places like Numéro Seize. She had just seven years in which to restore her fortune, depleted by her wartime generosity to the soldiers—seven years in which finally to secure Rogan's inheritance.

CHAPTER 51

1 9 1 9 ,   F R A N C E

The big salon at Numéro Seize had been cleared of the shabby tables and chairs that had seemed so smart in the candle-lit wartime years, and transformed at enormous expense into an intimate blue and silver supper club. The customers were entertained with smart cabaret acts recruited from Paris's best music halls and they danced to a jazz band brought over especially from New York. There was a glittering new cocktail bar to rival the one at the Ritz, all white leather, chrome, and plate-glass mirrors, that was considered the epitome of chic, though the quiet, paneled library and elegant formal dining room remained the same. Somehow Poppy had cleverly managed to span the generation gap between her old clients and the new young ones, who remembered her kindness to them in the war. Only now, of course, the cost was twice that of prewar years. You had to be very, very rich to afford membership at Numéro Seize.

Poppy also re-created Montespan as a "home" for Rogan. It wasn't just a question of new curtains; she tried to invent a past. She bought English antiques so she could say they came from his father's family home; she bought silver photograph frames and hunted in junk shops for old photos of anonymous faces she then claimed as relatives; she filled the shelves of his new study with costly rare books that she planned to tell him his father had collected. She bought "mementos" of his father —an old fountain pen she would say he had used, a heavy repeater pocketwatch that had been his "grandfather's," a gold signet ring with a worn family crest. She even found a beautiful old western saddle that she could tell him had belonged to her own father when she lived in California. And, in her mind, all these things became "Rogan's family inheritance."

"For a woman with no past," Netta said half admiringly, half despairingly as she looked around the new Montespan, "you've created an amazing illusion."

"And why not?" Poppy demanded proudly. "Why should Rogan be deprived of memories just because his father is dead?"

Netta stared at her worriedly; she was afraid Poppy was beginning to believe her own story. "But you know he's not dead," she said quietly. "Besides, I saw Franco just last month in Marseilles." She hadn't intended to tell her, but somehow she had to bring her back to reality.

Poppy's knees turned to jelly; even after all these years just hearing Franco's name could make her heart thump as wildly as that of a young girl in love. "How did he look?" she whispered.

"Older. His hair is completely gray. He looks thin, tired, worried. He's surrounded by bodyguards, they say even his house is armor-plated. He's . . ." She was going to say he was hated by everyone, but she couldn't bear to hurt her. "He's a very frightening man," she said somberly.

"*Why,* Netta?" Poppy asked piteously. "*Why* couldn't he just have been like any other man?" But she already knew the answer.

Netta had to admit, though, when Rogan came home for the holidays, that right or wrong, Poppy seemed to have worked a miracle. The boy held the watch he had been told had been first his grandfather's and then his father's as though it were the Holy Grail. "I'll treasure it always, Maman," he said reverently, "thank you for giving it to me." When she gave him the gold signet ring, he slid it proudly onto the little finger of his left hand, trying to decipher the worn crest, excited to think it had belonged to his English family, and making Poppy nervous when he talked about trying to trace the family tree.

Rogan examined every book in "his father's collection," marveling at their antiquity and beauty. "They must be worth a fortune," he exclaimed, awed. And he pored over the faces in the silver photograph frames, searching for a resemblance to himself—and finding it. "I think I have grandmother's eyes," he'd say to Poppy, or "Is my hair like yours or Grandpa's?"

"You are exactly like your father," she would tell him firmly, thanking God that he wasn't.

When Rogan expressed an interest in farming, she bought more acres for him; when he said he was intrigued by astronomy, she bought him an enormous telescope; when he wanted a boat, a dog, a small painting he'd admired by a new impressionist, she bought him it.

"I'm afraid to say I like anything," he complained, "because I know you'll buy it. You are too good to me, Maman."

"Nonsense," Poppy replied gaily. "I had to spend years without spoiling you and before I know it you'll be grown up and married. At least let me indulge myself now."

"I'll never leave you," Rogan said seriously, "you've been alone too long. I'll look after you, one day, Maman."

Poppy heeded the sound advice of the financiers and bankers who were her clients and her investments alone made her very wealthy. And with Numéro Seize again showing enormous profits, she knew that at last she was a rich woman. Though not yet as rich as she intended to be. Her secret plots of land were beginning to pay off. She had already sold two, at enormous profit, on the outskirts of Paris where new factories were being built. Of course, she hadn't sold all the land they'd wanted for their factories—she'd held some back so that when the factories needed to expand, she could ask an even more exorbitant price. Franco had taught her well!

When Rogan brought home his friends during the school holidays, she spent all her time with them at the farm, sending them out fishing, or to help with the haymaking, and feeding them enormous meals. When he was away she had to make do with Netta and Luchay, who now bore four jeweled rings on his tiny legs. "You must share in our happiness and good fortune, Luchay," she said, and, inspired, she picked up the telephone and called Bulgari in Rome to make a new cage for him. "Gold," she commanded, "like Scheherazade's palace. I want it to be *fabulous*! And I don't care what it costs." She wanted the best for Luchay, her bringer of luck, even though she had only ever bought a few simple jewels for herself.

"These are the happy years," she told the parrot as he rubbed his soft little head against her cheek. "And we've earned them, haven't we?"

Jacob Le Fanu's shrewd nose for an advantageous deal and his influential political contacts had taken him from the tenements of Algiers to a mansion in London's Belgravia. He had the reputation of driving a hard bargain, of being a man who never forgot, and of being a womanizer. He was an uneducated, self-made man whose massive fortune had gained him entrée into almost every level of society, except the one that counted—the top. He was short, dark-haired, and dark-eyed, and had a smooth Levantine sensuality that women seemed to fall for. Jacob considered himself a lover par excellence, and he prided himself that no woman could resist him for long, especially when she found the diamond bracelet hidden in the flowers he'd sent her, or a pair of ruby earrings among the chocolates. He knew every method there was of getting to a woman's heart; and he employed them all frequently.

When he was in Paris he patronized Numéro Seize not so much for its girls as for its contacts. Anyone who was anyone could be found there. He used it as his club, a place for private business discussions that he might not want to display publicly in a hotel or office. Numéro Seize was useful, but he also enjoyed the thrill of an afternoon spent with one of the special "society" girls because it made him feel good to see the upper classes—to which he could never belong—reduced to the status of whores.

In Jacob's view there was only one true lady at Numéro Seize—Poppy. Everyone had told him she was unattainable, but he'd thought he'd known better. He had wooed her with the diamond-bedecked flowers and ruby chocolates, but she'd sent them back with a polite little note saying she never accepted gifts. He'd sent baskets of out-of-season hothouse peaches and strawberries, and she'd thanked him and said she had forwarded them on to the children's hospital, where she was sure they would be enjoyed; he'd bought her an adorable white poodle puppy that he'd thought would entrance her, but he never knew if it did or not because she told him that, sadly, animals were not allowed at Numéro Seize and as she felt a puppy was something that couldn't be returned, she had given it to a friend in the country.

Jacob had run out of ideas, but he hadn't given up the battle. Poppy was a challenge and her evasive tactics only made her even more desirable. He was determined to be the man who cracked that beautiful icy facade.

The chance sighting of her at the Beau-Rivage had been sufficiently intriguing for him to make a few inquiries. His son was a pupil at La Rossant and it was easy to find out that Rogan's mother was "a widow"; that his father had been English, and that Rogan was a year younger than his own boy.

It was several months before he found himself in Paris again, checking into the Crillon because he always felt the hotel's discreet sumptuousness counterbalanced his own flamboyance. He ordered a hundred red roses to be sent immediately to Poppy at Numéro Seize, but this time he refrained from enclosing any jewelry. Instead he wrote a note saying that he was happy to be back in Paris and would be delighted if she would dine with him that evening, here at the Crillon or at Maxim's . . . anywhere she liked. He felt they had something "to discuss."

When the red roses arrived, Poppy read the note, and she knew what was coming. She sat at her desk, staring at the beautiful flowers, thinking of what to do. An hour later she sent a messenger to the Crillon with her reply.

When Jacob arrived back from his meeting at the Elysée Palace, her note was waiting and he read it with a pleased smile, though not quite as pleased as it might have been. Poppy would be happy to dine with him, it said, but in one of the private rooms at Numéro Seize, at nine that evening. Jacob had aspired to be the first man ever seen in public with the glamorous, elusive Poppy; he'd wanted to make it clear to all of Paris that Jacob Le Fanu had won where every other man had failed. Still, he thought with a pleased little smile of anticipation, she hadn't dared refuse him and it wouldn't be long before everyone knew—he would make sure of that.

Poppy was wearing a dress of soft dove-gray chiffon glinting with crystal beads. It left her creamy shoulders bare, and revealed a generous glimpse of her round breasts, and was almost deliberately tempting. She looked very lovely and Jacob tried to guess how old she was, but found it impossible. Poppy was ageless; she never seemed to grow any older, only more beautiful.

"Mr Le Fanu," she said gaily, "how pleasant to see you back in Paris. It's been a long time since we met . . . in Geneva, wasn't it? I hear you have a son at Le Rossant. Why don't you tell me all about him over dinner?"

Jacob was too clever to let her see how surprised he was that she had even mentioned the night when he'd seen her dining with her son. He'd thought it would be the one subject she would try her best to avoid, until he forced her into it.

"When a man works hard all his life, as I have done," he replied, "it's good to know there's a son to inherit the fruits of his labors. But, of course, I don't need to tell you that."

Poppy smiled pleasantly, ringing the bell to summon Watkins. "I chose tonight's menu myself," she told him. "I do hope you'll enjoy it. If I remember, you have a particular fondness for truffles. I had some especially delivered from the Périgord this afternoon. And Watkins has decanted the Château Haut-Brion you always enjoy when you are here."

You see, Jacob, Numéro Seize is even better than a grand hotel; we always remember what you like most and we do our best to provide it."

She kept up her chatter as Watkins served a beef consommé covered with a light pastry, watching as Jacob broke open the crust and breathed the delicious aroma. Fine food was one of his weaknesses and Poppy was baiting her trap with everything she could, luring him into a feeling of security, until she knew exactly what his game was.

She watched Jacob mellow under the influence of the wonderful food and the heady, powerful wine. She ate little, leaning forward instead with her chin propped on her hand, listening with a secret little smile as he told her about his talks at the Elysée Palace; she already knew where Jacob had been that afternoon and why. She, too, had her contacts.

"A little brandy?" she asked. "Or maybe the 1895 port?" Jacob was standing in front of the fire, looking as though he already owned the place, and he set the glass on the mantel and grabbed her hands in his.

"Poppy," he said thickly, "you know how I feel about you."

"I'm honored, Jacob," she replied calmly, "but many men feel like that about me. I'm sure it's because I'm the only woman not available at Numéro Seize. I've heard that some men have even taken bets on how quickly they could seduce Madame Poppy. It's sort of a game, by now." She smiled at him. "Sometimes grown men can be very childish."

"What I feel for you is not childish," he groaned, pulling her closer. "You are the most desirable woman in the world, Poppy. You are the only woman I want."

"Please let go of me, Jacob," she said quietly. "Watkins will be in any minute."

He let her go reluctantly as the butler appeared with a tray of petit fours and coffee; Watkins had been primed to interrupt them on any pretext every ten minutes or so.

"Of course, I realize that you wouldn't want certain facts to become public," Jacob said, picking a strawberry smothered in dark chocolate from the heaped silver tray and biting into it greedily. He wiped his fingers on a napkin. "I've decided to take an apartment in the rue de la Cour. It's a pleasant street on the Right Bank, and very discreet. And it's within easy reach of the government offices—as well as Numéro Seize, of course."

"Then you must be planning on spending a lot more time in Paris," Poppy said calmly.

"That depends on you, Poppy. The apartment is yours. I bought it for you this afternoon."

She stared at him silently, seeing his strong-boned face, his broad forehead and dark waving hair, his shiny brown eyes peering intently at her, and his fleshy lips, slightly parted as he licked them in anticipation.

"But I don't need an apartment, Jacob," she said at last. "I thought I'd already explained to you that it's my policy never to accept gifts from any man."

"But I am not 'any man,'" he said, a faint smile lifting the corners of his mouth. "I am a man who knows more about you than any other. I was surprised to find that you and I had something in common at Le Rossant. Something that could bring us closer together. Of course, I am discretion itself—when I choose to be."

"Then you were mistaken," Poppy said coldly. "I never mix business with pleasure. And certainly not with my family. I'm quite sure that Mrs. Le Fanu wouldn't want to hear about this . . . this little love nest in the rue de la Cour."

Jacob roared with laughter, pouring himself another brandy. "You can't blackmail *me*, Poppy," he told her, grinning appreciatively. "Just think, if it ever got out that Madame Poppy was threatening to tell her clients' secrets to their wives, or maybe even to their business rivals, Numéro Seize would be deserted faster than rats from a sinking ship! There wouldn't be a man left! So you see, you don't have much choice, my dear, do you? Why not let's be friends, Poppy? I'm a generous man; I shall look after you very well."

Jacob raised his beetling black eyebrows inquiringly, but he had the look of a man who already knew the answer, and the satisfied air of a man who had won.

Poppy looked him squarely in the eye. "It's a generous offer," she said coldly, "but you are not the first to make it. I have always refused, and I see no reason to change my mind now." She prayed he wouldn't hear the wobble of nervousness in her voice, or detect her racing pulse as she went on. "But you see, I too have *friends* in important places—the Elysée Palace, for instance. I've already had a word with these 'friends' and explained the delicacy of my problem to them. They were able to assure me, Jacob, that a man of your reputation and honor would never stoop to force a lady to do anything she didn't want to. But, of course, if he did try"—she shrugged her shoulders eloquently—"then he would no longer be welcome in their circles. You would be finished here in France, Jacob."

He lumbered clumsily to his feet, knocking the tray of sweets to the floor. "You're a clever woman, Poppy," he said, his face white with rage.

"In my business, I have to take care of myself," she replied. "But there's one more thing, Jacob. No one but you knows about my boy. If word gets out about him, or if Rogan ever hears about Numéro Seize, I shall know who it was. I'm warning you now, Jacob, it would be very unwise."

He picked up the brandy glass and drained it. "We shall call it quits then, Poppy," he said, managing his old smile. "I might have known you would be too smart for me. You're the only one who can ever say she's beaten Jacob Le Fanu."

"But of course I would never say that, Jacob," she said, pretending to be shocked.

"Friends, then?" he asked, holding out his hand.

"Friends," she agreed, smiling.

But even when several dozen more red roses arrived with a note of apology the following day, she knew he was an enemy.

CHAPTER 52

1925, FRANCE

It was Khalim Le Fanu's eighteenth birthday and his father had promised him the time of his life. "Bring a dozen of your young friends to
Paris for a weekend, Khalim," he'd told him generously, "we'll put them
all up at the Ritz; they'll have dinner at Maxim's, and then you can go
on to any nightclub you fancy. I want you to have a good time, son,"
he'd said, winking knowingly. "Oh, and Khalim, make sure you invite
that nice boy you told me about, Rogan."

Rogan was seventeen now, and a strong, husky-looking young man. He
stood six foot three in his socks with the broad-shouldered muscular body
of an athlete, and the deep voice of a man. He had been surprised but
thrilled to be included in Khalim's party; Khalim was a good-looking
popular boy in the class a year above him, and Rogan was especially
looking forward to it because somehow his mother didn't allow him to go
to Paris too often.

Mr. Le Fanu had taken over half a floor at the Ritz for his son's party.
He'd stocked it with champagne and food, and outside in the rue
Cambon was Khalim's present, a scarlet Bugatti sports car. His friends
were all treated to a set of diamond studs to commemorate the occasion
and at ten o'clock that night they set out for Maxim's in evening clothes
and high spirits.

They had been drinking champagne all evening and were all a little drunk when they arrived. As the waiters carried in a small mountain of caviar and slabs of smooth creamy pâté de foie gras, and a platter glistening with fresh oysters and seafoods, Khalim warned them to take it easy on the wine. "Wait till later," he said, grinning. "You're going to need all your strength for the girls."

The "girls" had been their main topic of conversation, after Khalim's new car, of course, and Rogan felt an anticipatory stirring in his loins as he contemplated the delights in store. Some of the boys claimed to have had a girl before, though he wasn't sure it was true, and they were all nervous. "It's easy," Khalim boasted, "and the girls at Numéro Seize will make it even easier for you. My father told me they're the best-looking women in the world."

Rogan ate another oyster because someone had told him it was an aphrodisiac, contemplating the thought of holding one of the best-looking women in the world in his arms, and praying she wouldn't find him inadequate.

"My father says they're so experienced," Khalim said, "they really know how to give a man a good time. We could have had dinner there too—he says it's one of the best restaurants in Paris, but he thought it would spoil the surprise. He said Maxim's was where you should go on your eighteenth birthday."

"He was right," they agreed enthusiastically, "this is great, Khalim."

"But first," he said, prolonging the delicious torture, "we're going to the Club Tombeau in Montmartre, we're going to watch the show and we're going to dance!"

There was more champagne at the Club Tombeau, though not as good as that at the Ritz and Maxim's; still, they managed to drink quite a lot of it and their confidence rose as they watched the half-naked girls in brief fringed skirts and high heels strutting across the stage.

It was two-thirty when they finally moved on to Numéro Seize, piling out of the cabs in front of the elegant town house, laughing and eager. "Don't expect a whorehouse," Khalim told them excitedly. "My father said this is the most exclusive club in Europe. If you haven't already lost your virginity, then this is the place to do it!"

They stared at the house uncertainly. "Are you sure this is the right place?" joked Rogan. "It looks more like somewhere your family might live."

They laughed again as Khalim rolled his eyes, grinning. "Imagine living here," he said, "you'd be exhausted."

"I'm Khalim Le Fanu," he said importantly to the gray-haired butler who answered the bell. "My father told you to expect us."

"Certainly, sir," Watkins replied, "would you please come in."

They crowded into the hall, staring around wide-eyed, expecting to see naked girls draped invitingly across velvet sofas, but there was only a bright green parrot on a stand. But what a stand! They gathered around admiringly. "It's gold," marveled Rogan. "Those stones can't be *real*," gasped someone else. "Just look at those emeralds and diamonds on his legs." Rogan stared at them, puzzled. He'd thought only Luchay had jeweled legs, but he supposed it must be the latest fashion now to decorate one's pet. Khalim poked a finger at the bird. "Come on, talk!" he commanded, but the parrot leaned forward and pecked him viciously. He jumped back with a howl of pain and Rogan said, surprised, "They're not usually vicious! Our parrot looks just like this and he's as gentle as a lamb."

"It's Khalim," the others laughed, "he took a dislike to you!"

A discreet murmur of conversation came from the candle-lit dining room on their right and they could see a fire burning brightly in the grate in the paneled library at the end of the hall.

"My father said summer or winter, there's always a fire in the library at Numéro Seize," Khalim told them as the butler took their black overcoats and white silk scarves. "He said we've got to see the cocktail bar and the nightclub."

"If you follow me, sir, I'll show you the way," Watkins said.

They hurried after him, jostling each other and whispering comments about the sumptuous decor. "Are you *sure* it's the right place?" they whispered to Khalim. "We haven't seen a single girl yet!"

They exclaimed in awe at the mirrored cocktail bar, and gasped when they saw the blue and silver nightclub. "It's a bit different from Le Tombeau, eh?" Khalim said, pleased.

"And just look at the girls," whispered Rogan. Suddenly it seemed there were dozens of them, tall and short, plump and rounded or elegantly sleek; blondes, brunettes, and redheads, and each one was as delectable as a chocolate and as terrifying as an alien from Mars.

A pretty young blonde in red chiffon came toward them. "I'm Olga," she said in a husky Russian accent. "Come and have some champagne with us and watch the cabaret. Tonight we have a rising new star, Gaby Delorges. She sings the naughtiest songs," she added with a wink, "but of course you young boys won't understand, will you?" She laughed as they protested, leading them across the midnight-blue carpeted room to a silver lamé table near the front. Soon each boy had a pretty girl next to him and the champagne was flowing once again.

"You'll like Gaby," Olga whispered in Rogan's ear, "she's the best dancer in Paris and she's very beautiful."

"Not more beautiful than you," he replied, dazzled by her flawless golden skin and short, silken blond hair.

She smiled prettily. "You certainly know the way to a girl's heart, Rogan," she murmured.

Gaby Delorges was delightful and alarming, bending her sinuous body into snakelike curves as she slithered on a black velvet chaise longue, singing huskily about how this lover liked her toes, this one her fingers, this one her thighs, this one her breasts . . . Rogan held his breath as Gaby's fingers absentmindedly caressed her breasts and he heard Olga laughing softly next to him. "More champagne, Rogan?" she whispered, refilling his glass.

Afterward, they danced and he held her close feeling his manhood stirring as she insinuated her body next to his. He glanced around the candle-lit room, and noticed that some of the boys had already disappeared. "This is a wonderful place," he told Olga, his voice blurred from the champagne.

"It's a place where we can make dreams come true," she whispered, resting her head against his chest. "I promise you your heart's desire tonight, Rogan."

The fresh, clean fragrance of her hair was in his nostrils, and impulsively, he bent his head and kissed her.

"I want to kiss you too, Rogan," she whispered as he nuzzled her neck, "but it's not permitted here. Come with me to my room."

Bemused from too much champagne and in an agony of desire, he walked hand in hand with her from the nightclub, stumbling as he emerged into the hall.

"Oops," Olga cried, laughing, "let me put my arm around you. Perhaps we'd better take the elevator instead of the stairs."

Rogan leaned against her happily as they waited for the elevator to descend, closing his eyes and envisioning the pleasure to come . . . just the touch of her hand on his waist gave him such an intense thrill of desire that he couldn't wait to undress her, to see her naked . . . to touch her . . .

With a little whirr the elevator came to a stop and the gilded cage doors opened onto the padded amber-velvet interior and the beautiful red-haired woman inside. She glanced up from the big ledger she was carrying, smiling at them. Suddenly her smile faded, and the color drained from her face, leaving even her lips bloodless.

"*Bonsoir,* Madame Poppy," Olga murmured, tugging at Rogan's hand, but it seemed he had turned to stone.

"Leave us, Olga," Poppy commanded, in her voice as thin as a whiplash, and Olga melted away as though she had never been.

"Rogan, I want to explain," Poppy said.

"*Explain?*" he cried, suddenly stone-cold sober. "*Explain what,* mother? That *you* are the madam of the famous Numéro Seize? God, I should have realized when I saw the parrot in the hall, but I was so naive, I thought it was just the fashion, that all the smart parrots were wearing jewels these days! But it's only the *whorehouse* parrots, isn't it, Mother?"

"Rogan," she pleaded, "I'm begging you to listen to me, to let me tell you the truth . . ."

"All the things you've ever bought me," he went on, horrified by the realization, "everything we own, the farm, Luchay's jewels, my education . . . everything was paid for with money from *this place.* My friends' fathers come here—*they* must know about you . . . Khalim Le Fanu . . ."

"Le Fanu?" she cried. "*He* brought you here?"

Rogan's blue eyes were glazed with horror as he looked at her. "I see now," he cried, agonized, "everybody must know about you. *About my mother!* All those stories about my dead father—why, I probably never even had one. I'll bet you didn't even *know who* he was! I've been living a lie, all these years!" His handsome young face crumpled with pain and Poppy stepped closer, putting her hand on his arm comfortingly.

Rogan jumped back as though he'd been burned. "*Don't touch me,* Mother," he said, his voice suddenly cold and menacing. "*Don't even come near me. I never in my life want to see you again.*"

"*Wait, Rogan,*" she exclaimed as he strode across the hall. "*Rogan, please . . .*" But he never once looked back at her as he flung open the door and ran into the night.

"*Rogan, come back,*" Poppy screamed, running down the steps after him, clinging to the railings for support, calling his name desperately as she watched him run to the end of the street and disappear around the corner.

She finally understood how Franco could murder people, because at that moment, she hated Jacob Le Fanu so much, she wanted to kill him. She wanted to see the life bleeding out of him as hers was now; she wanted to see him cry in agony, as she was. Jacob Le Fanu had waited six long years, but he had got his revenge.

CHAPTER 53

Of course, thought Mike, now it was obvious. In her journals, Poppy had a habit of bestowing names that meant something special to her . . . Luchay had been Poppy's "ray of light," and now he remembered that she had written that, to her, Rogan was her "little messenger from God." Rogan Messenger . . . He picked up the copy of Orlando's written statement that Lieber had sent him, and read it again.

"Grandfather Messenger was born in Paris," Orlando had said.

He came to live in England as a very young man. He was alone and penniless, but he finally managed to get a job playing piano in a night-club in Mayfair, one of those smart places they had in the 1920s where society people congregated to have fun. Apparently he was so poor, he even had to get an advance on his wages in order to buy a secondhand dinner jacket, and the first week he couldn't even afford to eat; he lived on coffee and hors d'oeuvres fed to him by a sympathetic waiter. He always joked that he was the only man who had almost starved to death on a diet of caviar and smoked salmon.

There was a woman who used to go there regularly, the wife of a famous financier, and she took quite a fancy to him. Grandfather was a very good-looking young man, very tall and blond—it seems I take after him. She started by asking him to play at her parties, at their big house in London, and then at their country place, Hawksfield Abbey in Sussex, and their "friendship" progressed from there. Nobody knows if there was anything really going on between them, but from what my father told me, I doubt it. Grandfather Messenger was a very moral man.

He was making a living at this point, but not much more, just scraping along. I think the country weekends, when he was playing for parties, were the only time he could rely on three square meals a day, and it must have felt like a bonus to him. Anyhow, Lady Melton kept telling him he was too good to be just a cocktail-piano player, especially when she discovered he'd been to school in Switzerland and spoke three languages fluently. *And* that he had a brain. She spoke to her husband and persuaded him to give him a try in his offices. He did well, earning really good money—and he was still only twenty-two.

Lady Melton saw that he mixed in all the right circles and that's where he met my grandmother, at a house party at Hawksfield Abbey. Grandma Messenger, Lydia Lyle as she was then, was quite well-off, though not "heavy" money, if you see what I mean. But they fell for each other and got married, and as a wedding present her father bought him a seat on the stock exchange. By the time their only son, my father, was born, a year later, Grandfather was already making a tidy fortune, playing the market very cleverly. There were no other children, I've never known why, because most people had large families in those days.

Grandfather Messenger died two years after I was born, and Grandmother a few months after him—it seems they were so devoted, she couldn't live without him. He left a nice little fortune that my father should have parlayed into a bigger one—God knows he had every chance; but he was weak and my mother was a gambler—she liked a flutter at the tables almost more than she liked her gin. When she'd get bored, she'd take off for Monte Carlo or Hong Kong, or on a long cruise—anywhere she could enjoy her two vices. She was very pretty and Father spent more time shepherding her around, afraid he would lose her, than he did looking after his business. What with the gambling and the extravagant life-style, by the time I was in school they were already scrambling to pay the fees.

When I was fourteen, my father told me what Grandfather Messenger had told him about his mother—I can quote him exactly. "Poppy Mallory was a whore," he said, "oh, not one of your smart society-whores who sleeps with a king, has half a dozen of his children 'under the blanket,' and gets herself a title and a country estate. Poppy's dead now, thank God," Grandfather had said, "and you'll never

need to meet her. I put her out of my mind forty years ago. Or almost
—because she wasn't a woman easily forgotten."

"And so you see, Mr. Lieber," he'd finished, "why I believe I am
Poppy Mallory's heir."

There was now no doubt in Mike's mind that Orlando was Poppy's
great-grandson, but then why had Poppy not even mentioned her son in
her will? All she'd talked about was her daughter. Had she cut Rogan out
of her will because he'd run away and left her? He called Lieber in
Geneva and told him the news.

Lieber wasn't really surprised about Orlando. "I thought there was
something about his story," he said. "And there was a note attached to
the will. I didn't think it was important at the time—Poppy seemed like
a dotty old lady who couldn't quite get her thoughts together . . . I just
assumed she was rambling. I thought it was someone in the lawyer's
office. It was for someone called 'Rogan,' telling him that she had written the will because he didn't know about the daughter, in case she
forgot later, because sometimes her memory defeated her. She'd said, 'I
wanted to make sure she was taken care of too. But, of course, you will
take care of that.'

"Of course," Lieber added, "we can't tell Orlando Messenger what we
know yet, until we find the true story about the daughters, and if there is
another heir, then the estate will be divided equally."

Mike thought over what he had said and then he placed a call to
Carraldo in Los Angeles.

There was one last notebook left to read, the one he hoped would give
him the final answer to what had happened to Poppy, and who her
daughter was. He thought about calling Aria to tell her, but decided he
would wait until he knew for sure. Walking over to Luchay, he stroked
the bird's soft wing and the parrot stared back at him unblinkingly.

"Poor Luchay," Mike said. "Poor boy. She left you, didn't she, and
she never came back."

Mike walked back to the desk and pored over the notebooks again.
When he was reading them, it was almost as if Poppy were here, in this
room. . . . He felt now he really knew her.

CHAPTER 54

1927, FRANCE

Poppy was alone again, at the farm at Montespan. It had been more than two years since Rogan had disappeared. Numéro Seize, rue des Arbres, was still shuttered and swathed in dust sheets, exactly as she had left it that night, and Simone told her that smart Parisians still mourned its passing.

"They say there'll never be another place like it," she told Poppy, "and they all swear you'll reopen it one day."

Poppy shook her head. "Never," she whispered. She had trekked the paths of her life a thousand times since that fateful night, telling herself that everything she had done had been done in order to survive. But she knew in her heart it wasn't true; there was one other reason. All her life she had thought of herself as the girl in Angel Konstant's shadow; finally at Numéro Seize, she had become Madame Poppy, one of the most courted and sought-after women in Paris, and one of the richest. Now she was just Poppy Mallory again, with a thousand acquaintances and millions of francs in the bank. And because of her false pride and her obsession to be rich she had lost the one thing that really mattered to her —the love and respect of her son.

If it hadn't been for Netta, she didn't know what she might have done. Netta had sold her business in Marseilles and come to live with Poppy at the farm. "I'm getting too old to go on playing the role of the gay madam," she'd sighed, "I'm almost fifty. I'm tired of having to hold in my stomach and cover the gray in my hair with dye!"

"I don't mind," Poppy said, absently touching the new white wings at her own temples, "each white hair means it's one day closer to the end."

Netta stared at her, horrified. Poppy scarcely ate, she looked as thin and brittle as a reed. Her face had lost all its softness and her prominent cheekbones threw shadows into the deep hollows of her cheeks. But somehow, she looked even more beautiful. And her eyes still blazed with the same old intensity as she charted the moves of the dozens of private detectives she employed in cities around the world, searching for her son. Their weekly reports, each as blank of information as the last, already filled a dozen filing cabinets in her study.

When Rogan had first disappeared, Poppy had waited for him to come back, and when she realized he wasn't going to come, she'd sought wildly for ways to find him. She'd thought of asking the help of the powerful men who'd patronized Numéro Seize and who had called her their friend, but even they would be powerless in this situation. She'd thought of going to the police, but that would have meant exposing herself and Rogan to a blaze of publicity, because she was a notorious woman and there would be no way to keep her secret. She had known at last that the only man who could find Rogan was Franco.

"But you *can't* ask him!" Netta had exclaimed. "Once Franco knew he had a son, he'd never let him go!"

"He won't know Rogan is his," she'd cried. "I'll tell him I had another lover . . ."

"All Franco has to do is count," Netta had said bluntly. "The boy is seventeen years old. Your only lover then was Franco." Poppy contemplated the bitter irony of the truth. Things hadn't changed. She still couldn't tell Franco about Rogan and she could never tell Rogan who his father was.

She had pinned her hopes on the private detectives, recruiting more and more as the months passed with still no trace of him. "But he's so distinctive-looking," she said despairingly as the empty weeks slid by, "he's so tall, six foot three, and he has this bright orangy-blond hair."

"There are thousands of tall young men, madame," they told her patiently, "and hair can be dyed, you know."

Netta had gone back to Marseilles for a vacation. She was driving back to Montespan in her brand-new little sports car when it went out of control on the rainswept road and struck a tree. She was killed instantly. Grief-stricken, Poppy buried her friend in the crowded graveyard on a hill overlooking the harbor at Marseilles, wishing it could have been her instead. She had lost her friend now, as well as her son—she felt as though the world was closing down.

The long winter months passed in solitude and unhappiness at Montespan, and for the first time she allowed herself to remember her daughter. She recalled the small baby she had held in her arms, her fuzz of fine blond hair and her soft pink-flushed skin, and she wondered what she looked like now. Twenty-eight years had passed, she remembered, shocked; the child would be a woman now. Suddenly she was racked with a desperate longing to see her. She paced the lonely, icy lanes around the farm, willing this strange new desire to go away. But it wouldn't, and the next week she found herself on the train to Venice.

The city was timeless under the blue May sky, floating against a Canaletto horizon, just as she remembered it. The smart hotels had put out their summer awnings, gondoliers took tourists along the canals, and the little orchestra still played in the Piazza San Marco.

Poppy peered through Florian's windows, half expecting to see Felipe waiting for her, and then with a feeling of déjà vu she took a seat at the same small marble-topped table, on the same red plush banquette, as the day she had met him. A young waiter served her iced tea, and she wondered what had happened to Carlo, the moustached old man who used to bring her chocolate *granita*. Felipe had told her he had come here as a child, that they knew him well. . . . It was ridiculous, she knew, but she couldn't help asking . . . after all, wouldn't Felipe have brought his own children here, the way he was brought as a child? "I wonder if you can help me," she said to the young waiter. "I used to know a family who came here years ago, but we've been out of touch. I just wondered whether you knew them. Their name is Rinardi . . . the Baronessa Rinardi."

He shook his head. "Sorry, Signora, I've only been working here a few months. But I'll ask one of the other waiters if you like."

He returned a few moments later with a gray-haired man who beamed at her kindly. "Ah, the Rinardis," he exclaimed, clasping his hands across his white apron, "such an *exquisite* family, so beautiful the children. And the Baronessa . . . a great beauty! When the children were small she used to bring them here all the time, when they were in residence at the palazzo. But no more, I'm afraid. We miss them."

"No more?" she asked. "But why?"

"I heard the Baronessa went back to America, Signora." He shrugged. "It happens in the best of families . . . unhappiness . . . separation.

Yes, the Baronessa had an *unhappy* face, even though she was a great beauty."

"And the children?" Poppy asked, her voice quavering.

"The girls were charming, both so pretty in such different ways, one so volatile, one so quiet. And the boy is handsome, like his father." He sighed. "Who knows, maybe the family will come back together again one day. If God wills it."

"Maybe," Poppy replied automatically. "Thank you, Signore."

"A pleasure, Signora. Enjoy your stay in Venice."

So Angel had a son, she thought, sipping her tea; she'd given Felipe his heir after all. And the two girls, one extrovert, one quiet—she could guess which one was her daughter. She stared despondently out of the window; she had been so sure she would see her, so sure she would *know* her immediately. But it was too late to bring back the past. And besides, Angel and her daughters were six thousand miles away in California. At the Rancho Santa Vittoria.

She hurried from Florian's to the office of Thomas Cook Ltd, travel agents. There was a ship, they told her, the *Michelangelo*, leaving Genoa for New York in three days time. Poppy booked a passage quickly before she could change her mind. She was going home at last.

CHAPTER 55

1927, CALIFORNIA

Poppy had ridden out to her old childish spy-place, up on the hill over-looking the Konstant House. The horse she'd rented from a local stable grazed contentedly nearby and the steady tearing of grass mingled with the twitter of the birds and the whirring of the cicadas.

She had gone to the Mallory House first, and found only a charred ruin. She'd waded horrified through the tangled waist-high grass that was once a lawn, and she'd sat once again on the broken front steps, remembering, with a familiar sinking feeling in her stomach, how she used to watch and wait for Jeb to return. She remembered the scary, blind old Indian in the adobe kitchen, and the dark anonymous room that had been her mother's, and her own desolate nursery that was full of shadows and fears when her father didn't come back. She recalled the shiny grand piano in the drawing room and the toys in the cupboard that she'd had to leave behind when she and Jeb began their trek around the cities, chasing a poker game; and she felt the same old terror of being alone and abandoned.

The Mallory House had never been a happy place, but it would have been hers if Jeb Mallory hadn't gambled it away; she would have had something real to give Rogan, instead of having to invent a past.

The only part of the house still standing was the adobe hut that had been there for two hundred years. Its foot-thick clay walls blocked out the sounds of the birds, and the sunlight barely filtered through the small high window onto the dusty floor. Closing her eyes, Poppy could see herself as a small child, holding her breath so the old Indian wouldn't hear her as she stole a hunk of the flat Indian cornbread. She'd been so afraid that the old man would catch her. Even now the place quivered with disturbed emotions, with feelings of loneliness and sadness . . . and of death. With a little cry of fear she ran from the musty adobe room, gulping the fresh air and pushing her way eagerly back through the tangled weeds. She turned instinctively to look at the hill, rising gently behind the ruined house. There were no poppies growing there.

She had taken the familiar shortcut to the Konstant House, automatically stopping at her old spy-place, just the way she had when she was a child, drawn there every day like a magnet to watch that magical, beautiful, happy family, yearning with all her heart to be a part of it.

It looked just the same, its white walls gleamed, its flowers bloomed, its fountain sparkled, and its red-tiled roofs glittered in the sun. Men were still working in the gardens and Arabian ponies still pranced in the paddock. And beyond that, the Konstant land stretched as far as the eye could see.

Poppy sank to the grass, her knees clasped under her chin, lost in her dreams. Suddenly a tall, gray-haired man hurried down the steps and across to the old barn. Her heart pounded and she thought she would faint as she recognized Greg. Of course he was older, but except for his gray hair he hadn't changed. He was still the tall, slender, handsome man she remembered. The man she had called her brother—the man she had found out too late she loved. A few minutes later Greg drove back into the courtyard at the wheel of a marine-blue Packard. His voice, as he called to someone to hurry up, sent remembered tremors of pleasure and pain through her, and she bit her lip to stop from crying out to him. Then a pretty woman ran down the steps, fanning herself with her big straw hat and laughing, and Poppy knew this must be his wife.

"Melissa, why are you always late?" she heard him complain.

"I suppose that after all these years I've just given up even trying," she laughed, climbing into the car.

"Come on, boys!" Greg yelled, hauling bags and valises into the trunk, and Poppy's heart jumped as three teenage boys hurtled down the steps. These were Greg's sons, the sons who might have been hers. They looked so like him, except the youngest one, dawdling behind; he was like his grandfather, Nik. "Hurry up, Hilliard," she heard Greg complain. And then behind them, walking slowly down the steps, came Angel! Poppy remembered the last time she had seen her . . . but the hair that she remembered as being moonlit blond seemed even fairer, and with a shock she realized Angel's hair was now pure white.

There was a flurry of good-bye hugs and kisses as they piled into the car and drove off. Angel waved them good-bye, and Poppy strained her eyes for a last glimpse of Greg and his sons. She felt again the old familiar pang of envy; she was back where she had started all those years ago, on the outside looking in. She had never really been part of the family after all. It was still only a dream.

She watched as Angel walked along the familiar grassy path to the little arbor she remembered so well; it was the place they had always gone to tell each other their secrets. She sat, agonized, wanting to go to Angel, but afraid . . . she knew she shouldn't, she knew she mustn't . . . but she so longed to go "home." Finally, she untethered her horse, and rode slowly down the hill toward the house.

Sitting on the carved bench in the vine-covered arbor, Angel opened the book she'd been carrying. It was her mother's journal; she'd discovered it just the other day, up in the attic amid a pile of her old schoolbooks. She'd hesitated about reading it, even now, twelve years after Rosalia's death, because somehow it had seemed like prying. Her own journal was such a personal thing; it recorded all her hopes and fears, her loves and sorrows, as well as the early parties and dances and visits to San Francisco. This would be like a private view into her mother's soul.

The first pages were all about her father, how they'd met, how much Rosalia loved him, about their wedding night . . . It was a young girl in love writing, not her mother, and Angel shut the book hurriedly. She would never read it now. She closed her eyes, half dozing, enjoying the warm sunlight filtering through the leaves and the special, alive silence of the countryside.

She had two precious weeks to herself. Two weeks before she had to return to Italy and the son who hated her almost as much as he'd hated his father; two weeks before she would have to decide what to do about her troubled daughters; just two weeks of rare solitude that she had never thought she'd want.

Angel's eyes flew open at the soft rustle of footsteps on the grass. Was it a dream? she wondered as Poppy walked toward her. Or maybe a ghost? Poppy's red hair was tied loosely with a ribbon the way she always used to wear it, but it was plumed with silver now. She was as slender as she had been at eighteen and still walked with the easy, long-striding grace that had always reminded Angel of a racehorse. She closed her eyes again, shocked. Poppy was real. She was here.

"I've come home, Angel," Poppy whispered. And then, covering her face with her hands, she sank to her knees and wept.

"Why are you here, Poppy?" Angel asked harshly, resisting the impulse to hold out her hand to comfort her. "This is no longer your home."

"I had to come," Poppy cried. "I've lost everything that matters to me . . . everything. Don't you see, Angel, I had to come back, I had to find you . . . I must know what happened to my daughter."

"You've broken your promise," Angel reminded her coldly. "You were never to contact any of us again."

"But it's so long ago," Poppy pleaded; "they say time heals old wounds—"

"Wounds!" Angel whispered, "wounds, Poppy? Those were not *wounds* you inflicted. *They were death blows!* You have no idea what disaster you brought upon me and my family! God, I wish my father had never met Jeb Mallory!"

Poppy's shocked tearstained eyes met hers. "You can't say that," she gasped. "Angel, we were like sisters. What happened was not my fault . . ."

"You didn't tell me the truth, did you, Poppy?" Angel asked icily. "But Felipe did. It was just *one* of the things he used to torture me with. He told me how you went to him that night, how passionate and insistent you were . . . he even told me how you felt in his arms—*Felipe was the secret lover you were seeing all those afternoons when you sneaked away from the hotel! And Felipe was the father of your child!"*

Poppy hung her head in silence. It was almost true. "He didn't make love to me, Angel; he raped me," she said quietly.

"You went to the Palazzo Rinardi in the middle of the night," Angel said scornfully. "He told me you had an assignation."

"It wasn't like that," she cried despairingly, "I swear to you it wasn't."

Angel shrugged coldly. "How and why it all happened scarcely matters anymore. But if it hadn't been for you, I would never have met Felipe." Her voice was filled with twenty-eight years of bitterness as she stared at Poppy. She wanted her to know everything so she would finally understand. "My whole life changed because of you, Poppy! I had to live for years with a man I despised and who loathed me. All Felipe ever wanted was the Konstants' money! When I could stand it no longer, I finally left. I took my two girls, but he kept the boy. And now my son hates me, Poppy, almost as much as he hated his father, because *he* had to stay there and live with him!"

Her wonderful clear eyes were full of pain as she remembered. "I had packed all our things," she said, "we were ready, in the hall; I had told Felipe the night before that we were leaving, that it was the end. Felipe came out of the gun room, it was autumn and I thought he was going out shooting pheasant. He was wearing a hunter-green jacket and he had a rifle under his arm. 'Aleksandr,' he said, 'come here to your father.' The boy looked at me, wondering what to do. I shook my head and put my arm around him. He was only nine years old . . . Felipe cocked the rifle and pointed it at him. 'I said come here, Aleksandr,' he repeated. I thrust the boy behind me, terrified. 'What are you doing?' I cried as he turned and pointed the rifle at the girls. 'If Aleksandr doesn't come here, to me, then I shall shoot one of the girls,' Felipe said . . . *and you know which one, Angel.*'

" 'You can't do that!' I cried. 'You can't murder your own child!' But Felipe always thought himself above the law.

" 'Murder?' he sneered. 'It will be a shooting accident, my dear . . . so terribly sad . . . everyone knows the Barone Rinardi adores his children.'

"Aleksandr pushed his way from my arms and walked toward his father. 'Please don't shoot them, Papa,' he said bravely. I'll never forget Felipe's smile of triumph as he put his hand on the boy's shoulder. 'You may go now,' he said, dismissing us. 'Aleksandr stays with me.'

"Aleksandr had always been a disappointment to Felipe; he was a delicate, shy, intellectual child, and he hated his father's showy display, he hated the way he always played the role of 'the Barone,' like a feudal lord. Felipe wanted his son to be an athlete, a sportsman, and he tortured Aleksandr about his frail physique, always pushing him to swim and to ride and to shoot, and taunting him about his spectacles because the boy was so nearsighted. Poor Aleksandr hated horses and he hated killing. Felipe never saw the beauty of Aleksandr's intelligence, he never read the poetry he wrote, or the stories. The tutors told me my son was a creative genius, that we should choose his schools carefully and make sure his talents were nurtured.

" 'Aleksandr stays with me,' Felipe said, 'he will be my hostage for the Konstants' money. As long as he is with me, the Konstants will pay.'

"My son stood there bravely while his father aimed the gun at us, watching as we left. 'I'll come back for you, Aleksandr,' I promised. But Felipe just laughed. 'It's your choice, Angel,' he called after me. 'You can stay here with me and your son.' Aleksandr's eyes looked at me so hopefully, though he still said not a word. But you see, now I knew how much Felipe hated his daughter—your daughter, Poppy. It was *she* he had aimed the gun at . . . I knew that if we stayed, one day he would surely kill her. Right now Aleksandr would be safe because he needed him. I would have to come back for him later. You see, I had no choice. It was to save your daughter, Poppy, that I sacrificed my son.

"I brought the girls here," she went on wearily. "For years we bargained with Felipe; my father offered him more and more money, but he just laughed and said it wasn't enough. He never let Aleksandr write to me. I was crazy with fear of what he must be doing to the child, how he must be torturing him. Finally, my father said he and Mama would go to Italy, they would confront him, they would bargain with him—a million dollars, two million—for my son. They were on the liner *Lusitania* when it was sunk by a German submarine."

Poppy felt as though she were dying inside. She remembered the day Nik and Rosalia had come to save her from the terror of the children's home in Pittsburgh, how they'd brought her here, and called her their daughter, how they'd loved her. She thought of Nik, so solid and strong, and Rosalia, so gay and charming, always laughing. They were so vivid in her memories that she couldn't believe they were lost beneath the cold green waves of the Atlantic Ocean.

"Greg took over the ranch," Angel went on. "If you'd seen how he suffered all those years, searching for you, you wouldn't have dared come back! I begged him not to go on looking for you, but how could I tell him the truth and hurt him even more? Finally he put it all behind him and married Melissa and now they have three fine sons. But the two eldest are at military school and it looks as though young Hilliard will follow them. So there is no one left who wants to take over the Rancho Santa Vittoria. Everything my father worked for now means nothing. Greg has already sold off hundreds of acres to developers—it seems they're prepared to pay a fortune for the land—the money is for his sons. In a few years you won't be able to recognize this place.

"Greg is content with Melissa," she added, "and he loves his boys. He's as happy as any man can expect to be. Don't think you can come back now and destroy that, Poppy."

Poppy shook her head. "I saw him once, in Paris years ago. He didn't see me. I could have gone to him, Angel, but I knew then it was too late." She hesitated. "I rode over to the Mallory House," she said quietly. "Angel, what happened to my father?"

"He died in the fire there, five years after you disappeared. He is buried in the Methodist chapel in Santa Barbara. Mama and Papa wouldn't let him lie in the same grave as your mother, I've never understood why." She glanced down at Rosalia's little blue leather journal on the seat beside her; it probably contained the answer, but she knew now she would never read it.

Poppy felt the old helpless feeling of rage against her father return once more, the flame of hatred that would burn in her forever. *He* had been the cause of all of this . . . *he* was the one who should be judged in heaven. If he had looked after his wife, his child, his land, none of this would have happened. Because of him she had lost her son. And so had Angel.

"Angel," she asked, half afraid of the answer, "what happened to Aleksandr?"

"Felipe refused to give him up, no matter how big the bribe. We even tried cutting off the money supply, but of course then he threatened the boy. We consulted international lawyers, but the law was adamant; when a man's wife leaves him, he is entitled to keep his children. They told me I was lucky to have my two girls. Felipe died suddenly, two years ago, and I went back to Italy to see Aleksandr at last. He refused to talk to me; he was hostile, alien. I tried to explain how I'd thought of him all the time, how I'd agonized over him, how I knew Felipe wanted to kill his sister and because of that we couldn't return. He wouldn't even listen. With Felipe dead, he was now the Barone Rinardi, but he refused to accept the title. For years Felipe had forced him to ride and shoot and do all the physical things he wanted him to be good at, until he got tired of the game. In revenge he got rid of Aleksandr's tutor; he refused to send the boy to school . . . *Aleksandr was uneducated!* But at least Felipe hadn't been able to deprive him of books, and he'd read his way through the vast library, teaching himself about the things he loved best. Aleksandr had escaped into a world of his own and now he would admit no one else into it. Especially the mother who had promised to come back for him . . . and failed."

Poppy hid her face in her hands; she knew that feeling, waiting and waiting for someone who never came . . .

"He wanted nothing more to do with the Rinardis or the Konstants; all he asked was enough money to buy a remote Italian villa on the slopes of the Dolomites. It's surrounded by acres of old-fashioned neglected gardens and he lives there alone, studying his books and creating order from the chaos in the grounds. He doesn't want to see me, or any of his family; all he wants is to be left alone. I like to think he is happy, at last."

Her voice was so wistful that instinctively Poppy took her hand. "I know how it feels, Angel," she cried. "I've lost my son too . . ."

"*Don't tell me*, Poppy," Angel cried, pulling her hand away. "I don't want to know anything about you. I just want you to go back to wherever you came from. My life is not yours, my children are not yours. You have nothing. You've brought enough grief to this family."

Poppy shrank from her, shocked by the quiet hatred in her voice. But she had to find out what she had come for. "I'll go," she said quietly. "But first I beg you, have pity on me, tell me about my daughter. How is she? Did you name her for me?"

"Like a fool, I named both girls for you—maybe because even though I loved you then and felt sorry for you, I knew one day you would come back and want her. I have *two* daughters, and their names are Maria-Cristina Poppy Rinardi, and Helena Mallory Rinardi. And you, Poppy, have none. Remember? *They are both mine.*"

"Angel," she begged, "please, let me see her, at least tell me which one is mine, and where she is. . . ."

"No! There is nothing else to say." A look of such deep sadness crossed Angel's face that Poppy felt frightened . . . what had happened to Maria-Cristina, to Helena, to make her look like that? But she knew Angel wouldn't tell her. "Will you let me come to see you again, Angel?" she asked humbly.

Angel shook her head, and they looked at each other for the last time, seeing each other as they were now, and as they had been when they were carefree girls, racing around the sunlit Rancho Santa Vittoria on their ponies, with never a thought for tomorrow.

Without another word, Poppy turned and walked down the grassy path. It seemed like the longest walk of her life, and she knew that the scent of the lantana bushes and the roses, the sounds of the cicadas, and the gay chirping of the little birds as she left the place and the family she loved, would linger in her memory, forever.

CHAPTER 56

1 9 3 1 ,   I T A L Y

Every time the bulletproof Mercedes limousine swept through the massive iron gates and he heard them clang shut behind him, Franco was reminded that he lived in a prison. But he didn't mind the isolation anymore; in a way, he almost preferred his solitude.

He had long since discovered that the only way to escape from his prison was through the mind. After the last meetings had finished and the final decisions of the day had been made, he would dine, always alone, at the long refectory table lit by priceless silver candelabra, eating meagerly from delicate china and drinking a single glass of fine wine from a beautiful Lalique glass. Then he would cross the hall to the library and close the doors softly behind him, shutting out at last the brutish faces of the guards, and all the tension and the responsibility. He was alone with his fine books, his old master paintings, and his memories.

Sometimes he would wander the vast beautiful room, looking at his collection of paintings, or he'd leaf through one or another of his fascinating collection of rare books, and sometimes he'd just sit in his usual deep chair, turn down the lamp, light a cigarette, and remember the way life used to be, when he was a happy man.

Tonight was different. He'd eaten slowly, even poured himself a second glass of wine in order to extend the pleasure of anticipation a little

longer, putting off the delicious moment when he could view his latest—
and most precious—acquisition.

At last, he drained the drops from his wineglass and, his heart pounding with excitement, he walked slowly across the hall into his sanctuary.
It was a hot night and the library's tall windows were thrown open to
catch the breeze. He could hear the footsteps of the guards patroling
outside as he turned off the lamps, all except the one beside a large easel
holding a painting, still covered by a dustcloth. He lit another cigarette
and sank into his chair, staring somberly at the shrouded painting. He
hadn't seen it in years, he'd just known he wanted it, at whatever cost,
and he'd instructed his agent to outbid all others at the auction.

Crushing out his cigarette, he walked to the easel and with a trembling hand removed the cloth. He gazed at the portrait of Poppy with
tears in his eyes; it was Poppy as he'd first known her, and Sargent had
captured all of youth's luminous arrogance and fears in her vivid face. He
seemed to have caught the nuances of a young animal eager to be let off
the leash, and yet afraid of the freedom. And there were the scars of
experience, too, in the wary insolence of the eyes and the challenging
smile. Poppy was wearing an ice-gray satin gown, sashed in pink, and
there was the famous rope of pearls at her neck and diamond stars
sparkling in her red hair, and in her hand she held a single white gardenia.

Franco sank back into his chair with a sigh of pleasure. After almost
twenty-five years, he was alone again with Poppy.

In an effort to exorcise her loneliness, Poppy had become a world
traveler; she had traveled on liners and on trains, on cargo boats and Nile
steamers, mules and camels. There was hardly a country left she hadn't
seen, or a ruin or historic monument she hadn't visited. And always
alone.

She was the mysterious, elegant woman traveling first class on the liner
Ile de France on her way to New York; she was the beautiful, aloof
stranger dining alone on the Orient Express on her way to Istanbul; she
was the slender, wary-eyed chic woman who spoke to no one on the river
cruise from Cairo to Luxor; she was one of the only women who braved
India's fierce daytime heat to view the Red Fort and the Taj Mahal in
sunlight, and again, alone, by moonlight. She was the only woman
aboard the freighter from Calcutta to Rangoon, and she was the only
woman in the bar at Raffles Hotel in Singapore. She was asked to dine, to
dance, to drink, in Hong Kong, Delhi, Vienna, Buenos Aires, and on top
of a mountain in Bolivia, as well as many places in between. She ac-

cepted no invitations. She spoke only to the guides, or to the chambermaids, stewards, and waiters in whatever ship or hotel she was staying.
She was running away from the world, and herself. And she wasn't
succeeding.

It had been four years since she'd seen Angel, and for four years she'd
been trying to forget. After she'd left Angel, she'd returned to her anonymous palatial suite at her hotel in San Francisco, wishing she could die.
Angel had laid the guilt and the blame for the disasters that had happened to the Konstant family on her, and she'd finally accepted it. Rogan
was her fault, too, as well as the poor child she had decided to abandon
even before it was born. Bitterly unhappy and uncertain what to do,
she'd wandered aimlessly south through California to Los Angeles, where
she took a suite at the Beverly Hills Hotel, and for a week she stayed
inside it, thinking.

At the end of that week she'd telephoned her lawyers in Paris and told
them to put the house and contents of Numéro Seize, rue des Arbres, up
for sale. She'd wanted to keep nothing. Then she telephoned the detectives who had been searching fruitlessly for so long for Rogan, and asked
them to find out everything they could about the Baronessa Angel
Rinardi's two daughters, telling them there was a rumor that one of
them had been adopted at birth—and she needed to know which one.
She had to know her own daughter, no matter how long it took. She
didn't want to take her away from Angel, but she needed to meet her,
because one day she intended to leave her her fortune. It would be all she
had ever done for her.

Los Angeles was a young, growing city and the warm sunshine and
sweet, orange blossom–laden air had beguiled her. She'd bought a car so
that she could drive herself around its wide, flat valleys and the sudden
ranges of hills, admiring the opulent estates and lavish white mansions of
the stars of the flourishing movie industry, Pickfair and Greystone and
the new forty-four-room Greenacres just being built at a cost of two
million dollars by Harold Lloyd. They'd looked so beautiful, sparkling in
the California sun, as though promising that the lives of those who lived
in them would be pleasant and tranquil and easy, and suddenly Poppy
had been tempted to buy land and build one herself. Why not, she
thought suddenly, after all, she was a rich woman, she could afford it; she
could afford anything she wanted, now. She knew she couldn't bear to go
home to Montespan and thought maybe she would find the peace she
was seeking, here in California.

She had bought a five-acre plot atop a hill at Beverly Drive north of
Sunset Boulevard and commissioned an architect to build her a Spanish-

style hacienda, which bore a strong resemblance to the Konstant House. The urge to buy more land took hold of her, and remembering Franco's advice, she skirted the periphery of the growing city, buying tracts of land that nobody wanted yet on Wilshire and Sunset, and Santa Monica; and she ventured even farther, buying useless scrubland in the San Fernando Valley, miles from anywhere. Then she instructed her agents to negotiate to buy the old Mallory House and as much of the surrounding land as the Konstants would sell. She intended to buy back her inheritance so that one day it would belong to her children.

Aching with loneliness, she embarked on a flurry of spending. She bought antiques and paintings for the house that was still only a blueprint in an architect's office; she bought whole groves of transplanted palm trees to line its yet unmarked driveway and hundreds of exotic shrubs and plants to landscape its future gardens. She bought a carved stone fountain for its courtyard and planned a turquoise-blue swimming pool enclosed by a clipped green yew hedge. And as she tossed and turned in bed at night she'd dreamed that one day, Rogan and her daughter would come to find her and she would say to them, "See, here is your home, it's been waiting for you all these years. This is all yours, and this, and this . . . all you have to do is to say you forgive me."

When the report came back from the detective, she'd opened it eagerly. Maybe now she would know the truth. They had been in touch with agents in Italy, they told her, where both young women were currently residing at the Villa d'Oro. Records had been searched and showed that they were twins, born on May 5, 1899, and baptized two months later at the Chapel at the Villa d'Oro. There was no evidence at all that they were anything other than twin sisters.

Poppy had drawn the curtains in her bright, cheerful, sunny suite at the Beverly Hills Hotel and cried into the darkness. When there were no more tears left, she had called the maid to pack her things and taken the train to Chicago and on to New York; her plan of a home in Beverly Hills was useless, she had no children to enjoy it. She was going home to Montespan. On the three-day train journey she asked herself why. First Franco had gone, then Rogan, then Netta . . . even the Joliots had finally retired and there was a new housekeeper in charge, who was looking after Luchay . . . without them Montespan was not a home anymore. There was no one left to welcome her with open arms. Only Luchay, and Luchay was no longer enough to ease her pain and make her forget. Then on an impulse she canceled her passage on the liner from New York to France and took one to Argentina instead.

Her travels had filled in her time and they'd cost her a great deal of money. Where once she had been prudent, saving her money for Rogan's inheritance, now she had spent lavishly. She had bought wonderful clothes that, carelessly, she had often left packed in steamer trunks in hotels around the world. She had bought rubies in Burma and emeralds in India and gold in Africa. And everywhere she went she had spied out the terrain, buying land shrewdly with an eye to the future. But wherever she went, whatever wonders of the world she saw, however much she spent, she never stopped thinking about Rogan and her daughter. She had no one to love, and no one who loved her.

It was while she was on a dilapidated little cargo boat, wallowing in the South China Sea, on her way from Manila to Singapore that she realized that there was only one person in the world who had truly known her, and who'd loved her despite all her faults and her flawed character. *If you ever need me,* he'd said, all those years ago, *just call me.* She remembered with a shiver Véronique and what had happened the last time she'd asked for his help. But this was different. All she wanted Franco to do was to find out about her daughter.

Three months later she was back at Montespan, surrounded by so many mementos and memories that she thought if it weren't for Luchay, she would go mad. Her four years of world-traveling seemed to have vanished like a dream and her plan that had seemed so fine and reasonable in the middle of the South China Sea suddenly seemed fraught with uncertainty and even danger. Now at night she dreamed of Franco in his villa fortress in Naples, and of the moonlight glinting on the evil black machine guns. She had left him that night nearly twenty-five years ago because he'd frightened her into believing there was no way their love could survive if she stayed. Franco had inherited the mantle of his father and he'd accepted it, but he hadn't wanted her to become a target of his enemies. How could she go to him now, after all these years? she wondered uncertainly. She had no idea of what his life was like now, or whether he even thought about her.

When she had ordered Numéro Seize to be sold she had told Drouot, the auctioneers, to sell off all its contents; she had wanted to keep nothing. Though she'd refused to attend, she'd heard that the auction had caused quite a stir in Paris with buyers and press searching for a glimpse of the legendary Poppy, and the excitement had forced up the prices spectacularly, netting her another fortune.

Now she ran her eye down the list Drouot's had sent her with the prices and the names of the purchasers, recognizing many of her old clients among them, touched that they had been willing to pay so generously for a memory of happy times spent at Numéro Seize. The sumptuous beds had gone for astonishing sums—people had even bought the satin sheets as souvenirs. And the fine antique pieces, the beautiful rugs, the silver and the china, all had brought far more than their worth. But it was her portrait by John Singer Sargent that had broken all records. It seemed everyone had wanted the painting of Paris's most famous and beautiful madam. The bidding had been pushed up by an Italian agent who had been instructed to buy it at whatever cost, and it had sold for more than a hundred times its estimate. When she called Drouot to ask about it, they told her that it was well known that the agent in question acted for the Mafia chief Franco Malvasi.

Now Poppy knew she could ask him a favor.

CHAPTER 57

1932, ITALY

Poppy had thought it all out carefully. Now she knew for certain what sort of man Franco was but she also knew that there was another side to him. The Franco she knew was the private man, caring, gentle, considerate, and *that* was the man she was about to appeal to now. Remembering the last time she'd gone to see him—the unanswered telephone messages, the frightened cabdrivers who wouldn't take her to the villa, and the sinister bodyguards, she decided this time she would do it differently.

She drove herself down to the south of France and through Italy in her latest extravagance, the new de Courmont coupe. It was long and low and sleek and in her favorite bottle-green color with buff leather upholstery, and she was wearing a matching green felt hat pulled low over her red hair. She pressed her foot to the accelerator, feeling its powerful engine respond, and the miles soon sped away under her wheels.

It wasn't until she reached Naples that she began to get nervous. She had never told Franco about Felipe and her daughter—though, of course, he knew she'd had a child—Franco had always said he knew everything about her, he'd told her that the first time they'd met. But she didn't believe he knew she'd given the child to Angel. Maybe he'd think she'd deliberately deceived him all these years, when the truth was, she had been bound by her promise to Angel not to tell. And, of course, he had never known about Rogan, because when he'd left her, he'd severed all ties. She knew Franco had cut her from his life as though she never existed. But those weren't the only things that were bothering her. She had been a young woman when they last met; what would Franco think of her now?

Naples was broiling under late-summer heat as she checked into a suite at the Grand Hotel, and she bathed and changed into a thin silk robe, pacing nervously between the silent waiting telephone and the tall mirror in her bedroom that showed her the truth. She had refused to cut her lavish red hair in a fashionable bob and it fell to her shoulders the way Franco would remember it, only now it was smoother, sleeker, and there were two fine sweeps of white at the temples. Her eyes were just as blue and maybe they still had that old insolent tilt, but there were small lines around them now, marks of past joys and sorrows. Throwing open her robe, she stared at her naked body, seeing it as he might; the curve of her breasts was a little deeper, her hips a little rounder, but her waist was still trim and her buttocks taut, and her long, elegant legs were as slender as they had always been.

She fastened the robe again with a sigh; she couldn't turn back the clock, even for Franco. And if she could have turned it back, she would have changed her whole life.

Nevertheless, she fussed endlessly over her appearance, choosing and discarding dresses until she found one that seemed right; she powdered the freckles on her nose and added a blush of color to her cheekbones, and a touch of coral lipstick to her lips. She sprayed on her favorite gardenia scent and finally, she was ready.

She could put off the moment no longer, and she picked up the telephone and dialed his number, tapping her nails nervously on the edge of the table as it rang.

"*Pronto*, Malvasi," he said.

Poppy's nails stopped tapping, her heart jumped, and her eyes widened with astonishment . . . "Franco!" she gasped. . . . "I didn't expect . . . I thought you wouldn't be there. . . ."

"Poppy," he said, "is it really you?"

"Yes . . . I'm sorry, I can't think . . . I hadn't expected to speak to you, I thought I'd have to talk to several secretaries, leave messages first . . ."

"You dialed my private number," he told her. "I always answer it myself. And I'm just as surprised, Poppy, to be talking to you."

"Franco," she whispered, cradling the telephone against her cheek as though it were his face, "you sound just the same."

She heard him sigh as he said, "After twenty-five years, Poppy, none of us are the same."

"I'm here—at the Grand in Naples," she cried eagerly. "I wanted to see you . . ."

There was a pause and then he said warningly, "It's better not to, Poppy. Remember?"

She nodded; she remembered only too well. "But it's important," she pleaded. "I *need* to see you, Franco. I'm here to ask your help."

"Then I'll send a car for you," he said abruptly, "it'll be there in half an hour."

She knew she couldn't bear the memory of the bulletproof black limousine with the shaded windows, and the guards and the guns. "I have my own car," she said quickly, "I'll drive myself, Franco. I know the way." She'd made it her business weeks ago to find out where the villa was.

"I'll tell the guards on the gate to expect you," he said quietly. "In an hour, Poppy?"

"In an hour." She waited until she heard the click as he replaced his receiver before she put down the phone.

The heat in Naples had been unbearable all day and even now, as dusk changed to midnight blue, the temperature had barely dropped. Poppy opened the car windows wide, letting the warm breeze rake through her hair, grateful for the breath of air. As the long green car climbed the hills she wondered what it would be like, seeing Franco again, touching his hand, looking into his eyes, and she shivered as though the breeze had turned cold.

The guards outside were different this time, they wore smart blue uniforms and peaked caps; there were no machine guns in evidence, and they manned a booth at the entrance linked to the house by telephone.

"We were expecting you, Signora," they told her politely, peering intently into the back seat and opening the trunk. But they didn't check her personally and she realized Franco must have asked them not to— still, she might be carrying one of those small neat pistols in her cream leather purse, the sort that didn't look nearly big enough to kill a man, but that she knew could.

The gates swung open, Poppy pressed her foot nervously on the gas. The big car prowled up the gravel driveway to where a butler was waiting on the white-columned portico. "Signor Malvasi is in the library, Signora," he told her.

"Wait," she said as he started to tap on the door and announce her. "I'll go in by myself."

She slid through the library door without a sound. The big room was filled with the scent of night-blooming flowers wafting in from the garden. There were pools of light from soft-shaded lamps, and a treasure house of paintings glowed on the walls. Franco was standing by an open window gazing out onto the moonlit garden. Of course he looked older, but he was the same lean, vigorous man she remembered and he was as immaculate as always, in a well-cut dinner jacket. His hair was now completely gray, though his heavy brows were still dark and his eyes as he turned and looked at her still had that same piercing quality, as though he could read her soul.

Franco stared at her silently; he'd been thinking about her, wondering what she would be like now, how it would feel being with her again . . . and now here she was. In the soft light, she was the Poppy of his dreams; a girl again, just as he always thought of her, in an apricot silk dress that brought out the peachy-red of her hair and made her skin glow like alabaster. She put her head to one side and looked at him with that old familiar insolent stare, and he wanted to kiss her.

"You look beautiful—as ever, Poppy," he said instead. "Time hasn't changed you."

"It's a trick of the light," she said, walking toward him and holding out her hands. "I've lived a dozen different lives, and it's all there on my face."

She was close to him now, and as he took her hands in his, he could see the truth. But even if life had been cruel to her, it had blessed her with a timelessness; she was more beautiful now than when she was a girl.

"I didn't think I'd ever feel this happy to see anyone," he said simply.

"Nor I," she said. And then she moved closer and the familiar scent of gardenias was in his nostrils as their lips met.

Poppy turned away, burying her face in his shoulder. "This isn't what I came here to tell you," she whispered, "but I'm quite sure now that I've never really loved any man but you, Franco. It's always been you . . . only you."

He stroked her hair gently. "It's too late for us," he said quietly. "It's always been too late. It was impossible right from the beginning. Nothing has changed, Poppy. It never will."

She nodded, "I know. I'm just glad to be here with you . . . now, for a little while."

Putting his hand under her chin, Franco lifted her face to his. "Then let's enjoy our stolen moments," he said, determinedly cheerful, "let's have champagne, let us talk the way we used to at Montespan, over dinner. You can tell me all about yourself."

He walked to the waiting silver wine cooler and pulled the cork, laughing like a boy as he filled the glasses until they foamed over with bubbles. "Poppy," he cried, "I think I've been old all my life; only you have the capacity to make me feel young."

She took the glass from him, laughing intoxicatedly though she hadn't yet drunk anything, elated at just being with him again. "It's our own party," she cried, "our *reunion* party, Franco! You and me—together again!"

They clinked glasses in a toast, laughing as the golden wine spilled.

"You were the champagne in my life," he told her, "you were always bubbling and full of fizz and vitality—"

"Except when I'm unhappy," she said abruptly, "which is all the time now."

They looked at each other soberly. "I wish that weren't true, Poppy," he said quietly.

She shrugged. "I've tried to run away from it. For four years I've chased around the world. There isn't a historic monument I haven't seen, an ocean I haven't crossed. And," she added with a short bitter laugh, "none of it mattered a damn!"

"I heard you closed Numéro Seize."

"A long time ago. I sold the contents recently. You bought my portrait. That's how I knew I could come back to you. I told you, I need your help," she said simply.

There was a small silence and then he said, "I'm always here when you need help, Poppy. I'm glad you remembered."

Franco drank his champagne quickly, wishing he didn't feel like crushing her in his arms, like begging her never to go away again . . . Of course he couldn't do that; he must take control of the situation, the way he always did. "You must be hungry," he said, taking her arm. "I thought we would have supper in here. It's my favorite room, where no one else is ever allowed. We'll get the breeze from those long windows."

Places were set at a small round table covered with a rich paisley shawl, and a serving trolley nearby groaned under the weight of platters of freshly poached salmon, pink shrimp, oysters and lobsters, iced soufflés, and a great crystal bowl of figs, melons, cherries, and wild strawberries.

"It's a still life, like one of your wonderful paintings," Poppy gasped, "a medieval feast fit for a prince!"

"Then tonight we are the royalty," he said with a smile. "After all, it's our celebration, isn't it?"

He refilled her glass and let her talk about her travels; noticing that the words spilled from her excitedly, the way they would from a woman too long alone. He put salmon on her plate and cut it into delicate little pieces for her, he plied her with fruits, slitting open the figs, revealing their soft pink inner skins bursting with sweet juices, and then he enjoyed watching her eat them. He tried with all his strength to keep her out of his heart and at the end of it all, when she fell silent and just looked at him with those wide, wonderful blue eyes, he knew he had failed. He still wanted her more than he'd ever wanted any other woman in the world.

Afterward they walked together to the window, and looked out onto the moonlit garden. "So," she said, meeting his glance, "nothing has changed, Franco?"

"Nothing's changed," he murmured. And as he took her in his arms and kissed her, he knew it never would.

She waited, still trembling from his kisses, while he picked up his house phone and dismissed the guards from inside the house; he told the butler that they would need nothing further and they were not to be disturbed. And when he was sure they were alone, he took her hand and they walked together up the grand staircase.

His room had the simplicity of absolute luxury. Priceless silk rugs, soft draperies, a beautifully carved antique headboard, and a single painting on the wall, a Botticelli Madonna. But then Franco pulled back a velvet curtain to reveal her portrait. "You see," he smiled, "now you are always with me. I see you first thing in the morning and last thing at night."

She sat nervously on the edge of the bed. "I know it's silly, Franco," she whispered, "but I feel as anxious as a new bride."

"Then that's what you shall be," he murmured, putting his arms around her.

But her body told her she wasn't his new bride, her body *remembered* his. The silk dress slid from her shoulders and she was naked underneath just the way he'd always liked her to be, but for pale peach silk French panties and her pearls. She felt him tremble as his lips moved slowly down her throat to her breasts. "Franco," she moaned, "oh, Franco, darling . . ."

Stripping himself naked, he lay beside her, turning her into his arms. They lay body against body, feeling their heartbeats, then he was kissing her again and the desire to possess her, to claim her again as his own, made him fierce. He thrust into her, again and again, until she shouted her passion, tossing her head frenziedly, demanding the final moment. "Poppy, oh, Poppy," he cried as he burst inside her, "ah, Poppy, my love . . ."

They lay quietly for a while, like dazed travelers returning from another world, reorienting themselves. "If you ever wondered how much I love you," he said at last, "surely now you know."

She turned to look into his eyes; their faces were so close that their breaths mingled. "I know," she said simply. "It will never change."

The night passed in moments of tenderness, wrapped in each other's arms—"Being in your arms is like coming home," she whispered—and in more lovemaking, longer this time, more drawn out, with tenderness as well as the frenzy of passion. As the hot sun rose again in the late-summer sky, jolting them from their private world into the public one, she begged him to let her stay. "Don't send me away, Franco, not yet . . . let's pretend just for a little while that life is the way it used to be."

Franco strode naked to the window, switching back the curtain on his world. Suddenly none of it mattered; he would trade it all for a week with the woman he loved. "I know a place," he said quietly, "an old villa . . . I haven't seen it in years and it's probably falling to rack and ruin by now. But there's no one there who knows us, no one who cares. Maybe, just for a few days . . ."

"A few days," Poppy whispered, "just a few days lost from our real lives. Who is there to care about that, Franco?"

She waited for him in the library while he summoned his top three men, telling them that he was leaving for a week, that they would not know where he was nor would they be able to get in touch with him. They stared at him mistrustfully, as he told them he was taking no one with him, no bodyguards, no bulletproof cars, no guns. "It's crazy," they warned. "You are Franco Malvasi, you'll be recognized anywhere you go. It's too dangerous." Franco just shrugged away their arguments; for the first time in almost twenty-five years he was doing exactly what he wanted, and he wanted it passionately, at any price.

"I expect you to carry on as normal," he told them. "See that the house is guarded as though I am still here. Have the doctor come here and let it be known that I have some minor illness and am confined to my bed—that will explain my absence." Their faces were worried as he left, but he didn't care. As he drove out of his prison in the long, low dark green de Courmont, all he cared about was Poppy.

The villa in the hills near Vicenza looked cool and white and dilapidated under its encroaching mantle of greenery. "Just the way Montespan was," Poppy cried delightedly, "when we first saw it."

The crumbling pillars flanking the entrance were surmounted by stone peacocks and overgrown with moss, and the iron gates bearing the name "Villa Castelletto" creaked rustily, refusing to open more than a crack. Laughing, they squeezed through, running up the winding overgrown driveway to where it ended in a circle in front of an imposing portico. Hand in hand they walked up the four wide shallow steps to the tall oaken doors. The handle gave under Franco's touch and she looked at him, surprised. "The caretaker is a village woman; she was told to come here this morning to clean up and make sure there was food in the kitchen. See, she left the key in the lock."

It felt deliciously cool after the heat outside, and slipping off her shoes, Poppy walked barefoot across the hall peering into rooms. The decor probably hadn't changed in a hundred years; there were heavy red velvet drapes with dangling gold tassels and massive pieces of gothic furniture, interspersed with fragile painted Venetian cabinets and intaglio tables. The floors were marble downstairs and polished wood upstairs, and the tall ceilings were painted with allegorical scenes of maidens and shepherds and cupids.

She thought of Montespan, the simple country farmhouse with its fake mementos of a life that never existed and its memories of sadness and loss. A little flicker of hope crept into her mind; maybe this wouldn't be for just a few days, maybe it would be a whole new beginning. . . .

"I'm starving," she cried, her eyes sparkling with happiness, "let's see what's in the kitchen."

There were baskets of produce, eggs, pasta, bread, and wine. Tying an apron around her waist, Poppy cooked omelets and pasta and salad, while Franco filled their wineglasses and munched the bread hungrily. They sat opposite each other at the kitchen table, eating their meal, looking up at each other now and then, and exclaiming how good it tasted. "It's like old times," Franco said, with a satisfied sigh.

"Better," Poppy replied, "because now we know the truth about ourselves." She remembered suddenly why she was here, and that they were not far from Venice—probably close to the Villa d'Oro—and she longed to tell him about her daughter, to ask his help. But the moment wasn't right. She would wait.

The days passed in dreamlike succession; they breakfasted on the sunny morning patio overlooking the tangled green gardens and sometimes afterward they would wander into the village to buy provisions and wine. Then they'd sleep away the hot afternoon, wrapped in each other's arms, still warm and moist from their lovemaking. The rusty iron gates still refused to open and the big green car stayed outside, awaiting their evening's pleasure, when, freshly bathed and cool again, they might drive to a country restaurant for a simple supper of salad and risotto and cool, prickly Venetian wine. The woman came to the house every morning to clean, but they never saw her. "She's the house ghost," Franco exclaimed, laughing as they returned home once again to find it immaculate; the beds were even turned down and there was a carafe of water on the bedside table.

But it was the nights that Poppy thought were so magical, lost from reality, together in their dusty, opulent green-shrouded villa. The soft night world outside their open windows seemed tangible as velvet and the moist warmth of her skin, the coolness of Franco's lips on her body, the scent of flowers and of their lovemaking, made her feel like a luxuriant jungle cat. She wanted nothing in the world more than Franco's arms around her, his body close to hers, his breath mingling with hers.

The scented nights slid by quickly; though she refused to count them. She had almost begun to believe that small flicker of hope that told her there was a life for them together, that Franco could escape from his world and she from her past, when he said to her, "It's time to go back, Poppy. Back to reality."

They were in bed. The sheets, crumpled from their lovemaking, were flung back and they lay side by side, hands touching, fingers entwined as their bodies had so recently been. The shrill continuous chirp of the cicadas filled the silence that fell on the room.

"After all," he said gently, "these were only stolen moments."

"Sometimes I think that's all there are—stolen moments. And dreams," Poppy answered bitterly. "When we are young we dream good dreams, we dream that we are going to have it all. As we grow older we realize that we're only going to get pieces of those dreams, little bits to treasure, here and there. The trick is to recognize the stolen moments, to take them when you can—and remember them. Because they are the only thing that makes life bearable."

He put his hand to her face, feeling the hot salt tears on his fingers. "No one gets it all, my Poppy," he murmured sadly.

She closed her eyes, trying to stop the tears, but they ran across her cheeks, into her ears, into her hair—and onto Franco's face as he held her close. She thought of what he had said . . . no one gets it all, and she remembered Angel, the girl who she had felt sure had it all, and she knew he was right. Dreams don't come true.

"When must we leave?" she asked brokenly.

"Tomorrow." He'd left himself no time to think about it, no time to change his mind.

Poppy nodded, drying her tears on a corner of the sheet. "Then we still have tonight," she said, her voice wobbling as she choked back a sob.

"Yes, we have tonight, my darling," he said, enfolding her in his safe, loving arms.

Poppy looked pale and weary-eyed the next morning as Franco closed the big oaken double doors for the final time, and they walked in silence down the winding gravel drive to the car. She watched somberly as he flung their bags into the trunk of the de Courmont and slammed it shut. "I'll drive," he said, "you don't look up to it."

She glanced back over her shoulder as they drove off; the villa looked just as it had when they'd arrived, cool and mysterious under the blue sky and its tangle of greenery. Only now it was different, now it contained their memories and the broken fragments of their dreams.

The car prowled smoothly back down the hills toward Verona. "We'll drive to Milan and then on to Genoa," Franco told her, his voice sounding different, brisker, more businesslike. "I've booked you into a hotel there for the night."

"And you?" she asked.

"I've arranged for a car to pick me up."

Poppy understood; he was deliberately changing himself into the other Franco, the one she didn't know.

"Very well," she said in a small voice.

The journey that had seemed to fly by before, now seemed long and tiring. It was raining when they got to Milan and stopped for lunch.

"Damn," Franco muttered, drumming his fingers nervously on the restaurant tablecloth, "the rain will make us late."

Poppy pushed away her uneaten food and stared at him sadly. It seemed he couldn't wait to get back to his fortress again.

She dozed uneasily as they drove through the long gray afternoon, aware of him by her side, but whenever she opened her eyes and glanced up at him, he was staring at the rainswept road, concentrating on his driving, lost in his own thoughts.

She awoke, startled, from a deep sleep as the car stopped suddenly. "We are almost at Genoa, Poppy," he said, "it's time to wake up."

"Franco," she said wildly, "couldn't we . . . isn't it possible . . ."

Her hands reached out and he pulled her to him. "Don't Poppy," he said quietly. "It's no good. Think of the reality of things. It's time to go back."

"I love you, Franco," she whispered, knowing it was the end.

"Thank you," he said simply. She noticed that his hand trembled as he turned the key in the ignition again and his face looked shuttered and withdrawn.

Franco knew the road he was looking for but in the heavy rain it was difficult to see exactly where he was. He drove slowly, checking off the landmarks as he came to them; they were an hour late and he knew his men would be anxious. At last he saw the glow of headlights ahead. "There they are," he told Poppy, half dozing at his side.

She'd just remembered that she hadn't yet asked him to help her find her daughter, somehow there hadn't been time . . . but the headlights were blinding; surely Franco couldn't see where he was going. "Don't you think they should turn out their lights now they've seen us?" she was asking. And then a hail of bullets shattered their windscreen and she knew no more.

CHAPTER 58

The telephone shrilled suddenly, breaking the silence that shrouded the Villa Castelletto. Mike leapt to answer it, his mind still on Poppy and Franco. He picked up the receiver, expecting Aria to be on the other end.

"Pronto," he said, feeling very Italian.

"Mr. Preston?"

The voice was vaguely familiar, but he couldn't place it, and he frowned. "Yeah, Mike Preston here."

"This is Pierluigi Galli."

"Galli! But—" He stopped suddenly; he'd been going to say, "But I thought you were in jail."

"I've been allowed out—on bail," Pierluigi said. "I called the Palazzo Rinardi, and Fiametta told me you were there. I'd like to talk to you, Mr. Preston. Unfortunately, I'm not supposed to leave the grounds of the Villa Velata, and as I'm not able to come to you, I would appreciate it if you could take the time to come here and see me. It's not too far from you."

Mike's eyebrows rose in surprise, first that they'd allowed Pierluigi out on bail—as far as he knew, the police had no other suspects for Claudia's murder; and second, after their abortive meeting in New York, he couldn't imagine what he wanted to tell him. It had been his opinion that beneath Pierluigi Galli's still facade ran very deep waters. The man was so secretive, he might have been cast in the mold of the perfect spy. Still, if he wanted to talk, Mike was surely going to listen—even though it was snowing like hell outside.

"Give me the directions," he told him. "I'll get there as soon as I can."

The drive took four hours in the snow and Mike had had no sleep—he'd been up all night with Poppy, and he was cold, tired, and hungry when he finally arrived at the Villa Velata. He parked the car and stood for a minute looking at the house. The snow-covered mountain cast a shadow over it, the shutters were closed and damp was creeping up the brown stucco; it was the most unprepossessing place Mike had ever seen, and he wondered if maybe Pierluigi hadn't traded one jail for another.

Pierluigi himself answered the bell. "No one will work at the villa," he told Mike with a faint sardonic smile, "not since Claudia died. So you see, I'm left to fend for myself."

Mike glanced at him, startled; he hadn't thought that they would be alone, and after all, this man was an accused murderer.

"Don't worry," Pierluigi said calmly, "I'm not going to kill you, Mr. Preston, I merely want to talk to you."

He showed Mike into the study. There was a large rolltop desk against one wall; its drawers had been flung open and there were piles of papers everywhere.

"Please forgive the mess," he said, "but I'm still searching for the evidence that will prove my claim—that I'm Poppy Mallory's legitimate heir. Take a seat, Mr. Preston. A drink? You probably need one after your long drive. It's freezing out today, though the temperature in here doesn't seem too much higher!"

He threw another log on the smoking fire and Mike watched him covertly. Despite his recent incarceration, Pierluigi was as immaculately dressed as the last time he'd seen him: pristine white shirt, dark suit, a plain black silk tie . . . in mourning for his sister, Claudia? But his time in jail had left its scars; he was thin, the well-cut suit hung on him, and his hand trembled as he poured the drinks.

"And have you found the evidence?" Mike asked, sipping the whiskey and waiting for it to reach his frozen fingers and toes.

"Not yet." Pierluigi looked him in the eye. "I really wanted to ask you the same question."

Mike stared at the amber-gold liquid in his glass; it was a beautiful glass, fine yet heavy—whoever had purchased it had had good taste. "If I had," he said quietly, "I wouldn't be at liberty to tell you."

Pierluigi sighed. "Mr. Preston," he said, choosing his words carefully. "I would be willing to be very generous to a man who could prove that my sister and I were the true heirs."

Mike glanced at him, surprised.

"Shall we say, half of Poppy Mallory's fortune?" Pierluigi suggested.

Mike placed his glass gently back on the table and stood up. "I think it's probably better if I leave now," he said coldly.

Pierluigi sighed. "This is not exactly the way it seems, and it's important to me, Mr. Preston."

"Poppy's fortune seems to be important to a great number of people," Mike said, walking to the door, "but that doesn't mean to say it necessarily belongs to them."

Pierluigi's pained dark eyes met his across the room. "You see," he said, "if it were decided that my sister and I were, in fact, the Mallory heirs, I would like the money to be used to create a charitable foundation in her memory—a charity to help young people . . . to see that they get to college. Education is the savior of all of us, Mr. Preston. It's only in the private power of the mind that we are finally free."

Mike shook his head, puzzled. "There's nothing I can do to help you," he said.

Pierluigi escorted him to the door in silence and their good-byes were brief. Mike looked back once as he drove away; the door was closed and the shuttered house, forever in shadow, looked even more brooding and secretive.

He thought about what had just happened. Pierluigi had offered him a bribe—an enormous bribe—to get his hands on Poppy's fortune, and yet, even though his business needed finance badly, he hadn't wanted the money for himself. He was willing to give it all away. But Pierluigi was also an accused killer; maybe he'd figured he wouldn't need the money now anyway . . . all he wanted was a memorial to Claudia. But if he'd loved his sister that much, then why would he have killed her? Mike remembered Pierluigi's haunted eyes. Maybe there was no motive, unless it was that he'd loved his sister very much—and maybe too well?

It was dark by the time he arrived back at the Villa Castelletto, and if he'd been cold before, now he was freezing. He needed a drink and he was starving. Fixing his usual ham and cheese on crusty bread, he lathered the sandwich with mustard and sent a silent prayer of thanks to Lieber for instructing the caretakers to keep the villa warm.

He ate standing at the kitchen table, sipping the red wine he liked, while his thoughts went back once more to Poppy. He was almost afraid to discover what had happened to her, and to Franco.

Finishing his sandwich, he grabbed the bottle of wine and carried it upstairs. The parrot blinked at him from his cage as he turned on the lamp, and Mike grinned at him. "Sorry, Luchay," he said, "didn't mean to startle you. I'll bet you're hungry too. Here you go." He filled the parrot's dish with seeds and then he laughed. Loneliness and the Villa Castelletto must be getting to him; he was talking to the parrot, just the way Poppy must have done.

He put a match to the fire that the caretaker had left ready in the grate, holding out his hands for a moment in the flames. Poppy's collection of notebooks lay on the pretty little desk, waiting for him. He let the parrot out of his cage and it fluttered onto the back of his chair as he sat down and began to read. "Just like old times, Luchay, isn't it?" Mike said.

CHAPTER 59

1 9 3 2 ,   I T A L Y

Franco's enemy had laid his plans well; it was no new territorial battle he
was after, only the settling of an old score. Revenge sometimes had to
wait a long time in their world, but simply because time had passed
didn't mean it was forgotten. An open sore remained open—until a
death healed it.

It took the top men in the Malvasi Family just hours to find out who
was the perpetrator of the deed, and just a few days to extract their own
revenge. The body of the thin-faced, sharp-suited Dottore was found
floating in the Bay of Naples, the puckered scar that ran from eye to
mouth making his bloated face even more grotesque in death than it had
been in life. He had been expelled from the Malvasi Family twenty years
before for what Franco had judged as unnecessary violence. He had
waited patiently for a chink in Franco's armor. And he had finally found
it.

The Dottore had had one of the servants at the villa in his pay for
many years, he'd known all Franco's moves. When he'd heard that
Franco had gone away—alone—he'd known that, at long last, he had a
chance. And when his spy had told him that the car was to meet Franco
on the road outside Genoa, he had driven there, parking a mile away
from the rendezvous point along the same road. He'd expected it to be
difficult; he would have to shoot Franco as he drove by, but the rain had

helped him. The Dottore had been forced to switch on his headlights in the heavy storm and, assuming it was his own car, Franco had slowed down. He'd been an easy target. The only miscalculation had been that he'd expected Franco to be in the passenger seat and that's where he'd directed his bullets.

Franco had thought it was the end. Shattered glass flew into his face and a bullet grazed his head. He felt the burn of hot metal in his chest and heard Poppy cry out next to him. The car skidded across the rain-slick road and, with blood streaming down his face and the terrible searing pain in his chest, he fought to stop it from turning over as it slid into the bank; it came to a stop with its front wheels in the ditch. The headlights of the waiting car had dipped and flickered as the engine was started, and Franco remembered hearing the tires squeal as it drove off. And then everything was silent and the night became even blacker as he slumped, unconscious, over the wheel.

He lost all concept of time, he had no idea whether minutes or even hours had passed. All he was aware of when he came to was the searing pain in his lungs and the warm blood trickling from his temple. And then he remembered Poppy.

"God, oh, God, what have I done to her?" he groaned, stretching out his hand to find her. He touched her arm; it was warm and he could feel the stickiness he knew was blood, but it was too dark to see anything. He fumbled desperately with the key in the ignition, willing it to turn, willing the lights to go on . . . the headlights beamed suddenly, illuminating the hedgerow, and the dashboard glowed green. He could see her —and he almost wished he couldn't. She was half sitting, half lying in her seat, just as she had been when he'd woken her to tell her they were almost there. As she'd turned to speak to him, the bullets had raked the right side of her head and body. "Oh, my darling," he groaned, touching her beautiful hair, matted with blood. He put his hand to her breast and felt the faint flutter of her heart . . . she was still alive, but she needed help, immediately.

Franco staggered from the car, staring wildly around him into the night. His assassin might still be lurking by the side of the road, waiting to take aim. But all that mattered was getting help for Poppy. He stumbled determinedly into the night, clutching a handkerchief to the wound on his head, wheezing as the bullet burned in his lungs.

The Malvasi guards had been patrolling near the waiting car almost a mile away when they'd heard the sound of gunfire through the storm. They were in the car in a flash, driving through the rain without headlights toward the sound of shooting. It was a miracle they didn't run Franco down as he loomed in front of the car in the middle of the road.

"Help," he cried as they ran toward him, "help her. Please help her."

The Sisters at the Ospedale Croce Rossa in Genoa were used to nursing all kinds of patients, and praying for them, too, but in their private chapel morning and night, they prayed extra hard for forgiveness for the crime boss Franco Malvasi and for the woman who'd been brought in with him, more dead than alive.

Franco had two bullet wounds to the head, but in both cases the bullets had just grazed the skull, shattering bone but not penetrating the brain. Nevertheless, it took skilled surgeons four hours to remove fragments of bone from the cerebrum, and another set of skilled men to remove the bullet from his left lung and attempt to repair the damage. Within days he was sitting up in his hospital bed, bandaged and weak, and asking after Poppy.

"She is gravely ill," they told him, "only time and God will tell now." A bullet had penetrated her brain on the right side—not deeply, but enough to do certain damage. Other bullets had penetrated her right arm and shoulder, but because she had been twisted onto her side, somehow she had protected her body with her arms and no vital organs had been damaged. There was a chance she would live, they said, but no one knew yet how badly damaged the brain was.

They wouldn't allow him to see her. "She is too ill to know you are there," they told him, "and you are too ill to go." He ordered bodyguards outside her door, night and day, but they were dismissed by the Sisters.

"This hospital is a house of God," they said sorrowfully, "we are saving lives, not killing them. There will be no guns and no violence in here." But they made no attempt to remove the men outside Franco's room; they understood the risk was too great.

When Franco was told two weeks later he could leave the hospital, Poppy still hadn't opened her eyes; she hadn't moved, she hadn't spoken. He went to see her, clutching a gardenia in his hand. She was lying in bed, her head swathed in bandages. Her eyes were tightly shut and he could hear her breathing. It was strange, he could see her there before him, but yet she wasn't there. Who knew where Poppy was in her dreams now? Placing the gardenia on her pillow, Franco kissed her gently and left her to her dreams.

He refused to leave the hospital until she awoke and he knew she was all right. "But Signore," they protested, "you can't stay; we shall need your room . . ."

"Let me stay," he said, "and I promise that next year your hospital will have a new wing with a hundred more rooms!"

It was three weeks before Poppy opened her eyes. He was sitting by her bedside and she gazed at him mistily. "Franco?" she asked. Her voice was faint and husky, but she'd recognized him.

Franco smiled at her. "It'll be all right now, Poppy. You'll see, everything will be all right. Soon you will be better. Then you can have whatever you want. Just tell me."

She smiled. "Gardenias," she said.

He filled her room with them until the Sisters protested that their overpowering scent was too much.

Poppy grew a little better day by day, but when the doctors told him it was going to take a long time—months, maybe even a year—he had her transferred by special ambulance to a private clinic in Naples.

He filled her suite with flowers, books, pretty nightdresses and robes, a silver mirror so she could check the progress of her poor shorn hair, shaved off when they operated; he gave her presents of all kinds and he went every day to see her, monitoring her progress personally with the doctors.

"There is some residual damage," they told him, "but the Signora has been lucky; the bullet didn't penetrate the part of the brain that affects movement, so there is no paralysis. But she will have some impairment of her memory . . . we don't yet know how drastic. By the way, she has no memory whatsoever of the accident. She thinks that the car skidded in the rain—and that she was driving. It would be wiser not to disillusion her."

Poppy made a quicker recovery than they had anticipated, and two months later they told her she could go home.

Franco sat by her bed, wishing he could keep her there, even if just another week. But it was time to let her go.

"What do you want to do?" he asked.

She smiled at him, looking like a young girl with her new short hair. "I'll go home," she said simply.

"To Montespan?"

"Montespan? Why of course not, to the Villa Castelletto." She frowned, puzzled. "Isn't that our home, Franco?"

He nodded gravely. "I suppose so."

"I always think of it as my home," she said, bewildered, "but then, I'm so confused about so many things these days."

"It's yours, Poppy," he said, "whatever you want is yours."

Her guileless blue eyes were suddenly shrewd again. "You?" she said softly.

He smiled. "That's the only thing I must deny you."

"Then it's good-bye again, Franco."

"This time it's good-bye."

She didn't seem to hear him. "I must go to Montespan first," she cried, "to get Luchay. Poor, poor darling, how could I have forgotten him! And to see if Rogan has returned."

"Rogan?"

Her eyes narrowed and she looked at him slyly. "What?" she murmured vaguely. "Poor Luchay, he must be so lonely. I hate being lonely. I'll fetch him and then we'll go back to the villa, for good." She smiled sweetly at him. "There's something so satisfying about those words Franco, 'for good, forever . . .' "

He gazed at her sadly; one moment she was his old Poppy, the next she was like an elusive piece of quicksilver as the thoughts and memories slid through her brain and scattered from her grasp. God forgive me, he said silently, for what I have done to her.

CHAPTER 60

Angel was sitting in the garden at the Villa d'Oro when she read the newspaper headline: ASSASSINATION ATTEMPT ON FRANCO MALVASI, CRIME CHIEF. But it was the final words of the report that riveted her attention. *Malvasi was with a female companion who was seriously injured in the hail of bullets. She has been identified as the Signora Poppy Mallory.*

The newspaper rustled to the grass as an image of Poppy's body, riddled with bullets, came to her mind, and she buried her face in her hands, overcome by pity and sadness. Why had Poppy been with a man like that? Everyone knew about him, everyone knew what he was. . . . "Oh, Poppy, Poppy," she groaned. "We had so much, how could it all have come to this?"

Impulsively she got to her feet; she must go to her, she couldn't just let her lie there, alone and maybe dying . . . after all, they'd loved each other like sisters once . . . Snatching up the newspaper she saw that Poppy was in the Croce Rossa Hospital in Genoa . . . she would go there right away.

"Mama? What are you doing out here, all alone?" her daughter Helena called to her from across the lawn, and Angel lifted her arm automatically in response. Sometimes Helena's voice sounded almost normal; she lip-read very well and if she could see a person, she always understood what they were saying, but as she'd grown older, her childhood memory of sound had diminished and now, at thirty-three, most of her words were just approximations of the correct vocal patterns. Now only Angel and Maria-Cristina could really understand what Helena was saying, and her frustration when they took her out shopping or for lunch made her childishly angry and tearful. Because she was so beautiful, tall and blond with heavenly blue eyes—deep as blue grottoes and beguilingly innocent —people would turn to stare at her, aiming sidelong glances of sympathy at her mother.

The trouble was that Helena had the mentality of a child; Angel's determination to protect her from the hurtful scorn of being different from other children had not only isolated her, it had retarded her. Helena had never gone to school like Maria-Cristina; she'd stayed home by her mother's side and for years Angel had kept up the pretense that there was nothing wrong. She'd smiled when people stared at Helena, puzzled, explaining that she was a very shy child; she'd answered the questions that Helena didn't hear; as a child she'd never allowed her to go to parties, and later to grown-up dances, saying she was too "fragile." She had refused to allow Helena to grow up. When they'd finally left Felipe and Aleksandr and returned to California, twelve-year-old Helena had been as dependent as a child of six.

At the Santa Vittoria ranch, Rosalia had noticed what was happening and she'd warned Angel about it. She'd thought, sympathetically, it was because Angel had lost her son that had made her so superprotective. Helena had grown from a sweet child into a childish young woman, still isolated from any normal life, but happy and cosseted within her own small world, where everybody understood her and everybody loved her. After all, she knew nothing else. She had the innocence of a child, but she also had the face and body of a lovely young woman. She never even met anyone outside the Abrego/Konstant family circle and friends, other than the doctors and specialists to whom she continued to go for treatment, and Angel was to blame herself forever afterward for not even noticing what was happening to her.

Helena strolled across the lawn swinging her tennis racquet lazily. She was wearing a short white dress and her bare legs were tanned by the summer sun. She was so graceful, Angel thought sadly, she walked like a dancer . . . and maybe she could have been one, if she hadn't held her back because of her own stupid fears.

"Mama? Why don't you come to the tennis court to watch me? You promised you would . . . I missed you, Mama," she added, but her words were only a jumble of discordant sounds.

"Sorry, darling, I was just reading the newspaper and I completely forgot about the time. I'll come right now."

"It's too late, Maria-Cristina got bored. She doesn't want to play anymore."

That was typical of her other daughter, Angel thought, she had the attention span of a butterfly—and a similar life-style, flitting from man to man the way a butterfly went from flower to flower.

Maria-Cristina had flirted her way through Santa Barbara's small society and then moved on to San Francisco. She had been the most popular debutante of 1916, and at the end of the season she'd become engaged to the prize among the eligible young men. Three months later she had broken it off and started on a career of parties and engagements that lasted until she was twenty-five years old and everyone was saying Maria-Cristina Rinardi had left it too late to marry, she was over the hill.

She'd paused long enough in her headlong pursuit of enjoyment to realize that what they were saying was probably true. Within a month she was re-engaged to the devoted young man who had asked her to marry him when she was still only eighteen. They were married three months later with full pomp and ceremony and four hundred guests had danced at their wedding. But Maria-Cristina had seen no reason why a husband should interfere with her usual round of parties and flirtations, and the only difference marriage had seemed to make to her was that now she entertained in her own home. Her young husband's devotion soon began to wear thin, but she scoffed at his requests that she settle down and behave like a responsible married woman. Their divorce three years later had caused a scandal that had necessitated a year abroad in order for things to calm down.

Maria-Cristina's life had reverted to that of a carefree single woman; she'd acted as though she hadn't a care in the world. But she'd also had no man who really cared about her. Until she met Bill Aston.

Bill was forty years old and a rich bachelor from the East Coast. He had a Manhattan apartment, a summer house in East Hampton, and a rambling old family place on the ocean at Palm Beach where he went to play polo. He was well educated and sophisticated and, for once, Maria-Cristina was overwhelmed. After they were married, Angel had thought with relief that at last her daughter had grown up.

For a while Maria-Cristina had played the fashionable East Coast wife; she'd seemed to enjoy giving the smart little cocktail parties in Manhattan, the charity luncheons in East Hampton, and the chic black-tie dinners in Palm Beach, and she'd basked in her new social fame as "the beautiful, elegant Mrs. Bill Aston." For a while it had seemed the perfect marriage—and then she'd had the baby: Paul.

Then just two months ago, she'd telephoned Angel to say that she was coming back to Italy—Bill was divorcing her. Hoping they could patch things up, Angel had asked her what the trouble was, but Maria-Cristina had just shrugged. "The same old thing, Mama," she'd sighed restlessly, "boredom."

When Aleksandr had refused the title after Felipe's death, seven-year-old Paul was next in succession, and he had become Paolo, the Barone Rinardi. But the fact that she had a child to look after seemed to make very little difference to Maria-Cristina's wild ways; as always, she'd just shrugged away her responsibilities. She never really looked after him; Fiametta did.

I'm as guilty as Poppy, Angel thought resignedly. I was unsuccessful as a wife and it seems I'm unsuccessful as a mother. All I ever gave my children was love, and it seems that wasn't enough. She remembered Poppy as she'd last seen her—slender and still elegant even in a linen shirt and jodhpurs, and the black sombrero she had always worn when riding. She thought of the question Poppy had asked her, and that she'd refused to answer. Oh, Poppy, she thought, sorrowfully. Don't you understand? That it really doesn't matter which daughter was yours. They don't belong to you or to me . . . they are themselves.

When she went to bed that night, she said her prayers, as she always did, for Aleksandr and Helena and Maria-Cristina, but this time she added a prayer for Poppy, too, asking for God's guidance. Should she go to Poppy as her heart told her she must? Or was the first priority still the safety of her secret? But no answer came from heaven, and in the end the decision was hers to make alone. She knew she could not risk seeing Poppy again. It could only lead to disaster.

CHAPTER *61*

1933, ITALY

The farm looked overgrown and neglected when the workmen came to Montespan and packed all the things. They ignored Luchay, crouching worriedly on his stand, as they crated the paintings and the clocks and the vases, the silver and the books, and the baskets of dried flowers. His sharp round eyes blinked nervously as they carried out the trunks with Poppy's vast collection of clothes and personal belongings, and they laughed when the parrot squawked in rage as they thrust him into his golden cage, throwing a hood over it, shutting out the light.

The truck rumbled through France and into Italy. Every now and then it stopped, and they thrust a bowl and some seeds into his cage, but they never took off his hood, and the parrot simply crouched on his perch, fluffing his feathers and hiding his head under his wing in fear. At last the truck stopped and the big doors were thrown open.

"*Allons-y,*" the burly French driver shouted, swinging the parrot's cage clumsily from the van.

As the man carried the cage, swinging violently, up the curving staircase, the parrot lifted his head tentatively, as though listening for Poppy's familiar voice, but there was only the sound of great activity: the whoosh of a broom on the ground and the slap of a wet mop on a marble floor, the squeak of chamois leather on a windowpane, and the tread of heavy feet. There was the smell of fresh paint and of soap . . . and the sweet familiar scent of gardenias.

"And what have we here?" a woman's voice demanded. The linen hood was whisked off and the parrot blinked its eyes in the bright sunlight fluttering its wings fearfully.

"Ah, the poor little creature, he is so frightened!" the woman exclaimed, opening the door and holding out her hand to him, but Luchay shied away, edging back along his perch to the farthest corner of the cage.

"Leave him," Franco said quietly, "he only likes Poppy. For now, just see that he has food and water and is kept quiet."

They placed Luchay's cage and his beautiful bejeweled stand near an open window in a large sunny bedroom. Men toiled in the garden below, cutting back the overgrown shrubs and creepers, pulling up weeds and re-creating lawns. The scents of the garden mingled with the gardenias and the bird peered around inquisitively, tilting his head from side to side, listening to the bird noises and the yapping somewhere of a little dog. A long white ambulance with a red cross on its side rolled smoothly to a stop by the steps and Franco hurried forward to help as they carried Poppy on a stretcher into the house.

"Are we home, then?" she asked in a clear voice as they brought her into the bedroom.

Luchay ruffled his feathers. "Poppy *cara*, Poppy *chérie*, Poppy darling!" he squawked, fluttering his wings excitedly.

"Luchay? Is that you, at last?" she called. "Ah, come here, my sweet, come to me . . ." Franco carried his cage across to the bed where they'd propped her against a mound of fresh white linen pillows, and the parrot fluttered unsteadily onto her outstretched hand. "Poppy, Poppy . . . Poppy . . ." he muttered.

"I missed you, too, Luchay," she said softly. "I need you, my friend."

Poppy's voice sounded tired, her shaven head was covered with the fluffy copper-amber sheen of new hair, and an angry red scar ran from her right temple across her skull. Her cheekbones jutted sharply and her blue eyes were sunken and tired; even her freckles seemed to have faded into the translucent whiteness of her skin. And the bony fingers that stroked the parrot's wing were trembling as though they'd never stop.

A woman in a rustling starched white uniform came to stand by the bed and Franco said, "Poppy, the nurse is here to take care of you. She will see that you have everything you need."

"I'd rather be alone," Poppy said wearily, "too many nurses, too many doctors . . . ask her to go away."

"Not yet, Poppy, you still need help."

Taking her hand in his, Franco gazed at her with a look of mingled tenderness and sadness and then he said, "I'll let you rest now. I'll be back to see you when you're feeling stronger."

"Am I home then, Franco?" she asked, her eyes closing wearily.

He nodded. "You're home now, Poppy," he said, bending to kiss her cheek.

For the first few weeks Poppy was quiet and listless, but with the arrival of spring she seemed to get stronger and she finally ventured outdoors. Luchay crouched on her shoulder as she wandered hesitantly through the newly immaculate gardens, with tears coursing down her cheeks. "This isn't 'home,' Luchay," she cried, "the garden there was all tangled and green and mysterious . . . it was a special place. Why are we here? This isn't the place."

The nurse came running; she looked anxious and later she telephoned Franco. The next day he came to see her. He'd noticed that sometimes she would welcome him with a look of joy, and at others she would just stare at him, puzzled, as though he were a stranger, disturbing her chosen solitude.

Today Poppy was haughty and autocratic. "I've dismissed the gardeners," she told him abruptly. "I don't want manicured lawns and flower beds. I want weeds and green-growing creepers that hide things." Her eyes grew puzzled again. "Isn't this the place, Franco?" she asked. "Isn't this 'home?' I thought it was . . ."

"Don't worry," he soothed her, "it will be exactly as you wish. Whatever makes you happy, Poppy."

The next person she fired was the nurse. "I don't need a nurse anymore," she told Franco when he came hurrying back to the villa. "Besides," she added with that sly, knowing look in her eyes, "she's not my nurse. She's my *keeper*."

He nodded. "You're right," he said, "it's time she went." The following week a new "housekeeper" appeared, but she, too, didn't last long.

"We don't need all these people around us," Poppy whispered to Luchay as they watched her march down the drive, suitcase in hand. "We shall be alone together, Luchay, just you and me. Until Rogan comes home."

Summer slipped into autumn, and autumn into winter. Franco came to see her at Christmas, his big car loaded with gaily wrapped parcels that she never even opened. She refused to talk to him and just sat by the fire all day, staring into its flames. But despite everything, he still came once a month to see her.

In the evenings Poppy would eat a simple meal prepared for her by the woman who came in from the village, and she'd drink a glass of wine. Then she'd walk slowly upstairs to her room and sit at her desk and begin to write. "Sometimes I know it all, Luchay," she'd say, looking at her scribbled words sorrowfully, "and sometimes nothing. I thought if I wrote it all down I could capture my memories, and when I forget, they'll be here to remind me."

The next time she was told Franco was coming, she went to a great deal of trouble to look nice. Her beautiful, rich red hair, streaked at the temples with white, had grown back again, and she washed it and brushed it until it shone, pinning it up with the diamond stars. She rummaged in the vast armoires that held a quarter of a century's worth of her clothes, until she found the ice-gray satin gown with the wide pink sash that she'd worn in her portrait. As always, she wore her pearls and she plucked a gardenia from the dozens of growing plants that Franco kept her supplied with, winter and summer.

When he arrived, she was standing by the window of the ornate salon, waiting for him, her head tilted to one side, a smile on her lips and the gardenia clutched in her hand.

"Franco," she said clearly, "I want you to see something. Come closer, darling. Look at me."

Luchay skittered agitatedly along his stand as Franco walked slowly toward her, his face as gray as the ice-satin gown.

"What is it, Poppy?" he asked. "Why are you dressed like this . . . ?"

"Don't I look like my portrait, Franco?" she asked softly. "Once I was that woman, painted by Sargent. But now look . . . see the scar on my skull, and here, this puckered red flesh on my neck, and here on my shoulders, and along my arm. . . . There are other scars, Franco, but you can't see them; nobody can, only me. But you see, I'm not that woman in the portrait anymore; she's gone, Franco, gone forever. For you, the reality is not this aging shell of a half-mad woman . . . she's the woman in the painting on your bedroom wall. That memory is *real*, Franco. Keep it. But the other one has gone forever. She has set you free."

"Poppy," he cried brokenly, "you don't know what you're saying."

"Oh, yes, Franco, darling, today I do know. I don't want you to come back here again. Please, Franco. Say good-bye to me now, while the memory of what we were still lingers. And then leave me to my solitude and my jumbled half-world. You see, I don't need anyone anymore."

Franco bent to kiss her hand, and then with a choked cry he turned and walked rapidly from the room. The gardenia she was holding, with its creamy petals that withered the moment it was plucked from the tree, fell unnoticed to the ground.

After a while, Poppy walked slowly through the ornate red and gold salon, across the empty marble hallway, and lifting her long skirts gracefully, she mounted the grand curving staircase under the painted cupola of nymphs and cupids, and walked back to her room.

"It's just you and me now, Luchay," she said wearily, "and the past, for that will never leave us alone." A puzzled frown crossed her face. "There's just one more thing to be done—if only I can remember what it is. . . ."

She remembered sometime later . . . was it the next week, the next year? She couldn't recall.

"I must write my will, Luchay," she said as they sat together at her desk after supper. "Of course, I don't need to worry about Rogan," she added confidently, "he'll take care of everything when he comes home. But I must write this while I remember—because you know, Luchay, sometimes I don't even recall that I have a daughter."

This is my Last Will and Testament, she wrote in her tremulous hand, *made this fourth day of November, 1933. I leave everything to my child. I've never known her, but she is my daughter. Angel Konstant Rinardi will tell you who she is.* She signed it in slow, careful letters, but the trembling hand betrayed her with a splutter of black ink.

"Oh, and a note for my son!" she cried, taking a fresh sheet of paper. *Rogan,* she wrote. *Sometimes my memory defeats me, and in case I don't remember when I see you, I've written this will because you didn't know about my daughter. I wanted to make sure she was taken care of too. But, of course, you will make sure of that.*

"I'm tired now, Luchay," she said, walking slowly to the big white bed. "Tomorrow we'll call the lawyer; we'll give him this to take care of, and then I know I can sleep without worrying about my children anymore. They will have their inheritance after all."

CHAPTER 62

As the Swissair flight circled Los Angeles, Mike stared at the familiar grid of neat houses and blue swimming pools glinting in the eternal sunshine, and the endless lines of cars snaking along the broad freeways that bound the city together. He'd spent two weeks in Venice, replaying his tape recordings and analyzing his notes made at the Villa Castelletto, thinking angrily that he'd come to another dead end. Had Poppy really gone to her grave without seeing Rogan again? And without knowing her daughter? And if she didn't know, then who did?

He'd recalled Hilliard Konstant's sardonic glance as he told him excitedly of his find in the attics. "Have a glass of manzanilla," he'd said gleefully, "and tell me all about it." Hilliard was Greg Konstant's son; he was the only person alive who'd known Angel and her three children, and yet he claimed he remembered nothing at all about them. He'd bet that the old man had been playing a game with him all along, giving him the freedom of his big mausoleum of a library and telling him to get on with it and find out for himself! Now he had most of the story—but he was sure that Hilliard knew the rest. And that's what he was in L.A. to find out.

He thought of the meeting he'd just had in Geneva with Lieber; the lawyer had confirmed that Orlando would not be informed that he was one of the heirs to Poppy's estate until they knew the identity of the daughter, and the name of the other heir or heiress—if, in fact, there was one.

"But let us not forget that when we tell Orlando that he is Poppy's great-grandson," he'd said, "we must also tell him the name of his great-grandfather. Franco Malvasi. One of the most notorious Mafia chiefs of the past century!"

Mike remembered Lauren Hunter, maybe still half hoping to inherit. He'd thought about her quite a lot over the past few weeks, and he'd tried to analyze why. It wasn't pity he felt for her, and Lauren wouldn't want that; she had shouldered her responsibilities and, with love as the motivating force in her life, Mike knew she would work things out. It would be tough, but Lauren would do it. All he knew was that he'd never felt like this before in his life, and, as the plane touched down on the tarmac and taxied toward the terminal, he knew that for once the past and Poppy Mallory would have to wait. He was going to see Lauren.

It was four in the afternoon and Denny's was pretty quiet. Mike saw her at once; she was taking an order from a customer with two small boys, and she was smiling at them as she carried the booster seats for their chairs. She wore her long reddish-blond hair loose today, swept up at the sides in a couple of tortoiseshell combs, and in her short black skirt and white blouse, she looked pretty and efficient. Lauren smiled again, patting the head of the smallest child as she turned away. Then she saw him and her beautiful smile grew wider. "Hi," she called, walking over to him. "What are you doing here?"

"I had to be in L.A., so I came to see you," Mike said honestly.

She blushed, but he could tell she was pleased. "Thanks again for the teddy bear," she said, "it really made Maria's Christmas."

"I'd like to meet Maria," he said, "she sounds like a great kid."

"Would you really?" Lauren asked eagerly, but then her eyes clouded. "Well, I'm not sure," she said, "you know how it is . . . Maria has her schedule and I have mine. It gets pretty complicated with the baby-sitters and all."

"What time d'you finish here?" Mike asked abruptly.

"At four-thirty—in half an hour."

"Good. I'll meet you then."

"Okay," she agreed, half reluctantly.

Even though the sunshine was bright, it was a cool day for Los Angeles and Lauren was wearing a red fake-fur bomber jacket. "My Christmas present to myself," she told him when he admired it.

Mike remembered Aria's beautiful sheared green beaver, which had cost a fortune and which, if she wasn't the heiress, Carraldo was going to have to pay for, and he thought how unfair fate could be. "Okay," he said, "what next?"

"I have to pick Maria up from the baby-minder."

"Great. Let's do it. I'll follow you in my car."

She lived in a walk-up apartment in an old block just off Ventura Boulevard in Studio City, and Mike helped her upstairs with Maria's stroller and baggage while she carried the baby.

"She sure is pretty," he called as the baby smiled at him over Lauren's shoulder.

"The prettiest," she agreed firmly.

It was one of those typical small L.A. apartments, open plan with a combination living/dining room and kitchen. "There's just one bedroom," Lauren told him, "and a bathroom. That's it. But it's big enough for us at the moment, isn't it, Maria? Would you like some coffee," she asked, "while I fix her supper?"

"Sure." He took a seat on a stool at the kitchen counter, watching as Lauren put a pot of coffee on and began preparing Maria's food. He thought she looked better, a little rounder and a bit glossier, as though she was looking after herself a bit more. It suited her. She was a lovely girl—or would be if she could ever lose that faint frown of worry.

Maria was in her playpen, crawling around and testing her budding teeth on her toys. She was surely a cute kid, Mike thought, with all that dark hair and such big blue eyes. Maria caught his glance and smiled at him, waving a small Raggedy Ann doll by its leg.

"Hi," he called, "hi there, Maria." She smiled at him again. "How old is she now?" he asked as Lauren placed a cup of coffee in front of him.

"Almost eighteen months."

"She's cute. So, where d'you want to go for dinner? French, Italian, Chinese, Japanese?"

Lauren laughed. "How did you know it was my night off?"

"I didn't," he grinned, "I was just hoping."

"I'll have to get a baby-sitter," she said doubtfully, "and I don't really have anything smart to wear."

"I hate getting dressed up, anywhere that takes blue jeans is good enough for me."

She sighed, but she was smiling at him. "You're a very kind man, Mike, you know that?"

"Not me." He grinned. "I'm the tough investigative journalist, remember?"

"I remember. I was going to ask you about Poppy, but now you can tell me over dinner." She put Maria in her high chair and he watched as she began to feed her. There was something puzzling about the baby, but he couldn't put his finger on it. Something that wasn't quite right . . .

"I'd better go," he told her. "I've got a few calls to make. I'll pick you up about seven-thirty?"

"Great," she said, "I'll be ready."

They went to a little French place on Melrose and Lauren was so obviously thrilled that it made him feel good. She was wearing a simple dark blue jersey dress with a wide leather belt that emphasized the smallness of her waist; her long reddish-blond hair was brushed into a smooth fall and she wore just enough makeup to enhance her gray-blue eyes.

"You can't imagine what a treat this is," she told him honestly. "I haven't been anywhere this nice since before Maria was born."

Mike noticed she didn't say "before my Mom died," but "before Maria was born." Lauren had a positive attitude and he hoped it would help when she heard that she wasn't the Mallory heiress. She listened, fascinated, as he told her the story of Poppy, or as much as he knew of it so far.

"Poor Poppy," she said at last, "everything seemed to go wrong for her. What happened in the end?"

"I don't know yet," he replied with a sigh, "but I think I know who does. That's why I'm back in California. I'm going to see him tomorrow. But you see, Lauren, I'm afraid there seems no hope now of your being related to Poppy. The Mallory name must have been just a coincidence."

"I didn't really expect it anyway," she told him honestly. "It was a long shot—sort of like winning at Las Vegas. I hope Aria gets the money; she sounds as though she needs it."

"Not more than you do," he said, thinking of the baby. "Lauren, what's wrong with Maria?"

She dropped her fork, shocked. "What do you mean?" she asked nervously.

He took her hand across the table. "There is something wrong with her, isn't there? Why don't you tell me?"

Lauren looked at their clasped hands and then at him. His eyes were understanding; she felt she could trust him with her secret. "I don't know exactly what it is," she said quietly. "I think there's something wrong with her mentally. She just doesn't respond, you see, and she doesn't try to talk. Most kids her age are already saying 'Mommy' and 'Daddy' and trying out new words and sounds, but Maria is so quiet."

Now he knew what had puzzled him. The baby had never made a sound the whole time he was there. "What are you doing about it?" he asked.

"Nothing. I've been afraid to admit it, even to myself, I even have nightmares about it. You're the first person I've told," she added, tears lurking at the corners of her eyes. "I'm afraid they'll take her away from me, you see, and put her in one of those homes. I can't afford to pay for treatment or special doctors. I suppose I'm just putting off the evil day, but I can't lose her, Mike, I just can't! Maria's all I have left." She looked at him pleadingly. "I suppose you're going to tell me I was wrong, but I don't think it's done any harm, after all, she's only a baby."

"I'm sure you haven't harmed her," he said, "but at some point it's only fair to find out what's wrong, and whether she can be helped."

Lauren hung her head, staring at the napkin she was twisting in her fingers. "I know," she said in a small voice. "It's just tough to face it alone."

"Look," he said, his heart melting under her glance. "I'll find out the name of the best doctor for her to see. I'll make an appointment for you, he'll examine her and maybe do a few tests—then at least you'll know what's wrong. It'll be my pleasure to pay for it, Lauren."

She looked at him hesitantly—in one way what he was offering was tempting, but in another it was frightening, because the truth might be more than she could face. But he was right, it was Maria's life she had to think of, not her own. "I couldn't let you pay," she said quickly, "that wouldn't be right."

"You're not letting me. Maria is. Let's call it a birthday present."

She smiled. "It's not her birthday."

"Let's pretend," Mike said, squeezing her hand. "I'll call you tomorrow about the appointment. And then I'm off to Santa Barbara and the Rancho Santa Vittoria, to get the truth out of old Hilliard Konstant."

Hilliard had aged in the three months since Mike had seen him. "I'm fine, just fine," he said even more irritably than Mike remembered. "What are you doing here? Come to tell me you've found Poppy Mallory's heiress, have you?" A malicious grin flickered across his face as he poured two glasses of manzanilla. "I missed you, you know, young man. I got used to having you in the library, poring over my books."

"Yeah, but I have the feeling you could have saved me a lot of time," Mike said bluntly.

"I suppose I've you to thank for sending that abominable Italian woman here to see me. Paolo Rinardi's wife?"

"Francesca," Mike said with a grin, imagining the two of them drinking sherry together. "But the bonus was that you got to meet Aria."

"She's a nice girl," Hilliard admitted thoughtfully. "Strange to think I still have some family after all. I wasn't much interested before, and I guess I just never gave much thought to the Italian side. Of course, she's Maria-Cristina's granddaughter, pretty like her, too, but I doubt if she has the same temperament. Aria doesn't look the wild sort to me."

"I thought you didn't remember Maria-Cristina," Mike said.

Hilliard's pale eyes narrowed slyly. "Well, you know, some days I remember things, some days I don't. It's one of the privileges of growing old."

"Okay, truth time, Hilliard." Mike put down his glass and faced him, challengingly. "I'm going to tell you exactly what I've found out about Poppy and then you can tell me what you know. *Exactly what you know.* Is it a deal?"

Hilliard drained his sherry, and then rubbed his hands together delightedly. "Go on then," he said. "I'm dying to hear."

He listened carefully as Mike told him the story, asking a question here and there, and nodding in agreement occasionally as though it tallied with things he already knew.

"And so you see," Mike said finally, "I'm at a dead end again, Hilliard. I know one daughter was Poppy's, but I still don't know which one. *But I believe you do.*"

"I didn't know about the son, Rogan," Hilliard replied slowly. "Does that mean there's someone else claiming the money now?"

"There is, and his claim is valid. He's Poppy's great-grandson."

"I didn't know about Numéro Seize and all that stuff either," Hilliard said. "And I'm sure my father and Angel didn't know. But she knew about the Mafia boss. Not the details, but she'd read about it in the newspapers. I heard her telling one of the daughters—Maria-Cristina, I guess."

"*Why* was she telling Maria-Cristina?" Mike asked quietly. "Was she Poppy's daughter?"

"Don't tell me you can't find that out for yourself." Hilliard grinned maliciously. "You've done a pretty good job so far. Besides, why should I tell you? Just so some avaricious bitch can get her hands on the money?"

"*Why should you tell me?*" Mike exclaimed angrily. "Because Poppy's money is lying there, *worthless,* when it could be put to good use! To one of these people it will mean a lot—freedom, education, love—it could mean everything. And a selfish old man like you has no right to deprive them of it. Look, Hilliard, one person is already dead, others may be in danger."

Hilliard stared at him, shocked. "Dead," he repeated, "who is dead? Not . . . young Aria?"

"No, not Aria, but she may be in danger. The game is over," Mike added firmly. "You must tell me the truth."

Hilliard sank back in his wheelchair, all the fight and game-playing gone out of him. He looked shriveled and old, and his hand shook as he poured himself another drink. "Very well, then, if it means that much, I'll tell you what I know." He sipped his drink in silence for a while, marshaling his thoughts.

"I'd better tell you *how* I know, first," he said finally. "Angel lived here, at the ranch, you know, in the latter part of her life. She'd always hated living in Italy; it had bad memories for her even though her two girls spent a great deal of their time there. Especially Helena, who'd finally broken away from her mother. Maria-Cristina was always on a plane or on a boat; she changed countries as often as she changed her boyfriends, but her son, Paolo, was brought up in Italy; the old woman you told me about, Fiametta, Aria's nurse, she looked after him.

"Anyway, it was 1939, I think. I was home on furlough from the army with my wife and a very young son of my own. Angel had complained of a bad cold she couldn't shake off, and suddenly it seemed to go to her chest. She was a beautiful woman, you know, Mike, truly beautiful, even then, when she was almost sixty. But it was as if suddenly a lamp inside her was turned out; she just shriveled and grew old in a couple of days. I remember going to see her, she was lying in bed and she smiled at me, even though she was so ill. She reminded me of the woman in a book I'd been reading—*Lost Horizon*—you remember, how the woman just crumbled to dust when her lover took her away from the enchanted valley of Shangri-la? Well, that's how Angel looked.

" 'Tell your father I want to see him, will you?' she asked in that clear, sweet voice of hers. I went to get my father and I remember the worried look in his eyes as I walked with him from the shearing sheds. 'Is it that bad then?' I asked. He nodded. 'It's pretty bad, Son,' he said grimly, 'but she's still refusing to go to the hospital.' "

Hilliard paused to sip his sherry, sinking back into his thoughts for a few moments. "I didn't go in with him," he said. "I understood it was something private between the two of them. But Dad hadn't quite closed the door and I was waiting out in the hall. Angel's voice always had that carrying quality, so I could hear clearly what she was saying.

" 'Greg, I want to tell you about Poppy,' she said. 'This may be my last chance, and I think you should know the truth.'

" 'You mustn't talk about last chances, Angel, that's silly,' he said to her in the sort of reproving voice he used to use to us when we were kids.

" 'You've got to listen, Greg,' she said, and she sounded panicky now.

" 'But I don't really want to know,' my father said. 'Not anymore. It's all in the past, you see. It's better forgotten.'

" 'I've lied to you, and to everyone,' she replied, 'and before I die I'm determined to wipe the slate clean. So sit down beside me, Greg, and listen.' I heard the chair scrape on the floor as he sat down, and then she began to tell him about Poppy and her husband, Felipe. My father heard her out and at the end, he said, 'Angel, I wish you hadn't told me.'

" 'I needed to,' she said, 'you had a right to know. You see, I knew one day she would come back to find her daughter, and when she finally did come to see me I refused to tell her.'

" 'I don't want to know,' he said, and I could tell he was crying, 'please don't tell me, Angel. To me they are both your girls and I don't even want to think about Poppy. Let's leave it that way.'

"There was a long silence and then Angel said, 'I have one more confession to make, and this time it's all my fault. No one else's but mine. You know I always protected Helena too much. She was such a sweet little girl, Greg, always smiling . . . and then we found out about her deafness. I couldn't bear seeing her hurt by the other children's impatience and taunts and so I began to take over her life. I answered questions for her, I refused to let her go out without me; you remember the governesses and the nurses . . . ? Oh, it was fine when she was still a child, but then that child became a woman, with a woman's feelings and emotions, but she knew nothing about men and love. After all, she never met any—I made sure of that.

" 'The only place Helena ever went without me was to see the ear doctor in San Francisco. I would leave her there while I went shopping, in the city. Dr. Barton had looked after her for years, ever since we came back from Italy. He'd operated on her once, but without much success. He was in his forties, married, with children of his own.

" 'I had to go to New York to rescue Maria-Cristina from one of her usual unfortunate entanglements, and of course I had to leave Helena here, so this time she had to go to San Francisco to see the doctor alone, though naturally I'd arranged for a chauffeured car. Dr. Barton was a very attractive man, and I hadn't realized just how lovely Helena was, I always thought of her as a child, you see. But Dr. Barton saw her in a different light, and she, poor girl, fell in love. She didn't even know what that sort of "love" was . . . she was as innocent as the child I'd tried to make her stay all her life!

" 'I was away for longer than I'd expected—almost two months. When I got back I noticed she was different, secretive . . . but it wasn't until later I noticed something else. I took her to another doctor, a gynecologist, and he confirmed that she was pregnant. Helena cried when I told her—she didn't understand it. She was like a child of twelve, mentally. "But I don't want a baby, Mama," she said, "all I want is Richard." Richard Barton, the doctor!

" 'I took her away to Arizona—I told everyone it was for her health. She had the baby there. The poor girl hardly knew what was going on. It was terrible, Greg, absolutely terrible for her. I wanted to kill Dr. Barton, but of course I could do nothing—except call to tell him to stay away from her. But I didn't tell him about the baby. I'd arranged for the child to be adopted and the couple came to pick her up. So that was the end; it was all over as though it had never happened.

" 'I took Helena back to Italy for a year or two to get her away from him, and to try to forget about the baby, and I'm afraid I began to treat her like a true invalid, cosseting her and always watching over her when she really didn't need it. And gradually she began to adapt to the role. She stopped speaking for almost a whole year, then when she started again, she said the strangest things . . . I knew there was nothing really wrong with her, but she was no longer "normal." I'd crippled her with my stupid overwhelming love, just as surely as if I'd harmed her in some physical accident. I'd never had the sense to let go of her and she would always be a childish innocent in a grown-up world.'

"Angel was crying and coughing and I heard my father trying to calm her down. 'You're only upsetting yourself talking about the past,' he told her.

" 'Helena's forgotten about the child,' Angel said, 'or at least I think she has. She never mentions it and I suppose it must have seemed like a bad dream to her. I have a copy of the signed adoption form and the name and address of the couple. Of course, I've never seen them since. But I've kept it hidden all these years, inside a copy of my favorite book in the library. And with it is a letter explaining the truth about Maria-Cristina and Helena. I want you to know where it is, Greg, in case I'm not here, and it is needed.'

" 'I don't want it,' Greg said—he was almost shouting, I remember. 'Leave the letter there, Angel. It's not important anymore. *Both* girls are your daughters.'

"She was coughing again, but when she'd finished she said to him,

'Well, Greg, you know where it is, when I'm gone. But I had to tell you, so you would understand about Helena and so you'll look after her.'

"I think they were both crying and I figured I'd better not stay around. I watched my father afterward to see if he would go to the library and find the book, but as far as I know he never did. Angel went into the hospital and died two weeks later of pneumonia. I've never seen my father so upset—he was devastated. But he still never looked in the book."

"And you did?" Mike asked.

Hilliard nodded. "Of course I looked. It meant very little to me then. I'd never known Poppy Mallory—or Angel's husband, Felipe." Wheeling his chair to the shelves, he took down an anthology of Keats's poetry. "You see," he said with his old malicious grin, "I didn't steer you wrong, if you'd looked hard enough, you would've found it."

"It would have taken me ten years, and you knew it," Mike retorted, watching as he took an envelope from between the pages.

"This is it," Hilliard said, offering it to him, "this is your answer. And much good it'll do you!"

The paper was crisp with age and falling apart at the creases. Mike opened it carefully. He read what Angel had written and looked at Hilliard. "Helena?" he asked, surprised.

"Helena," Hilliard said, with a triumphant grin. "So now you see, you're back to square one. You still don't know who your 'heiress' is!"

CHAPTER 63

A white mist hovered just inches above the Grand Canal, parting briefly as the watery noonday sun struggled through, giving a glimpse of the islands of Giudecca and San Giorgio, seemingly floating on clouds, before it closed in again.

It was the first day of *carnevale* and people were already in costume, though it was at nightime when the true festivities would begin. The *maschereri*, Venice's famous maskmakers, had been working overtime preparing the traditional *bauta* masks, the shiny white or black masks made from papier-mâché that covered the entire face, leaving just empty sockets for the eyes. It was the most sinister of all the carnival masks, and somehow the most anonymous. There were more elaborate masks: some looked like peacocks decorated with feathers and worn with feathered capes; there were lace masks studded with "diamonds," and golden parrot masks, and porcelain masks with doll-like features. But the old tradition of the *bauta*, worn with a black hood and a full-length black cape and topped by a tricorne hat, meant people could be completely anonymous—or they could become anyone else they wanted to be.

The Palazzo Rinardi was being groomed within an inch of its life; its marble floors glistened from much polishing, its woodwork shone, its silver and crystal sparkled, and its treasures glowed. Workmen were standing on stepladders, inserting hundreds of candles into the enormous chandeliers, and a team of a dozen caterers had taken over Fiametta's kitchen and were preparing exquisite food in readiness for the party that night. Francesca queened it over them all, issuing commands and countermanding them minutes later, and generally driving everyone crazy, while Aria lurked by the telephone in her room, praying for it to ring.

She wondered if she should call Orlando again, but she'd already called the *pensione* so many times since she got back, now her pride held her back. "*Si*, the Signore has returned," they'd told her patiently, "we will give him your message, Signorina." But Orlando still hadn't called her. She hadn't spoken to him since just before Christmas, when she'd told him she was going to Los Angeles with Carraldo. Surely he'd known it wasn't that she'd *wanted* to go. She'd had no choice, and once they were there, it seemed as though Carraldo never wanted to come back. Her mother had been no help, she'd been enjoying playing the rich society hostess too much. "No one could say Francesca Rinardi didn't leave her mark on Hollywood!" she'd exclaimed as they finally left a few days ago, her suitcases loaded down with new finery, and especially her dress for tonight's party. It was a fluid column of white silk chiffon, beaded from neck to hem with silver and crystal, and created especially for her by Bob Mackie, the king of Hollywood designers. She'd had a special mask made to go with it, with sweeping white plumes tipped in crystal, with the eye sockets outlined in crystal to match.

Tonight was to be Francesca's triumph, and she intended to look stunning. And tonight was Aria's despair, because at the party for three hundred people, her engagement to Antony Carraldo would be announced. Worse, he had told her he wanted to get married right away—next week, if she would agree. "Of course you will agree," Francesca had told her firmly. "It's your duty. And besides, Carraldo has been very patient. He's waited long enough—and so have I."

Aria had understood it was no use arguing, she'd just bided her time until she got back to Venice, and Orlando. She had lain awake at night, planning how they would run away together and how, if it took Mike a long time to find the evidence proving she was the heiress, she would get a job and take care of Orlando. He wouldn't have to worry about a thing, she told herself, he could just paint all day long. And, of course, when she finally got Poppy's money, he could have anything he wanted, anything at all. She just knew he would repay her by becoming a very great artist one day.

The phone rang and she grabbed it, almost dropping it in her haste. "*Pronto?*" she whispered.

"Aria, it's Mike."

"Mike! Where have you been? I haven't heard from you in so long. Is everything all right?"

"Yes . . . sure, everything's fine," Mike said, hating to deceive her, but on Lieber's instructions he had no choice. The matter of the heir and the heiress was now in the lawyer's hands. He had finally unraveled the rest of the story and it was Lieber who would contact the heirs and inform them officially that they were the true beneficiaries of Poppy's estate.

"I really need to know about Poppy," Aria said worriedly, "you don't know what's going on here . . . Mama and Carraldo are throwing a big carnival party tonight—*an engagement party!* I've been trying to get in touch with Orlando ever since we got back a couple of days ago. I'm afraid he must still be angry with me. . . ."

"Hold on, hold on," Mike interrupted quickly, "one thing at a time, Aria. Look, I'm at the Gritti Palace, why don't you come over and see me? We can talk about things."

"I'd love to," she said miserably, "but Mama's not letting me out of her sight. There's a hairdresser flying in from Rome at three o'clock to do our hair, and he's bringing a makeup person to paint our faces. I shall look like the virgin adorned for the sacrifice!" she added bitterly. "But what can I do? Mama just said it was my duty. Oh, Mike, do you have the proof about Poppy's daughter yet? Please say you do, and then I won't have to go through with this charade."

"I'm not sure yet," he said, wishing he could tell her the whole truth without hedging like this.

"Then you're still looking? It's so important. If I had Poppy's money now, I could give most of it to Mama and then I'd just run away with Orlando. He needs someone to take care of him, you see. An artist can't earn very much until he's established, and that could take time. I'd have to look after us both."

"Don't worry about Orlando," Mike said curtly. "I know he'll be all right."

"Of course he will," she wailed, "but will I? I've called him and called him, Mike, but he doesn't call me back. I can't believe he doesn't care about me anymore, not after the way things were between us. He's just angry with me, that's all, and I can't say that I blame him. Imagine how it looked to him, me jetting off to L.A. with Carraldo, leaving him all by himself at Christmastime . . ."

Mike sighed. "I guess he's not invited to the party?" he asked.

"Of course he's not! In fact, I suspect that Mama has asked Carraldo to dismiss him, so he's no longer my tutor. But *you* are invited," she added, "I'm inviting you now. The only thing is, I might not be there."

"Where will you be?" he demanded, alarmed.

"Oh, I don't know . . . I don't have anywhere to go. Without Orlando there's nowhere to turn, no escape . . ."

Her voice had the calm matter-of-factness of desperation and he said anxiously, "Don't do anything foolish, Aria. I'll be there tonight and we'll talk."

"Come at ten o'clock," she said, "and by the way, you're supposed to be in carnival costume."

It was odd, Mike thought as he dressed for the party in the hastily purchased knee breeches, brocade jacket, and buckled shoes, that the only claimant to Poppy's estate that he hadn't met should be a real heir; and never having met Orlando, he had no basis on which to judge Aria's infatuation for him. So far, all he knew about Orlando was hearsay. And he had never met Aria's other suitor, Carraldo. He thought of the long conversation he'd had with Carraldo just that afternoon, and he hoped he'd done the right thing.

Putting on the black velvet eye-mask, he stared at himself in the mirror. He looked like a seventeenth-century gentleman—except he'd drawn the line at the powdered wig. He threw the black cape over his shoulders and put on his black tricorne hat, and then he decided to have a drink at Harry's Bar en route to the Palazzo Rinardi.

The fog had rolled in at sunset. The cascading banks of cotton wool settled over the city by nightfall like a mysterious, intangible gray blanket, blurring the bold colors of the carnival revelers and muffling their shouts of laughter and music. Colored lights were strung from the trees and gaily decorated gondolas slid silently past in the mist, permitting a glimpse of Punchinellos and Harlequins, and exotic maidens in yards of multicolored tulle and satin and jewels, or gaudy tropical birds, and glittering fairylike creatures from other planets. Tonight, Venice was a city of illusion, and wrapped in its mantle of mist, it seemed to have recaptured the past.

Luchay perched on his jewel-encrusted stand in the hall of the Palazzo Rinardi, just the way he had all those years ago, at Numéro Seize, as Aria waited with her mother and Carraldo at the top of the marble staircase to greet their guests. She was wearing a full-skirted seventeenth-century dress of wine-red velvet, and a magnificent necklace of rubies and diamonds—Carraldo's present to her tonight. A silver mask hid the despairing expression in her eyes as Carraldo took her hand in his and smiled at her encouragingly. He was wearing a copy of the costume worn by Van Dyck's gentleman in the portrait at the Ca' d'Oro, and to Aria, he looked even more sinister.

Francesca, looking like a magnificent icicle in her crystal dress and diamonds, was in her element; she had achieved her life's ambition at last and tonight she was the queen of Venice! Candles flickered in the palazzo's great chandeliers and torches blazed on the rose-decorated landing stage, illuminating the guests as they arrived in their beribboned gondolas to the strains of a string quartet playing music by Vivaldi, Handel, and Albinoni. There was also a cocktail pianist in each of the two rooms where drinks were being served, and a band was waiting in the long-unused ballroom, to play for dancing after dinner.

Pierluigi Galli, anonymous in a *bauta* mask, black hood, and tricorne hat, stepped from his gondola onto the dock at the Palazzo Rinardi. Drawing his black cape around him to keep out the cold, he waited for a launch to disembark its glittering cargo of partygoers, tagging along behind as they entered the palazzo. In the general confusion, the butler checking the invitation cards never even noticed there was one extra person.

"My goodness," Francesca exclaimed as he bowed low over her hand, "I hardly recognize anyone tonight, the masks are so clever. But your game will be up, sir, at dinner. Everyone has a place card—and then we'll know who you are!"

Pierluigi merely smiled; he had no intention of having dinner.

"Smile, Aria, *please*," Francesca chided her daughter. "Look, here's Mike. You should have worn a wig," she told him reprovingly, "or at least a hood."

"You look great," Aria told him, "you've got the right legs for knee breeches. Can we talk?" she whispered as he kissed her. "I'll escape as soon as I can and meet you in the salon."

"Orlando hasn't called," she said when she joined him half an hour later. "What am I going to do? I think I'll call him just one more time."

"No!" Mike exclaimed sharply. "Don't do that."

"It's wrong, isn't it?" she said sorrowfully. "A girl shouldn't chase after a man like this. But you see, I love him—and I know now I can't go through with this engagement!"

"Aria," Francesca called, "come and say hello to the Contessa Mifori . . ."

"I'll speak to you later," she said miserably.

Mike decided he'd better keep an eye on her, there was no telling what she might do in her state. If only he could have told her she was the heiress, it would have been so much easier. . . .

"So, Mr. Preston," Carraldo interrupted his thoughts. "We finally meet, and I can thank you personally for giving me your trust. I think you understand now why it was necessary?" His dark, somber eyes, half hidden by the mask, searched Mike's face.

"I'm glad I was able to help," Mike said soberly. "I just wish I'd known earlier."

"Unfortunately none of us can put back the clock. But now your work is over and you must come and enjoy yourself. Let me worry about everything else."

The party was going with a swing, the champagne flowed, the dinner was delicious and the service impeccable, and Francesca had put Mike at a table next to a girl who he felt quite sure was very beautiful beneath her mysterious golden mask, and who had the sexiest voice and body, as well as an appealing Italian-English accent. She kept him so amused, he never saw the liveried footman in a powdered wig whisper in Aria's ear, and the room was so crowded that he never noticed her slip away. Not until some time later, when he finally went to look for her.

Aria took the phone call in the kitchen, the only place she could be sure her mother would never go.

"Orlando?" she said breathlessly. "Oh, at last! I've been trying and trying to get you . . ."

"I haven't called you before because I knew I couldn't compete with Carraldo," he said, sounding cold and distant over the phone. "I had no right to hold you back. I just wanted to tell you that it wasn't because I don't love you, but because I have nothing to offer you except the life of a struggling artist."

"But that's all I want," she whispered, "*you* are all I want. You've called just in time to save me, Orlando . . . why, oh, *why* didn't you call earlier?"

"I couldn't," he said abruptly. "We mustn't see each other again."

"Please, oh, *please*," she wailed, "I *must* see you. *I must talk to you.* Please, Orlando."

"Very well," he relented suddenly, "meet me in half an hour at the Church of Santa Maria della Pietà. I'll be waiting for you."

Aria threw a black cape over her velvet dress and putting on her mask, she tucked her hair beneath the tricorne hat. Then she sneaked down the back stairs, past the kitchen, and out onto the Calle San Vidal. It was cold outside and she wrapped the cape closer as she hurried through the dank, foggy alleys to meet Orlando.

A masked face loomed at her from the mist and she shrank back against the wall, her heart thumping wildly, as a man in the pointed-nosed mask of the Plague Doctor shook his beribboned stick playfully at her and then went on his way, laughing. The shrouded alleys seemed doubly silent as she hurried toward the Piazza San Marco, and she glanced fearfully over her shoulder, imagining she heard footsteps again. You're just being silly, she chided herself, no one's following you, it's just some other carnival reveler on his way to a party. But she quickened her step as she hurried along the Salizzada San Moise.

The deserted Piazza San Marco stretched before her in its shroud of fog, as silent and mysterious as an empty stage. Streetlamps shed a pale, diffused light, leaving patches of deep shadow under the colonnades, and she could hear the eerie strains of *The Four Seasons* relayed over loud-speakers from Vivaldi's church, where she was to meet Orlando. Something rustled in the darkness and her hand flew to her mouth, stifling a scream that turned into a relieved laugh as a cat brushed against her legs and scampered off into the mist.

The man stalked her in the shadow of the colonnade; he was wrapped in a black cape, with a tricorne hat pulled low over his mask. He knew exactly which way she would go . . . she was coming closer, closer . . .

He sprang at her suddenly from the shadow and Aria screamed, para-lyzed with fear. She just had time to catch a glimpse of his profile before she twisted from his grasp and fled back the way she'd come. The man was wearing a black hood and the sinister white *bauta* mask. And from the cavernous, empty eye socket dripped three scarlet teardrops, like gobbets of fresh blood.

She could hear him behind her as she fled toward the Piazzetta and the Grand Canal, praying that someone would be there, that there'd be a gondola or a launch . . . the fog seemed to be pressing on her eyelids, it caught in her throat, and her heart was pounding, harder and harder; she could hear him behind her, getting closer, closer . . . she was almost at the canal, she could hear something, people . . . they were laughing . . . oh, thank God, thank God . . .

He sprang at her again suddenly. A powerful arm was flung around her neck, her head jolted back painfully, and she stared terrified at the thin steel blade of a dagger . . . "No," she screamed, "no, no . . ."

"What is it?" someone called through the fog, "what's happening out there?"

"Help," she screamed, "help!"

"Just someone joking around," another voice said, laughing as they came toward her . . . she could see them . . .

The arm gripping her neck slackened suddenly and her attacker disappeared into the mist as though he'd never been. Gasping with relief, Aria ran toward the voices, but they'd already turned away, and she lost them again in the fog.

"Help," she cried, running through the Piazzetta, toward the canal, praying there'd be a boat waiting. "Oh, please, someone help me, please . . ." She spotted a gondola and waved it down frantically. Even the gondolier was wearing a carnival costume, a black *bauta* mask and cape. "Take me to the Church of Santa Maria della Pietà," she sobbed, sinking onto the cushions as they glided into the blank gray mist. Once she got to the church Orlando would be waiting for her and everything would be all right . . . except they weren't going the right way. The gondola had turned onto one of the narrow side canals. "Where are you going?" Aria called nervously. "This isn't the right way!" The gondolier turned to look at her and for the first time she saw that only one half of his mask was black. The other side was white, with three drops of blood spilling from the empty eye socket!

The sweat of fear trickled down her spine as she scrambled to her feet. "No," she screamed, "no . . . no . . . no . . ."

The masked gondolier came toward her, wielding the pole like a bludgeon. "Oh, God," Aria whispered, "please help me, *please help me . . .*"

There was a blare of music and laughter suddenly, and then the soft purr of an engine as a launch nosed its way through the fog toward them, filled with an aviary of bright carnival-costumed peacocks, drinking champagne, laughing and chattering. Distracted, her attacker turned to look, and in the split-second that the launch drew alongside them Aria hurled herself across the narrow gap of water and into the safety of the other boat.

"Oops," they cried, laughing as they helped her up, "couldn't stand him any longer, eh? Why don't you join us then?" And a glass of champagne was thrust into Aria's shaking hand. She turned, staring back at the canal, but there was only the swirling, empty gray fog.

"Where are you going, *carina*?" they asked her.

"To the Santa Maria della Pietà," she whispered, trembling.

"Church? At carnival? You must be crazy!" they exclaimed good-naturedly as the launch swung into the Grand Canal. "Is it okay if we drop you at the Molo? We're turning off here."

Aria jumped from the launch, watching as it disappeared again into the mist. She glanced around apprehensively, feeling a thousand imaginary eyes staring at her from the darkness, and then she turned and ran as fast as she could across the bridge onto the Riva degli Schiavoni.

The fog seemed even thicker here, swirling in from the lagoon and pressing against her eyes, blinding her . . . she was almost there, she told herself frantically as she ran, almost . . . only another few yards, just over that little bridge . . . Vivaldi's "Summer" music was louder now, its urgent beat matching the pounding of her heart. She stopped, her hand to her lips, listening . . . was it her imagination? Or had she heard footsteps behind her again? Oh, God, yes, yes . . . she could hear them distinctly now, footsteps running, coming closer, closer . . . closer . . . With a terrified scream she turned and ran full tilt into the masked man in front of her. As his powerful arms gripped her, she felt his breath on her face . . . and she saw again the three scarlet teardrops of blood.

"No!" she whispered helplessly, "please don't . . ." Her eyes were riveted on the dagger as his arm drew back, ready to plunge it into her breast.

His head jerked up suddenly at the sound of running footsteps. He drew back with an angry cry as a group of men cloaked and hooded like him, wearing the sinister tricorne hat and *bauta* mask, emerged from the fog. As he turned to run, Aria saw the dull gleam of a long, snub-nosed pistol, and she screamed again in terror as she heard a shot, and then, with a sharp cry, her attacker fell to the ground.

It had all happened in the space of a few seconds, and she stared horrified at the body lying on the ground, blood oozing from its chest, and then at the masked man who had shot him.

Carraldo looked at the man he had just killed. "Forgive me, Father," he said quietly. But it wasn't God he was asking for forgiveness, it was Franco Malvasi, whom he had always called simply "the man." "It's all right now, Aria," he said tiredly, "you're safe now."

Too numb even to speak, she stared at the gun in his hand and then she began to sob.

"There's no need to be afraid," Carraldo said gently, taking off his mask. His face looked as gray as the fog, and beads of perspiration were trickling down his temples and his eyes were full of pain. Quite suddenly and without even a sound, he slid to the ground at her feet. Aria knew she was screaming . . . she was screaming and screaming . . .

"Stop it, Aria, stop it!" Mike commanded, putting his arms around her. "Please stop now!"

She shivered in his arms. "Carraldo," she gasped, "what's wrong . . . ?"

"The launch will take him to the hospital," he said. "He'll be all right now."

"I was going to meet Orlando," she told him, sobbing into his chest, "he's waiting for me at the church . . . I could hear the music . . . I was almost there, I knew all I had to do was find him and then I'd be safe . . ."

Letting go of her, Mike walked across to the body still lying on the ground, with two of Carraldo's men standing guard over it. "Take off the hood and the mask," he told them quietly.

Aria watched in horrified fascination as they pulled off the hood, revealing a shock of bright blond hair. And then they took off the mask.

"My poor Aria," Mike said gently, "I'm afraid you'd already found Orlando."

CHAPTER 64

Aria had been given a sedative and she slept until the following afternoon. It wasn't until later that evening, after she'd answered questions from the police, that Mike was able to explain exactly what had happened.

She was sitting up in bed looking as pale as her pillows and with livid bruises on her arms and throat where Orlando had grabbed her.

"I don't understand," she whispered, "I thought he loved me. And I really, *really* loved him."

"You only loved what you thought he was," Mike said gently.

"But *why* would Orlando want to *kill* me?" she cried despairingly.

"I'm afraid he deceived you right from the beginning," Mike said. "He never told you that he was claiming to be Poppy Mallory's heir." Aria's stunned eyes met his. "And you have Carraldo to thank for finding out about him," he added. "He became suspicious when he realized Orlando hadn't told you, or him, about his claim to be the heir, and he decided to investigate his background. Orlando's stories about being thrown out of schools for boyish pranks and misbehavior turned out to be lies. He was a cruel bully who enjoyed torturing other boys. By the time he was thirteen he'd already attempted to kill a teacher by setting fire to his room. You see, the teacher had spotted the truth about him, and he'd let Orlando—and his parents—know it. Everything was hushed up on the condition his parents sent him for treatment, but the psychiatrist told them that Orlando's good looks were a useful facade behind which he hid a psychopathic personality. Orlando's parents didn't send him to Italy just to study art; they wanted to get rid of him.

"Carraldo became afraid for you and that was when he whisked you off to Los Angeles—out of harm's way—or so he thought. He'd found out that when Orlando was supposed to be in London, he was following you—the footsteps, and the man in the black Peugeot.

"Until Orlando made a move, there was nothing Carraldo could do— nothing he could accuse him of. After all, all he'd done so far was not tell you—and no doubt if questioned, he would have come up with a plausible excuse for that.

"Orlando had got hold of a copy of the list of possible heirs; obviously he thought Lauren Hunter's claim was too farfetched, yet he knew there must be a daughter somewhere, because that's what the will said, and either the Gallis or you must be descended from that daughter. In his warped mind he thought there were three serious rivals for his claim to Poppy's money. You, the favorite, and Claudia and Pierluigi Galli. Although Orlando believed—correctly—that his own claim was the true one, he now knew that there might be another heir, or possibly even three or four . . . who could tell? That meant he would have to share the estate. And Orlando wanted it all. He was tired of being a hanger-on in the international set he liked to mix with, now he wanted to be king. When Orlando finally had that money, he was going to get his revenge for all the insults he'd had to take with a smile all those years.

"Carraldo found out that Orlando had seen Claudia in Paris the week before she died, and that she'd left a message on her answering machine telling him she was going to the Villa Velata. Orlando went there, too, secretly . . . and it was he who severed the brakes on Claudia's car. The thing he hadn't expected was for Pierluigi to be there, too—he'd thought he would show up for the funeral later, when he planned to take care of him as well. Instead, Pierluigi was accused of the murder and put in jail. Even Orlando couldn't get to him there. He knew by then that I was on the trail, unraveling Poppy's story, and he decided to play the waiting game with Pierluigi—he'd find a way to get him later, if he had to.

"When Carraldo realized what had happened, he used his influence to get Pierluigi out of jail—he put up several millions in bail. But he warned him to lie low. Carraldo would never tell you this, but I think you should know that he has also arranged to help Pierluigi by backing him personally to the tune of millions of dollars—more than enough to save his company. I guess he thought Pierluigi had suffered enough, losing Claudia and having his name blackened, accused of murdering her. I think he understood only too well that for Pierluigi, his business life was the only life he had—without it he would be nothing. Carraldo is a compassionate man, Aria. Anyway, Pierluigi was at the party, and he was there at the end—if Carraldo hadn't shot Orlando, he would have. He'd come to take revenge for his sister—but Carraldo beat him to it. And that left just you, Aria, between Orlando and all that money."

"It's a curse," she wept, "Poppy Mallory's money is a curse!"

"That's not true," Mike replied quietly. "If Orlando had been sane, none of this would have happened. It's unfair to blame it on Poppy. Why don't I tell you the true story of what happened to her, and then maybe you'll understand about Orlando?"

Aria shook her head. "I don't want to know anymore," she whispered. "I just wish I'd never met him. And now because of me, Carraldo is ill. Mama told me he had a heart attack, he's in the hospital . . ."

"Carraldo's known for a long time that he had a serious heart problem, you mustn't blame yourself. It could have happened anytime, it was inevitable."

Aria twisted her ringless hands agitatedly. "But Carraldo saved my life, and it's because of me he might die." She looked at him, her eyes filled with tears. "I must go to him, Mike. I want to thank him."

"Tomorrow," he promised. "Now you must get some rest."

The hospital room was very quiet, just the faint humming of machinery and the nervous flickering of the screen monitoring his heartbeat. Carraldo could feel it fluttering uncontrollably in his chest and he knew that now the little white pills were no longer any use.

Closing his eyes, he thought about his life, wondering if he had made the right decision all those years ago, when he had agreed to become Franco Malvasi's legally adopted son. What had it brought him, he asked himself? He knew the answer. Riches that he'd never touched, and a conscience that he was unable to live with. But Franco had educated him; he'd given him the veneer of a civilized man over his crude slum-tenement beginnings; Franco had taught him all he knew about the things he loved most in the world, and with that knowledge he'd found success and a kind of happiness. He had made himself a legitimate fortune, the one he was leaving to Aria. He had done all he could to protect that fortune from falling into the hands of his enemies, but he knew it was too late now for the one thing that he felt would have secured it from all predators—marriage. Still, he was content, Aria would have enough for her freedom. She could fulfill her own destiny, the way her father Paolo should have.

He'd thought he'd been so clever when Franco died, imagining that by killing his enemies he'd bought his freedom. And in a way he had, for he'd never had to live like a prisoner in the villa in Naples, the way Franco had. He'd roamed the world freely on his powerful jet planes; he'd dined with princes, he was on speaking terms with people in high places, and he'd been a guest at all the grandest parties. And still he'd slept with the whores in the *bassi*, just the way he would have done if he'd remained a petty thief on the streets of Naples. And with all his social success, no man called him his friend. He was a prisoner of his loneliness just as surely as if he'd never left that villa, with its armed guards and snarling dogs, because he knew *what* he was, and there was never any escape from that.

Only with Paolo had he ever found the rapport of true, unjudging friendship, and in gratitude he'd wanted to take care of his daughter. What he hadn't expected was to fall in love with her. Aria had enchanted him with her vibrant youth and he'd wanted to capture her, to teach her about life, to watch her grow into the lovely woman he knew she could become, and he'd wanted to shield her from the cruel world with the power of his wealth. He'd known he didn't have long; maybe a year, maybe months, or even weeks . . . no one could tell. One day he would be alive and the next he would be dead, it was as quick and simple as that. But for that short while, he'd wanted Aria. It was unfair to her, he knew that now, but he also knew his selfishness would ensure her freedom.

The double irony was that the girl he loved should fall for Franco Malvasi's great-grandson. Because had Franco known he had a son, it would have been Orlando who would have inherited the Malvasi empire, not Carraldo. And he would have lived out his own life in Naples as an ordinary man. Such were the chances of fate.

He heard someone come into the room, and he knew it was Aria even before he opened his eyes . . . he knew her light step, and the fragrance of her hair as she bent over him.

His dark eyes opened suddenly and he looked at her with his familiar sardonic half smile. "It's kind of you to come to see me," he murmured, but she just stared at him, shocked by his gray pallor and his weak voice. "Sit beside me for a while," he said. "I want to talk to you."

Aria put her flowers on the table and took a seat by the bed. "How are you?" she asked anxiously.

"Who knows?" Carraldo said with a smile. "They tell me I've been dying for two years now."

"No!" she exclaimed, "it can't be true, there must be something they can do. We'll call the best specialists . . ."

"Aria," he said gently, "I've been to the best doctors in the world, if there was anything to be done, they would have done it."

She covered her face with her hands, weeping silently, and his eyes filled with sadness. "Don't cry," he said, "I've no intention of going just yet. Besides, I want to talk to you." He paused for a moment, catching his breath. "I've lived in a different world from you," he said at last, "a half-world, full of violence and evil, but I promise none of that will ever touch you. Your father knew the truth about me, and he gave me his friendship, man to man. I loved him for it, and now I love you, his daughter."

"I didn't know," she whispered, anguished, "I didn't understand. I realize now how selfish I've been, how unkind to you!"

"How could I expect anything else?" he asked. "You were a young girl looking for romance and true love. I knew I couldn't ask you for that."

Aria hung her head, staring at his hands lying limply on the white sheets; they looked fragile and vulnerable. Suddenly the powerful Carraldo seemed helpless.

"When I'm gone," he was saying, "my personal fortune will be yours —my art collection, the galleries, the houses—everything. Your mother will be taken care of—I've already arranged for that with my lawyers; and then you will be free. I should like to think that you were running the Carraldo Galleries, Aria, when I am no longer able. They were the one good thing in my life."

"Please," she whispered, taking his hand in hers, "don't talk like that. You'll get better and you'll be running the galleries for a long time yet. Promise me you'll get better?"

Her blue eyes met his anxiously and he thought how lovely she was, and how fortunate he was to have known her; she and her father had been like a breath of fresh air in his life. "I'm sorry about Orlando," he said at last.

"I didn't know he was Poppy's great-grandson," she whispered. "Mike told me."

"Orlando never had the evidence; it was Mike who found out."

"And I'm not the heiress after all," she said.

"It's not important now," Carraldo whispered. The pain was in his chest again, its iron bands were crushing him. Beads of sweat stood out on his forehead and he closed his eyes, breathing rapidly.

The green zigzag line on the monitor was jumping wildly and Aria glanced at it in alarm. "I'm tiring you," she said, gripping his hands, "you mustn't talk anymore."

After a while when he seemed easier, she said, "I came to thank you for saving my life, but words don't seem enough to repay such a debt. I've thought it over, and if you still want me, I'd like to marry you."

His pained dark eyes smiled at her. "You are like your father, after all, Aria," he said gently.

She sat for a long time, just holding his hands in hers until he seemed to be sleeping, and then, bending over him, she kissed him gently on the lips, before she left.

Antony Carraldo suffered a massive heart attack moments before dawn the next morning, and before the sun rose, he was dead. Many hundreds of people attended his funeral, though few mourned him. But there were tears of true sadness on Aria Rinardi's face as she placed a girlish posy of lily of the valley, baby's breath, and tiny cream rosebuds on his grave.

CHAPTER 65

Mike opened the bottle of champagne with a satisfactory pop and
Lauren hurried to hold the glass under the overflowing stream. "We
can't waste it," she said, laughing, "it tastes too good."

"Plenty more where that came from," he said. "Who do we toast first?
Maria? Poppy Mallory? Or you?"

She put her head on one side, considering. "None of them," she
decided finally. "We toast you, because without you, I never would have
found out the truth—about Maria, and about myself."

"Then we've got to toast Maria too," he argued, "because she gave me
the clue. Once I understood Helena's strange behavior was due to her
deafness, I realized that was probably what had puzzled me about Maria.
I could see the intelligence in her eyes, there seemed nothing wrong with
her intellect, and yet she was so silent. I called you and you told me the
doctor had confirmed her deafness. Then I remembered Helena had the
Mallory family name, and I thought about the names in your family
Bible . . . it didn't take long to track down the evidence, births, deaths,
marriages—I just started with you and worked backward to her daughter.

"Angel had said in her letter that the people who adopted Helena's
baby were named James, and they lived in Ventura County, here in
California. They'd told Angel they would call her Mary, and her middle

name would be Mallory. Mary Mallory James. It didn't take long to track it down after that.

"Maria-Cristina was killed in World War II, driving an ambulance, and Helena, who'd become a recluse, died years later. That's when Aria got the parrot. If she'd lived, then there would have been some family continuity, and all this wouldn't have been such a mystery. Still, it gave me an opportunity to know Poppy Mallory," he added thoughtfully, "and to tell the truth, it's an opportunity I wouldn't have missed. Poppy was a woman who lived by her heart rather than her head, and when it all went wrong, she glued the pieces back together somehow, and just carried on. *Indomitable*, that's the word I'd use to describe Poppy."

Lauren looked at him, her blue eyes serious. "This toast should be to Poppy," she said, raising her glass.

"To Poppy," Mike said. There was a silence and then he said, "So, now we'll drink to Miss Lauren Hunter, the Mallory heiress."

Lauren sighed. "I think I'm going to need quite a lot of champagne," she said, "because it's sobering thinking that now I own all that valuable real estate, and all those millions."

"You'll have good advice," he told her. "Lieber will take care of that."

"There's one thing I know I want to do with it, though," she said. "Remember you told me that if the money was his, Pierluigi had wanted to set up a foundation in his sister's memory? To help homeless young people and see that they get to college? I'd like to use some of those millions for that purpose. I'd like it to be called the Poppy Mallory Foundation. We could have special scholarships in Claudia's name."

"That's a fine thing to do, Lauren," he said quietly.

She shrugged. "I was one of those unfortunate young people myself, until last week."

They watched Maria, playing happily with her Christmas teddy. "I know her hearing problem is serious, but the doctor hopes that after the operation, she'll regain at least part of it." Lauren looked at him hopefully. "He tells me she'll be able to talk, and with lip-reading, she'll be fine. I'm just happy it wasn't anything worse."

"And what are *your* plans?" he asked, meeting her eyes.

"Maybe I can go to Stanford after all," she said eagerly. "I thought I'd buy a house nearby and I'm hoping they'll let me live off-campus, with Maria. I'll be able to afford to hire a nanny for her now, and to pay for her medical care." She sighed, looking at him gratefully. "Poppy Mallory will never know how much I appreciate her gift—because that's what it is, really. I didn't do anything to deserve all this money."

"Let's just say it found the right person, after all," Mike said, smiling at her. "Funny thing, you know, Lauren, I was just thinking how much I like it here in California, and about maybe getting a house myself. Poppy gave me a legacy too—a book—and California's as good a place as any to finish it. Maybe we'll be neighbors. And whenever you can shake off those eager young college guys, maybe you might have dinner with me, now and again?"

"I'd like that," Lauren said, her blue eyes shining, just the way Poppy's must have when she fell in love, all those years ago.

1957, EPILOGUE

Even now, when she was an old lady, alone in this gaudy, ornate Italian villa far from her childhood California home, Poppy could remember seeing the flowers she was named for the very week she was born. Of course, they'd always told her it was impossible, that an infant so young couldn't even see. Yet that same field, curving upward into the hills behind the old adobe house, had been plowed the following autumn and sown with barley for winter feed, and after the storms the graceful California poppies had never grown there again. How else, then, could she know them so well, unless they were imprinted on her memory?

If she closed her eyes, she could feel the floating, weightless sensation of being in her mother's arms, and smell the faint sweet fragrance of her skin as she waded, knee-deep, through the sea of blossoms. She remembered being held perilously forward to share her mother's pleasure at the sight of hundreds of heart-shaped petals scattering on the breeze like scarlet silk butterflies. And she could recall their deep, purple-black hearts and the golden fluff of pollen on the stamens as clearly as she knew her own mirror-image.

It was a story she would repeat often to Luchay. As she had grown older she'd talked to the parrot only about her *happy* memories, but then Luchay already knew her life story. *He knew all her secrets.*

She rarely spoke to the women who came from the village to clean the villa—all its thirty-two rooms filled with the curlicued gilded furniture she despised . . . "All red plush and tassels," she'd say to Luchay, cackling with self-mocking laughter. The women saw to her wants and prepared her solitary meals; and she supposed they stole from her, but she didn't really care—they probably had a dozen mouths to feed at home. And now, at the end, there was only her. A lonely old woman who was so very tired today, so tired, she might just take a little nap and dream her old dreams, hoping she could finally exorcise them. And then, just maybe, she might never wake again.

The tall foreigner stopped his car by the mossy stone pillars with their crumbling peacocks. He pushed the rusty iron gates tentatively, but they refused to open more than a crack. The villa was barely visible among its tangled greenery, and squaring his shoulders resolutely, he walked down the overgrown drive.

Hurrying up the front steps, he rang the bell, thrusting his hands into his pockets and pacing across the portico like a man undecided whether or not to change his mind. He took the newspaper clipping from his pocket and looked at it again. "Mallory," he read, "at the Villa Castelletto, Veneto, Italy. Poppy in her seventy-seventh year. Ever loved and missed by her friend, Franco." There was the sound of footsteps on the marble floor and then the door was opened. An old peasant woman, her head swathed in a black shawl, peered through the crack.

"Che desidera?" she demanded.

He told her he wanted to know about the woman who used to live there, he was a long-lost relative. He needed to know, he said, where she was buried.

The woman stared hard at him for a moment, her beady black eyes assessing him. Then slowly she opened the door. He peered past her into the gloomy hallway; the curtains were drawn and the mirrors were draped in black. "It's a pity you're too late for the funeral. She's buried in the graveyard by the village. The man came and took care of everything. He and I were the only two at the funeral. If you'd come earlier," she added chattily, "then there would have been three. Then the lawyer took the parrot away, they say he gave it to someone . . . I don't know who. All I know was it was the only thing she loved. Poor lonely soul." She crossed herself, muttering a blessing, as he turned away, and he walked quickly back down the drive.

"It's a pity you are too late," the woman called after him shrilly, "Madame never had any visitors . . . it would have been nice for her . . ."

The graveyard had four walls stacked with neat whitewashed tombs. Each had its saint or Madonna or a figure of Christ on the cross, and each was dotted with photographs of the dead person and a jar of flowers. In the center of the graveyard were several larger and more elaborate tombs and he walked around inspecting them, reading each name carefully; but none of the baroque edifices surmounted by spires and angels was Poppy's resting place.

He found it at last in a sunny corner by the far wall, just a simple plot, bordered in pinkish marble with a plain headstone with her name and the date of her birth and her death. *In Loving Memory,* it said. And on the grave lay a fresh gardenia plant; its dark green leaves were waxen and shiny, and its heady-scented flowers as creamy and smooth as new milk.

Rogan ran his hands wearily through his graying hair, staring down at the grave. After a few moments he walked quickly from the graveyard and without once glancing back, he climbed into his car and drove away.